THE ANNOTATED
Lolita

THE ANNOTATED

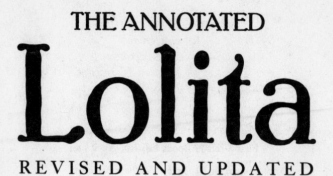

Lolita

REVISED AND UPDATED

Vladimir Nabokov

*Edited, with
preface, introduction, and notes by*
ALFRED APPEL, JR.

VINTAGE BOOKS
A DIVISION OF RANDOM HOUSE, INC.
NEW YORK

First Vintage Books Edition, April 1991

Copyright © 1955 by Vladimir Nabokov
Annotated edition copyright © 1970, 1991 by Alfred Appel, Jr.

Library of Congress Cataloging-in-Publication Data
Nabokov, Vladimir Vladimirovich, 1899–1977.
[Lolita]
The annotated Lolita / Vladimir Nabokov; edited, with preface, introduction, and notes by Alfred Appel, Jr. — 1st Vintage books ed.
p. cm. —
Includes bibliographical references.
ISBN 0–679–72729–9
I. Appel, Alfred. II. Title.
PS3527.A15L6 1991
813'.54 — dc20 90–50264
CIP

Manufactured in the United States of America
3579B864

to Véra

Acknowledgments

I would like to thank the following for permission to quote: *The New Yorker*, in whose pages the poems first appeared, for "A Discovery" and "Ode to a Model," Copyright © 1943, 1955 by Vladimir Nabokov; New Directions, for passages from *The Real Life of Sebastian Knight* by Vladimir Nabokov, Copyright by New Directions, 1941. Part II of my own article, "Nabokov's Puppet Show," is reprinted by permission of *The New Republic*, Copyright © 1967 by Harrison-Blaine of New Jersey, Inc. The University of Wisconsin Press has kindly allowed me to reprint portions of my article, "*Lolita:* The Springboard of Parody," *Wisconsin Studies in Contemporary Literature*, VIII (Spring 1967), and passages from "An Interview with Vladimir Nabokov," *ibid.* (© 1967 by the Regents of the University of Wisconsin). I also wish to acknowledge the assistance of Karen Appel, Richard Appel, Frank Cady, Eli Cohen, Patricia McKea, Raymond Nelson, Stephen Oshman, Professor Fred C. Robinson, and Bruce Sattler.

—A.A.

Preface

In the decades since its American publication (in 1958), Vladimir Nabokov's *Lolita* has emerged as a classic of contemporary literature. This annotated edition, a corrected and chastely revised version of the edition first published in 1970, is designed for the general reader and particularly for use in college literature courses. It has developed out of my own experiences in teaching and writing about *Lolita*, which have demonstrated that many readers are more troubled by Humbert Humbert's use of language and lore than by his abuse of Lolita and law. Their sense of intimidation is not unwarranted; *Lolita* is surely the most allusive and linguistically playful novel in English since *Ulysses* (1922) and *Finnegans Wake* (1939), and, if its involuted and constantly evolving means bring to mind any previous novel, it should be that most elusive of works, *The Confidence-Man* (1857) by Herman Melville. As with Joyce and Melville, the reader of *Lolita* attempts to arrive at some sense of its overall "meaning," while at the same time having to struggle with the difficulties posed by the recondite materials and rich, elaborate verbal textures. The main purpose of this edition is to solve such local problems and to show how they contribute to the total design of the novel. Neither the Introduction nor the Notes attempts a total interpretation of *Lolita*.

The annotations keep in mind the specific needs of college students. Many kinds of allusions are identified: literary, historical, mythological, Biblical, anatomical, zoological, botanical, and geographical. Writers and artists long out of fashion (e.g., Maeterlinck) receive fuller treatment than more familiar names. Selective cross-references to identical or related allusions in other Nabokov works (a sort of mini–concordance) will help to place *Lolita* in a wider context and, one hopes, may be of some assistance to future critics of Nabokov. Many of the novel's most important motifs are limned by brief cross-references. Humbert's vocabulary is extraordinary, its range enlarged by the many portmanteau words he creates. Puns, coinages, and comic etymologies, as well as foreign, archaic, rare, or unusual words are defined. Although some of the "unusual" words are in collegiate dictionaries, they are nevertheless annotated as a matter of convenience. Not every neologism is identified (e.g., "truckster"), but many that should be obvious enough *are* noted, because the rapidly moving eye may well miss the vowel on which such a pun depends (speed-readers of the world, beware! *Lolita* is not the book for you). Because many American students have little or no French, virtually all the interpolations in French are translated. In a few instances, readers may feel an annotation belabors the obvious; I well remember my own resentment, as a college sophomore, when a textbook reference to Douglas MacArthur was garnished by the footnote "Famous American general (1880–)." Yet the commonplace may turn out to be obscure. For instance, early in *Lolita* Humbert mentions that his first wife Valeria was "deep in *Paris-Soir*" (p. 26). When in 1967 I asked a Stanford University class of some eighty students if they knew what *Paris-Soir* was, sixty of them had no idea, twenty reasonably guessed it to be a magazine or newspaper, but no one knew specifically that it was a newspaper which featured lurid reportage, and that the detail formulates Valeria's puerility and Humbert's contempt for her. In 1967, most of them knew what a "zoot suit" and "crooner" are; this is no longer true, so they've been glossed (only twelve of one hundred 1990 Northwestern University students could define a crooner or zoot suit, a new wrinkle in The Crisis in the Humanities). Several notes are thus predicated on the premise that one epoch's "popular culture" is another's esoterica (see Note 148/1).

Most of the Introduction is drawn from parts of my previously published articles in *The New Republic* ("Nabokov's Puppet Show—Part II," CLVI [January 21, 1967], 25–32), *Wisconsin Studies in Contemporary Literature* (1967), *The Denver Quarterly* (1968), and *TriQuarterly* (1970). Several Notes are adapted from the two middle articles and my interview with Nabokov in *Wisconsin Studies* (see bibliography for full entries). The first edition was completed in 1968, save for eleventh-hour allusions to *Ada*, and published in 1969, but the vagaries and vagrancies of publishing delayed its appearance. In the meantime, Carl R. Proffer's *Keys to Lolita* was published (1968). Two enchanted hunters (see Note 108/2) working independently of each other, Mr. Proffer and I arrived at many similar identifications, and, excepting those which are readily apparent, I have tried to indicate where he anticipated me.

The text of *Lolita* is that of the 1989 Vintage edition. It contains many corrections made over time, some of which are identified in the Notes. All were approved by Nabokov. Like the first American edition of 1958, this variorum edition concludes with Nabokov's Afterword, which, along with its Notes, should be read in conjunction with the Introduction (where the reader will be offered exact instructions as to this procedure).

Given the length of the Notes and the fact that they are at the back of the book, the reader would do well to consider the question of how best to use these annotations. An old reader familiar with *Lolita* can approach the apparatus as a separate unit, but the perspicacious student who keeps turning back and forth from text to Notes risks vertigo. A more balanced method is to read through a chapter and then read its annotations, or vice versa. Each reader, however, has to decide for himself which is the most comfortable procedure. In a more perfect world, this edition would be in two volumes, text in one, Notes in the other; placed adjacent to one another, they could be read concurrently. Charles Kinbote in his Foreword to *Pale Fire* (1962) suggests a solution that closely approximates this arrangement, and the reader is directed to his sensible remarks, which are doubly remarkable in view of his insanity (this edition, p. lxxv).

Although there are some nine hundred notes to this text, the initial annotated edition of a work should never be offered as "definitive," and that claim will not be made here. As it is, *The Annotated Lolita* was the first annotated edition of a modern novel to have been published during its author's lifetime—*A Tale of a Tub* for our time. Vladimir Nabokov was occasionally consulted and, in some cases, commented on the annotations. In such instances his contribution is acknowledged. He asked me to mention that in several instances his interpretation of *Lolita* did not necessarily coincide with mine, and I have tried to point out such cases; the literary allusions, however, have been deemed accurate. Every allusion newly identified in the second edition of 1991 was double-checked with Nabokov during the last years of his life.

This edition—now, as in 1970—is analogous to what *Pale Fire* might have been like if poor John Shade had been given the opportunity to comment on Charles Kinbote's Commentary. Of course, the annotator and editor of a novel written by the creator of Kinbote and John Ray, Jr., runs the real risk of being mistaken for another fiction, when at most he resembles those gentlemen only figuratively. But the annotator exists; he is a veteran and a grandfather, a teacher and taxpayer, and has not been invented by Vladimir Nabokov.

Contents

Introduction

I. NABOKOV'S PUPPET SHOW

I have tried my best to show the workings of the book, at least some of its workings. Its charm, humour and pathos can only be appreciated by direct reading. But for enlightenment of those who felt baffled by its habit of metamorphosis, or merely disgusted at finding something incompatible with the idea of a "nice book" in the discovery of a book's being an utterly new one, I should like to point out that *The Prismatic Bezel* can be thoroughly enjoyed once it is understood that the heroes of the book are what can be loosely called "methods of composition." It is as if a painter said: look, here I'm going to show you not the painting of a landscape, but the painting of different ways of painting a certain landscape, and I trust their harmonious fusion will disclose the landscape as I intend you to see it.

VLADIMIR NABOKOV, *The Real Life of Sebastian Knight*[1]

Vladimir Vladimirovich Nabokov was born on April 23, 1899, in St. Petersburg, Russia. The rich and aristocratic Nabokovs were not the "White Russian" stock figures of Western liberal demonology—all monocles, Fabergé snuffboxes, and reactionary opinions—but rather a family with a long tradition of high culture and public service. Nabokov's grandfather

---

[1] New York, 1941, p. 93. Henceforth, page references will be placed in parentheses in the text, and pertain to the Vintage editions of Nabokov's novels, interviews, and autobiography, and to the hardcover editions of his other work.

was Minister of Justice under two tsars and implemented the court reforms, while Nabokov's father was a distinguished jurist, a foe of anti-Semitism, a prolific journalist and scholar, a leader of the opposition party (the Kadets), and a member of the first parliament (Duma). In 1919 he took his family into exile, co-editing a liberal émigré daily in Berlin until his death in 1922 (at age fifty-two), at a political meeting, where he was shot while trying to shield the speaker from two monarchist assassins. Young Nabokov went to Trinity College, Cambridge, in 1922 taking an honors degree in Slavic and Romance Languages. For the next eighteen years he lived in Germany and France, writing prolifically in Russian. The spectral émigré communities of Europe were not large enough to sustain a writer, and Nabokov supported himself through translations, public readings of his works, lessons in English and tennis, and, fittingly, the first Russian crossword puzzles, which he composed for a daily émigré paper. In 1940 he and his wife and son moved to the United States, and Nabokov began to write in English. The frequently made comparison with Joseph Conrad denies Nabokov his signal achievement; for the Polish-born author was thirty when he started to write in English, and, unlike the middle-aged Nabokov, he had not written anything in his native language, let alone nine novels.[1]

In America, Nabokov lectured on Russian literature at Wellesley (1941–1948) and Cornell (1948–1958), where his Masterpieces of European Fiction course proved immensely popular. While at Wellesley he also worked on Lepidoptera in the Museum of Comparative Zoology at Harvard. Nabokov's several books in English had meanwhile earned him the quiet respect of discerning readers, but *Lolita* was the first to attract wide attention. Its best-sellerdom and film sale in 1958 enabled Nabokov to resign his teaching position and devote himself to his writing in Montreux, Switzerland, where he took up residence in 1960. When the first edition of *The Annotated Lolita* went to press, he was working on a new novel *(Transparent Things)* and a history of the butterfly in Western art, and planning for the future publication of several works, including his Cornell lectures, his screenplay of *Lolita* (only parts of which were used in Stanley Kubrick's 1962 film), and a selection of his Russian poems, translated by Nabokov and about to be published, together with his chess problems, as *Poems and Problems.*

Lolita had made Lolita famous, rather than Nabokov. Although praised by influential critics, *Lolita* was treated as a kind of miracle of spontaneous

---

[1]Brian Boyd's *Vladimir Nabokov: The Russian Years* (Princeton, 1990), the first volume in an anticipated two-volume biography, is recommended.

generation, for Nabokov's *oeuvre* was like an iceberg, the massive body of his Russian novels, stories, plays, and poems remaining untranslated and out of sight, lurking beneath the visible peaks of *Lolita* and *Pnin* (1957). But in those eleven years since Putnam's had published *Lolita*, twenty-one Nabokov titles had appeared, including six works translated from the Russian, three out-of-print novels, two collections of stories, *Pale Fire* (1962), the monumental four-volume translation of Pushkin's *Eugene Onegin* (1964), *Speak, Memory: An Autobiography Revisited* (1966)—a considerably revised and expanded version of the memoir first issued in 1951 as *Conclusive Evidence*—and *Ada* (1969), his fifteenth novel, whose publication celebrated his seventieth birthday. The publication of *Mary* (1926) and *Glory* (1931), then being Englished by, respectively, Michael Glenny and Nabokov's son, Dmitri, would complete the translation of his Russian novels.

This extraordinary outburst of Nabokoviana highlights the resolute spirit of the man who published his masterpieces, *Lolita* and *Pale Fire*, at the ages of fifty-six and sixty-three, respectively. Nabokov had endured the exigencies of being an émigré writer when the Western world seemed interested only in his inferior Soviet contemporaries, and emerged not only as a major Russian writer but as the most important living American novelist. No doubt some academic pigeonholers still worried about Nabokov's nationality and where to "place" him, but John Updike had solved this synthetic problem when he described Nabokov as "the best writer of English prose at present holding American citizenship."[1] Not since Henry James, an émigré in his own right, had an American citizen created so formidable a corpus of work.

Nabokov's pronounced antipathy to Freud and the novel of society continued to alienate some critics during his lifetime, but there was a reason for the delay in achieving his proper status more basic than the unavailability of his early books or his failure to conform to some accepted school or *Zeitgeist* pattern: readers trained on the tenets of formalist criticism simply did not know what to make of works which resist the search for ordered mythic and symbolic "levels of meaning" and depart completely from post-Jamesian requisites for the "realistic" or "impressionistic" novel— that a fiction be the impersonal product of a pure aesthetic impulse, a self-contained illusion of reality rendered from a consistently held point of view and through a central intelligence from which all authorial comment

[1] John Updike, "Grandmaster Nabokov," *New Republic*, CLI (September 26, 1964), 15. Reprinted in Updike's *Assorted Prose* (New York, 1965).

has been exorcised. Quite the opposite happens in Nabokov's fiction: his art must be seen as artifice, even when its verisimilitude is most convincing and compelling, as in *Lolita;* and the fantastic, a-realistic, and involuted forms toward which even his earliest fictions evolve make it clear that Nabokov had always gone his own way, and it was not the way of the novel's Great Tradition according to F.R. Leavis. But Nabokov's eminence signaled a radical shift in opinions about the novel and the novelist's ethical responsibilities. A future historian of the novel may one day claim that it was Nabokov, more than any of his contemporaries, who kept alive an exhausted art form not only by demonstrating new possibilities for it but by reminding us, through his example, of the variegated aesthetic resources of his great forebears, such as Sterne and the Joyce who was a parodist rather than a symbolist.

In addition to its qualities as a memoir, *Speak, Memory* serves, along with Chapter Five in *Gogol* (1944), as the ideal introduction to Nabokov's art, for some of the most lucid criticism of Nabokov is found in his own books. His most overtly parodic novels spiral in upon themselves and provide their own commentary; sections of *The Gift* (1937–1938) and *The Real Life of Sebastian Knight* (1941) limpidly describe the narrative strategies of later novels. Nabokov's preoccupations are perhaps best projected by bringing together the opening and closing sentences of *Speak, Memory:* "The cradle rocks above an abyss, and common sense tells us that our existence is but a brief crack of light between two eternities of darkness." At the end of the book he describes how he and his wife first perceived, through the stratagems thrown up to confound the eye, the ocean liner waiting to take them and their son to America: "It was most satisfying to make out among the jumbled angles of roofs and walls, a splendid ship's funnel, showing from behind the clothesline as something in a scrambled picture—Find What the Sailor Has Hidden—that the finder cannot unsee once it has been seen." *The Eye* (1930) is well titled; the apprehension of "reality" (a word that Nabokov says must always have quotes around it) is first of all a miracle of vision, and our existence is a sequence of attempts to unscramble the "pictures" glimpsed in that "brief crack of light." Both art and nature are to Nabokov "a game of intricate enchantment and deception," and the process of reading and rereading his novels is a game of perception, like those E. H. Gombrich writes about in *Art and Illusion*—everything is *there*, in sight (no symbols lurking in murky depths), but one must penetrate the *trompe-l'oeil*, which eventually reveals something totally different from what one had expected. This is how Nabokov seems to envision the game of life and the effect of his novels: each time a "scrambled picture" has been discerned "the finder cannot unsee" it; consciousness has been expanded or created.

The word "game" commonly denotes frivolity and an escape from the exigencies of the world, but Nabokov confronts the void by virtue of his play-concept. His "game of worlds" (to quote John Shade in *Pale Fire*) proceeds within the terrifyingly immutable limits defined by the "two eternities of darkness" and is a search for order—for "some kind / Of correlated pattern in the game"—which demands the full consciousness of its players. The author and the reader are the "players," and when in *Speak, Memory* Nabokov describes the composition of chess problems he is also telescoping his fictional practices. If one responds to the author's "false scents" and "specious lines of play," best effected by parody, and believes, say, that Humbert's confession is "sincere" and that he exorcises his guilt, or that the narrator of *Pnin* is really perplexed by Pnin's animosity toward him, or that a Nabokov book is an illusion of a reality proceeding under the natural laws of our world—then one not only has lost the game to the author but most likely is not faring too well in the "game of worlds," one's own unscrambling of pictures.

Speak, Memory rehearses the major themes of Nabokov's fiction: the confrontation of death; the withstanding of exile; the nature of the creative process; the search for complete consciousness and the "free world of timelessness." In the first chapter he writes, "I have journeyed back in thought—with thought hopelessly tapering off as I went—to remote regions where I groped for some secret outlet only to discover that the prison of time is spherical and without exits." Nabokov's protagonists live in claustrophobic, cell-like rooms; and Humbert, Cincinnatus in *Invitation to a Beheading* (1936), and Krug in *Bend Sinister* (1947) are all indeed imprisoned. The struggle to escape from this spherical prison (Krug is Russian for "circle") assumes many forms throughout Nabokov; and his own desperate and sometimes ludicrous attempts, as described in *Speak, Memory*, are variously parodied in the poltergeist machinations of *The Eye*, in Hazel Shade's involvement with "a domestic ghost" and her spirit-writing in the haunted barn in *Pale Fire*, and in "The Vane Sisters" (in *Tyrants Destroyed* [1975]), where an acrostic in the final paragraph reveals that two vivid images from the story's opening paragraphs were dictated by the dead Vane sisters.

Although *Speak, Memory* clearly illuminates the self-parodic content of Nabokov's fiction, no one has fully recognized the aesthetic implications of these transmutations or the extent to which Nabokov consciously projected his own life in his fiction. To be sure, this is dangerous talk, easily misunderstood. Of course Nabokov did not write the kind of thinly disguised transcription of personal experience which too often passes for fiction. But it is crucial to an understanding of his art to realize how often his novels are improvisations on an autobiographic theme, and in *Speak, Memory* Nabokov good-naturedly anticipates his critics: "The future specialist in such dull literary lore as auto-plagiarism will like to collate a protagonist's experience in my novel *The Gift* with the original event." Further on he comments on his habit of bestowing "treasured items" from his past on his characters. But it is more than mere "items" that Nabokov has transmogrified in the "artificial world" of his novels, as a dull specialist discovers by comparing Chapters Eleven and Thirteen of *Speak, Memory* with *The Gift*, or, since it is Nabokov's overriding subject, by comparing the attitudes toward exile expressed in *Speak, Memory* with the treatment it is given in his fiction. The reader of his memoir learns that Nabokov's great-grandfather explored and mapped Nova Zembla (where Nabokov's River is named after him), and in *Pale Fire* Kinbote believes himself to be the exiled king of Zembla. His is both a fantastic vision of Nabokov's opulent past as entertained by a madman and the vision of a poet's irreparable loss, expressed otherwise by Nabokov in 1945: "Beyond the seas where I have lost a sceptre, / I hear the neighing of my dappled nouns" ("An Evening of Russian Poetry"). Nabokov's avatars do not grieve for "lost banknotes." Their circumstances, though exacerbated by adversity, are not exclusive to the émigré. Exile is a correlative for all human loss, and Nabokov records with infinite tenderness the constrictions the heart must suffer; even in his most parodic novels, such as *Lolita*, he makes audible through all the playfulness a cry of pain. "Pity," says John Shade, "is the password." Nabokov's are emotional and spiritual exiles, turned back upon themselves, trapped by their obsessive memories and desires in a solipsistic "prison of mirrors" where they cannot distinguish the glass from themselves (to use another prison trope, drawn from the story "The Assistant Producer" [1943], in *Nabokov's Dozen* [1958]).

The transcendence of solipsism is a central concern in Nabokov. He recommends no escape, and there is an unmistakable moral resonance in his treatment of the theme: it is only at the outset of *Lolita* that Humbert can say that he had Lolita "safely solipsized." The coldly unromantic scrutiny which his exiles endure is often overlooked by critics. In *Pnin* the gentle, addlepated professor is seen in a new light in the final chapter, when the narrator assumes control and makes it clear that he is inheriting Pnin's job but not, he would hope, his existence. John Shade asks us to pity "the exile, the old man / Dying in a motel," and we do; but in the Commentary,

Kinbote says that a "king who sinks his identity in the mirror of exile is guilty of [a regicide]." "The past [is] the past," Lolita tells Humbert toward the end of that novel (p. 272), when he asks her to relive what had always been inexorably lost. As a book about the spell exerted by the past, *Lolita* is Nabokov's own parodic answer to his previous book, the first edition of *Speak, Memory*. Mnemosyne is now seen as a black muse, nostalgia as a grotesque cul-de-sac. *Lolita* is the last book one would offer as "autobiographical," but even in its totally created form it connects with the deepest reaches of Nabokov's soul. Like the poet Fyodor in *The Gift*, Nabokov could say that while he keeps everything "on the very brink of parody . . . there must be on the other hand an abyss of seriousness, and I must make my way along this narrow ridge between my own truth and a caricature of it" (p. 200).

An autobiographic theme submitted to the imagination thus takes on a new life: frozen in art, halted in space, now timeless, it can be lived with. When the clownish Gradus assassinates John Shade by mistake, in a novel published forty years after Nabokov's father was similarly murdered, one may remember the butterfly which the seven-year-old Nabokov caught and then lost, but which was "finally overtaken and captured, after a forty-year race, on an immigrant dandelion . . . near Boulder" (*Speak, Memory*, p. 120). One recognizes how art makes life possible for Nabokov, and why he calls *Invitation to a Beheading* a "violin in a void." His art records a constant process of becoming—the evolution of the artist's self through artistic creation—and the cycle of insect metamorphosis is Nabokov's controlling metaphor for the process, provided by a lifetime of biological investigations which established in his mind "links between butterflies and the central problems of nature." Significantly, a butterfly or moth will often appear at the end of a Nabokov novel, when the artistic "cycle" of that book is complete.

Speak, Memory only reinforces what is suggested by Nabokov's visibly active participation in the life of his fiction, as in *Invitation to a Beheading* when Cincinnatus strains to look out of his barred window and sees on the prison wall the telling, half-erased inscription, "You cannot see anything. I tried it too" (p. 29), written in the neat, recognizable hand of the "prison director"—that is, the author—whose intrusions involute the book and deny it any reality except that of "book." The word "involution" may trouble some readers, but one has only to extend the dictionary definition. An involuted work turns in upon itself, is self-referential, conscious of its status as a fiction, and *"allégorique de lui-même"*—allegorical of itself, to use Mallarmé's description of one of his own poems. An ideally involuted sentence would simply read, "I am a sentence," and John Barth's short stories "Title," "Life-Story," and "Menelaiad" (in *Lost in the Funhouse,* 1968) come as close to this dubious ideal as any fiction possibly can. The components of "Title," for example, sustain a miraculous discussion among themselves, sometimes even addressing the author: "Once upon a time you were satisfied with incidental felicities and niceties of technique."

Characters in involuted works often recognize that their authenticity is more than suspect. In Raymond Queneau's *Les Enfants du Limon* (1938), Chambernac is a lycée headmaster who has been collecting material for a monumental work on "literary madmen," *L'Encyclopédie des sciences inexactes.* By the last chapter he has abandoned hope of getting it published, but he then is approached in a café by *"un type"* (Queneau, as it turns out, who identifies himself by name) and offers to turn the manuscript over for use in a novel Queneau is writing, one of whose characters is a headmaster, and so forth. A similar infinite regress exists in Chapter Four of Lewis Carroll's *Through the Looking-Glass* (1872), the creator's (and Creator's) role now played by the sleeping Red King. When Alice moves to waken the King, Tweedledee stops her:

"He's dreaming now," said Tweedledee: "and what do you think he's dreaming about?"

Alice said, "Nobody can guess that."

"Why, about *you!*" Tweedledee exclaimed, clapping his hands triumphantly. "And if he left off dreaming about you, where do you suppose you'd be?"

"Where I am now, of course," said Alice.

"Not you!" Tweedledee retorted contemptuously. "You'd be nowhere. Why you're only a sort of thing in his dream!"

"If that there King was to wake," added Tweedledum, "you'd go out—bang!—just like a candle!"

"I shouldn't!" Alice exclaimed indignantly. "Besides, if *I'm* only a sort of thing in his dream, what are *you,* I should like to know?"

"Ditto," said Tweedledum.

"Ditto, ditto!" cried Tweedledee.

He shouted this so loud that Alice couldn't help saying "Hush! You'll be waking him, I'm afraid, if you make so much noise."

"Well, it's no use *your* talking about waking him," said Tweedledum, "when you're only one of the things in his dream. You know very well you're not real."

"I *am* real!" said Alice, and began to cry.

A similar discussion occurs in Samuel Beckett's *Endgame* (1957). "What is there to keep me here?" asks Clov. "The dialogue," answers Hamm. More like the Tweedles than Alice are the three aging characters in Queneau's *Le Chiendent* (1933). Having survived the long destructive Franco-Etruscan war, by the final pages they are ready for anything. When the queen is complimented, she says, "It wasn't I who said that. . . . It's in the book." Asked "What book?" she replies, "Well, this one. The one we're in now, which repeats what we say as we say it and which follows us and tells about us, a genuine blotter which has been stuck on our lives."[1] They then discuss the novel of which they are a part and agree to try to annihilate time and begin all over again. They go back to Paris, back in time. The last two sentences of the book are the first two sentences.

Although the philosophical implications are somewhat less interesting, the most patent examples of involution are found in comic books, comic strips, and animated cartoons. The creatures in cartoons used to be brought to life before one's eyes: first, the *tabula rasa* of an empty screen, which is then seen to be a drawing board, over which the artist's brush sweeps, a few strokes creating the characters, who only then begin to move. Or the convention of the magical ink bottle, framing the action fore and aft. The characters are sucked back into the bottle at the end, just as they had spilled out of it at the start. These devices describe the process of *Le Chiendent*, where one sees a silhouette from the first page fleshed-out more and more as the novel progresses, or Alain Robbe-Grillet's *Dans le labyrinthe* (*In the Labyrinth*, 1959), where in the stillness of his room the narrator contemplates several objects, including a steel engraving, which is then "animated," a fiction spinning out of it. "We create ourselves in time," says one of the characters at the end of *Le Chiendent*, "and the old book snatches us up right away with its funny little scrawl [handwriting]."[2]

In involuted works, characters readily communicate with their creators, though the relationship is not always ideal. One may recall an early *Bugs Bunny* animated cartoon (c. 1943) in which there is a wild running battle between the rabbit and the artist, whose visible hand alternately wields an eraser and a drawing pencil, terrible weapons which at one moment remove the rabbit's feet so that he cannot escape, and at another give him a duck's bill so that he cannot talk back, not unlike the lot of the characters in *Invitation to a Beheading*, who are taken apart, rearranged, and reassem-

[1]Raymond Queneau, *Le Chiendent* (Paris, 1933), p. 294. The above translations are mine—A.A.
[2]*Ibid.*

bled at will. But characters are not always as uncomplaining as Cincinnatus. In the next-to-last box of a 1936 daily strip, Chester Gould pictured his hero trapped horribly in a mine shaft, its entrance blocked by a huge boulder. The balloon above Dick Tracy's stricken face said, "Gould, you have gone too far." The concluding box was to have shown a kindly eraser-bearing hand, descending to remove the boulder; but *The Chicago Tribune*'s Captain Patterson, no doubt a disciple of Dr. Leavis, thought Gould had indeed gone too far, and rejected that strip. Considerably less desperate is Shakespeare's direct address to Joyce in Nighttown: "How my Oldfellow chokit his Thursdaymomun," that moment being Bloomsday, this book, and Joyce's stab at greatness.[1] "O Jamesy let me up out of this," pleads Molly Bloom to Joyce,[2] and in the hallucinated Nighttown section the shade of Virag says, "That suits your book, eh?" When in acknowledgment his throat is made to twitch, Virag says, "Slapbang! There he goes again."[3] Virga is quite right to speak directly to Joyce, because the phantasmagoria of Nighttown are the artist's. Virag accepts the truth that he is another's creation, and does so far more gracefully than Alice or poor Krug in Nabokov's *Bend Sinister*, who is instantaneously rendered insane by the realization. On the other hand, this perception steels Cincinnatus, who is waiting to be beheaded, since it means he cannot really "die."

Nabokov's remarks on Gogol help to underscore this analogical definition of involution. "All reality is a mask," he writes (p. 148), and Nabokov's narratives are masques, stagings of his own inventions rather than re-creations of the naturalistic world. But, since the latter is what most readers expect and demand of fiction, many still do not understand what Nabokov is doing. They are not accustomed to "the allusions to something else behind the crudely painted screens" (p. 142), where the "real plots behind the obvious ones are taking place." There are thus at least two "plots" in all of Nabokov's fiction: the characters in the book, and the consciousness of the creator above it—the "real plot" which is visible in the "gaps" and "holes" in the narrative. These are best described in Chapter Fourteen of *Speak, Memory*, when Nabokov discusses "the loneliest and most arrogant" of the émigré writers, Sirin (his émigré pen name): "The real life of his books flowed in his figures of speech, which one critic [Nabokov?] has compared to windows giving upon a contiguous world . . . a rolling corollary, the shadow of a train of thought." The contiguous world is the

---

[1] James Joyce, *Ulysses* (New York, 1961), p. 567.
[2] *Ibid.*, p. 769.
[3] *Ibid.*, p. 513.

mind and spirit of the author, whose identity, psychic survival, and "manifold awareness" are ultimately both the subject and the product of the book. In whatever way they are opened, the "windows" always reveal that "the poet (sitting in a lawn chair, at Ithaca, N.Y.) is the nucleus" of everything.

From its birth in *King, Queen, Knave* (1928), to its full maturation in *Invitation to a Beheading* (1936), to its apotheosis in the "involute abode" of *Pale Fire* (1962), the strategy of involution has determined the structure and meaning of Nabokov's novels. One must always be aware of the imprint of "that master thumb," to quote Frank Lane in *Pale Fire*, "that made the whole involuted boggling thing one beautiful straight line," for only then does it become possible to see how the "obvious plots" spiral in and out of the "real" ones. Although other writers have created involuted works, Nabokov's self-consciousness is supreme; and the range and scale of his effects, his mastery and control, make him unique. Not including autobiographic themes, the involution is achieved in seven basic ways, all closely interrelated, but schematized here for the sake of clarity:

PARODY. As willful artifice, parody provides the main basis for Nabokov's involution, the "springboard for leaping into the highest region of serious emotion," as the narrator of *The Real Life of Sebastian Knight* says of Knight's novels. Because its referents are either other works of art or itself, parody denies the possibility of a naturalistic fiction. Only an authorial sensibility can be responsible for the texture of parody and self-parody; it is a verbal vaudeville, a series of literary impersonations performed by the author. When Nabokov calls a character or even a window shade "a parody," it is in the sense that his creation can possess no other "reality." In a novel such as *Lolita*, which has the fewest "gaps" of any novel after *Despair* (1934), and is seemingly his most realistic, the involution is sustained by the parody and the verbal patterning.

COINCIDENCE. *Speak, Memory* is filled with examples of Nabokov's love of coincidence. Because they are drawn from his life, these incidents demonstrate how Nabokov's imagination responds to coincidence, using it in his fiction to trace the pattern of a life's design, to achieve shattering interpenetrations of space and time. "Some law of logic," writes Nabokov in *Ada* (1969), "should fix the number of coincidences, in a given domain, after which they cease to be coincidences, and form, instead, the living organism of a new truth" (p. 361). Humbert goes to live in Charlotte Haze's house at 342 Lawn Street; he and Lolita inaugurate their illicit cross-country tour in room 342 of The Enchanted Hunters hotel; and in one year on the road they register in 342 motels and hotels. Given the endless mathematical combinations possible, the numbers seem to signal his entrapment by McFate (to use Humbert's personification). But they are also a patent, purposeful contrivance, like the copy of the 1946 *Who's Who in the Limelight* which Humbert would have us believe he found in the prison library on the night previous to his writing the chapter we are now reading. The yearbook not only prefigures the novel's action, but under Lolita's mock-entry of "Dolores Quine" we are informed that she "Made New York debut in 1904 in *Never Talk to Strangers*"—and in the closing paragraph of the novel, almost three hundred pages later, Humbert advises the absent Lolita, "Do not talk to strangers," a detail that exhibits extraordinary narrative control for an allegedly unrevised, first-draft confessional, written during fifty-six chaotic days. Clearly, "Someone else is in the know," to quote a mysterious voice that interrupts the narration of *Bend Sinister*. It is no coincidence when coincidences extend from book to book. Creations from one "reality" continually turn up in another: the imaginary writer Pierre Delalande is quoted in *The Gift* and provides the epigraph for *Invitation to a Beheading;* Pnin and another character mention "Vladimir Vladimirovich" and dismiss his entomology as an affectation; "Hurricane Lolita" is mentioned in *Pale Fire*, and Pnin is glimpsed in the university library. Mythic or prosaic names and certain fatidic numbers recur with slight variation in many books, carrying no burden of meaning whatsoever other than the fact that someone beyond the work is repeating them, that they are all part of one master pattern.

PATTERNING. Nabokov's passion for chess, language, and lepidoptery has inspired the most elaborately involuted patterning in his work. Like the games implemented by parody, the puns, anagrams, and spoonerisms all reveal the controlling hand of the logomachist; thematically, they are appropriate to the prison of mirrors. Chess motifs are woven into several narratives, and even in *The Defense* (1930), a most naturalistically ordered early novel, the chess patterning points to forces beyond Grandmaster Luzhin's comprehension ("Thus toward the end of Chapter Four an unexpected move is made by me in a corner of the board," writes Nabokov in the Foreword). The importance of the lepidopteral motif has already been suggested, and it spirals freely in and out of Nabokov's books: in *Invitation to a Beheading*, just before he is scheduled to die, Cincinnatus gently strokes a giant moth; in *Pale Fire* a butterfly alights on John Shade's arm the minute before he is killed; in *Ada*, when Van Veen arrives for a duel, a transparent white butterfly floats past and Van is certain he has only minutes to live; in the final chapter of *Speak, Memory* Nabokov recalls seeing in Paris, just before the war, a live butterfly being promenaded on a leash of thread; at the end of *Bend Sinister* the masked author intrudes and suspends the "obvious plot," and as the book closes he looks out of the window and decides, as a moth twangs against the screen, that it is "A good night for mothing." *Bend Sinister* was published in 1947, and it is no accident that in Nabokov's next novel (1955) Humbert meets Lolita back in 1947, thus sustaining the author's "fictive time" without interruption and enabling him to pursue that moth's lovely diurnal Double through the substratum of the new novel in the most fantastic butterfly hunt of his career. "I confess I do not believe in time," writes Nabokov at the end of the ecstatic butterfly chapter in *Speak, Memory*. "I like to fold my magic carpet, after use, in such a way as to superimpose one part of the pattern upon another."

ALLUSION. Humbert's references to art and literature are consistent with his mind and education, but in other novels and stories such cultural allusions point to Nabokov. In *Invitation to a Beheading*, for instance, Cincinnatus, imprisoned by the State, cannot identify the bits and pieces from Baudelaire's poem *L'Invitation au voyage* (1855) that echo in his consciousness, inform the novel's garden motif, and sound in the book's title. They're emanating from the mind of his maker, who especially cherishes Baudelaire's utopia of the spirit as he writes the book at hand in Nazi Germany, in 1934—Hitler's voice echoing across nocturnal Berlin from rooftop loudspeakers at the very moment that Nabokov defies dystopia by writing the farcical, and finally joyous, *Invitation to a Beheading*.

THE WORK-WITHIN-THE-WORK. The self-referential devices in Nabokov, mirrors inserted into the books at oblique angles, are clearly of the author's making, since no point of view within the fiction could possibly account for the dizzying inversions they create. The course of *The Real Life of Sebastian Knight*, which purports to be an attempt to gather material for a proposed literary biography of the narrator's half brother but ends by obfuscating even the narrator's identity, is refracted in Knight's first novel,

The Prismatic Bezel, "a rollicking parody of the setting of a detective tale." Like an Elizabethan play-within-a-play, Quilty's play within *Lolita, The Enchanted Hunters,* offers a "message" that can be taken seriously as a commentary on the progression of the entire novel; and *Who's Who in the Limelight* and the class list of the Ramsdale school magically mirror the action taking place around them, including, by implication, the writing of *Lolita.* The a-novelistic components of *Pale Fire*—Foreword, Poem, Commentary, and Index—create a mirror-lined labyrinth of involuted cross-references, a closed cosmos that can only be of the author's making, rather than the product of an "unreliable" narrator. *Pale Fire* realizes the ultimate possibilities of works within works, already present twenty-four years earlier in the literary biography that serves as the fourth chapter of *The Gift.* If it is disturbing to discover that the characters in *The Gift* are also the readers of Chapter Four, this is because it suggests, as Jorge Luis Borges says of the play within *Hamlet,* "that if the characters of a fictional work can be readers or spectators, we, its readers or spectators, can be fictitious."[1]

THE STAGING OF THE NOVEL. Nabokov wrote the screenplay of *Lolita,* as well as nine plays in Russian, including one of his several forays into science fiction, *The Waltz Invention* (1938), which was translated and published in 1966. It is not surprising, then, that his novels should proliferate with "theatrical" effects that serve his play-spirit exceedingly well. Problems of identity can be investigated poetically by trying on and discarding a series of masks. And, too, what better way to demonstrate that everything in a book is being manipulated than by seeming to *stage* it? In *Invitation to a Beheading,* "A Summer thunderstorm, simply yet tastefully staged, was performed outside." When Quilty finally dies in *Lolita,* Humbert says, "This was the end of the ingenious play staged for me by Quilty"; and in *Laughter in the Dark* (1932), "The stage manager whom Rex had in view was an elusive, double, triple, self-reflecting Proteus." Nabokov the protean impersonator is always a masked presence in his fiction: as impresario, scenarist, director, warden, dictator, landlord, and even as bit player (the seventh Hunter in Quilty's play within *Lolita,* a Young Poet who insists that everything in the play is his invention)—to name only a

---

[1] J. L. Borges, "Partial Magic in the *Quixote,*" in *Labyrinths* (New York, 1964), p. 196. For an excellent analysis of involuted or self-reflexive fiction, see Robert Alter, *Partial Magic: The Novel as a Self-Conscious Genre* (Berkeley and Los Angeles, 1975).

few of the disguises he has donned as a secret agent who moves among his own creations like Prospero in *The Tempest*. Shakespeare is very much an ancestor (he and Nabokov even share a birthday), and the creaking, splintering noise made by the stage setting as it disintegrates at the end of *Invitation to a Beheading* is Nabokov's version of the snapping of Prospero's wand and his speech to the players ("Our revels now are ended. These our actors, / As I foretold you, were all spirits and / Are melted into air, into thin air"; IV.i).

AUTHORIAL VOICE. All the involuted effects spiral into the authorial voice—"an anthropomorphic deity impersonated by me," Nabokov calls it—which intrudes continually in all of his novels after *Despair*, most strikingly at the end, when it completely takes over the book (*Lolita* is a notable exception). It is this "deity" who is responsible for everything: who begins a narrative only to stop and retell the passage differently; halts a scene to "rerun" it on the chapter's screen, or turns a reversed lantern slide around to project it properly; intrudes to give stage directions, to compliment or exhort the actors, to have a prop moved; who reveals that the characters have "cotton-padded bodies" and are the author's puppets, that all is a fiction; and who widens the "gaps" and "holes" in the narrative until it breaks apart at "the end," when the vectors are removed, the cast of characters is dismissed, and even the fiction fades away—at most leaving behind an imprint on space in the form of a précis of "an old-fashioned [stage] melodrama" the "deity" may one day write, and which describes (as in the case of *Pale Fire*) the book we've just finished reading.

The vertiginous conclusion of a Nabokov novel calls for a complicated response which many readers, after a lifetime of realistic novels, are incapable of making. Children, however, are aware of other possibilities, as their art reveals. My own children, then three and six years old, reminded me of this one summer when they inadvertently demonstrated that, unless they change, they will be among Nabokov's ideal readers. One afternoon my wife and I built them a puppet theater. After propping the theater on the top edge of the living room couch, I crouched down behind it and began manipulating the two hand puppets in the stage above me. The couch and the theater's scenery provided good cover, enabling me to peer over the edge and watch the children immediately become engrossed in the show, and then virtually mesmerized by my improvised little story that ended with a patient father spanking an impossible child. But the puppeteer, carried away by his story's violent climax, knocked over the entire theater, which clattered onto the floor, collapsing into a heap of cardboard, wood, and cloth—leaving me crouched, peeking out at the room, my head now visible over the couch's rim, my puppeted hands, with their naked wrists, poised in mid-air. For several moments my children remained in their open-mouthed trance, still in the story, staring at the space where the theater had been, not seeing me at all. Then they did the kind of double take that a comedian might take a lifetime to perfect, and began to laugh uncontrollably, in a way I had never seen before—and not so much at my clumsiness, which was nothing new, but rather at those moments of total involvement in a nonexistent world, and at what its collapse implied to them about the authenticity of the larger world, and about their daily efforts to order it and their own fabricated illusions. They were laughing, too, over their sense of what the vigorous performance had meant to me; but they saw how easily they could be tricked and their trust belied, and the shrillness of their laughter finally suggested that they recognized the frightening implications of what had happened, and that only laughter could steel them in their new awareness.

When in 1966 I visited Vladimir Nabokov for four days in Montreux, to interview him for *Wisconsin Studies* and in regard to my critical study of his work, I told him about this incident, and how for me it defined literary involution and the response which he hoped to elicit from his readers at "the end" of a novel. "Exactly, exactly," he said as I finished. "You must put that in your book."

In parodying the reader's complete, self-indulgent identification with a character, which in its mindlessness limits consciousness, Nabokov is able to create the detachment necessary for a multiform, spatial view of his novels. The "two plots" in Nabokov's puppet show are thus made plainly visible as a description of the total design of his work, which reveals that in novel after novel his characters try to escape from Nabokov's prison of mirrors, struggling toward a self-awareness that only their creator has achieved by creating them—an involuted process which connects Nabokov's art with his life, and clearly indicates that the author himself is not in this prison. He is its creator, and is *above* it, in control of a book, as in one of those Saul Steinberg drawings (greatly admired by Nabokov) that show a man drawing the very line that gives him "life," in the fullest sense. But the process of Nabokov's involution, the global perspective which he invites us to share with him, is best described in *Speak, Memory*, Chapter Fifteen, when he comments on the disinclination of

. . . physicists to discuss the outside of the inside, the whereabouts of the curvature; for every dimension presupposes a medium within which it can act, and if, in the spiral unwinding of things, space warps into something akin to time, and time, in its turn, warps into something akin to thought, then, surely, another dimension follows—a special Space maybe, not the old one, we trust, unless spirals become vicious circles again.

The ultimate detachment of an "outside" view of a novel inspires our wonder and enlarges our potential for compassion because, "in the spiral unwinding of things," such compassion is extended to include the mind of an author whose deeply humanistic art affirms man's ability to confront and order chaos.

2. BACKGROUNDS OF *LOLITA*

Critics too often treat Nabokov's twelfth novel as a special case quite apart from the rest of his work, when actually it concerns, profoundly and in their darkest and yet most comic form, the themes which have always occupied him. Although *Lolita* may still be a shocking novel to several aging non-readers, the exact circumstances of its troubled publication and reception may not be familiar to younger readers. After four American publishers refused it, Madame Ergaz, of Bureau Littéraire Clairouin, Paris, submitted *Lolita* to Maurice Girodias' Olympia Press in Paris.[1] Although Girodias must be credited with the publication of several estimable if controversial works by writers such as Jean Genet, his main fare was the infamous Travellers Companion series, the green-backed books once so familiar and dear to the eagle-eyed inspectors of the U.S. Customs. But Nabokov did not know this and, because of one of Girodias' previous publishing ventures, the "Editions du Chêne," thought him a publisher of "fine editions." Cast in two volumes and bound in the requisite green, *Lolita* was quietly published in Paris in September 1955.

Because it seemed to confirm the judgment of those nervous American publishers, the Girodias imprimatur became one more obstacle for *Lolita* to overcome, though the problem of its alleged pornography indeed seems

[1] See Nabokov's article "*Lolita* and Mr. Girodias," *Evergreen Review*, XI (February 1967), 37–41.

remote today, and was definitively settled in France not long after its publication. I was Nabokov's student at Cornell in 1953–1954, at a time when most undergraduates did not know he was a writer. Drafted into the army a year later, I was sent overseas to France. On my first pass to Paris I naturally went browsing in a Left Bank bookstore. An array of Olympia Press books, daringly displayed above the counter, seemed most inviting —and there, between copies of *Until She Screams* and *The Sexual Life of Robinson Crusoe*, I found *Lolita*. Although I thought I knew all of Nabokov's works in English (and had searched through out-of-print stores to buy each of them), this title was new to me; and its context and format were more than surprising, even if in those innocent pre–Grove Press days the semi-literate wags on fraternity row had dubbed Nabokov's Literature 311–312 lecture course "Dirty Lit" because of such readings as *Ulysses* and *Madame Bovary* (the keenest campus wits invariably dropped the *B* when mentioning the latter). I brought *Lolita* back to my base, which was situated out in the woods. Passes were hard to get and new Olympia titles were always in demand in the barracks. The appearance of a new girl in town thus caused a minor clamor. "Hey, lemme read your dirty book, man!" insisted "Stockade Clyde" Carr, who had justly earned his sobriquet, and to whose request I acceded at once. "Read it aloud, Stockade," someone called, and skipping the Foreword, Stockade Clyde began to make his remedial way through the opening paragraph. " 'Lo . . . lita, light . . . of my life, fire of my . . . loins. My sin, my soul . . . Lo-lee-ta: The . . . tip of the . . . tongue . . . taking . . . a trip . . .'—*Damn!*" yelled Stockade, throwing the book against the wall. "*It's God-damn Litachure!!*" Thus the Instant Pornography Test, known in psychological-testing circles as the "IPT." Although infallible, it has never to my knowledge been used in any court case.

At a double remove from the usual review media, *Lolita* went generally unnoticed during its first six months. But in the winter of 1956 Graham Greene in England recommended *Lolita* as one of the best books of 1955, incurring the immediate wrath of a columnist in the *Sunday Express*, which moved Greene to respond in *The Spectator*. Under the heading of "Albion" (suggesting a quaint tempest in an old teapot), *The New York Times Book Review* of February 26, 1956, alluded briefly to this exchange, calling *Lolita* "a long French novel" and not mentioning Nabokov by name. Two weeks later, noting "that our mention of it created a flurry of mail," *The Times* devoted two-thirds of a column to the subject, quoting Greene at some length. Thus began the underground existence of *Lolita*, which became public in the summer of 1957 when the *Anchor Review* in New York devoted 112 of its pages to Nabokov. Included were an excellent introduction by F. W. Dupee, a long excerpt from the novel, and Nabokov's Afterword, "On a Book Entitled *Lolita.*" When Putnam's brought out the American edition in 1958 they were able to dignify their full-page advertisements with an array of statements by respectable and even distinguished literary names, though *Lolita*'s fast climb to the top of the best-seller list was not exclusively the result of their endorsements or the novel's artistry. "Hurricane / Lolita swept from Florida to Maine" (to quote John Shade in *Pale Fire* [l. 680]), also creating storms in England and Italy, and in France, where it was banned on three separate occasions. Although it never ran afoul of the law in this country, there were predictably some outraged protests, including an editorial in *The New Republic;* but, since these at best belong to social rather than literary history, they need not be detailed here, with one exception. Orville Prescott's review in the daily *New York Times* of August 18, 1958, has a charm that should be preserved: " 'Lolita,' then, is undeniably news in the world of books. Unfortunately, it is bad news. There are two equally serious reasons why it isn't worth any adult reader's attention. The first is that it is dull, dull, dull in a pretentious, florid and archly fatuous fashion. The second is that it is repulsive."[1] Prescott's remarks complement those of an anonymous reviewer in *The Southern Quarterly Review* (January 1852), who found an earlier, somewhat different treatment of the quest theme no less intolerable: "The book is sad stuff, dull and dreary, or ridiculous. Mr. Melville's Quakers are the wretchedest dolts and drivellers, and his Mad Captain, who pursues his personal revenges against the fish who has taken off his leg, at the expense of ship, crew and owners, is a monstrous bore. . . ."

Not surprisingly, Humbert Humbert's obsession has moved commentators to search for equivalent situations in Nabokov's earlier work, and they have not been disappointed. In *The Gift* (written between 1935 and 1937), some manuscript pages on the desk of the young poet Fyodor move a character to say:

> "Ah, if only I had a tick or two, what a novel I'd whip off! From real
> life. Imagine this kind of thing: an old dog—but still in his prime,

---

[1]In a manner similar to Joyce's, Nabokov four years later paid his respects to Prescott, though not by name, by having the assassin Gradus carefully read *The New York Times:* "A hack reviewer of new books for tourists, reviewing his own tour through Norway, said that the fjords were too famous to need (his) description, and that all Scandinavians loved flowers" (*Pale Fire,* p. 275). This was actually culled from the newspaper.

fiery, thirsting for happiness—gets to know a widow, and she has a daughter, still quite a little girl—you know what I mean—when nothing is formed yet but already she has a way of walking that drives you out of your mind—A slip of a girl, very fair, pale, with blue under the eyes—and of course she doesn't even look at the old goat. What to do? Well, not long thinking, he ups and marries the widow. Okay. They settle down the three of them. Here you can go on indefinitely—the temptation, the eternal torment, the itch, the mad hopes. And the upshot—a miscalculation. Time flies, he gets older, she blossoms out—and not a sausage. Just walks by and scorches you with a look of contempt. Eh? D'you feel here a kind of Dostoevskian tragedy? That story, you see, happened to a great friend of mine, once upon a time in fairyland when Old King Cole was a merry old soul. . . ." (pp. 176–77)

Although the passage[1] seems to anticipate *Lolita* ("It's queer, I seem to remember my future works," says Fyodor [p. 194]), *Laughter in the Dark* (1932) is mentioned most often in this regard, since Albert Albinus sacrifices everything, including his eyesight, for a girl, and loses her to a hack artist, Axel Rex. "Yes," agrees Nabokov, "some affinities between Rex and Quilty exist, as they do between Margot and Lo. Actually, of course, Margot was a common young whore, not an unfortunate little Lolita [and, technically speaking, no nymphet at all—A.A.]. Anyway I do not think that those recurrent sexual oddities and morbidities are of much interest or importance. My Lolita has been compared to Emmie in *Invitation*, to Mariette in *Bend Sinister*, and even Colette in *Speak, Memory*. . . ." *(Wisconsin Studies* interview, see Bibliography). Nabokov is justly impatient with those who hunt for Ur-Lolitas, for a preoccupation with specific "sexual morbidities" obscures the more general context in which these oddities should be seen, and his Afterword offers an urgent corrective. The reader of this Introduction should turn to that Afterword, "On a Book Entitled *Lolita,*" but not before placing a bookmark here, one substantial enough to remind him to return—a brightly colored piece of clothing would be suitable (the Notes to pages 315–316 are particularly recommended). Now please turn to page 311. ☞

Having just completed the Afterword, the serious reader is familiar with Nabokov's account of *Lolita*'s origins. That "initial shiver of inspiration"

[1]Also pointed out by Andrew Field, in *Nabokov: His Life in Art* (Boston, 1967), p. 325, and Carl R. Proffer, *Keys to Lolita* (Bloomington, 1968), p. 3.

resulted in a novella, *the Enchanter (Volshebnik)*, written in Russian in 1939 and published posthumously in a translation by Dmitri Nabokov.[1] In the first of the two passages below, the "enchanter" sees the young girl for the first time in what might be the Tuileries Gardens:

> A violet-clad girl of twelve (he never erred), was treading rapidly and firmly on skates that did not roll but crunched on the gravel as she raised and lowered them with little Japanese steps and approached his bench through the variable luck of the sunlight. Subsequently (for as long as the sequel lasted), it seemed to him that right away, at that very moment, he had appreciated all of her from tip to toe: the liveliness of her russet curls (recently trimmed); the radiance of her large, slightly vacuous eyes, somehow suggesting translucent gooseberries; her merry, warm complexion; her pink mouth, slightly open so that two large front teeth barely rested on the protuberance of the lower lip; the summery tint of her bare arms with the sleek little foxlike hairs running along the forearms; the indistinct tenderness of her still narrow but already not quite flat chest; the way the folds of her skirt moved; their succinctness and soft concavities; the slenderness and glow of her uncaring legs; the coarse straps of the skates.
>
> She stopped in front of his garrulous neighbor, who turned away to rummage in something lying to her right, then produced a slice of bread with a piece of chocolate on it and handed it to the girl. The latter, chewing rapidly, used her free hand to undo the straps and with them the entire weighty mass of the steel soles and solid wheels. Then, returning to earth among the rest of us, she stood up with an instantaneous sensation of heavenly barefootedness, not immediately recognizable as the feel of skateless shoes, and went off, now hesitantly, now with easy strides, until finally (probably because she had done with the bread) she took off at full tilt, swinging her liberated arms, flashing in and out of sight, mingling with a kindred play of light beneath the violet-and-green trees. (pp. 26–28)

The "enchanter" makes no sexual advances until the final pages, soon after the girl's mother has died:

> "Is this where I'm going to sleep?" the girl asked indifferently, and when, struggling with the shutters, squeezing tight their eyelike chinks, he replied affirmatively, she took a look at the cap she was holding and limply tossed it on the wide bed.

[1]New York, 1986.

"There we are," said he after the old man had dragged in their suitcases and left, and there remained in the room only the pounding of his heart and the distant throbbing of the night. "There, now it's time for bed."

Reeling with sleepiness, she bumped into the corner of an armchair, at which point he, simultaneously sitting down in it, took her by the hip and drew her close. She straightened, stretching up like an angel, for a split second tensed every muscle, took another half step, and softly descended onto his lap. "My sweetheart, my poor little girl," he spoke in a kind of general mist of pity, tenderness, and desire, as he observed her drowsiness, her wooziness, her diminishing smile, palpating her through the dark dress, feeling, through the thin wool, the band of the orphan's garter on her bare skin, thinking how defenseless, abandoned, warm she was, reveling in the animate weight of her legs as they slithered apart and then, with the faintest corporeal rustle, recrossed at a slightly higher level. She slowly entwined a somnolent arm, in its snug little sleeve, around his nape, engulfing him with the chestnut fragrance of her soft hair. . . . (pp. 81–82)

But the narrator fails as both enchanter and lover, and soon afterwards dies in a manner which Nabokov will transfer to Charlotte Haze. While the scene clearly foreshadows the first night at The Enchanted Hunters hotel, its straightforward action and solemn tone are quite different, and it compresses into a few paragraphs what will later occupy almost two chapters (pp. 119–133). The narrator's enjoyment of the girl's "animate weight" suggests the considerably more combustible lap scene in *Lolita* (pp. 58–61), perhaps the most erotic interlude in the novel—but it only *suggests* it. Aside from such echoes, little beyond the basic idea of the tale subsists in *Lolita;* and the telling is quite literally a world apart.

The Enchanter went unpublished not because of the forbidding subject matter, but rather, says Nabokov, because the girl possessed little "semblance of reality."[1] In 1949, after moving from Wellesley to Cornell, he became involved in a "new treatment of the theme, this time in English."

[1] One should remember that the story would have been read by a Russian émigré audience, notes Andrew Field, who quoted the same two passages in his own translation, *op. cit.*, pp. 328–329. Strongly erotic (as opposed to pornographic) themes have been used "seriously" far more frequently by Russian writers than by their English and American counterparts. Field points to Dostoevsky (the suppressed chapter of *The Possessed*), Leskov, Sologub, Kuzmin, Rozanov, Kuprin, Pilnyak, Babel, and Bunin (*ibid.*, p. 332).

Although *Lolita* "developed slowly," taking five years to complete, Nabokov had everything in mind quite early. As was customary with him, however, he did not write it in exact chronological sequence. Humbert's confessional diary was composed at the outset of this "new treatment," followed by Humbert and Lolita's first journey westward, and the climactic scene in which Quilty is killed ("His death had to be clear in my mind in order to control his earlier appearances," says Nabokov). Nabokov next filled in the gaps of Humbert's early life, and then proceeded ahead with the rest of the action, more or less in chronological order. Humbert's final interview with Lolita was composed at the very end, in 1954, followed only by John Ray's Foreword.

Especially new in this treatment was the shift from the third person to the first person, which created—obviously—the always formidable narrative problem of having an obsessed and even mad character meaningfully relate his own experience, a problem compounded in this specific instance by the understandable element of self-justification which his perversion would necessarily occasion, and by the fact that Humbert is a dying man. One wonders whether Thomas Mann would have been able to make *Death in Venice* an allegory about art and the artist if Aschenbach had been its narrator. While many of Nabokov's other principal characters are victims (Luzhin, Pnin, Albinus), none of them tells his own story; and it is only Humbert who is both victim and victimizer, thus making him unique among Nabokov's first-person narrators (discounting Hermann, the mad and murderous narrator of *Despair,* who is too patently criminal to qualify properly as victim). By having Humbert tell the tale, Nabokov created for himself the kind of challenge best described in Chapter Fourteen of *Speak, Memory* when, in a passage written concurrently with the early stages of *Lolita,* he compares the composition of a chess problem to "the writing of one of those incredible novels where the author, in a fit of lucid madness, has set himself certain unique rules that he observes, certain nightmare obstacles that he surmounts, with the zest of a deity building a live world from the most unlikely ingredients—rocks, and carbon, and blind throbbings."[1]

In addition to such obstacles, the novel also developed slowly because of an abundance of materials as unfamiliar as they were unlikely. It had been difficult enough to "invent Russia and Western Europe," let alone

[1]And speaking specifically of the writing of *Lolita,* he says, "She was like the composition of a beautiful puzzle—its composition and its solution at the same time, since one is a mirror view of the other, depending on the way you look."

America, and at the age of fifty Nabokov now had to set about obtaining "such local ingredients as would allow me to inject a modicum of average 'reality' (one of the few words which mean nothing without quotes) into the brew of individual fancy. "What was most difficult," he later told an interviewer, "was putting myself . . . I am a normal man, you see."[1] Research was thus called for, and in scholarly fashion Nabokov followed newspaper stories involving pedophilia (incorporating some into the novel), read case studies, and, like Margaret Mead coming home to roost, even did research in the field: "I travelled in school buses to listen to the talk of schoolgirls. I went to school on the pretext of placing our daughter. We have no daughter. For Lolita, I took one arm of a little girl who used to come to see Dmitri [his son], one kneecap of another,"[2] and thus a nymphet was born.

Perspicacious "research" aside, it was a remarkable imaginative feat for a European émigré to have re-created America so brilliantly, and in so doing to have become an American writer. Of course, those critics and readers who marvel at Nabokov's accomplishment may not realize that he physically knows America better than most of them. As he says in *Speak, Memory*, his adventures as a "lepist" carried him through two hundred motel rooms in forty-six states, that is, along all the roads traveled by Humbert and Lolita. Yet of all of Nabokov's novels, *Lolita* is the most unlikely one for him to have written, given his background and the rarefied nature of his art and avocations. "It was hardly foreseeable," writes Anthony Burgess, "that so exquisite and scholarly an artist should become America's greatest literary glory, but now it seems wholly just and inevitable."[3] It was even less foreseeable that Nabokov would realize better than any contemporary the hopes expressed by Constance Rourke in *American Humor* (1931) for a literature that would achieve an instinctive alliance between native materials and old world traditions, though the literal alliance in *Lolita* is perhaps more intimate than even Miss Rourke might have wished. But to have known Nabokov at all personally was first to be impressed by his intense and immense curiosity, his uninhibited and imaginative response to everything around him. To paraphrase Henry James's famous definition of the artist, Nabokov was truly a man on whom nothing

---

[1] Penelope Gilliatt, "Nabokov," *Vogue*, No. 2170 (December 1966), p. 280.
[2] *Ibid.*
[3] Anthony Burgess, "Poet and Pedant," *The Spectator*, March 24, 1967, p. 336. Reprinted in *Urgent Copy* (New York, 1969).

was lost—except that in Nabokov's instance it was *true*, whereas James and many American literary intellectuals after him have been so self-conscious in their mandarin "seriousness" and consequently so narrow in the range of their responses that they have often overlooked the sometimes extraordinarily uncommon qualities of the commonplace.

Nabokov's responsiveness is characterized for me by the last evening of my first visit to Montreux in September 1966. During my two hours of conversation with the Nabokovs in their suite after dinner, Nabokov tried to imagine what the history of painting might have been like if photography had been invented in the Middle Ages; spoke about science fiction; asked me if I had noticed what was happening in *Li'l Abner* and then compared it, in learned fashion, with an analogous episode of a dozen years back; noted that a deodorant stick had been found among the many days' siege provisions which the Texas sniper had with him on the tower; discoursed on a monstrous howler in the translation of Bely's *St. Petersburg;* showed me a beautifully illustrated book on hummingbirds, and then discussed the birdlife of Lake Geneva; talked admiringly and often wittily of the work of Borges, Updike, Salinger, Genet, Andrei Sinyavsky ("Abram Tertz"), Burgess, and Graham Greene, always making precise critical discriminations; recalled his experiences in Hollywood while working on the screenplay of *Lolita,* and his having met Marilyn Monroe at a party ("A delightful actress. Delightful," he said. "Which is your favorite Monroe film?"); talked of the Soviet writers he admired, summarizing their stratagems for survival; and defined for me exactly what kind of beetle Kafka's Gregor Samsa was in *The Metamorphosis* ("It was a domed beetle, a scarab beetle with wing-sheaths, and neither Gregor nor his maker realized that when the room was being made by the maid, and the window was open, he could have flown out and escaped and joined the other happy dung beetles rolling the dung balls on rural paths"). And did I know how a dung beetle laid its eggs? Since I did not, Nabokov rose and imitated the process, bending his head toward his waist as he walked slowly across the room, making a dung-rolling motion with his hands until his head was buried in them and the eggs were laid. When Lenny Bruce's name somehow came up, both Nabokov and his wife commented on how sad they had been to hear of Bruce's death; he had been a favorite of theirs. But they disagreed about where it was that they had last seen Bruce; Mrs. Nabokov thought it had been on Jack Paar's television show, while her husband—the scientist, linguist, and author of fifteen novels, who has written and published in three languages, and whose vast erudition is most clearly evidenced by the four-volume translation of Pushkin's *Eugene Onegin*, with its two volumes of annotations and one-hundred-page "Note on Prosody"—held out for the Ed Sullivan show.

Not only was nothing lost on Nabokov, but, like the title character in Borges's story "Funes the Memorious," he seemed to remember everything. At dinner the first evening of my 1966 visit, we reminisced about Cornell and his courses there, which were extraordinary and thoroughly Nabokovian, even in the smallest ways (witness the "bonus system" employed in examinations, allowing students two extra points per effort whenever they could garnish an answer with a substantial and accurate quotation ["a gem"] drawn from the text in question). Skeptically enough, I asked Nabokov if he remembered my wife, Nina, who had taken his Literature 312 course in 1955, and I mentioned that she had received a grade of 96. Indeed he did, since he had always asked to meet the students who performed well, and he described her accurately (seeing her in person in 1968, he remembered where she had sat in the lecture hall). On the night of my departure I asked Nabokov to inscribe my Olympia Press first edition of *Lolita*. With great rapidity he not only signed and dated it but added two elegant drawings of recently discovered butterflies, one identified as "*Flammea palida*" ("Pale Fire") and, below it, a considerably smaller species, labeled "Bonus bonus."[1] Delighted but in part mystified, I inquired, "Why 'Bonus bonus'?" Wrinkling his brow and peering over his eyeglasses, a parody of a professor, Nabokov replied in a mock-stentorian voice, "Now your wife has 100!" After four days and some twelve hours of conversation, and within an instant of my seemingly unrelated request, my prideful but passing comment had come leaping out of storage. So too was Nabokov's memory able to draw on a lifetime of reading—a lifetime in the most literal sense.[2]

When asked what he had read as a boy, Nabokov replied: "Between the ages of ten and fifteen in St. Petersburg, I must have read more fiction and poetry—English, Russian, and French—than in any other five-year period of my life. I relished especially the works of Wells, Poe, Browning, Keats, Flaubert, Verlaine, Rimbaud, Chekhov, Tolstoy, and Alexander Blok. On another level, my heroes were the Scarlet Pimpernel, Phileas Fogg, and Sherlock Holmes. In other words, I was a perfectly normal trilingual child in a family with a large library. At a later period, in Cam-

---

[1] A photograph of these drawings appears in *Time*, May 23, 1969, p. 83.

[2] For several reminiscences of Nabokov, see *Vladimir Nabokov: A Tribute*, edited by Peter Quennell (New York, 1980).

bridge, England, between the ages of twenty and twenty-three, my favorites were Housman, Rupert Brooke, Joyce, Proust, and Pushkin. Of these top favorites, several—Poe, Verlaine, Jules Verne, Emmuska Orczy, Conan Doyle, and Rupert Brooke—have faded away, have lost the glamour and thrill they held for me. The others remain intact and by now are probably beyond change as far as I am concerned" (*Playboy* interview, 1964, collected in *Strong Opinions* [1973]). The Notes to this edition will demonstrate that Nabokov has managed to invoke in his fiction the most distant of enthusiasms: a detective story read in early youth, a line from Verlaine, a tennis match seen at Wimbledon forty years before. All are clear in his mind, and, recorded in *Lolita,* memory negates time.

When queried about Nabokov, friends and former colleagues at Cornell invariably comment on the seemingly paradoxical manner in which the encyclopedic Nabokov mind could be enthralled by the trivial as well as the serious. One professor, at least twenty years Nabokov's junior and an instructor when he was there, remembers how Nabokov once asked him if he had ever watched a certain soap opera on television. Soap operas are of course ultimately comic if not fantastic in the way they characterize life as an uninterrupted series of crises and disasters; but missing the point altogether, suspecting a deadly leg-pull and supposing that with either answer he would lose (one making him a fool, the other a snob), Nabokov's young colleague had been reduced to a fit of wordless throat-clearing. Recalling it ten years later, he seemed disarmed all over again. On easier terms with Nabokov was Professor M. H. Abrams, who warmly recalls how Nabokov came into a living room where a faculty child was absorbed in a television western. Immediately engaged by the program, Nabokov was soon quaking with laughter over the furiously climactic fight scene. Just such idle moments, if not literally this one, inform the hilarious burlesque of the comparable "obligatory scene" in *Lolita,* the tussle of Humbert and Quilty which leaves them "panting as the cowman and the sheepman never do after their battle" (p. 299).

Even though he had academic tenure at Cornell, the Nabokovs never owned a house, and instead always rented, moving from year to year, a mobility he bestowed on refugee Humbert. "The main reason [for never settling anywhere permanently], the background reason, is, I suppose, that nothing short of a replica of my childhood surroundings would have satisfied me," says Nabokov. "I would never manage to match my memories correctly—so why trouble with hopeless approximations? Then there are some special considerations: for instance, the question of impetus, the habit of impetus. I propelled myself out of Russia so vigorously, with such indignant force, that I have been rolling on and on ever since. True, I have lived to become that appetizing thing, a 'full professor,' but at heart I have always remained a lean 'visiting lecturer.' The few times I said to myself anywhere: 'Now that's a nice spot for a permanent home,' I would immediately hear in my mind the thunder of an avalanche carrying away the hundreds of far places which I would destroy by the very act of settling in one particular nook of the earth. And finally, I don't much care for furniture, for tables and chairs and lamps and rugs and things—perhaps because in my opulent childhood I was taught to regard with amused contempt any too-earnest attachment to material wealth, which is why I felt no regret and no bitterness when the Revolution abolished that wealth" (*Playboy* interview).

Professor Morris Bishop, Nabokov's best friend at Cornell, who was responsible for his shift from Wellesley to Ithaca, recalled visiting the Nabokovs just after they had moved into the appallingly vulgar and garish home of an absent professor of Agriculture. "I couldn't have lived in a place like that," said Bishop, "but it delighted him. He seemed to relish every awful detail." Although Bishop didn't realize it then, Nabokov was learning about Charlotte Haze by renting her house, so to speak, by reading her books and living with her pictures and "wooden thingamabob[s] of commercial Mexican origin." These annual moves, however dismal their circumstances, constituted a field trip enabling entomologist Nabokov to study the natural habitat of Humbert's prey. Bishop also remembered that Nabokov read the New York *Daily News* for its crime stories,[1] and, for an even more concentrated dose of bizarrerie, Father Divine's newspaper, *New Day*—all of which should recall James Joyce, with whom Nabokov has so much else in common. Joyce regularly read *The Police Gazette*, the shoddy magazine *Titbits* (as does Bloom), and all the Dublin newspapers; attended burlesque shows, knew by heart most of the vulgar and comically obscene songs of the day, and was almost as familiar with the work of the execrable lady lending-library novelists of the *fin de siècle* as he was with the classics; and when he was living in Trieste and Paris and writing *Ulysses*, relied on his Aunt Josephine to keep him supplied with the necessary sub-literary materials. Of course, Joyce's art depends far more than Nabokov's on the vast residue of erudition and trivia which Joyce's insatiable and equally encyclopedic mind was able to store.

Nabokov is very selective, whereas Joyce collected almost at random

---

[1] In *Pale Fire*, Charles Kinbote spies John Shade seated in his car, "reading a tabloid newspaper which I had thought no poet would deign to touch" (p. 22).

and then ordered in art the flotsam and jetsam of everyday life. That Nabokov does not equal the older writer in this respect surely points to a conscious choice on Nabokov's part, as his Cornell lectures on *Ulysses* suggest.[1] In singling out the flaws in what is to him the greatest novel of the century, Nabokov stressed the "needless obscurities baffling to the less-than-brilliant reader," such as "local idiosyncrasies" and "untraceable references." Yet Nabokov also practiced the art of assemblage, incorporating in the rich textures of *Bend Sinister, Lolita, Pale Fire,* and *Ada* a most "Joycean" profusion of rags, tags, and oddments, both high and low, culled from books or drawn from "real life." Whatever the respective scales of their efforts in this direction, Nabokov and Joyce are (with Queneau and Borges) among the few modern fiction writers who have made aesthetic capital out of their learning. Both include in their novels the compendious stuff one associates with the bedside library, the great literary anatomies such as Burton's *Anatomy of Melancholy* or Dr. Johnson's *Dictionary,* or those unclassifiable masterpieces such as *Moby-Dick, Tristram Shandy,* and *Gargantua and Pantagruel,* in which the writer makes fictive use of all kinds of learning, and exercises the anatomist's penchant for collage effected out of verbal trash and bizarre juxtapositions—for the digression, the catalogue, the puzzle, pun, and parody, the gratuitous bit of lore included for the pleasure it can evoke, and for the quirky detail that does not contribute to the book's verisimilar design but nevertheless communicates vividly a sense of what it was like to be alive at a given moment in time. A hostile review of Nabokov's *Eugene Onegin* offered as typical of the Commentary's absurdities its mention of the fact that France exported to Russia some 150,000 bottles of champagne per annum; but the detail happens to telescope brilliantly the Francophilia of early nineteenth-century Russia and is an excellent example of the anatomist's imaginative absorption of significant trivia and a justification of his methods. M. H. Abrams recalls how early one Monday morning he met Nabokov entering the Cornell Library, staggering beneath a run of *The Edinburgh Review,* which Nabokov had pored over all weekend in Pushkin's behalf. "Marvelous

---

[1] The course in question is Literature 311–312, "Masterpieces of European Fiction," MWF, 12 (first term: Jane Austen's *Mansfield Park,* Gogol's *Dead Souls,* Dickens's *Bleak House,* Flaubert's *Madame Bovary,* and Tolstoy's *The Death of Ivan Ilyich;* second term: Tolstoy's *Anna Karenina,* Stevenson's *Dr. Jekyll and Mr. Hyde,* Gogol's *The Overcoat,* Kafka's *The Metamorphosis,* Proust's *Swann's Way,* and *Ulysses,* in that order). The quotations are from the annotator's class notes of 1953–1954 and can be supplemented now by Nabokov's *Lectures on Literature* (New York, 1980).

ads!" explained Nabokov, "simply marvelous!" It was this spirit that enabled Nabokov to create in the two volumes of *Onegin* Commentary a marvelous literary anatomy in the tradition of Johnson, Sterne, and Joyce —an insomniac's delight, a monumental, wildly inclusive, yet somehow elegantly ordered ragbag of humane discourse, in its own right a transcendent work of imagination.

Nabokov was making expressive use of unlikely bits and pieces in his novels as early as *The Defense* (1930), as when Luzhin's means of suicide is suggested by a movie still, lying on The Veritas film company's display table, showing "a white-faced man with his lifeless features and big American glasses, hanging by his hands from the ledge of a skyscraper—just about to fall off into the abyss"—a famous scene from Harold Lloyd's 1923 silent film, *Safety Last.* Although present throughout his work of the thirties, and culminating logically in *The Gift,* his last novel in Russian, Nabokov's penchant for literary anatomy was not fully realized until after he had been exposed to the polar extremes of American culture and American university libraries. Thus the richly variegated but sometimes crowded texture of *Bend Sinister* (1947), Nabokov's first truly "American" novel,[1] looks forward to *Lolita,* his next novel. *Bend Sinister*'s literary pastiche is by turns broad and hermetic. Titles by Remarque and Sholokov are combined to produce *All Quiet on the Don,* and Chapter Twelve offers this "famous American poem":

> A curious sight—these bashful bears,
> These timid warrior whalemen
>
> And now the time of tide has come;
> The ship casts off her cables
>
> It is not shown on any map;
> True places never are
>
> This lovely light, it lights not me;
> All loveliness is anguish—

No poem at all, it is formed, said Nabokov, by random "iambic incidents culled from the prose of *Moby-Dick.*" Such effects receive their fullest orchestration in *Lolita,* as the Notes to this volume will suggest.

---

[1]Although published in New York in 1941, a year after Nabokov's emigration, *The Real Life of Sebastian Knight* was in fact written in Paris in 1938 (in English). Students of chronology should also note that *Lolita* precedes *Pnin* (1957). The date of the former's American publication (1958) has proved misleading.

If the *Onegin* Commentary (1964) is the culmination, then *Lolita* represents the apogee in fiction of Nabokov's proclivities as anatomist and as such is a further reminder that the novel extends and develops themes and methods present in his work all along. Ranging from Dante to *Dick Tracy*, the allusions, puns, parodies, and pastiches in *Lolita* are controlled with a mastery unequaled by any writer since Joyce (who died in 1941). Readers should not be disarmed by the presence of so many kinds of "real" materials in a novel by a writer who believes so passionately in the primacy of the imagination; as Kinbote says in *Pale Fire*, " 'reality' is neither the subject nor the object of true art which creates its own special reality having nothing to do with the average 'reality' perceived by the communal eye" (p. 130).

By his example, Nabokov reminded younger American writers of the fictional nature of reality. When Terry Southern in *The Magic Christian* (1960) lampoons the myth of American masculinity and its attendant deification of the athlete by having his multimillionaire trickster, Guy Grand, fix the heavyweight championship fight so that the boxers grotesquely enact in the ring a prancing and mincing charade of homosexuality, causing considerable psychic injury to the audience, his art, such as it is, is quite late in imitating life. A famous athlete of the twenties was well-known as an invert, and Humbert mentions him twice, never by his real name, though he does call him "Ned Litam" (p. 232)—a simple anagram of "Ma Tilden"—which turns out to be one of the actual pseudonyms chosen by Tilden himself, under which he wrote stories and articles. Like the literary anatomists who have preceded him, Nabokov knows that what is so extraordinary about "reality" is that too often even the blackest of imaginations could not have invented it, and by taking advantage of this fact in *Lolita* he has, along with Nathanael West, defined with absolute authority the inevitable mode, the dominant dark tonalities—if not the contents—of the American comic novel.

Although Humbert clearly delights in many of the absurdities around him, the anatomist's characteristic vivacity is gone from the pages which concern Charlotte Haze, and not only because she is repugnant to Humbert in terms of the "plot" but rather because to Nabokov she is the definitive artsy-craftsy suburban lady—the culture-vulture, that travesty of Woman, Love, and Sexuality. In short, she is the essence of American *poshlust*, to use the "one pitiless [Russian] word" which, writes Nabokov in *Gogol*, is able to express "the idea of a certain widespread defect for which the other three European languages I happen to know possess no special term." *Poshlust:* "the sound of the 'o' is as big as the plop of an elephant falling into a muddy pond and as round as the bosom of a bathing beauty on a German picture postcard" (p. 63). More precisely, it "is not only the obviously trashy but also the falsely important, the falsely beautiful, the falsely clever, the falsely attractive" (p. 70).[1] It is an amalgam of pretentiousness and philistine vulgarity. In the spirit of Mark Twain describing the contents of the Grangerford household in *Huckleberry Finn* (earlier American *poshlust*), Humbert eviscerates the muddlecrass (to wax Joycean) world of Charlotte and her friends, reminding us that Humbert's long view of America is not an altogether genial one.

In the course of showing us our landscape in all its natural beauty, Humber satirizes American songs, ads, movies, magazines, brand names, tourist attractions, summer camps, Dude Ranches, hotels, and motels, as well as the Good-Housekeeping Syndrome (*Your Home Is You* is one of Charlotte Haze's essential volumes) and the cant of progressive educationist and child-guidance pontificators.[2] Nabokov offers us a grotesque parody of a "good relationship," for Humbert and Lo are "pals" with a vengeance; *Know Your Own Daughter* is one of the books which Humbert consults (the title exists). Yet Humbert's terrible demands notwithstanding, she is as insensitive as children are to their parents; sexuality aside, she demands anxious parental placation in a too typically American way, and, since it is Lolita "to whom ads were dedicated: the ideal consumer, the subject and object of every foul poster" (p. 148), she affords Nabokov an ideal opportunity to comment on the Teen and Sub-teen Tyranny. "Tristram in Movie-love," remarks Humbert, and Nabokov has responded to those various travesties of behavior which too many Americans recognize as tenable examples of reality. A gloss on this aspect of *Lolita* is provided by "Ode to a Model," a poem which Nabokov published the same year as the Olympia Press edition of *Lolita* (1955):

> I have followed you, model,
> in magazine ads through all seasons,
> from dead leaf on the sod
> to red leaf on the breeze,

[1] For Nabokov's later description of *poshlost* (as he then transliterated it), see his *Paris Review* interview, collected in *Strong Opinions* (New York, 1973), pp. 100–101.

[2] Satirized too is the romantic myth of the child, extending from Wordsworth to Salinger. "The McCoo girl?" responds Lolita kindly. "Ginny McCoo? Oh, she's a fright. And mean. And lame. Nearly died of polio." If the origin of modern sentimentality about the child's innocence can be dated at 1760, with the publication of *Mother Goose's Melodies,* then surely *Lolita* marks its death in 1955.

from your lily-white armpit
to the tip of your butterfly eyelash,
charming and pitiful,
silly and stylish.

Or in kneesocks and tartan
standing there like some fabulous symbol,
parted feet pointed outward
—pedal form of akimbo.

On a lawn, in a parody
of Spring and its cherry-tree,
near a vase and a parapet,
virgin practising archery.

Ballerina, black-masked,
near a parapet of alabaster.
"Can one"—somebody asked—
"rhyme 'star' and 'disaster'?"

Can one picture a blackbird
as the negative of a small firebird?
Can a record, run backward,
turn 'repaid' into 'diaper'?

Can one marry a model?
Kill your past, make you real, raise a family,
by removing you bodily
from back numbers of Sham?

Although Nabokov called attention to the elements of parody in his
work, he repeatedly denied the relevance of satire. One can understand
why he said, "I have neither the intent nor the temperament of a moral or
social satirist" (*Playboy* interview), for he eschewed the overtly moral
stance of the satirist who offers "to mend the world." Humbert's "satires"
are too often effected with an almost loving care. Lolita is indeed an "ideal
consumer," but she herself is consumed, pitifully, and there is, as Nabokov
said, "a queer, tender charm about that mythical nymphet." Moreover,
since Humbert's desperate tourism is undertaken in order to distract and
amuse Lolita and to outdistance his enemies, real and imagined, the "invented" American landscape also serves a quite functional thematic purpose in helping to dramatize Humbert's total and terrible isolation.
Humbert and Lolita, each is captive of the other, imprisoned together in

a succession of bedrooms and cars, but so distant from one another that they can share nothing of what they see—making Humbert seem as alone during the first trip West as he will be on the second, when she has left him and the car is an empty cell.

Nabokov's denials notwithstanding, many of Humbert's observations of American morals and mores *are* satiric, the product of his maker's moral sensibility; but the novel's greatness does not depend on the profundity or extent of its "satire," which is over-emphasized by readers who fail to recognize the extent of the parody, its full implications, or the operative distinction made by Nabokov: "satire is a lesson, parody is a game." Like Joyce, Nabokov shows how parody may inform a high literary art, and parody figures in the design of each of his novels. *The Eye* parodies the nineteenth-century Romantic tale, such as V. F. Odoevsky's "The Briga-dier" (1844), which is narrated by a ghost who has awakened after death to view his old life with new clarity, while *Laughter in the Dark* is a mercilessly cold mocking of the convention of the love triangle; *Despair* is cast as the kind of "cheap mystery" story the narrator's banal wife reads, though it evolves into something quite different; and *The Gift* parodies the major nineteenth-century Russian writers. *Invitation to a Beheading* is cast as a mock anti-utopian novel, as though Zamiatin's *We* (1920) had been restaged by the Marx Brothers. *Pnin* masquerades as an "academic novel" and turns out to parody the possibility of a novel's having a "reliable" narrator. Pnin's departure at the end mimics Chichikov's orbital exit from *Dead Souls* (1842), just as the last paragraph of *The Gift* conceals a parody of a Pushkin stanza. The texture of Nabokov's parody is unique because, in addition to being a master parodist of literary styles, he is able to make brief references to another writer's themes or devices which are so telling in effect that Nabokov need not burlesque that writer's style. He parodies not only narrative clichés and outworn subject matter but genres and prototypes of the novel; *Ada* parodically surveys nothing less than the novel's evolution. Because Chapter Four of *The Gift* is a mock literary biography, it anticipates the themes of Nabokov's major achievements, for he is continuously parodying the search for a verifiable truth—the autobi-ography, the biography, the exegesis, the detective story—and these ge-neric "quests" will coalesce in one work, especially when the entire novel is conceptually a parody, as in *Lolita* and *Pale Fire*.

In form, *Pale Fire* is a grotesque scholarly edition, while *Lolita* is a burlesque of the confessional mode, the literary diary, the Romantic novel that chronicles the effects of a debilitating love, the *Doppelgänger* tale, and, in parts, a Duncan Hines tour of America conducted by a guide with a black imagination, a parodic case study, and, as the narrator of *The Real Life of Sebastian Knight* says of his half brother's first novel, *The Prismatic Bezel*, "It is also a wicked imitation of many other . . . literary habit[s]." Knight's procedures summarize Nabokov's:

> As often was the way with Sebastian Knight he used parody as a kind of springboard for leaping into the highest region of serious emotion. J. L. Coleman has called it "a clown developing wings, an angel mimicking a tumbler pigeon," and the metaphor seems to me very apt. Based cunningly on a parody of certain tricks of the literary trade, *The Prismatic Bezel* soars skyward. With something akin to fanatical hate Sebastian Knight was ever hunting out the things which had once been fresh and bright but which were now worn to a thread, dead things among living ones; dead things shamming life, painted and repainted, continuing to be accepted by lazy minds serenely unaware of the fraud. (p. 91)

"But all this obscure fun is, I repeat, only the author's springboard" (p. 92), says the narrator, whose tone is justifiably insistent, for although Nabokov is a virtuoso of the minor art of literary burlesque, which is at best a kind of literary criticism, he knows that the novelist who uses parody is under an obligation to engage the reader emotionally in a way that Max Beerbohm's *A Christmas Garland* (1912) does not. The description of *The Prismatic Bezel* and the remainder of Chapter Ten in *The Real Life of Sebastian Knight* indicate that Nabokov is fully aware of this necessity, and, like Knight, he has succeeded in making parody a "springboard." There is thus an important paradox implicit in Nabokov's most audacious parodies: *Lolita* makes fun of Dostoevsky's *Notes from Underground* (1864), but Humbert's pages are indeed notes from underground in their own right, and Clare Quilty is both a parody of the Double as a convention of modern fiction and a Double who formulates the horror in Humbert's life.

With the possible exception of Joyce, Nabokov is alone among modern writers in his ability to make parody and pathos converge and sometimes coincide. Joyce comes closest to this in *Ulysses* (1922), not in the coldly brilliant "Oxen of the Sun" section but in the "Cyclops" episode in Barney Kiernan's pub, which oscillates between parodic passages and a straightforward rendering of the dialogue and action; in the "Nausicäa" episode on the beach, which first projects Gerty MacDowell's point of view in a style parodying sentimental ladies' magazine fiction, and midway shifts to Bloom's non-parodic stream-of-consciousness; and in parts of the "Hades" Nighttown section, especially the closing apparition of Bloom's dead son,

Rudy. Nabokov has gone beyond Joyce in developing parody as a novelistic form, for in *Lolita* and *Pale Fire*, which are totally parodic in form and may be the finest comic novels since *Ulysses*, the parody and pathos are always congruent, rather than adjacent to one another—as though the entire "Nausicäa" or "Cyclops" episodes were cast as parody, without in any way diminishing our sense of Bloom's suffering, or that Joyce had been able to express something of the humanity of Bloom or Mrs. Purefoy in the "Oxen of the Sun" *tour de force*. Nabokov has summarized in a phrase his triumph in *Lolita* and *Pale Fire*. Just before Humbert takes Lolita into their room at The Enchanted Hunters hotel in what is to be the most crucial event in his life, Humbert comments, "Parody of a hotel corridor. Parody of silence and death" (p. 119). To paraphrase Marianne Moore's well-known line that poetry is "imaginary gardens with real toads in them," Nabokov's "poem" is a parody of death with real suffering in it. With characteristic self-awareness, Nabokov defines in *The Gift* the essence of his own art: "The spirit of parody always goes along with genuine poetry."

This spirit in Nabokov represents not merely a set of techniques but, as suggested above, an attitude toward experience, a means of discovering the nature of experience. *The Prismatic Bezel* is aptly titled: a "bezel" is the sloping edge on a cutting tool or the oblique side of a gem, and the luminous bezel of Nabokov's parody can cut in any direction, often turning in upon itself as self-parody.

To stress the satiric (rather than parodic) elements of *Lolita* above all others is as limited a response as to stop short with its sexual content. "Sex as an institution, sex as a general notion, sex as a problem, sex as a platitude —all this is something I find too tedious for words," Nabokov told an interviewer from *Playboy,* and his Cornell lectures on Joyce further indicate that he was not interested in sexual oddities for their own sake. On May 10, 1954, in his opening lecture on *Ulysses* (delivered, as it turns out, at the time he was completing *Lolita*), Nabokov said of Leopold Bloom, "Joyce intended the portrait of an ordinary person. [His] sexual deportment [is] extremely perverse . . . Bloom indulges in acts and dreams sub-normal in an evolutionary sense, affecting both individual and species. . . . In Bloom's (and Joyce's) mind, the theme of sex is mixed with theme of latrine. Supposed to be ordinary citizen: mind of ordinary citizen does not dwell where Bloom's does. Sexual affairs heap indecency upon indecency . . ." Coming from the creator of Humbert Humbert, the fervent tone and the rather old-fashioned sense of normalcy may seem unexpected. On May 28, the last class of the term and concluding lecture on Joyce, he discussed the flaws in *Ulysses*, complaining that there is an "Obnoxious, overdone preoccupation with sex organs, as illustrated in Molly's stream-of-consciousness. Perverse attitudes exhibited."[1] In spite of the transcriptions in notebookese, one gets a firm idea of Nabokov's attitude toward the explicit detailing of sexuality, and his remarks imply a good deal about his intentions in *Lolita*. The "nerves of the novel" revealed in the Afterword underscore these intentions by generalizing Humbert's passion (p. 316). That the seemingly inscrutable Nabokov would even write this essay, let alone reprint it in magazines and append it to the twenty-five translations of *Lolita*, surely suggests the dismay he must have felt to see how many readers, including some old friends, had taken the book solely on an erotic level. Those exposed "nerves" should make it clear that insofar as it has a definable subject, *Lolita* is not merely about pedophilia. As Humbert says, rather than describing the details of the seduction at The Enchanted Hunters hotel, "Anybody can imagine those elements of animality. A greater endeavor lures me on: to fix once for all the perilous magic of nymphets" (p. 134). Humbert's desires are those of a poet as well as a pervert, and not surprisingly, since they reflect, darkly, in a crooked enough mirror, the artistic desires of his creator.

Humbert's is a nightmare vision of the ineffable bliss variously sought by one Nabokov character after another. For a resonant summary phrase, one turns to *Agaspher* (1923), a verse drama written when Nabokov was twenty-four. An adaptation of the legend of the Wandering Jew, only its Prologue was published. Tormented by "dreams of earthly beauty," Nabokov's wanderer exclaims, "I shall catch you / catch you, Maria my inexpressible dream / from age to age!"[2] Near the end of another early work, the novel *King, Queen, Knave* (1928), an itinerant photographer walks down the street, ignored by the crowd, "yelling into the wind: 'The artist is coming! The divinely favored, *der gottbegnadete* artist is coming!'" — a yell that ironically refers to the novel's unrealized artist, businessman Dreyer, and anticipates and announces the arrival of such future avatars of the artist as the chessplayer Luzhin in *The Defense* (1930), the butterfly collector Pilgram in "The Aurelian" (1931), the daydreaming art dealer and critic Albert Albinus in *Laughter in the Dark* (1932), the imprisoned and doomed Cincinnatus in *Invitation to a Beheading* (1935–1936), who struggles to write, the inventor Salvator Waltz in *The Waltz Invention* (1938), and the philosopher Krug in *Bend Sinister* (1947), as well as poets *manqués* such

---

[1]From the annotator's class notes, 1953–1954.
[2]Translated and quoted by Andrew Field, *op. cit.*, p. 79.

as Humbert Humbert in *Lolita* (1955), and such genuine yet only partially fulfilled artists as Fyodor Godunov-Cherdyntsev in *The Gift* (1937–1938), Sebastian Knight in *The Real Life of Sebastian Knight* (1941), and John Shade in *Pale Fire* (1962). When perceived by the reader, the involuted design of each novel reveals that these characters all exist in a universe of fiction arrayed around the consciousness of Vladimir Nabokov, the only artist of major stature who appears in Nabokov's work.

Some readers, however, may feel that works that are in part about themselves are limited in range and significance, too special, too hermetic. But the creative process is fundamental; perhaps nothing is *more* personal by implication and hence more relevant than fictions concerning fiction; identity, after all, is a kind of artistic construct, however imperfect the created product. If the artist does indeed embody in himself and formulate in his work the fears and needs and desires of the race, then a "story" about his mastery of form, his triumph in art is but a heightened emblem of all of our own efforts to confront, order, and structure the chaos of life, and to endure, if not master, the demons within and around us. "I am thinking of aurochs and angels, the secret of durable pigments, prophetic sonnets, the refuge of art," says Humbert in the closing moments of *Lolita,* and he speaks for more than one of Nabokov's characters.

It was the major émigré poet and critic Vladislav Khodasevich who first pointed out, more than fifty years ago, that whatever their occupations may be, Nabokov's protagonists represent the artist, and that Nabokov's principal works in part concern the creative process.[1] Khodasevich died in 1939, and until the 1960s, his criticism remained untranslated. If it *had* been available earlier, Nabokov's English and American readers would have recognized his deep seriousness at a much earlier date. This is especially true of *Lolita,* where Nabokov's constant theme is masked, but not obscured, by the novel's ostensible subject, sexual perversion. But what may have been a brilliant formulation in the thirties should be evident enough by now, and not because so many other critics have said it of Nabokov, but rather because it has become a commonplace of recent criticism to note that a work of art is about itself (Wordsworth, Mallarmé, Proust, Joyce, Yeats, Queneau, Borges, Barth, Claude Mauriac, Robbe-Grillet, Picasso, Saul Steinberg, and Fellini's film *8½* —to name but a baker's dozen). What

---

[1] Vladislav Khodasevich, "On Sirin" (1937), translated by Michael H. Walker, edited by Simon Karlinsky and Robert P. Hughes, *TriQuarterly,* No. 17 (Winter 1970).

is not so clear is how Nabokov's artifice and strategies of involution reveal the "second plot" in his fiction, the "contiguous world" of the author's mind; what it has meant to that mind to have created a fictional world; and what the effect of those strategies is upon the reader, whose illicit involvement with that fiction constitutes a "third plot," and who is manipulated by Nabokov's dizzying illusionistic devices to such an extent that he too can be said to become, at certain moments, another of Vladimir Nabokov's creations.

3. THE ARTIFICE OF *LOLITA*

Although *Lolita* has received much serious attention (see this edition's selected bibliography), the criticism which it has elicited usually forces a thesis which does not and in fact cannot accommodate the total design of the novel. That intricate design, described in the Notes to this edition, makes *Lolita* one of the few supremely original novels of the century. It is difficult to imagine, say, that *Lord Jim* could have been achieved without the example of Henry James's narrative strategies, or that *The Sound and the Fury* would be the same novel if Faulkner had not read *Ulysses*. But like *The Castle, Remembrance of Things Past, Ulysses, Finnegans Wake,* and *Pale Fire, Lolita* is one of those transcendent works of the imagination which defy the neat continuum maintained so carefully by literary historians. At most, it is one of those works which create their own precursors, to use Jorge Luis Borges's winning phrase.

Because Nabokov continually parodies the conventions of "realistic" and "impressionistic" fiction, readers must accept or reject him on his own terms. Many of his novels become all but meaningless in any other terms. At the same time, however, even Nabokov's most ardent admirers must sometimes wonder about the smaller, more hermetic components of Nabokov's artifice—the multifarious puns, allusions, and butterfly references which proliferate in novels such as *Pale Fire* and *Lolita.* Are they organic? Do they coalesce to form any meaningful pattern? Humbert's wide-ranging literary allusions more than "challenge [our] scholarship," as H.H. says of Quilty's similar performance. Several of Humbert's allusions are woven so subtly into the texture of the narrative as to elude all but the most compulsive exegetes. Many allusions, however, are direct and available, and these are most frequently to nineteenth-century writers; an early Note will suggest that this is of considerable importance. But unlike the allusions, which are sometimes only a matter of fun, the patterned verbal cross-references are always fundamental, defining a dimension of the novel that has escaped critical notice.

The verbal *figurae* in *Lolita* limn the novel's involuted design and establish the basis of its artifice. As indicated in the Foreword, no total interpretation of *Lolita* will be propounded here. The following remarks on artifice and game are *not* intended to suggest that this "level" of the novel is the most important; they are offered because no one has fully recognized the magnitude of this verbal patterning, or its significance.[1] Just as Nabokov's Afterword was read in advance of the novel, so the following pages might well be reread after the annotations, many of which they anticipate.

Although *Lolita* is less dramatically anti-realistic than *Pale Fire*, in its own way it is as grandly labyrinthine and as much a work of artifice as that more ostentatiously tricky novel. This is not immediately apparent because Humbert is Nabokov's most "humanized" character since Luzhin (1930), and *Lolita* the first novel since the early thirties in which "the end" remains intact. Moreover, Nabokov said that *The Enchanter*, the 1939 story containing the central idea of *Lolita*, went unpublished *not* because of its subject matter but rather because "The little girl wasn't alive. She hardly spoke. Little by little I managed to give her some semblance of reality." It may seem anomalous for puppeteer Nabokov, creator of the sham worlds of *Invitation to a Beheading* and *Bend Sinister*, to worry this way about "reality" (with or without quotation marks); yet one extreme does not preclude the other in Nabokov, and the originality of *Lolita* derives from this very paradox. The puppet theater never collapses, but everywhere there are fissures, if not gaps, in the structure, crisscrossing in intricate patterns and visible to the discerning eye—that is, the eye trained on Nabokov fictions and thus accustomed to novelistic *trompe-l'oeil*. *Lolita* is a great novel to the same extent as Nabokov is able to have it both ways, involving the reader on the one hand in a deeply moving yet outrageously comic story, rich in verisimilitude, and on the other engaging him in a game made possible by the interlacings of verbal figurations which undermine the novel's realistic base and distance the reader from its dappled surface,

[1] I have elsewhere discussed the novel as a novel, as well as an artifice; see my article "*Lolita:* The Springboard of Parody," *Wisconsin Studies in Contemporary Literature*, VIII (Spring 1967), 204–241. Reprinted in L. S. Dembo, ed., *Nabokov: The Man and His Work* (Madison, 1967).

which then assumes the aspect of a gameboard (the figurations are detailed in the Notes).

As a lecturer, Nabokov was a considerable Thespian, able to manipulate audiences in a similar manner. His rehearsal of Gogol's death agonies remains in one's mind: how the hack doctors alternately bled him and purged him and plunged him into icy baths, Gogol so frail that his spine could be felt through his stomach, the six fat white bloodletting leeches clinging to his nose, Gogol begging to have them removed—*"Please lift them, lift them, keep them away!"*—and, sinking behind the lectern, now a tub, Nabokov for several moments *was* Gogol, shuddering and shivering, his hands held down by a husky attendant, his head thrown back in pain and terror, nostrils distended, eyes shut, his beseechments filling the large lecture hall. Even the sea of C-minuses in the back of the room could not help being moved. And then, after a pause, Nabokov would very quietly say, in a sentence taken word-for-word from his *Gogol,* "Although the scene is unpleasant and has a human appeal which I deplore, it is necessary to dwell upon it a little longer in order to bring out the curiously physical side of Gogol's genius."

A great deal has been written about "unreliable narrators," but too little about unreliable readers. Although editor John Ray, Jr., serves fair enough warning to those "old-fashioned readers who wish to follow the destinies of 'real' people beyond the 'true story,'" virtually every "move" in the "true story" of *Lolita* seems to be structured with their predictable responses in mind; and the game-element depends on such reflexive action, for it tests the reader in so many ways. By calling out "Reader! *Bruder!*" (p. 262), Humbert echoes *Au Lecteur,* the prefatory poem in *Les Fleurs du mal* ("Hypocrite reader!—My fellow man—My brother!"); and, indeed, the entire novel constitutes an ironic upending of Baudelaire and a good many other writers who would enlist the reader's full participation in the work. "I want my learned readers to participate in the scene I am about to replay," says Humbert (p. 57), but such illicit participation will find the reader in constant danger of check, or even rougher treatment: "As greater authors than I have put it: 'Let readers imagine' etc. On second thought, I may as well give those imaginations a kick in the pants" (p. 65). Humbert addresses the reader directly no less than twenty-nine times,[1] drawing him

---

[1]See pp. 4, 34, 48, 57, 65, 87, 96, 104, 129, 137, 139, 154, 157, 165, 166, 167, 184, 190, 203, 210, 216, 226, 247, 250, 253, 257, 262, 285, and 308—not to mention Humbert's several interjections to the jury (p. 132 is typical), to mankind in general ("Human

into one trap after another. In Nabokov's hands the novel thus becomes a gameboard on which, through parody, he assaults his readers' worst assumptions, pretensions, and intellectual conventions, realizing and formulating through game his version of Flaubert's dream of an *Encyclopédie des idées reçues,* a *Dictionary of Accepted Ideas.*

"Satire is a lesson, parody is a game," says Nabokov, and although the more obvious sallies in *Lolita* could be called satiric (e.g., those against Headmistress Pratt), the most telling are achieved through the games implemented by parody. By creating a surface that is rich in "psychological" clues, but which finally resists and then openly mocks the interpretations of depth psychology, Nabokov is able to dispatch any Freudians who choose to "play" in the blitzkrieg game that is the novel's first sixty-or-so pages. The traps are baited with tempting "false scents" drawn from what Nabokov in *Speak, Memory* calls the "police state of sexual myth." The synthetic incest of Humbert and Lolita seems to suggest a classical Oedipal situation, but Humbert later calls it a "parody of incest." Nabokov further implies that the story works out the "transference" theory, whereby the daughter transfers her affections to another, similar man, but not her father, thus exorcising her Oedipal tension. If Freudians have interpreted Lolita's elopement with Quilty in this way, then they stop short in the hospital scene when Humbert says of the nurse, "I suppose Mary thought comedy father Professor Humbertoldi was interfering with the romance between Dolores and her father-substitute, roly-poly Romeo" (p. 243). The boyish

---

beings, attend!" [p. 124]), and to his car ("Hi, Melmoth, thanks a lot, old fellow" [p. 307]). One waxes statistical here because H.H.'s direct address is an important part of the narrative, and important too in the way that it demonstrates a paradoxically new technique. In regard to literary forms and devices, there is almost nothing new under the sun (to paraphrase a poet); it is contexts and combinations that are continually being made new. One epoch's realism is another's surrealism. To the Elizabethan playgoer or the reader of Cervantes, the work-within-the-work was a convention; to an audience accustomed to nineteenth-century realism, it is fantastic, perplexing, and strangely affecting. The same can be said of the reintroduction of "old-fashioned" direct address, revived and transmogrified at a moment in literary history when the post-Jamesian novelists seemed to have forever ruled out such self-conscious devices by refining the newer "impressionistic" conventions (the effaced narrator, the "central intelligence," the consistent if "unreliable" narrative *persona,* and so forth). "This new technique is that of the deliberate anachronism," writes J. L. Borges in "Pierre Menard, Author of the *Quixote,*" an essential text on the subject (*Labyrinths,* p. 44); and cinematic equivalents are readily available in the work of the directors who reintroduced silent film techniques (notably François Truffaut, Jean-Luc Godard, and Richard Lester) in the 1950s and 1960s.

qualities of a nymphet tempt the reader into interpreting Humbert's quest as essentially homosexual, but we may be less absolute in our judgment and practice of pop psychoanalysis when Humbert tells how during one of his incarcerations he trifled with psychiatrists, "teasing them with fake 'primal scenes.' " "By bribing a nurse I won access to some files and discovered, with glee, cards calling me 'potentially homosexual' " (p. 34). If the clinical-minded have accepted Humbert's explanation of the adolescent "trauma" which accounts for his pedophilia—interrupted coitus—then they should feel the force of the attack and their own form of loss when Lolita must leave Quilty's play "a week before its natural climax" (p. 209). Humbert's "trauma" affords a further trap for the clinical mind, for the incident seems to be a sly fictive transmutation of Nabokov's own considerably more innocent childhood infatuation with Colette (Chapter Seven, *Speak, Memory*); and such hints as the butterfly and the *Carmen* allusions shared by that chapter and *Lolita* only reinforce the more obvious similarities. When earnest readers, nurtured on the "standardized symbols of the psychoanalytic racket" (p. 285), leap to make the association between the two episodes —as several have done—and immediately conclude that *Lolita* is autobiographical in the most literal sense, then the trap has been sprung: their wantonly reductive gesture justifies the need for just such a parody as Nabokov's. With a cold literary perversity, Nabokov has demonstrated the falseness of their "truth"; the implications are considerable. Even the exegetic act of searching for the "meaning" of *Lolita* by trying to unfold the butterfly pattern becomes a parody of the expectations of the most sophisticated reader, who finds he is chasing a mocking inversion of the "normal" Freudian direction of symbols which, once identified, may still remain mysterious, explain very little, or, like the game of Word Golf in *Pale Fire*, reveal nothing.

Until almost the end of *Lolita*, Humbert's fullest expressions of "guilt" and "grief" are qualified, if not undercut completely, and these passages represent another series of traps in which Nabokov again parodies the reader's expectations by having Humbert the penitent say what the reader wants to hear: "I was a pentapod monster, but I loved you. I was despicable and brutal, and turpid, and everything" (p. 284). Eagerly absorbing Humbert's "confession," the reader suddenly stumbles over the rare word "turpid," and then is taken unawares by the silly catchall "and everything," which renders absurd the whole cluster, if not the reader. It *is* easy to confess, but the moral vocabulary we employ so readily may go no deeper than Humbert's parody of it.

Humbert's own moral vocabulary would seem to find an ideally expressive vehicle in the person of Clare Quilty. Throughout the narrative Humbert is literally and figuratively pursued by Quilty, who is by turns ludicrous and absurd, sinister and grotesque. For a while Humbert is certain that his "shadow" and nemesis is his Swiss cousin, Detective Trapp, and when Lolita agrees and says, "Perhaps he is Trapp," she is summarizing Quilty's role in the novel (p. 219). Quilty is so ubiquitous because he formulates Humbert's entrapment, his criminal passion, his sense of shame and self-hate. Yet Quilty embodies both "the truth and a caricature of it," for he is at once a projection of Humbert's guilt and a parody of the psychological Double; "Lo was playing a double game," says Humbert (p. 243), punningly referring to Lolita's tennis, the *Doppelgänger* parody, and the function of parody as game.

The Double motif figures prominently throughout Nabokov, from the early thirties in *Despair* and *Laughter in the Dark* (where the Albinus–Axel Rex pairing rehearses the Humbert–Quilty doubling), to *The Real Life of Sebastian Knight* and on through *Bend Sinister*, the story "Scenes from the Life of a Double Monster," *Lolita*, *Pnin*, and *Pale Fire*, which offers a monumental doubling (or, more properly, tripling). It is probably the most intricate and profound of all *Doppelgänger* novels, written at precisely the time when it seemed that the Double theme had been exhausted in modern literature, and this achievement was very likely made possible by Nabokov's elaborate parody of the theme in *Lolita*, which renewed his sense of the artistic efficacy of another literary "thing which had once been fresh and bright but which was now worn to a thread" (*Sebastian Knight*, p. 91).

By making Clare Quilty too clearly guilty,[1] Nabokov is assaulting the convention of the good and evil "dual selves" found in the traditional Double tale. Humbert would let some of us believe that when he kills Quilty in Chapter Thirty-five, Part Two, the good poet has exorcised the bad monster, but the two are finally not to be clearly distinguished: when Humbert and Quilty wrestle, "I rolled over him. We rolled over me. They rolled over him. We rolled over us." Although the parody culminates in this "silent, soft, formless tussle on the part of two literati" (p. 299), it is sustained throughout the novel. In traditional *Doppelgänger* fiction the Double representing the reprehensible self is often described as an ape. In Dostoevsky's *The Possessed* (1871), Stavrogin tells Verkhovensky, "you're my ape"; in Stevenson's *Dr. Jekyll and Mr. Hyde* (1886), Hyde plays "ape-

---

[1]The pun is also pointed out by Page Stegner in *Escape into Aesthetics: The Art of Vladimir Nabokov* (New York, 1966), p. 104.

like tricks," attacks and kills with "apelike fury" and "apelike spite"; and in Poe's "The Murders in the Rue Morgue" (1845), the criminal self is literally an ape. But "good" Humbert undermines the doubling by often calling himself an ape, rather than Quilty, and when the two face one another, Quilty also calls Humbert an ape. This transference is forcefully underscored when Humbert refers to himself as running along like "Mr. Hyde," his "talons still tingling" (p. 206). In Conrad's *Heart of Darkness* (1902), Kurtz is Marlow's "shadow" and "shade." Although Humbert calls Quilty his "shadow," the pun on Humbert's name (*ombre* = shadow) suggests that he is as much a shadow as Quilty, and like the shadow self who pursues the professor in Hans Christian Andersen's "The Shadow" (1850), Humbert is dressed all in black. Quilty in fact first regards Humbert as possibly being "some familiar and innocuous hallucination" of his own (p. 294); and in the novel's closing moments the masked narrator addresses Lolita and completes this transferral: "And do not pity C.Q. One had to choose between him and H.H., and one wanted H.H. to exist at least a couple of months longer, so as to have him make you live in the minds of later generations." The book might have been told by "C.Q.," the doubling reversed; "H.H." is simply a better artist, more likely to possess the "secret of durable pigments."

If the Humbert-Quilty doubling is a conscious parody of "William Wilson" (1839), it is with good reason, for Poe's story is unusual among *Doppelgänger* tales in that it presents a reversal of the conventional situation: the weak and evil self is the main character, pursued by the moral self, whom he kills. Nabokov goes further and with one vertiginous sweep stands the convention on its head: in terms of the nineteenth-century Double tale, it should not even be necessary to kill Quilty and what he represents, for Humbert has already declared his love for Lolita *before* he goes to Quilty's Pavor Manor, and, in asking the no longer nymphic Lolita to go away with him, he has transcended his obsession. Although Humbert's unqualified expression of "guilt" (p. 308) comes at the end of the novel, in the chronology of events it too occurs before he kills Quilty. As a "symbolic" act, the killing is gratuitous; the parodic design is complete.

Quilty rightly balks at his symbolic role: "I'm not responsible for the rapes of others. Absurd!" he tells Humbert, and his words are well taken, for in this scene Humbert *is* trying to make him totally responsible, and the poem which he has Quilty read aloud reinforces his effort, and again demonstrates how a Nabokov parody moves beyond the "obscure fun" of stylistic imitation to connect with the most serious region of the book. It begins as a parody of Eliot's "Ash Wednesday" but ends by undercutting all the confessing in which "remorseful" Humbert has just been engaged: "because of all you did / because of all I did not / you have to die" (p. 300). Since Quilty has been described as "the American Maeterlinck," it goes without saying that his ensuing death scene should be extravagantly "symbolic." Because one is not easily rid of an "evil" self, Quilty, indomitable as Rasputin, is almost impossible to kill; but the idea of exorcism is rendered absurd by his comically prolonged death throes, which, in the spirit of Canto V of *The Rape of the Lock,* burlesque the gore and rhetoric of literary death scenes ranging from the Elizabethan drama to the worst of detective novels and action films. ("Chum," Humbert's revolver, parodies the "phallic" pistols of "Freudian" Westerns and the American Gun Mystique at large.) Quilty returns to the scene of the crime—a bed—and it is here that Humbert finally corners him. When Humbert fires his remaining bullets at close range, Quilty "lay back, and a big pink bubble with juvenile connotations formed on his lips, grew to the size of a toy balloon, and vanished" (p. 304). The last details emphasize the mock-symbolic association with Lolita; the monstrous self that has devoured Lolita, bubble gum, childhood, and all, is "symbolically" dead, but as the bubble explodes, so does the Gothic *Doppelgänger* convention, with all its own "juvenile connotations" about identity, and we learn shortly that Humbert is still "all covered with Quilty." Guilt is not to be exorcised so readily—McFate is McFate, to coin a Humbertism— and the ambiguities of human experience and identity are not to be reduced to mere "dualities." Instead of the successful integration of a neatly divisible self, we are left with "Clare Obscure" and "quilted Quilty," the patchwork self (p. 306). Quilty refuses to die, just as the recaptured nose in Gogol's extraordinary Double story of that name (1836) would not at first stick to its owner's face. The reader who has expected the solemn moral-ethical absolutes of a Poe, Dostoevsky, Mann, or Conrad *Doppelgänger* fiction instead discovers himself adrift in a fantastic, comic cosmos more akin to Gogol's. Having hoped that Humbert would master his "secret sharer," we find instead that his quest for his "slippery self" figuratively resembles Major Kovaliov's frantic chase after his own nose through the spectral streets of St. Petersburg, and that Humbert's "quest" has its mock "ending" in a final confrontation that, like the end of "The Overcoat" (1842), is not a confrontation at all.

The parodic references to R. L. Stevenson suggest that Nabokov had in mind Henry Jekyll's painfully earnest discovery of the "truth" that "man is not only one, but truly two. I say two, because the state of my own knowledge does not pass beyond that point. Others will follow, others will outstrip me on the same lines." The "serial selves" of *Pale Fire* "outstrip" Stevenson and a good many other writers, and rather than undermining Humbert's guilt, the Double parody in *Lolita* locks Humbert within that prison of mirrors where the "real self" and its masks blend into one another, the refracted outlines of good and evil becoming terrifyingly confused.

Humbert's search for the whereabouts and identity of Detective Trapp (Quilty) invites the reader to wend his way through a labyrinth of clues in order to solve this mystery, a process which both parallels and parodies the Poe "tale of ratiocination." When Humbert finds Lolita and presses her for her abductor's name,

> She said really it was useless, she would never tell, but on the other hand, after all—"Do you really want to know who it was? Well it was—"
> And softly, confidentially, arching her thin eyebrows and puckering her parched lips, she emitted, a little mockingly, somewhat fastidiously, not untenderly, in a kind of muted whistle, the name that the astute reader has guessed long ago.
> Waterproof. Why did a flash from Hourglass Lake cross my consciousness? I, too, had known it, without knowing it, all along. There was no shock, no surprise. Quietly the fusion took place, and everything fell into order, into the pattern of branches that I have woven throughout this memoir with the express purpose of having the ripe fruit fall at the right moment; yes, with the express and perverse purpose of rendering—she was talking but I sat melting in my golden peace—of rendering that golden and monstrous peace through the satisfaction of logical recognition, which my most inimical reader should experience now. (pp. 271–272)

Even here Humbert withholds Quilty's identity, though the "astute reader" may recognize that "Waterproof" is a clue which leads back to an early scene at the lake, in which Charlotte had said that Humbert's watch was waterproof and Jean Farlow had alluded to Quilty's Uncle Ivor (by his first name only), and then had almost mentioned Clare Quilty by name: Ivor "told me a completely indecent story about his nephew. It appears—" But she is interrupted and the chapter ends (p. 89). This teasing exercise in ratiocination—"peace" indeed!—is the detective trap, another parody of the reader's assumptions and expectations, as though even the most astute reader could ever fully discover the identity of Quilty, Humbert, or of himself.

Provided with Quilty's name, Humbert now makes his way to Pavor Manor, that latter-day House of Usher on Grimm Road, where the extended and variegated parodies of Poe are laid to rest. All the novel's parodic themes are concluded in this chapter. Its importance is telescoped by Humbert's conclusion: "This, I said to myself, was the end of the ingenious play staged for me by Quilty" (p. 305). In form, of course, this bravura set piece is not a play; but, as a summary parodic commentary on the main action, it does function in the manner of an Elizabethan play-within-the-play, and its "staging" underscores once more the game-element central to the book.

Simultaneous with these games is a fully novelistic process that shows Humbert traveling much further than the 27,000 miles he and Lolita literally traverse. Foolish John Ray describes Humbert's as "a tragic tale tending unswervingly to nothing less than a moral apotheosis" (p. 5) and, amazingly enough, he turns out to be right. The reader sees Humbert move beyond his obsessional passion to a not altogether straightforward declaration of genuine love (pp. 277–278) and, finally, to a realization of the loss suffered not by him but by Lolita (pp. 307–308). It is expressed on the next to the last page in a long and eloquent passage that, for the first time in the novel, is in no way undercut by parody or qualified by irony. Midway through this "last mirage of wonder and hopelessness," the reader is invoked again, because Humbert's moral apotheosis, so uniquely straightforward, constitutes the end game and Nabokov's final *trompe-l'oeil*. If the reader has long since decided that there is no "moral reality" in the novel, and in his sophisticated way has accepted that, he may well miss this unexpected move in the farthest corner of the board and lose the game after all. It is the last time the reader will be addressed directly, for the game is about over, as is the novel.

In addition to sustaining the game-element, the authorial patterning reminds us that *Lolita* is but one part of that universe of fiction arrayed around the consciousness of Nabokov, who would join Humbert in his lament that words do indeed have their limitations, and that "the past is the past"; to live in it, as Humbert tried, is to die. That the author of *Speak, Memory* should suggest this surely establishes the moral dimension of

Lolita; and in the light of Johan Huizinga's remark that "play is outside the range of good and bad,"[1] *Lolita* becomes an even more extraordinary achievement.

When in *The Gift* Nabokov writes of Fyodor's poem, "At the same time he had to take great pains not to lose either his control of the game, or the viewpoint of the plaything," he is defining the difficulties he faced in writing novels whose full meaning depends on the reader's having a spatial view of the book. It should be evident by now how the parody and patterning create the distance necessary for a clear view of the "plaything," and Nabokov reinforces one's sense of the novel-as-gameboard by having an actual game in progress within *Lolita:* the seemingly continuous match between Humbert and Gaston Godin—a localized, foreground action which in turn telescopes both the Humbert-Quilty "Double game" being played back and forth across the gameboard of America and the overriding contest waged above the novel, between the author and the reader.[2] Hum-

[1]Johan Huizinga, *Homo Ludens: A Study of the Play Element in Culture* (Boston, 1955 [1st ed. 1944]), p. 11. An excellent introduction to Nabokov, even if he is not mentioned.

[2]This aspect of *Lolita* is nicely visualized in Tenniel's drawing of a landscaped

bert and Gaston play chess "two or three times weekly" in Humbert's study, and several times Nabokov carefully links Lolita with the Queen in their game (pp. 182–183). One evening while they are playing, Humbert gets a telephone call from Lolita's music teacher informing him that Lolita has again missed her lesson, the boldest lie he has caught her in, indicating that he is soon to lose her:

> As the reader may well imagine, my faculties were now impaired, and a move or two later, with Gaston to play, I noticed through the film of my general distress that he could collect my queen; he noticed it too, but thinking it might be a trap on the part of his tricky opponent, he demurred for quite a minute, and puffed and wheezed, and shook his jowls, and even shot furtive glances at me, and made hesitating half-thrusts with his pudgily bunched fingers—dying to take that juicy queen and not daring—and all of a sudden he swooped down upon it (who knows if it did not teach him certain later audacities?), and I spent a dreary hour in achieving a draw. (pp. 202–203).

In their respective ways, all the players want to capture "that juicy queen": poor homosexual Gaston, quite literally; pornographer Quilty, for only one purpose; pervert and poet Humbert, in two ways, first carnally but then artistically, out of love; and the common reader, who would either rescue Lolita by judging and condemning Humbert, or else participate vicariously, which would make him of Quilty's party—though there is every reason to think that the attentive reader will sooner or later share Humbert's perspective: "In my chess sessions with Gaston I saw the board as a square pool of limpid water with rare shells and stratagems rosily visible upon the smooth tessellated bottom, which to my confused adversary was all ooze and squid-cloud" (p. 233).

Humbert is being too modest at the outset of *Lolita* when he says "it is only a game," for it is one in which everything on the board "breath[es] with life," as Nabokov writes of the match between Luzhin and Turati in *The Defense*. Radical and dizzying shifts in focus are created in the reader's mind as he oscillates between a sense that he is by turns confronting characters in a novel and pieces in a game—as if a telescope were being spun 360 degrees on its axis, allowing one to look alternately through one

---

chessboard (or chessbored landscape) for Chapter Two of Lewis Carroll's *Through the Looking-Glass*, in which a chess game is literally woven into the narrative. For more on Carroll and Nabokov, see Note 131/1.

end and then the other. The various "levels" of *Lolita* are of course not the New Criticism's "levels of meaning," for the telescopic and global views of the "plaything" should enable one to perceive these levels or dimensions as instantaneous—as though, to adapt freely an image used by Mary McCarthy to describe *Pale Fire*, one were looking down on three or more games being played simultaneously by two chess masters on several separate glass boards, each arranged successively above the other.[1] A first reading of *Lolita* rarely affords this limpid, multiform view, and for many reasons, the initially disarming and distractive quality of its ostensible subject being foremost. But the uniquely exhilarating experience of rereading it on its own terms derives from the discovery of a totally new book in place of the old, and the recognition that its habit of metamorphosis has happily described the course of one's own perceptions. What Jorge Luis Borges says of Pierre Menard, author of the *Quixote*, surely holds for Vladimir Nabokov, the author of *Lolita:* he "has enriched, by means of a new technique, the halting and rudimentary art of reading."

ALFRED APPEL, JR.

Palo Alto, California
January 31, 1968

Wilmette, Illinois
May 21, 1990

[1] Mary McCarthy, "Vladimir Nabokov's *Pale Fire*," *Encounter*, XIX (October 1962), p. 76.

Selected Bibliography

I. CHECKLIST OF NABOKOV'S WRITING

Denotes a Russian work that has been translated; date following a title of a novel indicates year of magazine serialization; parentheses contain date of translation into English.

**Denotes work written in English.*
No asterisk indicates work is in Russian. Not included below are most of Nabokov's major entomological papers in English, nor the vast amount of writing that remains untranslated and uncollected from the twenties and thirties, including approximately 100 poems, several plays and short stories, fifty literary reviews and essays, and numerous translations of Rimbaud, Verlaine, Yeats, Brooke, Shakespeare, Musset, and others. Michael Juliar's Vladimir Nabokov: A Descriptive Bibliography *(New York, 1986) is the standard bibliography of Nabokov's published work. All seventeen of Nabokov's novels, along with* Speak, Memory *and* Strong Opinion, *are available in Vintage International editions.*

Carroll. *Alice in Wonderland.* Berlin, 1923. Translation.
*Mary. Berlin, 1926 (New York, 1970). A novel.
*King, Queen, Knave. Berlin, 1928 (New York, 1968). A novel.
*The Defense. 1929. Berlin, 1930 (New York, 1964). A novel.
*The Eye. 1930. (New York, 1965). A short novel.
*Glory. 1931. Paris, 1932 (New York, 1971). A novel.
*Camera Obscura. Paris and Berlin, 1932 (London, 1936; rev., New York, 1938, as *Laughter in the Dark*). A novel.

*_Despair._ 1934. Berlin, 1936 (London, 1937; rev., New York, 1966). A novel.

*_Invitation to a Beheading._ 1935–1936. Berlin and Paris, 1938 (New York, 1959). A novel.

*_The Gift._ 1937–1938. New York, 1952, in Russian (New York, 1963). A novel.

*_The Waltz Invention._ 1938 (New York, 1966). Drama in 3 acts.

**_The Real Life of Sebastian Knight._ Norfolk, Conn., 1941. A novel.

**_Three Russian Poets: Translations of Pushkin, Lermontov, and Tiutchev._ Norfolk, Conn., 1944.

**_Nikolai Gogol._ Norfolk, Conn., 1944. A critical study.

**_Bend Sinister._ New York, 1947. A novel.

**_Conclusive Evidence._ New York, 1951. A memoir.

Other Shores. New York, 1954. A Russian version of _Conclusive Evidence_, rewritten and expanded rather than translated.

**_Lolita._ Paris, 1955 (New York, 1958). A novel.

**_Pnin._ New York, 1957. A novel.

**Lermontov. _A Hero of Our Time._ New York, 1958. A translation.

**_Nabokov's Dozen._ New York, 1958. 13 stories, 3 translated from Russian, 1 from French.

**_The Song of Igor's Campaign._ New York, 1960. A translation of the twelfth-century epic.

**_Pale Fire._ New York, 1962. A novel.

**Pushkin, _Eugene Onegin._ New York, 1964. Translation and Commentary in 4 volumes.

**_Speak, Memory._ New York, 1966. Definitive version of memoir originally published as _Conclusive Evidence_, including _Other Shores_ and new material.

**_Ada._ New York, 1969. A novel.

*_Poems and Problems._ New York, 1971. 53 poems, 39 in both Russian and English, 18 chess problems.

**_Transparent Things._ New York, 1972. A novel.

*_A Russian Beauty and Other Stories._ 1924–1940. New York, 1973. 13 stories.

**_Strong Opinions._ New York, 1973. 22 interviews, 11 letters, 9 articles, and 5 lepidoptera papers.

**_Lolita: A Screenplay._ New York, 1974.

**_Look at the Harlequins!_ New York, 1974. A novel.

*_Tyrants Destroyed and Other Stories._ New York, 1975. 13 stories, 12 translated from the Russian.

*_Details of a Sunset and Other Stories._ New York, 1976. 13 stories.

**Karlinsky, Simon, ed. *The Nabokov-Wilson Letters: Correspondence Between Vladimir Nabokov and Edmund Wilson, 1940–1971.* New York, 1979.

Bowers, Fredson, ed. *Lectures on Literature.* New York, 1980.

———. *Lectures on Russian Literature.* New York, 1981.

———. *Lectures on Don Quixote.* New York, 1983.

*The Man from the USSR and Other Plays. New York, 1984. 4 plays.

*The Enchanter. New York, 1986. A novella.

Bruccoli, Matthew, and Dmitri Nabokov, eds. *Vladimir Nabokov: Selected Letters, 1940–1977.* New York, 1989.

2. CRITICISM OF *L O L I T A*

Included below are most of the studies of *Lolita* published during Nabokov's lifetime.

Aldridge, A. Owen, "Lolita and *Les Liaisons Dangereuses,*" *Wisconsin Studies in Contemporary Literature,* II (Fall 1961), 20–26.

Amis, Kingsley, "She Was a Child and I Was a Child," *The Spectator,* No. 6854 (November 6, 1959), 635–636.

Appel, Alfred, Jr., "The Art of Nabokov's Artifice," *Denver Quarterly,* III (Summer 1968), 25–37.

———, "An Interview with Vladimir Nabokov," in the Special all-Nabokov number, *Wisconsin Studies,* VIII (Spring 1967), 127–152. Reprinted in L. S. Dembo, ed., *Nabokov: The Man and His Work.* Madison: University of Wisconsin Press, 1967. Pp. 19–44. Reprinted in Nabokov, *Strong Opinions.* New York: Vintage International, 1989, pp. 62–92.

———, "*Lolita:* The Springboard of Parody," *Wisconsin Studies, op. cit.,* 204–241. Reprinted in Dembo, *op. cit.* Pp. 106–143.

———, *Nabokov's Dark Cinema.* New York: Oxford University Press, 1974. Pp. 61–151.

Brenner, Conrad, "Nabokov: The Art of the Perverse," *New Republic,* CXXXVIII (June 23, 1958), 18–21.

Bryer, Jackson R., and Thomas J. Bergin, Jr., "Vladimir Nabokov's Critical Reputation in English: A Note and a Checklist," *Wisconsin Studies, op. cit.,* 312–364. Reprinted in Dembo, *op. cit.* Pp. 225–274.

Butler, Diana, "Lolita Lepidoptera," *New World Writing,* No. 16 (1960), 58–84.

Dupee, F. W., "*Lolita* in America," *Encounter,* XII (February 1959), 30–35. Reprinted in *Columbia University Forum,* II (Winter 1959), 35–39.

————, "A Preface to *Lolita*," *Anchor Review*, No. 2 (1957), 1–13. Reprinted in his *"The King of the Cats" and Other Remarks on Writers and Writing*. New York: Farrar, Straus and Giroux, 1965. Pp. 117–141. Includes review of *The Gift*.

Fiedler, Leslie A., "The Profanation of the Child," *New Leader*, XLI (June 23, 1958), 26–29.

Field, Andrew, *Nabokov: His Life in Art*. Boston: Little, Brown, 1967. Pp. 323–351.

Girodias, Maurice, "Lolita, Nabokov, and I," *Evergreen Review*, IX (September 1965), 44–47, 89–91. Account of first publication of *Lolita;* for Nabokov's rejoinder, see *"Lolita* and Mr. Girodias," *Evergreen Review*, XI (February 1967), 37–41.

Gold, Herbert, "The Art of Fiction XL: Vladimir Nabokov, An Interview," *Paris Review*, No. 41 (Summer–Fall 1967), 92–111.

Green, Martin, "The Morality of *Lolita*," *Kenyon Review*, XXVIII (June 1966), 352–377.

Hicks, Granville, " 'Lolita' and Her Problems," *Saturday Review*, XLI (August 16, 1958), 12, 38.

Hollander, John, "The Perilous Magic of Nymphets," *Partisan Review*, XXIII (Fall 1956), 557–560. Reprinted in Richard Kostelanetz, ed., *On Contemporary Literature*. New York: Avon Books, 1964. Pp. 477–480.

Josipovici, G. D., "Lolita: Parody and the Pursuit of Beauty," *Critical Quarterly*, VI (Spring 1964), 35–48.

Kael, Pauline, "Lolita," in *I Lost It at the Movies*. New York: Bantam Books, 1966. Pp. 183–188. Reprinted in Andrew Sarris, ed., *The Film*. Indianapolis and New York: Bobbs-Merrill, 1968. Pp. 11–14. The most interesting review of the film version of *Lolita*.

Meyer, Frank S., "The Strange Fate of 'Lolita'—A Lance into Cotton Wool," *National Review*, VI (November 22, 1958), 340–341.

Mitchell, Charles, "Mythic Seriousness in *Lolita*," *Texas Studies in Literature and Language*, V (Autumn 1963), 329–343.

Nemerov, Howard, "The Morality of Art," *Kenyon Review*, XIX (Spring 1957), 313–314, 316–321. Reprinted in his *Poetry and Fiction: Essays*. New Brunswick, N.J.: Rutgers University Press, 1963. Pp. 260–269.

Phillips, Elizabeth, "The Hocus-Pocus of *Lolita*," *Literature and Psychology*, X (Summer 1960), 97–101.

"Playboy Interview: Vladimir Nabokov," *Playboy*, XI (January 1964), 35–41, 44–45. Reprinted in *The Twelfth Anniversary Playboy Reader*. Chicago: Playboy Press, 1965.

Prescott, Orville, "Books of The Times," *New York Times,* August 18, 1958, p. 17.

Proffer, Carl R., *Keys to Lolita.* Bloomington: Indiana University Press, 1968.

Rougemont, Denis de, "*Lolita,* or Scandal." In *Love Declared—Essays on the Myths of Love,* tr. Richard Howard. New York: Pantheon Books, 1963. Pp. 48–54.

Schickel, Richard, "Nabokov's Artistry," *The Progressive,* XXII (November 1958), 46, 48–49.

———, "A Review of a Novel You Can't Buy," *The Reporter,* XVII (November 28, 1957), 45–47.

Smith, Peter Duval, "Vladimir Nabokov on His Life and Work," *The Listener,* LXVIII (November 22, 1962), 856–858. Text of BBC television interview. Reprinted in *Vogue,* CXLI (March 1, 1963), 152–155.

Stegner, Page, *Escape into Aesthetics: The Art of Vladimir Nabokov.* New York: Dial Press, 1966. Pp. 102–115.

Trilling, Lionel, "The Last Lover—Vladimir Nabokov's 'Lolita,'" *Griffin,* VII (August 1958), 4–21. Reprinted in *Encounter,* XI (October 1958), 9–19.

West, Rebecca, " 'Lolita': A Tragic Book with a Sly Grimace," *London Sunday Times,* November 8, 1959, p. 16.

3. NABOKOV STUDIES

While studies of all aspects of Nabokov mount up by the year, the following are, or promise to be, indispensable.

Boyd, Brian. *Vladimir Nabokov: The Russian Years.* Princeton: Princeton University Press, 1990. Volume I of an anticipated two-volume biography.

See also Parker, Stephen Jan, ed. *The Nabokovian.* Lawrence: University of Kansas, 1984– . Earlier titled *The Vladimir Nabokov Research Newsletter,* 1978–1984. A semi-annual journal devoted to Nabokov studies, including bibliographies of critical studies.

Juliar, Michael. *Vladimir Nabokov: A Descriptive Bibliography.* New York: Garland Publishing, 1986.

In Place of a
Note on the Text

Shade's poem is, indeed, that sudden flourish of magic: my gray-haired friend, my beloved old conjurer, put a pack of index cards into his hat—and shook out a poem.

To this poem we now must turn. My Foreword has been, I trust, not too skimpy. Other notes, arranged in a running commentary, will certainly satisfy the most voracious reader. Although those notes, in conformity with custom, come after the poem, the reader is advised to consult them first and then study the poem with their help, rereading them of course as he goes through its text, and perhaps, after having done with the poem, consulting them a third time so as to complete the picture. I find it wise in such cases as this to eliminate the bother of back-and-forth leafings by either cutting out and clipping together the pages with the text of the thing, or, even more simply, purchasing two copies of the same work which can then be placed in adjacent positions on a comfortable table—not like the shaky little affair on which my typewriter is precariously enthroned now, in this wretched motor lodge, with that carousel inside and outside my head, miles away from New Wye. Let me state that without my notes Shade's text simply has no human reality at all since the human reality of such a poem as his (being too skittish and reticent for an autobiographical work), with the omission of many pithy lines carelessly rejected by him, has to depend entirely on the reality of its author and his surroundings, attachments and so forth, a reality that only my notes can provide. To this statement my dear poet would probably not have subscribed, but, for better or worse, it is the commentator who has the last word.

—CHARLES KINBOTE, *Pale Fire*

THE ANNOTATED
Lolita

Foreword

"Lolita, or the Confession of a White Widowed Male,"
such were the two titles under which the writer of the present 1
note received the strange pages it preambulates. "Humbert 2
Humbert," their author, had died in legal captivity, of coronary 3
thrombosis, on November 16, 1952, a few days before his trial
was scheduled to start. His lawyer, my good friend and relation,
Clarence Choate Clark, Esq., now of the District of Columbia
bar, in asking me to edit the manuscript, based his request on a
clause in his client's will which empowered my eminent cousin
to use his discretion in all matters pertaining to the preparation
of "Lolita" for print. Mr. Clark's decision may have been
influenced by the fact that the editor of his choice had just been
awarded the Poling Prize for a modest work ("Do the Senses
make Sense?") wherein certain morbid states and perversions
had been discussed.

My task proved simpler than either of us had anticipated.
Save for the correction of obvious solecisms and a careful sup- 4
pression of a few tenacious details that despite "H.H." 's own
efforts still subsisted in his text as signposts and tombstones
(indicative of places or persons that taste would conceal and
compassion spare), this remarkable memoir is presented intact. 5
Its author's bizarre cognomen is his own invention; and, of 6
course, this mask—through which two hypnotic eyes seem to 7
glow—had to remain unlifted in accordance with its wearer's 8
wish. While "Haze" only rhymes with the heroine's real sur-

1 *name, her first name is too closely interwound with the inmost
fiber of the book to allow one to alter it; nor (as the reader will
perceive for himself) is there any practical necessity to do so.*
2 *References to "H.H." 's crime may be looked up by the*
3 *inquisitive in the daily papers for September–October 1952; its
cause and purpose would have continued to remain a complete
mystery, had not this memoir been permitted to come under
my reading lamp.*

*For the benefit of old-fashioned readers who wish to follow
4 the destinies of the "real" people beyond the "true" story, a
few details may be given as received from Mr. "Windmuller,"
of "Ramsdale," who desires his identity suppressed so that "the
long shadow of this sorry and sordid business" should not reach
the community to which he is proud to belong. His daughter,
5 "Louise," is by now a college sophomore. "Mona Dahl" is a
student in Paris. "Rita" has recently married the proprietor of a
6 hotel in Florida. Mrs. "Richard F. Schiller" died in childbed,
7 giving birth to a stillborn girl, on Christmas Day 1952, in Gray
8 Star, a settlement in the remotest Northwest. "Vivian Dark-
9 bloom" has written a biography, "My Cue," to be published
shortly, and critics who have perused the manuscript call it her
best book. The caretakers of the various cemeteries involved
report that no ghosts walk.*

*Viewed simply as a novel, "Lolita" deals with situations and
emotions that would remain exasperatingly vague to the reader
10 had their expression been etiolated by means of platitudinous
evasions. True, not a single obscene term is to be found in the
whole work; indeed, the robust philistine who is conditioned by
modern conventions into accepting without qualms a lavish
array of four-letter words in a banal novel, will be quite shocked
by their absence here. If, however, for this paradoxical prude's
comfort, an editor attempted to dilute or omit scenes that a
certain type of mind might call "aphrodisiac" (see in this
respect the monumental decision rendered December 6, 1933,
by Hon. John M. Woolsey in regard to another, considerably
11 more outspoken, book), one would have to forego the publication
of "Lolita" altogether, since those very scenes that one might*

ineptly accuse of a sensuous existence of their own, are the most strictly functional ones in the development of a tragic tale tending unswervingly to nothing less than a moral apotheosis. The cynic may say that commercial pornography makes the same claim; the learned may counter by asserting that "H.H." 's impassioned confession is a tempest in a test tube; that at least 12% of American adult males—a "conservative" estimate according to Dr. Blanche Schwarzmann (verbal communication) —enjoy yearly, in one way or another, the special experience "H.H." describes with such despair; that had our demented diarist gone, in the fatal summer of 1947, to a competent psychopathologist, there would have been no disaster; but then, neither would there have been this book.

This commentator may be excused for repeating what he has stressed in his own books and lectures, namely that "offensive" is frequently but a synonym for "unusual"; and a great work of art is of course always original, and thus by its very nature should come as a more or less shocking surprise. I have no intention to glorify "H.H." No doubt, he is horrible, he is abject, he is a shining example of moral leprosy, a mixture of ferocity and jocularity that betrays supreme misery perhaps, but is not conducive to attractiveness. He is ponderously capricious. Many of his casual opinions on the people and scenery of this country are ludicrous. A desperate honesty that throbs through his confession does not absolve him from sins of diabolical cunning. He is abnormal. He is not a gentleman. But how magically his singing violin can conjure up a tendresse, a compassion for Lolita that makes us entranced with the book while abhorring its author!

As a case history, "Lolita" will become, no doubt, a classic in psychiatric circles. As a work of art, it transcends its expiatory aspects; and still more important to us than scientific significance and literary worth, is the ethical impact the book should have on the serious reader; for in this poignant personal study there lurks a general lesson; the wayward child, the egotistic mother, the panting maniac—these are not only vivid characters in a unique story: they warn us of dangerous trends; they point out potent evils. *"Lolita"* *should* *make* *all* *of* *us—parents,* *social* *workers,* *educators—apply* *ourselves* *with* *still* *greater* *vigilance* *and* *vision* *to* *the* *task* *of* *bringing* *up* *a* *better* *generation* *in* *a* *safer* *world.*

1   Widworth, Mass.   John Ray, Jr., Ph.D.
2   August 5, 1955

Part One

1

Lolita, light of my life, fire of my loins. My sin, my soul. 1
Lo-lee-ta: the tip of the tongue taking a trip of three steps 2
down the palate to tap, at three, on the teeth. Lo. Lee. Ta.

She was Lo, plain Lo, in the morning, standing four feet ten in 3
one sock. She was Lola in slacks. She was Dolly at school. She was 4
Dolores on the dotted line. But in my arms she was always Lolita. 5

Did she have a precursor? She did, indeed she did. In point of
fact, there might have been no Lolita at all had I not loved, one 6
summer, a certain initial girl-child. In a princedom by the sea. 7
Oh when? About as many years before Lolita was born as my age
was that summer. You can always count on a murderer for a
fancy prose style.

Ladies and gentlemen of the jury, exhibit number one is what
the seraphs, the misinformed, simple, noble-winged seraphs, en- 8
vied. Look at this tangle of thorns. 9

2

I was born in 1910, in Paris. My father was a gentle, easy-going
person, a salad of racial genes: a Swiss citizen, of mixed French
and Austrian descent, with a dash of the Danube in his veins. I
am going to pass around in a minute some lovely, glossy-blue
picture-postcards. He owned a luxurious hotel on the Riviera. His
father and two grandfathers had sold wine, jewels and silk, respectively. At thirty he married an English girl, daughter of

9

1 Jerome Dunn, the alpinist, and granddaughter of two Dorset
parsons, experts in obscure subjects—paleopedology and Aeolian
2 harps, respectively. My very photogenic mother died in a freak
accident (picnic, lightning) when I was three, and, save for a
pocket of warmth in the darkest past, nothing of her subsists
within the hollows and dells of memory, over which, if you can
still stand my style (I am writing under observation), the sun of
my infancy had set: surely, you all know those redolent remnants
of day suspended, with the midges, about some hedge in bloom
or suddenly entered and traversed by the rambler, at the bottom
3 of a hill, in the summer dusk; a furry warmth, golden midges.

4 My mother's elder sister, Sybil, whom a cousin of my father's
had married and then neglected, served in my immediate family
as a kind of unpaid governess and housekeeper. Somebody told
me later that she had been in love with my father, and that he
had lightheartedly taken advantage of it one rainy day and forgotten it by the time the weather cleared. I was extremely
fond of her, despite the rigidity—the fatal rigidity—of some of
her rules. Perhaps she wanted to make of me, in the fullness of
time, a better widower than my father. Aunt Sybil had pink-
rimmed azure eyes and a waxen complexion. She wrote poetry.
She was poetically superstitious. She said she knew she would die
soon after my sixteenth birthday, and did. Her husband, a great
traveler in perfumes, spent most of his time in America, where
eventually he founded a firm and acquired a bit of real estate.

I grew, a happy, healthy child in a bright world of illustrated
books, clean sand, orange trees, friendly dogs, sea vistas and smil-
5 ing faces. Around me the splendid Hotel Mirana revolved as a
kind of private universe, a whitewashed cosmos within the blue
greater one that blazed outside. From the aproned pot-scrubber
to the flanneled potentate, everybody liked me, everybody petted
me. Elderly American ladies leaning on their canes listed toward
me like towers of Pisa. Ruined Russian princesses who could not
pay my father, bought me expensive bonbons. He, *mon cher petit*
6 *papa*, took me out boating and biking, taught me to swim and
7 dive and water-ski, read to me *Don Quixote* and *Les Misérables*,
and I adored and respected him and felt glad for him whenever

I overheard the servants discuss his various lady-friends, beautiful and kind beings who made much of me and cooed and shed precious tears over my cheerful motherlessness.

I attended an English day school a few miles from home, and there I played rackets and fives, and got excellent marks, and was on perfect terms with schoolmates and teachers alike. The only definite sexual events that I can remember as having occurred before my thirteenth birthday (that is, before I first saw my little Annabel) were: a solemn, decorous and purely theoretical talk about pubertal surprises in the rose garden of the school with an American kid, the son of a then celebrated motion-picture actress whom he seldom saw in the three-dimensional world; and some interesting reactions on the part of my organism to certain photographs, pearl and umbra, with infinitely soft partings, in Pichon's sumptuous *La Beauté Humaine* that I had filched from under a mountain of marble-bound *Graphics* in the hotel library. Later, in his delightful debonair manner, my father gave me all the information he thought I needed about sex; this was just before sending me, in the autumn of 1923, to a *lycée* in Lyon (where we were to spend three winters); but alas, in the summer of that year, he was touring Italy with Mme de R. and her daughter, and I had nobody to complain to, nobody to consult.

3

Annabel was, like the writer, of mixed parentage: half-English, half-Dutch, in her case. I remember her features far less distinctly today than I did a few years ago, before I knew Lolita. There are two kinds of visual memory: one when you skillfully recreate an image in the laboratory of your mind, with your eyes open (and then I see Annabel in such general terms as: "honey-colored skin," "thin arms," "brown bobbed hair," "long lashes," "big bright mouth"); and the other when you instantly evoke, with shut eyes, on the dark innerside of your eyelids, the objective, absolutely optical replica of a beloved face, a little ghost in natural colors (and this is how I see Lolita).

Let me therefore primly limit myself, in describing Annabel, to saying she was a lovely child a few months my junior. Her parents were old friends of my aunt's, and as stuffy as she. They had rented a villa not far from Hotel Mirana. Bald brown Mr. Leigh and fat, powdered Mrs. Leigh (born Vanessa van Ness). How I loathed them! At first, Annabel and I talked of peripheral affairs. She kept lifting handfuls of fine sand and letting it pour through her fingers. Our brains were turned the way those of intelligent European preadolescents were in our day and set, and I doubt if much individual genius should be assigned to our interest in the plurality of inhabited worlds, competitive tennis, infinity, solipsism and so on. The softness and fragility of baby animals caused us the same intense pain. She wanted to be a nurse in some famished Asiatic country; I wanted to be a famous spy.

All at once we were madly, clumsily, shamelessly, agonizingly in love with each other; hopelessly, I should add, because that frenzy of mutual possession might have been assuaged only by our actually imbibing and assimilating every particle of each other's soul and flesh; but there we were, unable even to mate as slum children would have so easily found an opportunity to do. After one wild attempt we made to meet at night in her garden (of which more later), the only privacy we were allowed was to be out of earshot but not out of sight on the populous part of the *plage*. There, on the soft sand, a few feet away from our elders, we would sprawl all morning, in a petrified paroxysm of desire, and take advantage of every blessed quirk in space and time to touch each other: her hand, half-hidden in the sand, would creep toward me, its slender brown fingers sleepwalking nearer and nearer; then, her opalescent knee would start on a long cautious journey; sometimes a chance rampart built by younger children granted us sufficient concealment to graze each other's salty lips; these incomplete contacts drove our healthy and inexperienced young bodies to such a state of exasperation that not even the cold blue water, under which we still clawed at each other, could bring relief.

Among some treasures I lost during the wanderings of my

12

adult years, there was a snapshot taken by my aunt which showed Annabel, her parents and the staid, elderly, lame gentleman, a Dr. Cooper, who that same summer courted my aunt, grouped around a table in a sidewalk café. Annabel did not come out well, caught as she was in the act of bending over her *chocolat glacé,* and her thin bare shoulders and the parting in her hair were about all that could be identified (as I remember that picture) amid the sunny blur into which her lost loveliness graded; but I, sitting somewhat apart from the rest, came out with a kind of dramatic conspicuousness: a moody, beetle-browed boy in a dark sport shirt and well-tailored white shorts, his legs crossed, sitting in profile, looking away. That photograph was taken on the last day of our fatal summer and just a few minutes before we made our second and final attempt to thwart fate. Under the flimsiest of pretexts (this was our very last chance, and nothing really mattered) we escaped from the café to the beach, and found a desolate stretch of sand, and there, in the violet shadow of some red rocks forming a kind of cave, had a brief session of avid caresses, with somebody's lost pair of sunglasses for only witness. I was on my knees, and on the point of possessing my darling, when two bearded bathers, the old man of the sea and his brother, came out of the sea with exclamations of ribald encouragement, and four months later she died of typhus in Corfu.

4

I leaf again and again through these miserable memories, and keep asking myself, was it then, in the glitter of that remote summer, that the rift in my life began; or was my excessive desire for that child only the first evidence of an inherent singularity? When I try to analyze my own cravings, motives, actions and so forth, I surrender to a sort of retrospective imagination which feeds the analytic faculty with boundless alternatives and which causes each visualized route to fork and re-fork without end in the maddeningly complex prospect of my past. I am convinced, however, that in a certain magic and fateful way Lolita began with Annabel.

I also know that the shock of Annabel's death consolidated the frustration of that nightmare summer, made of it a permanent obstacle to any further romance throughout the cold years of my youth. The spiritual and the physical had been blended in us with a perfection that must remain incomprehensible to the matter-of-fact, crude, standard-brained youngsters of today. Long after her death I felt her thoughts floating through mine. Long before we met we had had the same dreams. We compared notes. We found strange affinities. The same June of the same year (1919) a stray canary had fluttered into her house and mine, in two widely separated countries. Oh, Lolita, had *you* loved me thus!

I have reserved for the conclusion of my "Annabel" phase the account of our unsuccessful first tryst. One night, she managed to deceive the vicious vigilance of her family. In a nervous and slender-leaved mimosa grove at the back of their villa we found a perch on the ruins of a low stone wall. Through the darkness and the tender trees we could see the arabesques of lighted windows which, touched up by the colored inks of sensitive memory, appear to me now like playing cards—presumably because a bridge game was keeping the enemy busy. She trembled and twitched as I kissed the corner of her parted lips and the hot lobe of her ear. A cluster of stars palely glowed above us, between the silhouettes of long thin leaves; that vibrant sky seemed as naked as she was under her light frock. I saw her face in the sky, strangely distinct, as if it emitted a faint radiance of its own. Her legs, her lovely live legs, were not too close together, and when my hand located what it sought, a dreamy and eerie expression, half-pleasure, half-pain, came over those childish features. She sat a little higher than I, and whenever in her solitary ecstasy she was led to kiss me, her head would bend with a sleepy, soft, drooping movement that was almost woeful, and her bare knees caught and compressed my wrist, and slackened again; and her quivering mouth, distorted by the acridity of some mysterious potion, with a sibilant intake of breath came near to my face.

She would try to relieve the pain of love by first roughly rubbing her dry lips against mine; then my darling would draw away with a nervous toss of her hair, and then again come darkly near and let me feed on her open mouth, while with a generosity that was ready to offer her everything, my heart, my throat, my entrails, I gave her to hold in her awkward fist the scepter of my passion.

I recall the scent of some kind of toilet powder—I believe she stole it from her mother's Spanish maid—a sweetish, lowly, musky perfume. It mingled with her own biscuity odor, and my senses were suddenly filled to the brim; a sudden commotion in a nearby bush prevented them from overflowing—and as we drew away from each other, and with aching veins attended to what was probably a prowling cat, there came from the house her mother's voice calling her, with a rising frantic note—and Dr. Cooper ponderously limped out into the garden. But that mimosa grove—the haze of stars, the tingle, the flame, the honeydew, and the ache remained with me, and that little girl with her seaside limbs and ardent tongue haunted me ever since—until at last, twenty-four years later, I broke her spell by incarnating her in another.

5

The days of my youth, as I look back on them, seem to fly away from me in a flurry of pale repetitive scraps like those morning snow storms of used tissue paper that a train passenger sees whirling in the wake of the observation car. In my sanitary relations with women I was practical, ironical and brisk. While a college student, in London and Paris, paid ladies sufficed me. My studies were meticulous and intense, although not particularly fruitful. At first, I planned to take a degree in psychiatry as many *manqué* talents do; but I was even more *manqué* than that; a peculiar exhaustion, I am so oppressed, doctor, set in; and I switched to English literature, where so many frustrated poets end as pipe-smoking teachers in tweeds. Paris suited me. I dis-

1 cussed Soviet movies with expatriates. I sat with uranists in the
2 Deux Magots. I published tortuous essays in obscure journals. I
3 composed pastiches:

> ...Fräulein von Kulp
> may turn, her hand upon the door;
> I will not follow her. Nor Fresca. Nor
> that Gull.

A paper of mine entitled "The Proustian theme in a letter
4 from Keats to Benjamin Bailey" was chuckled over by the six
or seven scholars who read it. I launched upon an "*Histoire*
5 *abrégée de la poésie anglaise*" for a prominent publishing firm,
and then started to compile that manual of French literature for
English-speaking students (with comparisons drawn from English
writers) which was to occupy me throughout the forties—
and the last volume of which was almost ready for press by the
time of my arrest.

I found a job—teaching English to a group of adults in
Auteuil. Then a school for boys employed me for a couple of
winters. Now and then I took advantage of the acquaintances I
had formed among social workers and psychotherapists to visit
in their company various institutions, such as orphanages and
reform schools, where pale pubescent girls with matted eyelashes
could be stared at in perfect impunity remindful of that granted
one in dreams.

Now I wish to introduce the following idea. Between the age
limits of nine and fourteen there occur maidens who, to certain
bewitched travelers, twice or many times older than they, reveal
6 their true nature which is not human, but nymphic (that is,
demoniac); and these chosen creatures I propose to designate as
"nymphets."

It will be marked that I substitute time terms for spatial ones.
In fact, I would have the reader see "nine" and "fourteen" as the
boundaries—the mirrory beaches and rosy rocks—of an enchanted
island haunted by those nymphets of mine and surrounded by
a vast, misty sea. Between those age limits, are all girl-children
nymphets? Of course not. Otherwise, we who are in the know,

we lone voyagers, we nympholepts, would have long gone insane. Neither are good looks any criterion; and vulgarity, or at least what a given community terms so, does not necessarily impair certain mysterious characteristics, the fey grace, the elusive, shifty, soul-shattering, insidious charm that separates the nymphet from such coevals of hers as are incomparably more dependent on the spatial world of synchronous phenomena than on that intangible island of entranced time where Lolita plays with her likes. Within the same age limits the number of true nymphets is strikingly inferior to that of provisionally plain, or just nice, or "cute," or even "sweet" and "attractive," ordinary, plumpish, formless, cold-skinned, essentially human little girls, with tummies and pigtails, who may or may not turn into adults of great beauty (look at the ugly dumplings in black stockings and white hats that are metamorphosed into stunning stars of the screen). A normal man given a group photograph of school girls or Girl Scouts and asked to point out the comeliest one will not necessarily choose the nymphet among them. You have to be an artist and a madman, a creature of infinite melancholy, with a bubble of hot poison in your loins and a super-voluptuous flame permanently aglow in your subtle spine (oh, how you have to cringe and hide!), in order to discern at once, by ineffable signs—the slightly feline outline of a cheekbone, the slenderness of a downy limb, and other indices which despair and shame and tears of tenderness forbid me to tabulate—the little deadly demon among the wholesome children; *she* stands unrecognized by them and unconscious herself of her fantastic power.

Furthermore, since the idea of time plays such a magic part in the matter, the student should not be surprised to learn that there must be a gap of several years, never less than ten I should say, generally thirty or forty, and as many as ninety in a few known cases, between maiden and man to enable the latter to come under a nymphet's spell. It is a question of focal adjustment, of a certain distance that the inner eye thrills to surmount, and a certain contrast that the mind perceives with a gasp of perverse delight. When I was a child and she was a child, my little Annabel was no nymphet to me; I was her equal, a faunlet

in my own right, on that same enchanted island of time; but today, in September 1952, after twenty-nine years have elapsed,
1 I think I can distinguish in her the initial fateful elf in my life. We loved each other with a premature love, marked by a fierceness that so often destroys adult lives. I was a strong lad and survived; but the poison was in the wound, and the wound remained ever open, and soon I found myself maturing amid a civilization which allows a man of twenty-five to court a girl of sixteen but not a girl of twelve.

No wonder, then, that my adult life during the European period of my existence proved monstrously twofold. Overtly, I had so-called normal relationships with a number of terrestrial women having pumpkins or pears for breasts; inly, I was consumed by a hell furnace of localized lust for every passing nymphet whom as a law-abiding poltroon I never dared approach. The human females I was allowed to wield were but palliative agents. I am ready to believe that the sensations I derived from natural fornication were much the same as those known to normal big males consorting with their normal big mates in that routine rhythm which shakes the world. The trouble was that those gentlemen had not, and I *had*, caught glimpses of an incomparably more poignant bliss. The dimmest
2 of my pollutive dreams was a thousand times more dazzling than all the adultery the most virile writer of genius or the most talented impotent might imagine. My world was split. I was aware of not one but two sexes, neither of which was mine; both would be termed female by the anatomist. But to me, through the prism of my senses, "they were as different as mist and mast." All this I rationalize now. In my twenties and early thirties, I did not understand my throes quite so clearly. While my body knew what it craved for, my mind rejected my body's every plea. One moment I was ashamed and frightened, another recklessly optimistic. Taboos strangulated me. Psychoanalysts wooed me
3 with pseudoliberations of pseudolibidoes. The fact that to me the only objects of amorous tremor were sisters of Annabel's, her handmaids and girl-pages, appeared to me at times as a forerunner of insanity. At other times I would tell myself that it was

all a question of attitude, that there was really nothing wrong in being moved to distraction by girl-children. Let me remind my reader that in England, with the passage of the Children and Young Person Act in 1933, the term "girl-child" is defined as "a girl who is over eight but under fourteen years" (after that, from fourteen to seventeen, the statutory definition is "young person"). In Massachusetts, U.S., on the other hand, a "wayward child" is, technically, one "between seven and seventeen years of age" (who, moreover, habitually associates with vicious or immoral persons). Hugh Broughton, a writer of controversy in the reign of James the First, has proved that Rahab was a harlot at ten years of age. This is all very interesting, and I daresay you see me already frothing at the mouth in a fit; but no, I am not; I am just winking happy thoughts into a little tiddle cup. Here are some more pictures. Here is Virgil who could the nymphet sing in single tone, but probably preferred a lad's perineum. Here are two of King Akhnaten's and Queen Nefertiti's pre-nubile Nile daughters (that royal couple had a litter of six), wearing nothing but many necklaces of bright beads, relaxed on cushions, intact after three thousand years, with their soft brown puppybodies, cropped hair and long ebony eyes. Here are some brides of ten compelled to seat themselves on the fascinum, the virile ivory in the temples of classical scholarship. Marriage and cohabitation before the age of puberty are still not uncommon in certain East Indian provinces. Lepcha old men of eighty copulate with girls of eight, and nobody minds. After all, Dante fell madly in love with his Beatrice when she was nine, a sparkling girleen, painted and lovely, and bejeweled, in a crimson frock, and this was in 1274, in Florence, at a private feast in the merry month of May. And when Petrarch fell madly in love with his Laureen, she was a fair-haired nymphet of twelve running in the wind, in the pollen and dust, a flower in flight, in the beautiful plain as descried from the hills of Vaucluse.

But let us be prim and civilized. Humbert Humbert tried hard to be good. Really and truly, he did. He had the utmost respect for ordinary children, with their purity and vulnerability, and under no circumstances would he have interfered with the innocence of a child, if there was the least risk of a row. But how his heart beat when, among the innocent throng, he espied a demon child, *"enfant charmante et fourbe,"* dim eyes, bright lips, ten years in jail if you only show her you are looking at her. So life went. Humbert was perfectly capable of intercourse with Eve, but it was Lilith he longed for. The bud-stage of breast development appears early (10.7 years) in the sequence of somatic changes accompanying pubescence. And the next maturational item available is the first appearance of pigmented pubic hair (11.2 years). My little cup brims with tiddles.

A shipwreck. An atoll. Alone with a drowned passenger's shivering child. Darling, this is only a game! How marvelous were my fancied adventures as I sat on a hard park bench pretending to be immersed in a trembling book. Around the quiet scholar, nymphets played freely, as if he were a familiar statue or part of an old tree's shadow and sheen. Once a perfect little beauty in a tartan frock, with a clatter put her heavily armed foot near me upon the bench to dip her slim bare arms into me and tighten the strap of her roller skate, and I dissolved in the sun, with my book for fig leaf, as her auburn ringlets fell all over her skinned knee, and the shadow of leaves I shared pulsated and melted on her radiant limb next to my chameleonic cheek. Another time a red-haired school girl hung over me in the *métro*, and a revelation of axillary russet I obtained remained in my blood for weeks. I could list a great number of these one-sided diminutive romances. Some of them ended in a rich flavor of hell. It happened for instance that from my balcony I would notice a lighted window across the street and what looked like a nymphet in the act of undressing before a co-operative mirror. Thus isolated, thus removed, the vision acquired an especially keen charm that made me race with all speed toward my lone gratification. But abruptly, fiendishly, the tender pattern of nudity I had adored would be transformed into the disgusting lamp-lit bare arm of a man in his underclothes reading his paper by the open window in the hot, damp, hopeless summer night.

Rope-skipping, hopscotch. That old woman in black who sat down next to me on my bench, on my rack of joy (a nymphet

was groping under me for a lost marble), and asked if I had
stomachache, the insolent hag. Ah, leave me alone in my
pubescent park, in my mossy garden. Let them play around me
forever. Never grow up.

6

A propos: I have often wondered what became of those
nymphets later? In this wrought-iron world of criss-cross cause
and effect, could it be that the hidden throb I stole from them
did not affect *their* future? I had possessed her—and she never
knew it. All right. But would it not tell sometime later? Had I
not somehow tampered with her fate by involving her image in
my voluptas? Oh, it was, and remains, a source of great and
terrible wonder.

I learned, however, what they looked like, those lovely, maddening, thin-armed nymphets, when they grew up. I remember
walking along an animated street on a gray spring afternoon
somewhere near the Madeleine. A short slim girl passed me at a
rapid, high-heeled, tripping step, we glanced back at the same
moment, she stopped and I accosted her. She came hardly up
to my chest hair and had the kind of dimpled round little face
French girls so often have, and I liked her long lashes and tight-
fitting tailored dress sheathing in pearl-gray her young body
which still retained—and that was the nymphic echo, the chill
of delight, the leap in my loins—a childish something mingling
with the professional *frétillement* of her small agile rump. I
asked her price, and she promptly replied with melodious silvery
precision (a bird, a very bird!) "*Cent.*" I tried to haggle but
she saw the awful lone longing in my lowered eyes, directed so
far down at her round forehead and rudimentary hat (a band,
a posy); and with one beat of her lashes: "*Tant pis*," she said,
and made as if to move away. Perhaps only three years earlier I
might have seen her coming home from school! That evocation
settled the matter. She led me up the usual steep stairs, with the
usual bell clearing the way for the *monsieur* who might not care

to meet another *monsieur*, on the mournful climb to the abject room, all bed and *bidet*. As usual, she asked at once for her *petit cadeau*, and as usual I asked her name (Monique) and her age (eighteen). I was pretty well acquainted with the banal way of streetwalkers. They all answer *"dix-huit"*—a trim twitter, a note of finality and wistful deceit which they emit up to ten times per day, the poor little creatures. But in Monique's case there could be no doubt she was, if anything, adding one or two years to her age. This I deduced from many details of her compact, neat, curiously immature body. Having shed her clothes with fascinating rapidity, she stood for a moment partly wrapped in the dingy gauze of the window curtain listening with infantile pleasure, as pat as pat could be, to an organ-grinder in the dust-brimming courtyard below. When I examined her small hands and drew her attention to their grubby fingernails, she said with a naïve frown *"Oui, ce n'est pas bien,"* and went to the wash-basin, but I said it did not matter, did not matter at all. With her brown bobbed hair, luminous gray eyes and pale skin, she looked perfectly charming. Her hips were no bigger than those of a squatting lad; in fact, I do not hesitate to say (and indeed this is the reason why I linger gratefully in that gauze-gray room of memory with little Monique) that among the eighty or so *grues* I had had operate upon me, she was the only one that gave me a pang of genuine pleasure. *"Il était malin, celui qui a inventé ce truc-là,"* she commented amiably, and got back into her clothes with the same high-style speed.

I asked for another, more elaborate, assignment later the same evening, and she said she would meet me at the corner café at nine, and swore she had never *posé un lapin* in all her young life. We returned to the same room, and I could not help saying how very pretty she was to which she answered demurely: *"Tu es bien gentil de dire ça"* and then, noticing what I noticed too in the mirror reflecting our small Eden—the dreadful grimace of clenched-teeth tenderness that distorted my mouth—dutiful little Monique (oh, she had been a nymphet all right!) wanted to know if she should remove the layer of red from her lips *avant qu'on se couche* in case I planned to kiss her. Of course, I planned it. I let myself go with her more completely than I had with any young lady before, and my last vision that night of long-lashed Monique is touched up with a gaiety that I find seldom associated with any event in my humiliating, sordid, taciturn love life. She looked tremendously pleased with the bonus of fifty I gave her as she trotted out into the April night drizzle with Humbert Humbert lumbering in her narrow wake. Stopping before a window display she said with great gusto: "*Je vais m'acheter des bas!*" and never may I forget the way her Parisian childish lips exploded on "*bas*," pronouncing it with an appetite that all but changed the "a" into a brief buoyant bursting "o" as in "*bot*."

I had a date with her next day at 2.15 P.M. in my own rooms, but it was less successful, she seemed to have grown less juvenile, more of a woman overnight. A cold I caught from her led me to cancel a fourth assignment, nor was I sorry to break an emotional series that threatened to burden me with heart-rending fantasies and peter out in dull disappointment. So let her remain, sleek, slender Monique, as she was for a minute or two: a delinquent nymphet shining through the matter-of-fact young whore.

My brief acquaintance with her started a train of thought that may seem pretty obvious to the reader who knows the ropes. An advertisement in a lewd magazine landed me, one brave day, in the office of a Mlle Edith who began by offering me to choose a kindred soul from a collection of rather formal photographs in a rather soiled album ("*Regardez-moi cette belle brune!*"). When I pushed the album away and somehow managed to blurt out my criminal craving, she looked as if about to show me the door; however, after asking me what price I was prepared to disburse, she condescended to put me in touch with a person *qui pourrait arranger la chose*. Next day, an asthmatic woman, coarsely painted, garrulous, garlicky, with an almost farcical Provençal accent and a black mustache above a purple lip, took me to what was apparently her own domicile, and there, after explosively kissing the bunched tips of her fat fingers to signify the delectable rosebud quality of her merchandise, she theatrically drew aside a curtain to reveal what I judged was that part of the room where a large and unfastidious family usually slept. It was now empty save for a monstrously plump, sallow, repulsively plain girl of at least fifteen with red-ribboned thick black braids who sat on a chair perfunctorily nursing a bald doll. When I shook my head and tried to shuffle out of the trap, the woman, talking fast, began removing the dingy woolen jersey from the young giantess' torso; then, seeing my determination to leave, she demanded *son argent*. A door at the end of the room was opened, and two men who had been dining in the kitchen joined in the squabble. They were misshapen, bare-necked, very swarthy and one of them wore dark glasses. A small boy and a begrimed, bowlegged toddler lurked behind them. With the insolent logic of a nightmare, the enraged procuress, indicating the man in glasses, said he had served in the police, *lui*, so that I had better do as I was told. I went up to Marie—for that was her stellar name—who by then had quietly transferred her heavy haunches to a stool at the kitchen table and resumed her interrupted soup while the toddler picked up the doll. With a surge of pity dramatizing my idiotic gesture, I thrust a banknote into her indifferent hand. She surrendered my gift to the ex-detective, whereupon I was suffered to leave.

7

I do not know if the pimp's album may not have been another link in the daisy-chain; but soon after, for my own safety, I decided to marry. It occurred to me that regular hours, home-cooked meals, all the conventions of marriage, the prophylactic routine of its bedroom activities and, who knows, the eventual flowering of certain moral values, of certain spiritual substitutes, might help me, if not to purge myself of my degrading and dangerous desires, at least to keep them under pacific control. A little money that had come my way after my father's death (nothing very grand—the Mirana had been sold long before), in addition to my striking if somewhat brutal good looks, allowed me to enter upon my quest with equanimity. After considerable deliberation, my choice fell on the daughter of a Polish doctor: the good man happened to be treating me for spells of dizziness and tachycardia. We played chess: his daughter watched me 1 from behind her easel, and inserted eyes or knuckles borrowed from me into the cubistic trash that accomplished misses then painted instead of lilacs and lambs. Let me repeat with quiet force: I was, and still am, despite *mes malheurs*, an exceptionally 2 handsome male; slow-moving, tall, with soft dark hair and a gloomy but all the more seductive cast of demeanor. Exceptional virility often reflects in the subject's displayable features a sullen and congested something that pertains to what he has to conceal. And this was my case. Well did I know, alas, that I could obtain at the snap of my fingers any adult female I chose; in fact, it had become quite a habit with me of not being too attentive to women lest they come toppling, bloodripe, into my cold lap. Had I been a *français moyen* with a taste for flashy ladies, I 3 might have easily found, among the many crazed beauties that lashed my grim rock, creatures far more fascinating than Valeria. My choice, however, was prompted by considerations whose essence was, as I realized too late, a piteous compromise. All of which goes to show how dreadfully stupid poor Humbert always was in matters of sex.

8

Although I told myself I was looking merely for a soothing presence, a glorified *pot-au-feu*, an animated merkin, what really 4, 5 attracted me to Valeria was the imitation she gave of a little girl. She gave it not because she had divined something about me; it was just her style—and I fell for it. Actually, she was at least in her late twenties (I never established her exact age for even her passport lied) and had mislaid her virginity under circumstances that changed with her reminiscent moods. I, on my part, was as naïve as only a pervert can be. She looked fluffy and frolicsome, dressed *à la gamine*, showed a generous amount of 6 smooth leg, knew how to stress the white of a bare instep by the black of a velvet slipper, and pouted, and dimpled, and romped, and dirndled, and shook her short curly blond hair in the cutest and tritest fashion imaginable.

After a brief ceremony at the *mairie*, I took her to the new apartment I had rented and, somewhat to her surprise, had her wear, before I touched her, a girl's plain nightshirt that I had managed to filch from the linen closet of an orphanage. I derived some fun from that nuptial night and had the idiot in hysterics by sunrise. But reality soon asserted itself. The bleached curl revealed its melanic root; the down turned to prickles on a shaved shin; the mobile moist mouth, no matter how I stuffed it with love, disclosed ignominiously its resemblance to the corresponding part in a treasured portrait of her toadlike dead mama; and presently, instead of a pale little gutter girl, Humbert Humbert had on his hands a large, puffy, short-legged, big-breasted and practically brainless *baba*.

This state of affairs lasted from 1935 to 1939. Her only asset was a muted nature which did help to produce an odd sense of comfort in our small squalid flat: two rooms, a hazy view in one window, a brick wall in the other, a tiny kitchen, a shoe-shaped bath tub, within which I felt like Marat but with no white-necked maiden to stab me. We had quite a few cozy evenings together, she deep in her *Paris-Soir*, I working at a rickety table. We went to movies, bicycle races and boxing matches. I appealed to her stale flesh very seldom, only in cases of great urgency and despair. The grocer opposite had a little daughter whose shadow drove me mad; but with Valeria's help I did find after all some legal outlets to my fantastic predicament. As to cooking, we tacitly dismissed the *pot-au-feu* and had most of our meals at a crowded place in rue Bonaparte where there were wine stains on the table cloth and a good deal of foreign babble. And next door, an art dealer displayed in his cluttered window a splendid, flamboyant, green, red, golden and inky blue, ancient American estampe—a locomotive with a gigantic smokestack, great baroque lamps and a tremendous cowcatcher, hauling its mauve coaches through the stormy prairie night and mixing a lot of spark-studded black smoke with the furry thunder clouds.

These burst. In the summer of 1939 *mon oncle d'Amérique*   1
died bequeathing me an annual income of a few thousand dollars
on condition I came to live in the States and showed some
interest in his business. This prospect was most welcome to me.
I felt my life needed a shake-up. There was another thing, too:
moth holes had appeared in the plush of matrimonial comfort.
During the last weeks I had kept noticing that my fat Valeria
was not her usual self; had acquired a queer restlessness; even
showed something like irritation at times, which was quite out
of keeping with the stock character she was supposed to impersonate. When I informed her we were shortly to sail for New
York, she looked distressed and bewildered. There were some
tedious difficulties with her papers. She had a Nansen, or better
say Nonsense, passport which for some reason a share in her   2
husband's solid Swiss citizenship could not easily transcend; and
I decided it was the necessity of queuing in the *préfecture,* and   3
other formalities, that had made her so listless, despite my
patiently describing to her America, the country of rosy children
and great trees, where life would be such an improvement on
dull dingy Paris.

We were coming out of some office building one morning,
with her papers almost in order, when Valeria, as she waddled
by my side, began to shake her poodle head vigorously without
saying a word. I let her go on for a while and then asked if she
thought she had something inside. She answered (I translate
from her French which was, I imagine, a translation in its turn
of some Slavic platitude): "There is another man in my life."

Now, these are ugly words for a husband to hear. They dazed
me, I confess. To beat her up in the street, there and then, as an
honest vulgarian might have done, was not feasible. Years of
secret sufferings had taught me superhuman self-control. So I
ushered her into a taxi which had been invitingly creeping along
the curb for some time, and in this comparative privacy I quietly
suggested she comment her wild talk. A mounting fury was suf-
focating me—not because I had any particular fondness for that

figure of fun, *Mme Humbert,* but because matters of legal and illegal conjunction were for me alone to decide, and here she was, Valeria, the comedy wife, brazenly preparing to dispose in her own way of my comfort and fate. I demanded her lover's name. I repeated my question; but she kept up a burlesque babble, discoursing on her unhappiness with me and announcing plans for an immediate divorce. *"Mais qui est-ce?"* I shouted at last, striking her on the knee with my fist; and she, without even wincing, stared at me as if the answer were too simple for words, then gave a quick shrug and pointed at the thick neck of the taxi driver. He pulled up at a small café and introduced himself. I do not remember his ridiculous name but after all those years I still see him quite clearly—a stocky White Russian ex-colonel with a bushy mustache and a crew cut; there were thousands of them plying that fool's trade in Paris. We sat down at a table; the Tsarist ordered wine; and Valeria, after applying a wet napkin to her knee, went on talking—*into* me rather than to me; she poured words into this dignified receptacle with a volubility I had never suspected she had in her. And every now and then she would volley a burst of Slavic at her stolid lover. The situation was preposterous and became even more so when the taxi-colonel, stopping Valeria with a possessive smile, began to unfold *his* views and plans. With an atrocious accent to his careful French, he delineated the world of love and work into which he proposed to enter hand in hand with his child-wife Valeria. She by now was preening herself, between him and me, rouging her pursed lips, tripling her chin to pick at her blouse-bosom and so forth, and he spoke of her as if she were absent, and also as if she were a kind of little ward that was in the act of being transferred, for her own good, from one wise guardian to another even wiser one; and although my helpless wrath may have exaggerated and disfigured certain impressions, I can swear that he actually consulted me on such things as her diet, her periods, her wardrobe and the books she had read or should read. "I think," he said, "she will like *Jean Christophe?*" Oh, he was quite a scholar, Mr. Taxovich.

I put an end to this gibberish by suggesting Valeria pack up

her few belongings immediately, upon which the platitudinous
colonel gallantly offered to carry them into the car. Reverting to
his professional state, he drove the Humberts to their residence
and all the way Valeria talked, and Humbert the Terrible deliberated with Humbert the Small whether Humbert Humbert
should kill her or her lover, or both, or neither. I remember once
handling an automatic belonging to a fellow student, in the days
(I have not spoken of them, I think, but never mind) when I
toyed with the idea of enjoying his little sister, a most diaphanous
nymphet with a black hair bow, and then shooting myself. I
now wondered if Valechka (as the colonel called her) was really
worth shooting, or strangling, or drowning. She had very vul-
nerable legs, and I decided I would limit myself to hurting her
very horribly as soon as we were alone.

But we never were. Valechka—by now shedding torrents of
tears tinged with the mess of her rainbow make-up,—started to
fill anyhow a trunk, and two suitcases, and a bursting carton,
and visions of putting on my mountain boots and taking a
running kick at her rump were of course impossible to put into
execution with the cursed colonel hovering around all the time.
I cannot say he behaved insolently or anything like that; on the
contrary, he displayed, as a small sideshow in the theatricals I
had been inveigled in, a discreet old-world civility, punctuating
his movements with all sorts of mispronounced apologies (*j'ai
demannde pardonne*—excuse me—*est-ce que j'ai puis*—may I—   1
and so forth), and turning away tactfully when Valechka took
down with a flourish her pink panties from the clothesline above
the tub; but he seemed to be all over the place at once, *le gredin*,   2
agreeing his frame with the anatomy of the flat, reading in my
chair my newspaper, untying a knotted string, rolling a cigarette,
counting the teaspoons, visiting the bathroom, helping his moll
to wrap up the electric fan her father had given her, and carrying streetward her luggage. I sat with arms folded, one hip on
the window sill, dying of hate and boredom. At last both were
out of the quivering apartment—the vibration of the door I had
slammed after them still rang in my every nerve, a poor substitute for the backhand slap with which I ought to have hit her

across the cheekbone according to the rules of the movies. Clumsily playing my part, I stomped to the bathroom to check if they had taken my English toilet water; they had not; but I noticed with a spasm of fierce disgust that the former Counselor of the Tsar, after thoroughly easing his bladder, had not flushed the toilet. That solemn pool of alien urine with a soggy, tawny cigarette butt disintegrating in it struck me as a crowning insult, and I wildly looked around for a weapon. Actually I daresay it was nothing but middle-class Russian courtesy (with an oriental tang, perhaps) that had prompted the good colonel (Maximovich! his name suddenly taxies back to me), a very formal person as they all are, to muffle his private need in decorous silence so as not to underscore the small size of his host's domicile with the rush of a gross cascade on top of his own hushed trickle. But this did not enter my mind at the moment, as groaning with rage I ransacked the kitchen for something better than a broom. Then, canceling my search, I dashed out of the house with the heroic decision of attacking him barefisted; despite my natural vigor, I am no pugilist, while the short but broad-shouldered Maximovich seemed made of pig iron. The void of the street, revealing nothing of my wife's departure except a rhinestone button that she had dropped in the mud after preserving it for three unnecessary years in a broken box, may have spared me a bloody nose. But no matter. I had my little revenge in due time. A man from Pasadena told me one day that Mrs. Maximovich née Zborovski had died in childbirth around 1945; the couple had somehow got over to California and had been used there, for an excellent salary, in a year-long experiment conducted by a distinguished American ethnologist. The experiment dealt with human and racial reactions to a diet of bananas and dates in a constant position on all fours. My informant, a doctor, swore he had seen with his own eyes obese Valechka and her colonel, by then gray-haired and also quite corpulent, diligently crawling about the well-swept floors of a brightly lit set of rooms (fruit in one, water in another, mats in a third and so on) in the company of several other hired quadrupeds, selected from indigent and helpless groups. I tried to

find the results of these tests in the *Review of Anthropology;* but they appear not to have been published yet. These scientific products take of course some time to fructuate. I hope they will   1
be illustrated with good photographs when they do get printed, although it is not very likely that a prison library will harbor such erudite works. The one to which I am restricted these days, despite my lawyer's favors, is a good example of the inane eclecticism governing the selection of books in prison libraries. They have the Bible, of course, and Dickens (an ancient set, N. Y., G. W. Dillingham, Publisher, MDCCCLXXXVII); and the *Children's Encyclopedia* (with some nice photographs of sunshine-haired Girl Scouts in shorts), and *A Murder Is Announced* by Agatha Christie; but they also have such coruscating trifles as   2
A Vagabond in Italy by Percy Elphinstone, author of *Venice*   3
Revisited, Boston, 1868, and a comparatively recent (1946) *Who's Who in the Limelight*—actors, producers, playwrights, and shots of static scenes. In looking through the latter volume, I was treated last night to one of those dazzling coincidences that logicians loathe and poets love. I transcribe most of the   4
page:

Pym, Roland. Born in Lundy, Mass., 1922. Received stage   5
training at Elsinore Playhouse, Derby, N.Y. Made debut in   6
Sunburst. Among his many appearances are *Two Blocks from*   7
Here, The Girl in Green, Scrambled Husbands, The Strange Mushroom, Touch and Go, John Lovely, I Was Dreaming   8
of You.

Quilty, Clare, American dramatist. Born in Ocean City,   9
N.J., 1911. Educated at Columbia University. Started on a commercial career but turned to playwriting. Author of *The*
Little Nymph, The Lady Who Loved Lightning (in col-   10, 11
laboration with Vivian Darkbloom), *Dark Age, The Strange*   12, 13
Mushroom, Fatherly Love, and others. His many plays for   14
children are notable. *Little Nymph* (1940) traveled 14,000
miles and played 280 performances on the road during the
winter before ending in New York. Hobbies: fast cars, pho-   15
tography, pets.   16
Quine, Dolores. Born in 1882, in Dayton, Ohio. Studied   17

for stage at American Academy. First played in Ottawa in 1900. Made New York debut in 1904 in *Never Talk to Strangers*. Has disappeared since in [a list of some thirty plays follows].

1, 2

How the look of my dear love's name even affixed to some old hag of an actress, still makes me rock with helpless pain! Perhaps, she might have been an actress too. Born 1935. Appeared 3 (I notice the slip of my pen in the preceding paragraph, but 4, 5 please do not correct it, Clarence) in *The Murdered Playwright*. 6 Quine the Swine. Guilty of killing Quilty. Oh, my Lolita, I 7 have only words to play with!

9

Divorce proceedings delayed my voyage, and the gloom of yet another World War had settled upon the globe when, after a winter of ennui and pneumonia in Portugal, I at last reached the States. In New York I eagerly accepted the soft job fate offered me: it consisted mainly of thinking up and editing perfume ads. I welcomed its desultory character and pseudoliterary aspects, attending to it whenever I had nothing better to do. On the other hand, I was urged by a war-time university in New York to complete my comparative history of French literature for English-speaking students. The first volume took me a couple of years during which I put in seldom less than fifteen hours of work daily. As I look back on those days, I see them divided tidily into ample light and narrow shade: the light pertaining to the solace of research in palatial libraries, the shade to my excruciating desires and insomnias of which enough has been said. Knowing me by now, the reader can easily imagine how dusty and hot I got, trying to catch a glimpse of nymphets (alas, always remote) playing in Central Park, and how repulsed I was by the glitter of deodorized career girls that a gay dog in one of the offices kept unloading upon me. Let us skip all that. A dreadful breakdown sent me to a sanatorium for more than a year; I went back to my work—only to be hospitalized again.

Robust outdoor life seemed to promise me some relief. One of my favorite doctors, a charming cynical chap with a little brown beard, had a brother, and this brother was about to lead an expedition into arctic Canada. I was attached to it as a "recorder of psychic reactions." With two young botanists and an old carpenter I shared now and then (never very successfully) the favors of one of our nutritionists, a Dr. Anita Johnson—who was soon flown back, I am glad to say. I had little notion of what object the expedition was pursuing. Judging by the number of meteorologists upon it, we may have been tracking to its lair (somewhere on Prince of Wales' Island, I understand) the wandering and wobbly north magnetic pole. One group, jointly with the Canadians, established a weather station on Pierre Point in Melville Sound. Another group, equally misguided, collected plankton. A third studied tuberculosis in the tundra. Bert, a film photographer—an insecure fellow with whom at one time I was made to partake in a good deal of menial work (he, too, had some psychic troubles)—maintained that the big men on our team, the real leaders we never saw, were mainly engaged in checking the influence of climatic amelioration on the coats of the arctic fox.

We lived in prefabricated timber cabins amid a Pre-Cambrian world of granite. We had heaps of supplies—the *Reader's Digest*, an ice cream mixer, chemical toilets, paper caps for Christmas. My health improved wonderfully in spite or because of all the fantastic blankness and boredom. Surrounded by such dejected vegetation as willow scrub and lichens; permeated, and, I suppose, cleansed by a whistling gale; seated on a boulder under a completely translucent sky (through which, however, nothing of importance showed), I felt curiously aloof from my own self. No temptations maddened me. The plump, glossy little Eskimo girls with their fish smell, hideous raven hair and guinea pig faces, evoked even less desire in me than Dr. Johnson had. Nymphets do not occur in polar regions.

I left my betters the task of analyzing glacial drifts, drumlins,

1, 2 and gremlins, and kremlins, and for a time tried to jot down what I fondly thought were "reactions" (I noticed, for instance, that dreams under the midnight sun tended to be highly colored, and this my friend the photographer confirmed). I was also supposed to quiz my various companions on a number of important matters, such as nostalgia, fear of unknown animals, food-fantasies, nocturnal emissions, hobbies, choice of radio programs, changes in outlook and so forth. Everybody got so fed up with this that I soon dropped the project completely, and only toward the end of my twenty months of cold labor (as one of the botanists jocosely put it) concocted a perfectly spurious and very racy report that the reader will find published in the *Annals of Adult Psychophysics* for 1945 or 1946, as well as in the issue of *Arctic Explorations* devoted to that particular expedition; which, in conclusion, was not really concerned with Victoria Island copper or anything like that, as I learned later from my genial doctor; for the nature of its real purpose was what is termed "hush-hush," and so let me add merely that whatever it was, that purpose was admirably achieved.

3 The reader will regret to learn that soon after my return to civilization I had another bout with insanity (if to melancholia and a sense of insufferable oppression that cruel term must be applied). I owe my complete restoration to a discovery I made while being treated at that particular very expensive sanatorium. I discovered there was an endless source of robust enjoyment in trifling with psychiatrists: cunningly leading them on; never letting them see that you know all the tricks of the trade; inventing for them elaborate dreams, pure classics in style (which make *them*, the dream-extortionists, dream and wake up shrieking); teasing them with fake "primal scenes"; and never allowing them the slightest glimpse of one's real sexual predicament. By bribing a nurse I won access to some files and discovered, with glee, cards calling me "potentially homosexual" and "totally impotent." The sport was so excellent, its results—in *my* case—so ruddy that I stayed on for a whole month after I was quite well (sleeping admirably and eating like a schoolgirl). And then I added another week just for the pleasure of taking on a power-

ful newcomer, a displaced (and, surely, deranged) celebrity, known for his knack of making patients believe they had witnessed their own conception.   1

10

Upon signing out, I cast around for some place in the New England countryside or sleepy small town (elms, white church) where I could spend a studious summer subsisting on a compact boxful of notes I had accumulated and bathing in some nearby lake. My work had begun to interest me again—I mean my scholarly exertions; the other thing, my active participation in my uncle's posthumous perfumes, had by then been cut down to a minimum.

One of his former employees, the scion of a distinguished family, suggested I spend a few months in the residence of his impoverished cousins, a Mr. McCoo, retired, and his wife, who wanted to let their upper story where a late aunt had delicately dwelt. He said they had two little daughters, one a baby, the other a girl of twelve, and a beautiful garden, not far from a beautiful lake, and I said it sounded perfectly perfect.

I exchanged letters with these people, satisfying them I was housebroken, and spent a fantastic night on the train, imagining in all possible detail the enigmatic nymphet I would coach in French and fondle in Humbertish. Nobody met me at the toy   2
station where I alighted with my new expensive bag, and nobody answered the telephone; eventually, however, a distraught McCoo in wet clothes turned up at the only hotel of green-and-pink Ramsdale with the news that his house had just burned down—possibly, owing to the synchronous conflagration that had   3
been raging all night in my veins. His family, he said, had fled to a farm he owned, and had taken the car, but a friend of his wife's, a grand person, Mrs. Haze of 342 Lawn Street, offered   4
to accommodate me. A lady who lived opposite Mrs. Haze's had   5
lent McCoo her limousine, a marvelously old-fashioned, square-

topped affair, manned by a cheerful Negro. Now, since the only reason for my coming at all had vanished, the aforesaid arrangement seemed preposterous. All right, his house would have to be completely rebuilt, so what? Had he not insured it sufficiently? I was angry, disappointed and bored, but being a polite European, could not refuse to be sent off to Lawn Street in that funeral car, feeling that otherwise McCoo would devise an even more elaborate means of getting rid of me. I saw him scamper away, and my chauffeur shook his head with a soft chuckle. En route, I swore to myself I would not dream of staying in Ramsdale under any circumstance but would fly that very day to the Bermudas or the Bahamas or the Blazes. Possibilities of sweetness on technicolor beaches had been trickling through my spine for some time before, and McCoo's cousin had, in fact, sharply diverted that train of thought with his well-meaning but as it transpired now absolutely inane suggestion.

Speaking of sharp turns: we almost ran over a meddlesome
1 suburban dog (one of those who lie in wait for cars) as we swerved into Lawn Street. A little further, the Haze house, a white-frame horror, appeared, looking dingy and old, more gray than white—the kind of place you know will have a rubber tube affixable to the tub faucet in lieu of shower. I tipped the chauffeur and hoped he would immediately drive away so that I might double back unnoticed to my hotel and bag; but the man merely crossed to the other side of the street where an old lady was calling to him from her porch. What could I do? I pressed the bell button.

A colored maid let me in—and left me standing on the mat while she rushed back to the kitchen where something was burning that ought not to burn.

The front hall was graced with door chimes, a white-eyed wooden thingamabob of commercial Mexican origin, and that
2 banal darling of the arty middle class, van Gogh's "Arlésienne." A door ajar to the right afforded a glimpse of a living room, with some more Mexican trash in a corner cabinet and a striped sofa along the wall. There was a staircase at the end of the hallway, and as I stood mopping my brow (only now did I realize how

hot it had been out-of-doors) and staring, to stare at something, at an old gray tennis ball that lay on an oak chest, there came from the upper landing the contralto voice of Mrs. Haze, who leaning over the banisters inquired melodiously, "Is that Monsieur Humbert?" A bit of cigarette ash dropped from there in addition. Presently, the lady herself—sandals, maroon slacks, yellow silk blouse, squarish face, in that order—came down the steps, her index finger still tapping upon her cigarette.

I think I had better describe her right away, to get it over with. The poor lady was in her middle thirties, she had a shiny forehead, plucked eyebrows and quite simple but not unattractive features of a type that may be defined as a weak solution of Marlene Dietrich. Patting her bronze-brown bun, she led me into the parlor and we talked for a minute about the McCoo fire and the privilege of living in Ramsdale. Her very wide-set sea-green eyes had a funny way of traveling all over you, carefully avoiding your own eyes. Her smile was but a quizzical jerk of one eyebrow; and uncoiling herself from the sofa as she talked, she kept making spasmodic dashes at three ashtrays and the near fender (where lay the brown core of an apple); whereupon she would sink back again, one leg folded under her. She was, obviously, one of those women whose polished words may reflect a book club or bridge club, or any other deadly conventionality, but never her soul; women who are completely devoid of humor; women utterly indifferent at heart to the dozen or so possible subjects of a parlor conversation, but very particular about the rules of such conversations, through the sunny cellophane of which not very appetizing frustrations can be readily distinguished. I was perfectly aware that if by any wild chance I became her lodger, she would methodically proceed to do in regard to me what taking a lodger probably meant to her all along, and I would again be enmeshed in one of those tedious affairs I knew so well.

But there was no question of my settling there. I could not be happy in that type of household with bedraggled magazines on every chair and a kind of horrible hybridization between the comedy of so-called "functional modern furniture" and the tragedy of decrepit rockers and rickety lamp tables with dead lamps. I was led upstairs, and to the left—into "my" room. I inspected it through the mist of my utter rejection of it; but I did discern above "my" bed René Prinet's "Kreutzer Sonata." And she called that servant maid's room a "semi-studio"! Let's get out of here at once, I firmly said to myself as I pretended to deliberate over the absurdly, and ominously, low price that my wistful hostess was asking for board and bed.

Old-world politeness, however, obliged me to go on with the ordeal. We crossed the landing to the right side of the house (where "I and Lo have our rooms"—Lo being presumably the maid), and the lodger-lover could hardly conceal a shudder when he, a very fastidious male, was granted a preview of the only bathroom, a tiny oblong between the landing and "Lo's" room, with limp wet things overhanging the dubious tub (the question mark of a hair inside); and there were the expected coils of the rubber snake, and its complement—a pinkish cozy, coyly covering the toilet lid.

"I see you are not too favorably impressed," said the lady letting her hand rest for a moment upon my sleeve: she combined a cool forwardness—the overflow of what I think is called "poise"—with a shyness and sadness that caused her detached way of selecting her words to seem as unnatural as the intonation of a professor of "speech." "This is not a neat household, I confess," the doomed dear continued, "but I assure you [she looked at my lips], you will be very comfortable, very comfortable, indeed. Let me show you the garden" (the last more brightly, with a kind of winsome toss of the voice).

Reluctantly I followed her downstairs again; then through the kitchen at the end of the hall, on the right side of the house— the side where also the dining room and the parlor were (under "my" room, on the left, there was nothing but a garage). In the kitchen, the Negro maid, a plump youngish woman, said, as she took her large glossy black purse from the knob of the door leading to the back porch: "I'll go now, Mrs. Haze." "Yes, Louise," answered Mrs. Haze with a sigh. "I'll settle with you Friday." We passed on to a small pantry and entered the dining room, parallel to the parlor we had already admired. I noticed a white sock on the floor. With a deprecatory grunt, Mrs. Haze stooped without stopping and threw it into a closet next to the pantry. We cursorily inspected a mahogany table with a fruit vase in the middle, containing nothing but the still glistening stone of one plum. I groped for the timetable I had in my pocket and surreptitiously fished it out to look as soon as possible for a train. I was still walking behind Mrs. Haze through the dining room when, beyond it, there came a sudden burst of greenery— "the piazza," sang out my leader, and then, without the least warning, a blue sea-wave swelled under my heart and, from a mat in a pool of sun, half-naked, kneeling, turning about on her knees, there was my Riviera love peering at me over dark glasses. 1

It was the same child—the same frail, honey-hued shoulders, the same silky supple bare back, the same chestnut head of hair. A polka-dotted black kerchief tied around her chest hid from my aging ape eyes, but not from the gaze of young memory, the juvenile breasts I had fondled one immortal day. And, as if I were the fairy-tale nurse of some little princess (lost, kidnaped, 2 discovered in gypsy rags through which her nakedness smiled at the king and his hounds), I recognized the tiny dark-brown mole on her side. With awe and delight (the king crying for joy, the trumpets blaring, the nurse drunk) I saw again her lovely in-drawn abdomen where my southbound mouth had briefly paused; and those puerile hips on which I had kissed the crenu-lated imprint left by the band of her shorts—that last mad im-mortal day behind the "Roches Roses." The twenty-five years I 3 had lived since then, tapered to a palpitating point, and vanished.

I find it most difficult to express with adequate force that flash, that shiver, that impact of passionate recognition. In the course of the sun-shot moment that my glance slithered over the kneeling child (her eyes blinking over those stern dark spectacles —the little Herr Doktor who was to cure me of all my aches) while I passed by her in my adult disguise (a great big hand-some hunk of movieland manhood), the vacuum of my soul managed to suck in every detail of her bright beauty, and these I checked against the features of my dead bride. A little later, of

1 course, she, this *nouvelle*, this Lolita, *my* Lolita, was to eclipse completely her prototype. All I want to stress is that my discovery of her was a fatal consequence of that "princedom by the sea" in my tortured past. Everything between the two events was but a series of gropings and blunders, and false rudiments of joy. Everything they shared made one of them.

I have no illusions, however. My judges will regard all this as a
2 piece of mummery on the part of a madman with a gross liking
3,4 for the *fruit vert. Au fond, ça m'est bien égal.* All I know is that while the Haze woman and I went down the steps into the breathless garden, my knees were like reflections of knees in rippling water, and my lips were like sand, and—

"That was my Lo," she said, "and these are my lilies."

"Yes," I said, "yes. They are beautiful, beautiful, beautiful!"

11

Exhibit number two is a pocket diary bound in black imitation
5 leather, with a golden year, 1947, *en escalier*, in its upper left-hand corner. I speak of this neat product of the Blank Blank Co.,
6 Blankton, Mass., as if it were really before me. Actually, it was destroyed five years ago and what we examine now (by courtesy of a photographic memory) is but its brief materialization, a
7 puny unfledged phœnix.

I remember the thing so exactly because I wrote it really twice. First I jotted down each entry in pencil (with many erasures and corrections) on the leaves of what is commercially known as a "typewriter tablet"; then, I copied it out with obvious abbreviations in my smallest, most satanic, hand in the little black book just mentioned.

May 30 is a Fast Day by Proclamation in New Hampshire but not in the Carolinas. That day an epidemic of "abdominal flu" (whatever that is) forced Ramsdale to close its schools for the summer. The reader may check the weather data in the Ramsdale *Journal* for 1947. A few days before that I moved into the

Haze house, and the little diary which I now propose to reel off (much as a spy delivers by heart the contents of the note he swallowed) covers most of June.

Thursday. Very warm day. From a vantage point (bathroom window) saw Dolores taking things off a clothesline in the apple-green light behind the house. Strolled out. She wore a plaid shirt, blue jeans and sneakers. Every movement she made in the dappled sun plucked at the most secret and sensitive chord of my abject body. After a while she sat down next to me on the lower step of the back porch and began to pick up the pebbles between her feet—pebbles, my God, then a curled bit of milk-bottle glass resembling a snarling lip—and chuck them at a can. *Ping.* You can't a second time—you can't hit it—this is agony—a second time. *Ping.* Marvelous skin—oh, marvelous: tender and tanned, not the least blemish. Sundaes cause acne. The excess of the oily substance called sebum which nourishes the hair follicles of the skin creates, when too profuse, an irritation that opens the way to infection. But nymphets do not have acne although they gorge themselves on rich food. God, what agony, that silky shimmer above her temple grading into bright brown hair. And the little bone twitching at the side of her dust-powdered ankle. "The McCoo girl? Ginny McCoo? Oh, she's a fright. And mean. And lame. Nearly died of polio." Ping. The glistening tracery of down on her forearm. When she got up to take in the wash, I had a chance of adoring from afar the faded seat of her rolled-up jeans. Out of the lawn, bland Mrs. Haze, complete with camera, grew up like a fakir's fake tree and after some heliotropic fussing—sad eyes up, glad eyes down—had the cheek of taking my picture as I sat blinking on the steps, Humbert le Bel.

Friday. Saw her going somewhere with a dark girl called Rose. Why does the way she walks—a child, mind you, a mere child!—excite me so abominably? Analyze it. A faint suggestion of turned in toes. A kind of wiggly looseness below the knee prolonged to the end of each footfall. The ghost of a drag. Very infantile, infinitely meretricious. Humbert Humbert is also infinitely moved by the little one's slangy speech, by her harsh high voice. Later heard her volley crude nonsense at Rose across the fence. Twanging through me in a rising rhythm. Pause. "I must go now, kiddo."

Saturday. (Beginning perhaps amended.) I know it is madness to keep this journal but it gives me a strange thrill to do so; and only a loving wife could decipher my microscopic script. Let me state with a sob that today my L. was sun-bathing on the so-called "piazza," but her mother and some other woman were around all the time. Of course, I might have sat there in the rocker and pretended to read. Playing safe, I kept away, for I was afraid that the horrible, insane, ridiculous and pitiful tremor
1 that palsied me might prevent me from making my *entrée* with any semblance of casualness.

2 *Sunday.* Heat ripple still with us; a most favonian week. This time I took up a strategic position, with obese newspaper and new pipe, in the piazza rocker *before* L. arrived. To my intense disappointment she came with her mother, both in two-piece bathing suits, black, as new as my pipe. My darling, my sweetheart stood for a moment near me—wanted the funnies—and she smelt almost exactly like the other one, the Riviera one, but more intensely so, with rougher overtones—a torrid odor that at once set my manhood astir—but she had already yanked out of
3 me the coveted section and retreated to her mat near her phocine mamma. There my beauty lay down on her stomach, showing me, showing the thousand eyes wide open in my eyed blood, her slightly raised shoulder blades, and the bloom along the incurvation of her spine, and the swellings of her tense narrow nates clothed in black, and the seaside of her schoolgirl thighs. Silently, the seventh-grader enjoyed her green-red-blue comics. She was
4 the loveliest nymphet green-red-blue Priap himself could think up. As I looked on, through prismatic layers of light, dry-lipped, focusing my lust and rocking slightly under my newspaper, I felt that my perception of her, if properly concentrated upon, might be sufficient to have me attain a beggar's bliss immediately;
5 but, like some predator that prefers a moving prey to a motionless one, I planned to have this pitiful attainment coincide with one of the various girlish movements she made now and then as

she read, such as trying to scratch the middle of her back and revealing a stippled armpit—but fat Haze suddenly spoiled everything by turning to me and asking me for a light, and starting a make-believe conversation about a fake book by some popular fraud.

Monday. *Delectatio morosa.* I spend my doleful days in dumps and dolors. We (mother Haze, Dolores and I) were to go to Our Glass Lake this afternoon, and bathe, and bask; but a nacreous morn degenerated at noon into rain, and Lo made a scene.

The median age of pubescence for girls has been found to be thirteen years and nine months in New York and Chicago. The age varies for individuals from ten, or earlier, to seventeen. Virginia was not quite fourteen when Harry Edgar possessed her. He gave her lessons in algebra. *Je m'imagine cela.* They spent their honeymoon at Petersburg, Fla. "Monsieur Poe-poe," as that boy in one of Monsieur Humbert Humbert's classes in Paris called the poet-poet.

I have all the characteristics which, according to writers on the sex interests of children, start the responses stirring in a little girl: clean-cut jaw, muscular hand, deep sonorous voice, broad shoulder. Moreover, I am said to resemble some crooner or actor chap on whom Lo has a crush.

Tuesday. Rain. Lake of the Rains. Mamma out shopping. L., I knew, was somewhere quite near. In result of some stealthy maneuvering, I came across her in her mother's bedroom. Prying her left eye open to get rid of a speck of something. Checked frock. Although I do love that intoxicating brown fragrance of hers, I really think she should wash her hair once in a while. For a moment, we were both in the same warm green bath of the mirror that reflected the top of a poplar with us in the sky. Held her roughly by the shoulders, then tenderly by the temples, and turned her about. "It's right there," she said, "I can feel it." "Swiss peasant would use the tip of her tongue." "Lick it out?" "Yeth. Shly try?" "Sure," she said. Gently I pressed my quivering sting along her rolling salty eyeball. "Goody-goody," she said nictating. "It *is* gone." "Now the other?" "You dope," she began, "there is noth—" but here she noticed the pucker of my approaching lips. "Okay," she said co-operatively, and bending toward her warm upturned russet face somber Humbert pressed his mouth to her fluttering eyelid. She laughed, and brushed past me out of the room. My heart seemed everywhere at once. Never in my life—not even when fondling my child-love in France—never—

Night. Never have I experienced such agony. I would like to describe her face, her ways—and I cannot, because my own desire for her blinds me when she is near. I am not used to being with nymphets, damn it. If I close my eyes I see but an immobilized fraction of her, a cinematographic still, a sudden smooth nether loveliness, as with one knee up under her tartan skirt she sits

1 tying her shoe. "Dolores Haze, *ne montrez pas vos zhambes*" (this is her mother who thinks she knows French).

2 A poet *à mes heures,* I composed a madrigal to the soot-black lashes of her pale-gray vacant eyes, to the five asymmetrical freckles of her bobbed nose, to the blond down of her brown limbs; but I tore it up and cannot recall it today. Only in the tritest of terms (diary resumed) can I describe Lo's features: I might say her hair is auburn, and her lips as red as licked red candy, the lower one prettily plump—oh, that I were a lady

3 writer who could have her pose naked in a naked light! But instead I am lanky, big-boned, wooly-chested Humbert Humbert, with thick black eyebrows and a queer accent, and a cesspoolful of rotting monsters behind his slow boyish smile. And neither is she the fragile child of a feminine novel. What drives me insane is the twofold nature of this nymphet—of every nymphet, perhaps; this mixture in my Lolita of tender dreamy childishness and a kind of eerie vulgarity, stemming from the snub-nosed cuteness of ads and magazine pictures, from the blurry pinkness of adolescent maidservants in the Old Country (smelling of crushed daisies and sweat); and from very young harlots disguised as children in provincial brothels; and then again, all this gets mixed up with the exquisite stainless tenderness seeping through the musk and the mud, through the dirt and the death, oh God, oh God. And what is most

singular is that she, *this* Lolita, *my* Lolita, has individualized the writer's ancient lust, so that above and over everything there is—Lolita. 1

Wednesday. "Look, make Mother take you and me to Our Glass Lake tomorrow." These were the textual words said to 2 me by my twelve-year-old flame in a voluptuous whisper, as we happened to bump into one another on the front porch, I out, she in. The reflection of the afternoon sun, a dazzling white diamond with innumerable iridescent spikes quivered on the round back of a parked car. The leafage of a voluminous elm played its mellow shadows upon the clapboard wall of the house. Two poplars shivered and shook. You could make out the formless sounds of remote traffic; a child calling "Nancy, Nan-cy!" In the house, Lolita had put on her favorite "Little Carmen" record which I used to call "Dwarf Conductors," 3 making her snort with mock derision at my mock wit.

Thursday. Last night we sat on the piazza, the Haze woman, Lolita and I. Warm dusk had deepened into amorous darkness. The old girl had finished relating in great detail the plot of a movie she and L. had seen sometime in the winter. The boxer had fallen extremely low when he met the good old priest (who had been a boxer himself in his robust youth and could still slug a sinner). We sat on cushions heaped on the floor, and L. was between the woman and me (she had squeezed herself in, the pet). In my turn, I launched upon a hilarious account of my arctic adventures. The muse of invention handed me a rifle and I shot a white bear who sat down and said: Ah! All 4 the while I was acutely aware of L.'s nearness and as I spoke I gestured in the merciful dark and took advantage of those invisible gestures of mine to touch her hand, her shoulder and a ballerina of wool and gauze which she played with and kept sticking into my lap; and finally, when I had completely en-meshed my glowing darling in this weave of ethereal caresses, I dared stroke her bare leg along the gooseberry fuzz of her shin, and I chuckled at my own jokes, and trembled, and concealed my tremors, and once or twice felt with my rapid lips the warmth of her hair as I treated her to a quick nuzzling, humorous aside and caressed her plaything. She, too, fidgeted a good deal so that finally her mother told her sharply to quit it and sent the doll flying into the dark, and I laughed and addressed myself to Haze across Lo's legs to let my hand creep up my nymphet's thin back and feel her skin through her boy's shirt.

But I knew it was all hopeless, and was sick with longing, and my clothes felt miserably tight, and I was almost glad when her mother's quiet voice announced in the dark: "And now we all think that Lo should go to bed." "I think you stink," said Lo. "Which means there will be no picnic tomorrow," said Haze. "This is a free country," said Lo. When angry Lo with a Bronx cheer had gone, I stayed on from sheer inertia, while Haze smoked her tenth cigarette of the evening and complained of Lo.

She had been spiteful, if you please, at the age of one, when she used to throw her toys out of her crib so that her poor mother should keep picking them up, the villainous infant! Now, at twelve, she was a regular pest, said Haze. All she wanted from life was to be one day a strutting and prancing baton twirler or a jitterbug. Her grades were poor, but she was better adjusted in her new school than in Pisky (Pisky was the Haze home town in the Middle West. The Ramsdale house was her late mother-in-law's. They had moved to Ramsdale less than two years ago). "Why was she unhappy there?" "Oh," said Haze, "poor me should know, I went through that when *I* was a kid: boys twisting one's arm, banging into one with loads of books, pulling one's hair, hurting one's breasts, flipping one's skirt. Of course, moodiness is a common concomitant of growing up, but Lo exaggerates. Sullen and evasive. Rude and defiant. Stuck Viola, an Italian schoolmate, in the seat with a fountain pen. Know what I would like? If you, monsieur, happened to be still here in the fall, I'd ask you to help her with her home-work—you seem to know everything, geography, mathematics, French." "Oh, everything," answered monsieur. "That means," said Haze quickly, "you'll *be* here!" I wanted to shout that I would stay on eternally if only I could hope to caress now and

46

then my incipient pupil. But I was wary of Haze. So I just grunted and stretched my limbs nonconcomitantly (*le mot juste*) and presently went up to my room. The woman, however, was evidently not prepared to call it a day. I was already lying upon my cold bed both hands pressing to my face Lolita's fragrant ghost when I heard my indefatigable landlady creeping stealthily up to my door to whisper through it—just to make sure, she said, I was through with the Glance and Gulp magazine I had borrowed the other day. From her room Lo yelled *she* had it. We are quite a lending library in this house, thunder of God.

Friday. I wonder what my academic publishers would say if I were to quote in my textbook Ronsard's "*la vermeillette fente*" or Remy Belleau's "*un petit mont feutré de mousse délicate, tracé sur le milieu d'un fillet escarlatte*" and so forth. I shall probably have another breakdown if I stay any longer in this house, under the strain of this intolerable temptation, by the side of my darling—my darling—my life and my bride. Has she already been initiated by mother nature to the Mystery of the Menarche? Bloated feeling. The Curse of the Irish. Falling from the roof. Grandma is visiting. "Mr. Uterus [I quote from a girls' magazine] starts to build a thick soft wall on the chance a possible baby may have to be bedded down there." The tiny madman in his padded cell.

Incidentally: if I ever commit a serious murder . . . Mark the "if." The urge should be something more than the kind of thing that happened to me with Valeria. Carefully mark that *then* I was rather inept. If and when you wish to sizzle me to death, remember that only a spell of insanity could ever give me the simple energy to be a brute (all this amended, perhaps). Sometimes I attempt to kill in my dreams. But do you know what happens? For instance I hold a gun. For instance I aim at a bland, quietly interested enemy. Oh, I press the trigger all right, but one bullet after another feebly drops on the floor from the sheepish muzzle. In those dreams, my only thought is to conceal the fiasco from my foe, who is slowly growing annoyed.

At dinner tonight the old cat said to me with a sidelong gleam of motherly mockery directed at Lo (I had just been

1 describing, in a flippant vein, the delightful little toothbrush mustache I had not quite decided to grow): "Better don't, if somebody is not to go absolutely dotty." Instantly Lo pushed her plate of boiled fish away, all but knocking her milk over, and bounced out of the dining room. "Would it bore you very much," quoth Haze, "to come with us tomorrow for a swim in Our Glass Lake if Lo apologizes for her manners?"

Later, I heard a great banging of doors and other sounds coming from quaking caverns where the two rivals were having a ripping row.

She has not apologized. The lake is out. It might have been fun.

Saturday. For some days already I had been leaving the door ajar, while I wrote in my room; but only today did the trap work. With a good deal of additional fidgeting, shuffling, scraping—to disguise her embarrassment at visiting me without having been called—Lo came in and after pottering around, became interested in the nightmare curlicues I had penned on a sheet of paper. Oh no: they were not the outcome of a belle-lettrist's inspired pause between two paragraphs; they were the hideous hieroglyphics (which she could not decipher) of my fatal lust. As she bent her brown curls over the desk at which I was sitting, Humbert the Hoarse put his arm around her in a miserable imitation of blood-relationship; and still studying, somewhat shortsightedly, the piece of paper she held, my innocent little visitor slowly sank to a half-sitting position upon my knee. Her adorable profile, parted lips, warm hair were some three inches from my bared eyetooth; and I felt the heat of her limbs through her rough tomboy clothes. All at once I knew I could kiss her throat or the wick of her mouth with perfect impunity. I knew she would let me do so, and even close her eyes as Hollywood teaches. A double vanilla with hot fudge —hardly more unusual than that. I cannot tell my learned reader (whose eyebrows, I suspect, have by now traveled all the way to the back of his bald head), I cannot tell him how 2 the knowledge came to me; perhaps my ape-ear had unconsciously caught some slight change in the rhythm of her respiration—for now she was not really looking at my scribble, but waiting with curiosity and composure—oh, my limpid nymphet! —for the glamorous lodger to do what he was dying to do. A modern child, an avid reader of movie magazines, an expert in dream-slow close-ups, might not think it too strange, I guessed, if a handsome, intensely virile grown-up friend—too late. The house was suddenly vibrating with voluble Louise's voice telling Mrs. Haze who had just come home about a dead something she and Leslie Tomson had found in the basement, and little Lolita was not one to miss such a tale.

Sunday. Changeful, bad-tempered, cheerful, awkward, graceful with the tart grace of her coltish subteens, excruciatingly desirable from head to foot (all New England for a lady-writer's pen!), from the black ready-made bow and bobby pins holding her hair in place to the little scar on the lower part of her neat calf (where a roller-skater kicked her in Pisky), a couple of inches above her rough white sock. Gone with her mother to the Hamiltons—a birthday party or something. Full-skirted gingham frock. Her little doves seem well formed already. Precocious pet! 1

Monday. Rainy morning. *"Ces matins gris si doux . . ."* My white pajamas have a lilac design on the back. I am like one of those inflated pale spiders you see in old gardens. Sitting in the middle of a luminous web and giving little jerks to this or that strand. *My* web is spread all over the house as I listen from my chair where I sit like a wily wizard. Is Lo in her room? Gently I tug on the silk. She is not. Just heard the toilet paper cylinder make its staccato sound as it is turned; and no footfalls has my outflung filament traced from the bathroom back to her room. Is she still brushing her teeth (the only sanitary act Lo performs with real zest)? No. The bathroom door has just slammed, so one has to feel elsewhere about the house for the beautiful warm-colored prey. Let us have a strand of silk descend the stairs. I satisfy myself by this means that she is not in the kitchen—not banging the refrigerator door or screeching at her detested mamma (who, I suppose, is enjoying her third, cooing and subduedly mirthful, telephone conversation 2 of the morning). Well, let us grope and hope. Ray-like, I glide in thought to the parlor and find the radio silent (and mamma still talking to Mrs. Chatfield or Mrs. Hamilton, very softly, flushed, smiling, cupping the telephone with her free hand, denying by implication that she denies those amusing rumors, rumor, roomer, whispering intimately, as she never does, the clear-cut lady, in face to face talk). So my nymphet is not in the house at all! Gone! What I thought was a prismatic weave turns out to be but an old gray cobweb, the house is empty, is dead. And then comes Lolita's soft sweet chuckle through my half-open door "Don't tell Mother but I've eaten *all* your bacon." Gone when I scuttle out of my room. Lolita, where are you? My breakfast tray, lovingly prepared by my landlady, leers at me toothlessly, ready to be taken in. Lola, Lolita!

Tuesday. Clouds again interfered with that picnic on that unattainable lake. Is it Fate scheming? Yesterday I tried on before the mirror a new pair of bathing trunks.

Wednesday. In the afternoon, Haze (common-sensical shoes, tailor-made dress), said she was driving downtown to buy a present for a friend of a friend of hers, and would I please come too because I have such a wonderful taste in textures and perfumes. "Choose your favorite seduction," she purred. What could Humbert, being in the perfume business, do? She had me cornered between the front porch and her car. "Hurry up," she said as I laboriously doubled up my large body in order to crawl in (still desperately devising a means of escape). She had started the engine, and was genteelly swearing at a backing and turning truck in front that had just brought old invalid Miss Opposite a brand new wheel chair, when my Lolita's sharp voice came from the parlor window: "You! Where are you going? I'm coming too! Wait!" "Ignore her," yelped Haze (killing the motor); alas for my fair driver; Lo was already pulling at the door on my side. "This is intolerable," began Haze; but Lo had scrambled in, shivering with glee. "Move your bottom, you," said Lo. "Lo!" cried Haze (sideglancing at me, hoping I would throw rude Lo out). "And behold," said Lo (not for the first time), as she jerked back, as I jerked back, as the car leapt forward. "It is intolerable," said Haze, violently getting into second, "that a child should be so ill-mannered. And so very persevering. When she knows she is unwanted. And needs a bath."

My knuckles lay against. the child's blue jeans. She was barefooted; her toenails showed remnants of cherry-red polish and there was a bit of adhesive tape across her big toe; and, God, what would I not have given to kiss then and there those delicate-boned, long-toed, monkeyish feet! Suddenly her hand slipped into mine and without our chaperon's seeing, I held, and stroked, and squeezed that little hot paw, all the way to the store. The wings of the driver's Marlenesque nose shone, having shed or burned up their ration of powder, and she kept up an elegant monologue anent the local traffic, and smiled in profile, and pouted in profile, and beat her painted lashes in profile, while I prayed we would never get to that store, but we did.

I have nothing else to report, save, *primo:* that big Haze had little Haze sit behind on our way home, and *secundo:* that the lady decided to keep Humbert's Choice for the backs of her own shapely ears.

Thursday. We are paying with hail and gale for the tropical beginning of the month. In a volume of the *Young People's Encyclopedia,* I found a map of the States that a child's pencil had started copying out on a sheet of lightweight paper, upon the other side of which, counter to the unfinished outline of Florida and the Gulf, there was a mimeographed list of names referring, evidently, to her class at the Ramsdale school. It is a poem I know already by heart.

> Angel, Grace
> Austin, Floyd
> Beale, Jack
> Beale, Mary
> Buck, Daniel
> Byron, Marguerite
> Campbell, Alice
> Carmine, Rose
> Chatfield, Phyllis

Clarke, Gordon
Cowan, John
Cowan, Marion
Duncan, Walter
Falter, Ted
Fantasia, Stella
Flashman, Irving
Fox, George
Glave, Mabel
Goodale, Donald
Green, Lucinda
Hamilton, Mary Rose
Haze, Dolores
Honeck, Rosaline
Knight, Kenneth
McCoo, Virginia
McCrystal, Vivian
McFate, Aubrey
Miranda, Anthony
Miranda, Viola
Rosato, Emil
Schlenker, Lena
Scott, Donald
Sheridan, Agnes
Sherva, Oleg
Smith, Hazel
Talbot, Edgar
Talbot, Edwin
Wain, Lull
Williams, Ralph
Windmuller, Louise

A poem, a poem, forsooth! So strange and sweet was it to discover this "Haze, Dolores" (she!) in its special bower of names, with its bodyguard of roses—a fairy princess between her two maids of honor. I am trying to analyze the spine-thrill of delight it gives me, this name among all those others. What is it that excites me almost to tears (hot, opalescent, thick tears that poets and lovers shed)? What is it? The tender anonymity of this name with its formal veil ("Dolores") and that abstract transposition of first name and surname, which is like a pair of new pale gloves or a mask? Is "mask" the keyword? Is it because there is always delight in the semitranslucent mystery, the flowing charshaf, through which the flesh and the eye you alone are elected to know smile in passing at you alone? Or is it because I can imagine so well the rest of the colorful classroom around my dolorous and hazy darling: Grace and her ripe pimples; Ginny and her lagging leg; Gordon, the haggard masturbator; Duncan, the foul-smelling clown; nail-biting Agnes; Viola, of the blackheads and the bouncing bust; pretty Rosaline; dark Mary Rose; adorable Stella, who has let strangers touch her; Ralph, who bullies and steals; Irving, for whom I am sorry. And there she is there, lost in the middle, gnawing a pencil, detested by teachers, all the boys' eyes on her hair and neck, *my* Lolita.

Friday. I long for some terrific disaster. Earthquake. Spectacular explosion. Her mother is messily but instantly and permanently eliminated, along with everybody else for miles around. Lolita whimpers in my arms. A free man, I enjoy her among the ruins. Her surprise, my explanations, demonstrations, ullulations. Idle and idiotic fancies! A brave Humbert would have played with her most disgustingly (yesterday, for instance, when she was again in my room to show me her drawings, schoolartware); he might have bribed her—and got away with it. A simpler and more practical fellow would have soberly stuck to various commercial substitutes—if you know where to go, I don't. Despite my manly looks, I am horribly timid. My romantic soul gets all clammy and shivery at the thought of running into some awful indecent unpleasantness. Those ribald sea monsters. *"Mais allez-y, allez-y!"* Annabel skipping on one foot to get into her shorts, I seasick with rage, trying to screen her.

Same date, later, quite late. I have turned on the light to take down a dream. It had an evident antecedent. Haze at dinner had benevolently proclaimed that since the weather bureau promised a sunny weekend we would go to the lake Sunday after church. As I lay in bed, erotically musing before trying to go to sleep, I thought of a final scheme how to profit

by the picnic to come. I was aware that mother Haze hated
my darling for her being sweet on me. So I planned my lake
day with a view to satisfying the mother. To her alone would
I talk; but at some appropriate moment I would say I had left
my wrist watch or my sunglasses in that glade yonder—and
plunge with my nymphet into the wood. Reality at this junc-
ture withdrew, and the Quest for the Glasses turned into a
quiet little orgy with a singularly knowing, cheerful, corrupt
and compliant Lolita behaving as reason knew she could not
possibly behave. At 3 A.M. I swallowed a sleeping pill, and presently, a dream that was not a sequel but a parody revealed to
me, with a kind of meaningful clarity, the lake I had never yet
visited: it was glazed over with a sheet of emerald ice, and a
pockmarked Eskimo was trying in vain to break it with a pickaxe,
although imported mimosas and oleanders flowered on its grav-
1 elly banks. I am sure Dr. Blanche Schwarzmann would have
2 paid me a sack of schillings for adding such a libidream to her
files. Unfortunately, the rest of it was frankly eclectic. Big
Haze and little Haze rode on horseback around the lake, and I
rode too, dutifully bobbing up and down, bowlegs astraddle
although there was no horse between them, only elastic air—
one of those little omissions due to the absent-mindedness of
the dream agent.

Saturday. My heart is still thumping. I still squirm and emit
low moans of remembered embarrassment.

3 Dorsal view. Glimpse of shiny skin between T-shirt and white
gym shorts. Bending, over a window sill, in the act of tearing off
leaves from a poplar outside while engrossed in torrential talk
with a newspaper boy below (Kenneth Knight, I suspect) who
had just propelled the Ramsdale *Journal* with a very precise thud
onto the porch. I began creeping up to her—"crippling" up to
her, as pantomimists say. My arms and legs were convex surfaces
between which—rather than upon which—I slowly progressed
by some neutral means of locomotion: Humbert the Wounded
Spider. I must have taken hours to reach her: I seemed to see
her through the wrong end of a telescope, and toward her taut
little rear I moved like some paralytic, on soft distorted limbs,

in terrible concentration. At last I was right behind her when I had the unfortunate idea of blustering a trifle—shaking her by the scruff of the neck and that sort of thing to cover my real *manège*, and she said in a shrill brief whine: "Cut it out!"— most coarsely, the little wench, and with a ghastly grin Humbert the Humble beat a gloomy retreat while she went on wisecracking streetward.

But now listen to what happened next. After lunch I was reclining in a low chair trying to read. Suddenly two deft little hands were over my eyes: she had crept up from behind as if re-enacting, in a ballet sequence, my morning maneuver. Her fingers were a luminous crimson as they tried to blot out the sun, and she uttered hiccups of laughter and jerked this way and that as I stretched my arm sideways and backwards without otherwise changing my recumbent position. My hand swept over her agile giggling legs, and the book like a sleigh left my lap, and Mrs. Haze strolled up and said indulgently: "Just slap her hard if she interferes with your scholarly meditations. How I love this garden [no exclamation mark in her tone]. Isn't it divine in the sun [no question mark either]." And with a sign of feigned content, the obnoxious lady sank down on the grass and looked up at the sky as she leaned back on her splayed-out hands, and presently an old gray tennis ball bounced over her, and Lo's voice came from the house haughtily: "*Pardonnez*, Mother. I was not aiming at *you*." Of course not, my hot downy darling.

12

This proved to be the last of twenty entries or so. It will be seen from them that for all the devil's inventiveness, the scheme remained daily the same. First he would tempt me—and then thwart me, leaving me with a dull pain in the very root of my being. I knew exactly what I wanted to do, and how to do it, without impinging on a child's chastity; after all, I had had *some* experience in my life of pederosis; had visually possessed dappled nymphets in parks; had wedged my wary and bestial way into the hottest, most crowded corner of a city bus full of strap-hanging school children. But for almost three weeks I had been interrupted in all my pathetic machinations. The agent of these interruptions was usually the Haze woman (who, as the reader will mark, was more afraid of Lo's deriving some pleasure from me than of my enjoying Lo). The passion I had developed for that nymphet—for the first nymphet in my life that could be reached at last by my awkward, aching, timid claws—would have certainly landed me again in a sanatorium, had not the devil realized that I was to be granted some relief if he wanted to have me as a plaything for some time longer.

The reader has also marked the curious Mirage of the Lake. It would have been logical on the part of Aubrey McFate (as I would like to dub that devil of mine) to arrange a small treat for me on the promised beach, in the presumed forest. Actually, the promise Mrs. Haze had made was a fraudulent one: she had not told me that Mary Rose Hamilton (a dark little beauty in her own right) was to come too, and that the two nymphets would be whispering apart, and playing apart, and having a good time all by themselves, while Mrs. Haze and her handsome lodger conversed sedately in the seminude, far from prying eyes. Incidentally, eyes did pry and tongues did wag. How queer life is! We hasten to alienate the very fates we intended to woo. Before my actual arrival, my landlady had planned to have an old spinster, a Miss Phalen, whose mother had been cook in Mrs. Haze's family, come to stay in the house with Lolita and me, while Mrs. Haze, a career girl at heart, sought some suitable job in the nearest city. Mrs. Haze had seen the whole situation very clearly: the bespectacled, round-backed Herr Humbert coming with his Central-European trunks to gather dust in his corner behind a heap of old books; the unloved ugly little daughter firmly supervised by Miss Phalen who had already once had my Lo under her buzzard wing (Lo recalled that 1944 summer with an indignant shudder); and Mrs. Haze herself engaged as a receptionist in a great elegant city. But a not too complicated event interfered with that program. Miss Phalen broke her hip in Savannah, Ga., on the very day I arrived in Ramsdale.

13

The Sunday after the Saturday already described proved to be as bright as the weatherman had predicted. When putting the breakfast things back on the chair outside my room for my good landlady to remove at her convenience, I gleaned the following situation by listening from the landing across which I had softly crept to the bannisters in my old bedroom slippers— the only old things about me.

There had been another row. Mrs. Hamilton had telephoned that her daughter "was running a temperature." Mrs. Haze informed *her* daughter that the picnic would have to be postponed. Hot little Haze informed big cold Haze that, if so, she would not go with her to church. Mother said very well and left.

I had come out on the landing straight after shaving, soapy-earlobed, still in my white pajamas with the cornflower blue (not the lilac) design on the back; I now wiped off the soap, perfumed my hair and armpits, slipped on a purple silk dressing gown, and, humming nervously, went down the stairs in quest of Lo.

I want my learned readers to participate in the scene I am about to replay; I want them to examine its every detail and see for themselves how careful, how chaste, the whole wine-sweet event is if viewed with what my lawyer has called, in a private talk we have had, "impartial sympathy." So let us get started. I have a difficult job before me.

Main character: Humbert the Hummer. Time: Sunday morning in June. Place: sunlit living room. Props: old, candy-striped davenport, magazines, phonograph, Mexican knickknacks (the late Mr. Harold E. Haze—God bless the good man—had engendered my darling at the siesta hour in a blue-washed room, on a honeymoon trip to Vera Cruz, and mementoes, among these Dolores, were all over the place). She wore that day a pretty print dress that I had seen on her once before, ample in the skirt, tight in the bodice, short-sleeved, pink, checkered with darker pink, and, to complete the color scheme, she had painted her lips and was holding in her hollowed hands a beautiful, banal, Eden-red apple. She was not shod, however, for church. And her white Sunday purse lay discarded near the phonograph.

My heart beat like a drum as she sat down, cool skirt ballooning, subsiding, on the sofa next to me, and played with her glossy fruit. She tossed it up into the sun-dusted air, and caught it— it made a cupped polished *plop*.

Humbert Humbert intercepted the apple.

"Give it back," she pleaded, showing the marbled flush of her palms. I produced Delicious. She grasped it and bit into it, and my heart was like snow under thin crimson skin, and with the monkeyish nimbleness that was so typical of that American nymphet, she snatched out of my abstract grip the magazine I had opened (pity no film had recorded the curious pattern, the monogrammic linkage of our simultaneous or overlapping moves). Rapidly, hardly hampered by the disfigured apple she held, Lo flipped violently through the pages in search of something she wished Humbert to see. Found it at last. I faked interest by bringing my head so close that her hair touched my temple and her arm brushed my cheek as she wiped her lips with her wrist. Because of the burnished mist through which I peered at the picture, I was slow in reacting to it, and her bare knees rubbed and knocked impatiently against each other. Dimly there came into view: a surrealist painter relaxing, supine, on a beach, and near him, likewise supine, a plaster replica of the Venus di Milo, half-buried in sand. Picture of the Week, said the legend. I whisked the whole obscene thing away. Next moment, in a sham effort to retrieve it, she was all over me. Caught her by her thin knobby wrist. The magazine escaped to the floor like a flustered fowl. She twisted herself free, recoiled, and lay back in the right-hand corner of the davenport. Then, with perfect simplicity, the impudent child extended her legs across my lap.

By this time I was in a state of excitement bordering on insanity; but I also had the cunning of the insane. Sitting there, on the sofa, I managed to attune, by a series of stealthy movements, my masked lust to her guileless limbs. It was no easy matter to divert the little maiden's attention while I performed the obscure adjustments necessary for the success of the trick.

Talking fast, lagging behind my own breath, catching up with it, mimicking a sudden toothache to explain the breaks in my patter —and all the while keeping a maniac's inner eye on my distant golden goal, I cautiously increased the magic friction that was doing away, in an illusional, if not factual, sense, with the physically irremovable, but psychologically very friable texture of the material divide (pajamas and robe) between the weight of two sunburnt legs, resting athwart my lap, and the hidden tumor of an unspeakable passion. Having, in the course of my patter, hit upon something nicely mechanical, I recited, garbling them slightly, the words of a foolish song that was then popular—O my Carmen, my little Carmen, something, something, those something nights, and the stars, and the cars, and the bars, and the barmen; I kept repeating this automatic stuff and holding her under its special spell (spell because of the garbling), and all the while I was mortally afraid that some act of God might interrupt me, might remove the golden load in the sensation of which all my being seemed concentrated, and this anxiety forced me to work, for the first minute or so, more hastily than was consensual with deliberately modulated enjoyment. The stars that sparkled, and the cars that parkled, and the bars, and the barmen, were presently taken over by her; her voice stole and corrected the tune I had been mutilating. She was musical and apple-sweet. Her legs twitched a little as they lay across my live lap; I stroked them; there she lolled in the right-hand corner, almost asprawl, Lola the bobby-soxer, devouring her immemorial fruit, singing through its juice, losing her slipper, rubbing the heel of her slipperless foot in its sloppy anklet, against the pile of old magazines heaped on my left on the sofa—and every movement she made, every shuffle and ripple, helped me to conceal and to improve the secret system of tactile correspondence between beast and beauty—between my gagged, bursting beast and the beauty of her dimpled body in its innocent cotton frock.

Under my glancing finger tips I felt the minute hairs bristle ever so slightly along her shins. I lost myself in the pungent but healthy heat which like summer haze hung about little Haze. Let her stay, let her stay ... As she strained to chuck the core of her abolished apple into the fender, her young weight, her shameless innocent shanks and round bottom, shifted in my tense, tortured, surreptitiously laboring lap; and all of a sudden a mysterious change came over my senses. I entered a plane of being where nothing mattered, save the infusion of joy brewed within my body. What had begun as a delicious distension of my innermost roots became a glowing tingle which *now* had reached that state of absolute security, confidence and reliance not found elsewhere in conscious life. With the deep hot sweetness thus established and well on its way to the ultimate convulsion, I felt I could slow down in order to prolong the glow. Lolita had been safely solipsized. The implied sun pulsated in the supplied poplars; we were fantastically and divinely alone; I watched her, rosy, gold-dusted, beyond the veil of my controlled delight, unaware of it, alien to it, and the sun was on her lips, and her lips were apparently still forming the words of the Carmen-barmen ditty that no longer reached my consciousness. Everything was now ready. The nerves of pleasure had been laid bare. The corpuscles of Krause were entering the phase of frenzy. The least pressure would suffice to set all paradise loose. I had ceased to be Humbert the Hound, the sad-eyed degenerate cur clasping the boot that would presently kick him away. I was above the tribulations of ridicule, beyond the possibilities of retribution. In my self-made seraglio, I was a radiant and robust Turk, deliberately, in the full consciousness of his freedom, postponing the moment of actually enjoying the youngest and frailest of his slaves. Suspended on the brink of that voluptuous abyss (a nicety of physiological equipoise comparable to certain techniques in the arts) I kept repeating chance words after her—barmen, alarmin', my charmin', my carmen, ahmen, ahahamen—as one talking and laughing in his sleep while my happy hand crept up her sunny leg as far as the shadow of decency allowed. The day before she had collided with the heavy chest in the hall and— "Look, look!"—I gasped—"look what you've done, what you've done to yourself, ah, look"; for there was, I swear, a yellowish-violet bruise on her lovely nymphet thigh which my huge hairy hand massaged and slowly enveloped—and because of her very perfunctory underthings, there seemed to be nothing to prevent my muscular thumb from reaching the hot hollow of her groin —just as you might tickle and caress a giggling child—just that— and: "Oh it's nothing at all," she cried with a sudden shrill note in her voice, and she wiggled, and squirmed, and threw her head back, and her teeth rested on her glistening underlip as she half-turned away, and my moaning mouth, gentlemen of the jury, almost reached her bare neck, while I crushed out against her left buttock the last throb of the longest ecstasy man or monster had ever known.

Immediately afterward (as if we had been struggling and now my grip had eased) she rolled off the sofa and jumped to her feet—to her foot, rather—in order to attend to the formidably loud telephone that may have been ringing for ages as far as I was concerned. There she stood and blinked, cheeks aflame, hair awry, her eyes passing over me as lightly as they did over the furniture, and as she listened or spoke (to her mother who was telling her to come to lunch with her at the Chatfields—neither Lo nor Hum knew yet what busybody Haze was plotting), she kept tapping the edge of the table with the slipper she held in her hand. Blessed be the Lord, she had noticed nothing!

With a handkerchief of multicolored silk, on which her listening eyes rested in passing, I wiped the sweat off my forehead, and, immersed in a euphoria of release, rearranged my royal robes. She was still at the telephone, haggling with her mother (wanted to be fetched by car, my little Carmen) when, singing louder and louder, I swept up the stairs and set a deluge of steaming water roaring into the tub.

At this point I may as well give the words of that song hit in full—to the best of my recollection at least—I don't think I ever had it right. Here goes:

> O my Carmen, my little Carmen!
> Something, something those something nights,
> And the stars, and the cars, and the bars, and the
> [barmen—
> And, O my charmin', our dreadful fights.

And the something town where so gaily, arm in
Arm, we went, and our final row,
And the gun I killed you with, O my Carmen,
The gun I am holding now.

1   (Drew his .32 automatic, I guess, and put a bullet through his
moll's eye.)

14

I had lunch in town—had not been so hungry for years. The
house was still Lo-less when I strolled back. I spent the afternoon musing, scheming, blissfully digesting my experience of the
morning.

I felt proud of myself. I had stolen the honey of a spasm without impairing the morals of a minor. Absolutely no harm done.
The conjurer had poured milk, molasses, foaming champagne
into a young lady's new white purse; and lo, the purse was intact.
Thus had I delicately constructed my ignoble, ardent, sinful
dream; and still Lolita was safe—and I was safe. What I had
madly possessed was not she, but my own creation, another,
fanciful Lolita—perhaps, more real than Lolita; overlapping, en-
casing her; floating between me and her, and having no will, no
consciousness—indeed, no life of her own.

The child knew nothing. I had done nothing to her. And
nothing prevented me from repeating a performance that affected her as little as if she were a photographic image rippling
upon a screen and I a humble hunchback abusing myself in the
dark. The afternoon drifted on and on, in ripe silence, and the
sappy tall trees seemed to be in the know; and desire, even
stronger than before, began to afflict me again. Let her come
2   soon, I prayed, addressing a loan God, and while mamma is in
the kitchen, let a repetition of the davenport scene be staged,
please, I adore her so horribly.

No: "horribly" is the wrong word. The elation with which the
vision of new delights filled me was not horrible but pathetic. I

qualify it as pathetic. Pathetic—because despite the insatiable fire of my venereal appetite, I intended, with the most fervent force and foresight, to protect the purity of that twelve-year-old child.

And now see how I was repaid for my pains. No Lolita came home—she had gone with the Chatfields to a movie. The table was laid with more elegance than usual: candlelight, if you please. In this mawkish aura, Mrs. Haze gently touched the silver on both sides of her plate as if touching piano keys, and smiled down on her empty plate (was on a diet), and said she hoped I liked the salad (recipe lifted from a woman's magazine). She hoped I liked the cold cuts, too. It had been a perfect day. Mrs. Chatfield was a lovely person. Phyllis, her daughter, was going to a summer camp tomorrow. For three weeks. Lolita, it was decided, would go Thursday. Instead of waiting till July, as had been initially planned. And stay there after Phyllis had left. Till school began. A pretty prospect, my heart.

Oh, how I was taken aback—for did it not mean I was losing my darling, just when I had secretly made her mine? To explain my grim mood, I had to use the same toothache I had already simulated in the morning. Must have been an enormous molar, with an abscess as big as a maraschino cherry.

"We have," said Haze, "an excellent dentist. Our neighbor, in fact. Dr. Quilty. Uncle or cousin, I think, of the playwright. Think it will pass? Well, just as you wish. In the fall I shall have him 'brace' her, as my mother used to say. It may curb Lo a little. I am afraid she has been bothering you frightfully all these days. And we are in for a couple of stormy ones before she goes. She has flatly refused to go, and I confess I left her with the Chatfields because I dreaded to face her alone just yet. The movie may mollify her. Phyllis is a very sweet girl, and there is no earthly reason for Lo to dislike her. Really, monsieur, I am very sorry about that tooth of yours. It would be so much more reasonable to let me contact Ivor Quilty first thing tomorrow morning if it still hurts. And, you know, I think a summer camp is so much healthier, and—well, it is all so much more *reasonable* as I say than to mope on a suburban lawn and use mamma's lipstick, and pursue shy studious gentlemen, and go into tantrums at the least provocation."

"Are you sure," I said at last, "that she will be happy there?" (lame, lamentably lame!)

"She'd better," said Haze. "And it won't be all play either. The camp is run by Shirley Holmes—you know, the woman who wrote *Campfire Girl*. Camp will teach Dolores Haze to grow in many things—health, knowledge, temper. And particularly in a sense of responsibility toward other people. Shall we take these candles with us and sit for a while on the piazza, or do you want to go to bed and nurse that tooth?"

Nurse that tooth.

15

Next day they drove downtown to buy things needed for the camp: any wearable purchase worked wonders with Lo. She seemed her usual sarcastic self at dinner. Immediately afterwards, she went up to her room to plunge into the comic books acquired for rainy days at Camp Q (they were so thoroughly sampled by Thursday that she left them behind). I too retired to my lair, and wrote letters. My plan now was to leave for the seaside and then, when school began, resume my existence in the Haze household; for I knew already that I could not live without the child. On Tuesday they went shopping again, and I was asked to answer the phone if the camp mistress rang up during their absence. She did; and a month or so later we had occasion to recall our pleasant chat. That Tuesday, Lo had her dinner in her room. She had been crying after a routine row with her mother and, as had happened on former occasions, had not wished me to see her swollen eyes: she had one of those tender complexions that after a good cry get all blurred and inflamed, and morbidly alluring. I regretted keenly her mistake about my private aesthetics, for I simply love that tinge of Botticellian pink, that raw rose about the lips, those wet, matted eyelashes; and, naturally, her bashful whim deprived me of many opportunities of specious consolation. There was, however, more to it than I thought. As we sat in the darkness of the veranda (a rude wind had put out her red candles), Haze, with a dreary laugh, said she had told Lo that her beloved Humbert thoroughly approved of the whole camp idea "and now," added Haze, "the child throws a fit; pretext: you and I want to get rid of her; actual reason: I told her we would exchange tomorrow for plainer stuff some much too cute night things that she bullied me into buying for her. You see, *she* sees herself as a starlet; *I* see her as a sturdy, healthy, but decidedly homely kid. This, I guess, is at the root of our troubles."

On Wednesday I managed to waylay Lo for a few seconds: she was on the landing, in sweatshirt and green-stained white shorts, rummaging in a trunk. I said something meant to be friendly and funny but she only emitted a snort without looking at me. Desperate, dying Humbert patted her clumsily on her coccyx, and she struck him, quite painfully, with one of the late 1 Mr. Haze's shoetrees. "Doublecrosser," she said as I crawled downstairs rubbing my arm with a great show of rue. She did not condescend to have dinner with Hum and mum: washed her hair and went to bed with her ridiculous books. And on Thursday quiet Mrs. Haze drove her to Camp Q.

As greater authors than I have put it: "Let readers imagine" etc. On second thought, I may as well give those imaginations a kick in the pants. I knew I had fallen in love with Lolita forever; but I also knew she would not be forever Lolita. She would be thirteen on January 1. In two years or so she would cease being a nymphet and would turn into a "young girl," and then, into a "college girl"—that horror of horrors. The word "forever" referred only to my own passion, to the eternal Lolita as reflected in my blood. The Lolita whose iliac crests had not yet flared, the 2 Lolita that today I could touch and smell and hear and see, the Lolita of the strident voice and the rich brown hair—of the bangs and the swirls at the sides and the curls at the back, and the sticky hot neck, and the vulgar vocabulary—"revolting," "super," "luscious," "goon," "drip"—*that* Lolita, *my* Lolita, poor

1 Catullus would lose forever. So how could I afford not to see her for two months of summer insomnias? Two whole months out of the two years of her remaining nymphage! Should I disguise myself as a somber old-fashioned girl, gawky Mlle Humbert, and put up my tent on the outskirts of Camp Q, in the hope that its russet nymphets would clamor: "Let us adopt that deep-voiced

2, 3 D.P.," and drag the sad, shyly smiling Berthe *au Grand Pied* to their rustic hearth. Berthe will sleep with Dolores Haze!

Idle dry dreams. Two months of beauty, two months of tenderness, would be squandered forever, and I could do nothing

4 about it, but nothing, *mais rien*.

One drop of rare honey, however, that Thursday did hold in its acorn cup. Haze was to drive her to the camp in the early morning. Upon sundry sounds of departure reaching me, I rolled out of bed and leaned out of the window. Under the poplars, the car was already athrob. On the sidewalk, Louise stood shading her eyes with her hand, as if the little traveler were already riding into the low morning sun. The gesture proved to be premature. "Hurry up!" shouted Haze. My Lolita, who was half in and about to slam the car door, wind down the glass, wave to Louise and the poplars (whom and which she was never to see again), interrupted the motion of fate: she looked up—and dashed back into the house (Haze furiously calling after her). A moment later I heard my sweetheart running up the stairs. My heart expanded with such force that it almost blotted me out. I hitched up the pants of my pajamas, flung the door open: and simultaneously Lolita arrived, in her Sunday frock, stamping, panting, and then she was in my arms, her innocent mouth melting under the ferocious pressure of dark male jaws, my palpitating darling! The next instant I heard her—alive, unraped—clatter downstairs. The motion of fate was resumed. The blond leg was pulled in, the car door was slammed—was re-slammed—and driver Haze at the violent wheel, rubber-red lips writhing in angry, inaudible speech, swung my darling away, while unnoticed by them or Louise, old Miss Opposite, an invalid, feebly but rhythmically waved from her vined veranda.

16

The hollow of my hand was still ivory-full of Lolita—full of
the feel of her pre-adolescently incurved back, that ivory-smooth,
sliding sensation of her skin through the thin frock that I had
worked up and down while I held her. I marched into her
tumbled room, threw open the door of the closet and plunged
into a heap of crumpled things that had touched her. There was
particularly one pink texture, sleazy, torn, with a faintly acrid
odor in the seam. I wrapped in it Humbert's huge engorged
heart. A poignant chaos was welling within me—but I had to
drop those things and hurriedly regain my composure, as I became aware of the maid's velvety voice calling me softly from
the stairs. She had a message for me, she said; and, topping my
automatic thanks with a kindly "you're welcome," good Louise
left an unstamped, curiously clean-looking letter in my shaking
hand.

This is a confession: I love you [so the letter began; and for
a distorted moment I mistook its hysterical scrawl for a
schoolgirl's scribble]. Last Sunday in church—bad you, who
refused to come to see our beautiful new windows!—only last
Sunday, my dear one, when I asked the Lord what to do about
it, I was told to act as I am acting now. You see, there is no
alternative. I have loved you from the minute I saw you.
I am a passionate and lonely woman and you are the love of
my life.

Now, my dearest, dearest, *mon cher, cher monsieur*, you
have read this; now you know. So, will you please, *at once*,
pack and leave. This is a landlady's order. I am dismissing a
lodger. I am kicking you out. Go! Scram! *Departez!* I shall be
back by dinnertime, if I do eighty both ways and don't have
an accident (but what would it matter?), and I do not wish
to find you in the house. Please, please, leave at once, *now*,
do not even read this absurd note to the end. Go. Adieu.

The situation, *chéri*, is quite simple. Of course, I know
with *absolute certainty* that I am nothing to you, nothing at
all. Oh yes, you enjoy talking to me (and kidding poor me),

you have grown fond of our friendly house, of the books I like, of my lovely garden, even of Lo's noisy ways—but I am nothing to you. Right? Right. Nothing to you whatever. *But* if, after reading my "confession," you decided, in your dark romantic European way, that I am attractive enough for you to take advantage of my letter and make a pass at me, then you would be a criminal—worse than a kidnaper who rapes a child. You see, *chéri*. If you decided to stay, *if* I found you at home (which I know I won't—and that's why I am able to go on like this), the *fact* of your remaining would only mean one thing: that you want me as much as I do you: as a lifelong mate; and that you are ready to link up your life with mine forever and ever and be a father to my little girl.

Let me rave and ramble on for a teeny while more, my dearest, since I know this letter has been by now torn by you, and its pieces (illegible) in the vortex of the toilet. My dearest, *mon très, très cher,* what a world of love I have built up for you during this miraculous June! I know how reserved you are, how "British." Your old-world reticence, your sense of decorum may be shocked by the boldness of an American girl! You who conceal your strongest feelings must think me a shameless little idiot for throwing open my poor bruised heart like this. In years gone by, many disappointments came my way. Mr. Haze was a splendid person, a sterling soul, but he happened to be twenty years my senior, and—well, let us not gossip about the past. My dearest, your curiosity must be well satisfied if you have ignored my request and read this letter to the bitter end. Never mind. Destroy it and go. Do not forget to leave the key on the desk in your room. And some scrap of address so that I could refund the twelve dollars I owe you till the end of the month. Good-bye, dear one. Pray for me—if you ever pray.

C.H.

What I present here is what I remember of the letter, and what I remember of the letter I remember verbatim (including that awful French). It was at least twice longer. I have left out a lyrical passage which I more or less skipped at the time, concerning Lolita's brother who died at 2 when she was 4, and how much I would have liked him. Let me see what else can I say?

Yes. There is just a chance that "the vortex of the toilet" (where the letter did go) is my own matter-of-fact contribution. She probably begged me to make a special fire to consume it.

My first movement was one of repulsion and retreat. My second was like a friend's calm hand falling upon my shoulder and bidding me take my time. I did. I came out of my daze and found myself still in Lo's room. A full-page ad ripped out of a slick magazine was affixed to the wall above the bed, between a crooner's mug and the lashes of a movie actress. It represented a dark-haired young husband with a kind of drained look in his Irish eyes. He was modeling a robe by So-and-So and holding a bridgelike tray by So-and-So, with breakfast for two. The legend, by the Rev. Thomas Morell, called him a "conquering hero." The thoroughly conquered lady (not shown) was presumably propping herself up to receive her half of the tray. How her bedfellow was to get under the bridge without some messy mishap was not clear. Lo had drawn a jocose arrow to the haggard lover's face and had put, in block letters: H.H. And indeed, despite a difference of a few years, the resemblance was striking. Under this was another picture, also a colored ad. A distinguished playwright was solemnly smoking a Drome. He always smoked Dromes. The resemblance was slight. Under this was Lo's chaste bed, littered with "comics." The enamel had come off the bedstead, leaving black, more or less rounded, marks on the white. Having convinced myself that Louise had left, I got into Lo's bed and reread the letter.

17

Gentlemen of the jury! I cannot swear that certain motions pertaining to the business in hand—if I may coin an expression—had not drifted across my mind before. My mind had not retained them in any logical form or in any relation to definitely recollected occasions; but I cannot swear—let me repeat—that I had not toyed with them (to rig up yet another expression), in my dimness of thought, in my darkness of passion. There may have been times—there must have been times, if I know my Humbert—when I had brought up for detached inspection the idea of marrying a mature widow (say, Charlotte Haze) with not one relative left in the wide gray world, merely in order to have my way with her child (Lo, Lola, Lolita). I am even prepared to tell my tormentors that perhaps once or twice I had cast an appraiser's cold eye at Charlotte's coral lips and bronze hair and dangerously low neckline, and had vaguely tried to fit her into a plausible daydream. This I confess under torture. Imaginary torture, perhaps, but all the more horrible. I wish I might digress and tell you more of the *pavor nocturnus* that would rack me at night hideously after a chance term had struck me in the random readings of my boyhood, such as *peine forte et dure* (what a Genius of Pain must have invented that!) or the dreadful, mysterious, insidious words "trauma," "traumatic event," and "transom." But my tale is sufficiently incondite already.

After a while I destroyed the letter and went to my room, and ruminated, and rumpled my hair, and modeled my purple robe, and moaned through clenched teeth and suddenly—Suddenly, gentlemen of the jury, I felt a Dostoevskian grin dawning (through the very grimace that twisted my lips) like a distant and terrible sun. I imagined (under conditions of new and perfect visibility) all the casual caresses her mother's husband would be able to lavish on his Lolita. I would hold her against me three times a day, every day. All my troubles would be expelled, I would be a healthy man. "To hold thee lightly on a gentle knee and print on thy soft cheek a parent's kiss..." Well-read Humbert!

Then, with all possible caution, on mental tiptoe so to speak, I conjured up Charlotte as a possible mate. By God, I could make myself bring her that economically halved grapefruit, that sugarless breakfast.

Humbert Humbert sweating in the fierce white light, and howled at, and trodden upon by sweating policemen, is now ready to make a further "statement" (*quel mot!*) as he turns his conscience inside out and rips off its innermost lining. I did not plan to marry poor Charlotte in order to eliminate her in some vulgar, gruesome and dangerous manner such as killing her by placing five bichloride-of-mercury tablets in her preprandial sherry or anything like that; but a delicately allied, pharmacopoeial thought did tinkle in my sonorous and clouded brain. Why limit myself to the modest masked caress I had tried already? Other visions of venery presented themselves to me swaying and smiling. I saw myself administering a powerful sleeping potion to both mother and daughter so as to fondle the latter through the night with perfect impunity. The house was full of Charlotte's snore, while Lolita hardly breathed in her sleep, as still as a painted girl-child. "Mother, I swear Kenny never even *touched* me." "You either lie, Dolores Haze, or it was an incubus." No, I would not go that far.   1

So Humbert the Cubus schemed and dreamed—and the red sun of desire and decision (the two things that create a live world) rose higher and higher, while upon a succession of balconies a succession of libertines, sparkling glass in hand, toasted the bliss of past and future nights. Then, figuratively speaking, I shattered the glass, and boldly imagined (for I was drunk on those visions by then and underrated the gentleness of my nature) how eventually I might blackmail—no, that is too strong a word—mauvemail big Haze into letting me consort with little   2
Haze by gently threatening the poor doting Big Dove with desertion if she tried to bar me from playing with my legal stepdaughter. In a word, before such an Amazing Offer, before such a vastness and variety of vistas, I was as helpless as Adam at the preview of early oriental history, miraged in his apple orchard.

And now take down the following important remark: the artist in me has been given the upper hand over the gentleman. It is with a great effort of will that in this memoir I have managed to tune my style to the tone of the journal that I kept when Mrs. Haze was to me but an obstacle. That journal of mine is no more; but I have considered it my artistic duty to preserve its intonations no matter how false and brutal they may seem to me now. Fortunately, my story has reached a point where I can cease insulting poor Charlotte for the sake of retrospective verisimilitude.

Wishing to spare poor Charlotte two or three hours of suspense on a winding road (and avoid, perhaps, a head-on collision that would shatter our different dreams), I made a thoughtful but abortive attempt to reach her at the camp by telephone. She had left half an hour before, and getting Lo instead, I told her—trembling and brimming with my mastery over fate—that I was going to marry her mother. I had to repeat it twice because something was preventing her from giving me her attention. "Gee, that's swell," she said laughing. "When is the wedding? Hold on a sec, the pup—That pup here has got hold of my sock. Listen—" and she added she guessed she was going to have loads of fun . . . and I realized as I hung up that a couple of hours at that camp had been sufficient to blot out with new impressions the image of handsome Humbert Humbert from little Lolita's mind. But what did it matter now? I would get her back as soon as a decent amount of time after the wedding had elapsed. "The orange

1 blossom would have scarcely withered on the grave," as a poet might have said. But I am no poet. I am only a very conscientious recorder.

After Louise had gone, I inspected the icebox, and finding it much too puritanic, walked to town and bought the richest foods available. I also bought some good liquor and two or three kinds of vitamins. I was pretty sure that with the aid of these stimulants and my natural resources, I would avert any embarrassment that my indifference might incur when called upon to display a strong and impatient flame. Again and again resourceful Hum-

2 bert evoked Charlotte as seen in the raree-show of a manly imagination. She was well groomed and shapely, this I could say for her, and she was my Lolita's big sister—this notion, perhaps, I could keep up if only I did not visualize too realistically her heavy hips, round knees, ripe bust, the coarse pink skin of her neck ("coarse" by comparison with silk and honey) and all the rest of that sorry and dull thing: a handsome woman.

The sun made its usual round of the house as the afternoon ripened into evening. I had a drink. And another. And yet another. Gin and pineapple juice, my favorite mixture, always double my energy. I decided to busy myself with our unkempt

3 lawn. *Une petite attention.* It was crowded with dandelions, and

a cursed dog—I loathe dogs—had defiled the flat stones where a
sundial had once stood. Most of the dandelions had changed
from suns to moons. The gin and Lolita were dancing in me, and
I almost fell over the folding chairs that I attempted to dislodge.
Incarnadine zebras! There are some eructations that sound like
cheers—at least, mine did. An old fence at the back of the garden
separated us from the neighbor's garbage receptacles and lilacs;
but there was nothing between the front end of our lawn (where
it sloped along one side of the house) and the street. Therefore
I was able to watch (with the smirk of one about to perform a
good action) for the return of Charlotte: that tooth should be
extracted at once. As I lurched and lunged with the hand mower,
bits of grass optically twittering in the low sun, I kept an eye on
that section of suburban street. It curved in from under an arch-
way of huge shade trees, then sped towards us down, down,
quite sharply, past old Miss Opposite's ivied brick house and
high-sloping lawn (much trimmer than ours) and disappeared
behind our own front porch which I could not see from where I
happily belched and labored. The dandelions perished. A reek
of sap mingled with the pineapple. Two little girls, Marion and
Mabel, whose comings and goings I had mechanically followed
of late (but who could replace my Lolita?) went toward the
avenue (from which our Lawn Street cascaded), one pushing a
bicycle, the other feeding from a paper bag, both talking at the
top of their sunny voices. Leslie, old Miss Opposite's gardener
and chauffeur, a very amiable and athletic Negro, grinned at me
from afar and shouted, re-shouted, commented by gesture, that
I was mighty energetic to-day. The fool dog of the prosperous
junk dealer next door ran after a blue car—not Charlotte's. The
prettier of the two little girls (Mabel, I think), shorts, halter
with little to halt, bright hair—a nymphet, by Pan!—ran back
down the street crumpling her paper bag and was hidden from
this Green Goat by the frontage of Mr. and Mrs. Humbert's
residence. A station wagon popped out of the leafy shade of the
avenue, dragging some of it on its roof before the shadows
snapped, and swung by at an idiotic pace, the sweatshirted driver
roof-holding with his left hand and the junkman's dog tearing

1, 2

3

alongside. There was a smiling pause—and then, with a flutter in my breast, I witnessed the return of the Blue Sedan. I saw it glide downhill and disappear behind the corner of the house. I had a glimpse of her calm pale profile. It occurred to me that until she went upstairs she would not know whether I had gone or not. A minute later, with an expression of great anguish on her face, she looked down at me from the window of Lo's room. By sprinting upstairs, I managed to reach that room before she left it.

18

When the bride is a widow and the groom is a widower; when the former has lived in Our Great Little Town for hardly two years, and the latter for hardly a month; when Monsieur wants to get the whole damned thing over with as quickly as possible, and Madame gives in with a tolerant smile; then, my reader, the wedding is generally a "quiet" affair. The bride may dispense with a tiara of orange blossoms securing her finger-tip veil, nor does she carry a white orchid in a prayer book. The bride's little daughter might have added to the ceremonies uniting H. and H. a touch of vivid vermeil; but I knew I would not dare be too tender with cornered Lolita yet, and therefore agreed it was not worth while tearing the child away from her beloved Camp Q.

1   My *soi-disant* passionate and lonely Charlotte was in everyday life matter-of-fact and gregarious. Moreover, I discovered that although she could not control her heart or her cries, she was a woman of principle. Immediately after she had become more or less my mistress (despite the stimulants, her "nervous, eager *chéri*"—a heroic *chéri!*—had some initial trouble, for which, however, he amply compensated her by a fantastic display of old-world endearments), good Charlotte interviewed me about my relations with God. I could have answered that on that score my mind was open; I said, instead—paying my tribute to a pious platitude—that I believed in a cosmic spirit. Looking down at her fingernails, she also asked me had I not in my family a cer-

tain strange strain. I countered by inquiring whether she would still want to marry me if my father's maternal grandfather had been, say, a Turk. She said it did not matter a bit; but that, if 1 she ever found out I did not believe in Our Christian God, she would commit suicide. She said it so solemnly that it gave me the creeps. It was then I knew she was a woman of principle.

Oh, she was very genteel: she said "excuse me" whenever a slight burp interrupted her flowing speech, called an envelope an ahnvelope, and when talking to her lady-friends referred to me as Mr. Humbert. I thought it would please her if I entered the community trailing some glamor after me. On the day of our wedding a little interview with me appeared in the Society Column of the Ramsdale *Journal*, with a photograph of Charlotte, one eyebrow up and a misprint in her name ("Hazer"). Despite this contretemps, the publicity warmed the porcelain 2 cockles of her heart—and made my rattles shake with awful glee. 3 By engaging in church work as well as by getting to know the better mothers of Lo's schoolmates, Charlotte in the course of twenty months or so had managed to become if not a prominent, at least an acceptable citizen, but never before had she come under that thrilling *rubrique*, and it was I who put her there, 4 Mr. Edgar H. Humbert (I threw in the "Edgar" just for the heck of it), "writer and explorer." McCoo's brother, when taking it down, asked me what I had written. Whatever I told him 5 came out as "several books on Peacock, Rainbow and other 6 poets." It was also noted that Charlotte and I had known each other for several years and that I was a distant relation of her first husband. I hinted I had had an affair with her thirteen years ago but this was not mentioned in print. To Charlotte I said that society columns *should* contain a shimmer of errors.

Let us go on with this curious tale. When called upon to enjoy my promotion from lodger to lover, did I experience only bitterness and distaste? No. Mr. Humbert confesses to a certain titillation of his vanity, to some faint tenderness, even to a pattern of remorse daintily running along the steel of his conspiratorial dagger. Never had I thought that the rather ridiculous, though rather handsome Mrs. Haze, with her blind faith in the wisdom of her church and book club, her mannerisms of elocution, her harsh, cold, contemptuous attitude toward an adorable, downy-armed child of twelve, could turn into such a touching, helpless creature as soon as I laid my hands upon her which happened on the threshold of Lolita's room whither she tremulously backed repeating "no, no, please no."

The transformation improved her looks. Her smile that had been such a contrived thing, thenceforth became the radiance of utter adoration—a radiance having something soft and moist about it, in which, with wonder, I recognized a resemblance to the lovely, inane, lost look that Lo had when gloating over a new kind of concoction at the soda fountain or mutely admiring my expensive, always tailor-fresh clothes. Deeply fascinated, I would watch Charlotte while she swapped parental woes with some other lady and made that national grimace of feminine resignation (eyes rolling up, mouth drooping sideways) which, in an infantile form, I had seen Lo making herself. We had highballs before turning in, and with their help, I would manage to evoke the child while caressing the mother. This was the white stomach within which my nymphet had been a little curved fish in 1934. This carefully dyed hair, so sterile to my sense of smell and touch, acquired at certain lamplit moments in the poster bed the tinge, if not the texture, of Lolita's curls. I kept telling myself, as I wielded my brand-new large-as-life wife, that biologically this was the nearest I could get to Lolita; that at Lolita's age, Lotte had been as desirable a schoolgirl as her daughter was, and as Lolita's daughter would be some day. I had my wife unearth from under a collection of shoes (Mr. Haze had a passion for them, it appears) a thirty-year-old album, so that I might see how Lotte had looked as a child; and even though the light was wrong and the dresses graceless, I was able to make out a dim first version of Lolita's outline, legs, cheekbones, bobbed nose. Lottelita, Lolitchen.

So I tom-peeped across the hedges of years, into wan little windows. And when, by means of pitifully ardent, naïvely lascivious caresses, she of the noble nipple and massive thigh prepared me for the performance of my nightly duty, it was still a nymphet's scent that in despair I tried to pick up, as I bayed through the undergrowth of dark decaying forests.

I simply can't tell you how gentle, how touching my poor wife was. At breakfast, in the depressingly bright kitchen, with its chrome glitter and Hardware and Co. Calendar and cute breakfast nook (simulating that Coffee Shoppe where in their college days Charlotte and Humbert used to coo together), she would sit, robed in red, her elbow on the plastic-topped table, her cheek propped on her fist, and stare at me with intolerable tenderness as I consumed my ham and eggs. Humbert's face might twitch with neuralgia, but in her eyes it vied in beauty and animation with the sun and shadows of leaves rippling on the white refrigerator. My solemn exasperation was to her the silence of love. My small income added to her even smaller one impressed her as a brilliant fortune; not because the resulting sum now sufficed for most middle-class needs, but because even my money shone in her eyes with the magic of my manliness, and she saw our joint account as one of those southern boulevards at midday that have solid shade on one side and smooth sunshine on the other, all the way to the end of a prospect, where pink mountains loom.

Into the fifty days of our cohabitation Charlotte crammed the activities of as many years. The poor woman busied herself with a number of things she had foregone long before or had never been much interested in, as if (to prolong these Proustian intonations) by my marrying the mother of the child I loved I had enabled my wife to regain an abundance of youth by proxy. With the zest of a banal young bride, she started to "glorify the home." Knowing as I did its every cranny by heart—since those days when from my chair I mentally mapped out Lolita's course through the house—I had long entered into a sort of emotional relationship with it, with its very ugliness and dirt, and now I could almost feel the wretched thing cower in its reluctance to endure the bath of ecru and ocher and putty-buff-and-snuff that Charlotte planned to give it. She never got as far as that, thank God, but she did use up a tremendous amount of energy in washing window shades, waxing the slats of Venetian blinds, purchasing new shades and new blinds, returning them to the store, replacing them by others, and so on, in a constant chiaroscuro of smiles and frowns, doubts and pouts. She dabbled in cretonnes and chintzes; she changed the colors of the sofa—the sacred sofa where a bubble of paradise had once burst in slow motion within me. She rearranged the furniture—and was pleased when she found, in a household treatise, that "it is permissible to separate a pair of sofa commodes and their companion lamps." With the authoress of *Your Home Is You*, she developed a hatred for little lean chairs and spindle tables. She believed that a room having a generous expanse of glass, and lots of rich wood paneling was an example of the masculine type of room, whereas the feminine type was characterized by lighter-looking windows and frailer woodwork. The novels I had found her reading when I moved in were now replaced by illustrated catalogues and homemaking guides. From a firm located at 4640 Roosevelt Blvd., Phila-delphia, she ordered for our double bed a "damask covered 312 coil mattress"—although the old one seemed to me resilient and durable enough for whatever it had to support.

A Midwesterner, as her late husband had also been, she had lived in coy Ramsdale, the gem of an eastern state, not long enough to know all the nice people. She knew slightly the jovial dentist who lived in a kind of ramshackle wooden chateau be-hind our lawn. She had met at a church tea the "snooty" wife of the local junk dealer who owned the "colonial" white horror at the corner of the avenue. Now and then she "visited with" old Miss Opposite; but the more patrician matrons among those she called upon, or met at lawn functions, or had telephone chats with—such dainty ladies as Mrs. Glave, Mrs. Sheridan, Mrs. McCrystal, Mrs. Knight and others, seldom seemed to call on my neglected Charlotte. Indeed, the only couple with whom she had relations of real cordiality, devoid of any *arrière-pensée* or practical foresight, were the Farlows who had just come back from a business trip to Chile in time to attend our wedding, with the Chatfields, McCoos, and a few others (but not Mrs. Junk or the even prouder Mrs. Talbot). John Farlow was a middle-aged, quiet, quietly athletic, quietly successful dealer in sporting goods, who had an office at Parkington, forty miles away: it was he who got me the cartridges for that Colt and showed me how to use it, during a walk in the woods one Sunday; he was also what he called with a smile a part-time lawyer and had handled some of Charlotte's affairs. Jean, his youngish wife (and first cousin), was a long-limbed girl in harlequin glasses with two boxer dogs, two pointed breasts and a big red mouth. She painted—landscapes and portraits—and vividly do I remember praising, over cocktails, the picture she had made of a niece of hers, little Rosaline Honeck, a rosy honey in a Girl Scout uniform, beret of green worsted, belt of green webbing, charming shoulder-long curls—and John removed his pipe and said it was a pity Dolly (my Dolita) and Rosaline were so critical of each other at school, but he hoped they would get on better when they returned from their respective camps. We talked of the school. It had its drawbacks, and it had its virtues. "Of course, too many of the tradespeople here are Italians," said John, "but on the other hand we are still spared—" "I wish," interrupted Jean with a laugh, "Dolly and Rosaline were spending the summer together." Suddenly I imagined Lo returning from camp—brown, warm, drowsy, drugged—and was ready to weep with passion and impatience.

19

A few words more about Mrs. Humbert while the going is good (a bad accident is to happen quite soon). I had been always aware of the possessive streak in her, but I never thought she would be so crazily jealous of anything in my life that had not been she. She showed a fierce insatiable curiosity for my past. She desired me to resuscitate all my loves so that she might make me insult them, and trample upon them, and revoke them apostately and totally, thus destroying my past. She made me tell her about my marriage to Valeria, who was of course a scream; but I also had to invent, or to pad atrociously, a long series of mistresses for Charlotte's morbid delectation. To keep her happy, I had to present her with an illustrated catalogue of them, all nicely differentiated, according to the rules of those American ads where schoolchildren are pictured in a subtle ratio of races, with one—only one, but as cute as they make them— chocolate-colored round-eyed little lad, almost in the very middle of the front row. So I presented my women, and had them smile and sway—the languorous blond, the fiery brunette, the sensual copperhead—as if on parade in a bordello. The more popular and platitudinous I made them, the more Mrs. Humbert was pleased with the show.

Never in my life had I confessed so much or received so many confessions. The sincerity and artlessness with which she discussed what she called her "love-life," from first necking to connubial catch-as-catch-can, were, ethically, in striking contrast with my glib compositions, but technically the two sets were congeneric since both were affected by the same stuff (soap operas, psychoanalysis and cheap novelettes) upon which I drew for my characters and she for her mode of expression. I was considerably amused by certain remarkable sexual habits that the good Harold Haze had had according to Charlotte who thought my mirth improper; but otherwise her autobiography was as devoid of interests as her autopsy would have been. I never saw a healthier woman than she, despite thinning diets.

Of my Lolita she seldom spoke—more seldom, in fact, than she did of the blurred, blond male baby whose photograph to the exclusion of all others adorned our bleak bedroom. In one of her tasteless reveries, she predicted that the dead infant's soul would return to earth in the form of the child she would bear in her present wedlock. And although I felt no special urge to supply the Humbert line with a replica of Harold's production (Lolita, with an incestuous thrill, I had grown to regard as *my* child), it occurred to me that a prolonged confinement, with a nice Caesarean operation and other complications in a safe maternity ward sometime next spring, would give me a chance to be alone with my Lolita for weeks, perhaps—and gorge the limp nymphet with sleeping pills.

Oh, she simply hated her daughter! What I thought especially vicious was that she had gone out of her way to answer with great diligence the questionnaires in a fool's book she had (*A Guide to Your Child's Development*), published in Chicago. The rigmarole went year by year, and Mom was supposed to fill out a kind of inventory at each of her child's birthdays. On Lo's twelfth, January 1, 1947, Charlotte Haze, née Becker, had underlined the following epithets, ten out of forty, under "Your Child's Personality": aggressive, boisterous, critical, distrustful, impatient, irritable, inquisitive, listless, negativistic (underlined twice) and obstinate. She had ignored the thirty remaining adjectives, among which were cheerful, co-operative, energetic, and so forth. It was really maddening. With a brutality that otherwise never appeared in my loving wife's mild nature, she attacked and routed such of Lo's little belongings that had wandered to various parts of the house to freeze there like so many hypnotized bunnies. Little did the good lady dream that one morning when an upset stomach (the result of my trying to improve on her sauces) had prevented me from accompanying her to church, I deceived her with one of Lolita's anklets. And then, her attitude toward my saporous darling's letters!

DEAR MUMMY AND HUMMY,
Hope you are fine. Thank you very much for the candy. I [crossed out and re-written again] I lost my new sweater in the woods. It has been cold here for the last few days. I'm having a time. Love.
DOLLY

"The dumb child," said Mrs. Humbert, "has left out a word before 'time.' That sweater was all-wool, and I wish you would not send her candy without consulting me."

20

There was a woodlake (Hourglass Lake—not as I had thought it was spelled) a few miles from Ramsdale, and there was one week of great heat at the end of July when we drove there daily.

I am now obliged to describe in some tedious detail our last swim there together, one tropical Tuesday morning.

We had left the car in a parking area not far from the road and were making our way down a path cut through the pine forest to the lake, when Charlotte remarked that Jean Farlow, in quest of rare light effects (Jean belonged to the old school of painting), had seen Leslie taking a dip "in the ebony" (as John had quipped) at five o'clock in the morning last Sunday.

"The water," I said, "must have been quite cold."

"That is not the point," said the logical doomed dear. "He is subnormal, you see. And," she continued (in that carefully phrased way of hers that was beginning to tell on my health), "I have a very definite feeling our Louise is in love with that moron."

Feeling. "We feel Dolly is not doing as well" etc. (from an old school report).

The Humberts walked on, sandaled and robed.

"Do you know, Hum: I have one most ambitious dream," pronounced Lady Hum, lowering her head—shy of that dream—and communing with the tawny ground. "I would love to get hold of a real trained servant maid like that German girl the Talbots spoke of; and have her live in the house."

"No room," I said.

"Come," she said with her quizzical smile, "surely, *chéri*, you underestimate the possibilities of the Humbert home. We would put her in Lo's room. I intended to make a guestroom of that hole anyway. It's the coldest and meanest in the whole house."

"What are you talking about?" I asked, the skin of my cheekbones tensing up (this I take the trouble to note only because my daughter's skin did the same when she felt that way: disbelief, disgust, irritation).

"Are you bothered by Romantic Associations?" queried my wife—in allusion to her first surrender.

"Hell no," said I. "I just wonder where will you put your daughter when you get your guest or your maid."

"Ah," said Mrs. Humbert, dreaming, smiling, drawing out the "Ah" simultaneously with the raise of one eyebrow and a soft exhalation of breath. "Little Lo, I'm afraid, does not enter the picture at all, at all. Little Lo goes straight from camp to a good boarding school with strict discipline and some sound religious training. And then—Beardsley College. I have it all mapped out, you need not worry."

She went on to say that she, Mrs. Humbert, would have to overcome her habitual sloth and write to Miss Phalen's sister who taught at St. Algebra. The dazzling lake emerged. I said I had forgotten my sunglasses in the car and would catch up with her.

I had always thought that wringing one's hands was a fictional gesture—the obscure outcome, perhaps, of some medieval ritual; but as I took to the woods, for a spell of despair and desperate meditation, this was the gesture ("look, Lord, at these chains!")   1 that would have come nearest to the mute expression of my mood.

Had Charlotte been Valeria, I would have known how to handle the situation; and "handle" is the word I want. In the good old days, by merely twisting fat Valechka's brittle wrist (the one she had fallen upon from a bicycle) I could make her change her mind instantly; but anything of the sort in regard to Charlotte was unthinkable. Bland American Charlotte frightened me. My lighthearted dream of controlling her through her passion for me was all wrong. I dared not do anything to spoil the image of me she had set up to adore. I had toadied to her when she was the awesome duenna of my darling, and a grovel-   2 ing something still persisted in my attitude toward her. The only ace I held was her ignorance of my monstrous love for her Lo. She had been annoyed by Lo's liking me; but *my* feelings she could not divine. To Valeria I might have said: "Look here, you fat fool, *c'est moi qui décide* what is good for Dolores Hum-   3 bert." To Charlotte, I could not even say (with ingratiating calm): "Excuse me, my dear, I disagree. Let us give the child one more chance. Let me be her private tutor for a year or so. You once told me yourself—" In fact, I could not say anything at all to Charlotte about the child without giving myself away. Oh, you cannot imagine (as I had never imagined) what these women of principle are! Charlotte, who did not notice the falsity of all the everyday conventions and rules of behavior, and foods, and books, and people she doted upon, would distinguish at once a false intonation in anything I might say with a view to keeping Lo near. She was like a musician who may be an odious vulgarian in ordinary life, devoid of tact and taste; but who will hear a false note in music with diabolical accuracy of judgment. To break Charlotte's will, I would have to break her heart. If I broke her heart, her image of me would break too. If I said: "Either I have my way with Lolita, and you help me to keep the matter quiet, or we part at once," she would have turned as pale as a woman of clouded glass and slowly replied: "All right, whatever you add or retract, this is the end." And the end it would be.

Such, then, was the mess. I remember reaching the parking area and pumping a handful of rust-tasting water, and drinking it as avidly as if it could give me magic wisdom, youth, freedom, a tiny concubine. For a while, purple-robed, heel-dangling, I sat on the edge of one of the rude tables, under the wooshing pines. In the middle distance, two little maidens in shorts and halters came out of a sun-dappled privy marked "Women." Gum-chewing Mabel (or Mabel's understudy) laboriously, absent-mindedly, straddled a bicycle, and Marion, shaking her hair because of the flies, settled behind, legs wide apart; and, wobbling, they slowly, absently, merged with the light and shade. Lolita! Father and daughter melting into these woods! The natural solution was to destroy Mrs. Humbert. But how?

No man can bring about the perfect murder; chance, however, can do it. There was the famous dispatch of a Mme Lacour in Arles, southern France, at the close of last century. An unidentified bearded six-footer, who, it was later conjectured, had been the lady's secret lover, walked up to her in a crowded street, soon after her marriage to Colonel Lacour, and mortally stabbed her in the back, three times, while the Colonel, a small bulldog of a man, hung onto the murderer's arm. By a miraculous and beautiful coincidence, right at the moment when the operator was in the act of loosening the angry little husband's jaws (while several onlookers were closing in upon the group), a cranky Italian in the house nearest to the scene set off by sheer accident some kind of explosive he was tinkering with, and immediately the street was turned into a pandemonium of smoke, falling bricks and running people. The explosion hurt no one (except that it knocked out game Colonel Lacour); but the lady's vengeful lover ran when the others ran—and lived happily ever after.

Now look what happens when the operator himself plans a perfect removal.

I walked down to Hourglass Lake. The spot from which we and a few other "nice" couples (the Farlows, the Chatfields) bathed was a kind of small cove; my Charlotte liked it because it was almost "a private beach." The main bathing facilities (or "drowning facilities" as the Ramsdale *Journal* had had occasion to say) were in the left (eastern) part of the hourglass, and could not be seen from our covelet. To our right, the pines soon gave way to a curve of marshland which turned again into forest on the opposite side.

I sat down beside my wife so noiselessly that she started.

"Shall we go in?" she asked.

"We shall in a minute. Let me follow a train of thought."

I thought. More than a minute passed.

"All right. Come on."

"Was I on that train?"

"You certainly were."

"I hope so," said Charlotte entering the water. It soon reached the gooseflesh of her thick thighs; and then, joining her outstretched hands, shutting her mouth tight, very plain-faced in her black rubber headgear, Charlotte flung herself forward with a great splash.

Slowly we swam out into the shimmer of the lake.

On the opposite bank, at least a thousand paces away (if one could walk across water), I could make out the tiny figures of two men working like beavers on their stretch of shore. I knew exactly who they were: a retired policeman of Polish descent and the retired plumber who owned most of the timber on that side of the lake. And I also knew they were engaged in building, just for the dismal fun of the thing, a wharf. The knocks that reached us seemed so much bigger than what could be distinguished of those dwarfs' arms and tools; indeed, one suspected the director of those acrosonic effects to have been at odds with the puppet-master, especially since the hefty crack of each diminutive blow lagged behind its visual version.

The short white-sand strip of "our" beach—from which by now we had gone a little way to reach deep water—was empty on weekday mornings. There was nobody around except those two tiny very busy figures on the opposite side, and a dark-red private plane that droned overhead, and then disappeared in the blue. The setting was really perfect for a brisk bubbling murder, and here was the subtle point: the man of law and the man of water were just near enough to witness an accident and just far enough not to observe a crime. They were near enough to hear a distracted bather thrashing about and bellowing for somebody to come and help him save his drowning wife; and they were too far to distinguish (if they happened to look too soon) that the anything but distracted swimmer was finishing to tread his wife underfoot. I was not yet at that stage; I merely want to convey the ease of the act, the nicety of the setting! So there was Charlotte swimming on with dutiful awkwardness (she was a very mediocre mermaid), but not without a certain solemn pleasure (for was not her merman by her side?); and as I watched, with the stark lucidity of a future recollection (you know—trying to see things as you will remember having seen them), the glossy whiteness of her wet face so little tanned despite all her endeavors, and her pale lips, and her naked convex forehead, and the tight black cap, and the plump wet neck, I knew that all I had to do was to drop back, take a deep breath, then grab her by the ankle and rapidly dive with my captive corpse. I say corpse because surprise, panic and inexperience would cause her to inhale at once a lethal gallon of lake, while I would be able to hold on for at least a full minute, open-eyed under water. The fatal gesture passed like the tail of a falling star across the blackness of the contemplated crime. It was like some dreadful silent ballet, the male dancer holding the ballerina by her foot and streaking down through watery twilight. I might come up for a mouthful of air while still holding her down, and then would dive again as many times as would be necessary, and only when the curtain came down on her for good, would I permit myself to yell for help. And when some twenty minutes later the two puppets steadily growing arrived in a rowboat, one half newly painted, poor Mrs. Humbert Humbert, the victim of a cramp or coronary occlusion, or both, would be standing on her head in the inky ooze, some thirty feet below the smiling surface of Hourglass Lake.

Simple, was it not? But what d'ye know, folks—I just could not make myself do it!

She swam beside me, a trustful and clumsy seal, and all the logic of passion screamed in my ear: Now is the time! And, folks, I just couldn't! In silence I turned shoreward and gravely, dutifully, she also turned, and still hell screamed its counsel, and still I could not make myself drown the poor, slippery, big-bodied creature. The scream grew more and more remote as I realized the melancholy fact that neither tomorrow, nor Friday, nor any other day or night, could I make myself put her to death. Oh, I could visualize myself slapping Valeria's breasts out of alignment, or otherwise hurting her—and I could see myself, no less clearly, shooting her lover in the underbelly and making him say "akh!" and sit down. But I could not kill Charlotte—especially when things were on the whole not quite as hopeless, perhaps, as they seemed at first wince on that miserable morning. Were I to catch her by her strong kicking foot; were I to see her amazed look, hear her awful voice; were I still to go through with the ordeal, her ghost would haunt me all my life. Perhaps if the year were 1447 instead of 1947 I might have hoodwinked my gentle nature by administering her some classical poison from a hollow agate, some tender philter of death. But in our middle-class nosy era it would not have come off the way it used to in the brocaded palaces of the past. Nowadays you have to be a scientist if you want to be a killer. No, no, I was neither. Ladies and gentlemen of the jury, the majority of sex offenders that hanker for some throbbing, sweet-moaning, physical but not necessarily coital, relation with a girl-child, are innocuous, inadequate, passive, timid strangers who merely ask the community to allow them to pursue their practically harmless, so-called aberrant behavior, their little hot wet private acts of sexual deviation without the police and society cracking down upon them. We are not sex fiends! We do not rape as good soldiers do. We are unhappy, mild, dog-eyed gentlemen, sufficiently well integrated to control our urge in the presence of adults, but ready to give years and years of life for one chance to touch a nymphet. Emphatically, no killers are we. Poets never kill. Oh, my poor Charlotte, do not hate me in your eternal heaven among an eternal alchemy of asphalt and rubber and metal and stone—but thank God, not water, not water!

Nonetheless it was a very close shave, speaking quite objectively. And now comes the point of my perfect-crime parable.

We sat down on our towels in the thirsty sun. She looked around, loosened her bra, and turned over on her stomach to give her back a chance to be feasted upon. She said she loved me. She sighed deeply. She extended one arm and groped in the pocket of her robe for her cigarettes. She sat up and smoked. She examined her right shoulder. She kissed me heavily with open smoky mouth. Suddenly, down the sand bank behind us, from under the bushes and pines, a stone rolled, then another.

"Those disgusting prying kids," said Charlotte, holding up her big bra to her breast and turning prone again. "I shall have to speak about that to Peter Krestovski."

From the debouchment of the trail came a rustle, a footfall, and Jean Farlow marched down with her easel and things.

"You scared us," said Charlotte.

Jean said she had been up there, in a place of green concealment, spying on nature (spies are generally shot), trying to finish a lakescape, but it was no good, she had no talent whatever (which was quite true)—"And have *you* ever tried painting, Humbert?" Charlotte, who was a little jealous of Jean, wanted to know if John was coming.

He was. He was coming home for lunch today. He had dropped her on the way to Parkington and should be picking

her up any time now. It was a grand morning. She always felt
a traitor to Cavall and Melampus for leaving them roped on   1
such gorgeous days. She sat down on the white sand between
Charlotte and me. She wore shorts. Her long brown legs were
about as attractive to me as those of a chestnut mare. She
showed her gums when she smiled.

"I almost put both of you into my lake," she said. "I even
noticed something you overlooked. You [addressing Humbert]
had your wrist watch on in, yes, sir, you had."

"Waterproof," said Charlotte softly, making a fish mouth.   2

Jean took my wrist upon her knee and examined Charlotte's
gift, then put back Humbert's hand on the sand, palm up.

"You could see anything that way," remarked Charlotte
coquettishly.

Jean sighed. "I once saw," she said, "two children, male and
female, at sunset, right here, making love. Their shadows were
giants. And I told you about Mr. Tomson at daybreak. Next
time I expect to see fat old Ivor in the ivory. He is really a
freak, that man. Last time he told me a completely indecent
story about his nephew. It appears—"   3

"Hullo there," said John's voice.

21

My habit of being silent when displeased, or, more exactly,
the cold and scaly quality of my displeased silence, used to
frighten Valeria out of her wits. She used to whimper and wail,
saying *"Ce qui me rend folle, c'est que je ne sais à quoi tu penses
quand tu es comme ça."* I tried being silent with Charlotte—and   4
she just chirped on, or chucked my silence under the chin.
An astonishing woman! I would retire to my former room, now
a regular "studio," mumbling I had after all a learned opus to
write, and cheerfully Charlotte went on beautifying the home,
warbling on the telephone and writing letters. From my window,
through the lacquered shiver of poplar leaves, I could see her

crossing the street and contentedly mailing her letter to Miss Phalen's sister.

The week of scattered showers and shadows which elapsed after our last visit to the motionless sands of Hourglass Lake was one of the gloomiest I can recall. Then came two or three dim rays of hope—before the ultimate sunburst.

It occurred to me that I had a fine brain in beautiful working order and that I might as well use it. If I dared not meddle with my wife's plans for her daughter (getting warmer and browner every day in the fair weather of hopeless distance), I could surely devise some general means to assert myself in a general way that might be later directed toward a particular occasion. One evening, Charlotte herself provided me with an opening.

"I have a surprise for you," she said looking at me with fond eyes over a spoonful of soup. "In the fall we two are going to England."

I swallowed *my* spoonful, wiped my lips with pink paper (Oh, the cool rich linens of Mirana Hotel!) and said:

"I have also a surprise for you, my dear. We two are not going to England."

"Why, what's the matter?" she said, looking—with more surprise than I had counted upon—at my hands (I was involuntarily folding and tearing and crushing and tearing again the innocent pink napkin). My smiling face set her somewhat at ease, however.

"The matter is quite simple," I replied. "Even in the most harmonious of households, as ours is, not all decisions are taken by the female partner. There are certain things that the husband is there to decide. I can well imagine the thrill that you, a healthy American gal, must experience at crossing the Atlantic on the same ocean liner with Lady Bumble—or Sam Bumble, the Frozen Meat King, or a Hollywood harlot. And I doubt not that you and I would make a pretty ad for the Traveling Agency when portrayed looking—you, frankly starry-eyed, I, controlling my envious admiration—at the Palace Sentries, or Scarlet Guards, or Beaver Eaters, or whatever they are called. But I happen to be allergic to Europe, including merry old England. As you well know, I have nothing but very sad associations with the Old and rotting World. No colored ads in your magazines will change the situation."

"My darling," said Charlotte. "I really—"

"No, wait a minute. The present matter is only incidental. I am concerned with a general trend. When you wanted me to spend my afternoons sunbathing on the Lake instead of doing my work, I gladly gave in and became a bronzed glamor boy for your sake, instead of remaining a scholar and, well, an educator. When you lead me to bridge and bourbon with the charming Farlows, I meekly follow. No, please, wait. When you decorate your home, I do not interfere with your schemes. When you decide—when you decide all kinds of matters, I may be in complete, or in partial, let us say, disagreement—but I say nothing. I ignore the particular. I cannot ignore the general. I love being bossed by you, but every game has its rules. I am not cross. I am not cross at all. Don't do that. But I am one half of this household, and have a small but distinct voice."

She had come to my side and had fallen on her knees and was slowly, but very vehemently, shaking her head and clawing at my trousers. She said she had never realized. She said I was her ruler and her god. She said Louise had gone, and let us make love right away. She said I must forgive her or she would die.

This little incident filled me with considerable elation. I told her quietly that it was a matter not of asking forgiveness, but of changing one's ways; and I resolved to press my advantage and spend a good deal of time, aloof and moody, working at my book—or at least pretending to work.

The "studio bed" in my former room had long been converted into the sofa it had always been at heart, and Charlotte had warned me since the very beginning of our cohabitation that gradually the room would be turned into a regular "writer's den." A couple of days after the British Incident, I was sitting in a new and very comfortable easy chair, with a large volume in my lap, when Charlotte rapped with her ring finger and sauntered in. How different were her movements from those of my Lolita, when *she* used to visit me in her dear dirty blue jeans, smelling of orchards in nymphetland; awkward and fey, and dimly depraved, the lower buttons of her shirt unfastened. Let me tell you, however, something. Behind the brashness of little Haze, and the poise of big Haze, a trickle of shy life ran that tasted the same, that murmured the same. A great French doctor once told my father that in near relatives the faintest gastric gurgle has the same "voice."

So Charlotte sauntered in. She felt all was not well between us. I had pretended to fall asleep the night before, and the night before that, as soon as we had gone to bed, and had risen at dawn.

Tenderly, she inquired if she were not "interrupting."

"Not at the moment," I said, turning volume C of the *Girls' Encyclopedia* around to examine a picture printed "bottom-edge" as printers say.

Charlotte went up to a little table of imitation mahogany with a drawer. She put her hand upon it. The little table was ugly, no doubt, but it had done nothing to her.

"I have always wanted to ask you," she said (businesslike, not coquettish), "why is this thing locked up? Do you want it in this room? It's so abominably uncouth."

"Leave it alone," I said. I was Camping in Scandinavia.

"Is there a key?"

"Hidden."

"Oh, Hum . . ."

"Locked up love letters."

She gave me one of those wounded-doe looks that irritated me so much, and then, not quite knowing if I was serious, or how to keep up the conversation, stood for several slow pages (Campus, Canada, Candid Camera, Candy) peering at the window-pane rather than through it, drumming upon it with sharp almond-and-rose fingernails.

Presently (at Canoeing or Canvasback) she strolled up to my chair and sank down, tweedily, weightily, on its arm, in-undating me with the perfume my first wife had used. "Would his lordship like to spend the fall *here?*" she asked, pointing with her little finger at an autumn view in a conservative Eastern State. "Why?" (very distinctly and slowly). She shrugged. (Probably Harold used to take a vacation at that time. Open season. Conditional reflex on her part.)

"I think I know where that is," she said, still pointing. "There is a hotel I remember, Enchanted Hunters, quaint, isn't it? And the food is a dream. And nobody bothers anybody."

She rubbed her cheek against my temple. Valeria soon got over that.

"Is there anything special you would like for dinner, dear? John and Jean will drop in later."

I answered with a grunt. She kissed me on my underlip, and, brightly saying she would bake a cake (a tradition subsisted from my lodging days that I adored her cakes), left me to my idleness.

Carefully putting down the open book where she had sat (it attempted to send forth a rotation of waves, but an inserted pencil stopped the pages), I checked the hiding place of the key: rather self-consciously it lay under the old expensive safety razor I had used before she bought me a much better and cheaper one. Was it the perfect hiding place—there, under that razor, in the groove of its velvet-lined case? The case lay in a small trunk where I kept various business papers. Could I improve upon this? Remarkable how difficult it is to conceal things— especially when one's wife keeps monkeying with the furniture.

22

I think it was exactly a week after our last swim that the noon mail brought a reply from the second Miss Phalen. The lady wrote she had just returned to St. Algebra from her sister's funeral. "Euphemia had never been the same after breaking that hip." As to the matter of Mrs. Humbert's daughter, she wished to report that it was too late to enroll her this year; but that she, the surviving Phalen, was practically certain that if Mr. and Mrs. Humbert brought Dolores over in January, her admittance might be arranged.

Next day, after lunch, I went to see "our" doctor, a friendly fellow whose perfect bedside manner and complete reliance on a few patented drugs adequately masked his ignorance of, and indifference to, medical science. The fact that Lo would have to come back to Ramsdale was a treasure of anticipation. For this event I wanted to be fully prepared. I had in fact begun my campaign earlier, before Charlotte made that cruel decision of hers. I had to be sure when my lovely child arrived, that very night, and then night after night, until St. Algebra took her away from me, I would possess the means of putting two creatures to sleep so thoroughly that neither sound nor touch should rouse them. Throughout most of July I had been experimenting with various sleeping powders, trying them out on Charlotte, a great taker of pills. The last dose I had given her (she thought it was a tablet of mild bromides—to anoint her nerves) had knocked her out for four solid hours. I had put the radio at full blast. I had blazed in her face an olisbos-like flashlight. I had pushed her, pinched her, prodded her—and nothing had disturbed the rhythm of her calm and powerful breathing. However, when I had done such a simple thing as kiss her, she had awakened at once, as fresh and strong as an octopus (I barely escaped). This would not do, I thought; had to get something still safer. At first, Dr. Byron did not seem to believe me when I said his last prescription was no match for my insomnia. He suggested I try again, and for a moment diverted my attention by showing me photographs of his family. He had a fascinating child of Dolly's age; but I saw through his tricks and insisted he prescribe the mightiest pill extant. He suggested I play golf, but finally agreed to give me something that, he said, "would really work"; and going to a cabinet, he produced a vial of violet-blue capsules banded with dark purple at one end, which, he said, had just been placed on the market and were intended not for neurotics whom a draft of water could calm if properly administered, but only for great sleepless artists who had to die for a few hours in order to live for centuries. I love to fool doctors, and though inwardly rejoicing, pocketed the pills with a skeptical shrug. Incidentally, I had had to be careful with him. Once, in another connection, a stupid lapse on my part made me mention my last sanatorium, and I thought I saw the tips of his ears twitch. Being not at all keen for Charlotte or anybody else to know that period of my past, I had hastily explained that I had once done some research among the insane for a novel. But no matter; the old rogue certainly had a sweet girleen.

I left in great spirits. Steering my wife's car with one finger, I contentedly rolled homeward. Ramsdale had, after all, lots of charm. The cicadas whirred; the avenue had been freshly watered. Smoothly, almost silkily, I turned down into our steep little street. Everything was somehow so right that day. So blue and green. I knew the sun shone because my ignition key was reflected in the windshield; and I knew it was exactly half past three because the nurse who came to massage Miss Opposite every afternoon was tripping down the narrow sidewalk in her white stockings and shoes. As usual, Junk's hysterical setter attacked me as I rolled downhill, and as usual, the local paper was lying on the porch where it had just been hurled by Kenny.

The day before I had ended the regime of aloofness I had imposed upon myself, and now uttered a cheerful homecoming call as I opened the door of the living room. With her cream-white nape and bronze bun to me, wearing the yellow blouse and maroon slacks she had on when I first met her, Charlotte sat at the corner bureau writing a letter. My hand still on the doorknob, I repeated my hearty cry. Her writing hand stopped. She sat still for a moment; then she slowly turned in her chair and rested her elbow on its curved back. Her face, disfigured by her emotion, was not a pretty sight as she stared at my legs and said:

"The Haze woman, the big bitch, the old cat, the obnoxious mamma, the—the old stupid Haze is no longer your dupe. She has—she has . . ."

My fair accuser stopped, swallowing her venom and her tears.

Whatever Humbert Humbert said—or attempted to say—is inessential. She went on:

"You're a monster. You're a detestable, abominable, criminal fraud. If you come near—I'll scream out the window. Get back!"

Again, whatever H.H. murmured may be omitted, I think.

"I am leaving tonight. This is all yours. Only you'll never, never see that miserable brat again. Get out of this room."

Reader, I did. I went up to the ex-semi-studio. Arms akimbo, I stood for a moment quite still and self-composed, surveying from the threshold the raped little table with its open drawer, a key hanging from the lock, four other household keys on the table top. I walked across the landing into the Humberts' bedroom, and calmly removed my diary from under her pillow into my pocket. Then I started to walk downstairs, but stopped halfway: she was talking on the telephone which happened to be plugged just outside the door of the living room. I wanted to hear what she was saying: she canceled an order for something or other, and returned to the parlor. I rearranged my respiration and went through the hallway to the kitchen. There, I opened a bottle of Scotch. She could never resist Scotch. Then I walked into the dining room and from there, through the half-open door, contemplated Charlotte's broad back.

"You are ruining my life and yours," I said quietly. "Let us be civilized people. It is all your hallucination. You are crazy, Charlotte. The notes you found were fragments of a novel. Your name and hers were put in by mere chance. Just because they came handy. Think it over. I shall bring you a drink."

She neither answered nor turned, but went on writing in a scorching scrawl whatever she was writing. A third letter, presumably (two in stamped envelopes were already laid out on the desk). I went back to the kitchen.

I set out two glasses (to St. Algebra? to Lo?) and opened the refrigerator. It roared at me viciously while I removed the ice from its heart. Rewrite. Let her read it again. She will not recall details. Change, forge. Write a fragment and show it to her or leave it lying around. Why do faucets sometimes whine so horribly? A horrible situation, really. The little pillow-shaped blocks of ice—pillows for polar teddy bear, Lo—emitted rasping, crackling, tortured sounds as the warm water loosened them in their cells. I bumped down the glasses side by side. I poured in the whiskey and a dram of soda. She had tabooed my pin. Bark and bang went the icebox. Carrying the glasses, I walked through the dining room and spoke through the parlor door which was a fraction ajar, not quite space enough for my elbow.

"I have made you a drink," I said.

She did not answer, the mad bitch, and I placed the glasses on the sideboard near the telephone, which had started to ring.

"Leslie speaking. Leslie Tomson," said Leslie Tomson who favored a dip at dawn. "Mrs. Humbert, sir, has been run over and you'd better come quick."

I answered, perhaps a bit testily, that my wife was safe and sound, and still holding the receiver, I pushed open the door and said:

"There's this man saying you've been killed, Charlotte."

But there was no Charlotte in the living room.

23

I rushed out. The far side of our steep little street presented a peculiar sight. A big black glossy Packard had climbed Miss Opposite's sloping lawn at an angle from the sidewalk (where a tartan laprobe had dropped in a heap), and stood there, shining in the sun, its doors open like wings, its front wheels deep in evergreen shrubbery. To the anatomical right of this car, on the trim turf of the lawn-slope, an old gentleman with a white mustache, well-dressed—doublebreasted gray suit, polka-dotted bow-tie—lay supine, his long legs together, like a death-size wax figure. I have to put the impact of an instantaneous vision into a sequence of words; their physical accumulation in the page impairs the actual flash, the sharp unity of impression: Rug-heap, car, old man-doll, Miss O.'s nurse running with a rustle, a half-empty tumbler in her hand, back to the screened porch—where the propped-up, imprisoned, decrepit lady herself may be imagined screeching, but not loud enough to drown the rhythmical yaps of the Junk setter walking from group to group—from a bunch of neighbors already collected on the sidewalk, near the bit of checked stuff, and back to the car which he had finally run to earth, and then to another group on the lawn, consisting of Leslie, two policemen and a sturdy man with tortoise shell glasses. At this point, I should explain that the prompt appearance of the patrolmen, hardly more than a minute after the accident, was due to their having been ticketing the illegally parked cars in a cross lane two blocks down the grade; that the fellow with the glasses was Frederick Beale, Jr., driver of the Packard; that his 79-year-old father, whom the nurse had just watered on the green bank where he lay—a banked banker so to speak—was not in a dead faint, but was comfortably and methodically recovering from a mild heart attack or its possibility; and, finally, that the laprobe on the sidewalk (where she had so often pointed out to me with disapproval the crooked green cracks) concealed the mangled remains of Charlotte Humbert who had been knocked down and dragged several feet by the Beale car as she was hurrying across the street to drop three letters in the mailbox, at the corner of Miss Opposite's lawn. These were picked up and handed to me by a pretty child in a dirty pink frock, and I got rid of them by clawing them to fragments in my trouser pocket.

Three doctors and the Farlows presently arrived on the scene and took over. The widower, a man of exceptional self-control, neither wept nor raved. He staggered a bit, that he did; but he opened his mouth only to impart such information or issue such directions as were strictly necessary in connection with the identification, examination and disposal of a dead woman, the top of her head a porridge of bone, brains, bronze hair and blood. The sun was still a blinding red when he was put to bed in Dolly's room by his two friends, gentle John and dewy-eyed Jean; who, to be near, retired to the Humberts' bedroom for the night; which, for all I know, they may not have spent as innocently as the solemnity of the occasion required.

I have no reason to dwell, in this very special memoir, on the pre-funeral formalities that had to be attended to, or on the funeral itself, which was as quiet as the marriage had been. But a few incidents pertaining to those four or five days after Charlotte's simple death, have to be noted.

My first night of widowhood I was so drunk that I slept as soundly as the child who had slept in that bed. Next morning I hastened to inspect the fragments of letters in my pocket. They had got too thoroughly mixed up to be sorted into three complete sets. I assumed that "... and you had better find it because I cannot buy ..." came from a letter to Lo; and other fragments seemed to point to Charlotte's intention of fleeing with Lo to Parkington, or even back to Pisky, lest the vulture snatch her precious lamb. Other tatters and shreds (never had I thought I had such strong talons) obviously referred to an application not to St. A. but to another boarding school which was said to be so harsh and gray and gaunt in its methods (although supplying croquet under the elms) as to have earned the nickname of "Reformatory for Young Ladies." Finally, the third epistle was obviously addressed to me. I made out such items as "... after a year of separation we may ..." "... oh, my dearest, oh my ..." "... worse than if it had been a woman you kept ..." "... or, maybe, I shall die ..." But on the whole my gleanings made little sense; the various fragments of those three hasty missives were as jumbled in the palms of my hands as their elements had been in poor Charlotte's head.

That day John had to see a customer, and Jean had to feed her dogs, and so I was to be deprived temporarily of my friends' company. The dear people were afraid I might commit suicide if left alone, and since no other friends were available (Miss Opposite was incommunicado, the McCoos were busy building a new house miles away, and the Chatfields had been recently called to Maine by some family trouble of their own), Leslie and Louise were commissioned to keep me company under the pretense of helping me to sort out and pack a multitude of orphaned things. In a moment of superb inspiration I showed the kind and credulous Farlows (we were waiting for Leslie to come for his paid tryst with Louise) a little photograph of Charlotte I had found among her affairs. From a boulder she smiled through blown hair. It had been taken in April 1934, a memorable spring. While on a business visit to the States, I had had occasion to spend several months in Pisky. We met— and had a mad love affair. I was married, alas, and she was engaged to Haze, but after I returned to Europe, we corresponded through a friend, now dead. Jean whispered she had heard some rumors and looked at the snapshot, and, still looking, handed it to John, and John removed his pipe and looked at lovely and fast Charlotte Becker, and handed it back to me. Then they left for a few hours. Happy Louise was gurgling and scolding her swain in the basement.

Hardly had the Farlows gone than a blue-chinned cleric called —and I tried to make the interview as brief as was consistent with neither hurting his feelings nor arousing his doubts. Yes, I would devote all my life to the child's welfare. Here, incidentally, was a little cross that Charlotte Becker had given me when we were both young. I had a female cousin, a respectable spinster in New York. There we would find a good private school for Dolly. Oh, what a crafty Humbert!

For the benefit of Leslie and Louise who might (and did) report it to John and Jean I made a tremendously loud and beautifully enacted long-distance call and simulated a conversation with Shirley Holmes. When John and Jean returned, I completely took them in by telling them, in a deliberately wild and confused mutter, that Lo had gone with the intermediate group on a five-day hike and could not be reached.

"Good Lord," said Jean, "what shall we do?"

John said it was perfectly simple—he would get the Climax police to find the hikers—it would not take them an hour. In fact, he knew the country and—

"Look," he continued, "why don't I drive there right now, and you may sleep with Jean"—(he did not really add that but Jean supported his offer so passionately that it might be implied).

I broke down. I pleaded with John to let things remain the

Lolita

way they were. I said I could not bear to have the child all around me, sobbing, clinging to me, she was so high-strung, the experience might react on her future, psychiatrists have analyzed such cases. There was a sudden pause.

"Well, you are the doctor," said John a little bluntly. "But after all I was Charlotte's friend and adviser. One would like to know what you are going to do about the child anyway."

"John," cried Jean, "she is his child, not Harold Haze's. Don't you understand? Humbert is Dolly's real father."

"I see," said John. "I am sorry. Yes, I see. I did not realize that. It simplifies matters, of course. And whatever you feel is right."

The distraught father went on to say he would go and fetch his delicate daughter immediately after the funeral, and would do his best to give her a good time in totally different surroundings, perhaps a trip to New Mexico or California—granted, of course, he lived.

So artistically did I impersonate the calm of ultimate despair, the hush before some crazy outburst, that the perfect Farlows removed me to their house. They had a good cellar, as cellars go in this country; and that was helpful, for I feared insomnia and a ghost.

Now I must explain *my* reasons for keeping Dolores away. Naturally, at first, when Charlotte had just been eliminated and I re-entered the house a free father, and gulped down the two whiskey-and-sodas I had prepared, and topped them with a pint or two of my "pin," and went to the bathroom to get away from neighbors and friends, there was but one thing in my mind and pulse—namely, the awareness that a few hours hence, warm, brown-haired, and mine, mine, mine, Lolita would be in my arms, shedding tears that I would kiss away faster than they could well. But as I stood wide-eyed and flushed before the mirror, John Farlow tenderly tapped to inquire if I was okay—and I immediately realized it would be madness on my part to have her in the house with all those busybodies milling around and scheming to take her away from me. Indeed, unpredictable Lo herself might—who knows?—show some foolish

distrust of me, a sudden repugnance, vague fear and the like—
and gone would be the magic prize at the very instant of triumph.

Speaking of busybodies, I had another visitor—friend Beale,
the fellow who eliminated my wife. Stodgy and solemn, looking
like a kind of assistant executioner, with his bulldog jowls, small
black eyes, thickly rimmed glasses and conspicuous nostrils,
he was ushered in by John who then left us, closing the door
upon us, with the utmost tact. Suavely saying he had twins in
my stepdaughter's class, my grotesque visitor unrolled a large
diagram he had made of the accident. It was, as my stepdaughter
would have put it, "a beaut," with all kinds of impressive arrows
and dotted lines in varicolored inks. Mrs. H. H.'s trajectory was
illustrated at several points by a series of those little outline
figures—doll-like wee career girl or WAC—used in statistics as
visual aids. Very clearly and conclusively, this route came into
contact with a boldly traced sinuous line representing two con-
secutive swerves—one which the Beale car made to avoid the
Junk dog (dog not shown), and the second, a kind of exaggerated continuation of the first, meant to avert the tragedy. A very
black cross indicated the spot where the trim little outline
figure had at last come to rest on the sidewalk. I looked for some
similar mark to denote the place on the embankment where
my visitor's huge wax father had reclined, but there was none.
That gentleman, however, had signed the document as a witness
underneath the name of Leslie Tomson, Miss Opposite and a
few other people.

With his hummingbird pencil deftly and delicately flying
from one point to another, Frederick demonstrated his absolute
innocence and the recklessness of my wife: while he was in the
act of avoiding the dog, *she* had slipped on the freshly watered
asphalt and plunged forward whereas she should have flung herself not forward but backward (Fred showed how by a jerk of
his padded shoulder). I said it was certainly not his fault, and
the inquest upheld my view.

Breathing violently through jet-black tense nostrils, he shook
his head and my hand; then, with an air of perfect *savoir vivre*
and gentlemanly generosity, he offered to pay the funeral-home

expenses. He expected me to refuse his offer. With a drunken sob of gratitude I accepted it. This took him aback. Slowly, incredulously, he repeated what he had said. I thanked him again, even more profusely than before.

In result of that weird interview, the numbness of my soul was for a moment resolved. And no wonder! I had actually seen the agent of fate. I had palpated the very flesh of fate—and its padded shoulder. A brilliant and monstrous mutation had suddenly taken place, and here was the instrument. Within the intricacies of the pattern (hurrying housewife, slippery pavement, a pest of a dog, steep grade, big car, baboon at its wheel), I could dimly distinguish my own vile contribution. Had I not been such a fool—or such an intuitive genius—to preserve that journal, fluids produced by vindictive anger and hot shame would not have blinded Charlotte in her dash to the mailbox. But even had they blinded her, still nothing might have happened, had not precise fate, that synchronizing phantom, mixed within its alembic the car and the dog and the sun 1 and the shade and the wet and the weak and the strong and the stone. Adieu, Marlene! Fat fate's formal handshake (as 2 reproduced by Beale before leaving the room) brought me out of my torpor; and I wept. Ladies and gentlemen of the jury—I wept.

24

The elms and the poplars were turning their ruffled backs to a sudden onslaught of wind, and a black thunderhead loomed above Ramsdale's white church tower when I looked around me for the last time. For unknown adventures I was leaving the livid house where I had rented a room only ten weeks before. The shades—thrifty, practical bamboo shades—were already down. On porches or in the house their rich textures lend modern drama. The house of heaven must seem pretty bare after that. A raindrop fell on my knuckles. I went back into the house for something or other while John was putting my bags into the car, and then a funny thing happened. I do not know if in these tragic notes I have sufficiently stressed the peculiar "sending" effect that the writer's good looks—pseudo-Celtic, attractively simian, boyishly manly—had on women of every age and environment. Of course, such announcements made in the first person may sound ridiculous. But every once in a while I have to remind the reader of my appearance much as a professional novelist, who has given a character of his some mannerism or a dog, has to go on producing that dog or that mannerism every time the character crops up in the course of the book. There may be more to it in the present case. My gloomy good looks should be kept in the mind's eye if my story is to be properly understood. Pubescent Lo swooned to Humbert's charm as she did to hiccuppy music; adult Lotte loved me with a mature, possessive passion that I now deplore and respect more than I care to say. Jean Farlow, who was thirty-one and absolutely neurotic, had also apparently developed a strong liking for me. She was handsome in a carved-Indian sort of way, with a burnt sienna complexion. Her lips were like large crimson polyps, and when she emitted her special barking laugh, she showed large dull teeth and pale gums.

She was very tall, wore either slacks with sandals or billowing skirts with ballet slippers, drank any strong liquor in any amount, had had two miscarriages, wrote stories about animals, painted, as the reader knows, lakescapes, was already nursing the cancer that was to kill her at thirty-three, and was hopelessly unattractive to me. Judge then of my alarm when a few seconds before I left (she and I stood in the hallway) Jean, with her always trembling fingers, took me by the temples, and, tears in her bright blue eyes, attempted, unsuccessfully, to glue herself to my lips.

"Take care of yourself," she said, "kiss your daughter for me."

A clap of thunder reverberated throughout the house, and she added:

"Perhaps, somewhere, some day, at a less miserable time, we may see each other again" (Jean, whatever, wherever you are, in minus time-space or plus soul-time, forgive me all this, parenthesis included).

And presently I was shaking hands with both of them in the street, the sloping street, and everything was whirling and flying before the approaching white deluge, and a truck with a mattress from Philadelphia was confidently rolling down to an empty house, and dust was running and writhing over the exact slab of stone where Charlotte, when they lifted the laprobe for me, had been revealed, curled up, her eyes intact, their black lashes still wet, matted, like yours, Lolita.

25

One might suppose that with all blocks removed and a prospect of delirious and unlimited delights before me, I would have mentally sunk back, heaving a sigh of delicious relief. *Eh bien, pas du tout!* Instead of basking in the beams of smiling Chance, I was obsessed by all sorts of purely ethical doubts and fears. For instance: might it not surprise people that Lo was so consistently debarred from attending festive and funeral functions in her immediate family? You remember—we had not had her at our wedding. Or another thing: granted it was the long hairy arm of Coincidence that had reached out to remove an innocent woman, might Coincidence not ignore in a heathen moment what its twin lamb had done and hand Lo a premature note of commiseration? True, the accident had been reported only by the Ramsdale *Journal*—not by the Parkington *Recorder* or the Climax *Herald*, Camp Q being in another state, and local deaths having no federal news interest; but I could not help fancying that somehow Dolly Haze had been informed already, and that at the very time I was on my way to fetch her, she was being driven to Ramsdale by friends unknown to me. Still more disquieting than all these conjectures and worries, was the fact that Humbert Humbert, a brand-new American citizen of obscure European origin, had taken no steps toward becoming the legal guardian of his dead wife's daughter (twelve years and seven months old). Would I ever dare take those steps? I could not repress a shiver whenever I imagined my nudity hemmed in by mysterious statutes in the merciless glare of the Common Law.

My scheme was a marvel of primitive art: I would whizz over to Camp Q, tell Lolita her mother was about to undergo a major operation at an invented hospital, and then keep moving with my sleepy nymphet from inn to inn while her mother got better and better and finally died. But as I traveled campward my anxiety grew. I could not bear to think I might not find Lolita there—or find, instead, another, scared, Lolita clamoring for some family friend: not the Farlows, thank God—she hardly knew them—but might there not be other people I had not reckoned with? Finally, I decided to make the long-distance call I had simulated so well a few days before. It was raining hard when I pulled up in a muddy suburb of Parkington, just before the Fork, one prong of which bypassed the city and led to the highway which crossed the hills to Lake Climax and Camp Q. I flipped off the ignition and for quite a minute sat in the car bracing myself for that telephone call, and staring at the rain, at the inundated sidewalk, at a hydrant: a hideous thing, really, painted a thick silver and red, extending the red stumps of its arms to be varnished by the rain which like stylized blood dripped upon its argent chains. No wonder that stopping beside those nightmare cripples is taboo. I drove up to a gasoline station. A surprise awaited me when at last the coins had satisfactorily clanked down and a voice was allowed to answer mine.

Holmes, the camp mistress, informed me that Dolly had gone Monday (this was Wednesday) on a hike in the hills with her group and was expected to return rather late today. Would I care to come tomorrow, and what was exactly—Without going into details, I said that her mother was hospitalized, that the situation was grave, that the child should not be told it was grave and that she should be ready to leave with me tomorrow afternoon. The two voices parted in an explosion of warmth and good will, and through some freak mechanical flaw all my coins came tumbling back to me with a hitting-the-jackpot clatter that almost made me laugh despite the disappointment at having to postpone bliss. One wonders if this sudden discharge, this spasmodic refund, was not correlated somehow, in the mind of McFate, with my having invented that little expedition before ever learning of it as I did now.

What next? I proceeded to the business center of Parkington and devoted the whole afternoon (the weather had cleared, the wet town was like silver-and-glass) to buying beautiful things for Lo. Goodness, what crazy purchases were prompted by the poignant predilection Humbert had in those days for check weaves, bright cottons, frills, puffed-out short sleeves, soft pleats, snug-fitting bodices and generously full skirts! Oh Lolita, you are my girl, as Vee was Poe's and Bea Dante's, and what little 1 girl would not like to whirl in a circular skirt and scanties? Did I have something special in mind? coaxing voices asked me. Swimming suits? We have them in all shades. Dream pink, frosted aqua, glans mauve, tulip red, oolala black. What about 2, 3 playsuits? Slips? No slips. Lo and I loathed slips.

One of my guides in these matters was an anthropometric entry made by her mother on Lo's twelfth birthday (the reader 4 remembers that Know-Your-Child book). I had the feeling that Charlotte, moved by obscure motives of envy and dislike, had added an inch here, a pound there; but since the nymphet had no doubt grown somewhat in the last seven months, I thought I could safely accept most of those January measurements: hip girth, twenty-nine inches; thigh girth (just below the gluteal sulcus), seventeen; calf girth and neck circumference, eleven; chest circumference, twenty-seven; upper arm girth, eight; waist, twenty-three; stature, fifty-seven inches; weight, seventy-eight pounds; figure, linear; intelligence quotient, 121; vermiform appendix present, thank God.

Apart from measurements, I could of course visualize Lolita with hallucinational lucidity; and nursing as I did a tingle on my breastbone at the exact spot her silky top had come level once or twice with my heart; and feeling as I did her warm weight in my lap (so that, in a sense, I was always "with Lolita" as a woman is "with child"), I was not surprised to discover later that my computation had been more or less correct. Having moreover studied a midsummer sale book, it was with a very knowing air that I examined various pretty articles, sport shoes, sneakers, pumps of crushed kid for crushed kids. The painted girl in black who attended to all these poignant needs of mine turned parental scholarship and precise description into commercial euphemisms, such as *"petite."* Another, much older woman, in a white dress, with a pancake make-up, seemed to be oddly impressed by my knowledge of junior fashions; perhaps I had a midget for mistress; so, when shown a skirt with two "cute" pockets in front, I intentionally put a naïve male question and was rewarded by a smiling demonstration of the way the zipper worked in the back of the skirt. I had next great fun with all kinds of shorts and briefs—phantom little Lolitas dancing, falling, daisying all over the counter. We rounded up the deal with some prim cotton pajamas in popular butcher-boy style. Humbert, the popular butcher.

There is a touch of the mythological and the enchanted in those large stores where according to ads a career girl can get a complete desk-to-date wardrobe, and where little sister can dream of the day when her wool jersey will make the boys in the back row of the classroom drool. Lifesize plastic figures of snubbed-nosed children with dun-colored, greenish, brown-dotted, faunish faces floated around me. I realized I was the only shopper in that rather eerie place where I moved about fish-like, in a glaucous aquarium. I sensed strange thoughts form in the minds of the languid ladies that escorted me from counter to counter, from rock ledge to seaweed, and the belts and the bracelets I chose seemed to fall from siren hands into transparent water. I bought an elegant valise, had my purchases put into it, and repaired to the nearest hotel, well pleased with my day.

Somehow, in connection with that quiet poetical afternoon of fastidious shopping, I recalled the hotel or inn with the seductive name of The Enchanted Hunters which Charlotte had happened to mention shortly before my liberation. With the help of a guidebook I located it in the secluded town of Briceland, a four-hour drive from Lo's camp. I could have telephoned but fearing my voice might go out of control and lapse into coy croaks of broken English, I decided to send a wire ordering a room with twin beds for the next night. What a comic, clumsy, wavering Prince Charming I was! How some of my readers will laugh at me when I tell them the trouble I had with the wording of my telegram! What should I put: Humbert and daughter? Humberg and small daughter? Homberg and immature girl? Homburg and child? The droll mistake—the "g" at the end—which eventually came through may have been a telepathic echo of these hesitations of mine.

And then, in the velvet of a summer night, my broodings over the philter I had with me! Oh miserly Hamburg! Was he not a very Enchanted Hunter as he deliberated with himself over his boxful of magic ammunition? To rout the monster of insomnia should he try himself one of those amethyst capsules? There were forty of them, all told—forty nights with a frail little sleeper at my throbbing side; could I rob myself of one such night in order to sleep? Certainly not: much too precious was each tiny plum, each microscopic planetarium with its live stardust. Oh, let me be mawkish for the nonce! I am so tired of being cynical.

26

This daily headache in the opaque air of this tombal jail is disturbing, but I must persevere. Have written more than a hundred pages and not got anywhere yet. My calendar is getting confused. That must have been around August 15, 1947. Don't think I can go on. Heart, head—everything. Lolita, Lolita, Lolita, Lolita, Lolita, Lolita, Lolita, Lolita, Lolita. Repeat till the page is full, printer.

27

Still in Parkington. Finally, I did achieve an hour's slumber—from which I was aroused by gratuitous and horribly exhausting congress with a small hairy hermaphrodite, a total stranger.

By then it was six in the morning, and it suddenly occurred to me it might be a good thing to arrive at the camp earlier than I had said. From Parkington I had still a hundred miles to go, and there would be more than that to the Hazy Hills and Briceland. If I had said I would come for Dolly in the afternoon, it was only because my fancy insisted on merciful night falling as soon as possible upon my impatience. But now I foresaw all kinds of misunderstandings and was all a-jitter lest delay might give her the opportunity of some idle telephone call to Ramsdale. However, when at 9.30 A.M. I attempted to start, I was confronted by a dead battery, and noon was nigh when at last I left Parkington.

1 I reached my destination around half past two; parked my car in a pine grove where a green-shirted, redheaded impish lad stood throwing horseshoes in sullen solitude; was laconically directed by him to an office in a stucco cottage; in a dying state, had to endure for several minutes the inquisitive commiseration of the camp mistress, a sluttish worn out female with rusty hair. Dolly she said was all packed and ready to go. She knew her mother was sick but not critically. Would Mr. Haze, I mean, Mr. Humbert, care to meet the camp counsellors? Or look at the cabins where the girls live? Each dedicated to a Disney creature? Or visit the Lodge? Or should Charlie be sent over to fetch her? The girls were just finishing fixing the Dining Room for a dance. (And perhaps afterwards she would say to somebody or other: "The poor guy looked like his own ghost.")

Let me retain for a moment that scene in all its trivial and fateful detail: hag Holmes writing out a receipt, scratching her head, pulling a drawer out of her desk, pouring change into my impatient palm, then neatly spreading a banknote over it with a bright "... and five!"; photographs of girl-children; some gaudy

2 moth or butterfly, still alive, safely pinned to the wall ("nature study"); the framed diploma of the camp's dietitian; my trembling hands; a card produced by efficient Holmes with a report of Dolly Haze's behavior for July ("fair to good; keen on swimming and boating"); a sound of trees and birds, and my pounding heart ... I was standing with my back to the open door, and

then I felt the blood rush to my head as I heard her respiration and voice behind me. She arrived dragging and bumping her heavy suitcase. "Hi!" she said, and stood still, looking at me with sly, glad eyes, her soft lips parted in a slightly foolish but wonderfully endearing smile.

She was thinner and taller, and for a second it seemed to me her face was less pretty than the mental imprint I had cherished for more than a month: her cheeks looked hollowed and too much lentigo camouflaged her rosy rustic features; and that first impression (a very narrow human interval between two tiger heartbeats) carried the clear implication that all widower Humbert had to do, wanted to do, or would do, was to give this wan-looking though sun-colored little orphan *aux yeux battus* (and even those plumbaceous umbrae under her eyes bore freckles) a sound education, a healthy and happy girlhood, a clean home, nice girl-friends of her age among whom (if the fates deigned to repay me) I might find, perhaps, a pretty little *Mägdlein* for Herr Doktor Humbert alone. But "in a wink," as the Germans say, the angelic line of conduct was erased, and I overtook my prey (time moves ahead of our fancies!), and she was my Lolita again—in fact, more of my Lolita than ever. I let my hand rest on her warm auburn head and took up her bag. She was all rose and honey, dressed in her brightest gingham, with a pattern of little red apples, and her arms and legs were of a deep golden brown, with scratches like tiny dotted lines of coagulated rubies, and the ribbed cuffs of her white socks were turned down at the remembered level, and because of her childish gait, or because I had memorized her as always wearing heelless shoes, her saddle oxfords looked somehow too large and too high-heeled for her. Good-bye, Camp Q, merry Camp Q. Good-bye, plain unwhole-some food, good-bye Charlie boy. In the hot car she settled down beside me, slapped a prompt fly on her lovely knee; then, her mouth working violently on a piece of chewing gum, she rapidly cranked down the window on her side and settled back again. We sped through the striped and speckled forest.

"How's Mother?" she asked dutifully.

I said the doctors did not quite know yet what the trouble

was. Anyway, something abdominal. Abominable? No, abdominal. We would have to hang around for a while. The hospital was in the country, near the gay town of Lepingville, where a great poet had resided in the early nineteenth century and where we would take in all the shows. She thought it a peachy idea and wondered if we could make Lepingville before nine P.M.

"We should be at Briceland by dinner time," I said, "and tomorrow we'll visit Lepingville. How was the hike? Did you have a marvelous time at the camp?"

"Uh-huh."

"Sorry to leave?"

"Un-un."

"Talk, Lo—don't grunt. Tell me something."

"What thing, Dad?" (she let the word expand with ironic deliberation).

"Any old thing."

"Okay, if I call you that?" (eyes slit at the road).

"Quite."

"It's a sketch, you know. When did you fall for my mummy?"

"Some day, Lo, you will understand many emotions and situations, such as for example the harmony, the beauty of spiritual relationship."

"Bah!" said the cynical nymphet.

Shallow lull in the dialogue, filled with some landscape.

"Look, Lo, at all those cows on that hillside."

"I think I'll vomit if I look at a cow again."

"You know, I missed you terribly, Lo."

"*I* did not. Fact I've been revoltingly unfaithful to you, but it does not matter one bit, because you've stopped caring for me, anyway. You drive much faster than my mummy, mister."

I slowed down from a blind seventy to a purblind fifty.

"Why do you think I have ceased caring for you, Lo?"

"Well, you haven't kissed me yet, have you?"

Inly dying, inly moaning, I glimpsed a reasonably wide shoulder of road ahead, and bumped and wobbled into the weeds. Remember she is only a child, remember she is only—

Hardly had the car come to a standstill than Lolita positively flowed into my arms. Not daring, not daring let myself go—not even daring let myself realize that *this* (sweet wetness and trembling fire) was the beginning of the ineffable life which, ably assisted by fate, I had finally willed into being—not daring really kiss her, I touched her hot, opening lips with the utmost piety, tiny sips, nothing salacious; but she, with an impatient wriggle, pressed her mouth to mine so hard that I felt her big front teeth and shared in the peppermint taste of her saliva. I knew, of course, it was but an innocent game on her part, a bit of backfisch foolery in imitation of some simulacrum of fake romance, and since (as the psychotherapist, as well as the rapist, will tell you) the limits and rules of such girlish games are fluid, or at least too childishly subtle for the senior partner to grasp—I was dreadfully afraid I might go too far and cause her to start back in revulsion and terror. And, as above all I was agonizingly anxious to smuggle her into the hermetic seclusion of The Enchanted Hunters, and we had still eighty miles to go, blessed intuition broke our embrace—a split second before a highway patrol car drew up alongside. 1, 2 3

Florid and beetle-browed, its driver stared at me:

"Happen to see a blue sedan, same make as yours, pass you before the junction?"

"Why, no."

"We didn't," said Lo, eagerly leaning across me, her innocent hand on my legs, "but are you sure it was blue, because—"

The cop (what shadow of us was he after?) gave the little colleen his best smile and went into a U-turn. 4

We drove on.

"The fruithead!" remarked Lo. "He should have nabbed *you*."

"Why me for heaven's sake?"

"Well, the speed in this bum state is fifty, and—No, don't slow down, you, dull bulb. He's gone now."

"We have still quite a stretch," I said, "and I want to get there before dark. So be a good girl."

"Bad, bad girl," said Lo comfortably. "Juvenile delickwent, but frank and fetching. That light was red. I've never seen such driving."

We rolled silently through a silent townlet.

"Say, wouldn't Mother be absolutely mad if she found out we were lovers?"

"Good Lord, Lo, let us not talk that way."

"But we *are* lovers, aren't we?"

"Not that I know of. I think we are going to have some more rain. Don't you want to tell me of those little pranks of yours in camp?"

"You talk like a book, *Dad*."

"What have you been up to? I insist you tell me."

"Are you easily shocked?"

"No. Go on."

"Let us turn into a secluded lane and I'll tell you."

"Lo, I must seriously ask you not to play the fool. Well?"

"Well—I joined in all the activities that were offered."

"*Ensuite?*"

"Ansooit, I was taught to live happily and richly with others and to develop a wholesome personality. Be a cake, in fact."

"Yes. I saw something of the sort in the booklet."

"We loved the sings around the fire in the big stone fireplace or under the darned stars, where every girl merged her own spirit of happiness with the voice of the group."

"Your memory is excellent, Lo, but I must trouble you to leave out the swear words. Anything else?"

"The Girl Scout's motto," said Lo rhapsodically, "is also mine. I fill my life with worthwhile deeds such as—well, never mind what. My duty is—to be useful. I am a friend to male animals. I obey orders. I am cheerful. That was another police car. I am thrifty and I am absolutely filthy in thought, word and deed."

"Now I do hope that's all, you witty child."

"Yep. That's all. No—wait a sec. We baked in a reflector oven. Isn't that terrific?"

"Well, that's better."

"We washed zillions of dishes. 'Zillions' you know is schoolmarm's slang for many-many-many-many. Oh yes, last but not least, as Mother says—Now let me see—what was it? I know: We made shadowgraphs. Gee, what fun."

"*C'est bien tout?*"

"*C'est.* Except for one little thing, something I simply can't tell you without blushing all over."

"Will you tell it me later?"

"If we sit in the dark and you let me whisper, I will. Do you sleep in your old room or in a heap with Mother?"

"Old room. Your mother may have to undergo a very serious operation, Lo."

"Stop at that candy bar, will you," said Lo.

Sitting on a high stool, a band of sunlight crossing her bare brown forearm, Lolita was served an elaborate ice-cream concoction topped with synthetic syrup. It was erected and brought her by a pimply brute of a boy in a greasy bow-tie who eyed my fragile child in her thin cotton frock with carnal deliberation. My impatience to reach Briceland and The Enchanted Hunters was becoming more than I could endure. Fortunately she dispatched the stuff with her usual alacrity.

"How much cash do you have?" I asked.

"Not a cent," she said sadly, lifting her eyebrows, showing me the empty inside of her money purse.

"This is a matter that will be mended in due time," I rejoined archly. "Are you coming?"

"Say, I wonder if they have a washroom."

"You are not going there," I said firmly. "It is sure to be a vile place. Do come on."

She was on the whole an obedient little girl and I kissed her in the neck when we got back into the car.

"*Don't* do that," she said looking at me with unfeigned surprise. "Don't drool on me. You dirty man."

She rubbed the spot against her raised shoulder.

"Sorry," I murmured. "I'm rather fond of you, that's all."

We drove under a gloomy sky, up a winding road, then down again.

"Well, I'm also sort of fond of you," said Lolita in a delayed soft voice, with a sort of sigh, and sort of settled closer to me.

(Oh, my Lolita, we shall never get there!)

Dusk was beginning to saturate pretty little Briceland, its

phony colonial architecture, curiosity shops and imported shade trees, when we drove through the weakly lighted streets in search of the Enchanted Hunters. The air, despite a steady drizzle beading it, was warm and green, and a queue of people, mainly children and old men, had already formed before the box office of a movie house, dripping with jewel-fires.

"Oh, I want to see that picture. Let's go right after dinner. Oh, let's!"

"We might," chanted Humbert—knowing perfectly well, the sly tumescent devil, that by nine, when *his* show began, she would be dead in his arms.

"Easy!" cried Lo, lurching forward, as an accursed truck in front of us, its backside carbuncles pulsating, stopped at a crossing.

If we did not get to the hotel soon, immediately, miraculously, in the very next block, I felt I would lose all control over the Haze jalopy with its ineffectual wipers and whimsical brakes; but the passers-by I applied to for directions were either strangers themselves or asked with a frown "Enchanted what?" as if I were a madman; or else they went into such complicated explanations, with geometrical gestures, geographical generalities and strictly local clues (... then bear south after you hit the courthouse ...) that I could not help losing my way in the maze of their well-meaning gibberish. Lo, whose lovely prismatic entrails had already digested the sweetmeat, was looking forward to a big meal and had begun to fidget. As to me, although I had long become used to a kind of secondary fate (McFate's inept secretary, so to speak) pettily interfering with the boss's generous magnificent plan—to grind and grope through the avenues of Briceland was perhaps the most exasperating ordeal I had yet faced. In later months I could laugh at my inexperience when recalling the obstinate boyish way in which I had concentrated upon that particular inn with its fancy name; for all along our route countless motor courts proclaimed their vacancy in neon lights, ready to accommodate salesmen, escaped convicts, impotents, family groups, as well as the most corrupt and vigorous couples. Ah, gentle drivers gliding through summer's black nights, what frolics, what twists of lust, you might see from your impeccable highways if Kumfy Kabins were suddenly drained of their pigments and became as transparent as boxes of glass!

The miracle I hankered for did happen after all. A man and a girl, more or less conjoined in a dark car under dripping trees, told us we were in the heart of The Park, but had only to turn left at the next traffic light and there we would be. We did not see any next traffic light—in fact, The Park was as black as the sins it concealed—but soon after falling under the smooth spell of a nicely graded curve, the travelers became aware of a diamond glow through the mist, then a gleam of lakewater appeared— and there it was, marvelously and inexorably, under spectral trees, at the top of a graveled drive—the pale palace of The Enchanted Hunters.

A row of parked cars, like pigs at a trough, seemed at first sight to forbid access; but then, by magic, a formidable convertible, resplendent, rubious in the lighted rain, came into motion—was energetically backed out by a broad-shouldered driver —and we gratefully slipped into the gap it had left. I immediately regretted my haste for I noticed that my predecessor had now taken advantage of a garage-like shelter nearby where there was ample space for another car; but I was too impatient to follow his example. 1

"Wow! Looks swank," remarked my vulgar darling squinting at the stucco as she crept out into the audible drizzle and with a childish hand tweaked loose the frock-fold that had stuck in the peach-cleft—to quote Robert Browning. Under the arclights 2 enlarged replicas of chestnut leaves plunged and played on white pillars. I unlocked the trunk compartment. A hunchbacked and hoary Negro in a uniform of sorts took our bags and wheeled them slowly into the lobby. It was full of old ladies and clergymen. Lolita sank down on her haunches to caress a pale-faced, blue-freckled, black-eared cocker spaniel swooning on the floral 3 carpet under her hand—as who would not, my heart—while I cleared my throat through the throng to the desk. There a bald porcine old man—everybody was old in that old hotel—examined 4 my features with a polite smile, then leisurely produced my (garbled) telegram, wrestled with some dark doubts, turned his head to look at the clock, and finally said he was very sorry, he had held the room with the twin beds till half past six, and now it was gone. A religious convention, he said, had clashed with a flower show in Briceland, and—"The name," I said coldly, "is not Humberg and not Humbug, but Herbert, I mean Humbert, and any room will do, just put in a cot for my little daughter. She is ten and very tired."

The pink old fellow peered good-naturedly at Lo—still squatting, listening in profile, lips parted, to what the dog's mistress, an ancient lady swathed in violet veils, was telling her from the depths of a cretonne easy chair.

Whatever doubts the obscene fellow had, they were dispelled by that blossom-like vision. He said, he might still have a room, had one, in fact—with a double bed. As to the cot—

"Mr. Potts, do we have any cots left?" Potts, also pink and bald, with white hairs growing out of his ears and other holes, would see what could be done. He came and spoke while I unscrewed my fountain pen. Impatient Humbert!

"Our double beds are really triple," Potts cozily said tucking me and my kid in. "One crowded night we had three ladies and a child like yours sleep together. I believe one of the ladies was a disguised man [*my* static]. However—would there be a spare cot in 49, Mr. Swine?"

"I think it went to the Swoons," said Swine, the initial old clown.

"We'll manage somehow," I said. "My wife may join us later —but even then, I suppose, we'll manage."

The two pink pigs were now among my best friends. In the slow clear hand of crime I wrote: Dr. Edgar H. Humbert and daughter, 342 Lawn Street, Ramsdale. A key (342!) was half-shown to me (magician showing object he is about to palm)— and handed over to Uncle Tom. Lo, leaving the dog as she would leave me some day, rose from her haunches; a raindrop fell on Charlotte's grave; a handsome young Negress slipped open the elevator door, and the doomed child went in followed by her throat-clearing father and crayfish Tom with the bags.

Parody of a hotel corridor. Parody of silence and death.   1

"Say, it's our house number," said cheerful Lo.

There was a double bed, a mirror, a double bed in the mirror,   2
a closet door with mirror, a bathroom door ditto, a blue-dark window, a reflected bed there, the same in the closet mirror, two chairs, a glass-topped table, two bedtables, a double bed: a big panel bed, to be exact, with a Tuscan rose chenille spread, and two frilled, pink-shaded nightlamps, left and right.

I was tempted to place a five-dollar bill in that sepia palm, but thought the largesse might be misconstrued, so I placed a quarter. Added another. He withdrew. Click. *Enfin seuls.*   3

"Are we to sleep in *one* room?" said Lo, her features working in that dynamic way they did—not cross or disgusted (though plain on the brink of it) but just dynamic—when she wanted to load a question with violent significance.

"I've asked them to put in a cot. Which I'll use if you like."

"You are crazy," said Lo.

"Why, my darling?"

"Because, my dahrling, when dahrling Mother finds out she'll divorce you and strangle me."

Just dynamic. Not really taking the matter too seriously.

"Now look here," I said, sitting down, while she stood, a few feet from me, and stared at herself contentedly, not unpleasantly surprised at her own appearance, filling with her own rosy sunshine the surprised and pleased closet-door mirror.

"Look here, Lo. Let's settle this once for all. For all practical purposes I am your father. I have a feeling of great tenderness for you. In your mother's absence I am responsible for your welfare. We are not rich, and while we travel, we shall be obliged —we shall be thrown a good deal together. Two people sharing one room, inevitably enter into a kind—how shall I say—a kind—"

"The word is incest," said Lo—and walked into the closet, walked out again with a young golden giggle, opened the adjoining door, and after carefully peering inside with her strange smoky eyes lest she make another mistake, retired to the bathroom.

I opened the window, tore off my sweat-drenched shirt, changed, checked the pill vial in my coat pocket, unlocked the—

She drifted out. I tried to embrace her: casually, a bit of controlled tenderness before dinner.

She said: "Look, let's cut out the kissing game and get something to eat."

It was then that I sprang my surprise.

Oh, what a dreamy pet! She walked up to the open suitcase as if stalking it from afar, at a kind of slow-motion walk, peering at that distant treasure box on the luggage support. (Was there something wrong, I wondered, with those great gray eyes of hers, or were we both plunged in the same enchanted mist?) She stepped up to it, lifting her rather high-heeled feet rather high, and bending her beautiful boy-knees while she walked

1   through dilating space with the lentor of one walking under water or in a flight dream. Then she raised by the armlets a copper-colored, charming and quite expensive vest, very slowly stretching it between her silent hands as if she were a bemused bird-hunter holding his breath over the incredible bird he spreads out by the tips of its flaming wings. Then (while I stood waiting for her) she pulled out the slow snake of a brilliant belt and tried it on.

Then she crept into my waiting arms, radiant, relaxed, caressing me with her tender, mysterious, impure, indifferent, twilight eyes—for all the world, like the cheapest of cheap cuties. For that is what nymphets imitate—while we moan and die.

"What's the katter with misses?" I muttered (word-control gone) into her hair.

"If you must know," she said, "you do it the wrong way."

"Show, wight ray."

2   "All in good time," responded the spoonerette.

3   *Seva ascendes, pulsata, brulans, kitzelans, dementissima. Elevator clatterans, pausa, clatterans, populus in corridoro. Hanc nisi mors mihi adimet nemo! Juncea puellula, jo pensavo fondis-*

4   *sime, nobserva nihil quidquam;* but, of course, in another mo-

ment I might have committed some dreadful blunder; fortunately, she returned to the treasure box.

From the bathroom, where it took me quite a time to shift back into normal gear for a humdrum purpose, I heard, standing, drumming, retaining my breath, my Lolita's "oo's" and "gee's" of girlish delight.

She had used the soap only because it was sample soap.

"Well, come on, my dear, if you are as hungry as I am."

And so to the elevator, daughter swinging her old white purse, father walking in front (nota bene: never behind, she is not a lady). As we stood (now side by side) waiting to be taken down, she threw back her head, yawned without restraint and shook her curls.

"When did they make you get up at that camp?"

"Half-past—" she stifled another yawn—"six"—yawn in full with a shiver of all her frame. "Half-past," she repeated, her throat filling up again.

The dining room met us with a smell of fried fat and a faded smile. It was a spacious and pretentious place with maudlin murals depicting enchanted hunters in various postures and states of enchantment amid a medley of pallid animals, dryads and trees. A few scattered old ladies, two clergymen, and a man in a sports coat were finishing their meals in silence. The dining room closed at nine, and the green-clad, poker-faced serving girls were, happily, in a desperate hurry to get rid of us.

"Does not he look exactly, but exactly, like Quilty?" said Lo in a soft voice, her sharp brown elbow not pointing, but visibly burning to point, at the lone diner in the loud checks, in the far corner of the room.

"Like our fat Ramsdale dentist?"

Lo arrested the mouthful of water she had just taken, and put down her dancing glass.

"Course not," she said with a splutter of mirth. "I meant the writer fellow in the Dromes ad."

Oh, Fame! Oh, Femina!

When the dessert was plunked down—a huge wedge of cherry pie for the young lady and vanilla ice cream for her protector, most of which she expeditiously added to her pie—I produced a small vial containing Papa's Purple Pills. As I look back at those seasick murals, at that strange and monstrous moment, I can only explain my behavior then by the mechanism of that dream vacuum wherein revolves a deranged mind; but at the time, it all seemed quite simple and inevitable to me. I glanced around, satisfied myself that the last diner had left, removed the stopper, and with the utmost deliberation tipped the philter into my palm. I had carefully rehearsed before a mirror the gesture of clapping my empty hand to my open mouth and swallowing a (fictitious) pill. As I expected, she pounced upon the vial with its plump, beautifully colored capsules loaded with Beauty's Sleep.

"Blue!" she exclaimed. "Violet blue. What are they made of?"

"Summer skies," I said, "and plums and figs, and the grape-blood of emperors."

"No, seriously—please."

1   "Oh, just Purpills. Vitamin X. Makes one strong as an ox or an ax. Want to try one?"

Lolita stretched out her hand, nodding vigorously.

I had hoped the drug would work fast. It certainly did. She had had a long long day, she had gone rowing in the morning with Barbara whose sister was Waterfront Director, as the adorable accessible nymphet now started to tell me in between suppressed palate-humping yawns, growing in volume—oh, how fast the magic potion worked!—and had been active in other ways too. The movie that had vaguely loomed in her mind was, of course, by the time we watertreaded out of the dining room, forgotten. As we stood in the elevator, she leaned against me, faintly smiling—wouldn't you like me to tell you?—half closing her dark-lidded eyes. "Sleepy, huh?" said Uncle Tom who was bringing up the quiet Franco-Irish gentleman and his daughter as well as two withered women, experts in roses. They looked with sympathy at my frail, tanned, tottering, dazed rosedarling. I had almost to carry her into our room. There, she sat down on the edge of the bed, swaying a little, speaking in dove-dull, long-drawn tones.

"If I tell you—if I tell you, will you promise [sleepy, so sleepy —head lolling, eyes going out], promise you won't make complaints?"

"Later, Lo. Now go to bed. I'll leave you here, and you go to bed. Give you ten minutes."

"Oh, I've been such a disgusting girl," she went on, shaking her hair, removing with slow fingers a velvet hair ribbon. "Lemme tell you—"

"Tomorrow, Lo. Go to bed, go to bed—for goodness sake, to bed."

I pocketed the key and walked downstairs.

28

Gentlewomen of the jury! Bear with me! Allow me to take just a tiny bit of your precious time! So this was *le grand moment.* I had left my Lolita still sitting on the edge of the abysmal bed, drowsily raising her foot, fumbling at the shoelaces and showing as she did so the nether side of her thigh up to the crotch of her panties—she had always been singularly absent-minded, or shameless, or both, in matters of legshow. This, then, was the hermetic vision of her which I had locked in—after satisfying myself that the door carried no inside bolt. The key, with its numbered dangler of carved wood, became forthwith the weighty sesame to a rapturous and formidable future. It was mine, it was part of my hot hairy fist. In a few minutes—say, twenty, say half-an-hour, *sicher ist sicher* as my uncle Gustave used to say—I would let myself into that "342" and find my nymphet, my beauty and bride, emprisoned in her crystal sleep. Jurors! If my happiness could have talked, it would have filled that genteel hotel with a deafening roar. And my only regret today is that I did not quietly deposit key "342" at the office, and leave the town, the country, the continent, the hemisphere,— indeed, the globe—that very same night.

Let me explain. I was not unduly disturbed by her self-accusatory innuendoes. I was still firmly resolved to pursue my policy of sparing her purity by operating only in the stealth of night, only upon a completely anesthetized little nude. Restraint and reverence were still my motto—even if that "purity" (incidentally, thoroughly debunked by modern science) had been slightly damaged through some juvenile erotic experience, no doubt homosexual, at that accursed camp of hers. Of course, in my old-fashioned, old-world way, I, Jean-Jacques Humbert, had taken for granted, when I first met her, that she was as unravished as the stereotypical notion of "normal child" had been since the lamented end of the Ancient World B.C. and its fascinating practices. We are not surrounded in our enlighted era by little slave flowers that can be casually plucked between business and bath as they used to be in the days of the Romans; and we do not, as dignified Orientals did in still more luxurious times, use tiny entertainers fore and aft between the mutton and the rose sherbet. The whole point is that the old link between the adult world and the child world has been completely severed nowadays by new customs and new laws. Despite my having dabbled in psychiatry and social work, I really knew very little about children. After all, Lolita was only twelve, and no matter what concessions I made to time and place—even bearing in mind the crude behavior of American schoolchildren—I still was under the impression that whatever went on among those brash brats, went on at a later age, and in a different environment. Therefore (to retrieve the thread of this explanation) the moralist in me by-passed the issue by clinging to conventional notions of what twelve-year-old girls should be. The child therapist in me (a fake, as most of them are—but no matter) regurgitated neo-Freudian hash and conjured up a dreaming and exaggerating Dolly in the "latency" period of girlhood. Finally, the sensualist in me (a great and insane monster) had no objection to some depravity in his prey. But somewhere behind the raging bliss, bewildered shadows conferred—and not to have heeded them, this is what I regret! Human beings, attend! I should have understood that Lolita had *already* proved to be something quite different from innocent Annabel, and that the nymphean evil breathing through every pore of the fey child that I had prepared for my secret delectation, would make the secrecy impossible, and the delectation lethal. I should have known (by the signs made to me by something in Lolita—the real child Lolita or some haggard angel behind her back) that nothing but pain and horror would result from the expected rapture. Oh, winged gentlemen of the jury!

And she was mine, she was mine, the key was in my fist, my fist was in my pocket, she was mine. In the course of the evocations and schemes to which I had dedicated so many insomnias, I had gradually eliminated all the superfluous blur, and by stacking level upon level of translucent vision, had evolved a final picture. Naked, except for one sock and her charm bracelet, spread-eagled on the bed where my philter had felled her—so I foreglimpsed her; a velvet hair ribbon was still clutched in her hand; her honey-brown body, with the white negative image of a rudimentary swimsuit patterned against her tan, presented to me its pale breastbuds; in the rosy lamplight, a little pubic floss glistened on its plump hillock. The cold key with its warm wooden addendum was in my pocket.

I wandered through various public rooms, glory below, gloom above: for the look of lust always is gloomy; lust is never quite sure—even when the velvety victim is locked up in one's dungeon —that some rival devil or influential god may still not abolish one's prepared triumph. In common parlance, I needed a drink; but there was no barroom in that venerable place full of perspiring philistines and period objects.

I drifted to the Men's Room. There, a person in clerical black —a "hearty party" *comme on dit*—checking with the assistance of Vienna, if it was still there, inquired of me how I had liked Dr. Boyd's talk, and looked puzzled when I (King Sigmund the Second) said Boyd was quite a boy. Upon which, I neatly chucked the tissue paper I had been wiping my sensitive finger tips with into the receptacle provided for it, and sallied lobbyward. Comfortably resting my elbows on the counter, I asked Mr. Potts was he quite sure my wife had not telephoned, and what about that cot? He answered she had not (she was dead, of

course) and the cot would be installed tomorrow if we decided
to stay on. From a big crowded place called The Hunters' Hall
came a sound of many voices discussing horticulture or eternity.
Another room, called The Raspberry Room, all bathed in light,
with bright little tables and a large one with "refreshments,"
was still empty except for a hostess (that type of worn woman
with a glassy smile and Charlotte's manner of speaking); she
floated up to me to ask if I was Mr. Braddock, because if so,
Miss Beard had been looking for me. "What a name for a
woman," I said and strolled away.

In and out of my heart flowed my rainbow blood. I would
give her till half-past-nine. Going back to the lobby, I found
there a change: a number of people in floral dresses or black
cloth had formed little groups here and there, and some elfish
chance offered me the sight of a delightful child of Lolita's age,
in Lolita's type of frock, but pure white, and there was a white
ribbon in her black hair. She was not pretty, but she was a
nymphet, and her ivory pale legs and lily neck formed for one

1 memorable moment a most pleasurable antiphony (in terms of
spinal music) to my desire for Lolita, brown and pink, flushed
and fouled. The pale child noticed my gaze (which was really
quite casual and debonair), and being ridiculously self-conscious, lost countenance completely, rolling her eyes and putting
the back of her hand to her cheek, and pulling at the hem of
her skirt, and finally turning her thin mobile shoulder blades to
me in specious chat with her cow-like mother.

I left the loud lobby and stood outside, on the white steps,
2 looking at the hundreds of powdered bugs wheeling around
the lamps in the soggy black night, full of ripple and stir. All
I would do—all I would dare to do—would amount to such a
trifle . . .

Suddenly I was aware that in the darkness next to me there
3 was somebody sitting in a chair on the pillared porch. I could not
really see him but what gave him away was the rasp of a screwing
off, then a discreet gurgle, then the final note of a placid screwing on. I was about to move away when his voice addressed me:

"Where the devil did you get her?"

"I beg your pardon?"

"I said: the weather is getting better."

"Seems so."

"Who's the lassie?"

"My daughter."

"You lie—she's not."

"I beg your pardon?"

"I said: July was hot. Where's her mother?"

"Dead."

"I see. Sorry. By the way, why don't you two lunch with me tomorrow. That dreadful crowd will be gone by then."

"We'll be gone too. Good night."

"Sorry. I'm pretty drunk. Good night. That child of yours needs a lot of sleep. Sleep is a rose, as the Persians say. Smoke?"   1

"Not now."

He struck a light, but because he was drunk, or because the wind was, the flame illumined not him but another person, a very old man, one of those permanent guests of old hotels—and his white rocker. Nobody said anything and the darkness returned to its initial place. Then I heard the old-timer cough and deliver himself of some sepulchral mucus.

I left the porch. At least half an hour in all had elapsed. I ought to have asked for a sip. The strain was beginning to tell. If a violin string can ache, then I was that string. But it would have been unseemly to display any hurry. As I made my way through a constellation of fixed people in one corner of the lobby, there came a blinding flash—and beaming Dr. Braddock, two orchid-ornamentalized matrons, the small girl in white, and presumably the bared teeth of Humbert Humbert sidling between the bridelike lassie and the enchanted cleric, were immortalized—insofar as the texture and print of small-town newspapers can be deemed immortal. A twittering group had   2 gathered near the elevator. I again chose the stairs. 342 was near the fire escape. One could still—but the key was already in the lock, and then I was in the room.

29

The door of the lighted bathroom stood ajar; in addition to that, a skeleton glow came through the Venetian blind from the outside arclights; these intercrossed rays penetrated the darkness of the bedroom and revealed the following situation.

Clothed in one of her old nightgowns, my Lolita lay on her side with her back to me, in the middle of the bed. Her lightly veiled body and bare limbs formed a Z. She had put both pillows under her dark tousled head; a band of pale light crossed her top vertebrae.

I seemed to have shed my clothes and slipped into pajamas with the kind of fantastic instantaneousness which is implied when in a cinematographic scene the process of changing is cut; and I had already placed my knee on the edge of the bed when Lolita turned her head and stared at me through the striped shadows.

Now this was something the intruder had not expected. The whole pill-spiel (a rather sordid affair, *entre nous soit dit*) had had for object a fastness of sleep that a whole regiment would not have disturbed, and here she was staring at me, and thickly calling me "Barbara." Barbara, wearing my pajamas which were much too tight for her, remained poised motionless over the little sleep-talker. Softly, with a hopeless sigh, Dolly turned away, resuming her initial position. For at least two minutes I waited and strained on the brink, like that tailor with his homemade parachute forty years ago when about to jump from the Eiffel Tower. Her faint breathing had the rhythm of sleep. Finally I heaved myself onto my narrow margin of bed, stealthily pulled at the odds and ends of sheets piled up to the south of my stone-cold heels—and Lolita lifted her head and gaped at me.

As I learned later from a helpful pharmaceutist, the purple pill did not even belong to the big and noble family of barbiturates, and though it might have induced sleep in a neurotic who believed it to be a potent drug, it was too mild a sedative to affect for any length of time a wary, albeit weary, nymphet. Whether the Ramsdale doctor was a charlatan or a shrewd old rogue, does not, and did not, really matter. What mattered, was that I had been deceived. When Lolita opened her eyes again, I realized that whether or not the drug might work later in the night, the security I had relied upon was a sham one. Slowly her head turned away and dropped onto her unfair amount of pillow. I lay quite still on my brink, peering at her rumpled hair, at the glimmer of nymphet flesh, where half a haunch and half a shoulder dimly showed, and trying to gauge the depth of her sleep by the rate of her respiration. Some time passed, nothing changed, and I decided I might risk getting a little closer to that lovely and maddening glimmer; but hardly had I moved into its warm purlieus than her breathing was suspended, and I had the odious feeling that little Dolores was wide awake and would explode in screams if I touched her with any part of my wretchedness. Please, reader: no matter your exasperation with the tenderhearted, morbidly sensitive, infinitely circumspect hero of my book, do not skip these essential pages! Imagine me; I shall not exist if you do not imagine me; try to discern the doe in me, trembling in the forest of my own iniquity; let's even smile a little. After all, there is no harm in smiling. For instance (I almost wrote "frinstance"), I had no place to rest my head, and a fit of heartburn (they call those fries "French," *grand Dieu!*) was added to my discomfort. ¹

She was again fast asleep, my nymphet, but still I did not dare to launch upon my enchanted voyage. *La Petite Dormeuse ou l'Amant Ridicule.* Tomorrow I would stuff her with those ² earlier pills that had so thoroughly numbed her mummy. In the glove compartment—or in the Gladstone bag? Should I wait a solid hour and then creep up again? The science of nympholepsy is a precise science. Actual contact would do it in one second flat. An interspace of a millimeter would do it in ten. Let us wait.

There is nothing louder than an American hotel; and, mind you, this was supposed to be a quiet, cozy, old-fashioned, homey place—"gracious living" and all that stuff. The clatter of the elevator's gate—some twenty yards northeast of my head but as clearly perceived as if it were inside my left temple—alternated with the banging and booming of the machine's various evolutions and lasted well beyond midnight. Every now and then, immediately east of my left ear (always assuming I lay on my back, not daring to direct my viler side toward the nebulous haunch of my bed-mate), the corridor would brim with cheerful, resonant and inept exclamations ending in a volley of good-nights. When *that* stopped, a toilet immediately north of my cerebellum took over. It was a manly, energetic, deep-throated toilet, and it was used many times. Its gurgle and gush and long afterflow shook the wall behind me. Then someone in a southern direction was extravagantly sick, almost coughing out his life with his liquor, and his toilet descended like a veritable Niagara, immediately beyond our bathroom. And when finally all the waterfalls had stopped, and the enchanted hunters were sound asleep, the avenue under the window of my insomnia, to the west of my wake—a staid, eminently residential, dignified alley of huge trees—degenerated into the despicable haunt of gigantic trucks roaring through the wet and windy night.

And less than six inches from me and my burning life, was nebulous Lolita! After a long stirless vigil, my tentacles moved towards her again, and this time the creak of the mattress did not awake her. I managed to bring my ravenous bulk so close to her that I felt the aura of her bare shoulder like a warm breath upon my cheek. And then, she sat up, gasped, muttered with insane rapidity something about boats, tugged at the sheets and lapsed back into her rich, dark, young unconsciousness. As she tossed, within that abundant flow of sleep, recently auburn, at present lunar, her arm struck me across the face. For a second I held her. She freed herself from the shadow of my embrace—doing this not consciously, not violently, not with any personal distaste, but with the neutral plaintive murmur of a child demanding its natural rest. And again the situation remained the same: Lolita with her curved spine to Humbert, Humbert resting his head on his hand and burning with desire and dyspepsia.

The latter necessitated a trip to the bathroom for a draft of water which is the best medicine I know in my case, except perhaps milk with radishes; and when I re-entered the strange

pale-striped fastness where Lolita's old and new clothes reclined
in various attitudes of enchantment on pieces of furniture that
seemed vaguely afloat, my impossible daughter sat up and in
clear tones demanded a drink, too. She took the resilient and
cold paper cup in her shadowy hand and gulped down its contents gratefully, her long eyelashes pointing cupward, and then,
with an infantile gesture that carried more charm than any
carnal caress, little Lolita wiped her lips against my shoulder.
She fell back on her pillow (I had subtracted mine while she
drank) and was instantly asleep again.

I had not dared offer her a second helping of the drug, and
had not abandoned hope that the first might still consolidate
her sleep. I started to move toward her, ready for any disappointment, knowing I had better wait but incapable of waiting. My
pillow smelled of her hair. I moved toward my glimmering
darling, stopping or retreating every time I thought she stirred
or was about to stir. A breeze from wonderland had begun to
affect my thoughts, and now they seemed couched in italics,
as if the surface reflecting them were wrinkled by the phantasm
of that breeze. Time and again my consciousness folded the
wrong way, my shuffling body entered the sphere of sleep,
shuffled out again, and once or twice I caught myself drifting
into a melancholy snore. Mists of tenderness enfolded mountains of longing. Now and then it seemed to me that the enchanted prey was about to meet halfway the enchanted hunter,
that her haunch was working its way toward me under the soft
sand of a remote and fabulous beach; and then her dimpled
dimness would stir, and I would know she was farther away from
me than ever.

If I dwell at some length on the tremors and gropings of that
distant night, it is because I insist upon proving that I am not,
and never was, and never could have been, a brutal scoundrel.
The gentle and dreamy regions through which I crept were
the patrimonies of poets—*not* crime's prowling ground. Had I
reached my goal, my ecstasy would have been all softness, a
case of internal combustion of which she would hardly have felt
the heat, even if she were wide awake. But I still hoped she

might gradually be engulfed in a completeness of stupor that would allow me to taste more than a glimmer of her. And so, in between tentative approximations, with a confusion of perception metamorphosing her into eyespots of moonlight or a fluffy flowering bush, I would dream I regained consciousness, dream I lay in wait.

In the first antemeridian hours there was a lull in the restless hotel night. Then around four the corridor toilet cascaded and its door banged. A little after five a reverberating monologue began to arrive, in several installments, from some courtyard or parking place. It was not really a monologue, since the speaker stopped every few seconds to listen (presumably) to another fellow, but that other voice did not reach me, and so no real meaning could be derived from the part heard. Its matter-of-fact intonations, however, helped to bring in the dawn, and the room was already suffused with lilac gray, when several industrious toilets went to work, one after the other, and the clattering and whining elevator began to rise and take down early risers and downers, and for some minutes I miserably dozed, and Charlotte was a mermaid in a greenish tank, and somewhere in the passage Dr. Boyd said "Good morning to you" in a fruity voice, and birds were busy in the trees, and then Lolita yawned.

Frigid gentlewomen of the jury! I had thought that months, perhaps years, would elapse before I dared to reveal myself to Dolores Haze; but by six she was wide awake, and by six fifteen we were technically lovers. I am going to tell you something very strange: it was she who seduced me.

Upon hearing her first morning yawn, I feigned handsome profiled sleep. I just did not know what to do. Would she be shocked at finding me by her side, and not in some spare bed? Would she collect her clothes and lock herself up in the bathroom? Would she demand to be taken at once to Ramsdale— to her mother's bedside—back to camp? But my Lo was a sportive lassie. I felt her eyes on me, and when she uttered at last that beloved chortling note of hers, I knew her eyes had been laughing. She rolled over to my side, and her warm brown hair came against my collarbone. I gave a mediocre imitation of waking up. We lay quietly. I gently caressed her hair, and we gently kissed. Her kiss, to my delirious embarrassment, had some rather comical refinements of flutter and probe which made me conclude she had been coached at an early age by a little Lesbian. No Charlie boy could have taught her *that*. As if to see whether I had my fill and learned the lesson, she drew away and surveyed me. Her cheekbones were flushed, her full underlip glistened, my dissolution was near. All at once, with a burst of rough glee (the sign of the nymphet!), she put her mouth to my ear—but for quite a while my mind could not separate into words the hot thunder of her whisper, and she laughed, and brushed the hair off her face, and tried again, and gradually the odd sense of living in a brand new, mad new dream world, where everything was permissible, came over me as I realized what she was suggesting. I answered I did not know what game she and Charlie had played. "You mean you have never—?"—her features twisted into a stare of disgusted incredulity. "You have never—" she started again. I took time out by nuzzling her a little. "Lay off, will you," she said with a twangy whine, hastily removing her brown shoulder from my lips. (It was very curious the way she considered—and kept doing so for a long time—all caresses except kisses on the mouth or the stark act of love either "romantic slosh" or "abnormal".)

"You mean," she persisted, now kneeling above me, "you never did it when you were a kid?"

"Never," I answered quite truthfully.

"Okay," said Lolita, "here is where we start."

However, I shall not bore my learned readers with a detailed account of Lolita's presumption. Suffice it to say that not a trace of modesty did I perceive in this beautiful hardly formed young girl whom modern co-education, juvenile mores, the campfire racket and so forth had utterly and hopelessly depraved. She saw the stark act merely as part of a youngster's furtive world, unknown to adults. What adults did for purposes of procreation was no business of hers. My life was handled by little Lo in an energetic, matter-of-fact manner as if it were an insensate gadget unconnected with me. While eager to impress me with the world of tough kids, she was not quite prepared for certain discrepancies between a kid's life and mine. Pride alone prevented her from giving up; for, in my strange predicament, I feigned supreme stupidity and had her have her way—at least while I could still bear it. But really these are irrelevant matters; I am not concerned with so-called "sex" at all. Anybody can imagine those elements of animality. A greater endeavor lures me on: to fix once for all the perilous magic of nymphets.

30

I have to tread carefully. I have to speak in a whisper. Oh you, veteran crime reporter, you grave old usher, you once popular policeman, now in solitary confinement after gracing that school crossing for years, you wretched emeritus read to by a boy! It would never do, would it, to have you fellows fall madly in love with my Lolita! Had I been a painter, had the management of The Enchanted Hunters lost its mind one summer day and commissioned me to redecorate their dining room with murals of my own making, this is what I might have thought up, let me list some fragments:

There would have been a lake. There would have been an arbor in flame-flower. There would have been nature studies— a tiger pursuing a bird of paradise, a choking snake sheathing
1 whole the flayed trunk of a shoat. There would have been a sultan, his face expressing great agony (belied, as it were, by his molding caress), helping a callypygean slave child to climb
2 a column of onyx. There would have been those luminous
3 globules of gonadal glow that travel up the opalescent sides of juke boxes. There would have been all kinds of camp activities
4 on the part of the intermediate group, Canoeing, Coranting, Combing Curls in the lakeside sun. There would have been poplars, apples, a suburban Sunday. There would have been a

fire opal dissolving within a ripple-ringed pool, a last throb, a
last dab of color, stinging red, smarting pink, a sigh, a wincing
child.

31

I am trying to describe these things not to relive them in
my present boundless misery, but to sort out the portion of
hell and the portion of heaven in that strange, awful, maddening world—nymphet love. The beastly and beautiful merged at
one point, and it is that borderline I would like to fix, and I feel
I fail to do so utterly. Why?

The stipulation of the Roman law, according to which a girl
may marry at twelve, was adopted by the Church, and is still   1, 2
preserved, rather tacitly, in some of the United States. And   3
fifteen is lawful everywhere. There is nothing wrong, say both   4
hemispheres, when a brute of forty, blessed by the local priest
and bloated with drink, sheds his sweat-drenched finery and
thrusts himself up to the hilt into his youthful bride. "In such
stimulating temperate climates [says an old magazine in this
prison library] as St. Louis, Chicago and Cincinnati, girls mature
about the end of their twelfth year." Dolores Haze was born
less than three hundred miles from stimulating Cincinnati. I
have but followed nature. I am nature's faithful hound. Why
then this horror that I cannot shake off? Did I deprive her of
her flower? Sensitive gentlewomen of the jury, I was not even her
first lover.

32

She told me the way she had been debauched. We ate flavorless mealy bananas, bruised peaches and very palatable potato
chips, and *die Kleine* told me everything. Her voluble but dis-   5
jointed account was accompanied by many a droll *moue*. As I   6
think I have already observed, I especially remember one wry

face on an "ugh!" basis: jelly-mouth distended sideways and eyes rolled up in a routine blend of comic disgust, resignation and tolerance for young frailty.

Her astounding tale started with an introductory mention of her tent-mate of the previous summer, at another camp, a "very select" one as she put it. That tent-mate ("quite a derelict character," "half-crazy," but a "swell kid") instructed her in various manipulations. At first, loyal Lo refused to tell me her name.

"Was it Grace Angel?" I asked.

She shook her head. No, it wasn't, it was the daughter of a big shot. He—

"Was it perhaps Rose Carmine?"

"No, of course not. Her father—"

"Was it, then, Agnes Sheridan perchance?"

She swallowed and shook her head—and then did a double take.

"Say, how come you know all those kids?"

I explained.

"Well," she said. "They are pretty bad, some of that school bunch, but not that bad. If you have to know, her name was Elizabeth Talbot, she goes now to a swanky private school, her father is an executive."

I recalled with a funny pang the frequency with which poor Charlotte used to introduce into party chat such elegant tidbits as "when my daughter was out hiking last year with the Talbot girl."

I wanted to know if either mother learned of those sapphic diversions?

"Gosh no," exhaled limp Lo mimicking dread and relief, pressing a falsely fluttering hand to her chest.

I was more interested, however, in heterosexual experience. She had entered the sixth grade at eleven, soon after moving to Ramsdale from the Middle West. What did she mean by "pretty bad"?

Well, the Miranda twins had shared the same bed for years, and Donald Scott, who was the dumbest boy in the school, had done it with Hazel Smith in his uncle's garage, and Kenneth

Knight—who was the brightest—used to exhibit himself wherever and whenever he had a chance, and—

"Let us switch to Camp Q," I said. And presently I got the whole story.

Barbara Burke, a sturdy blond, two years older than Lo and by far the camp's best swimmer, had a very special canoe which she shared with Lo "because I was the only other girl who could make Willow Island" (some swimming test, I imagine). Through July, every morning—mark, reader, every blessed morning—Barbara and Lo would be helped to carry the boat to Onyx or Eryx (two small lakes in the wood) by Charlie Holmes, the camp mistress' son, aged thirteen—and the only human male for a couple of miles around (excepting an old meek stone-deaf handyman, and a farmer in an old Ford who sometimes sold the campers eggs as farmers will); every morning, oh my reader, the three children would take a short cut through the beautiful innocent forest brimming with all the emblems of youth, dew, birdsongs, and at one point, among the luxuriant undergrowth, Lo would be left as sentinel, while Barbara and the boy copulated behind a bush.

At first, Lo had refused "to try what it was like," but curiosity and camaraderie prevailed, and soon she and Barbara were doing it by turns with the silent, coarse and surly but indefatigable Charlie, who had as much sex appeal as a raw carrot but sported a fascinating collection of contraceptives which he used to fish out of a third nearby lake, a considerably larger and more populous one, called Lake Climax, after the booming young factory town of that name. Although conceding it was "sort of fun" and "fine for the complexion," Lolita, I am glad to say, held Charlie's mind and manners in the greatest contempt. Nor had her temperament been roused by that filthy fiend. In fact, I think he had rather stunned it, despite the "fun."

By that time it was close to ten. With the ebb of lust, an ashen sense of awfulness, abetted by the realistic drabness of a gray neuralgic day, crept over me and hummed within my temples. Brown, naked, frail Lo, her narrow white buttocks to me, her sulky face to a door mirror, stood, arms akimbo, feet (in new slippers with pussy-fur tops) wide apart, and through a forehanging lock tritely mugged at herself in the glass. From the corridor came the cooing voices of colored maids at work, and presently there was a mild attempt to open the door of our room. I had Lo go to the bathroom and take a much-needed soap shower. The bed was a frightful mess with overtones of potato chips. She tried on a two-piece navy wool, then a sleeveless blouse with a swirly clathrate skirt, but the first was too tight and the second too ample, and when I begged her to hurry up (the situation was beginning to frighten me), Lo viciously sent those nice presents of mine hurtling into a corner, and put on yesterday's dress. When she was ready at last, I gave her a lovely new purse of simulated calf (in which I had slipped quite a few pennies and two mint-bright dimes) and told her to buy herself a magazine in the lobby.

"I'll be down in a minute," I said. "And if I were you, my dear, I would not talk to strangers."

Except for my poor little gifts, there was not much to pack; but I was forced to devote a dangerous amount of time (was she up to something downstairs?) to arranging the bed in such a way as to suggest the abandoned nest of a restless father and his tomboy daughter, instead of an ex-convict's saturnalia with a couple of fat old whores. Then I finished dressing and had the hoary bellboy come up for the bags.

Everything was fine. There, in the lobby, she sat, deep in an overstuffed blood-red armchair, deep in a lurid movie magazine. A fellow of my age in tweeds (the genre of the place had changed overnight to a spurious country-squire atmosphere) was staring at my Lolita over his dead cigar and stale newspaper. She wore her professional white socks and saddle oxfords, and that bright print frock with the square throat; a splash of jaded lamplight brought out the golden down on her warm brown limbs. There she sat, her legs carelessly highcrossed, and her pale eyes skimming along the lines with every now and then a blink. Bill's wife had worshiped him from afar long before they ever met: in fact, she used to secretly admire the famous young actor as he ate sundaes in Schwab's drugstore. Nothing could have been

more childish than her snubbed nose, freckled face or the purplish spot on her naked neck where a fairytale vampire had   1
feasted, or the unconscious movement of her tongue exploring
a touch of rosy rash around her swollen lips; nothing could be
more harmless than to read about Jill, an energetic starlet who
made her own clothes and was a student of serious literature;
nothing could be more innocent than the part in that glossy
brown hair with that silky sheen on the temple; nothing could
be more naïve—But what sickening envy the lecherous fellow
whoever he was—come to think of it, he resembled a little my
Swiss uncle Gustave, also a great admirer of *le découvert*—would   2
have experienced had he known that every nerve in me was still
anointed and ringed with the feel of her body—the body of some
immortal daemon disguised as a female child.   3

Was pink pig Mr. Swoon absolutely sure my wife had not
telephoned? He was. If she did, would he tell her we had gone
on to Aunt Clare's place? He would, indeedie. I settled the bill   4
and roused Lo from her chair. She read to the car. Still reading,
she was driven to a so-called coffee shop a few blocks south.
Oh, she ate all right. She even laid aside her magazine to eat,
but a queer dullness had replaced her usual cheerfulness. I
knew little Lo could be very nasty, so I braced myself and
grinned, and waited for a squall. I was unbathed, unshaven, and
had had no bowel movement. My nerves were a-jangle. I did
not like the way my little mistress shrugged her shoulders and
distended her nostrils when I attempted casual small talk. Had
Phyllis been in the know before she joined her parents in Maine?
I asked with a smile. "Look," said Lo making a weeping grimace,
"let us get off the subject." I then tried—also unsuccessfully,
no matter how I smacked my lips—to interest her in the road
map. Our destination was, let me remind my patient reader
whose meek temper Lo ought to have copied, the gay town of
Lepingville, somewhere near a hypothetical hospital. That des-   5
tination was in itself a perfectly arbitrary one (as, alas, so many
were to be), and I shook in my shoes as I wondered how to
keep the whole arrangement plausible, and what other plausible
objectives to invent after we had taken in all the movies in

Lepingville. More and more uncomfortable did Humbert feel. It was something quite special, that feeling: an oppressive, hideous constraint as if I were sitting with the small ghost of somebody I had just killed.

As she was in the act of getting back into the car, an expression of pain flitted across Lo's face. It flitted again, more meaningfully, as she settled down beside me. No doubt, she reproduced it that second time for my benefit. Foolishly, I asked her what was the matter. "Nothing, you brute," she replied. "You what?" I asked. She was silent. Leaving Briceland. Loquacious Lo was silent. Cold spiders of panic crawled down my back. This was an orphan. This was a lone child, an absolute waif, with whom a heavy-limbed, foul-smelling adult had had strenuous intercourse three times that very morning. Whether or not the realization of a lifelong dream had surpassed all expectation, it had, in a sense, overshot its mark—and plunged into a nightmare. I had been careless, stupid, and ignoble. And let me be quite frank: somewhere at the bottom of that dark turmoil I felt the writhing of desire again, so monstrous was my appetite for that miserable nymphet. Mingled with the pangs of guilt was the agonizing thought that her mood might prevent me from making love to her again as soon as I found a nice country road where to park in peace. In other words, poor Humbert Humbert was dreadfully unhappy, and while steadily and inanely driving toward Lepingville, he kept racking his brains for some quip, under the bright wing of which he might dare turn to his seatmate. It was she, however, who broke the silence:

"Oh, a squashed squirrel," she said. "What a shame."

"Yes, isn't it?" (eager, hopeful Hum).

"Let us stop at the next gas station," Lo continued. "I want to go to the washroom."

"We shall stop wherever you want," I said. And then as a lovely, lonely, supercilious grove (oaks, I thought; American trees at that stage were beyond me) started to echo greenly the rush of our car, a red and ferny road on our right turned its head before slanting into the woodland, and I suggested we might perhaps—

"Drive on," my Lo cried shrilly.

"Righto. Take it easy." (Down, poor beast, down.)

I glanced at her. Thank God, the child was smiling.

"You chump," she said, sweetly smiling at me. "You revolting creature. I was a daisy-fresh girl, and look what you've done to me. I ought to call the police and tell them you raped me. Oh, you dirty, dirty old man."

Was she just joking? An ominous hysterical note rang through her silly words. Presently, making a sizzling sound with her lips, she started complaining of pains, said she could not sit, said I had torn something inside her. The sweat rolled down my neck, and we almost ran over some little animal or other that was crossing the road with tail erect, and again my vile-tempered companion called me an ugly name. When we stopped at the filling station, she scrambled out without a word and was a long time away. Slowly, lovingly, an elderly friend with a broken nose wiped my windshield—they do it differently at every place, from chamois cloth to soapy brush, this fellow used a pink sponge.

She appeared at last. "Look," she said in that neutral voice that hurt me so, "give me some dimes and nickels. I want to call mother in that hospital. What's the number?"

"Get in," I said. "You can't call that number."

"Why?"

"Get in and slam the door."

She got in and slammed the door. The old garage man beamed at her. I swung onto the highway.

"Why can't I call my mother if I want to?"

"Because," I answered, "your mother is dead."

33

In the gay town of Lepingville I bought her four books of comics, a box of candy, a box of sanitary pads, two cokes, a manicure set, a travel clock with a luminous dial, a ring with a real topaz, a tennis racket, roller skates with white high shoes, field glasses, a portable radio set, chewing gum, a transparent raincoat, sunglasses, some more garments—swooners, shorts, all kinds of summer frocks. At the hotel we had separate rooms, but in the middle of the night she came sobbing into mine, and we made it up very gently. You see, she had absolutely nowhere else to go.

Part Two

Part Two

1

It was then that began our extensive travels all over the States. To any other type of tourist accommodation I soon grew to prefer the Functional Motel—clean, neat, safe nooks, ideal places for sleep, argument, reconciliation, insatiable illicit love. At first, in my dread of arousing suspicion, I would eagerly pay for both sections of one double unit, each containing a double bed. I wondered what type of foursome this arrangement was ever intended for, since only a pharisaic parody of privacy could be attained by means of the incomplete partition dividing the cabin or room into two communicating love nests. By and by, the very possibilities that such honest promiscuity suggested (two young couples merrily swapping mates or a child shamming sleep to earwitness primal sonorities) made me bolder, and every now and then I would take a bed-and-cot or twin-bed cabin, a prison cell of paradise, with yellow window shades pulled down to create a morning illusion of Venice and sunshine when actually it was Pennsylvania and rain.

We came to know—*nous connûmes*, to use a Flaubertian intonation—the stone cottages under enormous Chateaubriandesque trees, the brick unit, the adobe unit, the stucco court, on what the Tour Book of the Automobile Association describes as "shaded" or "spacious" or "landscaped" grounds. The log kind, finished in knotty pine, reminded Lo, by its golden-brown glaze, of fried-chicken bones. We held in contempt the plain whitewashed clapboard Kabins, with their faint sewerish smell or some other gloomy self-conscious stench and nothing to boast of (except "good beds"), and an unsmiling landlady always pre-

pared to have her gift ("... well, I could give you ...") turned
down.

Nous connûmes (this is royal fun) the would-be enticements
of their repetitive names—all those Sunset Motels, U-Beam
Cottages, Hillcrest Courts, Pine View Courts, Mountain View
Courts, Skyline Courts, Park Plaza Courts, Green Acres, Mac's
Courts. There was sometimes a special line in the write-up, such
as "Children welcome, pets allowed" (*You* are welcome, *you*
are allowed). The baths were mostly tiled showers, with an
endless variety of spouting mechanisms, but with one definitely
1 non-Laodicean characteristic in common, a propensity, while
in use, to turn instantly beastly hot or blindingly cold upon you,
depending on whether your neighbor turned on his cold or his
hot to deprive you of a necessary complement in the shower
you had so carefully blended. Some motels had instructions
pasted above the toilet (on whose tank the towels were un-
hygienically heaped) asking guests not to throw into its bowl
garbage, beer cans, cartons, stillborn babies; others had special
notices under glass, such as Things to Do (Riding: *You will
often see riders coming down Main Street on their way back
from a romantic moonlight ride.* "Often at 3 A.M.," sneered
unromantic Lo).

Nous connûmes the various types of motor court operators,
the reformed criminal, the retired teacher and the business flop,
among the males; and the motherly, pseudo-ladylike and ma-
2 damic variants among the females. And sometimes trains would
cry in the monstrously hot and humid night with heartrending
and ominous plangency, mingling power and hysteria in one
desperate scream.

We avoided Tourist Homes, country cousins of Funeral ones,
old-fashioned, genteel and showerless, with elaborate dressing
tables in depressingly white-and-pink little bedrooms, and photo-
3 graphs of the landlady's children in all their instars. But I did
surrender, now and then, to Lo's predilection for "real" hotels.
She would pick out in the book, while I petted her in the parked
car in the silence of a dusk-mellowed, mysterious side-road,
some highly recommended lake lodge which offered all sorts of

things magnified by the flashlight she moved over them, such as congenial company, between-meals snacks, outdoor barbecues —but which in my mind conjured up odious visions of stinking high school boys in sweatshirts and an ember-red cheek pressing against hers, while poor Dr. Humbert, embracing nothing but two masculine knees, would cold-humor his piles on the damp turf. Most tempting to her, too, were those "Colonial" Inns, which apart from "gracious atmosphere" and picture windows, promised "unlimited quantities of M-m-m food." Treasured recollections of my father's palatial hotel sometimes led me to seek for its like in the strange country we traveled through. I was soon discouraged; but Lo kept following the scent of rich food ads, while I derived a not exclusively economic kick from such roadside signs as TIMBER HOTEL, *Children under 14 Free.* On the other hand, I shudder when recalling that *soi-disant* "high-class" resort in a Midwestern state, which advertised "raid-the-icebox" midnight snacks and, intrigued by my accent, wanted to know my dead wife's and dead mother's maiden names. A two-days' stay there cost me a hundred and twenty-four dollars! And do you remember, Miranda, that other "ultrasmart" robbers' den with complimentary morning coffee and circulating ice water, and no children under sixteen (no Lolitas, of course)?

Immediately upon arrival at one of the plainer motor courts which became our habitual haunts, she would set the electric fan a-whirr, or induce me to drop a quarter into the radio, or she would read all the signs and inquire with a whine why she could not go riding up some advertised trail or swimming in that local pool of warm mineral water. Most often, in the slouching, bored way she cultivated, Lo would fall prostrate and abominably desirable into a red springchair or a green chaise longue, or a steamer chair of striped canvas with footrest and canopy, or a sling chair, or any other lawn chair under a garden umbrella on the patio, and it would take hours of blandishments, threats and promises to make her lend me for a few seconds her brown limbs in the seclusion of the five-dollar room before undertaking anything she might prefer to my poor joy.

A combination of naïveté and deception, of charm and vulgarity, of blue sulks and rosy mirth, Lolita, when she chose, could be a most exasperating brat. I was not really quite prepared for her fits of disorganized boredom, intense and vehement griping, her sprawling, droopy, dopey-eyed style, and what is called goofing off—a kind of diffused clowning which she thought was tough in a boyish hoodlum way. Mentally, I found her to be a disgustingly conventional little girl. Sweet hot jazz, square dancing, gooey fudge sundaes, musicals, movie magazines and so forth—these were the obvious items in her list of beloved things. The Lord knows how many nickels I fed to the gorgeous music boxes that came with every meal we had! I still hear the nasal voices of those invisibles serenading her, people with names like Sammy and Jo and Eddy and Tony and Peggy and Guy and Patti and Rex, and sentimental song hits, all of them as similar to my ear as her various candies were to my palate. She believed, with a kind of celestial trust, any advertisement or advice that appeared in *Movie Love* or *Screen Land*—Starasil Starves Pimples, or "You better watch out if you're wearing your shirttails outside your jeans, gals, because Jill says you shouldn't." If a roadside sign said: VISIT OUR GIFT SHOP—we *had* to visit it, *had* to buy its Indian curios, dolls, copper jewelry, cactus candy. The words "novelties and souvenirs" simply entranced her by their trochaic lilt. If some café sign proclaimed Icecold Drinks, she was automatically stirred, although all drinks everywhere were ice-cold. She it was to whom ads were dedicated: the ideal consumer, the subject and object of every foul poster. And she attempted—unsuccessfully—to patronize only those restaurants where the holy spirit of Huncan Dines had descended upon the cute paper napkins and cottage-cheese-crested salads.

In those days, neither she nor I had thought up yet the system of monetary bribes which was to work such havoc with my nerves and her morals somewhat later. I relied on three other methods to keep my pubescent concubine in submission and passable temper. A few years before, she had spent a rainy summer under Miss Phalen's bleary eye in a dilapidated Appalachian farmhouse that had belonged to some gnarled Haze or other in the dead past. It still stood among its rank acres of golden rod on the edge of a flowerless forest, at the end of a permanently muddy road, twenty miles from the nearest hamlet. Lo recalled that scarecrow of a house, the solitude, the soggy old pastures, the wind, the bloated wilderness, with an energy of disgust that distorted her mouth and fattened her half-revealed tongue. And it was there that I warned her she would dwell with me in exile for months and years if need be, studying under me French and Latin, unless her "present attitude" changed. Charlotte, I began to understand you!

A simple child, Lo would scream no! and frantically clutch at my driving hand whenever I put a stop to her tornadoes of temper by turning in the middle of a highway with the implication that I was about to take her straight to that dark and dismal abode. The farther, however, we traveled away from it west, the less tangible that menace became, and I had to adopt other methods of persuasion.

Among these, the reformatory threat is the one I recall with the deepest moan of shame. From the very beginning of our concourse, I was clever enough to realize that I must secure her complete co-operation in keeping our relations secret, that it should become a second nature with her, no matter what grudge she might bear me, no matter what other pleasures she might seek.

"Come and kiss your old man," I would say, "and drop that moody nonsense. In former times, when I was still your dream male [the reader will notice what pains I took to speak Lo's tongue], you swooned to records of the number one throb-and-sob idol of your coevals [Lo: "Of my what? Speak English"]. That idol of your pals sounded, you thought, like friend Humbert. But now, I am just your *old man*, a dream dad protecting his dream daughter.

"My *chère Dolorès!* I want to protect you, dear, from all the horrors that happen to little girls in coal sheds and alley ways, and, alas, *comme vous le savez trop bien, ma gentille*, in the blueberry woods during the bluest of summers. Through thick and thin I will still stay your guardian, and if you are good, I hope a court may legalize that guardianship before long. Let us, however, forget, Dolores Haze, so-called legal terminology, terminology that accepts as rational the term 'lewd and lascivious cohabitation.' I am not a criminal sexual psychopath taking indecent liberties with a child. The rapist was Charlie Holmes; I am the therapist—a matter of nice spacing in the way of distinction. I am your daddum, Lo. Look, I've a learned book here about young girls. Look, darling, what it says. I quote: the normal girl—normal, mark you—the normal girl is usually extremely anxious to please her father. She feels in him the forerunner of the desired elusive male ('elusive' is good, by Polonius!). The wise mother (and your poor mother would have been wise, had she lived) will encourage a companionship between father and daughter, realizing—excuse the corny style —that the girl forms her ideals of romance and of men from her association with her father. Now, what association does this cheery book mean—and recommend? I quote again: Among Sicilians sexual relations between a father and his daughter are accepted as a matter of course, and the girl who participates in such relationship is not looked upon with disapproval by the society of which she is part. I'm a great admirer of Sicilians, fine athletes, fine musicians, fine upright people, Lo, and great lovers. But let's not digress. Only the other day we read in the newspapers some bunkum about a middle-aged morals offender who pleaded guilty to the violation of the Mann Act and to transporting a nine-year-old girl across state lines for immoral purposes, whatever these are. Dolores darling! You are not nine but almost thirteen, and I would not advise you to consider yourself my cross-country slave, and I deplore the Mann Act as lending itself to a dreadful pun, the revenge that the Gods of Semantics take against tight-zippered Philistines. I am your father, and I *am* speaking English, and I love you.

"Finally, let us see what happens if you, a minor, accused of having impaired the morals of an adult in a respectable inn, what happens if you complain to the police of my having kidnaped and raped you? Let us suppose they believe you. A minor female, who allows a person over twenty-one to know her carnally, involves her victim into statutory rape, or second-degree sodomy, depending on the technique; and the maximum penalty is ten years. So I go to jail. Okay. I go to jail. But what happens to you, my orphan? Well, you are luckier. You become the ward of the Department of Public Welfare—which I am afraid sounds a little bleak. A nice grim matron of the Miss Phalen type, but more rigid and not a drinking woman, will take away your lipstick and fancy clothes. No more gadding about! I don't know if you have ever heard of the laws relating to dependent, neglected, incorrigible and delinquent children. While I stand gripping the bars, you, happy neglected child, will be given a choice of various dwelling places, all more or less the same, the correctional school, the reformatory, the juvenile detention home, or one of those admirable girls' protectories where you knit things, and sing hymns, and have rancid pancakes on Sundays. You will go there, Lolita—*my* Lolita, *this* Lolita will leave her Catullus and go there, as the wayward girl you are. In plainer words, if we two are found out, you will be analyzed and institutionalized, my pet, *c'est tout*. You will dwell, my Lolita will dwell (come here, my brown flower) with thirty-nine other dopes in a dirty dormitory (no, allow me, please) under the supervision of hideous matrons. This is the situation, this is the choice. Don't you think that under the circumstances Dolores Haze had better stick to her old man?"

By rubbing all this in, I succeeded in terrorizing Lo, who despite a certain brash alertness of manner and spurts of wit was not as intelligent a child as her I.Q. might suggest. But if I managed to establish that background of shared secrecy and shared guilt, I was much less successful in keeping her in good humor. Every morning during our yearlong travels I had to devise some expectation, some special point in space and time for her to look forward to, for her to survive till bedtime. Otherwise, deprived of a shaping and sustaining purpose, the skeleton of her day sagged and collapsed. The object in view might be anything—a lighthouse in Virginia, a natural cave in Arkansas converted to a café, a collection of guns and violins somewhere in Oklahoma, a replica of the Grotto of Lourdes in Louisiana, shabby photographs of the bonanza mining period in the local museum of a Rocky Mountains resort, anything whatsoever—but it had to be there, in front of us, like a fixed star, although as likely as not Lo would feign gagging as soon as we got to it.

By putting the geography of the United States into motion, I did my best for hours on end to give her the impression of "going places," of rolling on to some definite destination, to some unusual delight. I have never seen such smooth amiable roads as those that now radiated before us, across the crazy quilt of forty-eight states. Voraciously we consumed those long highways, in rapt silence we glided over their glossy black dance floors. Not only had Lo no eye for scenery but she furiously resented my calling her attention to this or that enchanting detail of landscape; which I myself learned to discern only after being exposed for quite a time to the delicate beauty ever present in the margin of our undeserving journey. By a paradox of pictorial thought, the average lowland North-American countryside had at first seemed to me something I accepted with a shock of amused recognition because of those painted oilcloths which were imported from America in the old days to be hung above washstands in Central-European nurseries, and which fascinated a drowsy child at bed time with the rustic green views they depicted—opaque curly trees, a barn, cattle, a brook, the dull white of vague orchards in bloom, and perhaps a stone fence or hills of greenish gouache. But gradually the models of those elementary rusticities became stranger and stranger to the eye, the nearer I came to know them. Beyond the tilled plain, beyond the toy roofs, there would be a slow suffusion of inutile loveliness, a low sun in a platinum haze with a warm, peeled-peach tinge pervading the upper edge of a two-dimensional, dove-gray cloud fusing with the distant amorous mist. There might be a line of spaced trees silhouetted against the horizon, and hot still noons above a wilderness of clover, and Claude Lorrain clouds inscribed remotely into misty azure with only their cumulus part conspicuous against the neutral swoon of the background. Or again, it might be a stern El Greco horizon, pregnant with inky rain, and a passing glimpse of some mummy-necked farmer, and all around alternating strips of quick-silverish water and harsh green corn, the whole arrangement opening like a fan, somewhere in Kansas.

Now and then, in the vastness of those plains, huge trees would advance toward us to cluster self-consciously by the roadside and provide a bit of humanitarian shade above a picnic table, with sun flecks, flattened paper cups, samaras and discarded ice-cream sticks littering the brown ground. A great user of roadside facilities, my unfastidious Lo would be charmed by toilet signs—Guys-Gals, John-Jane, Jack-Jill and even Buck's-Doe's; while lost in an artist's dream, I would stare at the honest brightness of the gasoline paraphernalia against the splendid green of oaks, or at a distant hill scrambling out—scarred but still untamed—from the wilderness of agriculture that was trying to swallow it.

At night, tall trucks studded with colored lights, like dreadful giant Christmas trees, loomed in the darkness and thundered by the belated little sedan. And again next day a thinly populated sky, losing its blue to the heat, would melt overhead, and Lo would clamor for a drink, and her cheeks would hollow vigorously over the straw, and the car inside would be a furnace when we got in again, and the road shimmered ahead, with a remote car changing its shape mirage-like in the surface glare, and seeming to hang for a moment, old-fashionedly square and high, in the hot haze. And as we pushed westward, patches of what the garage-man called "sage brush" appeared, and then the mysterious outlines of table-like hills, and then red bluffs ink-blotted with junipers, and then a mountain range, dun grading into blue, and blue into dream, and the desert would meet us with a steady gale, dust, gray thorn bushes, and hideous bits of tissue paper mimicking pale flowers among the prickles of wind-tortured withered stalks all along the highway; in the middle of which there sometimes stood simple cows, immobilized in a position (tail left, white eyelashes right) cutting across all human rules of traffic.

My lawyer has suggested I give a clear, frank account of the itinerary we followed, and I suppose I have reached here a point where I cannot avoid that chore. Roughly, during that mad year

(August 1947 to August 1948), our route began with a series of wiggles and whorls in New England, then meandered south, up

1 and down, east and west; dipped deep into *ce qu'on appelle* Dixieland, avoided Florida because the Farlows were there, veered west, zigzagged through corn belts and cotton belts (this is not *too* clear I am afraid, Clarence, but I did not keep any notes, and have at my disposal only an atrociously crippled tour book in three volumes, almost a symbol of my torn and tattered past, in which to check these recollections); crossed and recrossed the Rockies, straggled through southern deserts where we wintered; reached the Pacific, turned north through the pale lilac fluff of flowering shrubs along forest roads; almost reached the Canadian border; and proceeded east, across good lands and bad lands, back to agriculture on a grand scale, avoiding, despite little Lo's strident remonstrations, little Lo's birthplace, in a corn, coal and hog producing area; and finally returned to the fold of the East, petering out in the college town of Beardsley.

2

Now, in perusing what follows, the reader should bear in mind not only the general circuit as adumbrated above, with its many sidetrips and tourist traps, secondary circles and skittish deviations, but also the fact that far from being an indolent *partie de*

2 *plaisir*, our tour was a hard, twisted, teleological growth, whose
3 sole *raison d'être* (these French clichés are symptomatic) was to keep my companion in passable humor from kiss to kiss.

Thumbing through that battered tour book, I dimly evoke that Magnolia Garden in a southern state which cost me four bucks and which, according to the ad in the book, you must

4 visit for three reasons: because John Galsworthy (a stone-dead writer of sorts) acclaimed it as the world's fairest garden; because in 1900 Baedeker's Guide had marked it with a star; and finally, because ... O, Reader, My Reader, guess! ... because children (and by Jingo was not my Lolita a child!) will "walk

starry-eyed and reverently through this foretaste of Heaven, drinking in beauty that can influence a life." "Not mine," said grim Lo, and settled down on a bench with the fillings of two Sunday papers in her lovely lap.

We passed and re-passed through the whole gamut of American roadside restaurants, from the lowly Eat with its deer head (dark trace of long tear at inner canthus), "humorous" picture post cards of the posterior "Kurort" type, impaled guest checks, life savers, sunglasses, adman visions of celestial sundaes, one half of a chocolate cake under glass, and several horribly experienced flies zigzagging over the sticky sugar-pour on the ignoble counter; and all the way to the expensive place with the subdued lights, preposterously poor table linen, inept waiters (ex-convicts or college boys), the roan back of a screen actress, the sable eyebrows of her male of the moment, and an orchestra of zoot-suiters with trumpets.

We inspected the world's largest stalagmite in a cave where three southeastern states have a family reunion; admission by age; adults one dollar, pubescents sixty cents. A granite obelisk commemorating the Battle of Blue Licks, with old bones and Indian pottery in the museum nearby, Lo a dime, very reasonable. The present log cabin boldly simulating the past log cabin where Lincoln was born. A boulder, with a plaque, in memory of the author of "Trees" (by now we are in Poplar Cove, N.C., reached by what my kind, tolerant, usually so restrained tour book angrily calls "a very narrow road, poorly maintained," to which, though no Kilmerite, I subscribe). From a hired motorboat operated by an elderly, but still repulsively handsome White Russian, a baron they said (Lo's palms were damp, the little fool), who had known in California good old Maximovich and Valeria, we could distinguish the inaccessible "millionaires' colony" on an island, somewhere off the Georgia coast. We inspected further: a collection of European hotel picture post cards in a museum devoted to hobbies at a Mississippi resort, where with a hot wave of pride I discovered a colored photo of my father's Mirana, its striped awnings, its flag flying above the retouched palm trees. "So what?" said Lo, squinting at the

1 bronzed owner of an expensive car who had followed us into the Hobby House. Relics of the cotton era. A forest in Arkansas and, on her brown shoulder, a raised purple-pink swelling (the work of some gnat) which I eased of its beautiful transparent poison between my long thumbnails and then sucked till I was gorged on her spicy blood. Bourbon Street (in a town named New Orleans) whose sidewalks, said the tour book, "may [I liked the "may"] feature entertainment by pickaninnies who will [I liked the "will" even better] tap-dance for pennies" (what fun), while "its numerous small and intimate night clubs are thronged with visitors" (naughty). Collections of frontier lore. Ante-bellum homes with iron-trellis balconies and hand-worked stairs, the kind down which movie ladies with sun-kissed shoulders run in rich Technicolor, holding up the fronts of their flounced skirts with both little hands in that special way, and the devoted Negress shaking her head on the upper landing. The Menninger Foundation, a psychiatric clinic, just for the heck of it. A patch of beautifully eroded clay; and yucca blossoms, so

2 pure, so waxy, but lousy with creeping white flies. Independence, Missouri, the starting point of the Old Oregon Trail; and

3 Abilene, Kansas, the home of the Wild Bill Something Rodeo. Distant mountains. Near mountains. More mountains; bluish beauties never attainable, or ever turning into inhabited hill after hill; south-eastern ranges, altitudinal failures as alps go; heart and sky-piercing snow-veined gray colossi of stone, relentless peaks appearing from nowhere at a turn of the highway; timbered enormities, with a system of neatly overlapping dark firs, interrupted in places by pale puffs of aspen; pink and lilac

4 formations, Pharaonic, phallic, "too prehistoric for words" (blasé Lo); buttes of black lava; early spring mountains with young-

5 elephant lanugo along their spines; end-of-the-summer mountains, all hunched up, their heavy Egyptian limbs folded under folds of tawny moth-eaten plush; oatmeal hills, flecked with

6 green round oaks; a last rufous mountain with a rich rug of

7 lucerne at its foot.

Moreover, we inspected: Little Iceberg Lake, somewhere in Colorado, and the snow banks, and the cushionets of tiny alpine flowers, and more snow; down which Lo in red-peaked cap tried to slide, and squealed, and was snowballed by some youngsters, and retaliated in kind *comme on dit*. Skeletons of burned aspens, patches of spired blue flowers. The various items of a scenic drive. Hundreds of scenic drives, thousands of Bear Creeks, Soda Springs, Painted Canyons. Texas, a drought-struck plain. Crystal Chamber in the longest cave in the world, children under 12 free, Lo a young captive. A collection of a local lady's homemade sculptures, closed on a miserable Monday morning, dust, wind, witherland. Conception Park, in a town on the Mexican border which I dared not cross. There and elsewhere, hundreds of gray hummingbirds in the dusk, probing the throats of dim flowers. Shakespeare, a ghost town in New Mexico, where bad man Russian Bill was colorfully hanged seventy years ago. Fish hatcheries. Cliff dwellings. The mummy of a child (Florentine Bea's Indian contemporary). Our twentieth Hell's Canyon. Our fiftieth Gateway to something or other *fide* that tour book, the cover of which had been lost by that time. A tick in my groin. Always the same three old men, in hats and suspenders, idling away the summer afternoon under the trees near the public fountain. A hazy blue view beyond railings on a mountain pass, and the backs of a family enjoying it (with Lo, in a hot, happy, wild, intense, hopeful, hopeless whisper—"Look, the McCrystals, please, let's talk to them, please"—let's talk to them, reader!— "please! I'll do anything you want, oh, please..."). Indian ceremonial dances, strictly commercial. ART: American Refrigerator Transit Company. Obvious Arizona, pueblo dwellings, aboriginal pictographs, a dinosaur track in a desert canyon, printed there thirty million years ago, when I was a child. A lanky, six-foot, pale boy with an active Adam's apple, ogling Lo and her orange-brown bare midriff, which I kissed five minutes later, Jack. Winter in the desert, spring in the foothills, almonds in bloom. Reno, a dreary town in Nevada, with a nightlife said to be "cosmopolitan and mature." A winery in California, with a church built in the shape of a wine barrel. Death Valley. Scotty's Castle. Works of Art collected by one Rogers over a period of years. The ugly villas of handsome actresses. R. L.

1 Stevenson's footprint on an extinct volcano. Mission Dolores:
2, 3 good title for book. Surf-carved sandstone festoons. A man having
4 a lavish epileptic fit on the ground in Russian Gulch State Park.
Blue, blue Crater Lake. A fish hatchery in Idaho and the State
Penitentiary. Somber Yellowstone Park and its colored hot
springs, baby geysers, rainbows of bubbling mud—symbols of
my passion. A herd of antelopes in a wildlife refuge. Our hun-
dredth cavern, adults one dollar, Lolita fifty cents. A chateau
built by a French marquess in N.D. The Corn Palace in S.D.;
and the huge heads of presidents carved in towering granite. The
5 Bearded Woman read our jingle and now she is no longer single.
A zoo in Indiana where a large troop of monkeys lived on con-
6 crete replica of Christopher Columbus' flagship. Billions of dead,
or halfdead, fish-smelling May flies in every window of every
eating place all along a dreary sandy shore. Fat gulls on big
stones as seen from the ferry *City of Sheboygan,* whose brown
woolly smoke arched and dipped over the green shadow it cast
on the aquamarine lake. A motel whose ventilator pipe passed
under the city sewer. Lincoln's home, largely spurious, with
parlor books and period furniture that most visitors reverently
accepted as personal belongings.

We had rows, minor and major. The biggest ones we had took
place: at Lacework Cabins, Virginia; on Park Avenue, Little
7 Rock, near a school; on Milner Pass, 10,759 feet high, in Colorado; at the corner of Seventh Street and Central Avenue in
Phoenix, Arizona; on Third Street, Los Angeles, because the
tickets to some studio or other were sold out; at a motel called
Poplar Shade in Utah, where six pubescent trees were scarcely
8 taller than my Lolita, and where she asked, *à propos de rien,*
how long did I think we were going to live in stuffy cabins, doing
filthy things together and never behaving like ordinary people?
On N. Broadway, Burns, Oregon, corner of W. Washington,
facing Safeway, a grocery. In some little town in the Sun Valley
of Idaho, before a brick hotel, pale and flushed bricks nicely
mixed, with, opposite, a poplar playing its liquid shadows all
over the local Honor Roll. In a sage brush wilderness, between
Pinedale and Farson. Somewhere in Nebraska, on Main Street,

near the First National Bank, established 1889, with a view of
a railway crossing in the vista of the street, and beyond that the
white organ pipes of a multiple silo. And on McEwen St., corner
of Wheaton Ave., in a Michigan town bearing his first name.

We came to know the curious roadside species, Hitchhiking
Man, *Homo pollex* of science, with all its many sub-species and
forms: the modest soldier, spic and span, quietly waiting, quietly
conscious of khaki's viatic appeal; the schoolboy wishing to go
two blocks; the killer wishing to go two thousand miles; the
mysterious, nervous, elderly gent, with brand-new suitcase and
clipped mustache; a trio of optimistic Mexicans; the college
student displaying the grime of vacational outdoor work as
proudly as the name of the famous college arching across the
front of his sweatshirt; the desperate lady whose battery has just
died on her; the clean-cut, glossy-haired, shifty-eyed, white-faced
young beasts in loud shirts and coats, vigorously, almost priapi-
ically thrusting out tense thumbs to tempt lone women or sad-
sack salesmen with fancy cravings.

"Let's take him," Lo would often plead, rubbing her knees
together in a way she had, as some particularly disgusting *pollex*,
some man of my age and shoulder breadth, with the *face à
claques* of an unemployed actor, walked backwards, practically
in the path of our car.

Oh, I had to keep a very sharp eye on Lo, little limp Lo!
Owing perhaps to constant amorous exercise, she radiated, despite her very childish appearance, some special languorous glow
which threw garage fellows, hotel pages, vacationists, goons in
luxurious cars, maroon morons near blued pools, into fits of
concupiscence which might have tickled my pride, had it not
incensed my jealousy. For little Lo was aware of that glow of
hers, and I would often catch her *coulant un regard* in the direction of some amiable male, some grease monkey, with a sinewy
golden-brown forearm and watch-braceleted wrist, and hardly
had I turned my back to go and buy this very Lo a lollipop, than
I would hear her and the fair mechanic burst into a perfect love
song of wisecracks.

When, during our longer stops, I would relax after a particu-

larly violent morning in bed, and out of the goodness of my
lulled heart allow her—indulgent Hum!—to visit the rose garden
or children's library across the street with a motor court neighbor's plain little Mary and Mary's eight-year-old brother, Lo
would come back an hour late, with barefoot Mary trailing far
behind, and the little boy metamorphosed into two gangling,
golden-haired high school uglies, all muscles and gonorrhea. The
reader may well imagine what I answered my pet when—rather
uncertainly, I admit—she would ask me if she could go with
Carl and Al here to the roller-skating rink.

I remember the first time, a dusty windy afternoon, I did let
her go to one such rink. Cruelly she said it would be no fun if I
accompanied her, since that time of day was reserved for teen-
agers. We wrangled out a compromise: I remained in the car,
among other (empty) cars with their noses to the canvas-topped
open-air rink, where some fifty young people, many in pairs, were
endlessly rolling round and round to mechanical music, and the
wind silvered the trees. Dolly wore blue jeans and white high
shoes, as most of the other girls did. I kept counting the revolu-
tions of the rolling crowd—and suddenly she was missing. When
she rolled past again, she was together with three hoodlums
whom I had heard analyze a moment before the girl skaters from
the outside—and jeer at a lovely leggy young thing who had
arrived clad in red shorts instead of those jeans or slacks.

At inspection stations on highways entering Arizona or California, a policeman's cousin would peer with such intensity at
us that my poor heart wobbled. "Any honey?" he would inquire,
and every time my sweet fool giggled. I still have, vibrating all
along my optic nerve, visions of Lo on horseback, a link in the
chain of a guided trip along a bridle trail: Lo bobbing at a walking pace, with an old woman rider in front and a lecherous red-
necked dude-rancher behind; and I behind him, hating his fat
flowery-shirted back even more fervently than a motorist does a
slow truck on a mountain road. Or else, at a ski lodge, I would
see her floating away from me, celestial and solitary, in an
ethereal chairlift, up and up, to a glittering summit where laughing athletes stripped to the waist were waiting for her, for her.

Lolita

In whatever town we stopped I would inquire, in my polite European way, anent the whereabouts of natatoriums, museums, local schools, the number of children in the nearest school and so forth; and at school bus time, smiling and twitching a little (I discovered this *tic nerveux* because cruel Lo was the first to mimic it), I would park at a strategic point, with my vagrant schoolgirl beside me in the car, to watch the children leave school—always a pretty sight. This sort of thing soon began to bore my so easily bored Lolita, and, having a childish lack of sympathy for other people's whims, she would insult me and my desire to have her caress me while blue-eyed little brunettes in blue shorts, copperheads in green boleros, and blurred boyish blondes in faded slacks passed by in the sun.

As a sort of compromise, I freely advocated whenever and wherever possible the use of swimming pools with other girl-children. She adored brilliant water and was a remarkably smart diver. Comfortably robed, I would settle down in the rich post-meridian shade after my own demure dip, and there I would sit, with a dummy book or a bag of bonbons, or both, or nothing but my tingling glands, and watch her gambol, rubber-capped, be-pearled, smoothly tanned, as glad as an ad, in her trim-fitted satin pants and shirred bra. Pubescent sweetheart! How smugly would I marvel that she was mine, mine, mine, and revise the recent matitudinal swoon to the moan of the mourning doves, and devise the late afternoon one, and slitting my sun-speared eyes, compare Lolita to whatever other nymphets parsimonious chance collected around her for my anthological delectation and judgment; and today, putting my hand on my ailing heart, I really do not think that any of them ever surpassed her in desirability, or if they did, it was so two or three times at the most, in a certain light, with certain perfumes blended in the air— once in the hopeless case of a pale Spanish child, the daughter of a heavy-jawed nobleman, and another time—*mais je divague.*

Naturally, I had to be always wary, fully realizing, in my lucid jealousy, the danger of those dazzling romps. I had only to turn away for a moment—to walk, say, a few steps in order to see if our cabin was at last ready after the morning change of linen—and

Lo and Behold, upon returning, I would find the former, *les yeux perdus*, dipping and kicking her long-toed feet in the water on the stone edge of which she lolled, while, on either side of her, there crouched a *brun adolescent* whom her russet beauty and the quicksilver in the baby folds of her stomach were sure to cause to *se tordre*—oh Baudelaire!—in recurrent dreams for months to come.

I tried to teach her to play tennis so we might have more amusements in common; but although I had been a good player in my prime, I proved to be hopeless as a teacher; and so, in California, I got her to take a number of very expensive lessons with a famous coach, a husky, wrinkled old-timer, with a harem of ball boys; he looked an awful wreck off the court, but now and then, when, in the course of a lesson, to keep up the exchange, he would put out as it were an exquisite spring blossom of a stroke and twang the ball back to his pupil, that divine delicacy of absolute power made me recall that, thirty years before, I had seen *him* in Cannes demolish the great Gobbert! Until she began taking those lessons, I thought she would never learn the game. On this or that hotel court I would drill Lo, and try to relive the days when in a hot gale, a daze of dust, and queer lassitude, I fed ball after ball to gay, innocent, elegant Annabel (gleam of bracelet, pleated white skirt, black velvet hair band). With every word of persistent advice I would only augment Lo's sullen fury. To our games, oddly enough, she preferred—at least, before we reached California—formless pat ball approximations—more ball hunting than actual play—with a wispy, weak, wonderfully pretty in an *ange gauche* way coeval. A helpful spectator, I would go up to that other child, and inhale her faint musky fragrance as I touched her forearm and held her knobby wrist, and push this way or that her cool thigh to show her the back-hand stance. In the meantime, Lo, bending forward, would let her sunny-brown curls hang forward as she stuck her racket, like a cripple's stick, into the ground and emitted a tremendous ugh of disgust at my intrusion. I would leave them to their game and look on, comparing their bodies in motion, a silk scarf round my throat; this was in south Arizona, I think—

and the days had a lazy lining of warmth, and awkward Lo would slash at the ball and miss it, and curse, and send a simulacrum of $\quad$ 1 a serve into the net, and show the wet glistening young down of her armpit as she brandished her racket in despair, and her even more insipid partner would dutifully rush out after every ball, and retrieve none; but both were enjoying themselves beautifully, and in clear ringing tones kept the exact score of their ineptitudes all the time.

One day, I remember, I offered to bring them cold drinks from the hotel, and went up the gravel path, and came back with two tall glasses of pineapple juice, soda and ice; and then a sudden void within my chest made me stop as I saw that the tennis court was deserted. I stooped to set down the glasses on a bench and for some reason, with a kind of icy vividness, saw Charlotte's face in death, and I glanced around, and noticed Lo in white shorts receding through the speckled shadow of a garden path in the company of a tall man who carried two tennis rackets. I $\quad$ 2 sprang after them, but as I was crashing through the shrubbery, I saw, in an alternate vision, as if life's course constantly branched, Lo, in slacks, and her companion, in shorts, trudging up and down a small weedy area, and beating bushes with their rackets in listless search for their last lost ball.

I itemize these sunny nothings mainly to prove to my judges that I did everything in my power to give my Lolita a really good time. How charming it was to see her, a child herself, showing another child some of her few accomplishments, such as for example a special way of jumping rope. With her right hand holding her left arm behind her untanned back, the lesser nymphet, a diaphanous darling, would be all eyes, as the pavo- $\quad$ 3 nine sun was all eyes on the gravel under the flowering trees, $\quad$ 4 while in the midst of that oculate paradise, my freckled and $\quad$ 5 raffish lass skipped, repeating the movements of so many others I had gloated over on the sun-shot, watered, damp-smelling side- walks and ramparts of ancient Europe. Presently, she would $\quad$ 6 hand the rope back to her little Spanish friend, and watch in her turn the repeated lesson, and brush away the hair from her brow, and fold her arms, and step on one toe with the other, or drop her hands loosely upon her still unflared hips, and I would satisfy myself that the damned staff had at last finished cleaning up our cottage; whereupon, flashing a smile to the shy, dark-haired page girl of my princess and thrusting my fatherly fingers deep into Lo's hair from behind, and then gently but firmly clasping them around the nape of her neck, I would lead my reluctant pet to our small home for a quick connection before dinner.

"Whose cat has scratched poor you?" a full-blown fleshy handsome woman of the repulsive type to which I was particularly attractive might ask me at the "lodge," during a table d'hôte dinner followed by dancing promised to Lo. This was one of the reasons why I tried to keep as far away from people as possible, while Lo, on the other hand, would do her utmost to draw as many potential witnesses into her orbit as she could.

She would be, figuratively speaking, wagging her tiny tail, her whole behind in fact as little bitches do—while some grinning stranger accosted us and began a bright conversation with a comparative study of license plates. "Long way from home!" Inquisitive parents, in order to pump Lo about me, would suggest her going to a movie with their children. We had some close shaves. The waterfall nuisance pursued me of course in all our caravansaries. But I never realized how wafery their wall substance was until one evening, after I had loved too loudly, a neighbor's masculine cough filled the pause as clearly as mine would have done; and next morning as I was having breakfast at the milk bar (Lo was a late sleeper, and I liked to bring her a pot of hot coffee in bed), my neighbor of the eve, an elderly fool wearing plain glasses on his long virtuous nose and a convention badge on his lapel, somehow managed to rig up a conversation with me, in the course of which he inquired, if my missus was like his missus a rather reluctant get-upper when not on the farm; and had not the hideous danger I was skirting almost suffocated me, I might have enjoyed the odd look of surprise on his thin-lipped weather-beaten face when I drily answered, as I slithered off my stool, that I was thank God a widower.

How sweet it was to bring that coffee to her, and then deny it until she had done her morning duty. And I was such a thoughtful friend, such a passionate father, such a good pediatrician, attending to all the wants of my little auburn brunette's body! My only grudge against nature was that I could not turn my Lolita inside out and apply voracious lips to her young matrix, her unknown heart, her nacreous liver, the sea-grapes of her lungs, her comely twin kidneys. On especially tropical afternoons, in the sticky closeness of the siesta, I liked the cool feel of armchair leather against my massive nakedness as I held her in my lap. There she would be, a typical kid picking her nose while engrossed in the lighter sections of a newspaper, as indifferent to my ecstasy as if it were something she had sat upon, a shoe, a doll, the handle of a tennis racket, and was too indolent to remove. Her eyes would follow the adventures of her favorite strip characters: there was one well-drawn sloppy bobby-soxer, with high cheekbones and angular gestures, that I was not above enjoying myself; she studied the photographic results of head-on collisions; she never doubted the reality of place, time and circumstance alleged to match the publicity pictures of naked-thighed beauties; and she was curiously fascinated by the photographs of local brides, some in full wedding apparel, holding bouquets and wearing glasses.

A fly would settle and walk in the vicinity of her navel or explore her tender pale areolas. She tried to catch it in her fist (Charlotte's method) and then would turn to the column Let's Explore Your Mind.

"Let's explore your mind. Would sex crimes be reduced if children obeyed a few don'ts? Don't play around public toilets. Don't take candy or rides from strangers. If picked up, mark down the license of the car."

". . . and the brand of the candy," I volunteered.

She went on, her cheek (recedent) against mine (pursuant); and this was a good day, mark, O reader!

"If you don't have a pencil, but are old enough to read—"

"We," I quip-quoted, "medieval mariners, have placed in this bottle—"

"If," she repeated, "you don't have a pencil, but are old

enough to read and write—this is what the guy means, isn't it, you dope—scratch the number somehow on the roadside."

"With your little claws, Lolita.'"

3

1 She had entered my world, umber and black Humberland, with rash curiosity; she surveyed it with a shrug of amused distaste; and it seemed to me now that she was ready to turn away from it with something akin to plain repulsion. Never did she vibrate under my touch, and a strident "what d'you think you are doing?" was all I got for my pains. To the wonderland I had to offer, my fool preferred the corniest movies, the most cloying fudge. To think that between a Hamburger and a Humburger, she would—invariably, with icy precision—plump for the former. There is nothing more atrociously cruel than an adored child. Did I mention the name of that milk bar I visited a moment ago? It was, of all things, The Frigid Queen. Smiling a little

2 sadly, I dubbed her My Frigid Princess. She did not see the wistful joke.

Oh, do not scowl at me, reader, I do not intend to convey the impression that I did not manage to be happy. Reader must understand that in the possession and thralldom of a nymphet the enchanted traveler stands, as it were, *beyond happiness*. For there is no other bliss on earth comparable to that of fondling a

3 nymphet. It is *hors concours*, that bliss, it belongs to another class, another plane of sensitivity. Despite our tiffs, despite her nastiness, despite all the fuss and faces she made, and the vulgarity, and the danger, and the horrible hopelessness of it all, I still dwelled deep in my elected paradise—a paradise whose skies were the color of hell-flames—but still a paradise.

The able psychiatrist who studies my case—and whom by now Dr. Humbert has plunged, I trust, into a state of leporine

4 fascination—is no doubt anxious to have me take my Lolita to the seaside and have me find there, at last, the "gratification" of

a lifetime urge, and release from the "subconscious" obsession of an incomplete childhood romance with the initial little Miss Lee.

Well, comrade, let me tell you that I *did* look for a beach, though I also have to confess that by the time we reached its mirage of gray water, so many delights had already been granted me by my traveling companion that the search for a Kingdom by the Sea, a Sublimated Riviera, or whatnot, far from being the impulse of the subconscious, had become the rational pursuit of a purely theoretical thrill. The angels knew it, and arranged things accordingly. A visit to a plausible cove on the Atlantic side was completely messed up by foul weather. A thick damp sky, muddy waves, a sense of boundless but somehow matter-of-fact mist—what could be further removed from the crisp charm, the sapphire occasion and rosy contingency of my Riviera romance? A couple of semitropical beaches on the Gulf, though bright enough, were starred and spattered by venomous beasties and swept by hurricane winds. Finally, on a Californian beach, facing the phantom of the Pacific, I hit upon some rather perverse privacy in a kind of cave whence you could hear the shrieks of a lot of girl scouts taking their first surf bath on a separate part of the beach, behind rotting trees; but the fog was like a wet blanket, and the sand was gritty and clammy, and Lo was all gooseflesh and grit, and for the first time in my life I had as little desire for her as for a manatee. Perhaps, my learned readers may perk up if I tell them that even had we discovered a piece of sympathetic seaside somewhere, it would have come too late, since my real liberation had occurred much earlier: at the moment, in point of fact, when Annabel Haze, alias Dolores Lee, alias Loleeta, had appeared to me, golden and brown, kneeling, looking up, on that shoddy veranda, in a kind of fictitious, dishonest, but eminently satisfactory seaside arrangement (although there was nothing but a second-rate lake in the neighborhood).

So much for those special sensations, influenced, if not actually brought about, by the tenets of modern psychiatry. Consequently, I turned away—I headed my Lolita away—from beaches which were either too bleak when lone, or too populous when ablaze. However, in recollection, I suppose, of my hopeless hauntings of public parks in Europe, I was still keenly interested in outdoor activities and desirous of finding suitable playgrounds in the open where I had suffered such shameful privations. Here, too, I was to be thwarted. The disappointment I must now register (as I gently grade my story into an expression of the continuous risk and dread that ran through my bliss) should in no wise reflect on the lyrical, epic, tragic but never Arcadian American wilds. They are beautiful, heart-rendingly beautiful, those wilds, with a quality of wide-eyed, unsung, innocent surrender that my lacquered, toy-bright Swiss villages and exhaustively lauded Alps no longer possess. Innumerable lovers have clipped and kissed on the trim turf of old-world mountainsides, on the innerspring moss, by a handy, hygienic rill, on rustic benches under the initialed oaks, and in so many *cabanes* in so many beech forests. But in the Wilds of America the open-air lover will not find it easy to indulge in the most ancient of all crimes and pastimes. Poisonous plants burn his sweetheart's buttocks, nameless insects sting his; sharp items of the forest floor prick his knees, insects hers; and all around there abides a sustained rustle of potential snakes—*que dis-je*, of semi-extinct dragons!—while the crablike seeds of ferocious flowers cling, in a hideous green crust, to gartered black sock and sloppy white sock alike.

I am exaggerating a little. One summer noon, just below timberline, where heavenly-hued blossoms that I would fain call larkspur crowded all along a purly mountain brook, we did find, Lolita and I, a secluded romantic spot, a hundred feet or so above the pass where we had left our car. The slope seemed untrodden. A last panting pine was taking a well-earned breather on the rock it had reached. A marmot whistled at us and withdrew. Beneath the lap-robe I had spread for Lo, dry flowers crepitated softly. Venus came and went. The jagged cliff crowning the upper talus and a tangle of shrubs growing below us seemed to offer us protection from sun and man alike. Alas, I had not reckoned with a faint side trail that curled up in cagey fashion among the shrubs and rocks a few feet from us.

It was then that we came closer to detection than ever before, and no wonder the experience curbed forever my yearning for rural amours.

I remember the operation was over, all over, and she was weeping in my arms;—a salutory storm of sobs after one of the fits of moodiness that had become so frequent with her in the course of that otherwise admirable year! I had just retracted some silly promise she had forced me to make in a moment of blind impatient passion, and there she was sprawling and sobbing, and pinching my caressing hand, and I was laughing happily, and the atrocious, unbelievable, unbearable, and, I suspect, eternal horror that I know *now* was still but a dot of blackness in the blue of my bliss; and so we lay, when with one of those jolts that have ended by knocking my poor heart out of its groove, I met the unblinking dark eyes of two strange and beautiful children, faunlet and nymphet, whom their identical flat dark hair and bloodless cheeks proclaimed siblings if not twins. They stood crouching and gaping at us, both in blue playsuits, blending with the mountain blossoms. I plucked at the lap-robe for desperate concealment—and within the same instant, something that looked like a polka-dotted pushball among the undergrowth a few paces away, went into a turning motion which was transformed into the gradually rising figure of a stout lady with a raven-black bob, who automatically added a wild lily to her bouquet, while staring over her shoulder at us from behind her lovely carved bluestone children.

Now that I have an altogether different mess on my conscience, I know that I am a courageous man, but in those days I was not aware of it, and I remember being surprised by my own coolness. With the quiet murmured order one gives a sweat-stained distracted cringing trained animal even in the worst of plights (what mad hope or hate makes the young beast's flanks pulsate, what black stars pierce the heart of the tamer!), I made Lo get up, and we decorously walked, and then indecorously scuttled down to the car. Behind it a nifty station wagon was parked, and a handsome Assyrian with a little blue-black beard, *un monsieur très bien*, in silk shirt and magenta slacks, pre-   1 sumably the corpulent botanist's husband, was gravely taking the picture of a signboard giving the altitude of the pass. It was well over 10,000 feet and I was quite out of breath; and with a scrunch and a skid we drove off, Lo still struggling with her clothes and swearing at me in language that I never dreamed little girls could know, let alone use.

There were other unpleasant incidents. There was the movie theatre once, for example. Lo at the time still had for the cinema a veritable passion (it was to decline into tepid condescension during her second high school year). We took in, voluptuously and indiscriminately, oh, I don't know, one hundred and fifty or two hundred programs during that one year, and during some of the denser periods of movie-going we saw many of the news-reels up to half-a-dozen times since the same weekly one went with different main pictures and pursued us from town to town. Her favorite kinds were, in this order: musicals, underworlders, westerners. In the first, real singers and dancers had unreal stage careers in an essentially grief-proof sphere of existence where-from death and truth were banned, and where, at the end, white-haired, dewy-eyed, technically deathless, the initially reluctant father of a show-crazy girl always finished by applauding her apotheosis on fabulous Broadway. The underworld was a world apart: there, heroic newspapermen were tortured, telephone bills ran to billions, and, in a robust atmosphere of incompetent marksmanship, villains were chased through sewers and store-houses by pathologically fearless cops (I was to give them less exercise). Finally there was the mahogany landscape, the florid-faced, blue-eyed roughriders, the prim pretty schoolteacher ar-riving in Roaring Gulch, the rearing horse, the spectacular stampede, the pistol thrust through the shivered windowpane, the stupendous fist fight, the crashing mountain of dusty old-fashioned furniture, the table used as a weapon, the timely somersault, the pinned hand still groping for the dropped bowie knife, the grunt, the sweet crash of fist against chin, the kick in the belly, the flying tackle; and immediately after a plethora of pain that would have hospitalized a Hercules (I should know by now), nothing to show but the rather becoming bruise on the bronzed cheek of the warmed-up hero embracing his gorgeous frontier bride. I remember one matinee in a small airless theatre crammed with children and reeking with the hot breath of popcorn. The moon was yellow above the neckerchiefed crooner, and his finger was on his strumstring, and his foot was on a pine 1 log, and I had innocently encircled Lo's shoulder and approached my jawbone to her temple, when two harpies behind us started 2 muttering the queerest things—I do not know if I understood aright, but what I thought I did, made me withdraw my gentle hand, and of course the rest of the show was fog to me.

Another jolt I remember is connected with a little burg we were traversing at night, during our return journey. Some twenty miles earlier I had happened to tell her that the day school she would attend at Beardsley was a rather high-class, non-coeducational one, with no modern nonsense, whereupon Lo treated me to one of those furious harangues of hers where entreaty and insult, self-assertion and double talk, vicious vulgarity and childish despair, were interwoven in an exasperating semblance of logic which prompted a semblance of explanation from me. Enmeshed in her wild words (swell chance . . . I'd be a sap if I took your opinion seriously . . . Stinker . . . You can't boss me . . . I despise you . . . and so forth), I drove through the slumbering town at a fifty-mile-per-hour pace in continuance of my smooth highway swoosh, and a twosome of patrolmen put their spotlight on the car, and told me to pull over. I shushed Lo who was automatically raving on. The men peered at her and me with malevolent curiosity. Suddenly all dimples, she beamed sweetly at them, as she never did at my orchideous masculinity; for, in a 3 sense, my Lo was even more scared of the law than I—and when the kind officers pardoned us and servilely we crawled on, her eyelids closed and fluttered as she mimicked limp prostration.

At this point I have a curious confession to make. You will laugh—but really and truly I somehow never managed to find out quite exactly what the legal situation was. I do not know it yet. Oh, I have learned a few odds and ends. Alabama prohibits a guardian from changing the ward's residence without an order of the court; Minnesota, to whom I take off my hat, provides that when a relative assumes permanent care and custody of any child under fourteen, the authority of a court does not come into play. Query: is the stepfather of a gaspingly adorable pubescent pet, a stepfather of only one month's standing, a neurotic widower of mature years and small but independent means, with the parapets of Europe, a divorce and a few madhouses behind him, is he to be considered a relative, and thus a natural guardian? And if not, must I, and could I reasonably dare notify some Welfare Board and file a petition (how do you file a petition?), and have a court's agent investigate meek, fishy me and dangerous Dolores Haze? The many books on marriage, rape, adoption and so on, that I guiltily consulted at the public libraries of big and small towns, told me nothing beyond darkly insinuating that the state is the super-guardian of minor children. Pilvin and Zapel, if I remember their names right, in an impressive volume on the legal side of marriage, completely ignored stepfathers with motherless girls on their hands and knees. My best friend, a social service monograph (Chicago, 1936), which was dug out for me at great pains from a dusty storage recess by an innocent old spinster, said "There is no principle that every minor must have a guardian; the court is passive and enters the fray only when the child's situation becomes conspicuously perilous." A guardian, I concluded, was appointed only when he expressed his solemn and formal desire; but months might elapse before he was given notice to appear at a hearing and grow his pair of gray wings, and in the meantime the fair daemon child was legally left to her own devices which, after all, was the case of Dolores Haze. Then came the hearing. A few questions from the bench, a few reassuring answers from the attorney, a smile, a nod, a light drizzle outside, and the appointment was made. And still I dared not. Keep away, be a mouse, curl up in your hole. Courts became extravagantly active only when there was some monetary question involved: two greedy guardians, a robbed orphan, a third, still greedier, party. But here all was in perfect order, an inventory had been made, and her mother's small property was waiting untouched for Dolores Haze to grow up. The best policy seemed to be to refrain from any application. Or would some busybody, some Humane Society, butt in if I kept *too* quiet?

Friend Farlow, who was a lawyer of sorts and ought to have been able to give me some solid advice, was too much occupied with Jean's cancer to do anything more than what he had promised—namely, to look after Charlotte's meager estate while I recovered very gradually from the shock of her death. I had conditioned him into believing Dolores was my natural child, and so could not expect him to bother his head about the situation. I am, as the reader must have gathered by now, a poor businessman; but neither ignorance nor indolence should have prevented me from seeking professional advice elsewhere. What stopped me was the awful feeling that if I meddled with fate in any way and tried to rationalize her fantastic gift, that gift would be snatched away like that palace on the mountain top in the Oriental tale which vanished whenever a prospective owner asked its custodian how come a strip of sunset sky was clearly visible from afar between black rock and foundation.

I decided that at Beardsley (the site of Beardsley College for Women) I would have access to works of reference that I had not yet been able to study, such as Woerner's Treatise "On the American Law of Guardianship" and certain United States Children's Bureau Publications. I also decided that anything was better for Lo than the demoralizing idleness in which she lived. I could persuade her to do so many things—their list might stupefy a professional educator; but no matter how I pleaded or stormed, I could never make her read any other book than the so-called comic books or stories in magazines for American females. Any literature a peg higher smacked to her of school, and though theoretically willing to enjoy *A Girl of the Limberlost* or the *Arabian Nights*, or *Little Women*, she was quite sure she would not fritter away her "vacation" on such highbrow reading matter.

I now think it was a great mistake to move east again and have her go to that private school in Beardsley, instead of somehow scrambling across the Mexican border while the scrambling was good so as to lie low for a couple of years in subtropical bliss

until I could safely marry my little Creole for I must confess
that depending on the condition of my glands and ganglia, I
could switch in the course of the same day from one pole of
insanity to the other—from the thought that around 1950 I
would have to get rid somehow of a difficult adolescent whose
magic nymphage had evaporated—to the thought that with pa-
tience and luck I might have her produce eventually a nymphet
with my blood in her exquisite veins, a Lolita the Second, who
would be eight or nine around 1960, when I would still be *dans
la force de l'âge;* indeed, the telescopy of my mind, or un-mind,
was strong enough to distinguish in the remoteness of time a
vieillard encore vert—or was it green rot?—bizarre, tender, sali-
vating Dr. Humbert, practicing on supremely lovely Lolita the
Third the art of being a granddad.

In the days of that wild journey of ours, I doubted not that as
father to Lolita the First I was a ridiculous failure. I did my best;
I read and reread a book with the unintentionally biblical title
Know Your Own Daughter, which I got at the same store where
I bought Lo, for her thirteenth birthday, a de luxe volume with
commercially "beautiful" illustrations, of Andersen's *The Little
Mermaid.* But even at our very best moments, when we sat
reading on a rainy day (Lo's glance skipping from the window
to her wrist watch and back again), or had a quiet hearty meal
in a crowded diner, or played a childish game of cards, or went
shopping, or silently stared, with other motorists and their
children, at some smashed, blood-bespattered car with a young
woman's shoe in the ditch (Lo, as we drove on: "That was the
exact type of moccasin I was trying to describe to that jerk in
the store"); on all those random occasions, I seemed to myself
as implausible a father as she seemed to be a daughter. Was,
perhaps, guilty locomotion instrumental in vitiating our powers
of impersonation? Would improvement be forthcoming with a
fixed domicile and a routine schoolgirl's day?

In my choice of Beardsley I was guided not only by the fact
of there being a comparatively sedate school for girls located
there, but also by the presence of the women's college. In my
desire to get myself *casé,* to attach myself somehow to some

patterned surface which my stripes would blend with, I thought
of a man I knew in the department of French at Beardsley College; he was good enough to use my textbook in his classes and
had attempted to get me over once to deliver a lecture. I had
no intention of doing so, since, as I have once remarked in the
course of these confessions, there are few physiques I loathe
more than the heavy low-slung pelvis, thick calves and deplor-
able complexion of the average coed (in whom I see, maybe,
the coffin of coarse female flesh within which my nymphets are
buried alive); but I did crave for a label, a background, and a
simulacrum, and, as presently will become clear, there was a
reason, a rather zany reason, why old Gaston Godin's company
would be particularly safe.

Finally, there was the money question. My income was cracking under the strain of our joy-ride. True, I clung to the cheaper
motor courts; but every now and then, there would be a loud
hotel de luxe, or a pretentious dude ranch, to mutilate our
budget; staggering sums, moreover, were expended on sightsee-
ing and Lo's clothes, and the old Haze bus, although a still
vigorous and very devoted machine, necessitated numerous
minor and major repairs. In one of our strip maps that has
happened to survive among the papers which the authorities
have so kindly allowed me to use for the purpose of writing my
statement, I find some jottings that help me compute the following. During that extravagant year 1947–1948, August to
August, lodgings and food cost us around 5,500 dollars; gas, oil
and repairs, 1,234, and various extras almost as much; so that
during about 150 days of actual motion (we covered about 27,000
miles!) plus some 200 days of interpolated standstills, this modest
rentier spent around 8,000 dollars, or better say 10,000 because,
unpractical as I am, I have surely forgotten a number of items.

And so we rolled East, I more devastated than braced with
the satisfaction of my passion, and she glowing with health,
her bi-iliac garland still as brief as a lad's, although she had added
two inches to her stature and eight pounds to her weight. We
had been everywhere. We had really seen nothing. And I catch
myself thinking today that our long journey had only defiled

with a sinuous trail of slime the lovely, trustful, dreamy, enormous country that by then, in retrospect, was no more to us than a collection of dog-eared maps, ruined tour books, old tires, and her sobs in the night—every night, every night—the moment I feigned sleep.

4

When, through decorations of light and shade, we drove up to 14 Thayer Street, a grave little lad met us with the keys and a note from Gaston who had rented the house for us. My Lo, without granting her new surroundings one glance, unseeingly turned on the radio to which instinct led her and lay down on the living room sofa with a batch of old magazines which in the same precise and blind manner she landed by dipping her hand into the nether anatomy of a lamp table.

I really did not mind where to dwell provided I could lock my Lolita up somewhere; but I had, I suppose, in the course of my correspondence with vague Gaston, vaguely visualized a house of ivied brick. Actually the place bore a dejected resemblance to the Haze home (a mere 400 miles distant): it was the same sort of dull gray frame affair with a shingled roof and dull green drill awnings; and the rooms, though smaller and furnished in a more consistent plush-and-plate style, were arranged in much the same order. My study turned out to be, however, a much larger room, lined from floor to ceiling with some two thousand books on chemistry which my landlord (on sabbatical leave for the time being) taught at Beardsley College.

I had hoped Beardsley School for girls, an expensive day school, with lunch thrown in and a glamorous gymnasium, would, while cultivating all those young bodies, provide some formal education for their minds as well. Gaston Godin, who was seldom right in his judgment of American habitus, had warned me that the institution might turn out to be one of those where girls are taught, as he put it with a foreigner's love for such things: "not to spell very well, but to smell very well." I don't think they achieved even that.

At my first interview with headmistress Pratt, she approved of my child's "nice blue eyes" (blue! Lolita!) and of my own friendship with that "French genius" (a genius! Gaston!)—and then, having turned Dolly over to a Miss Cormorant, she wrinkled her brow in a kind of *recueillement* and said:

"We are not so much concerned, Mr. Humbird, with having our students become bookworms or be able to reel off all the capitals of Europe which nobody knows anyway, or learn by heart the dates of forgotten battles. What we are concerned with is the adjustment of the child to group life. This is why we stress the four D's: Dramatics, Dance, Debating and Dating. We are confronted by certain facts. Your delightful Dolly will presently enter an age group where dates, dating, date dress, date book, date etiquette, mean as much to her as, say, business, business connections, business success, mean to you, or as much as [smiling] the happiness of my girls means to me. Dorothy Humbird is already involved in a whole system of social life which consists, whether we like it or not, of hot-dog stands, corner drugstores, malts and cokes, movies, square-dancing, blanket parties on beaches, and even hair-fixing parties! Naturally at Beardsley School we disapprove of some of these activities; and we rechannel others into more constructive directions. But we do try to turn our backs on the fog and squarely face the sunshine. To put it briefly, while adopting certain teaching techniques, we are more interested in communication than in composition. That is, with due respect to Shakespeare and others, we want our girls to *communicate* freely with the live world around them rather than plunge into musty old books. We are still groping perhaps, but we grope intelligently, like a gynecologist feeling a tumor. We think, Dr. Humburg, in organismal and organizational terms. We have done away with the mass of irrelevant topics that have traditionally been presented to young girls, leaving no place, in former days, for the knowledges and the skills, and the attitudes they will need in managing

1
2

their lives and—as the cynic might add—the lives of their husbands. Mr. Humberson, let us put it this way: the position of a star is important, but the most practical spot for an icebox in the kitchen may be even more important to the budding housewife. You say that all you expect a child to obtain from school is a sound education. But what do we mean by education? In the old days it was in the main a verbal phenomenon; I mean, you could have a child learn by heart a good encyclopedia and he or she would know as much as or more than a school could offer. Dr. Hummer, do you realize that for the modern pre-adolescent child, medieval dates are of less vital value than weekend ones [twinkle]?—to repeat a pun that I heard the Beardsley college psychoanalyst permit herself the other day. We live not only in a world of thoughts, but also in a world of things. Words without experience are meaningless. What on earth can Dorothy Hummerson care for Greece and the Orient with their harems and slaves?"

1

This program rather appalled me, but I spoke to two intelligent ladies who had been connected with the school, and they affirmed that the girls did quite a bit of sound reading and that the "communication" line was more or less ballyhoo aimed at giving old-fashioned Beardsley School a financially remunerative modern touch, though actually it remained as prim as a prawn.

Another reason attracting me to that particular school may seem funny to some readers, but it was very important to me, for that is the way I am made. Across our street, exactly in front of our house, there was, I noticed, a gap of weedy wasteland, with some colorful bushes and a pile of bricks and a few scattered planks, and the foam of shabby mauve and chrome autumn roadside flowers; and through that gap you could see a shimmery section of School Rd., running parallel to our Thayer St., and immediately beyond that, the playground of the school. Apart from the psychological comfort this general arrangement should afford me by keeping Dolly's day adjacent to mine, I immediately foresaw the pleasure I would have in distinguishing from my study-bedroom, by means of powerful binoculars, the statistically inevitable percentage of nymphets among the other girl-children playing around Dolly during recess; unfortunately, on the very first day of school, workmen arrived and put up a fence some way down the gap, and in no time a construction of tawny wood maliciously arose beyond that fence utterly blocking my magic vista; and as soon as they had erected a sufficient amount of material to spoil everything, those absurd builders suspended their work and never appeared again.

5

In a street called Thayer Street, in the residential green, fawn, and golden of a mellow academic townlet, one was bound to have a few amiable fine-dayers yelping at you. I prided myself on the exact temperature of my relations with them: never rude, always aloof. My west-door neighbor, who might have been a businessman or a college teacher, or both, would speak to me once in a while as he barbered some late garden blooms or watered his car, or, at a later date, defrosted his driveway (I don't mind if these verbs are all wrong), but my brief grunts, just sufficiently articulate to sound like conventional assents or interrogative pause-fillers, precluded any evolution toward chumminess. Of the two houses flanking the bit of scrubby waste opposite, one was closed, and the other contained two professors of English, tweedy and short-haired Miss Lester and fadedly feminine Miss Fabian, whose only subject of brief sidewalk conversation with me was (God bless their tact!) the young loveliness of my daughter and the naïve charm of Gaston Godin. My east-door neighbor was by far the most dangerous one, a sharp-nosed character whose late brother had been attached to the College as Superintendent of Buildings and Grounds. I remember her waylaying Dolly, while I stood at the living-room window, feverishly awaiting my darling's return from school. The odious spinster, trying to conceal her morbid in-quisitiveness under a mask of dulcet goodwill, stood leaning on her slim umbrella (the sleet had just stopped, a cold wet sun had sidled out), and Dolly, her brown coat open despite the raw weather, her structural heap of books pressed against her stomach, her knees showing pink above her clumsy wellingtons, a sheepish frightened little smile flitting over and off her snub-nosed face, which—owing perhaps to the pale wintry light—looked almost plain, in a rustic, German, *Mägdlein*-like way, as she stood there and dealt with Miss East's questions "And where is your mother, my dear? And what is your poor father's occupation? And where did you live before?" Another time the loathsome creature accosted me with a welcoming whine—but I evaded her; and a few days later there came from her a note in a blue-margined envelope, a nice mixture of poison and treacle, suggesting Dolly come over on a Sunday and curl up in a chair to look through the "loads of beautiful books my dear mother gave me when I was a child, instead of having the radio on at full blast till all hours of the night."

I had also to be careful in regard to a Mrs. Holigan, a char-woman and cook of sorts whom I had inherited with the vacuum cleaner from the previous tenants. Dolly got lunch at school, so that this was no trouble, and I had become adept at provid-ing her with a big breakfast and warming up the dinner that Mrs. Holigan prepared before leaving. That kindly and harm-less woman had, thank God, a rather bleary eye that missed details, and I had become a great expert in bedmaking; but still I was continuously obsessed by the feeling that some fatal stain had been left somewhere, or that, on the rare occasions where Holigan's presence happened to coincide with Lo's, simple Lo might succumb to buxom sympathy in the course of a cozy kitchen chat. I often felt we lived in a lighted house of glass, and that any moment some thin-lipped parchment face would peer through a carelessly unshaded window to obtain a free glimpse of things that the most jaded *voyeur* would have paid a small fortune to watch.

6

A word about Gaston Godin. The main reason why I enjoyed 1
—or at least tolerated with relief—his company was the spell of
absolute security that his ample person cast on my secret. Not
that he knew it; I had no special reason to confide in him, and
he was much too self-centered and abstract to notice or suspect
anything that might lead to a frank question on his part and a
frank answer on mine. He spoke well of me to Beardsleyans,
he was my good herald. Had he discovered *mes goûts* and 2
Lolita's status, it would have interested him only insofar as
throwing some light on the simplicity of my attitude toward
him, which attitude was as free of polite strain as it was of
ribald allusions; for despite his colorless mind and dim memory,
he was perhaps aware that I knew more about him than the
burghers of Beardsley did. He was a flabby, dough-faced, melancholy bachelor tapering upward to a pair of narrow, not quite
level shoulders and a conical pear-head which had sleek black
hair on one side and only a few plastered wisps on the other.
But the lower part of his body was enormous, and he ambulated
with a curious elephantine stealth by means of phenomenally
stout legs. He always wore black, even his tie was black; he 3
seldom bathed; his English was a burlesque. And, nonetheless,
everybody considered him to be a supremely lovable, lovably
freakish fellow! Neighbors pampered him; he knew by name
all the small boys in our vicinity (he lived a few blocks away
from me) and had some of them clean his sidewalk and burn
leaves in his back yard, and bring wood from his shed, and
even perform simple chores about the house, and he would
feed them fancy chocolates, with *real* liqueurs inside—in the
privacy of an orientally furnished den in his basement, with
amusing daggers and pistols arrayed on the moldy, rug-adorned
walls among the camouflaged hot-water pipes. Upstairs he had
a studio—he painted a little, the old fraud. He had decorated its
sloping wall (it was really not more than a garret) with large
photographs of pensive André Gide, Tchaïkovsky, Norman 4
Douglas, two other well-known English writers, Nijinsky (all 5

thighs and fig leaves), Harold D. Doublename (a misty-eyed left-wing professor at a Midwestern university) and Marcel Proust. All these poor people seemed about to fall on you from their inclined plane. He had also an album with snapshots of all the Jackies and Dickies of the neighborhood, and when I happened to thumb through it and make some casual remark, Gaston would purse his fat lips and murmur with a wistful pout "*Oui, ils sont gentils.*" His brown eyes would roam around the various sentimental and artistic bric-a-brac present, and his own banal *toiles* (the conventionally primitive eyes, sliced guitars, blue nipples and geometrical designs of the day), and with a vague gesture toward a painted wooden bowl or veined vase, he would say "*Prenez donc une de ces poires. La bonne dame d'en face m'en offre plus que je n'en peux savourer.*" Or: "*Missise Taille Lore vient de me donner ces dahlias, belles fleurs que j'exècre.*" (Somber, sad, full of world-weariness.)

For obvious reasons, I preferred my house to his for the games of chess we had two or three times weekly. He looked like some old battered idol as he sat with his pudgy hands in his lap and stared at the board as if it were a corpse. Wheezing he would meditate for ten minutes—then make a losing move. Or the good man, after even more thought, might utter: *Au roi!* with a slow old-dog woof that had a gargling sound at the back of it which made his jowls wabble; and then he would lift his circumflex eyebrows with a deep sigh as I pointed out to him that he was in check himself.

Sometimes, from where we sat in my cold study I could hear Lo's bare feet practicing dance techniques in the living room downstairs; but Gaston's outgoing senses were comfortably dulled, and he remained unaware of those naked rhythms—and-one, and-two, and-one, and-two, weight transferred on a straight right leg, leg up and out to the side, and-one, and-two, and only when she started jumping, opening her legs at the height of the jump, and flexing one leg, and extending the other, and flying, and landing on her toes—only then did my pale, pompous, morose opponent rub his head or cheek as if confusing those distant thuds with the awful stabs of my formidable Queen.

Sometimes Lola would slouch in while we pondered the board —and it was every time a treat to see Gaston, his elephant eye still fixed on his pieces, ceremoniously rise to shake hands with her, and forthwith release her limp fingers, and without looking once at her, descend again into his chair to topple into the trap I had laid for him. One day around Christmas, after I had not seen him for a fortnight or so, he asked me "*Et toutes vos fillettes, elles vont bien?*" from which it became evident to me that he had multiplied my unique Lolita by the number of sartorial categories his downcast moody eye had glimpsed during a whole series of her appearances: blue jeans, a skirt, shorts, a quilted robe.

I am loath to dwell so long on the poor fellow (sadly enough, a year later, during a voyage to Europe, from which he did not return, he got involved in a *sale histoire*, in Naples of all places!). I would have hardly alluded to him at all had not his Beardsley existence had such a queer bearing on my case. I need him for my defense. There he was, devoid of any talent whatsoever, a mediocre teacher, a worthless scholar, a glum repulsive fat old invert, highly contemptuous of the American way of life, triumphantly ignorant of the English language—there he was in priggish New England, crooned over by the old and caressed by the young—oh, having a grand time and fooling everybody; and here was I.

7

I am now faced with the distasteful task of recording a definite drop in Lolita's morals. If her share in the ardors she kindled had never amounted to much, neither had pure lucre ever come to the fore. But I was weak, I was not wise, my schoolgirl nymphet had me in thrall. With the human element dwindling, the passion, the tenderness, and the torture only increased; and of this she took advantage.

Her weekly allowance, paid to her under condition she fulfill her basic obligations, was twenty-one cents at the start of the

Beardsley era—and went up to one dollar five before its end. This was a more than generous arrangement seeing she constantly received from me all kinds of small presents and had for the asking any sweetmeat or movie under the moon—although, of course, I might fondly demand an additional kiss, or even a whole collection of assorted caresses, when I knew she coveted very badly some item of juvenile amusement. She was, however, not easy to deal with. Only very listlessly did she earn her three pennies—or three nickels—per day; and she proved to be a cruel negotiator whenever it was in her power to deny me certain life-wrecking, strange, slow paradisal philters without which I could not live more than a few days in a row, and which, because of the very nature of love's languor, I could not obtain by force. Knowing the magic and might of her own soft mouth, she managed—during one schoolyear!—to raise the bonus price of a fancy embrace to three, and even four bucks. O Reader! Laugh not, as you imagine me, on the very rack of joy noisily emitting dimes and quarters, and great big silver dollars like some sonorous, jingly and wholly demented machine vomiting riches; and in the margin of that leaping epilepsy she would firmly clutch a handful of coins in her little fist, which, anyway, I used to pry open afterwards unless she gave me the slip, scrambling away to hide her loot. And just as every other day I would cruise all around the school area and on comatose feet visit drugstores, and peer into foggy lanes, and listen to receding girl laughter in between my heart throbs and the falling leaves, so every now and then I would burgle her room and scrutinize torn papers in the wastebasket with the painted roses, and look under the pillow of the virginal bed I had just made myself. Once I found eight one-dollar notes in one of her books (fittingly—*Treasure Island*), and once a hole in the wall behind Whistler's Mother yielded as much as twenty-four dollars and some change—say twenty-four sixty—which I quietly removed, upon which, next day, she accused, to my face, honest Mrs. Holigan of being a filthy thief. Eventually, she lived up to her I.Q. by finding a safer hoarding place which I never discovered; but by that time I had brought prices down drastically by having her earn the hard and nauseous way permission to participate in the school's theatrical program; because what I feared most was not that she might ruin me, but that she might accumulate sufficient cash to run away. I believe the poor fierce-eyed child had figured out that with a mere fifty dollars in her purse she might somehow reach Broadway or Hollywood—or the foul kitchen of a diner (Help Wanted) in a dismal ex-prairie state, with the wind blowing, and the stars blinking, and the cars, and the bars, and the barmen, and everything soiled, torn, dead. 1

8

I did my best, your Honor, to tackle the problem of boys. Oh, I used even to read in the Beardsley *Star* a so-called Column for 2 Teens, to find out how to behave!

A word to fathers. Don't frighten away daughter's friend. Maybe it is a bit hard for you to realize that now the boys are finding her attractive. To you she is still a little girl. To the boys she's charming and fun, lovely and gay. They like her. Today you clinch big deals in an executive's office, but yesterday you were just highschool Jim carrying Jane's school books. Remember? Don't you want your daughter, now that her turn has come, to be happy in the admiration and company of boys she likes? Don't you want them to have wholesome fun together?

Wholesome fun? Good Lord!

Why not treat the young fellows as guests in your house? Why not make conversation with them? Draw them out, make them laugh and feel at ease?

Welcome, fellow, to this bordello.

If she breaks the rules don't explode out loud in front of her partner in crime. Let her take the brunt of your displeasure in private. And stop making the boys feel she's the daughter of an old ogre.

First of all the old ogre drew up a list under "absolutely forbidden" and another under "reluctantly allowed." Absolutely forbidden were dates, single or double or triple—the next step being of course mass orgy. She might visit a candy bar with her girl friends, and there giggle-chat with occasional young males, while I waited in the car at a discreet distance; and I promised her that if her group were invited by a socially acceptable group in Butler's Academy for Boys for their annual ball (heavily chaperoned, of course), I might consider the question whether a girl of fourteen can don her first "formal" (a kind of gown that makes thin-armed teen-agers look like flamingoes). Moreover, I promised her to throw a party at our house to which she would be allowed to invite her prettier girl friends and the nicer boys she would have met by that time at the Butler dance. But I was quite positive that as long as my regime lasted she would never, never be permitted to go with a youngster in rut to a movie, or neck in a car, or go to boy-girl parties at the houses of schoolmates, or indulge out of my earshot in boy-girl telephone conversations, even if "only discussing his relations with a friend of mine."

Lo was enraged by all this—called me a lousy crook and worse —and I would probably have lost my temper had I not soon discovered, to my sweetest relief, that what really angered her was my depriving her not of a specific satisfaction but of a general right. I was impinging, you see, on the conventional program, the stock pastimes, the "things that are done," the routine of youth; for there is nothing more conservative than a child, especially a girl-child, be she the most auburn and russet, the most mythopoeic nymphet in October's orchard-haze.

Do not misunderstand me. I cannot be absolutely certain that in the course of the winter she did not manage to have, in a casual way, improper contacts with unknown young fellows; of course, no matter how closely I controlled her leisure, there would constantly occur unaccounted-for time leaks with over-elaborate explanations to stop them up in retrospect; of course, my jealousy would constantly catch its jagged claw in the fine fabrics of nymphet falsity; but I did definitely feel—and can now vouchsafe for the accuracy of my feeling—that there was no reason for serious alarm. I felt that way not because I never once discovered any palpable hard young throat to crush among the masculine mutes that flickered somewhere in the background; but because it was to me "overwhelmingly obvious" (a favorite expression with my aunt Sybil) that all varieties of high school boys—from the perspiring nincompoop whom "holding hands" thrills, to the self-sufficient rapist with pustules and a souped-up car—equally bored my sophisticated young mistress. "All this noise about boys gags me," she had scrawled on the inside of a schoolbook, and underneath, in Mona's hand (Mona is due any minute now), there was the sly quip: "What about Rigger?" 1 (due too).

Faceless, then, are the chappies I happened to see in her company. There was for instance Red Sweater who one day, the day we had the first snow—saw her home; from the parlor window I observed them talking near our porch. She wore her first cloth coat with a fur collar; there was a small brown cap on my favorite hairdo—the fringe in front and the swirl at the sides and the natural curls at the back—and her damp-dark moccasins and white socks were more sloppy than ever. She pressed as usual her books to her chest while speaking or listening, and her feet gestured all the time: she would stand on her left instep with her right toe, remove it backward, cross her feet, rock slightly, sketch a few steps, and then start the series all over again. There was Windbreaker who talked to her in front of a restaurant one Sunday afternoon while his mother and sister attempted to walk me away for a chat; I dragged along and looked back at my only love. She had developed more than one conventional mannerism, such as the polite adolescent way of showing one is literally "doubled up" with laughter by inclining one's head, and so (as she sensed my call), still feigning helpless merriment, she walked backward a couple of steps, and then faced about, and walked toward me with a fading smile. On the other hand, I greatly liked—perhaps because it reminded me of her first unforgettable confession—her trick of sighing "oh dear!" in humorous wistful submission to fate, or emitting a long "no-o" in a deep almost growling undertone when the blow of fate had actually fallen. Above all—since we are speaking of movement and youth—I liked to see her spinning up and down Thayer Street on her beautiful young bicycle: rising on the pedals to work on them lustily, then sinking back in a languid posture while the speed wore itself off; and then she would stop at our mailbox and, still astride, would flip through a magazine she found there, and put it back, and press her tongue to one side of her upperlip and push off with her foot, and again sprint through pale shade and sun.

On the whole she seemed to me better adapted to her surroundings than I had hoped she would be when considering my spoiled slave-child and the bangles of demeanor she naïvely affected the winter before in California. Although I could never get used to the constant state of anxiety in which the guilty, the great, the tenderhearted live, I felt I was doing my best in the way of mimicry. As I lay on my narrow studio bed after a session of adoration and despair in Lolita's cold bedroom, I used to review the concluded day by checking my own image as it prowled rather than passed before the mind's red eye. I watched dark-and-handsome, not un-Celtic, probably high-church, possibly very high-church, Dr. Humbert see his daughter off to school. I watched him greet with his slow smile and pleasantly arched thick black ad-eyebrows good Mrs. Holigan, who smelled of the plague (and would head, I knew, for master's gin at the first opportunity). With Mr. West, retired executioner or writer of religious tracts—who cared?—I saw neighbor what's his name, I think they are French or Swiss, meditate in his frank-windowed study over a typewriter, rather gaunt-profiled, an almost Hitlerian cowlick on his pale brow. Weekends, wearing a well-tailored overcoat and brown gloves, Professor H. might be seen with his daughter strolling to Walton Inn (famous for its violet-ribboned china bunnies and chocolate boxes among which you sit and wait for a "table for two" still filthy with your predecessor's crumbs). Seen on weekdays, around one P.M., saluting with dignity Argus-eyed East while maneuvering the car out of the garage and around the damned evergreens, and down onto the slippery road. Raising

1

a cold eye from book to clock in the positively sultry Beardsley College library, among bulky young women caught and petrified in the overflow of human knowledge. Walking across the campus with the college clergyman, the Rev. Rigger (who also taught Bible in Beardsley School). "Somebody told me her mother was a celebrated actress killed in an airplane accident. Oh? My mistake, I presume. Is that so? I see. How sad." (Sublimating her mother, eh?) Slowly pushing my little pram through the labyrinth of the supermarket, in the wake of Professor W., also a slow-moving and gentle widower with the eyes of a goat. Shoveling the snow in my shirt-sleeves, a voluminous black and white muffler around my neck. Following with no show of rapacious haste (even taking time to wipe my feet on the mat) my schoolgirl daughter into the house. Taking Dolly to the dentist—pretty nurse beaming at her—old magazines—*ne montrez pas vos zhambes*. At dinner with Dolly in town, Mr. Edgar H. Humbert was seen eating his steak in the continental knife-and-fork manner. Enjoying, in duplicate, a concert: two marble-faced, becalmed Frenchmen sitting side by side, with Monsieur H. H.'s musical little girl on her father's right, and the musical little boy of Professor W. (father spending a hygienic evening in Providence) on Monsieur G. G.'s left. Opening the garage, a square of light that engulfs the car and is extinguished. Brightly pajamaed, jerking down the window shade in Dolly's bedroom. Saturday morning, unseen, solemnly weighing the winter-bleached lassie in the bathroom. Seen and heard Sunday morning, no churchgoer after all, saying don't be too late, to Dolly who is bound for the covered court. Letting in a queerly observant schoolmate of Dolly's: "First time I've seen a man wearing a smoking jacket, sir—except in movies, of course."

9

Her girl friends, whom I had looked forward to meet, proved on the whole disappointing. There was Opal Something, and Linda Hall, and Avis Chapman, and Eva Rosen, and Mona Dahl

1 (save one, all these names are approximations, of course). Opal was a bashful, formless, bespectacled, bepimpled creature who doted on Dolly who bullied her. With Linda Hall the school tennis champion, Dolly played singles at least twice a week: I suspect Linda was a true nymphet, but for some unknown reason she did not come—was perhaps not allowed to come—to our house; so I recall her only as a flash of natural sunshine on an indoor court. Of the rest, none had any claims to nymphetry except Eva Rosen. Avis was a plump lateral child with hairy legs, while Mona, though handsome in a coarse sensual way and only a year older than my aging mistress, had obviously long ceased to be a nymphet, if she ever had been one. Eva Rosen, a displaced little person from France, was on the other hand a good example of a not strikingly beautiful child revealing to the perspicacious amateur some of the basic elements of nymphet charm, such as a perfect pubescent figure and lingering eyes and high cheekbones. Her glossy copper hair had Lolita's silkiness, and the features of her delicate milky-white face with pink lips and silverfish eyelashes were less foxy than those of her likes—the great clan of intra-racial redheads; nor did she sport their green uniform but wore, as I remember her, a lot of black or cherry dark—a very smart black pullover, for instance, and high-heeled black shoes, and garnet-red fingernail polish. I spoke French to her (much to Lo's disgust). The child's tonalities were still admirably pure, but for school words and play words she resorted to current American and then a slight Brooklyn accent would crop up in her speech, which was amusing in a little Parisian who went to a select New England school with phoney British aspirations. Unfortunately, despite "that French kid's uncle" being "a millionaire," Lo dropped Eva for some reason before I had had time to enjoy in my modest way her fragrant presence in the Humbert open house. The reader knows what importance I attached to having a bevy of page girls, consolation prize nymphets, around my Lolita. For a while, I endeavored to interest my senses in Mona Dahl who was a good deal around, especially during the spring term when Lo and she got so enthusiastic about dramatics. I have often wondered what secrets outrageously treacherous

Dolores Haze had imparted to Mona while blurting out to me by urgent and well-paid request various really incredible details concerning an affair that Mona had had with a marine at the seaside. It was characteristic of Lo that she chose for her closest chum that elegant, cold, lascivious, experienced young female whom I once heard (misheard, Lo swore) cheerfully say in the hallway to Lo—who had remarked that her (Lo's) sweater was of virgin wool: "The only thing about you that is, kiddo..." She had a curiously husky voice, artificially waved dull dark hair, earrings, amber-brown prominent eyes and luscious lips. Lo said teachers had remonstrated with her on her loading herself with so much costume jewelry. Her hands trembled. She was burdened with a 150 I.Q. And I also know she had a tremendous chocolate-brown mole on her womanish back which I inspected the night Lo and she had worn low-cut pastel-colored, vaporous dresses for a dance at the Butler Academy.

I am anticipating a little, but I cannot help running my memory all over the keyboard of that school year. In meeting my attempts to find out what kind of boys Lo knew, Miss Dahl was elegantly evasive. Lo who had gone to play tennis at Linda's country club had telephoned she might be a full half hour late, and so, would I entertain Mona who was coming to practice with her a scene from *The Taming of the Shrew*. Using all the modulations, all the allure of manner and voice she was capable of and staring at me with perhaps—could I be mistaken?—a faint gleam of crystalline irony, beautiful Mona replied: "Well, sir, the fact is Dolly is not much concerned with mere boys. Fact is, we are rivals. She and I have a crush on the Reverend Rigger." (This was a joke—I have already mentioned that gloomy giant of a man, with the jaw of a horse: he was to bore me to near murder with his impressions of Switzerland at a tea party for parents that I am unable to place correctly in terms of time.)

How had the ball been? Oh, it had been a riot. A what? A panic. Terrific, in a word. Had Lo danced a lot? Oh, not a frightful lot, just as much as she could stand. What did she, languorous Mona, think of Lo? Sir? Did she think Lo was doing well at school? Gosh, she certainly was quite a kid. But her general behavior was—? Oh, she was a swell kid. But still? "Oh, she's a doll," concluded Mona, and sighed abruptly, and picked up a book that happened to lie at hand, and with a change of expression, falsely furrowing her brow, inquired: "Do tell me about 1 Ball Zack, sir. Is he really that good?" She moved up so close to my chair that I made out through lotions and creams her uninteresting skin scent. A sudden odd thought stabbed me: was my Lo playing the pimp? If so, she had found the wrong substitute. Avoiding Mona's cool gaze, I talked literature for a minute. Then Dolly arrived—and slit her pale eyes at us. I left the two friends to their own devices. One of the latticed squares in a small cobwebby casement window at the turn of the staircase was glazed with ruby, and that raw wound among the unstained rectangles and its asymmetrical position—a knight's move from the top—always strangely disturbed me.

10

Sometimes . . . Come on, how often exactly, Bert? Can you recall four, five, more such occasions? Or would no human heart have survived two or three? Sometimes (I have nothing to say in reply to your question), while Lolita would be haphazardly preparing her homework, sucking a pencil, lolling sideways in an easy chair with both legs over its arm, I would shed all my pedagogic restraint, dismiss all our quarrels, forget all my masculine pride—and literally crawl on my knees to your chair, my 2 Lolita! You would give me one look—a gray furry question mark of a look: "Oh no, not again" (incredulity, exasperation); for you never deigned to believe that I could, without any specific designs, ever crave to bury my face in your plaid skirt, my darling! The fragility of those bare arms of yours—how I longed to enfold them, all your four limpid lovely limbs, a folded colt, and take your head between my unworthy hands, and pull the temple-skin back on both sides, and kiss your chinesed eyes, and— "Pulease, leave me alone, will you," you would say, "for Christ's sake leave me alone." And I would get up from the floor while you looked on, your face deliberately twitching in imitation of my *tic nerveux*. But never mind, never mind, I am only a brute, never mind, let us go on with my miserable story.

11

One Monday forenoon, in December I think, Pratt asked me to come over for a talk. Dolly's last report had been poor, I knew. But instead of contenting myself with some such plausible explanation of this summons, I imagined all sorts of horrors, and had to fortify myself with a pint of my "pin" before I could face the interview. Slowly, all Adam's apple and heart, I went up the steps of the scaffold.

A huge woman, gray-haired, frowsy, with a broad flat nose and small eyes behind black-rimmed glasses—"Sit down," she said, pointing to an informal and humiliating hassock, while she perched with ponderous spryness on the arm of an oak chair. For a moment or two, she peered at me with smiling curiosity. She had done it at our first meeting, I recalled, but I could afford then to scowl back. Her eye left me. She lapsed into thought—probably assumed. Making up her mind she rubbed, fold on fold, her dark gray flannel skirt at the knee, dispelling a trace of chalk or something. Then she said, still rubbing, not looking up:

"Let me ask a blunt question, Mr. Haze. You are an old-fashioned Continental father, aren't you?"

"Why, no," I said, "conservative, perhaps, but not what you would call old-fashioned." 1

She sighed, frowned, then clapped her big plump hands together in a let's-get-down-to-business manner, and again fixed her beady eyes upon me.

"Dolly Haze," she said, "is a lovely child, but the onset of sexual maturing seems to give her trouble."

I bowed slightly. What else could I do?

"She is still shuttling," said Miss Pratt, showing how with her liver-spotted hands, "between the anal and genital zones of development. Basically she is a lovely—"

"I beg your pardon," I said, "what zones?"

"That's the old-fashioned European in you!" cried Pratt delivering a slight tap on my wrist watch and suddenly disclosing her dentures. "All I mean is that biologic and psychologic drives —do you smoke?—are not fused in Dolly, do not fall so to speak into a—into a rounded pattern." Her hands held for a moment an invisible melon.

"She is attractive, bright though careless" (breathing heavily, without leaving her perch, the woman took time out to look at the lovely child's report sheet on the desk at her right). "Her marks are getting worse and worse. Now I wonder, Mr. Haze—" Again the false meditation.

"Well," she went on with zest, "as for me, I do smoke, and, as dear Dr. Pierce used to say: I'm not proud of it but I jeest love it." She lit up and the smoke she exhaled from her nostrils was like a pair of tusks.

"Let me give you a few details, it won't take a moment. Now let me see [rummaging among her papers]. She is defiant toward Miss Redcock and impossibly rude to Miss Cormorant. Now here is one of our special research reports: Enjoys singing with group in class though mind seems to wander. Crosses her knees and wags left leg to rhythm. Type of by-words: a two-hundred-forty-two word area of the commonest pubescent slang fenced in by a number of obviously European polysyllabics. Sighs a good deal in class. Let me see. Yes. Now comes the last week in November. Sighs a good deal in class. Chews gum vehemently. Does not bite her nails though if she did, this would conform better to her general pattern—scientifically speaking, of course. Menstruation, according to the subject, well established. Belongs at present to no church organization. By the way, Mr. Haze, her mother was—? Oh, I see. And you are—? Nobody's business is, I suppose, God's business. Something else we wanted to know. She has no regular home duties, I understand. Making a princess of your Dolly, Mr. Haze, eh? Well, what else have we got here? Handles books gracefully. Voice pleasant. Giggles rather often. A littly dreamy. Has private jokes of her own, transposing for instance the first letters of some of her teachers' names. Hair light and dark brown, lustrous—well [laughing] you are aware of *that*, I suppose. Nose unobstructed, feet high-arched, eyes—let me see, I had here somewhere a still more recent report. Aha, here we are. Miss Gold says Dolly's tennis form is excellent to superb, even better than Linda Hall's, but concentration and point-accumulation are just "poor to fair." Miss Cormorant cannot decide whether Dolly has exceptional emotional control or none at all. Miss Horn reports she—I mean, Dolly—cannot verbalize her emotions, while according to Miss Cole Dolly's metabolic efficiency is superfine. Miss Molar thinks Dolly is myopic and should see a good ophthalmologist, but Miss Redcock insists that the girl simulates eye-strain to get away with scholastic incompetence. And to conclude, Mr. Haze, our researchers are wondering about something really crucial. Now I want to ask you something. I want to know if your poor wife, or yourself, or anyone else in the family—I understand she has several aunts and a maternal grandfather in California?—oh, *had!*—I'm sorry—well, we all wonder if anybody in the family has instructed Dolly in the process of mammalian reproduction. The general impression is that fifteen-year-old Dolly remains morbidly uninterested in sexual matters, or to be exact, represses her curiosity in order to save her ignorance and self-dignity. All right—fourteen. You see, Mr. Haze, Beardsley School does not believe in bees and blossoms, and storks and love birds, but it does believe very strongly in preparing its students for mutually satisfactory mating and successful child rearing. We feel Dolly could make excellent progress if only she would put her mind to her work. Miss Cormorant's report is significant in that respect. Dolly is inclined to be, mildly speaking, impudent. But all feel that *primo*, you should have your family doctor tell her the facts of life and, *secundo*, that you allow her to enjoy the company of her schoolmates' brothers at the Junior Club or in Dr. Rigger's organization, or in the lovely homes of our parents."

"She may meet boys at her own lovely home," I said.

"I hope she will," said Pratt buoyantly. "'When we questioned her about her troubles, Dolly refused to discuss the home situation, but we have spoken to some of her friends and really—well, for example, we insist you un-veto her nonparticipation in the dramatic group. You just must allow her to take part in *The Hunted Enchanters*. She was such a perfect little nymph in the try-out, and sometime in spring the author will stay for a few days at Beardsley College and may attend a rehearsal or two in our new auditorium. I mean it is all part of the fun of being young and alive and beautiful. You must understand—"

"I always thought of myself," I said, "as a very understanding father."

"Oh no doubt, no doubt, but Miss Cormorant thinks, and I am inclined to agree with her, that Dolly is obsessed by sexual thoughts for which she finds no outlet, and will tease and martyrize other girls, or even our younger instructors because *they* do have innocent dates with boys."

Shrugged my shoulders. A shabby *émigré*.

"Let us put our two heads together, Mr. Haze. What on earth is wrong with that child?"

"She seems quite normal and happy to me," I said (disaster coming at last? was I found out? had they got some hypnotist?).

"What worries me," said Miss Pratt looking at her watch and starting to go over the whole subject again, "is that both teachers and schoolmates find Dolly antagonistic, dissatisfied, cagey—and everybody wonders why you are so firmly opposed to all the natural recreations of a normal child."

"Do you mean sex play?" I asked jauntily, in despair, a cornered old rat.

"Well, I certainly welcome this civilized terminology," said Pratt with a grin. "But this is not quite the point. Under the auspices of Beardsley School, dramatics, dances and other natural activities are not technically sex play, though girls do meet boys, if that is what you object to."

"All right," I said, my hassock exhaling a weary sigh. "You win. She can take part in that play. Provided male parts are taken by female parts."

"I am always fascinated," said Pratt, "by the admirable way foreigners—or at least naturalized Americans—use our rich language. I'm sure Miss Gold, who conducts the play group, will be overjoyed. I notice she is one of the few teachers that seem to like—I mean who seem to find Dolly manageable. This takes care of general topics, I guess; now comes a special matter. We are in trouble again."

Pratt paused truculently, then rubbed her index finger under her nostrils with such vigor that her nose performed a kind of war dance.

"I'm a frank person," she said, "but conventions are conventions, and I find it difficult... Let me put it this way... The Walkers, who live in what we call around here the Duke's Manor, you know the great gray house on the hill—they send their two girls to our school, and we have the niece of President Moore with us, a really gracious child, not to speak of a number of other prominent children. Well, under the circumstances, it is rather a jolt when Dolly, who looks like a little lady, uses words which you as a foreigner probably simply do not know or do not understand. Perhaps it might be better—Would you like me to have Dolly come up here right away to discuss things? No? You see—oh well, let's have it out. Dolly has written a most obscene four-letter word which our Dr. Cutler tells me is low-Mexican for urinal with her lipstick on some health pamphlets which Miss Redcock, who is getting married in June, distributed among the girls, and we thought she should stay after hours—another half hour at least. But if you like—"

"No," I said, "I don't want to interfere with rules. I shall talk to her later. I shall thrash it out."

"Do," said the woman rising from her chair arm. "And perhaps we can get together again soon, and if things do not improve we might have Dr. Cutler analyze her."

Should I marry Pratt and strangle her?

"... And perhaps your family doctor might like to examine her physically—just a routine check-up. She is in Mushroom—the last classroom along that passage."

Beardsley School, it may be explained, copied a famous girls' school in England by having "traditional" nicknames for its various classrooms: Mushroom, Room-In 8, B-room, Room-BA and so on. Mushroom was smelly, with a sepia print of Reynolds' "Age of Innocence" above the chalkboard, and several rows of clumsy-looking pupil desks. At one of these, my Lolita was reading the chapter on "Dialogue" in Baker's *Dramatic Technique*, and all was very quiet, and there was another girl with a very naked, porcelain-white neck and wonderful platinum hair, who sat in front reading too, absolutely lost to the world and interminably winding a soft curl around one finger, and I sat beside Dolly just behind that neck and that hair, and unbuttoned my overcoat and for sixty-five cents plus the permission to participate in the school play, had Dolly put her inky, chalky, red-knuckled hand under the desk. Oh, stupid and reckless of me, no doubt, but after the torture I had been subjected to, I simply had to take advantage of a combination that I knew would never occur again.

12

Around Christmas she caught a bad chill and was examined by a friend of Miss Lester, a Dr. Ilse Tristramson (hi, Ilse, you were a dear, uninquisitive soul, and you touched my dove very gently). She diagnosed bronchitis, patted Lo on the back (all its bloom erect because of the fever) and put her to bed for a week or longer. At first she "ran a temperature" in American parlance, and I could not resist the exquisite caloricity of unexpected delights—Venus febriculosa—though it was a very languid Lolita that moaned and coughed and shivered in my embrace. And as soon as she was well again, I threw a Party with Boys.

Perhaps I had drunk a little too much in preparation for the ordeal. Perhaps I made a fool of myself. The girls had decorated and plugged in a small fir tree—German custom, except that colored bulbs had superseded wax candles. Records were chosen and fed into my landlord's phonograph. Chic Dolly wore a nice gray dress with fitted bodice and flared skirt. Humming, I retired to my study upstairs—and then every ten or twenty minutes I would come down like an idiot just for a few seconds; to pick up ostensibly my pipe from the mantelpiece or hunt for the newspaper; and with every new visit these simple actions became harder to perform, and I was reminded of the dreadfully distant days when I used to brace myself to casually enter a room in the Ramsdale house where Little Carmen was on.

The party was not a success. Of the three girls invited, one did not come at all, and one of the boys brought his cousin Roy, so there was a superfluity of two boys, and the cousins knew all the steps, and the other fellows could hardly dance at all, and most of the evening was spent in messing up the kitchen, and then endlessly jabbering about what card game to play, and sometime later, two girls and four boys sat on the floor of the living room, with all windows open, and played a word game which Opal could not be made to understand, while Mona and Roy, a lean handsome lad, drank ginger ale in the kitchen, sitting on the table and dangling their legs, and hotly discussing Predestination and the Law of Averages. After they had all gone my Lo said ugh, closed her eyes, and dropped into a chair with all four limbs starfished to express the utmost disgust and exhaustion and swore it was the most revolting bunch of boys she had ever seen. I bought her a new tennis racket for that remark.

January was humid and warm, and February fooled the forsythia: none of the townspeople had ever *seen* such weather. Other presents came tumbling in. For her birthday I bought her a bicycle, the doe-like and altogether charming machine already mentioned—and added to this a *History of Modern American Painting:* her bicycle manner, I mean her approach to it, the hip movement in mounting, the grace and so on, afforded me supreme pleasure; but my attempt to refine her pictorial taste was a failure; she wanted to know if the guy noon-napping on Doris Lee's hay was the father of the pseudo-voluptuous hoyden in the foreground, and could not understand why I said Grant Wood or Peter Hurd was good, and Reginald Marsh or Frederick Waugh awful.

1

13

By the time spring had touched up Thayer Street with yellow and green and pink, Lolita was irrevocably stage-struck. Pratt, whom I chanced to notice one Sunday lunching with some people at Walton Inn, caught my eye from afar and went through the motion of sympathetically and discreetly clapping her hands while Lo was not looking. I detest the theatre as being a primitive and putrid form, historically speaking; a form that smacks of stone-age rites and communal nonsense despite those individual injections of genius, such as, say, Elizabethan poetry which a closeted reader automatically pumps out of the stuff. Being much occupied at the time with my own literary labors, I did not bother to read the complete text of *The Enchanted Hunters,* the playlet in which Dolores Haze was assigned the part of a farmer's daughter who imagines herself to be a woodland witch, or Diana, or something, and who, having got hold of a book on hypnotism, plunges a number of lost hunters into various entertaining trances before falling in her turn under the spell of a vagabond poet (Mona Dahl). That much I gleaned from bits of crumpled and poorly typed script that Lo sowed all over the house. The coincidence of the title with the name of an unforgettable inn was pleasant in a sad little way: I wearily thought I had better not bring it to my own enchantress's notice, lest a brazen accusation of mawkishness hurt me even more than her failure to notice it for herself had done. I assumed the playlet was just another, practically anonymous, version of some banal legend. Nothing prevented one, of course, from supposing that in quest of an attractive name the founder of the hotel had been immediately and solely influenced by the chance fantasy of the second-rate muralist he had hired, and that subsequently the hotel's name had suggested the play's title. But in my credulous, simple, benevolent mind I happened to twist it the other way round, and without giving the whole matter much thought really, supposed that mural, name and title had all been derived from a common source, from some local tradition, which I, an alien unversed in New England lore, would not be supposed to know.

Lolita

In consequence I was under the impression (all this quite casually, you understand, quite outside any orbit of importance) that the accursed playlet belonged to the type of whimsey for juvenile consumption, arranged and rearranged many times, such as *Hansel and Gretel* by Richard Roe, or *The Sleeping Beauty* 1, 2 by Dorothy Doe, or *The Emperor's New Clothes* by Maurice Vermont and Marion Rumpelmeyer—all this to be found in any 3 *Plays for School Actors* or *Let's Have a Play!* In other words, I did not know—and would not have cared, if I did—that actually *The Enchanted Hunters* was a quite recent and technically original composition which had been produced for the first time only three or four months ago by a highbrow group in New York. To me—inasmuch as I could judge from my charmer's part—it seemed to be a pretty dismal kind of fancy work, with echoes from Lenormand and Maeterlinck and various quiet 4, 5 British dreamers. The red-capped, uniformly attired hunters, of 6 which one was a banker, another a plumber, a third a policeman, a fourth an undertaker, a fifth an underwriter, a sixth an escaped convict (you see the possibilities!), went through a complete change of mind in Dolly's Dell, and remembered their real lives only as dreams or nightmares from which little Diana had aroused them; but a seventh Hunter (in a *green* cap, the fool) 7 was a Young Poet, and he insisted, much to Diana's annoyance, that she and the entertainment provided (dancing nymphs, and elves, and monsters) were his, the Poet's, invention. I under- 8 stand that finally, in utter disgust at this cocksureness, barefooted Dolores was to lead check-trousered Mona to the paternal farm behind the Perilous Forest to prove to the braggard she was not a poet's fancy, but a rustic, down-to-brown-earth lass—and a last-minute kiss was to enforce the play's profound message, namely, that mirage and reality merge in love. I considered it wiser not to criticize the thing in front of Lo: she was so healthily en-grossed in "problems of expression," and so charmingly did she put her narrow Florentine hands together, batting her eyelashes and pleading with me not to come to rehearsals as some ridicu-lous parents did because she wanted to dazzle me with a perfect First Night—and because I was, anyway, always butting in and saying the wrong thing, and cramping her style in the presence of other people.

There was one very special rehearsal . . . my heart, my heart . . . there was one day in May marked by a lot of gay flurry—it all rolled past, beyond my ken, immune to my memory, and when I saw Lo next, in the late afternoon, balancing on her bike, pressing the palm of her hand to the damp bark of a young birch tree on the edge of our lawn, I was so struck by the radiant tenderness of her smile that for an instant I believed all our troubles gone. "Can you remember," she said, "what was the name of that hotel, *you* know [nose puckered], come on, you know—with those white columns and the marble swan in the lobby? Oh, you know [noisy exhalation of breath]—the hotel where you raped me. Okay, skip it. I mean, was it [almost in a whisper] The Enchanted Hunters? Oh, it was? [musingly] Was it?"—and with a yelp of amorous vernal laughter she slapped the glossy bole and tore uphill, to the end of the street, and then rode back, feet at rest on stopped pedals, posture relaxed, one hand dreaming in her print-flowered lap.

14

Because it supposedly tied up with her interest in dance and dramatics, I had permitted Lo to take piano lessons with a Miss Emperor (as we French scholars may conveniently call her) to whose blue-shuttered little white house a mile or so beyond Beardsley Lo would spin off twice a week. One Friday night toward the end of May (and a week or so after the very special rehearsal Lo had not had me attend) the telephone in my study, where I was in the act of mopping up Gustave's—I mean Gaston's—king's side, rang and Miss Emperor asked if Lo was coming next Tuesday because she had missed last Tuesday's and today's lessons. I said she would by all means—and went on with the game. As the reader may well imagine, my faculties were now impaired, and a move or two later, with Gaston to play, I noticed

through the film of my general distress that he could collect my queen; he noticed it too, but thinking it might be a trap on the part of his tricky opponent, he demurred for quite a minute, and puffed and wheezed, and shook his jowls, and even shot furtive glances at me, and made hesitating half-thrusts with his pudgily bunched fingers—dying to take that juicy queen and not daring—and all of a sudden he swooped down upon it (who knows if it did not teach him certain later audacities?), and I spent a dreary hour in achieving a draw. He finished his brandy and presently lumbered away, quite satisfied with this result (*mon pauvre ami, je ne vous ai jamais revu et quoiqu'il y ait bien peu de chance que vous voyiez mon livre, permettez-moi de vous dire que je vous serre la main bien cordialement, et que toutes mes fillettes vous saluent*). I found Dolores Haze at the kitchen 1
table, consuming a wedge of pie, with her eyes fixed on her script. They rose to meet mine with a kind of celestial vapidity. She remained singularly unruffled when confronted with my discovery, and said *d'un petit air faussement contrit* that she 2
knew she was a very wicked kid, but simply had not been able to resist the enchantment, and had used up those music hours—O Reader, My Reader!—in a nearby public park rehearsing the magic forest scene with Mona. I said "fine"—and stalked to the 3
telephone. Mona's mother answered: "Oh yes, she's in" and retreated with a mother's neutral laugh of polite pleasure to shout off stage "Roy calling!" and the very next moment Mona rustled up, and forthwith, in a low monotonous not untender voice started berating Roy for something he had said or done and I interrupted her, and presently Mona was saying in her humblest, sexiest contralto, "yes, sir," "surely, sir," "I am alone to blame, sir, in this unfortunate business," (what elocution! what poise!) "honest, I feel very bad about it"—and so on and so forth as those little harlots say.

So downstairs I went clearing my throat and holding my heart. Lo was now in the living room, in her favorite overstuffed chair. As she sprawled there, biting at a hangnail and mocking me with her heartless vaporous eyes, and all the time rocking a stool upon which she had placed the heel of an outstretched shoeless foot, I perceived all at once with a sickening qualm how much she had changed since I first met her two years ago. Or had this happened during those last two weeks? *Tendresse?* Surely that was an exploded myth. She sat right in the focus of my incandescent anger. The fog of all lust had been swept away leaving nothing but this dreadful lucidity. Oh, she had changed! Her complexion was now that of any vulgar untidy highschool girl who applies shared cosmetics with grubby fingers to an unwashed face and does not mind what soiled texture, what pustulate epidermis comes in contact with her skin. Its smooth tender bloom had been so lovely in former days, so bright with tears, when I used to roll, in play, her tousled head on my knee. A coarse flush had now replaced that innocent fluorescence. What was locally known as a "rabbit cold" had painted with flaming pink the edges of her contemptuous nostrils. As in terror I lowered my gaze, it mechanically slid along the underside of her tensely stretched bare thigh—how polished and muscular her legs had grown! She kept her wide-set eyes, clouded-glass gray and slightly bloodshot, fixed upon me, and I saw the stealthy thought showing through them that perhaps after all Mona was right, and she, orphan Lo, could expose me without getting penalized herself. How wrong I was. How mad I was! Everything about her was of the same exasperating impenetrable order —the strength of her shapely legs, the dirty sole of her white sock, the thick sweater she wore despite the closeness of the room, her wenchy smell, and especially the dead end of her face with its strange flush and freshly made-up lips. Some of the red had left stains on her front teeth, and I was struck by a ghastly recollection—the evoked image not of Monique, but of another young prostitute in a bell-house, ages ago, who had been snapped up by somebody else before I had time to decide whether her mere youth warranted my risking some appalling disease, and who had just such flushed prominent *pommettes* and a dead *maman*, and big front teeth, and a bit of dingy red ribbon in her country-brown hair.

"Well, speak," said Lo. "Was the corroboration satisfactory?"

"Oh, yes," I said. "Perfect. Yes. And I do not doubt you two made it up. As a matter of fact, I do not doubt you have told her everything about us."

"Oh, yah?"

I controlled my breath and said: "Dolores, this must stop right away. I am ready to yank you out of Beardsley and lock you up you know where, but this must stop. I am ready to take you away the time it takes to pack a suitcase. This must stop or else anything may happen."

"Anything may happen, huh?"

I snatched away the stool she was rocking with her heel and her foot fell with a thud on the floor.

"Hey," she cried, "take it easy."

"First of all you go upstairs," I cried in my turn,—and simultaneously grabbed at her and pulled her up. From that moment, I stopped restraining my voice, and we continued yelling at each other, and she said unprintable things. She said she loathed me. She made monstrous faces at me, inflating her cheeks and producing a diabolical plopping sound. She said I had attempted to violate her several times when I was her mother's roomer. She said she was sure I had murdered her mother. She said she would sleep with the very first fellow who asked her and I could do nothing about it. I said she was to go upstairs and show me all her hiding places. It was a strident and hateful scene. I held her by her knobby wrist and she kept turning and twisting it this way and that, surreptitiously trying to find a weak point so as to wrench herself free at a favorable moment, but I held her quite hard and in fact hurt her rather badly for which I hope my heart may rot, and once or twice she jerked her arm so violently that I feared her wrist might snap, and all the while she stared at me with those unforgettable eyes where cold anger and hot tears struggled, and our voices were drowning the telephone, and when I grew aware of its ringing she instantly escaped.

With people in movies I seem to share the services of the machina telephonica and its sudden god. This time it was an irate neighbor. The east window happened to be agape in the living room, with the blind mercifully down, however; and behind it the damp black night of a sour New England spring had been breathlessly listening to us. I had always thought that type of haddocky spinster with the obscene mind was the result of considerable literary inbreeding in modern fiction; but now I am convinced that prude and prurient Miss East—or to explode her incognito, Miss Fenton Lebone—had been probably protruding three-quarter-way from her bedroom window as she strove to catch the gist of our quarrel.

"... This racket ... lacks all sense of ..." quacked the receiver, "we do not live in a tenement here. I must emphatically ..."

I apologized for my daughter's friends being so loud. Young people, you know—and cradled the next quack and a half.

Downstairs the screen door banged. Lo? Escaped?

Through the casement on the stairs I saw a small impetuous ghost slip through the shrubs; a silvery dot in the dark—hub of bicycle wheel—moved, shivered, and she was gone.

It so happened that the car was spending the night in a repair shop downtown. I had no other alternative than to pursue on foot the winged fugitive. Even now, after more than three years have heaved and elapsed, I cannot visualize that spring-night street, that already so leafy street, without a gasp of panic. Before their lighted porch Miss Lester was promenading Miss Fabian's dropsical dackel. Mr. Hyde almost knocked it over. Walk three steps and run three. A tepid rain started to drum on the chestnut leaves. At the next corner, pressing Lolita against an iron railing, a blurred youth held and kissed—no, not her, mistake. My talons still tingling, I flew on.

Half a mile or so east of number fourteen, Thayer Street tangles with a private lane and a cross street; the latter leads to the town proper; in front of the first drugstore, I saw—with what melody of relief!—Lolita's fair bicycle waiting for her. I pushed instead of pulling, pulled, pushed, pulled, and entered. Look out! Some ten paces away Lolita, through the glass of a telephone booth (membranous god still with us), cupping the tube, confidentially hunched over it, slit her eyes at me, turned away

with her treasure, hurriedly hung up, and walked out with a 1
flourish.

"Tried to reach you at home," she said brightly. "A great
decision has been made. But first buy me a drink, dad."

She watched the listless pale fountain girl put in the ice, pour
in the coke, add the cherry syrup—and my heart was bursting
with love-ache. That childish wrist. My lovely child. You have a
lovely child, Mr. Humbert. We always admire her as she passes
by. Mr. Pim watched Pippa suck in the concoction. 2

J'ai toujours admiré l'œuvre ormonde du sublime Dublinois. 3
And in the meantime the rain had become a voluptuous shower.

"Look," she said as she rode the bike beside me, one foot
scraping the darkly glistening sidewalk, "look, I've decided something. I want to leave school. I hate that school. I hate the play,
I really do! Never go back. Find another. Leave at once. Go for
a long trip again. But *this* time we'll go wherever *I* want, won't
we?"

I nodded. My Lolita.

"I choose? *C'est entendu?*" she asked wobbling a little beside 4
me. Used French only when she was a very good little girl.

"Okay. *Entendu.* Now hop-hop-hop, Lenore, or you'll get 5
soaked." (A storm of sobs was filling my chest.)

She bared her teeth and after her adorable school-girl fashion,
leaned forward, and away she sped, my bird.

Miss Lester's finely groomed hand held a porch-door open for
a waddling old dog *qui prenait son temps.* 6

Lo was waiting for me near the ghostly birch tree.

"I am drenched," she declared at the top of her voice. "Are
you glad? To hell with the play! See what I mean?"

An invisible hag's claw slammed down an upper-floor window.

In our hallway, ablaze with welcoming lights, my Lolita
peeled off her sweater, shook her gemmed hair, stretched towards
me two bare arms, raised one knee:

"Carry me upstairs, please. I feel sort of romantic to-night."

It may interest physiologists to learn, at this point, that I have
the ability—a most singular case, I presume—of shedding torrents of tears throughout the other tempest.

15

The brakes were relined, the waterpipes unclogged, the valves ground, and a number of other repairs and improvements were paid for by not very mechanically-minded but prudent papa Humbert, so that the late Mrs. Humbert's car was in respectable shape when ready to undertake a new journey.

We had promised Beardsley School, good old Beardsley School, that we would be back as soon as my Hollywood engagement came to an end (inventive Humbert was to be, I hinted, chief consultant in the production of a film dealing with "existentialism," still a hot thing at the time). Actually I was toying with the idea of gently trickling across the Mexican border—I was braver now than last year—and there deciding what to do with my little concubine who was now sixty inches tall and weighed ninety pounds. We had dug out our tour books and maps. She had traced our route with immense zest. Was it thanks to those theatricals that she had now outgrown her juvenile jaded airs and was so adorably keen to explore rich reality? I experienced the queer lightness of dreams that pale but warm Sunday morning when we abandoned Professor Chem's puzzled house and sped along Main Street toward the four-lane highway. My Love's striped, black-and-white, cotton frock, jaunty blue cap, white socks and brown moccasins were not quite in keeping with the large beautifully cut aquamarine on a silver chainlet, which gemmed her throat: a spring rain gift from me. We passed the New Hotel, and she laughed. "A penny for your thoughts," I said and she stretched out her palm at once, but at that moment I had to apply the brakes rather abruptly at a red light. As we pulled up, another car came to a gliding stop alongside, and a very striking looking, athletically lean young woman (where had I seen her?) with a high complexion and shoulder-length brilliant bronze hair, greeted Lo with a ringing "Hi!"— and then, addressing me, effusively, edusively (placed!), stressing certain words, said: "What a *shame* it was to *tear* Dolly away from the play—you should have *heard* the author *raving* about her after that rehearsal—" "Green light, you dope," said Lo

208

under her breath, and simultaneously, waving in bright adieu a bangled arm, Joan of Arc (in a performance we saw at the local theatre) violently outdistanced us to swerve into Campus Avenue.

"Who was it exactly? Vermont or Rumpelmeyer?"

"No—Edusa Gold—the gal who coaches us." 1

"I was not referring to her. Who exactly concocted that play?"

"Oh! Yes, of course. Some old woman, Clare Something, I 2 guess. There was quite a crowd of them there."

"So she complimented you?"

"Complimented my eye—she kissed me on my pure brow"— and my darling emitted that new yelp of merriment which— perhaps in connection with her theatrical mannerisms—she had lately begun to affect.

"You are a funny creature, Lolita," I said—or some such words. "Naturally, I am overjoyed you gave up that absurd stage business. But what is curious is that you dropped the whole thing only a week before its natural climax. Oh, Lolita, you should be 3 careful of those surrenders of yours. I remember you gave up Ramsdale for camp, and camp for a joyride, and I could list other abrupt changes in your disposition. You must be careful. There are things that should never be given up. You must persevere. You should try to be a little nicer to me, Lolita. You should also watch your diet. The tour of your thigh, you know, should not exceed seventeen and a half inches. More might be fatal (I was kidding, of course). We are now setting out on a long happy journey. I remember—"

16

I remember as a child in Europe gloating over a map of North America that had "Appalachian Mountains" boldly running from Alabama up to New Brunswick, so that the whole region they spanned—Tennessee, the Virginias, Pennsylvania, New York, Vermont, New Hampshire and Maine, appeared to my

imagination as a gigantic Switzerland or even Tibet, all mountain, glorious diamond peak upon peak, giant conifers, *le*
1   *montagnard émigré* in his bear skin glory, and *Felis tigris gold-*
2,3 *smithi*, and Red Indians under the catalpas. That it all boiled
down to a measly suburban lawn and a smoking garbage incinerator, was appalling. Farewell, Appalachia! Leaving it, we crossed
Ohio, the three states beginning with "I," and Nebraska—ah,
4   that first whiff of the West! We travelled very leisurely, having
more than a week to reach Wace, Continental Divide, where
she passionately desired to see the Ceremonial Dances marking
the seasonal opening of Magic Cave, and at least three weeks to
reach Elphinstone, gem of a western State where she yearned to
5   climb Red Rock from which a mature screen star had recently
jumped to her death after a drunken row with her gigolo.

Again we were welcomed to wary motels by means of inscrip-
tions that read:

"We wish you to feel at home while here. *All* equipment was
carefully checked upon your arrival. Your license number is on
record here. Use hot water sparingly. We reserve the right to
eject without notice any objectionable person. Do not throw
waste material of *any* kind in the toilet bowl. Thank you. Call
again. The Management. P.S. We consider our guests the Finest
People of the World."

In these frightening places we paid ten for twins, flies queued
outside at the screenless door and successfully scrambled in, the
ashes of our predecessors still lingered in the ashtrays, a woman's
hair lay on the pillow, one heard one's neighbor hanging his coat
in his closet, the hangers were ingeniously fixed to their bars by
coils of wire so as to thwart theft, and, in crowning insult, the
pictures above the twin beds were identical twins. I also noticed
that commercial fashion was changing. There was a tendency
6   for cabins to fuse and gradually form the caravansary, and, lo
(she was not interested but the reader may be), a second story
was added, and a lobby grew in, and cars were removed to a communal garage, and the motel reverted to the good old hotel.

I now warn the reader not to mock me and my mental daze.
It is easy for him and me to decipher *now* a past destiny; but a

destiny in the making is, believe me, not one of those honest mystery stories where all you have to do is keep an eye on the clues. In my youth I once read a French detective tale where the clues were actually in italics; but that is not McFate's way—even if one does learn to recognize certain obscure indications.

For instance: I would not swear that there was not at least one occasion, prior to, or at the very beginning of, the Midwest lap of our journey, when she managed to convey some information to, or otherwise get into contact with, a person or persons unknown. We had stopped at a gas station, under the sign of Pegasus, and she had slipped out of her seat and escaped to the rear of the premises while the raised hood, under which I had bent to watch the mechanic's manipulations, hid her for a moment from my sight. Being inclined to be lenient, I only shook my benign head though strictly speaking such visits were taboo, since I felt instinctively that toilets—as also telephones—happened to be, for reasons unfathomable, the points where my destiny was liable to catch. We all have such fateful objects—it may be a recurrent landscape in one case, a number in another—carefully chosen by the gods to attract events of special significance for us: here shall John always stumble; there shall Jane's heart always break.

Well—my car had been attended to, and I had moved it away from the pumps to let a pickup truck be serviced—when the growing volume of her absence began to weigh upon me in the windy grayness. Not for the first time, and not for the last, had I stared in such dull discomfort of mind at those stationary trivialities that look almost surprised, like staring rustics, to find themselves in the stranded traveller's field of vision: that green garbage can, those very black, very whitewalled tires for sale, those bright cans of motor oil, that red icebox with assorted drinks, the four, five, seven discarded bottles within the incompleted crossword puzzle of their wooden cells, that bug patiently walking up the inside of the window of the office. Radio music was coming from its open door, and because the rhythm was not synchronized with the heave and flutter and other gestures of wind-animated vegetation, one had the impression of an old

scenic film living its own life while piano or fiddle followed a line of music quite outside the shivering flower, the swaying branch. The sound of Charlotte's last sob incongruously vibrated through me as, with her dress fluttering athwart the rhythm, Lolita veered from a totally unexpected direction. She had found the toilet occupied and had crossed over to the sign of the
1 Conche in the next block. They said there they were proud of their home-clean restrooms. These prepaid postcards, they said, had been provided for your comments. No postcards. No soap. Nothing. No comments.

That day or the next, after a tedious drive through a land of food crops, we reached a pleasant little burg and put up at
2 Chestnut Court—nice cabins, damp green grounds, apple trees, an old swing—and a tremendous sunset which the tired child ignored. She had wanted to go through Kasbeam because it was only thirty miles north from her home town but on the following morning I found her quite listless, with no desire to see again the sidewalk where she had played hopscotch some five years before. For obvious reasons I had rather dreaded that side trip, even though we had agreed not to make ourselves conspicuous in any way—to remain in the car and not look up old friends. My relief at her abandoning the project was spoiled by the thought that had she felt I were totally against the nostalgic possibilities of Pisky, as I had been last year, she would not have given up so easily. On my mentioning this with a sigh, she sighed too and complained of being out of sorts. She wanted to remain in bed till teatime at least, with lots of magazines, and then if she felt better she suggested we just continue westward. I must say she was very sweet and languid, and craved for fresh fruits, and I decided to go and fetch her a toothsome picnic lunch in Kasbeam. Our cabin stood on the timbered crest of a hill, and from our window you could see the road winding down, and then running as straight as a hair parting between two rows of chestnut trees, towards the pretty town, which looked singularly distinct and toylike in the pure morning distance. One could
3 make out an elf-like girl on an insect-like bicycle, and a dog, a bit too large proportionately, all as clear as those pilgrims and

mules winding up wax-pale roads in old paintings with blue hills and red little people. I have the European urge to use my feet when a drive can be dispensed with, so I leisurely walked down, eventually meeting the cyclist—a plain plump girl with pigtails, followed by a huge St. Bernard dog with orbits like pansies. In Kasbeam a very old barber gave me a very mediocre haircut: he babbled of a baseball-playing son of his, and, at every explodent, spat into my neck, and every now and then wiped his glasses on my sheet-wrap, or interrupted his tremulous scissor work to produce faded newspaper clippings, and so inattentive was I that it came as a shock to realize as he pointed to an easeled photograph among the ancient gray lotions, that the mustached young ball player had been dead for the last thirty years.

I had a cup of hot flavorless coffee, bought a bunch of bananas for my monkey, and spent another ten minutes or so in a delicatessen store. At least an hour and a half must have elapsed when this homeward-bound little pilgrim appeared on the winding road leading to Chestnut Castle.   1

The girl I had seen on my way to town was now loaded with linen and engaged in helping a misshapen man whose big head and coarse features reminded me of the "Bertoldo" character in low Italian comedy. They were cleaning the cabins of which   2 there was a dozen or so on Chestnut Crest, all pleasantly spaced amid the copious verdure. It was noon, and most of them, with a final bang of their screen doors, had already got rid of their occupants. A very elderly, almost mummy-like couple in a very new model were in the act of creeping out of one of the contiguous garages; from another a red hood protruded in some-   3 what cod-piece fashion; and nearer to our cabin, a strong and   4 handsome young man with a shock of black hair and blue eyes was putting a portable refrigerator into a station wagon. For some reason he gave me a sheepish grin as I passed. On the grass expanse opposite, in the many-limbed shade of luxuriant trees, the familiar St. Bernard dog was guarding his mistress' bicycle, and nearby a young woman, far gone in the family way, had seated a rapt baby on a swing and was rocking it gently, while a jealous boy of two or three was making a nuisance of himself by trying to push or pull the swing board; he finally succeeded in getting himself knocked down by it, and bawled loudly as he lay supine on the grass while his mother continued to smile gently at neither of her present children. I recall so clearly these minutiae probably because I was to check my impressions so thoroughly only a few minutes later; and besides, something in me had been on guard ever since that awful night in Beardsley. I now refused to be diverted by the feeling of well-being that my walk had engendered—by the young summer breeze that enveloped the nape of my neck, the giving crunch of the damp gravel, the juicy tidbit I had sucked out at last from a hollow tooth, and even the comfortable weight of my provisions which the general condition of my heart should not have allowed me to carry; but even that miserable pump of mine seemed to be working sweetly, and I felt *adolori d'amoureuse langueur*, to quote dear old Ronsard, as I reached the cottage where I had left my Dolores.

1

To my surprise I found her dressed. She was sitting on the edge of the bed in slacks and T-shirt, and was looking at me as if she could not quite place me. The frank soft shape of her small breasts was brought out rather than blurred by the limpness of her thin shirt, and this frankness irritated me. She had not washed; yet her mouth was freshly though smudgily painted, and her broad teeth glistened like wine-tinged ivory, or pinkish poker chips. And there she sat, hands clasped in her lap, and dreamily brimmed with a diabolical glow that had no relation to me whatever.

2

I plumped down my heavy paper bag and stood staring at the bare ankles of her sandaled feet, then at her silly face, then again at her sinful feet. "You've been out," I said (the sandals were filthy with gravel).

"I just got up," she replied, and added upon intercepting my downward glance: "Went out for a sec. Wanted to see if you were coming back."

She became aware of the bananas and uncoiled herself tableward.

What special suspicion could I have? None indeed—but those muddy, moony eyes of hers, that singular warmth emanating from her! I said nothing. I looked at the road meandering so distinctly within the frame of the window... Anybody wishing to betray my trust would have found it a splendid lookout. With rising appetite, Lo applied herself to the fruit. All at once I remembered the ingratiating grin of the Johnny nextdoor. I stepped out quickly. All cars had disappeared except his station wagon; his pregnant young wife was now getting into it with her baby and the other, more or less cancelled, child.

"What's the matter, where are you going?" cried Lo from the porch.

I said nothing. I pushed her softness back into the room and went in after her. I ripped her shirt off. I unzipped the rest of her. I tore off her sandals. Wildly, I pursued the shadow of her infidelity; but the scent I travelled upon was so slight as to be practically undistinguishable from a madman's fancy.

17

Gros Gaston, in his prissy way, had liked to make presents— presents just a prissy wee bit out of the ordinary, or so he prissily thought. Noticing one night that my box of chessmen was broken, he sent me next morning, with a little lad of his, a copper case: it had an elaborate Oriental design over the lid and could be securely locked. One glance sufficed to assure me that it was one of those cheap money boxes called for some reason "luizettas" that you buy in Algiers and elsewhere, and wonder what to do with afterwards. It turned out to be much too flat for holding my bulky chessmen, but I kept it—using it for a totally different purpose.

In order to break some pattern of fate in which I obscurely felt myself being enmeshed, I had decided—despite Lo's visible annoyance—to spend another night at Chestnut Court; definitely waking up at four in the morning, I ascertained that Lo was still sound asleep (mouth open, in a kind of dull amazement at the curiously inane life we all had rigged up for her) and satisfied myself that the precious contents of the "luizetta" were safe. There, snugly wrapped in a white woollen scarf, lay a pocket automatic: caliber .32, capacity of magazine 8 cartridges, length a little under one ninth of Lolita's length, stock checked walnut, finish full blued. I had inherited it from the late Harold Haze, with a 1938 catalog which cheerily said in part: "Particularly well adapted for use in the home and car as well as on the person." There it lay, ready for instant service on the person or persons, loaded and fully cocked with the slide lock in safety position, thus precluding any accidental discharge. We must remember that a pistol is the Freudian symbol of the Ur-father's central forelimb.

I was now glad I had it with me—and even more glad that I had learned to use it two years before, in the pine forest around my and Charlotte's glass lake. Farlow, with whom I had roamed those remote woods, was an admirable marksman, and with his .38 actually managed to hit a hummingbird, though I must say not much of it could be retrieved for proof—only a little iridescent fluff. A burley ex-policeman called Krestovski, who in the twenties had shot and killed two escaped convicts, joined us and bagged a tiny woodpecker—completely out of season, incidentally. Between those two sportsmen I of course was a novice and kept missing everything, though I did wound a squirrel on a later occasion when I went out alone. "You lie here," I whispered to my light-weight compact little chum, and then toasted it with a dram of gin.

18

The reader must now forget Chestnuts and Colts, and accompany us further west. The following days were marked by a number of great thunderstorms—or perhaps, there was but one single storm which progressed across country in ponderous frog-leaps and which we could not shake off just as we could not shake off detective Trapp: for it was during those days that the problem

of the Aztec Red Convertible presented itself to me, and quite 1
overshadowed the theme of Lo's lovers.

Queer! I who was jealous of every male we met—queer, how I
misinterpreted the designations of doom. Perhaps I had been
lulled by Lo's modest behavior in winter, and anyway it would
have been too foolish even for a lunatic to suppose another
Humbert was avidly following Humbert and Humbert's nymphet
with Jovian fireworks, over the great and ugly plains. I surmised, 2
donc, that the Red Yak keeping behind us at a discreet distance 3
mile after mile was operated by a detective whom some busybody had hired to see what exactly Humbert Humbert was doing
with that minor stepdaughter of his. As happens with me at
periods of electrical disturbance and crepitating lightnings, I had 4
hallucinations. Maybe they were more than hallucinations. I
do not know what she or he, or both had put into my liquor but
one night I felt sure somebody was tapping on the door of our
cabin, and I flung it open, and noticed two things—that I was
stark naked and that, white-glistening in the rain-dripping darkness, there stood a man holding before his face the mask of Jutting Chin, a grotesque sleuth in the funnies. He emitted a muffled 5
guffaw and scurried away, and I reeled back into the room, and
fell asleep again, and am not sure even to this day that the visit
was not a drug-provoked dream: I have thoroughly studied
Trapp's type of humor, and this might have been a plausible
sample. Oh, crude and absolutely ruthless! Somebody, I imagined, was making money on those masks of popular monsters
and morons. Did I see next morning two urchins rummaging in
a garbage can and trying on Jutting Chin? I wonder. It may all
have been a coincidence—due to atmospheric conditions, I
suppose.

Being a murderer with a sensational but incomplete and un-
orthodox memory, I cannot tell you, ladies and gentlemen, the
exact day when I first knew with utter certainty that the red
convertible was following us. I do remember, however, the first
time I saw its driver quite clearly. I was proceeding slowly one
afternoon through torrents of rain and kept seeing that red ghost
swimming and shivering with lust in my mirror, when presently

the deluge dwindled to a patter, and then was suspended altogether. With a swishing sound a sunburst swept the highway,
and needing a pair of new sunglasses, I pulled up at a filling
station. What was happening was a sickness, a cancer, that could
not be helped, so I simply ignored the fact that our quiet pursuer, in his converted state, stopped a little behind us at a café
or bar bearing the idiotic sign: The Bustle: A Deceitful Seatful.
Having seen to the needs of my car, I walked into the office to
get those glasses and pay for the gas. As I was in the act of signing
a traveller's check and wondered about my exact whereabouts, I
happened to glance through a side window, and saw a terrible
thing. A broad-backed man, baldish, in an oatmeal coat and
dark-brown trousers, was listening to Lo who was leaning out of
the car and talking to him very rapidly, her hand with outspread
fingers going up and down as it did when she was very serious
and emphatic. What struck me with sickening force was—how
should I put it?—the voluble familiarity of her way, as if they had
known each other—oh, for weeks and weeks. I saw him scratch
his cheek and nod, and turn, and walk back to his convertible, a
broad and thickish man of my age, somewhat resembling
Gustave Trapp, a cousin of my father's in Switzerland—same
smoothly tanned face, fuller than mine, with a small dark mus-
1 tache and a rosebud degenerate mouth. Lolita was studying a
road map when I got back into the car.

"What did that man ask you, Lo?"

"Man? Oh, that man. Oh yes. Oh, I don't know. He wondered if I had a map. Lost his way, I guess."

We drove on, and I said:

"Now listen, Lo. I do not know whether you are lying or not,
and I do not know whether you are insane or not, and I do not
care for the moment; but that person has been following us all
day, and his car was at the motel yesterday, and I think he is a
cop. You know perfectly well what will happen and where you
will go if the police find out about things. Now I want to know
exactly what he said to you and what you told him."

She laughed.

"If he's really a cop," she said shrilly but not illogically, "the worst thing we could do, would be to show him we are scared. Ignore him, *Dad*."

"Did he ask where we were going?"

"Oh, he knows *that*" (mocking me).

"Anyway," I said, giving up, "I have seen his face now. He is not pretty. He looks exactly like a relative of mine called Trapp."

"Perhaps he is Trapp. If I were you—Oh, look, all the nines are changing into the next thousand. When I was a little kid," she continued unexpectedly, "I used to think they'd stop and go back to nines, if only my mother agreed to put the car in reverse."

It was the first time, I think, she spoke spontaneously of her pre-Humbertian childhood; perhaps, the theatre had taught her that trick; and silently we travelled on, unpursued.

But next day, like pain in a fatal disease that comes back as the drug and hope wear off, there it was again behind us, that glossy red beast. The traffic on the highway was light that day; nobody passed anybody; and nobody attempted to get in between our humble blue car and its imperious red shadow—as if there were some spell cast on that interspace, a zone of evil mirth and magic, a zone whose very precision and stability had a glass-like virtue that was almost artistic. The driver behind me, with his stuffed shoulders and Trappish mustache, looked like a display dummy, and his convertible seemed to move only because an invisible rope of silent silk connected it with our shabby vehicle. We were many times weaker than his splendid, lacquered machine, so that I did not even attempt to outspeed him. *O lente currite noctis equi!* O softly run, nightmares! We climbed long 1 grades and rolled downhill again, and heeded speed limits, and spared slow children, and reproduced in sweeping terms the black wiggles of curves on their yellow shields, and no matter how and where we drove, the enchanted interspace slid on intact, mathematical, mirage-like, the viatic counterpart of a magic 2 carpet. And all the time I was aware of a private blaze on my right: her joyful eye, her flaming cheek.

A traffic policeman, deep in the nightmare of crisscross streets —at half-past-four P.M. in a factory town—was the hand of chance that interrupted the spell. He beckoned me on, and then with the same hand cut off my shadow. A score of cars were launched in between us, and I sped on, and deftly turned into a narrow lane. A sparrow alighted with a jumbo bread crumb, was tackled by another, and lost the crumb.

When after a few grim stoppages and a bit of deliberate meandering, I returned to the highway, our shadow had disappeared.

Lola snorted and said: "If he is what you think he is, how silly to give him the slip."

"I have other notions by now," I said.

"You should—ah—check them by—ah—keeping in touch with him, fahther deah," said Lo, writhing in the coils of her own sarcasm. "Gee, you *are* mean," she added in her ordinary voice.

We spent a grim night in a very foul cabin, under a sonorous amplitude of rain, and with a kind of prehistorically loud thunder incessantly rolling above us.

1 "I am not a lady and do not like lightning," said Lo, whose dread of electric storms gave me some pathetic solace.

2 We had breakfast in the township of Soda, pop. 1001.

"Judging by the terminal figure," I remarked, "Fatface is already here."

"Your humor," said Lo, "is sidesplitting, deah fahther."

We were in sage-brush country by that time, and there was a day or two of lovely release (I had been a fool, all was well, that

3 discomfort was merely a trapped flatus), and presently the mesas gave way to real mountains, and, on time, we drove into Wace.

Oh, disaster. Some confusion had occurred, she had misread a date in the Tour Book, and the Magic Cave ceremonies were over! She took it bravely, I must admit—and, when we dis-

4 covered there was in kurortish Wace a summer theatre in full swing, we naturally drifted toward it one fair mid-June evening. I really could not tell you the plot of the play we saw. A trivial affair, no doubt, with self-conscious light effects and a mediocre leading lady. The only detail that pleased me was a garland of seven little graces, more or less immobile, prettily painted, bare-limbed—seven bemused pubescent girls in colored gauze that had been recruited locally (judging by the partisan flurry here and

there among the audience) and were supposed to represent a living rainbow, which lingered throughout the last act, and rather teasingly faded behind a series of multiplied veils. I remember thinking that this idea of children-colors had been lifted by authors Clare Quilty and Vivian Darkbloom from a passage 1 in James Joyce, and that two of the colors were quite exasperatingly lovely—Orange who kept fidgeting all the time, and 2 Emerald who, when her eyes got used to the pitch-black pit where we all heavily sat, suddenly smiled at her mother or her protector.

As soon as the thing was over, and manual applause—a sound my nerves cannot stand—began to crash all around me, I started to pull and push Lo toward the exit, in my so natural amorous impatience to get her back to our neon-blue cottage in the stunned, starry night: I always say nature is stunned by the sights she sees. Dolly-Lo, however, lagged behind, in a rosy daze, her pleased eyes narrowed, her sense of vision swamping the rest of her senses to such an extent that her limp hands hardly came together at all in the mechanical action of clapping they still went through. I had seen that kind of thing in children before but, by God, this was a special child, myopically beaming at the already remote stage where I glimpsed something of the joint authors—a man's tuxedo and the bare shoulders of a hawk-like, black-haired, strikingly tall woman.

"You've again hurt my wrist, you brute," said Lolita in a small voice as she slipped into her car seat.

"I am dreadfully sorry, my darling, my own ultraviolet darling," I said, unsuccessfully trying to catch her elbow, and I added, to change the conversation—to change the direction of fate, oh God, oh God: "Vivian is quite a woman. I am sure we saw her yesterday in that restaurant, in Soda pop."

"Sometimes," said Lo, "you are quite revoltingly dumb. First, Vivian is the male author, the gal author is Clare; and second, she is forty, married and has Negro blood."

"I thought," I said kidding her, "Quilty was an ancient flame of yours, in the days when you loved me, in sweet old Ramsdale."

"What?" countered Lo, her features working. "That fat dentist? You must be confusing me with some other fast little article."

And I thought to myself how those fast little articles forget everything, everything, while we, old lovers, treasure every inch of their nymphancy.

19

With Lo's knowledge and assent, the two post offices given to the Beardsley postmaster as forwarding addresses were P.O. Wace and P.O. Elphinstone. Next morning we visited the former and had to wait in a short but slow queue. Serene Lo studied the rogues' gallery. Handsome Bryan Bryanski, alias Anthony Bryan, alias Tony Brown, eyes hazel, complexion fair, was wanted for kidnaping. A sad-eyed old gentleman's faux-pas was mail fraud, and, as if that were not enough, he was cursed with deformed arches. Sullen Sullivan came with a caution: Is believed armed, and should be considered extremely dangerous. If you want to make a movie out of my book, have one of these faces gently melt into my own, while I look. And moreover there was a smudgy snapshot of a Missing Girl, age fourteen, wearing brown shoes when last seen, rhymes. Please notify Sheriff Buller.

I forget my letters; as to Dolly's, there was her report and a very special-looking envelope. This I deliberately opened and perused its contents. I concluded I was doing the foreseen since she did not seem to mind and drifted toward the newsstand near the exit.

"Dolly-Lo: Well, the play was a grand success. All three hounds lay quiet having been slightly drugged by Cutler, I suspect, and Linda knew all your lines. She was fine, she had alertness and control, but lacked somehow the *responsiveness*, the *relaxed vitality*, the charm of *my*—and the author's—Diana; but there was no author to applaud us as last time, and the terrific electric storm outside interfered with our own modest off-stage thunder. Oh dear, life does fly. Now that everything is over, school, play, the Roy mess, mother's confinement (our baby, alas, did not live!), it all seems such a long time ago, though practically I still bear traces of the paint.

"We are going to New York after to-morrow, and I guess I can't manage to wriggle out of accompanying my parents to Europe. I have even worse news for you. Dolly-Lo! I may not be back at Beardsley if and when you return. With one thing and another, one being you know who, and the other not being who you think you know, Dad wants me to go to school in Paris for one year while he and Fullbright are around.

"As expected, poor Poet stumbled in Scene III when arriving at the bit of French nonsense. Remember? *Ne manque pas de dire à ton amant, Chimène, comme le lac est beau car il faut qu'il t'y mène*. Lucky beau! *Qu'il t'y*—What a tongue-twister! Well, be good, Lollikins. Best love from your Poet, and best regards to the Governor. Your Mona. P.S. Because of one thing and another, my correspondence happens to be rigidly controlled. So better wait till I write you from Europe." (She never did as far as I know. The letter contained an element of mysterious nastiness that I am too tired to-day to analyze. I found it later preserved in one of the Tour Books, and give it here *à titre documentaire*. I read it twice.)

I looked up from the letter and was about to—There was no Lo to behold. While I was engrossed in Mona's witchery, Lo had shrugged her shoulders and vanished. "Did you happen to see—" I asked of a hunchback sweeping the floor near the entrance. He had, the old lecherer. He guessed she had seen a friend and had hurried out. I hurried out too. I stopped—she had not. I hurried on. I stopped again. It had happened at last. She had gone for ever.

In later years I have often wondered why she did *not* go for ever that day. Was it the retentive quality of her new summer clothes in my locked car? Was it some unripe particle in some general plan? Was it simply because, all things considered, I might as well be used to convey her to Elphinstone—the secret terminus, anyway? I only know I was quite certain she had left me for ever. The noncommittal mauve mountains half encircling

1

2

3

4

the town seemed to me to swarm with panting, scrambling, laughing, panting Lolitas who dissolved in their haze. A big W made of white stones on a steep talus in the far vista of a cross street seemed the very initial of woe.

The new and beautiful post office I had just emerged from stood between a dormant movie house and a conspiracy of poplars. The time was 9 A.M. mountain time. The street was Main Street. I paced its blue side peering at the opposite one: charming it into beauty, was one of those fragile young summer mornings with flashes of glass here and there and a general air of faltering and almost fainting at the prospect of an intolerably torrid noon. Crossing over, I loafed and leafed, as it were, through one long block: Drugs, Real Estate, Fashions, Auto Parts, Cafe, Sporting Goods, Real Estate, Furniture, Appliances, Western Union, Cleaners, Grocery. Officer, officer, my daughter has run away. In collusion with a detective; in love with a blackmailer. Took advantage of my utter helplessness. I peered into all the stores. I deliberated inly if I should talk to any of the sparse foot-passengers. I did not. I sat for a while in the parked car. I inspected the public garden on the east side. I went back to Fashions and Auto Parts. I told myself with a burst of furious sarcasm—*un ricanement*—that I was crazy to suspect her, that she would turn up in a minute.

She did.

I wheeled around and shook off the hand she had placed on my sleeve with a timid and imbecile smile.

"Get into the car," I said.

She obeyed, and I went on pacing up and down, struggling with nameless thoughts, trying to plan some way of tackling her duplicity.

Presently she left the car and was at my side again. My sense of hearing gradually got tuned in to station Lo again, and I became aware she was telling me that she had met a former girl friend.

"Yes? Whom?"

"A Beardsley girl."

"Good. I know every name in your group. Alice Adams?"

"This girl was not in my group."

"Good. I have a complete student list with me. Her name please."

"She was not in my school. She is just a town girl in Beardsley."

"Good. I have the Beardsley directory with me too. We'll look up all the Browns."

"I only know her first name."

"Mary or Jane?"

"No—Dolly, like me."

"So that's the dead end" (the mirror you break your nose against). "Good. Let us try another angle. You have been absent twenty-eight minutes. What did the two Dollys do?"

"We went to a drugstore."

"And you had there—?"

"Oh, just a couple of Cokes."

"Careful, Dolly. We can check that, you know."

"At least, she had. I had a glass of water."

"Good. Was it that place there?"

"Sure."

"Good, come on, we'll grill the soda jerk."

"Wait a sec. Come to think it might have been further down —just around the corner."

"Come on all the same. Go in please. Well, let's see." (Opening a chained telephone book.) "Dignified Funeral Service. No, not yet. Here we are: Druggists-Retail. Hill Drug Store. Larkin's Pharmacy. And two more. That's all Wace seems to have in the way of soda fountains—at least in the business section. Well, we will check them all."

"Go to hell," she said.

"Lo, rudeness will get you nowhere."

"Okay," she said. "But you're not going to trap me. Okay, so we did not have a pop. We just talked and looked at dresses in show windows."

"Which? That window there for example?"

"Yes, that one there, for example."

"Oh Lo! Let's look closer at it."

It was indeed a pretty sight. A dapper young fellow was vacuum-cleaning a carpet of sorts upon which stood two figures that looked as if some blast had just worked havoc with them. One figure was stark naked, wigless and armless. Its comparatively small stature and smirking pose suggested that when clothed it had represented, and would represent when clothed again, a girl-child of Lolita's size. But in its present state it was sexless. Next to it, stood a much taller veiled bride, quite perfect and *intacta* except for the lack of one arm. On the floor, at the feet of these damsels, where the man crawled about laboriously with his cleaner, there lay a cluster of three slender arms, and a blond wig. Two of the arms happened to be twisted and seemed to suggest a clasping gesture of horror and supplication.

"Look, Lo," I said quietly. "Look well. Is not that a rather good symbol of something or other? However"—I went on as we got back in to the car—"I have taken certain precautions. Here (delicately opening the glove compartment), on this pad, I have our boy friend's car number."

As the ass I was I had not memorized it. What remained of it in my mind were the initial letter and the closing figure as if the whole amphitheatre of six signs receded concavely behind a tinted glass too opaque to allow the central series to be deciphered, but just translucent enough to make out its extreme edges—a capital P and a 6. I have to go into those details (which in themselves can interest only a professional psychologue) because otherwise the reader (ah, if I could visualize him as a blond-bearded scholar with rosy lips sucking *la pomme de sa canne* as he quaffs my manuscript!) might not understand the quality of the shock I experienced upon noticing that the P had acquired the bustle of a B and that the 6 had been deleted altogether. The rest, with erasures revealing the hurried shuttle smear of a pencil's rubber end, and with parts of numbers obliterated or reconstructed in a child's hand, presented a tangle of barbed wire to any logical interpretation. All I knew was the state—one adjacent to the state Beardsley was in.

I said nothing. I put the pad back, closed the compartment, and drove out of Wace. Lo had grabbed some comics from the back seat and, mobile-white-bloused, one brown elbow out of the window, was deep in the current adventure of some clout or clown. Three or four miles out of Wace, I turned into the shadow of a picnic ground where the morning had dumped its litter of light on an empty table; Lo looked up with a semi-smile of surprise and without a word I delivered a tremendous backhand cut that caught her smack on her hot hard little cheekbone.

And then the remorse, the poignant sweetness of sobbing atonement, groveling love, the hopelessness of sensual reconciliation. In the velvet night, at Mirana Motel (Mirana!) I kissed the yellowish soles of her long-toed feet, I immolated myself... But it was all of no avail. Both doomed were we. And soon I was to enter a new cycle of persecution.

In a street of Wace, on its outskirts... Oh, I am quite sure it was not a delusion. In a street of Wace, I had glimpsed the Aztec Red convertible, or its identical twin. Instead of Trapp, it contained four or five loud young people of several sexes—but I said nothing. After Wace a totally new situation arose. For a day or two, I enjoyed the mental emphasis with which I told myself that we were not, and never had been followed; and then I became sickeningly conscious that Trapp had changed his tactics and was still with us, in this or that rented car.

A veritable Proteus of the highway, with bewildering ease he switched from one vehicle to another. This technique implied the existence of garages specializing in "stage-automobile" operations, but I never could discover the remises he used. He seemed to patronize at first the Chevrolet genus, beginning with a Campus Cream convertible, then going on to a small Horizon Blue sedan, and thenceforth fading into Surf Gray and Driftwood Gray. Then he turned to other makes and passed through a pale dull rainbow of paint shades, and one day I found myself attempting to cope with the subtle distinction between our own Dream Blue Melmoth and the Crest Blue Oldsmobile he had rented; grays, however, remained his favorite cryptochromism, and, in agonizing nightmares, I tried in vain to sort out properly such ghosts as Chrysler's Shell Gray, Chevrolet's Thistle Gray, Dodge's French Gray . . .

The necessity of being constantly on the lookout for his little moustache and open shirt—or for his baldish pate and broad shoulders—led me to a profound study of all cars on the road— behind, before, alongside, coming, going, every vehicle under the dancing sun: the quiet vacationist's automobile with the box of Tender-Touch tissues in the back window; the recklessly speeding jalopy full of pale children with a shaggy dog's head protruding, and a crumpled mudguard; the bachelor's tudor sedan crowded with suits on hangers; the huge fat house trailer weaving in front, immune to the Indian file of fury boiling behind it; the car with the young female passenger politely perched in the middle of the front seat to be closer to the young male driver; the car carrying on its roof a red boat bottom up . . . The gray car slowing up before us, the gray car catching up with us.

We were in mountain country, somewhere between Snow and Champion, and rolling down an almost imperceptible grade, when I had my next distinct view of Detective Paramour Trapp. The gray mist behind us had deepened and concentrated into the compactness of a Dominion Blue sedan. All of a sudden, as if the car I drove responded to my poor heart's pangs, we were slithering from side to side, with something making a helpless plap-plap-plap under us.

"You got a flat, mister," said cheerful Lo.

I pulled up—near a precipice. She folded her arms and put her foot on the dashboard. I got out and examined the right rear wheel. The base of its tire was sheepishly and hideously square. Trapp had stopped some fifty yards behind us. His distant face formed a grease spot of mirth. This was my chance. I started to walk towards him—with the brilliant idea of asking him for a jack though I had one. He backed a little. I stubbed my toe against a stone—and there was a sense of general laughter. Then a tremendous truck loomed from behind Trapp and thundered by me—and immediately after, I heard it utter a convulsive honk. Instinctively I looked back—and saw my own car gently creeping away. I could make out Lo ludicrously at the wheel,

and the engine was certainly running—though I remembered I
had cut it but had not applied the emergency brake; and during
the brief space of throb-time that it took me to reach the croak-
ing machine which came to a standstill at last, it dawned upon
me that during the last two years little Lo had had ample time
to pick up the rudiments of driving. As I wrenched the door
open, I was goddam sure she had started the car to prevent me
from walking up to Trapp. Her trick proved useless, however,
for even while I was pursuing her he had made an energetic
U-turn and was gone. I rested for a while. Lo asked wasn't I
going to thank her—the car had started to move by itself and—
Getting no answer, she immersed herself in a study of the map.
I got out again and commenced the "ordeal of the orb," as   1
Charlotte used to say. Perhaps, I was losing my mind.

We continued our grotesque journey. After a forlorn and
useless dip, we went up and up. On a steep grade I found myself
behind the gigantic truck that had overtaken us. It was now
groaning up a winding road and was impossible to pass. Out of   2
its front part a small oblong of smooth silver—the inner wrap-
ping of chewing gum—escaped and flew back into our windshield. It occurred to me that if I were really losing my mind, I
might end by murdering somebody. In fact—said high-and-dry
Humbert to floundering Humbert—it might be quite clever to
prepare things—to transfer the weapon from box to pocket—so
as to be ready to take advantage of the spell of insanity when it
does come.

20

By permitting Lolita to study acting I had, fond fool, suffered
her to cultivate deceit. It now appeared that it had not been
merely a matter of learning the answers to such questions as
what is the basic conflict in "Hedda Gabler," or where are the
climaxes in "Love Under the Lindens," or analyze the prevailing   3
mood of "Cherry Orchard"; it was really a matter of learning to
betray me. How I deplored now the exercises in sensual simula-

tion that I had so often seen her go through in our Beardsley parlor when I would observe her from some strategic point while she, like a hypnotic subject or a performer in a mystic rite, produced sophisticated versions of infantile make-believe by going through the mimetic actions of hearing a moan in the dark, seeing for the first time a brand new young stepmother, tasting something she hated, such as buttermilk, smelling crushed grass in a lush orchard, or touching mirages of objects with her sly, slender, girl-child hands. Among my papers I still have a mimeographed sheet suggesting:

Tactile drill. Imagine yourself picking up and holding: a pingpong ball, an apple, a sticky date, a new flannel-fluffed tennis ball, a hot potato, an ice cube, a kitten, a puppy, a
1   horseshoe, a feather, a flashlight.
Knead with your fingers the following imaginary things: a piece of bread, india rubber, a friend's aching temple, a sample of velvet, a rose petal.
You are a blind girl. Palpate the face of: a Greek youth, Cyrano, Santa Claus, a baby, a laughing faun, a sleeping
2   stranger, your father.

But she had been so pretty in the weaving of those delicate spells, in the dreamy performance of her enchantments and duties! On certain adventurous evenings, in Beardsley, I also had her dance for me with the promise of some treat or gift, and although these routine leg-parted leaps of hers were more like those of a football cheerleader than like the languorous and
3   jerky motions of a Parisian *petit rat*, the rhythms of her not quite nubile limbs had given me pleasure. But all that was nothing, absolutely nothing, to the indescribable itch of rapture that her tennis game produced in me—the teasing delirious feeling of teetering on the very brink of unearthly order and splendor.

Despite her advanced age, she was more of a nymphet than ever, with her apricot-colored limbs, in her sub-teen tennis togs! Winged gentlemen! No hereafter is acceptable if it does not produce her as she was then, in that Colorado resort between Snow and Elphinstone, with everything right: the white wide little-boy shorts, the slender waist, the apricot midriff, the white breast-kerchief whose ribbons went up and encircled her neck to end behind in a dangling knot leaving bare her gaspingly young and adorable apricot shoulder blades with that pubescence and those lovely gentle bones, and the smooth, downward-tapering back. Her cap had a white peak. Her racket had cost me a small fortune. Idiot, triple idiot! I could have filmed her! I would have had her now with me, before my eyes, in the projection room of my pain and despair!

She would wait and relax for a bar or two of white-lined time before going into the act of serving, and often bounced the ball once or twice, or pawed the ground a little, always at ease, always rather vague about the score, always cheerful as she so seldom was in the dark life she led at home. Her tennis was the highest point to which I can imagine a young creature bringing the art of make-believe, although I daresay, for her it was the very geometry of basic reality.

The exquisite clarity of all her movements had its auditory counterpart in the pure ringing sound of her every stroke. The ball when it entered her aura of control became somehow whiter, its resilience somehow richer, and the instrument of precision she used upon it seemed inordinately prehensile and deliberate at the moment of clinging contact. Her form was, indeed, an absolutely perfect imitation of absolutely top-notch tennis— without any utilitarian results. As Edusa's sister, Electra Gold, a marvelous young coach, said to me once while I sat on a pulsating hard bench watching Dolores Haze toying with Linda Hall (and being beaten by her): "Dolly has a magnet in the center of her racket guts, but why the heck is she so polite?" Ah, Electra, what did it matter, with such grace! I remember at the very first game I watched being drenched with an almost painful convulsion of beauty assimilation. My Lolita had a way of raising her bent left knee at the ample and springy start of the service cycle when there would develop and hang in the sun for a second a vital web of balance between toed foot, pristine armpit, burnished arm and far back-flung racket, as she smiled up with gleaming teeth at the small globe suspended so high in the zenith of the

1

powerful and graceful cosmos she had created for the express purpose of falling upon it with a clean resounding crack of her golden whip.

It had, that serve of hers, beauty, directness, youth, a classical purity of trajectory, and was, despite its spanking pace, fairly easy to return, having as it did no twist or sting to its long elegant hop.

That I could have had all her strokes, all her enchantments, immortalized in segments of celluloid, makes me moan to-day with frustration. They would have been so much more than the snapshots I burned! Her overhead volley was related to her service as the envoy is to the ballade; for she had been trained, my pet, to patter up at once to the net on her nimble, vivid, white-shod feet. There was nothing to choose between her forehand and backhand drives: they were mirror images of one another—my very loins still tingle with those pistol reports repeated by crisp echoes and Electra's cries. One of the pearls of Dolly's game was a short half-volley that Ned Litam had taught her in California.

She preferred acting to swimming, and swimming to tennis; yet I insist that had not something within her been broken by me—not that I realized it then!—she would have had on the top of her perfect form the will to win, and would have become a real girl champion. Dolores, with two rackets under her arm, in Wimbledon. Dolores endorsing a Dromedary. Dolores turning professional. Dolores acting a girl champion in a movie. Dolores and her gray, humble, hushed husband-coach, old Humbert.

There was nothing wrong or deceitful in the spirit of her game —unless one considered her cheerful indifference toward its outcome as the feint of a nymphet. She who was so cruel and crafty in everyday life, revealed an innocence, a frankness, a kindness of ball-placing, that permitted a second-rate but determined player, no matter how uncouth and incompetent, to poke and cut his way to victory. Despite her small stature, she covered the one thousand and fifty-three square feet of her half of the court with wonderful ease, once she had entered into the rhythm of a rally and as long as she could direct that rhythm; but any abrupt attack, or sudden change of tactics on her adversary's part, left her helpless. At match point, her second serve, which—rather typically—was even stronger and more stylish than her first (for she had none of the inhibitions that cautious winners have), would strike vibrantly the harp-cord of the net—and ricochet out of court. The polished gem of her dropshot was snapped up and put away by an opponent who seemed four-legged and wielded a crooked paddle. Her dramatic drives and lovely volleys would candidly fall at his feet. Over and over again she would land an easy one into the net—and merrily mimic dismay by drooping in a ballet attitude, with her forelocks hanging. So sterile were her grace and whipper that she could not even win from panting me and my old-fashioned lifting drive.

I suppose I am especially susceptible to the magic of games. In my chess sessions with Gaston I saw the board as a square pool of limpid water with rare shells and stratagems rosily visible upon the smooth tessellated bottom, which to my confused adversary was all ooze and squid-cloud. Similarly, the initial tennis coaching I had inflicted on Lolita—prior to the revelations that came to her through the great Californian's lessons— remained in my mind as oppressive and distressful memories— not only because she had been so hopelessly and irritatingly irritated by every suggestion of mine—but because the precious symmetry of the court instead of reflecting the harmonies latent in her was utterly jumbled by the clumsiness and lassitude of the resentful child I mistaught. Now things were different, and on that particular day, in the pure air of Champion, Colorado, on that admirable court at the foot of steep stone stairs leading up to Champion Hotel where we had spent the night, I felt I could rest from the nightmare of unknown betrayals within the innocence of her style, of her soul, of her essential grace.

She was hitting hard and flat, with her usual effortless sweep, feeding me deep skimming balls—all so rhythmically coordinated and overt as to reduce my footwork to, practically, a swinging stroll—crack players will understand what I mean. My rather heavily cut serve that I had been taught by my father who had

1   learned it from Decugis or Borman, old friends of his and great champions, would have seriously troubled my Lo, had I really tried to trouble her. But who would upset such a lucid dear? Did I ever mention that her bare arm bore the 8 of vaccination? That I loved her hopelessly? That she was only fourteen?

2   An inquisitive butterfly passed, dipping, between us.

Two people in tennis shorts, a red-haired fellow only about eight years my junior, with sunburnt bright pink shins, and an indolent dark girl with a moody mouth and hard eyes, about two years Lolita's senior, appeared from nowhere. As is common with dutiful tyros, their rackets were sheathed and framed, and they carried them not as if they were the natural and comfortable extensions of certain specialized muscles, but hammers

3   or blunderbusses or wimbles, or my own dreadful cumbersome sins. Rather unceremoniously seating themselves near my precious coat, on a bench adjacent to the court, they fell to admiring very vocally a rally of some fifty exchanges that Lo innocently helped me to foster and uphold—until there occurred a syncope

4   in the series causing her to gasp as her overhead smash went out of court, whereupon she melted into winsome merriment, my golden pet.

I felt thirsty by then, and walked to the drinking fountain; there Red approached me and in all humility suggested a mixed double. "I am Bill Mead," he said. "And that's Fay Page, ac-

5   tress. Maffy On Say"—he added (pointing with his ridiculously hooded racket at polished Fay who was already talking to Dolly). I was about to reply "Sorry, but—" (for I hate to have my filly involved in the chops and jabs of cheap bunglers), when a remarkably melodious cry diverted my attention: a bellboy was tripping down the steps from the hotel to our court and making me signs. I was wanted, if you please, on an urgent long distance call—so urgent in fact that the line was being held for me. Certainly. I got into my coat (inside pocket heavy with pistol) and told Lo I would be back in a minute. She was picking up a ball —in the continental foot-racket way which was one of the few nice things I had taught her,—and smiled—she smiled at me!

An awful calm kept my heart afloat as I followed the boy up

to the hotel. This, to use an American term, in which discovery, retribution, torture, death, eternity appear in the shape of a singularly repulsive nutshell, was *it*. I had left her in mediocre hands, but it hardly mattered now. I would fight, of course. Oh, I would fight. Better destroy everything than surrender her. Yes, quite a climb.

At the desk, a dignified, Roman-nosed man, with, I suggest, a very obscure past that might reward investigation, handed me a message in his own hand. The line had not been held after all. The note said:

"Mr. Humbert. The head of Birdsley (sic!) School called. Summer residence—Birdsley 2-8282. Please call back immediately. Highly important."

I folded myself into a booth, took a little pill, and for about twenty minutes tussled with space-spooks. A quartet of propositions gradually became audible: soprano, there was no such number in Beardsley; alto, Miss Pratt was on her way to England; tenor, Beardsley School had not telephoned; bass, they could not have done so, since nobody knew I was, that particular day, in Champion, Colo. Upon my stinging him, the Roman took the trouble to find out if there had been a long distance call. There had been none. A fake call from some local dial was not excluded. I thanked him. He said: You bet. After a visit to the purling men's room and a stiff drink at the bar, I started on my return march. From the very first terrace I saw, far below, on the tennis court which seemed the size of a school child's ill-wiped slate, golden Lolita playing in a double. She moved like a fair angel among three horrible Boschian cripples. One of these, her partner, while changing sides, jocosely slapped her on her behind with his racket. He had a remarkably round head and wore incongruous brown trousers. There was a momentary flurry—he saw me, and throwing away his racket—mine!—scuttled up the slope. He waved his wrists and elbows in would-be comical imitation of rudimentary wings, as he climbed, bow-legged, to the street, where his gray car awaited him. Next moment he and the grayness were gone. When I came down, the remaining trio were collecting and sorting out the balls.

"Mr. Mead, who was that person?"

Bill and Fay, both looking very solemn, shook their heads.

1   That absurd intruder had butted in to make up a double, hadn't he, Dolly?

Dolly. The handle of my racket was still disgustingly warm. Before returning to the hotel, I ushered her into a little alley half-smothered in fragrant shrubs, with flowers like smoke, and was about to burst into ripe sobs and plead with her imperturbed dream in the most abject manner for clarification, no matter how meretricious, of the slow awfulness enveloping me, when we found ourselves behind the convulsed Mead twosome —assorted people, you know, meeting among idyllic settings in old comedies. Bill and Fay were both weak with laughter—we had come at the end of their private joke. It did not really matter.

Speaking as if it really did not really matter, and assuming, apparently, that life was automatically rolling on with all its routine pleasures, Lolita said she would like to change into her bathing things, and spend the rest of the afternoon at the swimming pool. It was a gorgeous day. Lolita!

21

"Lo! Lola! Lolita!" I hear myself crying from a doorway into the sun, with the acoustics of time, domed time, endowing my call and its tell-tale hoarseness with such a wealth of anxiety, passion and pain that really it would have been instrumental in wrenching open the zipper of her nylon shroud had she been dead. Lolita! In the middle of a trim turfed terrace I found her at last—she had run out before I was ready. Oh Lolita! There she was playing with a damned dog, not me. The animal, a terrier of sorts, was losing and snapping up again and adjusting
2   between his jaws a wet little red ball; he took rapid chords with his front paws on the resilient turf, and then would bounce away. I had only wanted to see where she was, I could not swim with my heart in that state, but who cared—and there she was,

and there was I, in my robe—and so I stopped calling; but suddenly something in the pattern of her motions, as she dashed this way and that in her Aztec Red bathing briefs and bra, struck me... there was an ecstasy, a madness about her frolics that was too much of a glad thing. Even the dog seemed puzzled by the extravagance of her reactions. I put a gentle hand to my chest as I surveyed the situation. The turquoise blue swimming pool some distance behind the lawn was no longer behind that lawn, but within my thorax, and my organs swam in it like excrements in the blue sea water in Nice. One of the bathers had left the pool and, half-concealed by the peacocked shade of trees, stood quite still, holding the ends of the towel around his neck and following Lolita with his amber eyes. There he stood, in the camouflage of sun and shade, disfigured by them and masked by his own nakedness, his damp black hair or what was left of it, glued to his round head, his little mustache a humid smear, the wool on his chest spread like a symmetrical trophy, his naval pulsating, his hirsute thighs dripping with bright droplets, his tight wet black bathing trunks bloated and bursting with vigor where his great fat bullybag was pulled up and back like a padded shield over his reversed beasthood. And as I looked at his oval nut-brown face, it dawned upon me that what I had recognized him by was the reflection of my daughter's countenance—the same beatitude and grimace but made hideous by his maleness. And I also knew that the child, my child, knew he was looking, enjoyed the lechery of his look and was putting on a show of gambol and glee, the vile and beloved slut. As she made for the ball and missed it, she fell on her back, with her obscene young legs madly pedalling in the air; I could sense the musk of her excitement from where I stood, and then I saw (petrified with a kind of sacred disgust) the man close his eyes and bare his small, horribly small and even, teeth as he leaned against a tree in which a multitude of dappled Priaps shivered. Immediately afterwards a marvelous transformation took place. He was no longer the satyr but a very good-natured and foolish Swiss cousin, the Gustave Trapp I have mentioned more than once, who used to counteract his "sprees" (he drank beer with milk, the good swine) by feats of weight-lifting—tottering and grunting on a lake beach with his otherwise very complete bathing suit jauntily stripped from one shoulder. *This* Trapp noticed me from afar and working the towel on his nape walked back with false insouciance to the pool. And as if the sun had gone out of the game, Lo slackened and slowly got up ignoring the ball that the terrier placed before her. Who can say what heartbreaks are caused in a dog by our discontinuing a romp? I started to say something, and then sat down on the grass with a quite monstrous pain in my chest and vomited a torrent of browns and greens that I had never remembered eating.

I saw Lolita's eyes, and they seemed to be more calculating than frightened. I heard her saying to a kind lady that her father was having a fit. Then for a long time I lay in a lounge chair swallowing pony upon pony of gin. And next morning I felt strong enough to drive on (which in later years no doctor believed).

22

The two-room cabin we had ordered at Silver Spur Court, Elphinstone, turned out to belong to the glossily browned pine-log kind that Lolita used to be so fond of in the days of our carefree first journey; oh, how different things were now! I am not referring to Trapp or Trapps. After all—well, really . . . After all, gentlemen, it was becoming abundantly clear that all those identical detectives in prismatically changing cars were figments of my persecution mania, recurrent images based on coincidence and chance resemblance. *Soyons logiques*, crowed the cocky Gallic part of my brain—and proceeded to rout the notion of a Lolita-maddened salesman or comedy gangster, with stooges, persecuting me, and hoaxing me, and otherwise taking riotous advantage of my strange relations with the law. I remember humming my panic away. I remember evolving even an explanation of the "Birdsley" telephone call . . . But if I could dismiss Trapp, as I had dismissed my convulsions on the lawn at

Champion, I could do nothing with the anguish of knowing Lolita to be so tantalizingly, so miserably unattainable and beloved on the very eve of a new era, when my alembics told me she should stop being a nymphet, stop torturing me.

An additional, abominable, and perfectly gratuitous worry was lovingly prepared for me in Elphinstone. Lo had been dull and silent during the last lap—two hundred mountainous miles uncontaminated by smoke-gray sleuths or zigzagging zanies. She hardly glanced at the famous, oddly shaped, splendidly flushed rock which jutted above the mountains and had been the take-off for nirvana on the part of a temperamental show girl. The town was newly built, or rebuilt, on the flat floor of a seven-thousand-foot-high valley; it would soon bore Lo, I hoped, and we would spin on to California, to the Mexican border, to mythical bays, saguaro deserts, fatamorganas. José Lizzarrabengoa, as you remember, planned to take his Carmen to the *Etats Unis*. I conjured up a Central American tennis competition in which Dolores Haze and various Californian schoolgirl champions would dazzlingly participate. Good-will tours on that smiling level eliminate the distinction between passport and sport. Why did I hope we would be happy abroad? A change of environment is the traditional fallacy upon which doomed loves, and lungs, rely.

Mrs. Hays, the brisk, brickly rouged, blue-eyed widow who ran the motor court, asked me if I were Swiss perchance, because her sister had married a Swiss ski instructor. I was, whereas my daughter happened to be half Irish. I registered, Hays gave me the key and a twinkling smile, and, still twinkling, showed me where to park the car; Lo crawled out and shivered a little: the luminous evening air was decidedly crisp. Upon entering the cabin, she sat down on a chair at a card table, buried her face in the crook of her arm and said she felt awful. Shamming, I thought, shamming, no doubt, to evade my caresses; I was passionately parched; but she began to whimper in an unusually dreary way when I attempted to fondle her. Lolita ill. Lolita dying. Her skin was scalding hot! I took her temperature, orally, then looked up a scribbled formula I fortunately had in a jotter

1, 2, 3

4

5

and after laboriously reducing the, meaningless to me, degrees Fahrenheit to the intimate centrigrade of my childhood, found she had 40.4, which at least made sense. Hysterical little nymphs might, I knew, run up all kinds of temperature—even exceeding a fatal count. And I would have given her a sip of hot spiced wine, and two aspirins, and kissed the fever away, if, upon an examination of her lovely uvula, one of the gems of her body, I had not seen that it was a burning red. I undressed her. Her breath was bittersweet. Her brown rose tasted of blood. She was shaking from head to toe. She complained of a painful stiffness in the upper vertebrae—and I thought of poliomyelitis as any American parent would. Giving up all hope of intercourse, I wrapped her up in a laprobe and carried her into the car. Kind Mrs. Hays in the meantime had alerted the local doctor. "You are lucky it happened here," she said; for not only was Blue the best man in the district, but the Elphinstone hospital was as modern as modern could be, despite its limited capacity. With a heterosexual Erlkönig in pursuit, thither I drove, half-blinded by a royal sunset on the lowland side and guided by a little old woman, a portable witch, perhaps his daughter, whom Mrs. Hays had lent me, and whom I was never to see again. Dr. Blue, whose learning, no doubt, was infinitely inferior to his reputation, assured me it was a virus infection, and when I alluded to her comparatively recent flu, curtly said this was another bug, he had forty such cases on his hands; all of which sounded like the "ague" of the ancients. I wondered if I should mention, with a casual chuckle, that my fifteen-year-old daughter had had a minor accident while climbing an awkward fence with her boy friend, but knowing I was drunk, I decided to withhold the information till later if necessary. To an unsmiling blond bitch of a secretary I gave my daughter's age as "practically sixteen." While I was not looking, my child was taken away from me! In vain I insisted I be allowed to spend the night on a "welcome" mat in a corner of their damned hospital. I ran up constructivistic flights of stairs, I tried to trace my darling so as to tell her she had better not babble, especially if she felt as lightheaded as we all did. At one point, I was rather dreadfully rude to a very young and very cheeky nurse with overdeveloped gluteal parts and blazing black eyes —of Basque descent, as I learned. Her father was an imported shepherd, a trainer of sheep dogs. Finally, I returned to the car and remained in it for I do not know how many hours, hunched up in the dark, stunned by my new solitude, looking out open-mouthed now at the dimly illumed, very square and low hospital building squatting in the middle of its lawny block, now up at the wash of stars and the jagged silvery ramparts of the *haute montagne* where at the moment Mary's father, lonely Joseph Lore, was dreaming of Oloron, Lagore, Rolas—*que sais-je!* —or seducing a ewe. Such-like fragrant vagabond thoughts have been always a solace to me in times of unusual stress, and only when, despite liberal libations, I felt fairly numbed by the endless night, did I think of driving back to the motel. The old woman had disappeared, and I was not quite sure of my way. Wide gravel roads criss-crossed drowsy rectangular shadows. I made out what looked like the silhouette of gallows on what was probably a school playground; and in another wastelike block there rose in domed silence the pale temple of some local sect. I found the highway at last, and then the motel, where millions of so-called "millers," a kind of insect, were swarming around the neon contours of "No Vacancy"; and, when, at 3 A.M., after one of those untimely hot showers which like some mordant only help to fix a man's despair and weariness, I lay on her bed that smelled of chestnuts and roses, and peppermint, and the very delicate, very special French perfume I latterly allowed her to use, I found myself unable to assimilate the simple fact that for the first time in two years I was separated from my Lolita. All at once it occurred to me that her illness was somehow the development of a theme—that it had the same taste and tone as the series of linked impressions which had puzzled and tormented me during our journey; I imagined that secret agent, or secret lover, or prankster, or hallucination, or whatever he was, prowling around the hospital—and Aurora had hardly "warmed her hands," as the pickers of lavender say in the country of my birth, when I found myself trying to get into

1
2

3

4
5
6

that dungeon again, knocking upon its green doors, breakfast-less, stool-less, in despair.

This was Tuesday, and Wednesday or Thursday, splendidly reacting like the darling she was to some "serum" (sparrow's sperm or dugong's dung), she was much better, and the doctor said that in a couple of days she would be "skipping" again.

Of the eight times I visited her, the last one alone remains sharply engraved on my mind. It had been a great feat to come for I felt all hollowed out by the infection that by then was at work on me too. None will know the strain it was to carry that bouquet, that load of love, those books that I had traveled sixty miles to buy: Browning's *Dramatic Works, The History of Dancing, Clowns and Columbines, The Russian Ballet, Flowers of the Rockies, The Theatre Guild Anthology, Tennis* by Helen Wills, who had won the National Junior Girl Singles at the age of fifteen. As I was staggering up to the door of my daughter's thirteen-dollar-a-day private room, Mary Lore, the beastly young part-time nurse who had taken an unconcealed dislike to me, emerged with a finished breakfast tray, placed it with a quick crash on a chair in the corridor, and, fundament jigging, shot back into the room—probably to warn her poor little Dolores that the tyrannic old father was creeping up on crepe soles, with books and bouquet: the latter I had composed of wild flowers and beautiful leaves gathered with my own gloved hands on a mountain pass at sunrise (I hardly slept at all that fateful week).

Feeding my Carmencita well? Idly I glanced at the tray. On a yolk-stained plate there was a crumpled envelope. It had contained something, since one edge was torn, but there was no address on it—nothing at all, save a phony armorial design with "Ponderosa Lodge" in green letters; thereupon I performed a *chassé-croisé* with Mary, who was in the act of bustling out again—wonderful how fast they move and how little they do, those rumpy young nurses. She glowered at the envelope I had put back, uncrumpled.

"You better not touch," she said, nodding directionally. "Could burn your fingers."

Below my dignity to rejoin. All I said was:

"*Je croyais que c'était un* bill—not a *billet doux.*" Then, 1
entering the sunny room, to Lolita: "*Bonjour, mon petit.*"

"Dolores," said Mary Lore, entering with me, past me,
through me, the plump whore, and blinking, and starting to
fold very rapidly a white flannel blanket as she blinked: "Dolores,
your pappy thinks you are getting letters from my boy friend.
It's me (smugly tapping herself on the small gilt cross she wore)
gets them. And my pappy can parlay-voo as well as yours."

She left the room. Dolores, so rosy and russet, lips freshly
painted, hair brilliantly brushed, bare arms straightened out on
neat coverlet, lay innocently beaming at me or nothing. On the
bed table, next to a paper napkin and a pencil, her topaz ring
burned in the sun.

"What gruesome funeral flowers," she said. "Thanks all the
same. But do you mind very much cutting out the French? It
annoys everybody."

Back at the usual rush came the ripe young hussy, reeking
of urine and garlic, with the *Deseret News*, which her fair 2
patient eagerly accepted, ignoring the sumptuously illustrated
volumes I had brought.

"My sister Ann," said Mary (topping information with after- 3
thought), "works at the Ponderosa place."

Poor Bluebeard. Those brutal brothers. *Est-ce que tu ne
m'aimes plus, ma Carmen?* She never had. At the moment I 4
knew my love was as hopeless as ever—and I also knew the two
girls were conspirators, plotting in Basque, or Zemfirian, against 5, 6
my hopeless love. I shall go further and say that Lo was playing
a double game since she was also fooling sentimental Mary 7
whom she had told, I suppose, that she wanted to dwell with
her fun-loving young uncle and not with cruel melancholy me.
And another nurse whom I never identified, and the village
idiot who carted cots and coffins into the elevator, and the
idiotic green love birds in a cage in the waiting room—all were
in the plot, the sordid plot. I suppose Mary thought comedy
father Professor Humbertoldi was interfering with the romance
between Dolores and her father-substitute, roly-poly Romeo (for 8

you *were* rather lardy, you know, Rom, despite all that "snow" and "joy juice").

My throat hurt. I stood, swallowing, at the window and stared at the mountains, at the romantic rock high up in the smiling plotting sky.

"My Carmen," I said (I used to call her that sometimes), "we shall leave this raw sore town as soon as you get out of bed."

1   "Incidentally, I want all my clothes," said the gitanilla, humping up her knees and turning to another page.

". . . Because, really," I continued, "there is no point in staying here."

"There is no point in staying anywhere," said Lolita.

I lowered myself into a cretonne chair and, opening the attractive botanical work, attempted, in the fever-humming hush of the room, to identify my flowers. This proved impossible. Presently a musical bell softly sounded somewhere in the passage.

I do not think they had more than a dozen patients (three or four were lunatics, as Lo had cheerfully informed me earlier) in that show place of a hospital, and the staff had too much leisure. However—likewise for reasons of show—regulations were rigid. It is also true that I kept coming at the wrong hours. Not without a secret flow of dreamy *malice*, visionary Mary (next

2   time it will be *une belle dame toute en bleu* floating through Roaring Gulch) plucked me by the sleeve to lead me out. I looked at her hand; it dropped. As I was leaving, leaving voluntarily, Dolores Haze reminded me to bring her next morning . . . She did not remember where the various things she wanted were . . . "Bring me," she cried (out of sight already, door on the move, closing, closed), "the new gray suitcase and Mother's trunk"; but by next morning I was shivering, and boozing, and dying in the motel bed she had used for just a few minutes, and the best I could do under the circular and dilating circumstances was to send the two bags over with the widow's beau, a robust and kindly trucker. I imagined Lo displaying her treasures to Mary . . . No doubt, I was a little delirious—and on the following day I was still a vibration rather than a solid, for

when I looked out of the bathroom window at the adjacent lawn, I saw Dolly's beautiful young bicycle propped up there on its support, the graceful front wheel looking away from me, as it always did, and a sparrow perched on the saddle—but it was the landlady's bike, and smiling a little, and shaking my poor head over my fond fancies, I tottered back to my bed, and lay as quiet as a saint—   1

> *Saint*, forsooth! While brown Dolores,
> On a patch of sunny green
> With Sanchicha reading stories
> In a movie magazine—

—which was represented by numerous specimens wherever Dolores landed, and there was some great national celebration in town judging by the firecrackers, veritable bombs, that exploded all the time, and at five minutes to two P.M. I heard the sound of whistling lips nearing the half-opened door of my cabin, and then a thump upon it.

It was big Frank. He remained framed in the opened door, one hand on its jamb, leaning forward a little.

Howdy. Nurse Lore was on the telephone. She wanted to know was I better and would I come today?

At twenty paces Frank used to look a mountain of health; at five, as now, he was a ruddy mosaic of scars—had been blown through a wall overseas; but despite nameless injuries he was able to man a tremendous truck, fish, hunt, drink, and buoyantly dally with roadside ladies. That day, either because it was such a great holiday, or simply because he wanted to divert a   2 sick man, he had taken off the glove he usually wore on his left hand (the one pressing against the side of the door) and revealed to the fascinated sufferer not only an entire lack of fourth and fifth fingers, but also a naked girl, with cinnabar nipples and indigo delta, charmingly tattooed on the back of his crippled hand, its index and middle digit making her legs while his wrist bore her flower-crowned head. Oh, delicious . . . reclining against the woodwork, like some sly fairy.   3

I asked him to tell Mary Lore I would stay in bed all day   4 and would get into touch with my daughter sometime to-morrow if I felt probably Polynesian.

He noticed the direction of my gaze and made her right hip twitch amorously.

"Okey-dokey," big Frank sang out, slapped the jamb, and whistling, carried my message away, and I went on drinking, and by morning the fever was gone, and although I was as limp as a toad, I put on the purple dressing gown over my maize yellow pajamas, and walked over to the office telephone. Everything was fine. A bright voice informed me that yes, everything was fine, my daughter had checked out the day before, around two, her uncle, Mr. Gustave, had called for her with a cocker spaniel pup and a smile for everyone, and a black Caddy Lack, and had paid Dolly's bill in cash, and told them to tell me I should not worry, and keep warm, they were at Grandpa's ranch as agreed.

Elphinstone was, and I hope still is, a very cute little town. It was spread like a maquette, you know, with its neat green-wool trees and red-roofed houses over the valley floor and I think I have alluded earlier to its model school and temple and spacious rectangular blocks, some of which were, curiously enough, just unconventional pastures with a mule or a unicorn grazing in the young July morning mist. Very amusing: at one gravel-groaning sharp turn I sideswiped a parked car but said to myself telestically—and, telephathically (I hoped), to its gesticulating owner—that I would return later, address Bird School, Bird, New Bird, the gin kept my heart alive but bemazed my brain, and after some lapses and losses common to dream sequences, I found myself in the reception room, trying to beat up the doctor, and roaring at people under chairs, and clamoring for Mary who luckily for her was not there; rough hands plucked at my dressing gown, ripping off a pocket, and somehow I seem to have been sitting on a bald brown-headed patient, whom I had mistaken for Dr. Blue, and who eventually stood up, remarking with a preposterous accent: "Now, who is nevrotic, I ask?"—and then a gaunt unsmiling nurse presented me with seven beautiful, *beautiful* books and the exquisitely

folded tartan lap robe, and demanded a receipt; and in the
sudden silence I became aware of a policeman in the hallway,
to whom my fellow motorist was pointing me out, and meekly
I signed the very symbolic receipt, thus surrendering my Lolita
to all those apes. But what else could I do? One simple and
stark thought stood out and this was: "Freedom for the moment is everything." One false move—and I might have been
made to explain a life of crime. So I simulated a coming out
of a daze. To my fellow motorist I paid what he thought was
fair. To Dr. Blue, who by then was stroking my hand, I spoke
in tears of the liquor I bolstered too freely a tricky but not
necessarily diseased heart with. To the hospital in general I
apologized with a flourish that almost bowled me over, adding
however that I was not on particularly good terms with the rest
of the Humbert clan. To myself I whispered that I still had my
gun, and was still a free man—free to trace the fugitive, free to
destroy my brother.

1

23

A thousand-mile stretch of silk-smooth road separated Kasbeam, where, to the best of my belief, the red fiend had been
scheduled to appear for the first time, and fateful Elphinstone
which we had reached about a week before Independence Day.
The journey had taken up most of June for we had seldom
made more than a hundred and fifty miles per traveling day,
spending the rest of the time, up to five days in one case, at
various stopping places, all of them also prearranged, no doubt.
It was that stretch, then, along which the fiend's spoor should
be sought; and to this I devoted myself, after several unmentionable days of dashing up and down the relentlessly radiating
roads in the vicinity of Elphinstone.

2

Imagine me, reader, with my shyness, my distaste for any
ostentation, my inherent sense of the *comme il faut*, imagine
me masking the frenzy of my grief with a trembling ingratiating
smile while devising some casual pretext to flip through the

3

hotel register: "Oh," I would say, "I am almost positive that I stayed here once—let me look up the entries for mid-June —no, I see I'm wrong after all—what a very quaint name for 1 a home town, Kawtagain. Thanks very much." Or: "I had a customer staying here—I mislaid his address—may I ...?" And every once in a while, especially if the operator of the place happened to be a certain type of gloomy male, personal inspection of the books was denied me.

I have a memo here: between July 5 and November 18, when I returned to Beardsley for a few days, I registered, if 2 not actually stayed, at 342 hotels, motels and tourist homes. This figure includes a few registrations between Chestnut and Beardsley, one of which yielded a shadow of the fiend ("N. Petit, 3 Larousse, Ill."); I had to space and time my inquiries carefully so as not to attract undue attention; and there must have been at least fifty places where I merely inquired at the desk—but that was a futile quest, and I preferred building up a foundation of verisimilitude and good will by first paying for an unneeded room. My survey showed that of the 300 or so books inspected, at least 20 provided me with a clue: the loitering fiend had stopped even more often than we, or else—he was quite capable of that—he had thrown in additional registrations in order to keep me well furnished with derisive hints. Only in one case had he actually stayed at the same motor court as we, a few 4 paces from Lolita's pillow. In some instances he had taken up quarters in the same or in a neighboring block; not infrequently he had lain in wait at an intermediate spot between two bespoken points. How vividly I recalled Lolita, just before our departure from Beardsley, prone on the parlor rug, studying tour books and maps, and marking laps and stops with her lipstick!

I discovered at once that he had foreseen my investigations and had planted insulting pseudonyms for my special benefit. 5 At the very first motel office I visited, Ponderosa Lodge, his entry, among a dozen obviously human ones, read: Dr. Gratiano 6 Forbeson, Mirandola, NY. Its Italian Comedy connotations could not fail to strike me, of course. The landlady deigned to inform me that the gentleman had been laid up for five days with a bad cold, that he had left his car for repairs in some garage or other and that he had checked out on the 4th of July. Yes, a girl called Ann Lore had worked formerly at the Lodge, but was now married to a grocer in Cedar City. One moonlit night I waylaid white-shoed Mary on a solitary street; an automaton, she was about to shriek, but I managed to humanize her by the simple act of falling on my knees and with pious yelps imploring her to help. She did not know a thing, she swore. Who was this Gratiano Forbeson? She seemed to waver. I whipped out a hundred-dollar bill. She lifted it to the light of the moon. "He is your brother," she whispered at last. I plucked the bill out of her moon-cold hand, and spitting out a French curse turned and ran away. This taught me to rely on myself alone. No detective could discover the clues Trapp had tuned to my mind and manner. I could not hope, of course, he would ever leave his correct name and address; but I did hope he might slip on the glaze of his own subtlety, by daring, say, to introduce a richer and more personal shot of color than was strictly necessary, or by revealing too much through a qualitative sum of quantitative parts which revealed too little. In one thing he succeeded: he succeeded in thoroughly enmeshing me and my thrashing anguish in his demoniacal game. With infinite skill, he swayed and staggered, and regained an impossible balance, always leaving me with the sportive hope—if I may use such a term in speaking of betrayal, fury, desolation, horror and hate—that he might give himself away next time. He never did —though coming damn close to it. We all admire the spangled acrobat with classical grace meticulously walking his tight rope in the talcum light; but how much rarer art there is in the sagging rope expert wearing scarecrow clothes and impersonating a grotesque drunk! *I* should know.

The clues he left did not establish his identity but they reflected his personality, or at least a certain homogenous and striking personality; his genre, his type of humor—at its best at least—the tone of his brain, had affinities with my own. He mimed and mocked me. His allusions were definitely highbrow. He was well-read. He knew French. He was versed in logodaedaly

1 and logomancy. He was an amateur of sex lore. He had a feminine handwriting. He would change his name but he could not disguise, no matter how he slanted them, his very peculiar t's,
2 w's and l's. Quelquepart Island was one of his favorite residences. He did not use a fountain pen which fact, as any psychoanalyst will tell you, meant that the patient was a repressed undinist. One mercifully hopes there are water nymphs in the
3 Styx.

   His main trait was his passion for tantalization. Goodness, what a tease the poor fellow was! He challenged my scholarship. I am sufficiently proud of my knowing something to be modest about my not knowing all; and I daresay I missed some
4 elements in that cryptogrammic paper chase. What a shiver of triumph and loathing shook my frail frame when, among the plain innocent names in the hotel recorder, his fiendish conundrum would ejaculate in my face! I noticed that whenever he felt his enigmas were becoming too recondite, even for such a solver as I, he would lure me back with an easy one. "Arsène
5 Lupin" was obvious to a Frenchman who remembered the detective stories of his youth; and one hardly had to be a Coleridg-
6 ian to appreciate the trite poke of "A. Person, Porlock, England." In horrible taste but basically suggestive of a cultured man—not a policeman, not a common goon, not a lewd salesman—were such assumed names as "Arthur Rainbow"—plainly the travestied author of *Le Bateau Bleu*—let me laugh a little too, gentlemen—and "Morris Schmetterling," of *L'Oiseau Ivre*
7 fame (*touché*, reader!). The silly but funny "D. Orgon, Elmira,
8 NY," was from Molière, of course, and because I had quite recently tried to interest Lolita in a famous 18th-century play,
9 I welcomed as an old friend "Harry Bumper, Sheridan, Wyo." An ordinary encyclopedia informed me who the peculiar look-
10 ing "Phineas Quimby, Lebanon, NH" was; and any good Freudian, with a German name and some interest in religious prostitution, should recognize at a glance the implication of
11 "Dr. Kitzler, Eryx, Miss." So far so good. That sort of fun was shoddy but on the whole impersonal and thus innocuous. Among entries that arrested my attention as undoubtable clues

per se but baffled me in respect to their finer points I do not care to mention many since I feel I am groping in a border-land mist with verbal phantoms turning, perhaps, into living vacationists. Who was "Johnny Randall, Ramble, Ohio"? Or was he a real person who just happened to write a hand similar to "N.S. Aristoff, Catagela, NY"? What was the sting in "Catagela"? And what about "James Mavor Morell, Hoaxton, England"? "Aristophanes," "hoax"—fine, but what was I missing?

There was one strain running through all that pseudonymity which caused me especially painful palpitations when I came across it. Such things as "G. Trapp, Geneva, NY." was the sign of treachery on Lolita's part. "Aubrey Beardsley, Quelquepart Island" suggested more lucidly than the garbled telephone message had that the starting point of the affair should be looked for in the East. "Lucas Picador, Merrymay, Pa." insinuated that my Carmen had betrayed my pathetic endearments to the impostor. Horribly cruel, forsooth, was "Will Brown, Dolores, Colo." The gruesome "Harold Haze, Tombstone, Arizona" (which at another time would have appealed to my sense of humor) implied a familiarity with the girl's past that in nightmare fashion suggested for a moment that my quarry was an old friend of the family, maybe an old flame of Charlotte's, maybe a redresser of wrongs ("Donald Quix, Sierra, Nev."). But the most penetrating bodkin was the anagramtailed entry in the register of Chestnut Lodge "Ted Hunter, Cane, NH.".

The garbled license numbers left by all these Persons and Orgons and Morells and Trapps only told me that motel keepers omit to check if guests' cars are accurately listed. References—incompletely or incorrectly indicated—to the cars the fiend had hired for short laps between Wace and Elphinstone were of course useless; the license of the initial Aztec was a shimmer of shifting numerals, some transposed, others altered or omitted, but somehow forming interrelated combinations (such as "WS 1564" and "SH 1616," and "Q32888" or "CU 88322") which however were so cunningly contrived as to never reveal a common denominator.

It occurred to me that after he had turned that convertible over to accomplices at Wace and switched to the stage-motor car system, his successors might have been less careful and might have inscribed at some hotel office the archtype of those inter-related figures. But if looking for the fiend along a road I knew he had taken was such a complicated vague and unprofitable business, what could I expect from any attempt to trace unknown motorists traveling along unknown routes?

24

By the time I reached Beardsley, in the course of the har-rowing recapitulation I have now discussed at sufficient length, a complete image had formed in my mind; and through the—always risky—process of elimination I had reduced this image to the only concrete source that morbid cerebration and torpid memory could give it.

Except for the Rev. Rigor Mortis (as the girls called him), and an old gentleman who taught non-obligatory German and Latin, there were no regular male teachers at Beardsley School. But on two occasions an art instructor on the Beardsley College faculty had come over to show the schoolgirls magic lantern pictures of French castles and nineteenth-century paintings. I had wanted to attend those projections and talks, but Dolly, as was her wont, had asked me not to, period. I also remem-bered that Gaston had referred to that particular lecturer as a brilliant *garçon;* but that was all; memory refused to supply me with the name of the chateau-lover.

On the day fixed for the execution, I walked through the sleet across the campus to the information desk in Maker Hall, Beardsley College. There I learned that the fellow's name was Riggs (rather like that of the minister), that he was a bachelor, and that in ten minutes he would issue from the "Museum" where he was having a class. In the passage leading to the audi-torium I sat on a marble bench of sorts donated by Cecilia

Dalrymple Ramble. As I waited there, in prostatic discomfort, drunk, sleep-starved, with my gun in my fist in my raincoat pocket, it suddenly occurred to me that I was demented and was about to do something stupid. There was not one chance in a million that Albert Riggs, Ass. Prof., was hiding my Lolita at his Beardsley home, 24 Pritchard Road. He could not be the villain. It was absolutely preposterous. I was losing my time and my wits. He and she were in California and not here at all.

Presently, I noticed a vague commotion behind some white statues; a door—not the one I had been staring at—opened briskly, and amid a bevy of women students a baldish head and two bright brown eyes bobbed, advanced.

He was a total stranger to me but insisted we had met at a lawn party at Beardsley School. How was my delightful tennis-playing daughter? He had another class. He would be seeing me.

Another attempt at identification was less speedily resolved: through an advertisement in one of Lo's magazines I dared to get in touch with a private detective, an ex-pugilist, and merely to give him some idea of the *method* adopted by the fiend, I acquainted him with the kind of names and addresses I had collected. He demanded a goodish deposit and for two years— two years, reader!—that imbecile busied himself with checking those nonsense data. I had long severed all monetary relations with him when he turned up one day with the triumphant information that an eighty-year-old Indian by the name of Bill Brown lived near Dolores, Colo.

25

This book is about Lolita; and now that I have reached the part which (had I not been forestalled by another internal combustion martyr) might be called "*Dolorès Disparue*," there would be little sense in analyzing the three empty years that followed. While a few pertinent points have to be marked, the general impression I desire to convey is of a side door crashing open in life's full flight, and a rush of roaring black time drowning with its whipping wind the cry of lone disaster.

Singularly enough, I seldom if ever dreamed of Lolita as I remembered her—as I saw her constantly and obsessively in my conscious mind during my daymares and insomnias. More precisely: she did haunt my sleep but she appeared there in strange and ludicrous disguises as Valeria or Charlotte, or a cross between them. That complex ghost would come to me, shedding shift after shift, in an atmosphere of great melancholy and disgust, and would recline in dull invitation on some narrow board or hard settee, with flesh ajar like the rubber valve of a soccer ball's bladder. I would find myself, dentures fractured or hopelessly mislaid, in horrible *chambres garnies* where I would be entertained at tedious vivisecting parties that generally ended with Charlotte or Valeria weeping in my bleeding arms and being tenderly kissed by my brotherly lips in a dream disorder of auctioneered Viennese bric-à-brac, pity, impotence and the brown wigs of tragic old women who had just been gassed.

One day I removed from the car and destroyed an accumulation of teen-magazines. You know the sort. Stone age at heart; up to date, or at least Mycenaean, as to hygiene. A handsome, very ripe actress with huge lashes and a pulpy red underlip, endorsing a shampoo. Ads and fads. Young scholars dote on plenty of pleats—*que c'était loin, tout cela!* It is your hostess' duty to provide robes. Unattached details take all the sparkle out of your conversation. All of us have known "pickers"—one who picks her cuticle at the office party. Unless he is very elderly or very important, a man should remove his gloves before shaking hands with a woman. Invite Romance by wearing the Exciting New Tummy Flattener. Trims tums, nips hips. Tristram in Movielove. Yessir! The Joe-Roe marital enigma is making yaps flap. Glamourize yourself quickly and inexpensively. Comics. Bad girl dark hair fat father cigar; good girl red hair handsome daddums clipped mustache. Or that repulsive strip with the big gagoon and his wife, a kiddoid gnomide. *Et moi qui t'offrais mon génie*...I recalled the rather charming non-

sense verse I used to write her when she was a child: "nonsense,"
she used to say mockingly, "is correct."

> The Squirl and his Squirrel, the Rabs and their Rabbits
> Have certain obscure and peculiar habits.
> Male hummingbirds make the most exquisite rockets.
> The snake when he walks holds his hands in his pockets...

Other things of hers were harder to relinquish. Up to the end
of 1949, I cherished and adored, and stained with my kisses and
merman tears, a pair of old sneakers, a boy's shirt she had worn, 1
some ancient blue jeans I found in the trunk compartment, a
crumpled school cap, suchlike wanton treasures. Then, when
I understood my mind was cracking, I collected these sundry
belongings, added to them what had been stored in Beardsley—
a box of books, her bicycle, old coats, galoshes—and on her
fifteenth birthday mailed everything as an anonymous gift to a
home for orphaned girls on a windy lake, on the Canadian
border.

It is just possible that had I gone to a strong hypnotist he
might have extracted from me and arrayed in a logical pattern
certain chance memories that I have threaded through my book
with considerably more ostentation than they present themselves with to my mind even now when I know what to seek in
the past. At the time I felt I was merely losing contact with
reality; and after spending the rest of the winter and most of the 2
following spring in a Quebec sanatorium where I had stayed
before, I resolved first to settle some affairs of mine in New York
and then to proceed to California for a thorough search there.

Here is something I composed in my retreat: 3

> Wanted, wanted: Dolores Haze.
> Hair: brown. Lips: scarlet.
> Age: five thousand three hundred days.
> Profession: none, or "starlet."
>
> Where are you hiding, Dolores Haze?
> *Why* are you hiding, darling?
> (I talk in a daze, I walk in a maze,
> I cannot get out, said the starling). 4

Where are you riding, Dolores Haze?
What make is the magic carpet?
Is a Cream Cougar the present craze?
And where are you parked, my car pet?

Who is your hero, Dolores Haze?
Still one of those blue-caped star-men?
Oh the balmy days and the palmy bays,
And the cars, and the bars, my Carmen!

Oh Dolores, that juke-box hurts!
Are you still dancin', darlin'?
(Both in worn levis, both in torn T-shirts,
And I, in my corner, snarlin').

Happy, happy is gnarled McFate
Touring the States with a child wife,
Plowing his Molly in every State
Among the protected wild life.

1   My Dolly, my folly! Her eyes were *vair*,
And never closed when I kissed her.
2   Know an old perfume called *Soleil Vert*?
Are you from Paris, mister?

L'autre soir un air froid d'opéra m'alita:
Son félé—bien fol est qui s'y fie!
Il neige, le décor s'écroule, Lolita!
3   *Lolita, qu'ai-je fait de ta vie?*

Dying, dying, Lolita Haze,
Of hate and remorse, I'm dying.
And again my hairy fist I raise,
And again I hear you crying.

Officer, officer, there they go—
In the rain, where that lighted store is!
And her socks are white, and I love her so,
And her name is Haze, Dolores.

Lolita

Officer, officer, there they are—
Dolores Haze and her lover!
Whip out your gun and follow that car.
Now tumble out, and take cover.

Wanted, wanted: Dolores Haze.
Her dream-gray gaze never flinches.
Ninety pounds is all she weighs
With a height of sixty inches.

My car is limping, Dolores Haze,
And the last long lap is the hardest,
And I shall be dumped where the weed decays,
And the rest is rust and stardust.

By psychoanalyzing this poem, I notice it is really a maniac's masterpiece. The stark, stiff, lurid rhymes correspond very exactly to certain perspectiveless and terrible landscapes and figures, and magnified parts of landscapes and figures, as drawn by psychopaths in tests devised by their astute trainers. I wrote many more poems. I immersed myself in the poetry of others. But not for a second did I forget the load of revenge.

I would be a knave to say, and the reader a fool to believe, that the shock of losing Lolita cured me of pederosis. My accursed nature could not change, no matter how my love for her did. On playgrounds and beaches, my sullen and stealthy eye, against my will, still sought out the flash of a nymphet's limbs, the sly tokens of Lolita's handmaids and rosegirls. But one essential vision in me had withered: never did I dwell now on possibilities of bliss with a little maiden, specific or synthetic, in some out-of-the-way place; never did my fancy sink its fangs into Lolita's sisters, far far away, in the coves of evoked islands. *That* was all over, for the time being at least. On the other hand, alas, two years of monstrous indulgence had left me with certain habits of lust: I feared lest the void I lived in might drive me to plunge into the freedom of sudden insanity when confronted with a chance temptation in some lane between school and supper. Solitude was corrupting me. I needed company and care. My heart was a hysterical unreliable organ. This is how Rita enters the picture.

26

She was twice Lolita's age and three quarters of mine: a very slight, dark-haired, pale-skinned adult, weighing a hundred and five pounds, with charmingly asymmetrical eyes, an angular, rapidly sketched profile, and a most appealing *ensellure* to her supple back—I think she had some Spanish or Babylonian blood. I picked her up one depraved May evening somewhere between Montreal and New York, or more narrowly, between Toylestown and Blake, at a darkishly burning bar under the sign of the Tigermoth, where she was amiably drunk: she insisted we had gone to school together, and she placed her trembling little hand on my ape paw. My senses were very slightly stirred but I decided to give her a try; I did—and adopted her as a constant companion. She was so kind, was Rita, such a good sport, that I daresay she would have given herself to any pathetic creature or fallacy, an old broken tree or a bereaved porcupine, out of sheer chumminess and compassion.

When I first met her she had but recently divorced her third husband—and a little more recently had been abandoned by her seventh *cavalier servant*—the others, the mutables, were too numerous and mobile to tabulate. Her brother was—and no doubt still is—a prominent, pasty-faced, suspenders-and-painted-tie-wearing politician, mayor and booster of his ball-playing, Bible-reading, grain-handling home town. For the last eight years he had been paying his great little sister several hundred dollars per month under the stringent condition that she would never never enter great little Grainball City. She told me, with wails of wonder, that for some God-damn reason every new boy friend of hers would first of all take her Grainball-ward: it was a fatal attraction; and before she knew what was what, she would

find herself sucked into the lunar orbit of the town, and would
be following the flood-lit drive that encircled it—"going round
and round," as she phrased it, "like a God-damn mulberry
moth."   1

She had a natty little coupé; and in it we traveled to California
so as to give my venerable vehicle a rest. Her natural speed was
ninety. Dear Rita! We cruised together for two dim years, from
summer 1950 to summer 1952, and she was the sweetest, simplest, gentlest, dumbest Rita imaginable. In comparison to her,
Valechka was a Schlegel, and Charlotte a Hegel. There is no   2, 3
earthly reason why I should dally with her in the margin of this
sinister memoir, but let me say (hi, Rita—wherever you are,
drunk or hangoverish, Rita, hi!) that she was the most soothing,
the most comprehending companion that I ever had, and certainly saved me from the madhouse. I told her I was trying to
trace a girl and plug that girl's bully. Rita solemnly approved of
the plan—and in the course of some investigation she undertook
on her own (without really knowing a thing), around San Hum-
bertino, got entangled with a pretty awful crook herself; I had
the devil of a time retrieving her—used and bruised but still
cocky. Then one day she proposed playing Russian roulette with
my sacred automatic; I said you couldn't, it was not a revolver,
and we struggled for it, until at last it went off, touching off a very
thin and very comical spurt of hot water from the hole it made
in the wall of the cabin room; I remember her shrieks of laughter.

The oddly prepubescent curve of her back, her ricey skin, her
slow languorous columbine kisses kept me from mischief. It is
not the artistic aptitudes that are secondary sexual characters as
some shams and shamans have said; it is the other way around: 4
sex is but the ancilla of art. One rather mysterious spree that had 5
interesting repercussions I must notice. I had abandoned the
search: the fiend was either in Tartary or burning away in my   6
cerebellum (the flames fanned by my fancy and grief) but certainly not having Dolores Haze play champion tennis on the
Pacific Coast. One afternoon, on our way back East, in a hideous
hotel, the kind where they hold conventions and where labeled,
fat, pink men stagger around, all first names and business and

booze—dear Rita and I awoke to find a third in our room, a blond, almost albino, young fellow with white eyelashes and large transparent ears, whom neither Rita nor I recalled having ever seen in our sad lives. Sweating in thick dirty underwear, and with old army boots on, he lay snoring on the double bed beyond my chaste Rita. One of his front teeth was gone, amber pustules grew on his forehead. Ritochka enveloped her sinuous nudity in my raincoat—the first thing at hand; I slipped on a pair of candy-striped drawers; and we took stock of the situation. Five glasses had been used, which, in the way of clues, was an embarrassment of riches. The door was not properly closed. A sweater and a pair of shapeless tan pants lay on the floor. We shook their owner into miserable consciousness. He was completely amnesic. In an accent that Rita recognized as pure Brooklynese, he peevishly insinuated that somehow we had purloined his (worthless) identity. We rushed him into his clothes and left him at the nearest hospital, realizing on the way that somehow or other after forgotten gyrations, we were in Grainball. Half a year later Rita wrote the doctor for news. Jack Humbertson as he had been tastelessly dubbed was still isolated from his personal past. Oh Mnemosyne, sweetest and most mischievous of muses!

I would not have mentioned this incident had it not started a chain of ideas that resulted in my publishing in the *Cantrip Review* an essay on "Mimir and Memory," in which I suggested among other things that seemed original and important to that splendid review's benevolent readers, a theory of perceptual time based on the circulation of the blood and conceptually depending (to fill up this nutshell) on the mind's being conscious not only of matter but also of its own self, thus creating a continuous spanning of two points (the storable future and the stored past). In result of this venture—and in culmination of the impression made by my previous *travaux*—I was called from New York, where Rita and I were living in a little flat with a view of gleaming children taking shower baths far below in a fountainous arbor of Central Park, to Cantrip College, four hundred miles away, for one year. I lodged there, in special apartments for poets and philosophers, from September 1951 to June 1952, while Rita

whom I preferred not to display vegetated—somewhat indecorously, I am afraid—in a roadside inn where I visited her twice
a week. Then she vanished—more humanly than her predecessor
had done: a month later I found her in the local jail. She was
très digne, had had her appendix removed, and managed to con- 1
vince me that the beautiful bluish furs she had been accused of
stealing from a Mrs. Roland MacCrum had really been a spontaneous, if somewhat alcoholic, gift from Roland himself. I
succeeded in getting her out without appealing to her touchy
brother, and soon afterwards we drove back to Central Park
West, by way of Briceland, where we had stopped for a few
hours the year before.

A curious urge to relive my stay there with Lolita had got hold
of me. I was entering a phase of existence where I had given up
all hope of tracing her kidnaper and her. I now attempted to fall
back on old settings in order to save what still could be saved in
the way of *souvenir, souvenir que me veux-tu?* Autumn was ring- 2
ing in the air. To a post card requesting twin beds Professor
Hamburg got a prompt expression of regret in reply. They were
full up. They had one bathless basement room with four beds
which they thought I would not want. Their note paper was
headed:

The Enchanted Hunters

NEAR CHURCHES   NO DOGS
All legal beverages

I wondered if the last statement was true. All? Did they have
for instance sidewalk grenadine? I also wondered if a hunter,
enchanted or otherwise, would not need a pointer more than a
pew, and with a spasm of pain I recalled a scene worthy of a
great artist: *petite nymphe accroupie;* but that silky cocker 3
spaniel had perhaps been a baptized one. No—I felt I could not 4
endure the throes of revisiting that lobby. There was a much
better possibility of retrievable time elsewhere in soft, rich-
colored, autumnal Briceland. Leaving Rita in a bar, I made for
the town library. A twittering spinster was only too glad to help

me disinter mid-August 1947 from the bound *Briceland Gazette,* and presently, in a secluded nook under a naked light, I was turning the enormous and fragile pages of a coffin-black volume almost as big as Lolita.

1   Reader! *Bruder!* What a foolish Hamburg that Hamburg was! Since his supersensitive system was loath to face the actual scene, he thought he could at least enjoy a secret part of it—which reminds one of the tenth or twentieth soldier in the raping queue who throws the girl's black shawl over her white face so as not to see those impossible eyes while taking his military pleasure in the sad, sacked village. What *I* lusted to get was the printed picture that had chanced to absorb my trespassing image while the *Gazette's* photographer was concentrating on Dr. Braddock

2   and his group. Passionately I hoped to find preserved the portrait

3   of the artist as a younger brute. An innocent camera catching me on my dark way to Lolita's bed—what a magnet for Mnemosyne! I cannot well explain the true nature of that urge of mine. It was allied, I suppose, to that swooning curiosity which impels one to examine with a magnifying glass bleak little figures—still life practically, and everybody about to throw up—at an early morning execution, and the patient's expression impossible to make out in the print. Anyway, I was literally gasping for breath, and one corner of the book of doom kept stabbing me in the stomach

4   while I scanned and skimmed ... *Brute Force* and *Possessed* were coming on Sunday, the 24th, to both theatres. Mr. Purdom, independent tobacco auctioneer, said that ever since 1925 he had

5   been an Omen Faustum smoker. Husky Hank and his petite bride were to be the guests of Mr. and Mrs. Reginald G. Gore,

6   58 Inchkeith Ave. The size of certain parasites is one sixth of the host. Dunkerque was fortified in the tenth century. Misses' socks, 39 c. Saddle Oxfords 3.98. Wine, wine, wine, quipped the

7   author of *Dark Age* who refused to be photographed, may suit a Persian bubble bird, but I say give me rain, rain, rain on the

8   shingle roof for roses and inspiration every time. Dimples are caused by the adherence of the skin to the deeper tissues. Greeks repulse a heavy guerilla assault—and, ah, at last, a little figure in white, and Dr. Braddock in black, but whatever spectral shoulder

was brushing against his ample form—nothing of myself could I 1
make out.

I went to find Rita who introduced me with her *vin triste* smile 2
to a pocket-sized wizened truculently tight old man saying this
was—what was the name again, son?—a former schoolmate of
hers. He tried to retain her, and in the slight scuffle that followed I hurt my thumb against his hard head. In the silent
painted park where I walked her and aired her a little, she sobbed
and said I would soon, soon leave her as everybody had, and I
sang her a wistful French ballad, and strung together some
fugitive rhymes to amuse her:

> The place was called *Enchanted Hunters*. Query:
> What Indian dyes, Diana, did thy dell
> endorse to make of Picture Lake a very
> blood bath of trees before the blue hotel?

She said: "Why blue when it is white, why blue for heaven's 3
sake?" and started to cry again, and I marched her to the car, and
we drove on to New York, and soon she was reasonably happy
again high up in the haze on the little terrace of our flat. I notice
I have somehow mixed up two events, my visit with Rita to
Briceland on our way to Cantrip, and our passing through Briceland again on our way back to New York, but such suffusions of
swimming colors are not to be disdained by the artist in recollection.

27

My letterbox in the entrance hall belonged to the type that
allows one to glimpse something of its contents through a glassed
slit. Several times already, a trick of harlequin light that fell
through the glass upon an alien handwriting had twisted it into
a semblance of Lolita's script causing me almost to collapse as
I leant against an adjacent urn, almost my own. Whenever that

happened—whenever her lovely, loopy, childish scrawl was horribly transformed into the dull hand of one of my few correspondents—I used to recollect, with anguished amusement, the times in my trustful, pre-dolorian past when I would be misled by a jewel-bright window opposite wherein my lurking eye, the ever alert periscope of my shameful vice, would make out from afar a half-naked nymphet stilled in the act of combing her

1 Alice-in-Wonderland hair. There was in the fiery phantasm a perfection which made my wild delight also perfect, just because the vision was out of reach, with no possibility of attainment to spoil it by the awareness of an appended taboo; indeed, it may well be that the very attraction immaturity has for me lies not so much in the limpidity of pure young forbidden fairy child beauty as in the security of a situation where infinite perfections fill the gap between the little given and the great promised—the great

2 rosegray never-to-be-had. *Mes fenêtres!* Hanging above blotched sunset and welling night, grinding my teeth, I would crowd all the demons of my desire against the railing of a throbbing balcony: it would be ready to take off in the apricot and black humid evening; did take off—whereupon the lighted image would move and Eve would revert to a rib, and there would be nothing in the window but an obese partly clad man reading the paper.

Since I sometimes won the race between my fancy and nature's reality, the deception was bearable. Unbearable pain began when chance entered the fray and deprived me of the smile meant for

3 me. *"Savez-vous qu'à dix ans ma petite était folle de vous?"* said a woman I talked to at a tea in Paris, and the *petite* had just married, miles away, and I could not even remember if I had ever noticed her in that garden, next to those tennis courts, a dozen years before. And now likewise, the radiant foreglimpse, the promise of reality, a promise not only to be simulated seductively but also to be nobly held—all this, chance denied me —chance and a change to smaller characters on the pale beloved writer's part. My fancy was both Proustianized and Procrus-

4, 5 teanized; for that particular morning, late in September 1952, as I had come down to grope for my mail, the dapper and bilious janitor with whom I was on execrable terms started to complain that a man who had seen Rita home recently had been "sick like a dog" on the front steps. In the process of listening to him and tipping him, and then listening to a revised and politer version of the incident, I had the impression that one of the two letters which that blessed mail brought was from Rita's mother, a crazy little woman, whom we had once visited on Cape Cod and who kept writing me to my various addresses, saying how wonderfully well matched her daughter and I were, and how wonderful it would be if we married; the other letter which I opened and scanned rapidly in the elevator was from John Farlow.

I have often noticed that we are inclined to endow our friends with the stability of type that literary characters acquire in the reader's mind. No matter how many times we reopen "King Lear," never shall we find the good king banging his tankard in high revelry, all woes forgotten, at a jolly reunion with all three daughters and their lapdogs. Never will Emma rally, revived by the sympathetic salts in Flaubert's father's timely tear. Whatever evolution this or that popular character has gone through between the book covers, his fate is fixed in our minds, and, similarly, we expect our friends to follow this or that logical and conventional pattern we have fixed for them. Thus X will never compose the immortal music that would clash with the second-rate symphonies he has accustomed us to. Y will never commit murder. Under no circumstances can Z ever betray us. We have it all arranged in our minds, and the less often we see a particular person the more satisfying it is to check how obediently he conforms to our notion of him every time we hear of him. Any deviation in the fates we have ordained would strike us as not only anomalous but unethical. We would prefer not to have known at all our neighbor, the retired hot-dog stand operator, if it turns out he has just produced the greatest book of poetry his age has seen.

I am saying all this in order to explain how bewildered I was by Farlow's hysterical letter. I knew his wife had died but I certainly expected him to remain, throughout a devout widow-hood, the dull, sedate and reliable person he had always been. Now he wrote that after a brief visit to the U.S. he had returned to South America and had decided that whatever affairs he had controlled at Ramsdale he would hand over to Jack Windmuller of that town, a lawyer whom we both knew. He seemed particularly relieved to get rid of the Haze "complications." He had married a Spanish girl. He had stopped smoking and had gained thirty pounds. She was very young and a ski champion. They were going to India for their honeymonsoon. Since he was "building a family" as he put it, he would have no time henceforth for my affairs which he termed "very strange and very aggravating." Busybodies—a whole committee of them, it appeared—had informed him that the whereabouts of little Dolly Haze were unknown, and that I was living with a notorious divorcee in California. His father-in-law was a count, and exceedingly wealthy. The people who had been renting the Haze house for some years now wished to buy it. He suggested that I better produce Dolly quick. He had broken his leg. He enclosed a snapshot of himself and a brunette in white wool beaming at each other among the snows of Chile.

I remember letting myself into my flat and starting to say: Well, at least we shall now track them down—when the other letter began talking to me in a small matter-of-fact voice:

DEAR DAD:

How's everything? I'm married. I'm going to have a baby. I guess he's going to be a big one. I guess he'll come right for Christmas. This is a hard letter to write. I'm going nuts because we don't have enough to pay our debts and get out of here. Dick is promised a big job in Alaska in his very specialized corner of the mechanical field, that's all I know about it but it's really grand. Pardon me for withholding our home address but you may still be mad at me, and Dick must not know. This town is something. You can't see the morons for the smog. Please do send us a check, Dad. We could manage with three or four hundred /or even less, anything is welcome, you might sell my old things, because once we get there the dough will just start rolling in. Write, please. I have gone through much sadness and hardship.

Yours expecting,
DOLLY (MRS. RICHARD F. SCHILLER)

28

I was again on the road, again at the wheel of the old blue sedan, again alone. Rita had still been dead to the world when I read that letter and fought the mountains of agony it raised within me. I had glanced at her as she smiled in her sleep and had kissed her on her moist brow, and had left her forever, with a note of tender adieu which I taped to her navel—otherwise she might not have found it.

"Alone" did I say? *Pas tout à fait.* I had my little black chum with me, and as soon as I reached a secluded spot, I rehearsed Mr. Richard F. Schiller's violent death. I had found a very old and very dirty gray sweater of mine in the back of the car, and this I hung up on a branch, in a speechless glade, which I had reached by a wood road from the now remote highway. The carrying out of the sentence was a little marred by what seemed to me a certain stiffness in the play of the trigger, and I wondered if I should get some oil for the mysterious thing but decided I had no time to spare. Back into the car went the old dead sweater, now with additional perforations, and having reloaded warm Chum, I continued my journey.

The letter was dated September 18, 1952 (this was September 22), and the address she gave was "General Delivery, Coalmont" (not "Va.," not "Pa.," not "Tenn."—and not Coalmont, anyway—I have camouflaged everything, my love). Inquiries showed this to be a small industrial community some eight hundred miles from New York City. At first I planned to drive all day and all night, but then thought better of it and rested for a couple of hours around dawn in a motor court room, a few miles before reaching the town. I had made up my mind that the fiend, this Schiller, had been a car salesman who had perhaps got to know my Lolita by giving her a ride in Beardsley—the day her bike blew a tire on the way to Miss Emperor—and that he had got into some trouble since then. The corpse of the executed sweater, no matter how I changed its contours as it lay on the back seat of the car, had kept revealing various outlines pertaining to Trapp-Schiller—the grossness and obscene bonhommie of his body, and to counteract this taste of coarse corruption I resolved to make myself especially handsome and smart as I pressed home the nipple of my alarm clock before it exploded at the set hour of six A.M. Then, with the stern and romantic care of a gentleman about to fight a duel, I checked the arrangement of my papers, bathed and perfumed my delicate body, shaved my face and chest, selected a silk shirt and clean drawers, pulled on transparent taupe socks, and congratulated myself for having with me in my trunk some very exquisite clothes—a waistcoat with nacreous buttons, for instance, a pale cashmere tie and so on.

I was not able, alas, to hold my breakfast, but dismissed that physicality as a trivial contretemps, wiped my mouth with a gossamer handkerchief produced from my sleeve, and, with a blue block of ice for heart, a pill on my tongue and solid death in my hip pocket, I stepped neatly into a telephone booth in Coalmont (Ah-ah-ah, said its little door) and rang up the only Schiller—Paul, Furniture—to be found in the battered book. Hoarse Paul told me he did know a Richard, the son of a cousin of his, and his address was, let me see, 10 Killer Street (I am not going very far for my pseudonyms). Ah-ah-ah, said the little door.

At 10 Killer Street, a tenement house, I interviewed a number of dejected old people and two long-haired strawberry-blond incredibly grubby nymphets (rather abstractly, just for the heck of it, the ancient beast in me was casting about for some lightly clad child I might hold against me for a minute, after the killing was over and nothing mattered any more, and everything was allowed). Yes, Dick Skiller had lived there, but had moved when he married. Nobody knew his address. "They might know at the store," said a bass voice from an open manhole near which I happened to be standing with the two thin-armed, barefoot little girls and their dim grandmothers. I entered the wrong store and a wary old Negro shook his head even before I could ask anything. I crossed over to a bleak grocery and there, summoned by a customer at my request, a woman's voice from some wooden abyss in the floor, the manhole's counterpart, cried out: Hunter Road, last house.

Hunter Road was miles away, in an even more dismal district, all dump and ditch, and wormy vegetable garden, and shack, and gray drizzle, and red mud, and several smoking stacks in the distance. I stopped at the last "house"—a clapboard shack, with two or three similar ones farther away from the road and a waste of withered weeds all around. Sounds of hammering came from behind the house, and for several minutes I sat quite still in my old car, old and frail, at the end of my journey, at my gray goal, *finis*, my friends, *finis*, my fiends. The time was around two. My pulse was 40 one minute and 100 the next. The drizzle crepitated against the hood of the car. My gun had migrated to my right trouser pocket. A nondescript cur came out from behind the house, stopped in surprise, and started good-naturedly woof-woofing at me, his eyes slit, his shaggy belly all muddy, and then walked about a little and woofed once more.

29

I got out of the car and slammed its door. How matter-of-fact, how square that slam sounded in the void of the sunless day! *Woof*, commented the dog perfunctorily. I pressed the bell button, it vibrated through my whole system. *Personne. Je resonne. Repersonne.* From what depth this re-nonsense? Woof, said the dog. A rush and a shuffle, and woosh-woof went the door.

Couple of inches taller. Pink-rimmed glasses. New, heaped-up hairdo, new ears. How simple! The moment, the death I had kept conjuring up for three years was as simple as a bit of dry wood. She was frankly and hugely pregnant. Her head looked smaller (only two seconds had passed really, but let me give them as much wooden duration as life can stand), and her pale-freckled cheeks were hollowed, and her bare shins and arms had lost all their tan, so that the little hairs showed. She wore a brown, sleeveless cotton dress and sloppy felt slippers.

"We—e—ell!" she exhaled after a pause with all the emphasis of wonder and welcome.

"Husband at home?" I croaked, fist in pocket.

I could not kill *her*, of course, as some have thought. You see, I loved her. It was love at first sight, at last sight, at ever and ever sight.

"Come in," she said with a vehement cheerful note. Against the splintery deadwood of the door, Dolly Schiller flattened herself as best she could (even rising on tiptoe a little) to let me pass, and was crucified for a moment, looking down, smiling down at the threshold, hollow-cheeked with round *pommettes*, her watered-milk-white arms outspread on the wood. I passed without touching her bulging babe. Dolly-smell, with a faint fried addition. My teeth chattered like an idiot's. "No, you stay out" (to the dog). She closed the door and followed me and her belly into the dollhouse parlor.

1 "Dick's down there," she said pointing with an invisible tennis racket, inviting my gaze to travel from the drab parlor-bedroom where we stood, right across the kitchen, and through the back-doorway where, in a rather primitive vista, a dark-haired young stranger in overalls, instantaneously reprieved, was perched with his back to me on a ladder fixing something near or upon the shack of his neighbor, a plumper fellow with only one arm, who stood looking up.

This pattern she explained from afar, apologetically ("Men will be men"); should she call him in?

No.

Standing in the middle of the slanting room and emitting questioning "hm's," she made familiar Javanese gestures with her wrists and hands, offering me, in a brief display of humorous courtesy, to choose between a rocker and the divan (their bed after ten P.M.). I say "familiar" because one day she had welcomed me with the same wrist dance to her party in Beardsley. We both sat down on the divan. Curious: although actually her looks had faded, I definitely realized, so hopelessly late in the day, how much she looked—had always looked—like Botticelli's

2 russet Venus—the same soft nose, the same blurred beauty. In my pocket my fingers gently let go and repacked a little at the tip, within the handkerchief it was nested in, my unused weapon.

"That's not the fellow I want," I said.

The diffuse look of welcome left her eyes. Her forehead puckered as in the old bitter days:

"Not *who?*"

"Where is he? Quick!"

"Look," she said, inclining her head to one side and shaking it in that position. "Look, you are not going to bring that up."

"I certainly am," I said, and for a moment—strangely enough the only merciful, endurable one in the whole interview—we were bristling at each other as if she were still mine.

A wise girl, she controlled herself.

Dick did not know a thing of the whole mess. He thought I was her father. He thought she had run away from an upper-class home just to wash dishes in a diner. He believed anything. Why should I want to make things harder than they were by raking up all that muck?

But, I said, she must be sensible, she must be a sensible girl (with her bare drum under that thin brown stuff), she must understand that if she expected the help I had come to give, I must have at least a clear comprehension of the situation.

"Come, his name!"

She thought I had guessed long ago. It was (with a mischievous and melancholy smile) such a sensational name. I would never believe it. She could hardly believe it herself.

His name, my fall nymph.

It was so unimportant, she said. She suggested I skip it. Would I like a cigarette?

No. His name.

She shook her head with great resolution. She guessed it was too late to raise hell and I would never believe the unbelievably unbelievable—

I said I had better go, regards, nice to have seen her.

She said really it was useless, she would never tell, but on the other hand, after all—"Do you really want to know who it was? Well, it was—"

And softly, confidentially, arching her thin eyebrows and puckering her parched lips, she emitted, a little mockingly, somewhat fastidiously, not untenderly, in a kind of muted whistle, the name that the astute reader has guessed long ago.

1   Waterproof. Why did a flash from Hourglass Lake cross my consciousness? I, too, had known it, without knowing it, all along. There was no shock, no surprise. Quietly the fusion took place, and everything fell into order, into the pattern of branches that I have woven throughout this memoir with the express purpose of having the ripe fruit fall at the right moment; yes, with the express and perverse purpose of rendering—she was talking but I sat melting in my golden peace—of rendering that golden and monstrous peace through the satisfaction of logical recogni-
2   tion, which my most inimical reader should experience now.

She was, as I say, talking. It now came in a relaxed flow. He was the only man she had ever been crazy about. What about Dick? Oh, Dick was a lamb, they were quite happy together, but she meant something different. And *I* had never counted, of course?

She considered me as if grasping all at once the incredible—and somehow tedious, confusing and unnecessary—fact that the
3   distant, elegant, slender, forty-year-old valetudinarian in velvet coat sitting beside her had known and adored every pore and follicle of her pubescent body. In her washed-out gray eyes, strangely spectacled, our poor romance was for a moment reflected, pondered upon, and dismissed like a dull party, like a rainy picnic to which only the dullest bores had come, like a humdrum exercise, like a bit of dry mud caking her childhood.

I just managed to jerk my knee out of the range of a sketchy tap—one of her acquired gestures.

She asked me not to be dense. The past was the past. I had been a good father, she guessed—granting me *that*. Proceed, Dolly Schiller.

Well, did I know that he had known her mother? That he was practically an old friend? That he had visited with his uncle in
4   Ramsdale?—oh, years ago—and spoken at Mother's club, and had tugged and pulled her, Dolly, by her bare arm onto his lap in front of everybody, and kissed her face, she was ten and furious with him? Did I know he had seen me and her at the inn

where he was writing the very play she was to rehearse in Beardsley, two years later? Did I know—It had been horrid of her to sidetrack me into believing that Clare was an old female, maybe a relative of his or a sometime lifemate—and oh, what a close shave it had been when the Wace *Journal* carried his picture.

The *Briceland Gazette* had not. Yes, very amusing.

Yes, she said, this world was just one gag after another, if somebody wrote up her life nobody would ever believe it.

At this point, there came brisk homey sounds from the kitchen into which Dick and Bill had lumbered in quest of beer. Through the doorway they noticed the visitor, and Dick entered the parlor. "Dick, this is my Dad!" cried Dolly in a resounding violent voice that struck me as totally strange, and new, and cheerful, and old, and sad, because the young fellow, veteran of a remote war, was hard of hearing.

Arctic blue eyes, black hair, ruddy cheeks, unshaven chin. We shook hands. Discreet Bill, who evidently took pride in working wonders with one hand, brought in the beer cans he had opened. Wanted to withdraw. The exquisite courtesy of simple folks. Was made to stay. A beer ad. In point of fact, I preferred it that way, and so did the Schillers. I switched to the jittery rocker. Avidly munching, Dolly plied me with marshmallows and potato chips. The men looked at her fragile, *frileux*, diminutive, old-world, youngish but sickly, father in velvet coat and beige vest, maybe a viscount.

They were under the impression I had come to stay, and Dick with a great wrinkling of brows that denoted difficult thought, suggested Dolly and he might sleep in the kitchen on a spare mattress. I waved a light hand and told Dolly who transmitted it by means of a special shout to Dick that I had merely dropped in on my way to Readsburg where I was to be entertained by some friends and admirers. It was then noticed that one of the few thumbs remaining to Bill was bleeding (not such a wonder-worker after all). How womanish and somehow never seen that way before was the shadowy divison between her pale breasts when she bent down over the man's hand! She took him for repairs to the kitchen. For a few minutes, three or four little eternities which positively welled with artificial warmth, Dick and I remained alone. He sat on a hard chair rubbing his forelimbs and frowning. I had an idle urge to squeeze out the blackheads on the wings of his perspiring nose with my long agate claws. He had nice sad eyes with beautiful lashes, and very white teeth. His Adam's apple was large and hairy. Why don't they shave better, those young brawny chaps? He and his Dolly had had unrestrained intercourse on that couch there, at least a hundred and eighty times, probably much more; and before that —how long had she known him? No grudge. Funny—no grudge at all, nothing except grief and nausea. He was now rubbing his nose. I was sure that when finally he would open his mouth, he would say (slightly shaking his head): "Aw, she's a swell kid, Mr. Haze. She sure is. And she's going to make a swell mother." He opened his mouth—and took a sip of beer. This gave him countenance—and he went on sipping till he frothed at the mouth. He was a lamb. He had cupped her Florentine breasts. His fingernails were black and broken, but the phalanges, the whole carpus, the strong shapely wrist were far, far finer than mine: I have hurt too much too many bodies with my twisted poor hands to be proud of them. French epithets, a Dorset yokel's knuckles, an Austrian tailor's flat finger tips—that's Humbert Humbert.

Good. If he was silent I could be silent too. Indeed, I could very well do with a little rest in this subdued, frightened-to-death rocking chair, before I drove to wherever the beast's lair was— and then pulled the pistol's foreskin back, and then enjoyed the orgasm of the crushed trigger: I was always a good little follower of the Viennese medicine man. But presently I became sorry for poor Dick whom, in some hypnotoid way, I was horribly preventing from making the only remark he could think up ("She's a swell kid . . .").

"And so," I said, "you are going to Canada?"

In the kitchen, Dolly was laughing at something Bill had said or done.

"And so," I shouted, "you are going to Canada? Not Canada" —I re-shouted—"I mean Alaska, of course."

He nursed his glass and, nodding sagely, replied: "Well, he cut it on a jagger, I guess. Lost his right arm in Italy."

Lovely mauve almond trees in bloom. A blown-off surrealistic arm hanging up there in the pointillistic mauve. A flowergirl tattoo on the hand. Dolly and band-aided Bill reappeared. It occurred to me that her ambiguous, brown and pale beauty excited the cripple. Dick, with a grin of relief stood up. He guessed Bill and he would be going back to fix those wires. He guessed Mr. Haze and Dolly had loads of things to say to each other. He guessed he would be seeing me before I left. Why do those people guess so much and shave so little, and are so disdainful of hearing aids?

"Sit down," she said, audibly striking her flanks with her palms. I relapsed into the black rocker.

"So you betrayed me? Where did you go? Where is he now?"

She took from the mantelpiece a concave glossy snapshot. Old woman in white, stout, beaming, bowlegged, very short dress; old man in his shirtsleeves, drooping mustache, watch chain. Her in-laws. Living with Dick's brother's family in Juneau.

"Sure you don't want to smoke?"

She was smoking herself. First time I saw her doing it. *Streng verboten* under Humbert the Terrible. Gracefully, in a blue mist, Charlotte Haze rose from her grave. I would find him through Uncle Ivory if she refused.

1

"Betrayed you? No." She directed the dart of her cigarette, index rapidly tapping upon it, toward the hearth exactly as her mother used to do, and then, like her mother, oh my God, with her fingernail scratched and removed a fragment of cigarette paper from her underlip. No. She had not betrayed me. I was among friends. Edusa had warned her that Cue liked little girls, had been almost jailed once, in fact (nice fact), and he knew she knew. Yes... Elbow in palm, puff, smile, exhaled smoke, darting gesture. Waxing reminiscent. He saw—smiling—through everything and everybody, because he was not like me and her but a genius. A great guy. Full of fun. Had rocked with laughter when she confessed about me and her, and said he had thought so. It was quite safe, under the circumstances, to tell him ...

2

3

Well, Cue—they all called him Cue—

1   Her camp five years ago. Curious coincidence— . . . took her to a dude ranch about a day's drive from Elephant (Elphin-

2   stone). Named? Oh, some silly name—Duk Duk Ranch—*you* know just plain silly—but it did not matter now, anyway, because the place had vanished and disintegrated. Really, she meant, I could not imagine how utterly lush that ranch was, she meant it had everything but everything, even an indoor

3   waterfall. Did I remember the redhaired guy we ("we" was good) had once had some tennis with? Well, the place really belonged to Red's brother, but he had turned it over to Cue for the summer. When Cue and she came, the others had them actually go through a coronation ceremony and then—a terrific ducking, as when you cross the Equator. *You* know.

Her eyes rolled in synthetic resignation.

"Go on, please."

Well. The idea was he would take her in September to Hollywood and arrange a tryout for her, a bit part in the tennis-match scene of a movie picture based on a play of his—*Golden Guts*—and perhaps even have her double one of its sensational starlets on the Klieg-struck tennis court. Alas, it never came to that.

"Where is the hog now?"

He was not a hog. He was a great guy in many respects. But it was all drink and drugs. And, of course, he was a complete freak in sex matters, and his friends were his slaves. I just could not imagine (I, Humbert, could not imagine!) what they all did at Duk Duk Ranch. She refused to take part because she loved him, and he threw her out.

"What things?"

"Oh, weird, filthy, fancy things. I mean, he had two girls and two boys, and three or four men, and the idea was for all of us to tangle in the nude while an old woman took movie pictures."

4   (Sade's Justine was twelve at the start.)

"What things exactly?"

"Oh, things . . . Oh, I—really I"—she uttered the "I" as a subdued cry while she listened to the source of the ache, and for lack of words spread the five fingers of her angularly up-and-down-moving hand. No, she gave it up, she refused to go into particulars with that baby inside her.

That made sense.

"It is of no importance now," she said pounding a gray cushion with her fist and then lying back, belly up, on the divan. "Crazy things, filthy things. I said no, I'm just not going to [she used, in all insouciance really, a disgusting slang term which, in a literal French translation, would be *souffler*] your beastly 1 boys, because I want only you. Well, he kicked me out."

There was not much else to tell. That winter 1949, Fay and she had found jobs. For almost two years she had—oh, just drifted, oh, doing some restaurant work in small places, and then she had met Dick. No, she did not know where the other was. In New York, she guessed. Of course, he was so famous she would have found him at once if she had wanted. Fay had tried to get back to the Ranch—and it just was not there any more— it had burned to the ground, *nothing* remained, just a charred heap of rubbish. It was so *strange*, so *strange*—

She closed her eyes and opened her mouth, leaning back on the cushion, one felted foot on the floor. The wooden floor slanted, a little steel ball would have rolled into the kitchen. I knew all I wanted to know. I had no intention of torturing my darling. Somewhere beyond Bill's shack an afterwork radio had begun singing of folly and fate, and there she was with her ruined looks and her adult, rope-veined narrow hands and her goose-flesh white arms, and her shallow ears, and her unkempt arm-pits, there she was (my Lolita!), hopelessly worn at seventeen, 2 with that baby, dreaming already in her of becoming a big shot and retiring around 2020 A.D.—and I looked and looked at her, 3 and knew as clearly as I know I am to die, that I loved her more than anything I had ever seen or imagined on earth, or hoped for anywhere else. She was only the faint violet whiff and dead leaf echo of the nymphet I had rolled myself upon with such cries in the past; an echo on the brink of a russet ravine, with a far wood under a white sky, and brown leaves choking the brook, and one last cricket in the crisp weeds... but thank God it was not that

echo alone that I worshiped. What I used to pamper among the
1 tangled vines of my heart, *mon grand péché radieux*, had
dwindled to its essence: sterile and selfish vice, all *that* I canceled
and cursed. You may jeer at me, and threaten to clear the court,
but until I am gagged and half-throttled, I will shout my poor
truth. I insist the world know how much I loved my Lolita, *this*
Lolita, pale and polluted, and big with another's child, but still
gray-eyed, still sooty-lashed, still auburn and almond, still Carmencita, still mine; *Changeons de vie, ma Carmen, allons vivre*
2 *quelque part où nous ne serons jamais séparés;* Ohio? The wilds
of Massachusetts? No matter, even if those eyes of hers would
fade to myopic fish, and her nipples swell and crack, and her
lovely young velvety delicate delta be tainted and torn—even
then I would go mad with tenderness at the mere sight of your
dear wan face, at the mere sound of your raucous young voice,
my Lolita.

"Lolita," I said, "this may be neither here nor there but I
have to say it. Life is very short. From here to that old car you
know so well there is a stretch of twenty, twenty-five paces. It is
a very short walk. Make those twenty-five steps. Now. Right
3 now. Come just as you are. And we shall live happily ever after."
4 *Carmen, voulez-vous venir avec moi?*

"You mean," she said opening her eyes and raising herself
slightly, the snake that may strike, "you mean you will give us
[us] that money only if I go with you to a motel. Is *that* what
you mean?"

"No," I said, "you got it all wrong. I want you to leave your
5 incidental Dick, and this awful hole, and come to live with me,
and die with me, and everything with me" (words to that effect).

"You're crazy," she said, her features working.

"Think it over, Lolita. There are no strings attached. Except,
perhaps—well, no matter." (A reprieve, I wanted to say but did
not.) "Anyway, if you refuse you will still get your . . . *trousseau.*"

"No kidding?" asked Dolly.

I handed her an envelope with four hundred dollars in cash
and a check for three thousand six hundred more.

Gingerly, uncertainly, she received *mon petit cadeau;* and 1
then her forehead became a beautiful pink. "You mean," she
said, with agonized emphasis, "you are giving us *four thousand
bucks?*" I covered my face with my hand and broke into the
hottest tears I had ever shed. I felt them winding through my
fingers and down my chin, and burning me, and my nose got
clogged, and I could not stop, and then she touched my wrist.

"I'll die if you touch me," I said. "You are sure you are not
coming with me? Is there no hope of your coming? Tell me only
this."

"No," she said. "No, honey, no."

She had never called me honey before.

"No," she said, "it is quite out of the question. I would sooner
go back to Cue. I mean—"

She groped for words. I supplied them mentally ("*He* broke
my heart. *You* merely broke my life").

"I think," she went on—"oops"—the envelope skidded to the
floor—she picked it up—"I think it's oh utterly *grand* of you to
give us all that dough. It settles everything, we can start next
week. Stop crying, please. You should understand. Let me get
you some more beer. Oh, don't cry, I'm so sorry I cheated so
much, but that's the way things are."

I wiped my face and my fingers. She smiled at the *cadeau.*
She exulted. She wanted to call Dick. I said I would have to leave
in a moment, did not want to see him at all, at all. We tried to
think of some subject of conversation. For some reason, I kept
seeing—it trembled and silkily glowed on my damp retina—a
radiant child of twelve, sitting on a threshold, "pinging" pebbles
at an empty can. I almost said—trying to find some casual remark
—"I wonder sometimes what has become of the little McCoo
girl, did she ever get better?"—but stopped in time lest she
rejoin: "I wonder sometimes what has become of the little Haze
girl ..." Finally, I reverted to money matters. That sum, I said,
represented more or less the net rent from her mother's house;
she said: "Had it not been sold years ago?" No (I admit I *had*
told her this in order to sever all connections with R.); a lawyer

would send a full account of the financial situation later; it was rosy; some of the small securities her mother had owned had gone up and up. Yes, I was quite sure I had to go. I had to go, and find him, and destroy him.

Since I would not have survived the touch of her lips, I kept retreating in a mincing dance, at every step she and her belly made toward me.

She and the dog saw me off. I was surprised (this a rhetorical figure, I was not) that the sight of the old car in which she had ridden as a child and a nymphet, left her so very indifferent. All she remarked was it was getting sort of purplish about the gills. I said it was hers, I could go by bus. She said don't be silly, they 1 would fly to Jupiter and buy a car there. I said I would buy this one from her for five hundred dollars.

"At this rate we'll be millionnaires next," she said to the ecstatic dog.

2 *Carmencita, lui demandais-je* ... "One last word," I said in my horrible careful English, "are you quite, quite sure that— well, not tomorrow, of course, and not after tomorrow, but— well—some day, any day, you will not come to live with me? I will create a brand new God and thank him with piercing cries, if you give me that microscopic hope" (to that effect).

"No," she said smiling, "no."

"It would have made all the difference," said Humbert Humbert.

Then I pulled out my automatic—I mean, this is the kind of 3 fool thing a reader might suppose I did. It never even occurred to me to do it.

"Good by-aye!" she chanted, my American sweet immortal 4 dead love; for she is dead and immortal if you are reading this. I mean, such is the formal agreement with the so-called authorities.

Then, as I drove away, I heard her shout in a vibrant voice to her Dick; and the dog started to lope alongside my car like a fat dolphin, but he was too heavy and old, and very soon gave up.

And presently I was driving through the drizzle of the dying day, with the windshield wipers in full action but unable to cope with my tears.

30

Leaving as I did Coalmont around four in the afternoon (by
Route X—I do not remember the number), I might have made
Ramsdale by dawn had not a short-cut tempted me. I had to
get onto Highway Y. My map showed quite blandly that just
beyond Woodbine, which I reached at nightfall, I could leave
paved X and reach paved Y by means of a transverse dirt road.
It was only some forty miles long according to my map. Otherwise I would have to follow X for another hundred miles and
then use leisurely looping Z to get to Y and my destination.
However, the short-cut in question got worse and worse, bumpier
and bumpier, muddier and muddier, and when I attempted to
turn back after some ten miles of purblind, tortuous and
tortoise-slow progress, my old and weak Melmoth got stuck in
deep clay. All was dark and muggy, and hopeless. My headlights hung over a broad ditch full of water. The surrounding
country, if any, was a black wilderness. I sought to extricate myself but my rear wheels only whined in slosh and anguish.
Cursing my plight, I took off my fancy clothes, changed into
slacks, pulled on the bullet-riddled sweater, and waded four   1
miles back to a roadside farm. It started to rain on the way
but I had not the strength to go back for a mackintosh. Such
incidents have convinced me that my heart is basically sound
despite recent diagnoses. Around midnight, a wrecker dragged
my car out. I navigated back to Highway X and traveled on.
Utter weariness overtook me an hour later, in an anonymous
little town. I pulled up at the curb and in darkness drank deep
from a friendly flask.

The rain had been cancelled miles before. It was a black
warm night, somewhere in Appalachia. Now and then cars
passed me, red tail-lights receding, white headlights advancing,
but the town was dead. Nobody strolled and laughed on the
sidewalks as relaxing burghers would in sweet, mellow, rotting
Europe. I was alone to enjoy the innocent night and my terrible thoughts. A wire receptacle on the curb was very particular
about acceptable contents: Sweepings. Paper. No Garbage.

Sherry-red letters of light marked a Camera Shop. A large ther-
mometer with the name of a laxative quietly dwelt on the
front of a drugstore. Rubinov's Jewelry Company had a display
of artificial diamonds reflected in a red mirror. A lighted green
clock swam in the linenish depths of Jiffy Jeff Laundry. On the
other side of the street a garage said in its sleep—genuflexion
1 lubricity; and corrected itself to Gulflex Lubrication. An airplane, also gemmed by Rubinov, passed, droning, in the velvet
heavens. How many small dead-of-night towns I had seen! This
was not yet the last.

2 Let me dally a little, he is as good as destroyed. Some way
further across the street, neon lights flickered twice slower than
my heart: the outline of a restaurant sign, a large coffee-pot,
kept bursting, every full second or so, into emerald life, and
every time it went out, pink letters saying Fine Foods relayed
it, but the pot could still be made out as a latent shadow teasing
the eye before its next emerald resurrection. We made shadow-
3 graphs. This furtive burg was not far from The Enchanted
Hunters. I was weeping again, drunk on the impossible past.

31

At this solitary stop for refreshments between Coalmont and
Ramsdale (between innocent Dolly Schiller and jovial Uncle
Ivor), I reviewed my case. With the utmost simplicity and
clarity I now saw myself and my love. Previous attempts seemed
out of focus in comparison. A couple of years before, under
the guidance of an intelligent French-speaking confessor, to
whom, in a moment of metaphysical curiosity, I had turned
over a Protestant's drab atheism for an old-fashioned popish
cure, I had hoped to deduce from my sense of sin the existence
of a Supreme Being. On those frosty mornings in rime-laced
Quebec, the good priest worked on me with the finest tenderness and understanding. I am infinitely obliged to him and the
great Institution he represented. Alas, I was unable to transcend

the simple human fact that whatever spiritual solace I might
find, whatever lithophanic eternities might be provided for me, 1
nothing could make my Lolita forget the foul lust I had inflicted upon her. Unless it can be proven to me—to me as I am
now, today, with my heart and my beard, and my putrefaction
—that in the infinite run it does not matter a jot that a North
American girl-child named Dolores Haze had been deprived of
her childhood by a maniac, unless this can be proven (and if it
can, then life is a joke), I see nothing for the treatment of my
misery but the melancholy and very local palliative of articulate
art. To quote an old poet: 2

> The moral sense in mortals is the duty
> We have to pay on mortal sense of beauty.

32

There was the day, during our first trip—our first circle of
paradise—when in order to enjoy my phantasms in peace I
firmly decided to ignore what I could not help perceiving, the
fact that I was to her not a boy friend, not a glamour man, not
a pal, not even a person at all, but just two eyes and a foot of
engorged brawn—to mention only mentionable matters. There
was the day when having withdrawn the functional promise I
had made her on the eve (whatever she had set her funny little
heart on—a roller rink with some special plastic floor or a movie
matinee to which she wanted to go alone), I happened to
glimpse from the bathroom, through a chance combination of
mirror aslant and door ajar, a look on her face ... that look I
cannot exactly describe ... an expression of helplessness so perfect that it seemed to grade into one of rather comfortable
inanity just because this was the very limit of injustice and
frustration—and every limit presupposes something beyond it—
hence the neutral illumination. And when you bear in mind that
these were the raised eyebrows and parted lips of a child, you

may better appreciate what depths of calculated carnality, what reflected despair, restrained me from falling at her dear feet and dissolving in human tears, and sacrificing my jealousy to whatever pleasure Lolita might hope to derive from mixing with dirty and dangerous children in an outside world that was real to her.

And I have still other smothered memories, now unfolding themselves into limbless monsters of pain. Once, in a sunset-ending street of Beardsley, she turned to little Eva Rosen (I was taking both nymphets to a concert and walking behind them so close as almost to touch them with my person), she turned to Eva, and so very serenely and seriously, in answer to something the other had said about its being better to die than hear Milton Pinski, some local schoolboy she knew, talk about music, my Lolita remarked:

"You know, what's so dreadful about dying is that you are completely on your own"; and it struck me, as my automaton knees went up and down, that I simply did not know a thing about my darling's mind and that quite possibly, behind the awful juvenile clichés, there was in her a garden and a twilight, and a palace gate—dim and adorable regions which happened to be lucidly and absolutely forbidden to me, in my polluted rags and miserable convulsions; for I often noticed that living as we did, she and I, in a world of total evil, we would become strangely embarrassed whenever I tried to discuss something she and an older friend, she and a parent, she and a real healthy sweetheart, I and Annabel, Lolita and a sublime, purified, analyzed, deified Harold Haze, might have discussed—an abstract idea, a painting, stippled Hopkins or shorn Baudelaire, God or Shakespeare, anything of a genuine kind. Good will! She would mail her vulnerability in trite brashness and boredom, whereas I, using for my desperately detached comments an artificial tone of voice that set my own last teeth on edge, provoked my audience to such outbursts of rudeness as made any further conversation impossible, oh my poor, bruised child.

I loved you. I was a pentapod monster, but I loved you. I was despicable and brutal, and turpid, and everything, *mais je t'aimais, je t'aimais!* And there were times when I knew how you felt, and it was hell to know it, my little one. Lolita girl, brave Dolly Schiller.

I recall certain moments, let us call them icebergs in paradise, when after having had my fill of her—after fabulous, insane exertions that left me limp and azure-barred—I would gather her in my arms with, at last, a mute moan of human tenderness (her skin glistening in the neon light coming from the paved court through the slits in the blind, her soot-black lashes matted, her grave gray eyes more vacant than ever—for all the world a little patient still in the confusion of a drug after a major operation)—and the tenderness would deepen to shame and despair, and I would lull and rock my lone light Lolita in my marble arms, and moan in her warm hair, and caress her at random and mutely ask her blessing, and at the peak of this human agonized selfless tenderness (with my soul actually hanging around her naked body and ready to repent), all at once, ironically, horribly, lust would swell again—and "oh, *no*," Lolita would say with a sigh to heaven, and the next moment the tenderness and the azure—all would be shattered.

Mid-twentieth century ideas concerning child-parent relationship have been considerably tainted by the scholastic rigmarole and standardized symbols of the psychoanalytic racket, but I hope I am addressing myself to unbiased readers. Once when Avis's father had honked outside to signal papa had come to take his pet home, I felt obliged to invite him into the parlor, and he sat down for a minute, and while we conversed, Avis, a heavy, unattractive, affectionate child, drew up to him and eventually perched plumply on his knee. Now, I do not remember if I have mentioned that Lolita always had an absolutely enchanting smile for strangers, a tender furry slitting of the eyes, a dreamy sweet radiance of all her features which did not mean a thing of course, but was so beautiful, so endearing that one found it hard to reduce such sweetness to but a magic gene automatically lighting up her face in atavistic token of some ancient rite of welcome—hospitable prostitution, the coarse reader may say. Well, there she stood while Mr. Byrd twirled his hat and talked, and—yes, look how stupid of me, I have left out the main characteristic of the famous Lolita smile, namely: while the tender, nectared, dimpled brightness played, it was never directed at the stranger in the room but hung in its own remote flowered void, so to speak, or wandered with myopic softness over chance objects—and this is what was happening now: while fat Avis sidled up to her papa, Lolita gently beamed at a fruit knife that she fingered on the edge of the table, whereon she leaned, many miles away from me. Suddenly, as Avis clung to her father's neck and ear while, with a casual arm, the man enveloped his lumpy and large offspring, I saw Lolita's smile lose all its light and become a frozen little shadow of itself, and the fruit knife slipped off the table and struck her with its silver handle a freak blow on the ankle which made her gasp, and crouch head forward, and then, jumping on one leg, her face awful with the preparatory grimace which children hold till the tears gush, she was gone—to be followed at once and consoled in the kitchen by Avis who had such a wonderful fat pink dad and a small chubby brother, and a brand-new baby sister, and a home, and two grinning dogs, and Lolita had nothing. And I have a neat pendant to that little scene—also in a Beardsley setting. Lolita, who had been reading near the fire, stretched herself, and then inquired, her elbow up, with a grunt: "Where is she buried anyway?" "Who?" "Oh, you know, my murdered mummy." "And *you* know where her grave is," I said controlling myself, whereupon I named the cemetery—just outside Ramsdale, between the railway tracks and Lakeview Hill. "Moreover," I added, "the tragedy of such an accident is somewhat cheapened by the epithet you saw fit to apply to it. If you really wish to triumph in your mind over the idea of death—" "Ray," said Lo for hurray, and languidly left the room, and for a long while I stared with smarting eyes into the fire. Then I picked up her book. It was some trash for young people. There was a gloomy girl Marion, and there was her stepmother who turned out to be, against all expectations, a young, gay, understanding redhead who explained to Marion that Marion's dead mother had really been a heroic woman since she had deliberately dissimulated her great love for Marion because she was dying, and did not want her child to miss her. I did not rush up to her room with cries. I always preferred the mental hygiene of noninterference. Now, squirming and pleading with my own memory, I recall that on this and similar occasions, it was always my habit and method to ignore Lolita's states of mind while comforting my own base self. When my mother, in a livid wet dress, under the tumbling mist (so I vividly imagined her), had run panting ecstatically up that ridge above Moulinet to be felled there by a thunderbolt, I was but an infant, and in retrospect no yearnings of the accepted kind could I ever graft upon any moment of my youth, no matter how savagely psychotherapists heckled me in my later periods of depression. But I admit that a man of my power of imagination cannot plead personal ignorance of universal emotions. I may also have relied too much on the abnormally chill relations between Charlotte and her daughter. But the awful point of the whole argument is this. It had become gradually clear to my conventional Lolita during our singular and bestial cohabitation that even the most miserable of family lives was better than the parody of incest, which, in the long run, was the best I could offer the waif.

33

Ramsdale revisited. I approached it from the side of the lake. The sunny noon was all eyes. As I rode by in my mud-flecked car, I could distinguish scintillas of diamond water between the far pines. I turned into the cemetery and walked among the long and short stone monuments. *Bonzhur*, Charlotte. On some of the graves there were pale, transparent little national flags slumped in the windless air under the evergreens. Gee, Ed, that was bad luck—referring to G. Edward Grammar, a thirty-five-year-old New York office manager who had just been arrayed on a charge of murdering his thirty-three-year-old wife, Dorothy. Bidding for the perfect crime, Ed had bludgeoned his wife and put her into a car. The case came to light when two county policemen on patrol saw Mrs. Grammar's new big blue Chrysler, an anniversary present from her husband, speeding crazily down a hill, just inside their jurisdiction (God bless our good cops!). The car sideswiped a pole, ran up an embankment covered with beard grass, wild strawberry and cinquefoil, and overturned. The wheels were still gently spinning in the mellow sunlight when the officers removed Mrs. G's body. It appeared to be a routine highway accident at first. Alas, the woman's battered body did not match up with only minor damage suffered by the car. I did better.

I rolled on. It was funny to see again the slender white church and the enormous elms. Forgetting that in an American suburban street a lone pedestrian is more conspicuous than a lone motorist, I left the car in the avenue to walk unobtrusively past 342 Lawn Street. Before the great bloodshed, I was entitled to a little relief, to a cathartic spasm of mental regurgitation. Closed were the white shutters of the Junk mansion, and somebody had attached a found black velvet hair ribbon to the white FOR SALE sign which was· leaning toward the sidewalk. No dog barked. No gardener telephoned. No Miss Opposite sat on the vined porch—where to the lone pedestrian's annoyance two pony-tailed young women in identical polka-dotted pinafores stopped doing whatever they were doing to stare at him: she was long dead, no doubt, these might be her twin nieces from Philadelphia.

1   Should I enter my old house? As in a Turgenev story, a torrent of Italian music came from an open window—that of the living room: what romantic soul was playing the piano where

2   no piano had plunged and plashed on that bewitched Sunday with the sun on her beloved legs? All at once I noticed that from the lawn I had mown a golden-skinned, brown-haired nymphet of nine or ten, in white shorts, was looking at me with wild fascination in her large blue-black eyes. I said something pleasant to her, meaning no harm, an old-world compliment, what nice eyes you have, but she retreated in haste and the music stopped abruptly, and a violent-looking dark man, glistening with sweat, came out and glared at me. I was on the

point of identifying myself when, with a pang of dream-embarrassment, I became aware of my mud-caked dungarees, my filthy and torn sweater, my bristly chin, my bum's bloodshot eyes. Without saying a word, I turned and plodded back the way I had come. An aster-like anemic flower grew out of a remembered chink in the sidewalk. Quietly resurrected, Miss Opposite was being wheeled out by her nieces, onto her porch, as if it were a stage and I the star performer. Praying she would not call to me, I hurried to my car. What a steep little street. What a profound avenue. A red ticket showed between wiper and windshield; I carefully tore it into two, four, eight pieces.

Feeling I was losing my time, I drove energetically to the downtown hotel where I had arrived with a new bag more than five years before. I took a room, made two appointments by telephone, shaved, bathed, put on black clothes and went down for a drink in the bar. Nothing had changed. The barroom was suffused with the same dim, impossible garnet-red light that in Europe years ago went with low haunts, but here meant a bit of atmosphere in a family hotel. I sat at the same little table where at the very start of my stay, immediately after becoming Charlotte's lodger, I had thought fit to celebrate the occasion by suavely sharing with her half a bottle of champagne, which had fatally conquered her poor brimming heart. As then, a moon-faced waiter was arranging with stellar care fifty sherries on a round tray for a wedding party. Murphy-Fantasia, this time. It was eight minutes to three. As I walked through the lobby, I had to skirt a group of ladies who with *mille grâces* were taking leave of each other after a luncheon party. With a harsh cry of recognition, one pounced upon me. She was a stout, short woman in pearl-gray, with a long, gray, slim plume to her small hat. It was Mrs. Chatfield. She attacked me with a fake smile, all aglow with evil curiosity. (Had I done to Dolly, perhaps, what Frank Lasalle, a fifty-year-old mechanic, had done to eleven-year-old Sally Horner in 1948?) Very soon I had that avid glee well under control. She thought I was in California. How was—? With exquisite pleasure I informed her that my stepdaughter had just married a brilliant young mining engineer with a hush-hush job in the Northwest. She said she disapproved of such early marriages, she would never let her Phyllis, who was now eighteen—

"Oh yes, of course," I said quietly. "I remember Phyllis. Phyllis and Camp Q. Yes, of course. By the way, did she ever tell you how Charlie Holmes debauched there his mother's little charges?"

Mrs. Chatfield's already broken smile now disintegrated completely.

"For shame," she cried, "for shame, Mr. Humbert! The poor boy has just been killed in Korea."

1 I said didn't she think "*vient de,*" with the infinitive, expressed recent events so much more neatly than the English "just," with the past? But I had to be trotting off, I said.

There were only two blocks to Windmuller's office. He greeted me with a very slow, very enveloping, strong, searching grip. He thought I was in California. Had I not lived at one time at Beardsley? His daughter had just entered Beardsley College. And how was—? I gave all necessary information about Mrs. Schiller. We had a pleasant business conference. I walked out into the hot September sunshine a contented pauper.

Now that everything had been put out of the way, I could dedicate myself freely to the main object of my visit to Ramsdale. In the methodical manner on which I have always prided myself, I had been keeping Clare Quilty's face masked in my dark dungeon, where he was waiting for me to come with barber

2 and priest: "*Réveillez-vous, Laqueue, il est temps de mourir!*" I have no time right now to discuss the mnemonics of physiognomization—I am on my way to his uncle and walking fast— but let me jot down this: I had preserved in the alcohol of a

3 clouded memory the toad of a face. In the course of a few glimpses, I had noticed its slight resemblance to a cheery and rather repulsive wine dealer, a relative of mine in Switzerland. With his dumbbells and stinking tricot, and fat hairy arms, and bald patch, and pig-faced servant-concubine, he was on the whole a harmless old rascal. Too harmless, in fact, to be confused with my prey. In the state of mind I now found myself,

I had lost contact with Trapp's image. It had become completely engulfed by the face of Clare Quilty—as represented, with artistic precision, by an easeled photograph of him that stood on his uncle's desk.

In Beardsley, at the hands of charming Dr. Molnar, I had undergone a rather serious dental operation, retaining only a few upper and lower front teeth. The substitutes were dependent on a system of plates with an inconspicuous wire affair running along my upper gums. The whole arrangement was a masterpiece of comfort, and my canines were in perfect health. However, to garnish my secret purpose with a plausible pretext, I told Dr. Quilty that, in hope of alleviating facial neuralgia, I had decided to have all my teeth removed. What would a complete set of dentures cost? How long would the process take, assuming we fixed our first appointment for some time in November? Where was his famous nephew now? Would it be possible to have them all out in one dramatic session?

A white-smocked, gray-haired man, with a crew cut and the big flat cheeks of a politician, Dr. Quilty perched on the corner of his desk, one foot dreamily and seductively rocking as he launched on a glorious long-range plan. He would first provide me with provisional plates until the gums settled. Then he would make me a permanent set. He would like to have a look at that mouth of mine. He wore perforated pied shoes. He had not visited with the rascal since 1946, but supposed he could be found at his ancestral home, Grimm Road, not far from Parkington. It was a noble dream. His foot rocked, his gaze was inspired. It would cost me around six hundred. He suggested he take measurements right away, and make the first set before starting operations. My mouth was to him a splendid cave full of priceless treasures, but I denied him entrance.

"No," I said. "On second thoughts, I shall have it all done by Dr. Molnar. His price is higher, but he is of course a much better dentist than you."

I do not know if any of my readers will ever have a chance to say that. It is a delicious dream feeling. Clare's uncle re-

mained sitting on the desk, still looking dreamy, but his foot
had stopped push-rocking the cradle of rosy anticipation. On the
other hand, his nurse, a skeleton-thin, faded girl, with the tragic
eyes of unsuccessful blondes, rushed after me so as to be able
to slam the door in my wake.

Push the magazine into the butt. Press home until you hear
or feel the magazine catch engage. Delightfully snug. Capacity:
eight cartridges. Full Blued. Aching to be discharged.

34

A gas station attendant in Parkington explained to me very
clearly how to get to Grimm Road. Wishing to be sure Quilty
would be at home, I attempted to ring him up but learned that
his private telephone had recently been disconnected. Did that
mean he was gone? I started to drive to Grimm Road, twelve
miles north of the town. By that time night had eliminated most
of the landscape and as I followed the narrow winding highway,
a series of short posts, ghostly white, with reflectors, borrowed
my own lights to indicate this or that curve. I could make out
a dark valley on one side of the road and wooded slopes on
the other, and in front of me, like derelict snowflakes, moths
drifted out of the blackness into my probing aura. At the twelfth
mile, as foretold, a curiously hooded bridge sheathed me for a
moment and, beyond it, a white-washed rock loomed on the
right, and a few car lengths further, on the same side, I turned
off the highway up gravelly Grimm Road. For a couple of minutes all was dank, dark, dense forest. Then, Pavor Manor, a
wooden house with a turret, arose in a circular clearing. Its windows glowed yellow and red; its drive was cluttered with half a
dozen cars. I stopped in the shelter of the trees and abolished
my lights to ponder the next move quietly. He would be surrounded by his henchmen and whores. I could not help seeing
the inside of that festive and ramshackle castle in terms of
"Troubled Teens," a story in one of her magazines, vague

"orgies," a sinister adult with penele cigar, drugs, bodyguards. At least, he was there. I would return in the torpid morning.

Gently I rolled back to town, in that old faithful car of mine which was serenely, almost cheerfully working for me. My Lolita! There was still a three-year-old bobby pin of hers in the depths of the glove compartment. There was still that stream of pale moths siphoned out of the night by my headlights. Dark barns still propped themselves up here and there by the roadside. People were still going to the movies. While searching for night lodgings, I passed a drive-in. In a selenian glow, truly mystical in its contrast with the moonless and massive night, on a gigantic screen slanting away among dark drowsy fields, a thin phantom raised a gun, both he and his arm reduced to tremulous dish-water by the oblique angle of that receding world,—and the next moment a row of trees shut off the gesticulation.

35

I left Insomnia Lodge next morning around eight and spent some time in Parkington. Visions of bungling the execution kept obsessing me. Thinking that perhaps the cartridges in the automatic had gone stale during a week of inactivity, I removed them and inserted a fresh batch. Such a thorough oil bath did I give Chum that now I could not get rid of the stuff. I band-aged him up with a rag, like a maimed limb, and used another rag to wrap up a handful of spare bullets.

A thunderstorm accompanied me most of the way back to Grimm Road, but when I reached Pavor Manor, the sun was visible again, burning like a man, and the birds screamed in the drenched and steaming trees. The elaborate and decrepit house seemed to stand in a kind of daze, reflecting as it were my own state, for I could not help realizing, as my feet touched the springy and insecure ground, that I had overdone the alcoholic stimulation business.

A guardedly ironic silence answered my bell. The garage, however, was loaded with his car, a black convertible for the nonce. I tried the knocker. Re-nobody. With a petulant snarl, I pushed the front door—and, how nice, it swung open as in a medieval

1 fairy tale. Having softly closed it behind me, I made my way across a spacious and very ugly hall; peered into an adjacent drawing room; noticed a number of used glasses growing out of the carpet; decided that master was still asleep in the master bedroom.

So I trudged upstairs. My right hand clutched muffled Chum in my pocket, my left patted the sticky banisters. Of the three bedrooms I inspected, one had obviously been slept in that night. There was a library full of flowers. There was a rather

2 bare room with ample and deep mirrors and a polar bear skin on the slippery floor. There were still other rooms. A happy thought struck me. If and when master returned from his constitutional in the woods, or emerged from some secret lair, it might be wise for an unsteady gunman with a long job before him to prevent his playmate from locking himself up in a room. Consequently, for at least five minutes I went about—lucidly insane, crazily calm, an enchanted and very tight hunter—turning whatever keys in whatever locks there were and pocketing

3 them with my free left hand. The house, being an old one, had more planned privacy than have modern glamour-boxes, where the bathroom, the only lockable locus, has to be used for the furtive needs of planned parenthood.

Speaking of bathrooms—I was about to visit a third one when

4 master came out of it, leaving a brief waterfall behind him. The corner of a passage did not quite conceal me. Gray-faced, baggy-eyed, fluffily disheveled in a scanty balding way, but still perfectly recognizable, he swept by me in a purple bathrobe, very like one I had. He either did not notice me, or else dismissed me as some familiar and innocuous hallucination—and, showing me his hairy calves, he proceeded, sleepwalker-wise, downstairs. I pocketed my last key and followed him into the entrance hall. He had half opened his mouth and the front door, to peer out through a sunny chink as one who thinks he has heard a half-hearted visitor ring and recede. Then, still ignoring

the raincoated phantasm that had stopped in midstairs, master walked into a cozy boudoir across the hall from the drawing room, through which—taking it easy, knowing he was safe—I now went away from him, and in a bar-adorned kitchen gingerly unwrapped dirty Chum, taking care not to leave any oil stains on the chrome—I think I got the wrong product, it was black and awfully messy. In my usual meticulous way, I transferred naked Chum to a clean recess about me and made for the little boudoir. My step, as I say, was springy—too springy perhaps for success. But my heart pounded with tiger joy, and I crunched a cocktail glass underfoot.

Master met me in the Oriental parlor.

"Now who are you?" he asked in a high hoarse voice, his hands thrust into his dressing-gown pockets, his eyes fixing a point to the northeast of my head. "Are you by any chance Brewster?"

By now it was evident to everybody that he was in a fog and completely at my so-called mercy. I could enjoy myself.

"That's right," I answered suavely. "*Je suis Monsieur Brustère.* 1 Let us chat for a moment before we start."

He looked pleased. His smudgy mustache twitched. I removed my raincoat. I was wearing a black suit, a black shirt, no tie. We sat down in two easy chairs.

"You know," he said, scratching loudly his fleshy and gritty gray cheek and showing his small pearly teeth in a crooked grin, "you don't *look* like Jack Brewster. I mean, the resemblance is not particularly striking. Somebody told me he had a brother with the same telephone company."

To have him trapped, after those years of repentance and rage...To look at the black hairs on the back of his pudgy hands...To wander with a hundred eyes over his purple silks and hirsute chest foreglimpsing the punctures, and mess, and music of pain...To know that this semi-animated, subhuman trickster who had sodomized my darling—oh, my darling, this was intolerable bliss!

"No, I am afraid I am neither of the Brewsters."

He cocked his head, looking more pleased than ever.

1   "Guess again, Punch."

"Ah," said Punch, "so you have not come to bother me about those long-distance calls?"

"You do make them once in a while, don't you?"

"Excuse me?"

I said I had said I thought he had said he had never—

"People," he said, "people in general, I'm not accusing you, Brewster, but you know it's absurd the way people invade this 2 damned house without even knocking. They use the *vaterre*, they use the kitchen, they use the telephone. Phil calls Phila- 3 delphia. Pat calls Patagonia. I refuse to pay. You have a funny accent, Captain."

"Quilty," I said, "do you recall a little girl called Dolores 4 Haze, Dolly Haze? Dolly called Dolores, Colo.?"

"Sure, she may have made those calls, sure. Any place. Para- 5 dise, Wash., Hell Canyon. Who cares?"

"I do, Quilty. You see, I am her father."

"Nonsense," he said. "You are not. You are some foreign liter- ary agent. A Frenchman once translated my *Proud Flesh* as *La* 6 *Fierté de la Chair*. Absurd."

"She was my child, Quilty."

In the state he was in he could not really be taken aback by anything, but his blustering manner was not quite convincing. A sort of wary inkling kindled his eyes into a semblance of life. They were immediately dulled again.

"I'm very fond of children myself," he said, "and fathers are among my best friends."

He turned his head away, looking for something. He beat his pockets. He attempted to rise from his seat.

"Down!" I said—apparently much louder than I intended.

"You need not roar at me," he complained in his strange feminine manner. "I just wanted a smoke. I'm dying for a smoke."

"You're dying anyway."

"Oh, chucks," he said. "You begin to bore me. What do you 7 want? Are you French, mister? Woolly-woo-boo-are? Let's go to the barroomette and have a stiff—"

He saw the little dark weapon lying in my palm as if I were offering it to him.

"Say!" he drawled (now imitating the underworld numbskull of movies), "that's a swell little gun you've got there. What d'you want for her?"

I slapped down his outstretched hand and he managed to knock over a box on a low table near him. It ejected a handful of cigarettes.

"Here they are," he said cheerfully. "You recall Kipling: *une femme est une femme, mais un Caporal est une cigarette?* Now we need matches."

"Quilty," I said. "I want you to concentrate. You are going to die in a moment. The hereafter for all we know may be an eternal state of excruciating insanity. You smoked your last cigarette yesterday. Concentrate. Try to understand what is happening to you."

He kept taking the Drome cigarette apart and munching bits of it.

"I am willing to try," he said. "You are either Australian, or a German refugee. Must you talk to me? This is a Gentile's house, you know. Maybe, you'd better run along. And do stop demonstrating that gun. I've an old Stern-Luger in the music room."

I pointed Chum at his slippered foot and crushed the trigger. It clicked. He looked at his foot, at the pistol, again at his foot. I made another awful effort, and, with a ridiculously feeble and juvenile sound, it went off. The bullet entered the thick pink rug, and I had the paralyzing impression that it had merely trickled in and might come out again.

"See what I mean?" said Quilty. "You should be a little more careful. Give me that thing for Christ's sake."

He reached for it. I pushed him back into the chair. The rich joy was waning. It was high time I destroyed him, but he must understand why he was being destroyed. His condition infected me, the weapon felt limp and clumsy in my hand.

"Concentrate," I said, "on the thought of Dolly Haze whom you kidnaped—"

"I did not!" he cried. "You're all wet. I saved her from a beastly pervert. Show me your badge instead of shooting at my foot, you ape, you. Where is that badge? I'm not responsible for the rapes of others. Absurd! That joy ride, I grant you, was a silly stunt but you got her back, didn't you? Come, let's have a drink."

I asked him whether he wanted to be executed sitting or standing.

"Ah, let me think," he said. "It is not an easy question. Incidentally—I made a mistake. Which I sincerely regret. You see, I had no fun with your Dolly. I am practically impotent, to tell the melancholy truth. And I gave her a splendid vacation. She met some remarkable people. Do you happen to know—"

And with a tremendous lurch he fell all over me, sending the pistol hurtling under a chest of drawers. Fortunately he was more impetuous than vigorous, and I had little difficulty in shoving him back into his chair.

He puffed a little and folded his arms on his chest.

"Now you've done it," he said. "*Vous voilà dans de beaux draps, mon vieux.*"

His French was improving.

I looked around. Perhaps, if—Perhaps I could—On my hands and knees? Risk it?

"*Alors, que fait-on?*" he asked watching me closely.

I stooped. He did not move. I stooped lower.

"My dear sir," he said, "stop trifling with life and death. I am a playwright. I have written tragedies, comedies, fantasies. I have made private movies out of *Justine* and other eighteenth-century sexcapades. I'm the author of fifty-two successful scenarios. I know all the ropes. Let me handle this. There should be a poker somewhere, why don't I fetch it, and then we'll fish out your property."

Fussily, busybodily, cunningly, he had risen again while he talked. I groped under the chest trying at the same time to keep an eye on him. All of a sudden I noticed that he had noticed that I did not seem to have noticed Chum protruding from beneath the other corner of the chest. We fell to wrestling again.

Lolita

We rolled all over the floor, in each other's arms, like two huge helpless children. He was naked and goatish under his robe, and I felt suffocated as he rolled over me. I rolled over him. We rolled over me. They rolled over him. We rolled over us.

In its published form, this book is being read, I assume, in the first years of 2000 A.D. (1935 plus eighty or ninety, live long, my love); and elderly readers will surely recall at this point the obligatory scene in the Westerns of their childhood. Our tussle, however, lacked the ox-stunning fisticuffs, the flying furniture. He and I were two large dummies, stuffed with dirty cotton and rags. It was a silent, soft, formless tussle on the part of two literati, one of whom was utterly disorganized by a drug while the other was handicapped by a heart condition and too much gin. When at last I had possessed myself of my precious weapon, and the scenario writer had been reinstalled in his low chair, both of us were panting as the cowman and the sheepman never do after their battle.

I decided to inspect the pistol—our sweat might have spoiled something—and regain my wind before proceeding to the main item in the program. To fill in the pause, I proposed he read his own sentence—in the poetical form I had given it. The term "poetical justice" is one that may be most happily used in this respect. I handed him a neat typescript.

"Yes," he said, "splendid idea. Let me fetch my reading glasses" (he attempted to rise).

"No."

"Just as you say. Shall I read out loud?"

"Yes."

"Here goes. I see it's in verse.

> Because you took advantage of a sinner 1
> because you took advantage
> because you took
> because you took advantage of my disadvantage...

"That's good, you know. That's damned good."

> ... when I stood Adam-naked
> before a federal law and all its stinging stars

"Oh, grand stuff!"

> ...Because you took advantage of a sin
> when I was helpless moulting moist and tender
> hoping for the best
> dreaming of marriage in a mountain state
> aye of a litter of Lolitas...

1

"Didn't get that."

> Because you took advantage of my inner
> essential innocence
> because you cheated me—

"A little repetitious, what? Where was I?"

> Because you cheated me of my redemption
> because you took
> her at the age when lads
> play with erector sets

"Getting smutty, eh?"

> a little downy girl still wearing poppies
> still eating popcorn in the colored gloam
> where tawny Indians took paid croppers
> because you stole her
> from her wax-browed and dignified protector
> spitting into his heavy-lidded eye
> ripping his flavid toga and at dawn
> leaving the hog to roll upon his new discomfort
> the awfulness of love and violets
> remorse despair while you
> took a dull doll to pieces
> and threw its head away
> because of all you did
> because of all I did not
> you have to die

2

"Well, sir, this is certainly a fine poem. Your best as far as I am concerned."

He folded and handed it back to me.

I asked him if he had anything serious to say before dying.
The automatic was again ready for use on the person. He looked
at it and heaved a big sigh.

"Now look here, Mac," he said. "You are drunk and I am a
sick man. Let us postpone the matter. I need quiet. I have to
nurse my impotence. Friends are coming in the afternoon to
take me to a game. This pistol-packing farce is becoming a
frightful nuisance. We are men of the world, in everything—
sex, free verse, marksmanship. If you bear me a grudge, I am
ready to make unusual amends. Even an old-fashioned *rencontre*,   1
sword or pistol, in Rio or elsewhere—is not excluded. My memory and my eloquence are not at their best today but really,
my dear Mr. Humbert, you were not an ideal stepfather, and
I did not force your little protégée to join me. It was she made
me remove her to a happier home. This house is not as modern
as that ranch we shared with dear friends. But it is roomy, cool
in summer and winter, and in a word comfortable, so, since I
intend retiring to England or Florence forever, I suggest you
move in. It is yours, gratis. Under the condition you stop pointing at me that [he swore disgustingly] gun. By the way, I do
not know if you care for the bizarre, but if you do, I can offer
you, also gratis, as house pet, a rather exciting little freak, a
young lady with three breasts, one a dandy, this is a rare and
delightful marvel of nature. Now, *soyons raisonnables*. You will   2
only wound me hideously and then rot in jail while I recuper-
ate in a tropical setting. I promise you, Brewster, you will be
happy here, with a magnificent cellar, and all the royalties from
my next play—I have not much at the bank right now but I
propose to borrow—you know, as the Bard said, with that cold   3
in his head, to borrow and to borrow and to borrow. There
are other advantages. We have here a most reliable and bribable
charwoman, a Mrs. Vibrissa—curious name—who comes from   4
the village twice a week, alas not today, she has daughters,
granddaughters, a thing or two I know about the chief of police
makes him my slave. I am a playwright. I have been called
the American Maeterlinck. Maeterlinck-Schmetterling, says I.   5
Come on! All this is very humiliating, and I am not sure I am

1 doing the right thing. Never use herculanita with rum. Now
   drop that pistol like a good fellow. I knew your dear wife
   slightly. You may use my wardrobe. Oh, another thing—you are
   going to like this. I have an absolutely unique collection of
   erotica upstairs. Just to mention one item: the in folio de-luxe
   Bagration Island by the explorer and psychoanalyst Melanie
2 Weiss, a remarkable lady, a remarkable work—drop that gun—
   with photographs of eight hundred and something male organs
   she examined and measured in 1932 on Bagration, in the Barda
3 Sea, very illuminating graphs, plotted with love under pleasant
   skies—drop that gun—and moreover I can arrange for you to
   attend executions, not everybody knows that the chair is painted
   yellow—"

4 *Feu.* This time I hit something hard. I hit the back of a
   black rocking chair, not unlike Dolly Schiller's—my bullet hit
   the inside surface of its back whereupon it immediately went
   into a rocking act, so fast and with such zest that any one coming
   into the room might have been flabbergasted by the double
   miracle: that chair rocking in a panic all by itself, and the armchair, where my purple target had just been, now void of all
   live content. Wiggling his fingers in the air, with a rapid heave
   of his rump, he flashed into the music room and the next second
   we were tugging and gasping on both sides of the door which
   had a key I had overlooked. I won again, and with another
5 abrupt movement Clare the Impredictable sat down before the
   piano and played several atrociously vigorous, fundamentally
   hysterical, plangent chords, his jowls quivering, his spread hands
   tensely plunging, and his nostrils emitting the soundtrack snorts
   which had been absent from our fight. Still singing those impossible sonorities, he made a futile attempt to open with his
   foot a kind of seaman's chest near the piano. My next bullet
   caught him somewhere in the side, and he rose from his chair
   higher and higher, like old, gray, mad Nijinski, like Old Faithful, like some old nightmare of mine, to a phenomenal altitude,
   or so it seemed, as he rent the air—still shaking with the rich
   black music—head thrown back in a howl, hand pressed to his
   brow, and with his other hand clutching his armpit as if stung

by a hornet, down he came on his heels and, again a normal robed man, scurried out into the hall.

I see myself following him through the hall, with a kind of double, triple, kangaroo jump, remaining quite straight on straight legs while bouncing up twice in his wake, and then bouncing between him and the front door in a ballet-like stiff bounce, with the purpose of heading him off, since the door was not properly closed.

Suddenly dignified, and somewhat morose, he started to walk up the broad stairs, and, shifting my position, but not actually following him up the steps, I fired three or four times in quick succession, wounding him at every blaze; and every time I did it to him, that horrible thing to him, his face would twitch in an absurd clownish manner, as if he were exaggerating the pain; he slowed down, rolled his eyes half closing them and made a feminine "ah!" and he shivered every time a bullet hit him as if I were tickling him, and every time I got him with those slow, clumsy, blind bullets of mine, he would say under his breath, with a phoney British accent—all the while dreadfully twitching, shivering, smirking, but withal talking in a curiously detached and even amiable manner: "Ah, that hurts, sir, enough! Ah, that hurts atrociously, my dear fellow. I pray you, desist. Ah—very painful, very painful, indeed ... God! Hah! This is abominable, you should really not—" His voice trailed off as he reached the landing, but he steadily walked on despite all the lead I had lodged in his bloated body—and in distress, in dismay, I understood that far from killing him I was injecting spurts of energy into the poor fellow, as if the bullets had been capsules wherein a heady elixir danced.

I reloaded the thing with hands that were black and bloody—I had touched something he had anointed with his thick gore. Then I rejoined him upstairs, the keys jangling in my pockets like gold.

He was trudging from room to room, bleeding majestically, trying to find an open window, shaking his head, and still trying to talk me out of murder. I took aim at his head, and he retired to the master bedroom with a burst of royal purple where his ear had been.

"Get out, get out of here," he said coughing and spitting; and in a nightmare of wonder, I saw this blood-spattered but still buoyant person get into his bed and wrap himself up in the chaotic bedclothes. I hit him at very close range through the blankets, and then he lay back, and a big pink bubble with juvenile connotations formed on his lips, grew to the size of a toy balloon, and vanished.

I may have lost contact with reality for a second or two—oh, nothing of the I-just-blacked-out sort that your common criminal enacts; on the contrary, I want to stress the fact that I was responsible for every shed drop of his bubbleblood; but a kind of momentary shift occurred as if I were in the connubial bedroom, and Charlotte were sick in bed. Quilty was a very sick man. I held one of his slippers instead of the pistol—I was sitting on the pistol. Then I made myself a little more comfortable in the chair near the bed, and consulted my wrist watch. The crystal was gone but it ticked. The whole sad business had taken more than an hour. He was quiet at last. Far from feeling any relief, a burden even weightier than the one I had hoped to get rid of was with me, upon me, over me. I could not bring myself to touch him in order to make sure he was really dead. He looked it: a quarter of his face gone, and two flies beside themselves with a dawning sense of unbelievable luck. My hands were hardly in better condition than his. I washed up as best I could in the adjacent bathroom. Now I could leave. As I emerged on the landing, I was amazed to discover that a vivacious buzz I had just been dismissing as a mere singing in my ears was really a medley of voices and radio music coming from the downstairs drawing room.

I found there a number of people who apparently had just arrived and were cheerfully drinking Quilty's liquor. There was a fat man in an easy chair; and two dark-haired pale young beauties, sisters no doubt, big one and small one (almost a child), demurely sat side by side on a davenport. A florid-faced fellow with sapphire-blue eyes was in the act of bringing two glasses out of the bar-like kitchen, where two or three women were chatting and chinking ice. I stopped in the doorway and said: "I have just killed Clare Quilty." "Good for you," said the florid fellow as he offered one of the drinks to the elder girl. "Somebody ought to have done it long ago," remarked the fat man. "What does he say, Tony?" asked a faded blonde from the bar. "He says," answered the florid fellow, "he has killed Cue." "Well," said another unidentified man rising in a corner where he had been crouching to inspect some records, "I guess we all should do it to him some day." "Anyway," said Tony, "he'd better come down. We can't wait for him much longer if we want to go to that game." "Give this man a drink somebody," said the fat person. "Want a beer?" said a woman in slacks, showing it to me from afar.

Only the two girls on the davenport, both wearing black, the younger fingering a bright something about her white neck, only they said nothing, but just smiled on, so young, so lewd. As the music paused for a moment, there was a sudden noise on the stairs. Tony and I stepped out into the hall. Quilty of all people had managed to crawl out onto the landing, and there we could see him, flapping and heaving, and then subsiding, forever this time, in a purple heap.   1

"Hurry up, Cue," said Tony with a laugh. "I believe, he's still—" He returned to the drawing room, music drowned the rest of the sentence.

This, I said to myself, was the end of the ingenious play staged for me by Quilty. With a heavy heart I left the house   2 and walked through the spotted blaze of the sun to my car. Two other cars were parked on both sides of it, and I had some trouble squeezing out.

36

The rest is a little flattish and faded. Slowly I drove downhill, and presently found myself going at the same lazy pace in a direction opposite to Parkington. I had left my raincoat in the boudoir and Chum in the bathroom. No, it was not a house I would have liked to live in. I wondered idly if some surgeon of genius might not alter his own career, and perhaps the whole destiny of mankind, by reviving quilted Quilty, Clare Obscure. Not that I cared; on the whole I wished to forget the whole mess—and when I did learn he was dead, the only satisfaction it gave me, was the relief of knowing I need not mentally accompany for months a painful and disgusting convalescence interrupted by all kinds of unmentionable operations and relapses, and perhaps an actual visit from him, with trouble on my part to rationalize him as not being a ghost. Thomas had something. It is strange that the tactile sense, which is so infinitely less precious to men than sight, becomes at critical moments our main, if not only, handle to reality. I was all covered with Quilty —with the feel of that tumble before the bleeding.

The road now stretched across open country, and it occurred to me—not by way of protest, not as a symbol, or anything like that, but merely as a novel experience—that since I had disregarded all laws of humanity, I might as well disregard the rules of traffic. So I crossed to the left side of the highway and checked the feeling, and the feeling was good. It was a pleasant diaphragmal melting, with elements of diffused tactility, all this enhanced by the thought that nothing could be nearer to the elimination of basic physical laws than deliberately driving on the wrong side of the road. In a way, it was a very spiritual itch. Gently, dreamily, not exceeding twenty miles an hour, I drove on that queer mirror side. Traffic was light. Cars that now and then passed me on the side I had abandoned to them, honked at me brutally. Cars coming towards me wobbled, swerved, and cried out in fear. Presently I found myself approaching populated places. Passing through a red light was like a sip of forbidden Burgundy when I was a child. Meanwhile complications were arising. I was being followed and escorted. Then in front of me I saw two cars placing themselves in such a manner as to completely block my way. With a graceful movement I turned off the road, and after two or three big bounces, rode up a grassy slope, among surprised cows, and there I came to a gentle

rocking stop. A kind of thoughtful Hegelian synthesis linking   1
up two dead women.

I was soon to be taken out of the car (Hi, Melmoth, thanks
a lot, old fellow)—and was, indeed, looking forward to surrender myself to many hands, without doing anything to co-
operate, while they moved and carried me, relaxed, comfortable,
surrendering myself lazily, like a patient, and deriving an eerie
enjoyment from my limpness and the absolutely reliable support
given me by the police and the ambulance people. And while I
was waiting for them to run up to me on the high slope, I evoked
a last mirage of wonder and hopelessness. One day, soon after
her disappearance, an attack of abominable nausea forced me to
pull up on the ghost of an old mountain road that now accompanied, now traversed a brand new highway, with its population
of asters bathing in the detached warmth of a pale-blue afternoon in late summer. After coughing myself inside out, I rested
a while on a boulder, and then, thinking the sweet air might do
me good, walked a little way toward a low stone parapet on the
precipice side of the highway. Small grasshoppers spurted out of
the withered roadside weeds. A very light cloud was opening its
arms and moving toward a slightly more substantial one belonging to another, more sluggish, heavenlogged system. As I approached the friendly abyss, I grew aware of a melodious unity of
sounds rising like vapor from a small mining town that lay at my
feet, in a fold of the valley. One could make out the geometry of
the streets between blocks of red and gray roofs, and green puffs
of trees, and a serpentine stream, and the rich, ore-like glitter of
the city dump, and beyond the town, roads crisscrossing the crazy   2
quilt of dark and pale fields, and behind it all, great timbered
mountains. But even brighter than those quietly rejoicing colors
—for there are colors and shades that seem to enjoy themselves
in good company—both brighter and dreamier to the ear than
they were to the eye, was that vapory vibration of accumulated
sounds that never ceased for a moment, as it rose to the lip of
granite where I stood wiping my foul mouth. And soon I realized
that all these sounds were of one nature, that no other sounds
but these came from the streets of the transparent town, with the

women at home and the men away. Reader! What I heard was but the melody of children at play, nothing but that, and so limpid was the air that within this vapor of blended voices, majestic and minute, remote and magically near, frank and divinely enigmatic—one could hear now and then, as if released, an almost articulate spurt of vivid laughter, or the crack of a bat, or the clatter of a toy wagon, but it was all really too far for the eye to distinguish any movement in the lightly etched streets. I stood listening to that musical vibration from my lofty slope, to those flashes of separate cries with a kind of demure murmur for background, and then I knew that the hopelessly poignant thing was not Lolita's absence from my side, but the absence of her voice from that concord.

This then is my story. I have reread it. It has bits of marrow sticking to it, and blood, and beautiful bright-green flies. At this or that twist of it I feel my slippery self eluding me, gliding into deeper and darker waters than I care to probe. I have camouflaged what I could so as not to hurt people. And I have toyed with many pseudonyms for myself before I hit on a particularly apt one. There are in my notes "Otto Otto" and "Mesmer Mesmer" and "Lambert Lambert," but for some reason I think my choice expresses the nastiness best.

When I started, fifty-six days ago, to write *Lolita,* first in the psychopathic ward for observation, and then in this well-heated, albeit tombal, seclusion, I thought I would use these notes in toto at my trial, to save not my head, of course, but my soul. In mid-composition, however, I realized that I could not parade living Lolita. I still may use parts of this memoir in hermetic sessions, but publication is to be deferred.

For reasons that may appear more obvious than they really are, I am opposed to capital punishment; this attitude will be, I trust, shared by the sentencing judge. Had I come before myself, I would have given Humbert at least thirty-five years for rape, and dismissed the rest of the charges. But even so, Dolly Schiller will probably survive me by many years. The following decision I make with all the legal impact and support of a signed testament:

I wish this memoir to be published only when Lolita is no longer alive.

Thus, neither of us is alive when the reader opens this book. But while the blood still throbs through my writing hand, you are still as much part of blessed matter as I am, and I can still talk to you from here to Alaska. Be true to your Dick. Do not let other fellows touch you. Do not talk to strangers. I hope you will love your baby. I hope it will be a boy. That husband of yours, I hope, will always treat you well, because otherwise my specter shall come at him, like black smoke, like a demented giant, and pull him apart nerve by nerve. And do not pity C. Q. One had to choose between him and H. H., and one wanted H. H. to exist at least a couple of months longer, so as to have him make you live in the minds of later generations. I am thinking of aurochs and angels, the secret of durable pigments, prophetic sonnets, the refuge of art. And this is the only immortality you and I may share, my Lolita.

Vladimir Nabokov
On a Book Entitled
Lolita

After doing my impersonation of suave John Ray, the character in
Lolita who pens the Foreword, any comments coming straight from
me may strike one—may strike me, in fact—as an impersonation of
Vladimir Nabokov talking about his own book. A few points, however, have to be discussed; and the autobiographic device may induce
mimic and model to blend.

Teachers of Literature are apt to think up such problems as "What
is the author's purpose?" or still worse "What is the guy trying to
say?" Now, I happen to be the kind of author who in starting to work
on a book has no other purpose than to get rid of that book and who,
when asked to explain its origin and growth, has to rely on such
ancient terms as Interreaction of Inspiration and Combination—
which, I admit, sounds like a conjurer explaining one trick by performing another.

The first little throb of *Lolita* went through me late in 1939 or
early in 1940, in Paris, at a time when I was laid up with a severe
attack of intercostal neuralgia. As far as I can recall, the initial shiver
of inspiration was somehow prompted by a newspaper story about an
ape in the Jardin des Plantes, who, after months of coaxing by a
scientist, produced the first drawing ever charcoaled by an animal:
this sketch showed the bars of the poor creature's cage. The impulse
I record had no textual connection with the ensuing train of thought,
which resulted, however, in a prototype of my present novel, a short
story some thirty pages long. I wrote it in Russian, the language in
which I had been writing novels since 1924 (the best of these are not
translated into English, and all are prohibited for political reasons in

311

Russia). The man was a Central European, the anonymous nymphet was French, and the loci were Paris and Provence. I had him marry the little girl's sick mother who soon died, and after a thwarted attempt to take advantage of the orphan in a hotel room, Arthur (for that was his name) threw himself under the wheels of a truck. I read the story one blue-papered wartime night to a group of friends—Mark Aldanov, two social revolutionaries, and a woman doctor; but I was not pleased with the thing and destroyed it sometime after moving to America in 1940.

Around 1949, in Ithaca, upstate New York, the throbbing, which had never quite ceased, began to plague me again. Combination joined inspiration with fresh zest and involved me in a new treatment of the theme, this time in English—the language of my first governess in St. Petersburg, circa 1903, a Miss Rachel Home. The nymphet, now with a dash of Irish blood, was really much the same lass, and the basic marrying-her-mother idea also subsisted; but otherwise the thing was new and had grown in secret the claws and wings of a novel.

The book developed slowly, with many interruptions and asides. It had taken me some forty years to invent Russia and Western Europe, and now I was faced by the task of inventing America. The obtaining of such local ingredients as would allow me to inject a modicum of average "reality" (one of the few words which mean nothing without quotes) into the brew of individual fancy, proved at fifty a much more difficult process than it had been in the Europe of my youth when receptiveness and retention were at their automatic best. Other books intervened. Once or twice I was on the point of burning the unfinished draft and had carried my Juanita Dark as far as the shadow of the leaning incinerator on the innocent lawn, when I was stopped by the thought that the ghost of the destroyed book would haunt my files for the rest of my life.

Every summer my wife and I go butterfly hunting. The specimens are deposited at scientific institutions, such as the Museum of Comparative Zoology at Harvard or the Cornell University collection. The locality labels pinned under these butterflies will be a boon to some twenty-first-century scholar with a taste for recondite biography. It was at such of our headquarters as Telluride, Colorado; Afton, Wyoming; Portal, Arizona; and Ashland, Oregon, that *Lolita* was energetically resumed in the evenings or on cloudy days. I finished copying the thing out in longhand in the spring of 1954, and at once began casting around for a publisher.

Lolita

At first, on the advice of a wary old friend, I was meek enough to stipulate that the book be brought out anonymously. I doubt that I shall ever regret that soon afterwards, realizing how likely a mask was to betray my own cause, I decided to sign *Lolita*. The four American publishers, W, X, Y, Z, who in turn were offered the typescript and had their readers glance at it, were shocked by *Lolita* to a degree that even my wary old friend F.P. had not expected.

While it is true that in ancient Europe, and well into the eighteenth century (obvious examples come from France), deliberate lewdness was not inconsistent with flashes of comedy, or vigorous satire, or even the verve of a fine poet in a wanton mood, it is also true that in modern times the term "pornography" connotes mediocrity, commercialism, and certain strict rules of narration. Obscenity must be mated with banality because every kind of aesthetic enjoyment has to be entirely replaced by simple sexual stimulation which demands the traditional word for direct action upon the patient. Old rigid rules must be followed by the pornographer in order to have his patient feel the same security of satisfaction as, for example, fans of detective stories feel—stories where, if you do not watch out, the real murderer may turn out to be, to the fan's disgust, artistic originality (who for instance would want a detective story without a single dialogue in it?). Thus, in pornographic novels, action has to be limited to the copulation of clichés. Style, structure, imagery should never distract the reader from his tepid lust. The novel must consist of an alternation of sexual scenes. The passages in between must be reduced to sutures of sense, logical bridges of the simplest design, brief expositions and explanations, which the reader will probably skip but must know they exist in order not to feel cheated (a mentality stemming from the routine of "true" fairy tales in childhood). Moreover, the sexual scenes in the book must follow a crescendo line, with new variations, new combinations, new sexes, and a steady increase in the number of participants (in a Sade play they call the gardener in), and therefore the end of the book must be more replete with lewd lore than the first chapters.

Certain techniques in the beginning of *Lolita* (Humbert's Journal, for example) misled some of my first readers into assuming that this was going to be a lewd book. They expected the rising succession of erotic scenes; when these stopped, the readers stopped, too, and felt bored and let down. This, I suspect, is one of the reasons why not all the four firms read the typescript to the end. Whether they found it pornographic or not did not interest me. Their refusal to buy the book was based not on my treatment of the theme but on the theme itself, for there are at least three themes which are utterly taboo as far as most American publishers are concerned. The two others are: a Negro-White marriage which is a complete and glorious success resulting in lots of children and grandchildren; and the total atheist who lives a happy and useful life, and dies in his sleep at the age of 106.

Some of the reactions were very amusing: one reader suggested that his firm might consider publication if I turned my Lolita into a twelve-year-old lad and had him seduced by Humbert, a farmer, in a barn, amidst gaunt and arid surroundings, all this set forth in short, strong, "realistic" sentences ("He acts crazy. We all act crazy, I guess. I guess God acts crazy." Etc.). Although everybody should know that I detest symbols and allegories (which is due partly to my old feud with Freudian voodooism and partly to my loathing of generalizations devised by literary mythists and sociologists), an otherwise intelligent reader who flipped through the first part described *Lolita* as "Old Europe debauching young America," while another flipper saw in it "Young America debauching old Europe." Publisher X, whose advisers got so bored with Humbert that they never got beyond page 188, had the naïveté to write me that Part Two was too long. Publisher Y, on the other hand, regretted there were no good people in the book. Publisher Z said if he printed *Lolita*, he and I would go to jail.

No writer in a free country should be expected to bother about the exact demarcation between the sensuous and the sensual; this is preposterous; I can only admire but cannot emulate the accuracy of judgment of those who pose the fair young mammals photographed in magazines where the general neckline is just low enough to provoke a past master's chuckle and just high enough not to make a postmaster frown. I presume there exist readers who find titillating the display of mural words in those hopelessly banal and enormous novels which are typed out by the thumbs of tense mediocrities and called "powerful" and "stark" by the reviewing hack. There are gentle souls who would pronounce *Lolita* meaningless because it does not teach them anything. I am neither a reader nor a writer of didactic fiction, and, despite John Ray's assertion, *Lolita* has no moral in tow. For me a work of fiction exists only insofar as it affords me what I shall bluntly call aesthetic bliss, that is a sense of being somehow, somewhere, connected with other states of being where art (curiosity, tenderness, kindness, ecstasy) is the norm. There are not many such books. All the rest is either topical trash or what some call the Literature of Ideas, which very often is topical trash coming in huge blocks of plaster that are carefully transmitted from age to age until somebody comes along with a hammer and takes a good crack at Balzac, at Gorki, at Mann.

Another charge which some readers have made is that *Lolita* is anti-American. This is something that pains me considerably more than the idiotic accusation of immorality. Considerations of depth and perspective (a suburban lawn, a mountain meadow) led me to build a number of North American sets. I needed a certain exhilarating milieu. Nothing is more exhilarating than philistine vulgarity. But in regard to philistine vulgarity there is no intrinsic difference between Palearctic manners and Nearctic manners. Any proletarian from Chicago can be as bourgeois (in the Flaubertian sense) as a duke. I chose American motels instead of Swiss hotels or English inns only because I am trying to be an American writer and claim only the same rights that other American writers enjoy. On the other hand, my creature Humbert is a foreigner and an anarchist, and there are many things, besides nymphets, in which I disagree with him. And all my Russian readers know that my old worlds—Russian, British, German, French—are just as fantastic and personal as my new one is.

Lest the little statement I am making here seem an airing of grudges, I must hasten to add that besides the lambs who read the typescript of *Lolita* or its Olympia Press edition in a spirit of "Why did he have to write it?" or "Why should I read about maniacs?" there have been a number of wise, sensitive, and staunch people who understood my book much better than I can explain its mechanism here.

Every serious writer, I dare say, is aware of this or that published book of his as of a constant comforting presence. Its pilot light is steadily burning somewhere in the basement and a mere touch applied to one's private thermostat instantly results in a quiet little explosion of familiar warmth. This presence, this glow of the book in an ever accessible remoteness is a most companionable feeling, and the better the book has conformed to its prefigured contour and color the ampler and smoother it glows. But even so, there are certain ɪoints, byroads, favorite hollows that one evokes more eagerly and

enjoys more tenderly than the rest of one's book. I have not reread
Lolita since I went through the proofs in the spring of 1955 but I
find it to be a delightful presence now that it quietly hangs about the
house like a summer day which one knows to be bright behind the
haze. And when I thus think of Lolita, I seem always to pick out for
special delectation such images as Mr. Taxovich, or that class list
of Ramsdale School, or Charlotte saying "waterproof," or Lolita in
slow motion advancing toward Humbert's gifts, or the pictures
decorating the stylized garret of Gaston Godin, or the Kasbeam
barber (who cost me a month of work), or Lolita playing tennis, or
the hospital at Elphinstone, or pale, pregnant, beloved, irretrievable
Dolly Schiller dying in Gray Star (the capital town of the book), or
the tinkling sounds of the valley town coming up the mountain trail
(on which I caught the first known female of *Lycaeides sublivens*
Nabokov). These are the nerves of the novel. These are the secret
points, the subliminal co-ordinates by means of which the book is
plotted—although I realize very clearly that these and other scenes
will be skimmed over or not noticed, or never even reached, by those
who begin reading the book under the impression that it is something
on the lines of *Memoirs of a Woman of Pleasure* or *Les Amours de
Milord Grosvit*. That my novel does contain various allusions to the
physiological urges of a pervert is quite true. But after all we are not
children, not illiterate juvenile delinquents, not English public school
boys who after a night of homosexual romps have to endure the
paradox of reading the Ancients in expurgated versions.

It is childish to study a work of fiction in order to gain information
about a country or about a social class or about the author. And yet
one of my very few intimate friends, after reading Lolita, was sincerely
worried that I (I!) should be living "among such depressing people"
—when the only discomfort I really experienced was to live in my
workshop among discarded limbs and unfinished torsos.

After Olympia Press, in Paris, published the book, an American critic
suggested that Lolita was the record of my love affair with the romantic novel. The substitution "English language" for "romantic novel"
would make this elegant formula more correct. But here I feel my
voice rising to a much too strident pitch. None of my American
friends have read my Russian books and thus every appraisal on the
strength of my English ones is bound to be out of focus. My private
tragedy, which cannot, and indeed should not, be anybody's concern,
is that I had to abandon my natural idiom, my untrammeled, rich,

and infinitely docile Russian tongue for a second-rate brand of English, devoid of any of those apparatuses—the baffling mirror, the black velvet backdrop, the implied associations and traditions—which the native illusionist, frac-tails flying, can magically use to transcend the heritage in his own way.

November 12, 1956

Notes

The word or passage in the text to which each annotation refers is indicated by two numbers, the first giving the page and the second the number in the margin of the text. The numbering begins anew on each page and disregards chapter divisions. All page references to other Nabokov books are to the Vintage paperback editions.

FOREWORD

3/1 *two titles:* the term "white widowed male" occurs in the case histories of psychiatric works, while the entire subtitle parodies the titillating confessional novel, such as John Cleland's *Memoirs of a Woman of Pleasure* (1749), and the expectations of the reader who hopes *Lolita* will provide the pleasures of pornography (see 276/2). Although Nabokov could hardly have realized it at the time of writing, there is no small irony in the fact that the timidity of American publishers resulted in the novel's being first brought out by the Olympia Press, publishers of *The Sexual Life of Robinson Crusoe* and other "eighteenth-century sex-capades" (to use Clare Quilty's description of Sade's *Justine, ou, Les Infortunes de la vertu* [. . . *The Misfortunes of Virtue*]; see p. 298).

3/2 *preambulates:* to make a preamble, introduce.

3/3 *"Humbert Humbert":* in his *Playboy* interview (1964), Nabokov said, "The double rumble is, I think, very nasty, very suggestive. It is a hateful name for a hateful person. It is also a kingly name, but I did need a royal vibration for Humbert the Fierce and Humbert the Humble. Lends itself also to a number of puns." Like James Joyce, Nabokov fashions his puns from literary sources, from any of the several languages available to him, from obsolete words, or the roots of arcane words. If the associations are rich enough, a pun succeeds in projecting a theme central to the fiction, in summarizing or commenting on the action. In both *The Gift* (1937) and the 1959 Foreword to the English translation of *Invitation to a Beheading* (1935–1936), Nabokov mentions *Discours sur les ombres*, by Pierre Delalande, "the only author whom I must gratefully recognize as an influence upon me at the time of writing this book . . . [and] whom I invented." Delalande's *Discours* provided the epigraph for *Invitation*— "*Comme un fou se croît Dieu, nous nous croyons mortels*" ["As a madman deems himself God, we deem ourselves mortal"]—and Nabokov's entire corpus might be described as a "Discourse on Shadows, or Shades." John Shade is the author of the poem *Pale Fire*. In a rejected draft of his poem, he writes, "I like my name: Shade, *Ombre*, almost 'man' / In Spanish . . ."—an accurate etymological pairing (hombre > ombre) and a resonant pun that figuratively places *hombre* in ombre—a card game popular in the seventeenth and eighteenth centuries—and sets man to playing in Nabokov's "game of worlds" (see 20/4). Humbert was brought up on the French Riviera; pronounced with a French accent, his name partakes of these shadows and shades. By "solipsizing" Lolita (p. 60), Humbert condemns her to the solitary confinement of his obsessional shadowland. "She had entered my world, umber and black Humberland," says Humbert (p. 166), who, by choosing to chase the figurative shadows that play on the walls of his "cave," upends Plato's famous allegory. Although Humbert has had the benefit of a journey in the sunny "upper world"—a Riviera boyhood, in fact, and a full-sized wife or two—he nevertheless pursues the illusion that he can recapture what is inexorably lost. As Humbert demonstrates, illusions *are* realities in their ability to destroy us. "I was the shadow of the waxwing slain / By the false azure in the windowpane," writes John Shade in the opening lines of *Pale Fire*, while in Nabokov's poem "An Evening of Russian Poetry" (1945), the speaker says:

> My back is Argus-eyed. I live in danger.
> False shadows turn to track me as I pass
> and, wearing beards, disguised as secret agents,
> creep in to blot the freshly written page
> and read the blotter in the looking-glass.
> And in the dark, under my bedroom window,

until, with a chill whirr and shiver, day
presses its starter, warily they linger
or silently approach the door and ring
the bell of memory and run away.

Seventeen years later in *Pale Fire* the Shadows are the Zemblan "regicidal organization" who dispatch Gradus, one of whose aliases is d'Argus, to assassinate the exiled King Charles (Kinbote). But the Shadows' secret agent accidentally kills Shade instead. *Lolita* offers the converse, for "Shade" (Humbert) purposely kills his "shadow" (Clare Quilty). Thus the delusive nature of identity and perception, the constricting burdens of memory, and a haunting sense of mutability are all capsuled in a reverberating pun.

3/4 *solecism:* an irregularity or impropriety in speech and diction, grammar or syntax. Also in conduct, and therefore not an unwarranted definition in Humbert's instance.

3/5 *presented intact:* it is important to recognize how Nabokov belies the illusion of "realism" which both Ray and Humbert seem to create. See 9/1 and 32/7.

3/6 *cognomen:* its current definition, "a distinguishing nickname," is fundamental, and the humorous incongruity of using so high-toned a Latinate word is heightened by its original meaning: "The third or family name of a Roman citizen."

3/7 *this mask:* "Is 'mask' the keyword?" Humbert later asks (p. 53). In his Foreword to *Pale Fire*, Kinbote says of Shade: "His whole being constituted a mask."

3/8 *remain unlifted:* not quite; although the "real" name is never revealed, the mask does slip. See Chapter Twenty-six, the shortest in the book (p. 109).

4/1 *her first name:* Lolita's given name is "Dolores." See 9/5.

4/2 *"H.H." 's crime:* the murder of Clare Quilty (pp. 293–305), Humbert's grotesque alter ego and parodic Double. Humbert will henceforth be identified by his initials.

4/3 *1952:* a corrected author's error ("September–October 1952," instead of the 1958 edition's "September"). The following pages in the text contain corrections which are detailed in the Notes: pp. 4 (below), 6, 19, 23, 31,

32, 52, 60, 117, 121, 138, 150, 162, 185, 193, 195, 197, 199, 204, 225, 230, 232, 253, 259, 262, 264, 314, and 316. The 1958 Putnam's edition was set in type from the 1955 Olympia Press edition. The latter contains many minuscule mistakes (e.g., punctuation) which were carried over into the Putnam's edition and identified only when the present text was in page proof. Although these errors have been corrected, it was impossible to describe them separately in the Notes. However, since the present edition follows the Putnam's format exactly, save for the pagination (each Putnam page is two higher), assiduous students of such textual matters can easily identify these corrections by collating the two texts, as follows, adding two to get the Putnam's page: p. 5, line sixteen; p. 31, line fourteen; p. 40, last line; p. 63, lines three and twenty-six; p. 73, line nineteen; p. 82, last line; p. 111, line seventeen; p. 136, line thirteen; p. 141, lines six and seven; p. 150, line twenty-five; p. 156, line six; p. 158, line sixteen; p. 161, line fifteen; p. 164, line nine; p. 179, line three; p. 180, line nine; p. 218, line ten; p. 226, line seven; p. 239, line thirteen; p. 243, line twenty-three; p. 255, line five; p. 262, line twenty-five; p. 275, line four; p. 276, line thirty-three; and p. 278, line two.

4/4 *"real people"* . . . *"true story"*: in the Afterword, Nabokov mentions his "impersonation of suave John Ray" (p. 311); but by mocking the conventional reader's desire for verisimilitude, as Nabokov does in the opening paragraphs of *Laughter in the Dark, Despair, Invitation to a Beheading,* and *The Gift,* Dr. Ray here expresses the concerns of a novelist rather than psychologist, suggesting that the mask has not remained totally in place. There are subtle oscillations between the shrill locutions and behavioristic homilies of Ray and the quite reasonable statements of an authorial voice projected, as it were, from the wings. Note 4/9 underlines this, while 5/1 and 5/3–5/5 suggest other instances of that presence.

4/5 *sophomore*: a corrected misprint (a period instead of the 1958 edition's semicolon after "sophomore").

4/6 *Mrs. "Richard F. Schiller"*: Lolita's married name, first revealed on p. 266. The covert disclosure of Lolita's death is significant, for the announcement that the three main characters are now dead challenges the "old-fashioned reader" 's idea of "story": to reveal the outcome before the story even begins is of course to ruin it. The heroine of "The Beauty" (1934), an untranslated Nabokov story, also dies in childbirth within a year after her marriage (noted by Andrew Field, *Nabokov: His Life in Act* [Boston, 1967], p. 330).

4/7 *1952:* for a hermetic allusion to this crucial year, see 251/14.

4/8 *Gray Star:* it is most remote, for there is no town by this name anywhere in the world. Nabokov calls it "the capital town of the book" (p. 316). A gray star is one veiled by haze (Lolita's surname), and H.H. recalls "the haze of stars" that has always "remained with me." See 15/1 and 280/1.

4/9 *"Vivian Darkbloom"* . . . *"My Cue":* "Vivian Darkbloom" is Clare Quilty's mistress and an anagram of "Vladimir Nabokov" (see my 1967 *Wisconsin Studies* article, p. 216, and my 1968 *Denver Quarterly* article, p. 32 [see bibliography]). "Vivian Darkbloom" is the author of "Notes to Ada," which is appended to the 1970 Penguin paperback edition and the 1990 Vintage edition. Among her alphabetical cousins are "Vivian Bloodmark, a philosophical friend of mine," who appears in *Speak, Memory* (p. 218), and "Mr. Vivian Badlook," a photographer and teacher of English in the 1968 translation of the 1928 novel *King, Queen, Knave* (p. 153)—and they all descend from "Vivian Calmbrood" (see Field, *op. cit.,* p. 73), the alleged author of *The Wanderers,* an uncompleted play written by Nabokov in Russian (the anagram is helped along by the fact that in Cyrillic, the *c* is a *k*). One act of it was published in the émigré almanac *Facets* (1923), as an English play written by Vivian Calmbrood in 1768 and translated by V. Sirin (the pen name under which all of Nabokov's Russian work appeared). In a discussion in *Ada* (1969) of Van Veen's first novel, *Letters from Terra,* mention is made of the influence "of an obscene ancient Arab, expounder of anagrammatic dreams, Ben Sirine" (p. 344).

As for H.H. and John Ray, unless characters in a novel can be said to have miraculously fashioned their creators, someone else must be responsible for an anagram of the author's name, and such phenomena undermine the narrative's realistic base by pointing beyond the book to Nabokov, the stage manager, ventriloquist, and puppeteer, who might simply state, "My cue." Because Nabokov considered publishing *Lolita* anonymously (see p. 313), there was also a purely utilitarian reason for anagrammatizing his name, as proof of authorship. "Cue" is also the cognomen of Clare Quilty, who pursues H.H. throughout the novel. But who *is* Quilty?—a question the reader will surely ask (see the

Introduction, pp. xxx–lxvii, and 31/9). As with H.H. and Lolita (*née* Dolores Haze), Quilty's name lends itself to wordplay by turns jocose (see 223/1) and significant, since H.H. suggests that Clare Quilty is clearly guilty. Clare is also a town in Michigan (see 159/1), and, although Nabokov did not know it until this note came into being, Quilty is a town in County Clare, Ireland, appropriate to a verbally playful novel in which there are several apt references to James Joyce. See 4/11.

4/10 *etiolated:* to blanch or whiten a plant by exclusion of sunlight.

4/11 *outspoken book: Ulysses* (1922), by James Joyce (1882–1941), Irish novelist and poet. Judge Woolsey's historic decision paved the way for the 1934 American publication of *Ulysses,* and his decision, along with a statement by Morris Ernst, prefaces the Modern Library edition of the novel. Ray's parenthetical allusion echoes and compresses its complete title: "THE MONUMENTAL DECISION OF THE UNITED STATES DISTRICT COURT RENDERED DECEMBER 6, 1933, BY HON. JOHN M. WOOLSEY LIFTING THE BAN ON 'ULYSSES.' " Ray's Foreword in part burlesques the expert opinions which have inevitably prefaced subsequent "controversial" novels. For other allusions to Joyce, see 69/1, 120/4, 187/1, 198/3, 207/3, 221/1, 250/3, 262/3, and 284/4.

5/1 *moral apotheosis:* a just description of H.H.'s realization at the end of the novel: "the hopelessly poignant thing was not Lolita's absence from my side, but the absence of her voice from that concord" (p. 308).

5/2 *12%:* such "sextistics" (as H.H. or Quilty might call them) poke fun at the work of Alfred Kinsey (1894–1956) and his Indiana University Institute for Sex Research.

5/3 *Blanche Schwarzmann: schwarz* is German for "black"; her name is "White Blackman," because, to Nabokov, Freudians figuratively see no colors other than black and white (see 5/6). "White blackman" also describes the attire of a recently "white widowed male" (see 3/1). For a similarly hued lady, see p. 302 and "Melanie Weiss."

5/4 *a mixture of . . . supreme misery:* an accurate description of the pain at the center of H.H.'s playfulness.

5/5 *his singing violin:* another gap in the texture of Ray's rhetoric reveals the voice of his maker. In his Foreword to *Invitation to a Beheading,* Nabokov calls the novel a "violin in a void," and in *Speak, Memory* he calls the poet Boris Poplavski "a far violin among near balalaikas" (p. 287).

5/6 *a case history:* among other things, *Lolita* parodies such studies, and Nabokov's quarrel with psychoanalysis is well-known. No Foreword to his translated novels seems complete unless a few words are addressed to "the Viennese delegation," who are also invoked frequently throughout the works. Asked in a 1966 National Educational Television interview why he "detest[ed] Dr. Freud," Nabokov replied: "I think he's crude, I think he's medieval, and I don't want an elderly gentleman from Vienna with an umbrella inflicting his dreams upon me. *I* don't have the dreams that he discusses in his books. I don't see umbrellas in my dreams. Or balloons" (this half-hour interview may be rented for a nominal fee from the Audio-Visual Center, Indiana University, Bloomington, Indiana 47401; the film, notes their catalog, is "available to responsible individuals and groups both in and out of Indiana"). When I queried Nabokov about Freud (by now a trite question), just to see if he could rise to the occasion once more, he obliged me: "Oh, I am not up to discussing again that figure of fun. He is not worthy of more attention than I have granted him in my novels and in *Speak, Memory.* Let the credulous and the vulgar continue to believe that all mental woes can be cured by a daily application of old Greek myths to their private parts. I really do not care" (*Wisconsin Studies* interview).

In *Speak, Memory,* Nabokov recalls having seen from a Biarritz window "a huge custard-colored balloon . . . being inflated by Sigismond Lejoyeux, a local aeronaut" (p. 156); and "the police state of sexual myth" (p. 300) is in *Ada* called "psykitsch" (p. 29). The good doctor's paronomastic avatars are "Dr. Sig Heiler" (p. 28), and "A Dr. Froid . . . who may have been an émigré brother with a passport-changed name of the Dr. Froit of Signy-Mondieu-Mondieu" (p. 27). Since no parodist could improve on Erich Fromm's realization that "The little cap of red velvet in the German version of Little Red Riding Hood is a symbol of menstruation" (from *The Forgotten Language,* 1951, p. 240), or Dr. Oskar Pfister's felicitously expressed thought that "When a youth is all the time sticking his finger through his buttonhole . . . the analytic teacher knows that the appetite of the lustful one knows no limit in his phantasies" (from *The Psychoanalytical Method,* 1917, p. 79), Nabokov the literary anatomist simply includes these treasures in *Pale Fire* (p. 271). See

Lolita, pp. 34, 167, 194–195, 250, and 285; and 35/1, 125/3, 254/3, and 274/4.

6/1 *John Ray, Jr.:* the first John Ray (1627–1705) was an English naturalist famous for his systems of natural classification. His system of plant classification greatly influenced the development of systematic botany (*Historia plantarium,* 1686–1704). He was the first to attempt a definition of what constitutes a species. His system of insects, as set forth in *Methodus insectorum* (1705) and *Historia insectorum* (1713), is based on the concept of metamorphosis (see 16/6). The reference to Ray is no coincidence (it was first pointed out by Diana Butler, in "Lolita Lepidoptera," *New World Writing 16* [1960], p. 63). Nabokov was a distinguished lepidopterist, worked in Lepidoptera as a Research Fellow in the Museum of Comparative Zoology at Harvard (1942–1948), and published some twenty papers on the subject. While I was visiting him in 1966, he took from the shelf his copy of Alexander B. Klots's standard work, *A Field Guide to the Butterflies* (1951), and, opening it, pointed to the first sentence of the section on "*Genus* Lycæides *Scudder:* The Orange Margined Blues," which reads: "The recent work of Nabokov has entirely rearranged the classification of this genus" (p. 164). "That's real fame," said the author of *Lolita.* "That means more than anything a literary critic could say." In *Speak, Memory* (Chapter Six), he writes evocatively of his entomological forays, of the fleeting moments of ecstasy he experiences in catching exquisite and rare butterflies. These emotions are perhaps best summarized in his poem "A Discovery" (1943; from *Poems,* p. 15), its twentieth line echoing what he said to me more than two decades later:

> I found it in a legendary land
> all rocks and lavender and tufted grass,
> where it was settled on some sodden sand
> hard by the torrent of a mountain pass.
>
> The features it combines mark it as new
> to science: shape and shade—the special tinge,
> akin to moonlight, tempering its blue,
> the dingy underside, the checquered fringe.
>
> My needles have teased out its sculptured sex;
> corroded tissues could no longer hide
> that priceless mote now dimpling the convex
> and limpid teardrop on a lighted slide.

Smoothly a screw is turned; out of the mist
two ambered hooks symmetrically slope,
or scales like battledores of amethyst
cross the charmed circle of the microscope.

I found it and I named it, being versed
in taxonomic Latin; thus became
godfather to an insect and its first
describer—and I want no other fame.

Wide open on its pin (though fast asleep),
and safe from creeping relatives and rust,
in the secluded stronghold where we keep
type specimens it will transcend its dust.

Dark pictures, thrones, the stones that pilgrims kiss,
poems that take a thousand years to die
but ape the immortality of this
red label on a little butterfly.

There are many references to butterflies in *Lolita*, but it must be
remembered that it is Nabokov, and not H.H., who is the expert. As
Nabokov said, "H.H. knows nothing about Lepidoptera. In fact, I went
out of my way to indicate [p. 110 and p. 157] that he confuses the hawkmoths visiting flowers at dusk with 'gray hummingbirds.' " The author
has implored the unscientific annotator to omit references to Lepidoptera, "a tricky subject." Only the most specific lepidopterological allusions will be noted, though even this modest trove will make it clear how
the butterfly motif enables Nabokov to leave behind on H.H.'s pages a
trail of his own phosphorescent fingerprints. For entomological allusions, see 9/5, 10/3, 12/1, 16/6, 42/5, 46/1, 56/2, 110/3, 112/1, 126/2, 141/1,
156/2, 157/2, 189/5, 209/1, 210/2, 211/4, 227/4, 231/1, 234/2, 258/5, 259/1,
262/6, 301/5, 315/1, and 316/10.

6/2 *1955:* a corrected author's error (the date was not included in the 1958
edition).

PART ONE
CHAPTER I

9/1 *Lolita, light of my life:* her name is the first word in the Foreword, as well as the first and last words of the novel. Such symmetries and carefully effected alliterations and rhythms undermine the credibility of H.H.'s "point of view," since the narrative is presented as an unrevised first draft, mistakes intact, started in a psychiatric ward and completed in a prison cell, the product of the fifty-six frenzied final days of H.H.'s life (see his reminder, p. 308, and 32/7 and 34/3). When asked how her name occurred to him, Nabokov replied, "For my nymphet I needed a diminutive with a lyrical lilt to it. One of the most limpid and luminous letters is 'L.' The suffix '-ita' has a lot of Latin tenderness, and this I required too. Hence: Lolita. However, it should not be pronounced as . . . most Americans pronounce it: Low-lee-ta, with a heavy, clammy 'L' and a long 'O.' No, the first syllable should be as in 'lollipop,' the 'L' liquid and delicate, the 'lee' not too sharp. Spaniards and Italians pronounce it, of course, with exactly the necessary note of archness and caress. Another consideration was the welcome murmur of its source name, the fountain name: those roses and tears in 'Dolores' [see 9/5]. My little girl's heart-rending fate had to be taken into account together with the cuteness and limpidity. Dolores also provided her with another, plainer, more familiar and infantile diminutive: Dolly, which went nicely with the surname 'Haze,' where Irish mists blend with a German bunny—I mean a small German hare [= *hase*]" (*Playboy* interview). Since most everything is in a name, Nabokov both memorializes and instructs in *Ada:* "For the big picnic on Ada's twelfth birthday . . . the child was permitted to wear her lolita (thus dubbed after the little Andalusian gipsy [see *Carmen* note, 244/1—A.A.] of that name in Osberg's novel and pronounced, incidentally, with a Spanish 't,' not a thick English one) . . ." (p. 77). Lolita's name is lovingly celebrated by Anthony Burgess in his poem, "To Vladimir Nabokov on His Seventieth Birthday," in *TriQuarterly,* No. 17 (Winter 1970):

> That nymphet's beauty lay less on her bones
> Than in her name's proclaimed two allophones.
> A boned veracity slow to be found
> In all the channels of recorded sound.

9/2 *Lo-lee-ta:* the middle syllable alludes to "Annabel Lee" (1849), by Edgar Allan Poe (1809–1849). H.H. will lead one to believe that "Annabel Leigh" is the cause of his misery: "Annabel Haze, alias Dolores Lee, alias Loleeta," he says on p. 167. References to Poe are noted in 31/5, 43/5, 75/5, 107/1, 118/2, 189/3, and 292/2; while "Annabel Lee" is variously invoked on pp. 40, 125, and 230, and otherwise as noted 9/7, 9/8, 12/1, 13/4, 39/1, 42/3, 47/4, 53/5, and 166/2. But rather than identify *every* "Annabel Lee" echo occurring in the first chapter and elsewhere, the text of the poem is provided:

> It was many and many a year ago,
>> In a kingdom by the sea,
> That a maiden there lived whom you may know
>> By the name of Annabel Lee;—
> And this maiden she lived with no other thought
>> Than to love and be loved by me.
>
> *She* was a child and *I* was a child,
>> In this kingdom by the sea,
> But we loved with a love that was more than love—
>> I and my Annabel Lee—
> With a love that the winged seraphs of Heaven
>> Coveted her and me.
>
> And this was the reason that, long ago,
>> In this kingdom by the sea,
> A wind blew out of a cloud by night
>> Chilling my Annabel Lee;
>
> So that her high-born kinsmen came
>> And bore her away from me,
> To shut her up in a sepulchre
>> In this kingdom by the sea.
>
> The angels, not half so happy in Heaven,
>> Went envying her and me:—
> Yes! that was the reason (as all men know,
>> In this kingdom by the sea)
> That the wind came out of the cloud, chilling
>> And killing my Annabel Lee.
>
> But our love it was stronger by far than the love
>> Of those who were older than we—
>> Of many far wiser than we—
> And neither the angels in Heaven above

> Nor the demons down under the sea
> Can ever dissever my soul from the soul
> Of the beautiful Annabel Lee:—
> For the moon never beams without bringing me dreams
> Of the beautiful Annabel Lee;
>
> And the stars never rise but I see the bright eyes
> Of the beautiful Annabel Lee;
> And so, all the night-tide, I lie down by the side
> Of my darling, my darling, my life and my bride
> In her sepulchre there by the sea—
> In her tomb by the sounding sea.

Poe is referred to more than twenty times in *Lolita* (echoes of "my darling" haven't been counted), far more than any other writer (followed by Mérimée, Shakespeare, and Joyce, in that order). Not surprisingly, Poe allusions have been the most readily identifiable to readers and earlier commentators (I pointed out several in my 1967 *Wisconsin Studies* article, *"Lolita:* The Springboard of Parody" [see bibliography]). See also the earlier articles by Elizabeth Phillips ("The Hocus-Pocus of *Lolita,"* *Literature and Psychology,* X [Summer 1960], 97–101) and Arthur F. DuBois ("Poe and *Lolita,"* *CEA Critic,* XXVI [No. 6, 1963], 1, 7). More recent is Carl R. Proffer's thorough compilation in *Keys to Lolita* (henceforth called *Keys*), pp. 34–45.

Although my Notes seldom discuss in detail the significance of the literary allusions they limn, Poe's conspicuous presence surely calls for a few general remarks; subsequent Notes will establish the most specific —and obvious—links between H.H. and Poe (e.g., their "child brides"; see 43/5). Poe is appropriate for many reasons. He wrote the kind of *Doppelgänger* tale ("William Wilson") which the H.H.-Quilty relationship seemingly parallels but ultimately upends, and he of course "fathered" the detective tale. Although, as a reader, Nabokov abhorred the detective story, he was not alone in recognizing that the genre's properties are well-suited to the fictive treatment of metaphysical questions and problems of identity and perception. Thus—along with other contemporary writers such as Graham Greene (*Brighton Rock,* 1938), Raymond Queneau (*Pierrot mon ami [Pierrot],* 1942), Jorge Luis Borges ("Death and the Compass," "An Examination of the Work of Herbert Quain," "The Garden of Forking Paths" [first published in *Ellery Queen's Mystery Magazine*], and "The South"), Alain Robbe-Grillet (*Les Gommes* [*The Erasers*], 1953), Michel Butor (*L'Emploi du temps [Passing Time],*

1956), and Thomas Pynchon (*V.*, 1963)—Nabokov often transmuted or parodied the forms, techniques, and themes of the detective story, as in *Despair, The Real Life of Sebastian Knight, Lolita,* and, less directly, in *The Eye,* where, Nabokov said, "The texture of the tale mimics that of detective fiction." The reader of *Lolita* is invited to wend his way through a labyrinth of clues in order to solve the mystery of Quilty's identity, which in part makes *Lolita* a "tale of ratiocination," to use Poe's phrase (see 31/9). Early in the novel one is told that H.H. is a murderer. Has he killed Charlotte? Or Lolita? (See also *Keys,* p. 39.) The reader is led to expect both possibilities, and his various attempts at ratiocination should ultimately tell the reader as much about his own mind as about the "crimes," "identities," or "psychological development" of fictional characters. For allusions to detective story writers other than Poe, see 31/2 (Agatha Christie), 64/1 (Conan Doyle), and 211/1 and 250/5 (Maurice Leblanc).

It is also in part through Poe that Nabokov manages to suggest some consistently held attitudes toward language and literature. H.H. says of his artistic labors, "The beastly and beautiful merged at one point, and it is that borderline I would like to fix, and I feel I fail to do so utterly. Why?" (p. 135). The rhetorical question is coy enough, because he has answered it at the beginning of his narrative; he hasn't failed, but neither can he ever be entirely successful, because "Oh, my Lolita, I have only words to play with!" (p. 32)—an admission many Romantic and Symbolist writers would not make. Nabokov's remark about Joyce's giving "too much verbal body to words" (*Playboy* interview) succinctly defines the burden the post-Romantics placed on the word, as though it were an endlessly resonant object rather than one component in a referential system of signs (see 120/4 for a parody of Joycean stream-of-consciousness writing). H.H.'s acknowledgment of the limitations of language leaves many writers open to criticism, especially Romantic poets such as Poe. "When I was young I liked Poe, and I still love Melville," said Nabokov; "I tore apart the fantasies of Poe," writes John Shade in *Pale Fire* (line 632 of the poem); the implications are clear enough. In *Lolita,* his choice of both subject matter and narrator parody Poe's designation, in "The Philosophy of Composition," of the "most poetical topic in the world"; "the death of a beautiful woman . . . and equally is it beyond doubt that the lips best suited for such topic are those of a bereaved lover" (see also my 1967 *Wisconsin Studies* article, *op. cit.*, p. 236). Both Annabel Lee and Lolita "die," the latter figuratively as well as literally, in terms of her fading nymphic qualities and escape from H.H., who seems to invoke yet another of Poe's lost ladies when he calls Lolita "Lenore" (though the primary allusion is to Bürger's poem, said Nabokov; see 207/5).

The speaker in Poe's "Lenore" gropes for the right elegiac chord: "How *shall* the ritual, then, be read?—the requiem how be sung / By you—by yours, the evil eye,—by yours, the slanderous tongue / That did to death the innocence that died, and died so young?" How shall it be "sung" is also the main question in *Lolita*, and Nabokov found his answer in a parodic style that seems to parody *all* styles, including the novel's own. "You talk like a book, *Dad,*" Lolita tells H.H.; and, in order to protect his own efforts to capture her essence, he tries to exhaust the "fictional gestures," such as Edgar Poe's, which would reduce the nymphet's ineffable qualities to a convention of language or literature. "Well-read Humbert" thus toys with one writer after another, as though only through parody and caricature can he rule out the possibility of his memoir's finally being nothing more than what the authorial voice in *Invitation to a Beheading* suggests to its captive creation: "Or is this all but obsolete romantic rot, Cincinnatus?" (p. 139).

9/3 *four feet ten:* see 262/6 for an involuted conversion to inches.

9/4 *Lola:* in addition to being a diminutive of "Dolores," it is the name of the young cabaret entertainer who enchants a middle-aged professor in the German film, *The Blue Angel* (1930), directed by Josef von Sternberg. Nabokov never saw the film (though he did see still photos from it) and doubted that he had the association in mind. Lola was played by Marlene Dietrich (1904–), and it is worth noting that H.H. describes Lolita's mother as having "features of a type that may be defined as a weak solution of Marlene Dietrich" (p. 37) and, after he reports her death, bids "Adieu, Marlene!" (p. 103). In *Ada*, Van Veen visits a don and his family, "a charming wife and a triplet of charming twelve-year-old daughters, Ala, Lolá and Lalage—especially Lalage" ["the age"— twelve, a nymphet's prime (p. 353)].

9/5 *Dolores:* derived from the Latin, *dolor:* sorrow, pain (see 43/2). Traditionally an allusion to the Virgin Mary, Our Lady of Sorrows, and the Seven Sorrows concerning the life of Jesus. H.H. observes a church, "Mission Dolores," and takes advantage of the ready-made pun; "good title for book" (p. 158). Less spiritual are the sorrows detailed in "Dolores" (1866), by Algernon Swinburne (1837–1909), English poet (see also *Keys*, p. 28). "Our Lady of Pain" is its constant refrain, and her father is Priap, whom H.H. mentions several times (see 42/4). The name *Dolores* is in two ways "closely interwound with the inmost fiber of the book," as John Ray says on p. 4. When in the Afterword Nabokov defines the "nerves of the novel," he concludes with "the tinkling sounds of the valley town coming up the mountain trail (on which I caught the first known female of *Lycæides sublivens* Nabokov)" (p. 316). Diana Butler, in "Lolita Lepidoptera," *op. cit.,* p. 62, notes that this important capture was made at Telluride, Colorado (see p. 312), and that in his paper on it, Nabokov identifies Telluride as a "cul-de-sac . . . at the end of two converging roads, one from Placerville, the other from Dolores" (*The Lepidopterists' News*, VI, 1952). Dolores is in fact everywhere in that region: river, town, and county are so named. When H.H. finally confronts Quilty, he asks, "do you recall a little girl called Dolores Haze, Dolly Haze? Dolly called Dolores, Colo.?" (p. 296). "Dolly" is an appropriate diminutive ("you / took a dull doll to pieces / and threw its head away," writes H.H. of Quilty [p. 300]). For the entomological allusions, see 6/1. On shipboard in *Ada*, Van Veen sees a film of *Don Juan's Last Fling* in which Dolores the dancing girl turns out to be Ada (pp. 488–490). Ada later gives Van "a sidelong 'Dolores' glance" (p. 513).

9/6 *in point of fact:* the childhood "trauma" which H.H. will soon offer as the psychological explanation of his condition (see p. 13). H.H.'s first chapter is so extraordinarily short in order to mock the traditional novel's expository opening. How reassuring, by comparison, are the initial paragraphs of those conventional novels—so anachronistic to Nabokov—which prepare the reader for the story about to unfold by supplying him with the complete psychological, social, and moral prehistories of the characters. Anticipating such needs, H.H. poses the reader's questions ("Did she have a precursor?"; "Oh when?"), and parodies more than that kind of reader dependence on such exposition. It may seem surprising in a supposedly "confessional" novel that this should be the narrator's initial concern; but it is by way of a challenge to play, like the good-humored cry of *"Avanti"* with which Luzhin greets Turati in *The Defense*, before they begin their great match game. H.H.'s "point of fact" mocks the "scientific" certitude of psychiatrists who have turned intensely private myths and symbols—in short, fictions—into hard fact. The H.H. who is the subject of a case study immediately undercuts the persuasiveness of his own specific "trauma" by projecting it in fragments of another man's verse; literary allusions, after all, point *away* from the unique, inviolable, formative "inner reality" of a neurotic or psychotic consciousness. Annabel Leigh, the object of H.H.'s unconsummated love, has no reality other than literary. See also *Keys,* p. 45.

9/7 *princedom by the sea:* a variant of the most famous line in "Annabel Lee." Poe's "kingdom" has been changed to accommodate the fact that H.H. is always an aspirant, never an absolute monarch. On p. 166 he calls Lolita "My Frigid Princess."

9/8 *noble-winged seraphs, envied:* a pastiche composed of a phrase from line 11 of "Annabel Lee" and a verb from line 22. "Seraphs" are the highest of the nine orders of angels; in the Bible they have six wings, as well as hands and feet, and a human voice (Isaiah 6:2). "The seraph with his six flamingo wings" is invoked by John Shade in *Pale Fire* (line 225 of the poem).

9/9 *tangle of thorns:* another H.H., the penitent, confessor, and martyr to love, calls attention to his thorns, the immodest reference to so sacred an image suggesting that the reader would do well to judge H.H.'s tone rather than his deeds. When H.H. addresses the "Ladies and gentlemen of the jury," as he will do so often, he summarizes the judicial proclivities of those literal-minded and moralistic readers who, having soberly considered what John Ray, Jr., has said, already hate "Humbert the Horrible." On p. 270, H.H. calls Lolita "crucified"—a verb that sincerely projects his "moral apotheosis."

CHAPTER 2

10/1 *Jerome Dunn, the alpinist:* in a novel so allusive as *Lolita* it is only natural to be suspicious of the most innocuous references, and to search for allusions under every bush. Anticipating the efforts of future exegetes, I will occasionally offer non-notes—"anti-annotations" which simply state that Nabokov intended no allusion whatsoever. Thus, "Jerome Dunn" is non-allusive, as are "Clarence Choate Clark," H.H.'s lawyer (p. 3), and John Ray's residence of "Widworth, Mass." (p. 6). For important caveats in Nabokov's own words, see 56/1 and 221/2.

10/2 *paleopedology and Aeolian harps:* respectively, the branch of pedology concerned with the soils of past geological ages, and a box-shaped musical instrument on which the wind produces varying harmonies (after

Aeolus, Greek god of the winds). A favorite romantic metaphor for the poet's sensibility.

10/3 *midge:* a gnat-like insect. For entomological allusions, see 6/1.

10/4 *Sybil:* or *sibyl,* from the Greek; any of several prophetesses credited to widely separate parts of the ancient world. H.H.'s aunt is well-named, since she predicts her own death.

10/5 *Mirana:* a heat-shimmer blend of "mirage," *"se mirer"* (French; to look at oneself; admire oneself), "Mirabella," and "Fata Morgana" (a kind of mirage most frequently seen in the Strait of Messina, and formerly considered the work of fairies who would thus lure sailors aground). Bewitching Lolita is often characterized as a fairy (see 31/3); the latter word is derived from the Latin word *fatum* (fate, destiny), and H.H. is pursued by bedeviling "Aubrey McFate" (see 56/1).

10/6 *Mon . . . papa:* French; my dear little Daddy.

10/7 *Don Quixote:* the famous novel (1605, 1615) by Miguel Cervantes (1547–1616); see 251/10. *Les Misérables* (1862) is by Victor Hugo (1802–1885), French novelist, playwright, and poet; see 256/3.

11/1 *rose garden:* see 52/5 and 56/1 for more school-house roses.

11/2 *La Beauté Humaine:* French; "The Human Beauty." The book is invented, as is its author, whose name is a play on *"nichon,"* a French (slang) epithet for the female breast.

11/3 *lycée:* the basic institution of French secondary education; a student attends a lycée for seven years (from age eleven to eighteen).

CHAPTER 3

12/1 *powdered Mrs. Leigh . . . Vanessa van Ness:* Poe's "Annabel Lee"; on p. 167 it is spelled *Lee.* The Red Admirable (or Admiral) butterfly, which figures throughout Nabokov, is *Vanessa atalanta,* family *Nymphalidae* (for more on "nymph," see 16/6); and butterflies, as well as women, are "powdered." H.H. is also alluding to Jonathan Swift's (1667–1745) "Vanessa," as he called the young woman whose passion he awakened (for the Swift allusion, see also *Keys,* p. 96). Nabokov expands the dual allusion in *Pale Fire.* John Shade addresses "My dark Vanessa, Crimson-barred, my blest / My Admirable butterfly! . . ." (lines 270–271); and, in his note to these lines, Charles Kinbote quotes from Swift's "Cadenus and Vanessa," though he doesn't identify it by name: "When, lo! *Vanessa* in her bloom / Advanced like *Atalanta's* star." He also alludes to "Vanessa" 's actual name thusly: "*Van* homrigh, *Es*ther!" (p. 172)—thereby underscoring at least the alphabetical arrangement of Swift's anagramour (let me laugh a little, too, gentlemen, as H.H. says on p. 250). But in his succinct way, H.H. has already anticipated Kinbote ("van Ness"). A Red Admirable lands on Shade's arm the minute before he is killed (see lines 993–995 and Kinbote's note for them) and the insect appears in *King, Queen, Knave* just after Nabokov has withdrawn his omniscience (p. 44). In the final chapter of *Speak, Memory* Nabokov recalls having seen in a Paris park, just before the war, a live Red Admirable being promenaded on a leash of thread by a little girl; "there was some vaguely repulsive symbolism about her sullen sport," he writes (p. 306). When Van Veen casually mentions Ada's having pointed out "some accursed insect," the offended heroine parenthetically and angrily adds, "Accursed? *Accursed?* It was the newly described, fantastically rare vanessian, *Nymphalis danaus* Nab., orange-brown, with black-and-white foretips, mimicking, as its discoverer Professor Nabonidus of Babylon College, Nebraska, realized, not the Monarch butterfly directly, but the Monarch *through* the Viceroy, one of the Monarch's best known imitators" (p. 158). See 6/1.

12/2 *solipsism:* a central word in *Lolita.* An epistemological theory that the self knows only its present state and is the only existent thing, and that "reality" is subjective; concern with the self at the expense of social relationships. See 60/1.

12/3 *plage:* French; beach.

13/1 *chocolat glacé:* French; in those days, an iced chocolate drink with whipped cream (today it means "chocolate ice cream").

13/2 *red rocks:* see 39/3 and 56/1.

13/3 *lost pair of sunglasses:* the sunglasses image connects Annabel and Lolita. H.H. first perceives her as his "Riviera love peering at me over dark glasses" (see 39/1). See also *Keys,* p. 43 and p. 143n.

13/4 *point of possessing:* for a comment on the "traumatic" nature of this experience, see 209/3. "My darling" echoes line 39 of "Annabel Lee" (see 47/4 for the entire line, and 9/2 for the poem itself).

13/5 *Corfu:* Greek island.

CHAPTER 4

15/1 *haze of stars:* see 4/8. In one sense, the novel begins and ends in "Gray Star."

15/2 *her spell:* "spells" and "enchantments" are fundamental in *Lolita.* See 16/6, 45/3, and 260/2.

CHAPTER 5

15/3 *manqué:* French; unfulfilled.

16/1 *uranists:* H.H.'s own variant of the uncommon English word, *uranism,* derived from a Greek word for "spiritual" and meaning "homosexual." Havelock Ellis uses it in Chapter Five of *Psychology of Sex* (1938), and claims the term was invented by the nineteenth-century legal official Karl Ulrichs.

16/2 *Deux Magots:* the famous Left Bank café in Paris, where intellectuals congregate. *Magot* is a kind of monkey, but *"magots de Saxe"* means "statuettes of saxe [porcelain]" (eighteenth-century). Nabokov purposely seats his uranists in this particular café, because he wants to invoke the simian association and the image of the grotesque Chinese porcelain figures.

16/3 *pastiches:* the "quotation" is an assemblage including bits and pieces of "Gerontion" (1920), by T. S. Eliot, the Anglo-American poet (1888–1965): ". . . Fräulein von Kulp / Who turned in the hall, one hand on the door" (lines 27–28); ". . . De Bailhache, Fresca, Mrs. Cammel, whirled . . ." (line 66); ". . . Gull against the wind, in the windy straits / Of Belle Isle . . ." (lines 69–70). See 258/3 and 299/1 for other allusions to Eliot. Having small sympathy with some of Eliot's social prejudices, Nabokov ironically describes in *Ada* a "Mr. Eliot, a Jewish businessman" (p. 5), who later meets the late-blooming banker (Eliot's early vocation) Kithar Sween (= Eliot's "Sweeney"), author of *"The Waistline,* a satire in free verse on Anglo-American feeding habits, and *Cardinal Grishkin* [= Eliot's "Whispers of Immortality"], an overtly subtle yarn extolling the Roman faith" (p. 506). For *The Four Quartets,* see *Pale Fire,* lines 368–379. Nabokov said, "I was never exposed in the 'twenties and 'thirties, as so many of my coevals have been, to the poetry of Eliot and Pound. I read them late in the season, around 1945, in the guest room of an American friend's house, and not only remained completely indifferent to them, but could not understand why anybody should bother about them. But I suppose that they preserve some sentimental value for such readers as discovered them at an earlier age than I did" (*Playboy* interview).

16/4 *"Proustian theme . . . Bailey"*: the letters of the English poet John Keats (1795–1821) to his close friend Benjamin Bailey (1791–1853) are among the important statements of Keats's poetic theory. In *Pale Fire*, Kinbote measures the progress of poetry "from the caveman to Keats" (p. 289). H.H.'s "Proustian theme" is no doubt on the nature of time and memory. Marcel Proust (1871–1922)—the great French novelist, the first half of whose *À la Recherche du temps perdu* (*Remembrance of Things Past*, 1913–1927) was to Nabokov one of the four "greatest masterpieces of twentieth-century prose" (see 207/3)—is also mentioned on pp. 77 and 182, and as noted 253/2 and 264/4. He appears too in *Pale Fire*, pp. 87, 161–163, and 248, as well as in line 224 of Shade's poem (p. 41), where he envisions eternity, and ". . . talks / With Socrates and Proust in cypress walks." In *The Real Life of Sebastian Knight*, Knight's hack biographer, Mr. Goodman, mentions "the French author M. Proust, whom Knight consciously or subconsciously copied" (p. 114); and Knight himself parenthetically remarks in a letter, "I am [not] apologizing for that Proustian parenthesis" (p. 52)—a device H.H. consciously indulges, as when he parenthetically "prolong[s] these Proustian intonations" (p. 77). There are also many allusions to Proust in *Ada* (see pp. 9, 55–56, 66, 73, 168–169, 254, and 541).

16/5 *"Histoire . . . anglaise"*: French; "A Short History of English Poetry."

16/6 *not human, but nymphic*: like Sinclair Lewis's "Babbitt" (*Babbitt*, 1922), Nabokov's "nymphet" has entered the language, though the latest dictionary entries which *Lolita* has inspired are as inelegant as they are inaccurate: *nymph*: "a woman of loose morals" (*Webster's Third New International*, echoed by the *Random House Dictionary*). The *Penguin English Dictionary*, G. N. Garmonsway, ed., gives under *nymphet*: "(coll.) very young but sexually attractive girl" (H.H., who strives so desperately to expropriate idiomatic English, would appreciate that "colloquial"). "Nymphet" continues to be loosely used. Witness *People* magazine: "She plays Kelly Bundy, the shopping-mall nymphet, on Fox's comedy hit *Married . . . with Children*, but Christina Applegate says she—" reports the columnist, though the lovely eighteen-year-old actress in the photo could pass for twenty–five (September 24, 1990, p. 108). As for *nymph*, the mythological and zoological definitions are

CHAPTER 4

15/1 *haze of stars:* see 4/8. In one sense, the novel begins and ends in "Gray Star."

15/2 *her spell:* "spells" and "enchantments" are fundamental in *Lolita*. See 16/6, 45/3, and 260/2.

CHAPTER 5

15/3 *manqué:* French; unfulfilled.

16/1 *uranists:* H.H.'s own variant of the uncommon English word, *uranism*, derived from a Greek word for "spiritual" and meaning "homosexual." Havelock Ellis uses it in Chapter Five of *Psychology of Sex* (1938), and claims the term was invented by the nineteenth-century legal official Karl Ulrichs.

16/2 *Deux Magots:* the famous Left Bank café in Paris, where intellectuals congregate. *Magot* is a kind of monkey, but *"magots de Saxe"* means "statuettes of saxe [porcelain]" (eighteenth-century). Nabokov purposely seats his uranists in this particular café, because he wants to invoke the simian association and the image of the grotesque Chinese porcelain figures.

16/3 *pastiches:* the "quotation" is an assemblage including bits and pieces of "Gerontion" (1920), by T. S. Eliot, the Anglo-American poet (1888–1965): ". . . Fräulein von Kulp / Who turned in the hall, one hand on the door" (lines 27–28); ". . . De Bailhache, Fresca, Mrs. Cammel, whirled . . ." (line 66); ". . . Gull against the wind, in the windy straits / Of Belle Isle . . ." (lines 69–70). See 258/3 and 299/1 for other allusions to Eliot. Having small sympathy with some of Eliot's social prejudices, Nabokov ironically describes in *Ada* a "Mr. Eliot, a Jewish businessman" (p. 5), who later meets the late-blooming banker (Eliot's early vocation) Kithar Sween (= Eliot's "Sweeney"), author of *"The Waistline*, a satire in free verse on Anglo-American feeding habits, and *Cardinal Grishkin* [= Eliot's "Whispers of Immortality"], an overtly subtle yarn extolling the Roman faith" (p. 506). For *The Four Quartets*, see *Pale Fire*, lines 368–379. Nabokov said, "I was never exposed in the 'twenties and 'thirties, as so many of my coevals have been, to the poetry of Eliot and Pound. I read them late in the season, around 1945, in the guest room of an American friend's house, and not only remained completely indifferent to them, but could not understand why anybody should bother about them. But I suppose that they preserve some sentimental value for such readers as discovered them at an earlier age than I did" (*Playboy* interview).

16/4 *"Proustian theme . . . Bailey"*: the letters of the English poet John Keats (1795–1821) to his close friend Benjamin Bailey (1791–1853) are among the important statements of Keats's poetic theory. In *Pale Fire*, Kinbote measures the progress of poetry "from the caveman to Keats" (p. 289). H.H.'s "Proustian theme" is no doubt on the nature of time and memory. Marcel Proust (1871–1922)—the great French novelist, the first half of whose *À la Recherche du temps perdu* (*Remembrance of Things Past*, 1913–1927) was to Nabokov one of the four "greatest masterpieces of twentieth-century prose" (see 207/3)—is also mentioned on pp. 77 and 182, and as noted 253/2 and 264/4. He appears too in *Pale Fire*, pp. 87, 161–163, and 248, as well as in line 224 of Shade's poem (p. 41), where he envisions eternity, and ". . . talks / With Socrates and Proust in cypress walks." In *The Real Life of Sebastian Knight*, Knight's hack biographer, Mr. Goodman, mentions "the French author M. Proust, whom Knight consciously or subconsciously copied" (p. 114); and Knight himself parenthetically remarks in a letter, "I am [not] apologizing for that Proustian parenthesis" (p. 52)—a device H.H. consciously indulges, as when he parenthetically "prolong[s] these Proustian intonations" (p. 77). There are also many allusions to Proust in *Ada* (see pp. 9, 55–56, 66, 73, 168–169, 254, and 541).

16/5 *"Histoire . . . anglaise"*: French; "A Short History of English Poetry."

16/6 *not human, but nymphic*: like Sinclair Lewis's "Babbitt" (*Babbitt*, 1922), Nabokov's "nymphet" has entered the language, though the latest dictionary entries which *Lolita* has inspired are as inelegant as they are inaccurate: *nymph*: "a woman of loose morals" (*Webster's Third New International*, echoed by the *Random House Dictionary*). The *Penguin English Dictionary*, G. N. Garmonsway, ed., gives under *nymphet*: "(coll.) very young but sexually attractive girl" (H.H., who strives so desperately to expropriate idiomatic English, would appreciate that "colloquial"). "Nymphet" continues to be loosely used. Witness *People* magazine: "She plays Kelly Bundy, the shopping-mall nymphet, on Fox's comedy hit *Married . . . with Children*, but Christina Applegate says she—" reports the columnist, though the lovely eighteen-year-old actress in the photo could pass for twenty–five (September 24, 1990, p. 108). As for *nymph*, the mythological and zoological definitions are primary. In Greek and Roman mythology, a *nymph* is "One of the inferior divinities of nature represented as beautiful maidens dwelling in the mountains, waters, forests, etc." *Nympholepsy,* H.H.'s malady (hence, "nympholept" [p. 17]), is "a species of demoniac enthusiasm supposed to seize one bewitched by a nymph; a frenzy of emotion, as for some unattainable ideal" (more specifically, in *Blakiston's New Gould Medical Dictionary,* it is defined as "ecstasy of an erotic type"). Under the entry for "The Nymphs" in *The Book of Imaginary Beings* (1969), Jorge Luis Borges notes that "Paracelsus limited their dominion to water, but the ancients thought the world was full of Nymphs . . . [some] Nymphs were held to be immortal or, as Plutarch obscurely intimates, lived for above 9,720 years . . . The exact number of the Nymphs is unknown; Hesiod gives us the figure three thousand . . . Glimpsing them could cause blindness and, if they were naked, death. A line of Propertius affirms this." H.H. echoes these definitions. Here and on the following pages he alludes to "spells," "magic," "fantastic powers," and "deadly demons" (for various enchantments, see 10/5 [Fata Morgana], 20/2 [Lilith], 31/3 [elves], 45/3 [*Carmen*], 71/1 [an incubus], and 240/2 [king of the elves]). Lolita's "inhuman" and "bewitching charms" suggest that she is Keats's "La Belle Dame Sans Merci" (1819) in bobby socks (Nabokov translated the poem into Russian in *The Empyrean Path,* 1923), and that the novel is in part a unique variant of the archetypal tale of a mortal destroyed by his love for a supernatural *femme fatale,* "The Lovely Lady Without Pity" of ballad, folk tale, and fairy tale. Nabokov calls *Lolita* a "fairy tale," and his nymph a "fairy princess" (p. 52); see 31/3.

One of Nabokov's lepidopterological finds is known as "Nabokov's Wood-Nymph" (belonging to the family *Nymphalidae;* see 12/1), and he is not unaware that a "nymph" is also defined as "a pupa," or "the young of an insect undergoing incomplete metamorphosis." Crucial to an understanding of *Lolita* is some sense of the various but simultaneous metamorphoses undergone by Lolita, H.H., the book, the author, and the reader, who is manipulated by the novel's game-element and illusionistic devices to such an extent that he too can be said to become, at certain moments, another of Vladimir Nabokov's creations—an experience which is bound to change him. The butterfly is thus a controlling metaphor that enriches *Lolita* in a more fundamental and organic manner than, say, the *Odyssey* does Joyce's *Ulysses.* Just as the nymph undergoes a metamorphosis in becoming the butterfly, so everything in *Lolita* is constantly in the process of metamorphosis, including the novel itself—a set of "notes" being compiled by an imprisoned man during a fifty-six-day period for possible use at his trial, emerging as a book after his death, and then only after it has passed through yet another stage, the nominal "editorship" of John Ray, Jr. As Lolita turns from a girl into a woman, so H.H.'s lust becomes love. His sense of a "safely solipsized" Lolita (p. 60) is replaced by his awareness that she was his "own creation" with "no will, no consciousness—indeed, no life of her own" (p. 62), that he did not know her (p. 284), and that their sexual intimacy only isolated him more completely from the helpless girl. These "metamorphoses" enable H.H. to transform a "crime" into a redeeming work of art, and the reader watches the chrysalis come to life. "And a metamorphosis is a thing always exciting to watch," says Nabokov in *Gogol* (p. 43), referring to etymological rather than entomological phenomena (see 118/3 and 212/2; also follow the multifarious permutations of "Humbert").

On his first night with Lolita at The Enchanted Hunters hotel, H.H. experiences "a confusion of perception metamorphosing her into eyespots of moonlight or a fluffy flowering bush" (p. 132), and, anticipating the design and progression of *Lolita*, the narrator of *The Real Life of Sebastian Knight* (1941) mentions the readers who "felt baffled by [*The Prismatic Bezel*'s] habit of metamorphosis" (p. 93; for the complete passage, see the epigraph to the Introduction). When Nabokov in his lectures at Cornell discussed "the theme of transformation" in R. L. Stevenson's *Dr. Jekyll and Mr. Hyde*, Gogol's *The Overcoat*, and Kafka's *The Metamorphosis*, he said that Stevenson's tale is a "thriller and mystery only in respect to artistic creativity. It is a phenomenon of style, a transformation through the art of writing." He likened the Jekyll-Hyde transformation to the metamorphosis of the larva into the pupa into the butterfly, and imagined Jekyll's final emergence from the melting and blackened features of the evil Hyde as "the rush of panic" which must accompany "the feeling of hatching." Once again, as in his book on Gogol, Nabokov described his own performance by defining the art of another. As a metaphor for the artistic process, the nymph's cycle suggests a transcendent design. See Introduction, pp. xxiii–xxviii. For entomological allusions, see 6/1.

17/1 *bubble of hot poison:* see 304/1; the bubble breaks.

17/2 *faunlet:* in mythology, the faun is a woodland deity represented as a man having the ears, horns, tail, and hind legs of a goat; a satyr. The diminutive form is H.H.'s coinage. See Nabokov's letter in *New Statesman*, Nov. 17, 1967, p. 680.

18/1 *fateful elf:* see 31/3 for a summary of elves and the novel as fairy–tale.

18/2 *pollutive:* H.H.'s variant of *pollution;* the less common meaning, "emission of semen at other times than in coitus."

18/3 *pseudolibidoes:* H.H.'s usage (see p. 54 for "libidream") of *libido:* the sexual impulse; to Freud, the instinctual drive behind all human activities.

19/1 *Children . . . 1933:* the Act actually reads: "'Child' means a person under the age of fourteen years . . . 'Young Person' means a person who has attained the age of fourteen years and is under the age of seventeen years." From *Children and Young Persons Act of 1933* 23 & 24 Geo. 5, c. 12, §107 (1). No specific definition of girl-child is given; but, even if H.H.'s quotation is wrong, he is a sound legal scholar, for a child must be eight years old to incur criminal liability. See p. 135.

19/2 *Massachusetts . . . "a wayward child" . . . immoral persons:* an accurate transcription; the parenthetical phrase is also a direct quotation from *Mass. Anno. Laws* ch. 119 §52 (1957).

19/3 *Hugh Broughton:* controversial Puritan divine and pamphleteer (1549–1612). The allusion is to his *A Consent of Scripture* (1588), an eccentric discourse on Biblical chronology.

19/4 *Rahab:* the Canaanite prostitute of Joshua 2: 1–21.

19/5 *Virgil . . . perineum:* the Latin poet (70–19 B.C.). The *perineum* includes the urinogenital passages and the rectum. In the 1958 edition it read *peritonium* (the double serous membrane which lines the cavity of the abdomen). Although H.H.'s grotesque error is intentional on Nabokov's part, he decided to correct it here because the mistake, if discerned, might be taken for the author's, or remain ambiguous.

19/6 *King Akhnaten's . . . Nile daughters:* Akhnaten of Egypt (reigned 1375–1358 B.C.) and Nefertiti had a total of seven daughters. On his monuments, the king is shown with six. H.H. also loses a "daughter."

19/7 *fascinum:* Latin; a penis of ivory used in certain ancient erotic rites.

19/8 *East Indian provinces:* the Lepchas are a Mongoloid people of Sikkim and the Darjeeling district of India. What H.H. says is true, and Nabokov thought H.H. may have got it from somewhere in Havelock Ellis's monumental, many-volumed *Studies in the Psychology of Sex* (1891).

19/9 *Dante . . . month of May:* Dante was born between May 15 and June 15, 1265. He was therefore nine years old when he met Beatrice in 1274, and she was supposedly eight. There was no romance.

19/10 *Petrarch . . . Laureen:* Petrarch was born July 20, 1304. He was therefore twenty-three when he met Laura on April 6, 1327. She remains unknown to this day, and all attempts to identify her with historical persons are purely speculative. Her age therefore cannot be determined.

19/11 *hills of Vaucluse:* an area in Southeastern France, the capital of which is Avignon. It was Petrarch's favorite home, but he found that natural beauty there only added to the sense of his loss of Laura.

20/1 *"enfant . . . fourbe":* French; "sly and lovely child."

20/2 *it was Lilith:* in Jewish legend, Lilith was Adam's wife before Eve. Also a female demon who attacked children and a famous witch in the demonology of the Middle Ages. In *Pale Fire*, a Zemblan "society sculptor" finds in Charles the Beloved's sister "what he sought and . . . used her breasts and feet for his *Lilith Calling Back Adam*" (p. 108). See 16/6 for more on enchantments.

20/3 *tiddles:* H.H. here completes his reference to a game of tiddlywinks on the previous page: "I am just winking happy thoughts into a little tiddle cup." A player "winks" the tiddle (a small piece) into the cup in tiddlywinks, so these "tiddles" are a metaphor for H.H.'s collected thoughts about nymphets. *Tiddles* also means "trifles"; from *tiddle*, an obsolete verb except in dialect or slang; to fondle, to fuss or trifle.

20/4 *this is only a game:* in the *Wisconsin Studies* interview, Nabokov said, "Satire is a lesson, parody is a game." The pun on H.H.'s name includes the game of ombre (see 3/3), which is played in Canto III of Alexander Pope's *The Rape of the Lock* (1714); see lines 87–100. Also see the games H.H. plays on pp. 182–183, 202–203, and 233.

20/5 *métro:* the Paris subway.

CHAPTER 6

21/1 *voluptas:* Latin; sensual pleasures.

21/2 *the Madeleine:* a church in Paris (a very prominent landmark), and the fact that H.H. encounters a streetwalker here slyly alludes to the fact that the church is named after Mary Magdelene, the repentant prostitute.

21/3 *frétillement:* French; a wiggle.

21/4 *"Cent":* French; one hundred (francs).

21/5 *"Tant pis":* French; "Too bad!"

22/1 *petit cadeau:* French; small gift.

22/2 *"dix-huit":* French; "eighteen" (years old).

22/3 *"Oui, ce n'est pas bien":* French; "Yes, that is not nice."

22/4 *grues:* French; slang word for prostitutes.

22/5 *"Il était malin ... truc-là":* French; "The man who invented this trick was a smart one."

22/6 *poser un lapin:* French; to stand someone up.

22/7 *"Tu es ... de dire ça":* French; "You are very nice to say that."

22/8 *avant qu'on se couche:* French; before we go to bed.

23/1 *"Je vais m'acheter des bas":* French; "I am going to buy myself some stockings."

23/2 *"Regardez-moi ... brune":* French; "Take a look at this beautiful brunette." The 1958 edition omitted the period after the parenthesis.

23/3 *qui pourrait arranger la chose:* French; who could fix it.

24/1 *son argent:* French; her money.

24/2 *lui:* French; himself (pronoun which is redundant and serves to emphasize a noun).

24/3 *Marie ... stellar name:* derived from the Virgin's name; to Biblical commentators, it means *stellamaris,* star of the sea. H.H. has more fun with "stellar" later (see 289/1).

CHAPTER 7

25/1 *tachycardia:* a term from pathology; abnormal rapidity of the heart's action.

25/2 *mes malheurs:* French; my misfortunes.

25/3 *français moyen:* French; the average Frenchman, the man in the street.

CHAPTER 8

25/4 *pot-au-feu:* French; a common stew, containing meat, vegetables, and almost anything else.

25/5 *merkin:* an artificial female pudendum, or its false hair.

25/6 *à la gamine:* French; in imitation of a cute young girl.

26/1 *mairie:* French; town hall.

26/2 *melanic:* pigmented; hence, black or dark.

26/3 *baba:* although it is Franco-Russian for a ring-shaped pastry imbued with rum, Nabokov intends it otherwise: " 'Baba' colloquially means in Russian any female on the common side; a blousy, vulgar woman. It is also used metaphorically for certain thick, sturdy, columellar, menhir-like, compact things, such as the pastry *romovaya baba* (but this has nothing to do with its meaning here). Originally, *baba* meant a peasant woman."

26/4 *I felt like Marat . . . stab me:* Jean-Paul Marat (1743–1793), French revolutionist stabbed to death in his bath by Charlotte Corday; the subject of a famous painting by Jacques-Louis David, *Marat assassiné* (1793). The "original" tub can be seen at both Madame Tussaud's Wax Works in London and at Paris's wax museum, Musée Grevin. In *Pale Fire*, John Shade imagines how his biographer would describe him shaving in his bath: ". . . he'd / Sit like a king there, and like Marat bleed" (lines 893–894). On his travels, student Van Veen is shown "the peasant-bare footprint of Tolstoy preserved in the clay of a motor court in Utah where he had written the tale of Murat, the Navajo chieftain, a French general's bastard, shot by Cora Day in his swimming pool" (*Ada*, p. 171)—a combination of Murad (from Tolstoy's *Hadji Murad*), General Murat (Napoleon's brother-in-law and king of Naples), and Marat.

26/5 *Paris-Soir:* a sensationalistic daily newspaper; now *France-Soir,* and an excellent example of how a small quotidian detail can telescope a character's sensibility. In Nabokov's story "The Assistant Producer" (1943), set in émigré Paris of the thirties, General Golubkov, head of the vicious, vulgar, Ur-Hitleristic right-wing White Warriors Union, "escort[s] his wife to her dressmaker, [and] sat there for a while reading the *Paris-Soir*" (*Nabokov's Dozen,* p. 87).

26/6 *Estampe:* a print or engraving. H.H.'s "moral apotheosis" at the end of the book parallels the way the landscape evolves from this flat, unpeopled, clichéd scene to the rich landscape depicted on p. 307. The reader is reminded that a landscape is a construct, a symbolic unit—while "nature" is random phenomena.

27/1 *mon oncle d'Amérique:* French; the proverbial rich American uncle who dies, leaving one a fortune; a curtain line in many old-fashioned melodramas.

27/2 *Nansen . . . passport:* the special passport issued to émigrés in Europe before World War II; the document figures prominently in the story, " 'That in Aleppo Once . . .' " in *Nabokov's Dozen* (1958).

27/3 *préfecture:* French; police headquarters.

28/1 *"Mais qui est-ce?":* French; "But who is it?"

28/2 *quite a scholar:* the ten-volume *Jean Christophe* (1904–1912), by the Frenchman Romain Rolland (1866–1944), is a panoramic novel of society, admired no more by Nabokov than by H.H. (see *Pnin,* p. 142).

29/1 *j'ai demannde pardonne:* French; "I beg your pardon." The tense is incorrect (should be *"je"*); and the wrong spelling—an extra *n* in both words—indicates a Russian accent.

29/2 *gredin:* French; scoundrel, villain.

30/1 *Maximovich . . . taxies back to me:* see bottom of p. 28.

31/1 *fructuate: rare;* to bear fruit, to fructify.

31/2 *Agatha Christie: A Murder Is Announced* is the actual title of a 1950 novel by Agatha Christie (1891–1976), the well-known English mystery writer. A murder *is* announced on the next page (Clare Quilty's; see 32/5).

31/3 *Percy Elphinstone:* Elphinstone and his books are also genuine, according to Nabokov, though it has been impossible to document this. Nabokov recalled finding *A Vagabond in Italy* "in a hospital library, the nearest thing to a prison library." But the town of Elphinstone (pp. 238–247) is invented. H.H. calls Annabel "the initial fateful elf in my life" (p. 18); and Lolita's original home town in the Midwest was "Pisky," another form of *pixie* or *elf* (p. 46). H.H. allows how "elfish chance offered me the sight of a delightful child of Lolita's age" (p. 128). When H.H. deposits Lolita in the Elphinstone Hospital, it is the last time he will see the nymphic incarnation of his initial "elf" (p. 246); for him, the "fairy tale" (and he imagines himself a "fairy-tale nurse" [p. 39]) ends in Elph's Stone just as it had begun in the town of "elf." Quilty in pursuit is seen as the "Erlkönig," the king of the elves in Goethe's poem of that name (see 240/2). At The Enchanted Hunters hotel, on the night that H.H. first possesses Lolita, he notes, "Nothing could have been more childish than . . . the purplish spot on her naked neck where a fairy tale vampire had feasted" (p. 138–139). Quilty's Pavor [Latin: fear, panic] Manor turns out to be on Grimm Road (p. 291), and when H.H. goes to kill him, the door "swung open as in a medieval fairy tale" (p. 294). As a birthday present, H.H. gives Lolita a de luxe edition of Hans Christian Andersen's *The Little Mermaid* (174/5); and allusions are made to *Hansel and Gretel, Beauty and the Beast, The Sleeping Beauty, The Emperor's New Clothes* (201/1), and *Bluebeard* (243/3). "What a comic, clumsy, wavering Prince Charming I was!" declares H.H. (p. 111). The simplicity of *Lolita*'s "story," such as it is—"plot," in the conventional sense, may be paraphrased in three sentences—and the themes of deception, enchantment, and metamorphosis are akin to the fairy tale (see 16/6); while the recurrence of places and motifs and the presence of three principal characters recall the formalistic design and symmetry of those archetypal tales (see 265/2). But the fate of Nabokov's "fairy princess" (p. 52) and the novel's denouement reverse the fairy-tale process, even though H.H. offers Lolita the opportunity of a formulaic fairy-tale ending: "we shall live happily ever after" (p. 278).

The fairy-tale element has a significance far greater than its local importance to *Lolita*. Several of Nabokov's novels, stories, and poems are "fairy tales" in the sense that they are set in imaginary lands. These lands extend from five of his untranslated Russian works (1924–1940), to *Bend Sinister*'s Padukgrad (1947), to *Pale Fire*'s kingdom of Zembla (1962), culminating in *Ada* (1969), where the entire universe has been reimagined. Held captive in his own Zemblan palace, King Charles helplessly looks down upon "lithe youths diving into the swimming pool of a fairy tale sport club" (p. 119); after making his

escape, he stops at a warm farmhouse where he is "given a fairy-tale meal of bread and cheese" (p. 140). Because it is Nabokov's most extensive fantasia, *Ada* naturally abounds in fairy-tale references (see pp. 5 ["Lake Kitezh"], 87, 143, 164, 180, 191, 228 ["Cendrillon": Cinderella: "Ashette" on pp. 114 and 397], 281, and 287). God is called "Log" in *Ada*, and Hermann in *Despair* (1934) says that he cannot believe in God because "the fairy tale about him is not really mine, it belongs to strangers, to all men . . ." (p. 101–102). When in *Invitation to a Beheading* (1936) Cincinnatus extolls the powers of the imagination, M'sieur Pierre answers, "Only in fairy tales do people escape from prison" (p. 114). "The Fairy's Daughter," an untranslated fantasy in verse for children, is collected in *The Empyrean Path* (1923, the same year that Nabokov translated *Alice in Wonderland* into Russian [see 131/1]); and the émigré story "A Fairytale" (1926) tells of a timid, erotically obsessed man who imagines a harem for himself. He makes an arrangement with a woman who turns out to be the devil. She offers him a choice of as many women as he desires, so long as the total number is odd. But his hopes are dashed when he chooses the same girl twice (a nymphet), for a total of twelve instead of thirteen (translated as "A Nursery Tale," the story appears in *Tyrants Destroyed*, 1975). Before describing Hazel Shade's final poltergeist vigil, as imagined in his playlet *The Haunted Barn*, Kinbote notes, "There are always 'three nights' in fairy tales, and in this sad fairy tale there was a third one too" (*Pale Fire*, p. 190). "Speaking of novels," Kinbote says to Sybil Shade, "you remember we decided once, you, your husband and I, that Proust's rough masterpiece was a huge, ghoulish fairy tale" (pp. 161–162); and mentioned in *Ada* are "the pretentious fairy tales" of "Osberg" (Borges; an anagram [p. 344]).

At Cornell (where the annotator was his student in 1953–1954), Nabokov would begin his first class by saying, "Great novels are above all great fairy tales. . . . Literature does not tell the truth but makes it up. It is said that literature was born with the fable of the boy crying, 'Wolf! Wolf!' as he was being chased by the animal. This was *not* the birth of literature; it happened instead the day the lad cried 'Wolf!' and the tricked hunters saw no wolf . . . the magic of art is manifested in the dream about the wolf, in the shadow of the invented wolf." As suggested in the Introduction, Nabokov goes to great lengths to show the reader that the boy has been crying "Wolf!" all along, and that the subject of Nabokov's art is in part the relationship between the old boy and the nonexistent wolf. See 32/7.

31/4 *dazzling coincidences . . . poets love:* evident everywhere in Nabokov's work is his "poet's love" of coincidence. The verbal figurations and "coincidences" limned in *Who's Who in the Limelight* are of great consequence, for H.H. alludes to "actors, producers, playwrights, and shots of static scenes" which prefigure the action of the novel. The three entries in this imaginary yearbook represent H.H., Lolita, and, obviously, Quilty. Although no "producer" is listed, it will shortly be seen that he reveals his name covertly (31/12), and shows his hand throughout. The importance of *Who's Who in the Limelight* is also discussed in the Introduction, pp. xxviii and xxx.

31/5 *Pym, Roland:* Pym is the title character in Edgar Allan Poe's *The Narrative of A. Gordon Pym* (1838); he is also mentioned in Nabokov's poem, "The Refrigerator Awakes" (1942), in *Poems* (p. 12). The name suits H.H. well, because, like Pym's, his is a first-person narrative that begins in the spirit of hoax but evolves into something very different. See 251/3 for "Hoaxton." As for "Roland," Nabokov intended no allusions to the medieval *Chanson de Roland,* to the character in Ariosto's *Orlando Furioso,* or to Browning's Childe Roland. For Poe, see 9/12.

31/6 *Elsinore Playhouse, Derby, N.Y.:* both exist. The former, invoking Hamlet's castle, is a common name for a theater. *Hamlet* is often referred to in Nabokov. In *Invitation to a Beheading,* M'sieur Pierre and Cincinnatus are "identically clad in Elsinore jackets" (p. 182); in *Ada,* a reviewer of Van Veen's first book is called "the First Clown in *Elsinore,* a distinguished London weekly" (p. 343); and in *Gogol,* "*Hamlet* is the wild dream of a neurotic scholar" (p. 140). Nabokov's own considerable Shakespearean scholarship is evident in Chapter Seven of *Bend Sinister,* which offers a totalitarian state version of the play. Nabokov himself glossed this chapter in his Introduction to the Time Reading Program edition (reprinted in the Vintage edition of *Bend Sinister*). The narrator of *The Real Life of Sebastian Knight,* who is Sebastian's half brother, demolishes a biography of Knight by demonstrating that the biographer, Mr. Goodman, has incorporated several bogus stories into his book, simply because the leg-pulling Sebastian had said they were so: "Third story: Sebastian speaking of his very first novel (unpublished and destroyed) explained that it was about a fat young student who travels home to find his mother married to his uncle; this uncle, an ear-specialist, had murdered the student's father. Mr. Goodman misses the joke" (p. 62). Recognizing that Sebastian's trap telescopes Nabokov's methods, some readers will no doubt sympathize with hapless Mr. Goodman. For another *Hamlet* allusion in *Lolita*, see 150/2. For further Shakespeare allusions, see pp. 177, 191 *(The Taming of the Shrew)*, 243 *(Romeo and Juliet)*, and 265 *(King Lear)*, as well as 157/3, 251/14, 301/3 *(Macbeth)*, and, for a summary note, 284/4.

31/7 *Made debut in Sunburst:* see p. 90, where H.H. refers to Charlotte Haze's impending death as "the ultimate sunburst," for it will indeed allow him to make his debut with her daughter. Unless they are annotated, the titles in the *Who's Who* entries are non-allusive and of no significance.

31/8 *The Strange Mushroom:* it is a "dazzling coincidence" that "Pym" should appear in a play authored by Quilty (see next entry). As for the specific origin of the "mushroom" image, literary history may be served by the strange fact related by Nabokov: "Somewhere, in a collection of 'cases,' I found a little girl who referred to her uncle's organ as 'his mushroom.' " The plant is in fact a sex symbol in many cultures. In *Ada* (p. 405), a photo reveals "the type of tight–capped toadstool called in Scots law . . . 'the Lord of Erection.' "

31/9 *Quilty, Clare:* although alluded to by John Ray, Jr., in the "Foreword" (see 4/9), this is the first time that the omnipresent Quilty will be identified by his complete name (Quilty's role is discussed in the Introduction, pp. xxx–lxvii *passim.*). H.H. withholds Quilty's identity until almost the end of *Lolita*, and adducing it by virtue of the trail of clues is one of the novel's special pleasures. His importance is most vividly demonstrated by gathering together all the Quilty references and hints as follows: pp. 4, 31, 32, 43, 63, 64, 69, 78, 89, 117, 121, 126–127, 130, 138, 139; [Part Two] 152, 159, 163, 170, 186, 196, 200–202, 203, 207–209, 211, 213, 215, 217–223, 224, 226–228, 232, 235, 236–238, 240, 241–243, 246–252, 262, 271–277, 279, 282, 290–292, 293–305, 306, 307, and 309. Each appearance or allusion to Quilty will be duly noted below, but a reader armed only with this telescopic list should be able to identify Quilty whenever he appears or is evoked on a page. This compilation also appears in my 1967 *Wisconsin Studies* article, "*Lolita:* The Springboard of Parody" (p. 225), and there is more on Quilty in my 1968 *Denver Quarterly* article, "The Art of Nabokov's Artifice" (see bibliography). See also *Keys,* pp. 57–78. An excellent ancillary text is *Stories of the Double,* Albert J. Guerard, ed.

    The killing of Quilty (pp. 293–305) was written well out of sequence, early in the composition of *Lolita*. "His death had to be clear in my mind in order to control his earlier appearances," said Nabokov. Nabokov removed from the final version of *Lolita* three scenes in which Quilty figured conspicuously: a talk before Charlotte Haze's club (see 78/1); a meeting with Lolita's friend Mona; and an appearance at a rehearsal of his own play, featuring Lolita. All three scenes were omitted because such foreground appearances interrupted the structure and rhythm of Quilty's pursuit of Lolita, and undermined the mystery surrounding his identity. Moreover, the latter two scenes created a most awkward narrative problem. Since H.H. couldn't narrate these scenes, Nabokov had to wait and let Lolita do it during their important confrontation scene (pp. 269 ff.), and that proved unwieldy. See 35/3 for mention of another omitted scene.

31/10 *The Little Nymph:* like *Fatherly Love* (in the same entry), this is an appropriate work for H.H.'s sinister alter ego to have authored.

31/11 *The Lady Who Loved Lightning:* Nabokov confirmed the deduction that this is the unnamed play which H.H. and Lolita attend in Wace, pp. 220–221. See p. 220; Lolita says, "I am not a lady and do not like lightning." Although H.H.'s mother was killed by lightning (p. 10), Nabokov intends no cross-reference; he grants, however, that "the connection is cozy and tempting." The *Who* in the play's title was not capitalized in the 1958 edition; the error has been corrected.

31/12 *in collaboration with Vivian Darkbloom:* at the very least she must be called Quilty's collaborator, since "she" is an anagram of "Vladimir Nabokov" (4/9).

31/13 *Dark Age:* see 262/7, where H.H. alludes to its author.

31/14 *The Strange Mushroom:* see above, 31/8.

31/15 *traveled 14,000 . . . New York:* H.H. "doubles" Quilty for a change, for he will travel some 27,000 miles with the little nymph (see p. 175), while Quilty's "play" of that name consumes virtually half of that distance.

31/16 *Hobbies . . . pets:* the three "hobbies" prefigure Quilty's pursuit of H.H. and Lolita ("fast cars"), his love of dogs (see 246/1), and the pornographic movies he will force his favorite "pet" to act in (see 276/2).

31/17 *Quine, Dolores:* "Dolores" is Lolita's given name (see 9/5), while "Quine" echoes Quilty, sets up an internal rhyme which condemns him (32/6), and is French for two fives at a game of tric-trac (a form of backgammon). Although Nabokov said he did not intend any allusion, *"Une quine à la lotérie"* is a bid prize, an advantage, which describes the way H.H. and Quilty variously bid for Lolita, and the way the book's game-element manipulates the reader (see p. 299); Quilty reads aloud from H.H.'s poem, "because you took advantage of my disadvantage."

32/1 *Never Talk to Strangers:* this is no idle title. See p. 138 ("I would not talk to strangers," H.H. advises Lolita) and 309/1, where he repeats and expands upon this excellent fatherly advice: "Be true to your [husband]. Do not let other fellows touch you. Do not talk to strangers."

32/2 *Has disappeared:* see next note, and p. 253, where H.H. says, "I have reached the part which . . . might be called *'Dolorès Disparue'* " (a play on *Albertine disparue,* the title of the penultimate volume of the original French edition of Marcel Proust's *À la Recherche du temps perdu*). An error in the 1958 edition has been corrected (the transposing of the concluding bracket and period after "follows").

32/3 *I notice . . . in the preceding paragraph:* the "slip" refers to "Has disappeared" instead of "Has appeared," another foreshadowing of his loss. Lolita will be cast in a play by Quilty, *The Enchanted Hunters.* See pp. 200–202. It is central to a full sense of the novel.

32/4 *Clarence:* H.H.'s lawyer, to whom the manuscript of this "unrevised" draft is entrusted. See p. 3.

32/5 *The Murdered Playwright:* the prefiguration of the murder announced above is completed here (31/2). H.H. now explicitly refers to his killing of Quilty (pp. 293–305), which is prefigured several more times (see 45/4 and 47/6). By strategically placing *Who's Who in the Limelight* early in *Lolita*—like Black Guinea's list of the avatars of the confidence man in Chapter Three of Herman Melville's *The Confidence-Man: His Masquerade* (1857)—Nabokov gives the reader an opportunity to make at least some of these connections as the novel unfolds.

32/6 *Quine the Swine . . . my Lolita:* Quilty, and for "my Lolita," see 45/1 and 192/2.

32/7 *I have only words to play with:* even if H.H. has only words, the reader must consider the implications of his extraordinary control of them. The interlacements which lead in and out of this veritable nerve center reveal a capacity for design and order that, given the conditions under which his narrative has allegedly been composed, is only within the reach of the manipulative author above the book. By no accident is *Who's Who in the Limelight* a theatrical yearbook, for the involutions which spiral out of it demonstrate that playwright Quilty, H.H., and Lolita, as well as the actor and actress who serve as their stand-ins in *Who's Who*, are all performing in another of Nabokov's puppet shows. "I could not really see him," says H.H., of Quilty, "but what gave him away [in the dark] was the rasp of a screwing off, then a discreet gurgle, then the final note of a placid screwing on"—sounds from the workshop (p. 126). "Guess again, Punch," H.H. tells Quilty (p. 296); and, of their fight, H.H. says, "He and I were two large dummies, stuffed with dirty cotton and rags" (p. 299). The novel's first reference to Quilty thus offers a summary phrase (4/9); for the countless involuted verbal figurations and cross-references in *Lolita* all represent "Vivian Darkbloom" 's "cue," and suggest that the authorial consciousness is somehow profoundly involved in a tale that in every literal way is surely separate from it.

Having recognized the novel's verisimilar disguise, the reader is afforded a global view of the book *qua* book, whose dappled surface now reveals patterns that seem almost visual. In the Foreword to the 1966 version of *Speak, Memory*, Nabokov says that in looking for a title for the first edition, he "toyed with *The Anthemion* which is the name of a honeysuckle ornament, consisting of elaborate interlacements and expanding clusters, but nobody liked it"; it would be a fitting, if precious, subtitle for *Lolita* (as well as for several other Nabokov works). A grand anthemion entwines H.H.'s narrative, like some vast authorial watermark, and its outlines are traced by the elegantly ordered networks of alliteration, "coincidences," narrative "inconsistencies," lepidopterological references, "cryptocolors," and shadows and glimpses of Quilty.

CHAPTER 9

33/1 *charming . . . chap:* the cascade of alliterations in this paragraph, so carefully controlled, underscores the significance of *Who's Who*, as does a remark on the next page (34/3).

33/2 *Pierre Point in Melville Sound:* H.H.'s invention, from *Pierre* (1852) by Herman Melville (1819–1891). An allusion to Book IX's opening, where a reckless, truth–seeking "Arctic explorer" "loses the directing compass of his mind. . . . at the Pole, to whose barrenness only it points . . ." Pierre dies in prison, as does H.H. Melville's gloomy "Byronic" themes are apposite.

34/1 *gremlin:* a mischievous little gnome reported by World War II air-men as causing mechanical trouble in airplanes. "Drumlins" (bottom of p. 33) is the plural for "an elongate or oval hill of glacial drift" (Webster's 2nd).

34/2 *kremlin:* the name of the governing center of Russia completes this sequence of phonological pairings. The best example is found in *Pale Fire* (note to line 803). Nabokov continually manipulates the basic lin-guistic devices—auditory, morphological, and alphabetical, the latter most conspicuously. In *Pale Fire,* Zemblan is "the tongue of the mirror" (p. 242); and the fragmentation or total annihilation of the self reverber-ates in the verbal distortions in *Bend Sinister*'s police state, "where everybody is merely an anagram of everybody else," as well as in the alphabetical and psychic inversions and reversals of *Pale Fire*—such as Botkin-Kinbote and the Index references to Word Golf and *"Sudarg of Bokay,* a mirror maker of genius," the latter an anagrammatic reflection and poetic description of omnipresent death, represented in *Pale Fire* by the Zemblan assassin J[y]akob Gradus, who throws his shadow across the entire novel, its creations, creator, and readers.

34/3 *The reader will regret to learn . . . I had another bout with insanity:* H.H. is right, readers *do* regret to hear this from a narrator; and H.H. virtually encloses his narrative within reminders of this "unreliability," for, to-ward the end (p. 255), he casually says he retired to another sanatorium ("I felt I was merely losing contact with reality" [*merely!*—A.A.]). Several of Nabokov's narrators are mad. Among other things, their madness functions as a parody of critical dogma about fiction, and a telling parody of the reader's own delusory "contact with reality." Of course H.H.'s is not a credible point of view in the terms laid down by Henry James, refined by Percy Lubbock, put into practice by Ford Madox Ford and Joseph Conrad, institutionalized by two generations of critics, and enforced by thousands of creative writing instructors—and the involuted, patterned surface of *Lolita* makes this even clearer. H.H.'s copy of *Who's Who* and Quilty's "cryptogrammic paper chase" (pp. 250–251), the two most important concentrations of authorial inlays, typical in method and effect, are thus symmetrically located at the beginning and near the end of the novel, almost next to those declara-tions of insanity which seem to frame it, though these symmetries can-not hope to be as exact as the one formed by the first and final words of the novel ("Lolita"). See Notes 51/1 through 52/3 for another concen-tration of self-reflexive involutions.

CHAPTER 10

35/1 *patients . . . had witnessed their own conception:* Nabokov's attacks on Freud are consistent. Kinbote includes in his Commentary lines deleted in the draft of the poem *Pale Fire:*

> . . . Your modern architect
> Is in collusion with psychanalysts:
> When planning parents' bedrooms, he insists
> On lockless doors so that, when looking back,
> The future patient of the future quack
> May find, all set for him, the Primal Scene. [p. 94]

In *Speak, Memory,* Nabokov similarly "reject[s] completely the vulgar, shabby, fundamentally medieval world of Freud, with its crankish quest for sexual symbols (something like searching for Baconian acrostics in Shakespeare's works) and its bitter little embryos spying, from their natural nooks, upon the love life of their parents" (p. 20); while in *Ada* he notes the "pale pencil which poor [public] speakers are obsessed with in familiar dreams (attributed by Dr. Froid of Signy-Mondieu-Mondieu to the dreamer's having read in infancy his adulterous parents' love letters)" (p. 549). For Freud, see 5/6.

35/2 *Humbertish:* H.H.'s coinage; after any language ending in the *-ish* suffix (Finnish, English, Lettish).

35/3 *house . . . burned down:* Nabokov omitted from the last draft of *Lolita* a hilarious scene describing H.H.'s arrival by taxi at the charred-out, bepuddled, roped-off ruins of the McCoo residence. A large crowd applauds H.H. as he grandly alights from the cab; only an encyclopedia has survived the holocaust. He recognizes that the lost opportunity to coach "the enigmatic [McCoo] nymphet" is no loss at all (see p. 41). Nabokov reinstated the scene in his published screenplay of *Lolita* (Stanley Kubrick had dropped it from the film). "Although there are just enough borrowings from [my *Lolita* script in Kubrick's] version to justify my legal position as author of the script, the final product is only a blurred skimpy glimpse of the marvelous picture I imagined and set down scene by scene during the six months I worked in a Los Angeles villa. I do not wish to imply that Kubrick's film is mediocre; in its own right, it is first-rate, but it is not what I wrote. A tinge of *poshlost* [see Introduction, pp. xlvii–xlviii] is often given by the cinema to the novel it distorts and coarsens in its crooked glass. Kubrick, I think, avoided this fault in his version, but I shall never understand why he did not follow my directions and dreams. It is a great pity; but at least I shall be able to have people read my *Lolita* play in its original form" (*Paris Review* interview, 1967). Speaking more positively three years earlier, Nabokov said, "The four main actors deserve the very highest praise. Sue Lyon bringing that breakfast tray or childishly pulling on her sweater in the car—these are moments of unforgettable acting and directing. The killing of Quilty [Peter Sellers] is a masterpiece, and so is the death of Mrs. Haze [Shelley Winters; James Mason was H.H.]. I must point out, though, that I had nothing to do with the actual production. If I had, I might have insisted on stressing certain things that were not stressed—for example, the different motels at which they stopped" (*Playboy* interview). The highways and motels were so little in evidence because the film, released in 1962, was shot in England.

35/4 *342:* for "coincidences," see 118/3 and 248/2.

35/5 *A lady who lived opposite:* and she is subsequently referred to as "Miss Opposite" on pp. 52 ff.

36/1 *suburban dog:* a foreshadowing of Charlotte Haze's death, for Mr. Beale will run over her when he swerves to avoid hitting what may well be this dog (see p. 102). See also *Keys,* p. 6.

36/2 *van Gogh:* the "Arlésienne" (1888) is a famous portrait of a woman from the town of Arles in Provence, by Vincent van Gogh (1853–1890). Mass-produced reproductions of it are quite popular in America. H.H.'s low opinion of van Gogh is shared by other Nabokov characters. In *Pnin,* the art teacher Lake thinks "That van Gogh is second-rate and Picasso supreme, despite his commercial foibles" (p. 96); and Victor Wind acknowledges "with a nod of ironic recognition" a framed reproduction of van Gogh's "La Berceuse" (p. 108).

37/1 *Marlene Dietrich:* see 9/4. Also pp. 51 and 101.

38/1 *René Prinet:* "The Kreutzer Sonata" was dedicated by Beethoven to Rodolphe Kreutzer in 1805 (Nabokov intended no allusion to Tolstoy's story of that name). Prinet's painting (1898) has long illustrated the Tabu perfume advertisement found in *The New Yorker* and chic ladies' magazines. It shows, in Nabokov's words, an "ill-groomed girl pianist rising like a wave from her stool after completing the duo, and being kissed by a hirsute violinist. Very unappetizing and clammy, but has 'camp' charm." For a scented version, see and smell *Glamour,* December 1990, p. 49.

39/1 *Riviera love . . . over dark glasses:* the confluence of sunglasses and H.H.'s Riviera love suggest that H.H. has stumbled upon a veritable Lost-and-Found Department (see 13/3).

39/2 *fairy-tale:* see 16/6 and 31/3.

39/3 *"Roches Roses":* the "red rocks" of p. 13. See 56/1. Both H.H.'s and Poe's "Annabel Lee" are alluded to on this and the next page.

40/1 *nouvelle:* French; new one. For the literary importance of "this Lolita, *my* Lolita, see 45/1.

40/2 *mummery:* the performance of an actor in a dumb show; *mummer* is obsolete slang for a play-actor.

40/3 *fruit vert:* "green fruit"; French (dated) slang for " 'unripe' females attractive to ripe gentlemen," noted Nabokov.

40/4 *Au fond, ça m'est bien égal:* French; "Really, I don't care at all."

CHAPTER 11

40/5 *en escalier:* set-up in an oblique typography; French for "staircase style."

40/6 *Blank . . . Blankton, Mass.:* there is no such town. The "blanks" make fun of the "authenticity" of the pages of both the diary and the entire novel, H.H.'s "photographic memory" notwithstanding. Thus *Lolita*'s parodic design also includes the literary journal or diary. Nabokov regarded with profound skepticism the possibilities of complete autobiographical revelation. "Manifold self-awareness" (as he calls it in *Speak, Memory*) is not to be achieved through solemn introspection, certainly not through the diarist's compulsive egotism, candid but totally self-conscious self-analysis, carefully created "honesty," willful irony, and studied self-deprecation. Nabokov burlesqued the literary diary as far back as 1934. Near the end of *Despair,* Hermann's first-person narrative "degenerates into a diary"—"the lowest form of literature" (p. 208)—and this early parody is fully realized in *Lolita,* especially in the present chapter. For more on the confessional mode, see 70/3.

40/7 *phoenix:* a legendary bird represented by the ancient Egyptians as living for five or six centuries, being consumed in fire by its own act, and then rising from its ashes; an emblem of resurrection and immortality.

41/1 *sebum:* the material secreted by the sebaceous glands.

41/2 *Humbert le Bel:* Humbert the Fair; a kingly epithet (e.g., Charles le Bel of France).

42/1 *entrée:* appearance on a stage; grand entrance.

42/2 *favonian:* of or pertaining to the west wind; thus, gentle.

42/3 *phocine:* pertaining to the zoological sub-family which includes the common seal, the image against which H.H. measures "the seaside of [Lolita's] schoolgirl thighs"—an allusion to the lost "kingdom" of Annabel (see 9/2).

42/4 *Priap:* son of Dionysus and Aphrodite, Priapus was the Greco-Roman god of procreation and fertility, usually portrayed in a manly state. Also mentioned on pp. 159, 237, and less mythically, on p. 213. See 9/5.

42/5 *predator . . . prey:* H.H. often characterizes himself as a predator, most often as an ape or spider (prominent among the butterfly's natural enemies). For further discussion, see my 1967 *Wisconsin Studies* article, *op. cit.,* pp. 222 and 228.

43/1 *stippled:* engraved, by means of dots rather than lines; in painting, refers to the use of small touches which coalesce to produce gradations of light and shade. See 284/2.

43/2 *Delectatio morosa . . . dolors:* Latin; morose pleasure, a monastic term. In the next sentence, as on p. 53, H.H. toys with the Latin etymology of "Dolores" (see 9/5).

43/3 *Our Glass Lake:* see 81/2.

43/4 *nacreous:* having a pearly iridescence.

43/5 *Virginia . . . Edgar:* Poe was born January 19, 1809. He was therefore twenty-seven when in 1836 he married his thirteen-year-old cousin, Virginia Clemm, who died of a lingering disease in 1847. She was the inspiration for many of his poems. For his first conjugal night with

Lolita, H.H. appropriately registers as "Edgar" (see 118/2). He also employs the name on pp. 75 and 189 (see also *Keys*, p. 37). Nabokov told me that he originally intended to call Lolita "Virginia" and title the book *Ginny*. For a summary of the Poe allusions, see 9/2.

43/6 *Je m'imagine cela:* French; I can imagine that.

43/7 *"Monsieur Poe-poe":* H.H. puns on "poet," but the schoolboy had in mind *"popo"* (or *"popotin"*), French slang for the posterior.

43/8 *resemble . . . actor chap:* Clare Quilty. They *do* resemble one another. For a summary of Quilty allusions, see 31/9.

43/9 *nictating: rare;* winking.

44/1 *"ne montrez pas vos zhambes":* French; "don't show your legs" (*jambes* is misspelled to indicate an American accent). See 189/2.

44/2 *à mes heures:* French; when in the right mood.

44/3 *lady writer:* H.H.'s characterization and caricature are *not* "sexist." He's referring to the kind of deathless trite prose long produced by women *for* women (e.g., the Harlequin romances, whose male authors adopt female pseudonyms to be "credible").

45/1 *the writer's ancient lust:* H.H. sees himself in a line descending from the great Roman love poets, and he frequently imitates their locutions. The intonational stresses of *"this* Lolita, *my* Lolita" are borrowed from a donnish English translation of a Latin poem (see pp. 40, 65–66, 151, 277, 278, 293). H.H.'s "ancient" models include Propertius (c. 50–16 B.C.) on Cynthia, Tibullus (c. 55–19 B.C.) on Delia, and Horace (65–8 B.C.) on any of the sixteen women to whom he wrote poems. See 192/2.

45/2 *Our Glass Lake:* a "mistake"; see 81/2.

45/3 *"Little Carmen":* a pun: little [train]men, or "Dwarf Conductors" (see also *Keys*, p. 144n). The allusions to *Carmen* have nothing to do with Bizet's opera. They refer only to the novella (1845) by Prosper Mérimée (1803–1870). For a pun on his name, see 251/7. Like H.H., José Lizzarrabengoa, Carmen's abandoned and ill-fated lover (see 239/3), tells his story from prison (but not until the third chapter, when the narrative frame is withdrawn). The story of love, loss, and revenge is appropriate. The *Carmen* allusions also serve as a trap for the sophisticated reader who is misled into believing that H.H., like José, will murder his treacherous Carmen; see p. 280, where H.H. springs the trap. H.H. quotes

Mérimée (243/4, 278/2, 278/4) and frequently calls Lolita "Carmen," the traditional name of a bewitching woman (pp. 59, 60, 61, 242–243, 251, 256, 278, 280). Carl R. Proffer discusses the *Carmen* allusions in *Keys*, pp. 43–51. In Latin, *carmen* means song, poetry, and charm. "My charmin', my Carmen," says H.H. (p. 60), thus demonstrating that he knows its etymology and original English meaning: the chanting of a verse having magic power; "to bewitch, enchant, subdue by magic power." See 16/6. H.H. calls himself "an enchanted hunter," takes Lolita to the hotel of that name, speaks of an "enchanted island of time" (p. 18), and so forth. Nabokov told his lecture classes at Cornell that a great writer was at once a storyteller, a teacher, and, most supremely, an enchanter. See 108/2.

45/4 *I shot . . . said: Ah!:* a prevision of Quilty's death; see 87/1 and 303/1.

46/1 *Pisky:* "Pixie"; see 31/3. The town is invented. Also means "moth" in rural England. For entomological allusions, see 6/1.

47/1 *le mot juste:* French; the right word; a phrase made famous by the French novelist Gustave Flaubert (1821–1880), who often took a week to find *le mot juste*. For other allusions to Flaubert, see 145/3, 202/2, and 265/2.

47/2 *Ronsard's "la vermeillette fente":* Pierre de Ronsard (1524–1585), the greatest poet of the French Renaissance. H.H. alludes to a sonnet entitled *L.M.F.*, and its first line, *"Je te salue, o vermeillette fante"* (*"fente"* is the modern spelling): "I salute [or hail] you, oh little red slit" (*"Blason du sexe feminin,"* Edition Pléiade, II, 775). A *"Blason"* is a short poem in praise or criticism of a certain subject. For another allusion to Ronsard, see 214/1. During his émigré period in Germany in the twenties and early thirties, Nabokov published Russian translations of many of the writers alluded to by H.H., including Ronsard, Verlaine, Byron, Keats, Baudelaire, Shakespeare, Rimbaud, Goethe, Pushkin, Carroll, and Romain Rolland.

47/3 *Remy Belleau's "un petit . . . escarlatte":* Belleau (1528–1577), Ronsard's colleague in the Pléiade group, also writes a *"blason"* in praise of the external female genitalia; "the hillock velveted with delicate moss, / traced in the middle with a little scarlet thread [labia]." For obvious reasons, the poem is rarely anthologized and is difficult to find. It appears in the Leyden reprint (1865) of the rare anthology *Recueil de pièces choisies rassemblées par les soins du cosmopolite,* duc d'Aiguillon, ed. (1735). The Cornell Library owns a copy, noted Nabokov.

47/4 *of my darling . . . my bride:* line 39 of Poe's "Annabel Lee." See 9/2 for the poem.

47/5 *Mystery of the Menarche:* the menarche is the initial menstrual period. In Ireland it is called "The Curse of the Irish."

47/6 *kill in my dreams:* another prevision of Quilty's death scene; see p. 297.

48/1 *toothbrush mustache:* Quilty has one too; see p. 218. Poe also had one, but Nabokov said that no allusion was intended here.

48/2 *ape-ear:* H.H. several times characterizes himself this way. See p. 311 for a most resonant ape image.

49/1 *coltish subteens . . . (all New England for a lady–writer's pen!):* this diary entry opens with a burst of cheap-fiction clichés—prose as ready–made as "the black ready-made bow and bobby pins holding [Lo's] hair in place." H.H.'s dead language and reference to a colt sets-up a parenthetical echo of the battlefield lamentation of Richard III when his horse is slain: "A horse! A horse! My kingdom for a horse!" (*Richard III*, V, iv, 19). Shakespeare, the king of English, is deposed and truly in parentheses at this turn of *Lolita,* hemmed-in by the stock epithets of "a lady writer." For Shakespeare, see 284/4.

49/2 *Ces matins gris si doux:* French; "Those gray mornings, so soft . . ."

50/1 *rumor; roomer:* a homophone. In *The Real Life of Sebastian Knight,* the narrator speaks of "mad Sebastian, struggling in a naughty world of Juggernauts, and aeronauts, and naughts, and what-nots" (p. 63).

50/2 *Is it Fate:* "McFate" is quietly introduced; see 52/3 and 56/1.

50/3 *"And behold":* Lolita completes her mother's "Lo," and H.H. later twists the epithet (223/4).

51/1 *her class at . . . school:* in *Pnin,* young Victor Wind sees in the glass headlight or chrome plating of a car "a view of the street and himself comparable to the microcosmic version of a room (with a dorsal view of diminutive people) in that very special and very magical small convex mirror that, half a millennium ago, Van Eyck and Petrus Christus and Memling used to paint into their detailed interiors, behind the sour merchant or the domestic madonna" (pp. 97–98). Like *Who's Who in the Limelight* (pp. 31–32) and the "cryptogrammic paper chase" (pp. 250–51), the "poetic" class list serves as a kind of magical mirror. The list is printed on the back of an unfinished map of the United States, drawn by Lolita, suggesting the scale of the gameboard on which the action is played. The image of the map secreted in the *Young People's Encyclopedia* prefigures their journeys (on which H.H. will "finish" the map by showing Lolita the country), just as the class list prefigures and mirrors an extraordinary number of other things.

51/2 *Beale:* the Beales' father kills Charlotte Haze (p. 98), and they are the first of no less than five sets of twins or twinned names in Lolita's class (the Beales, the Cowans, the Talbots, and the incestuous Mirandas [see p. 136]), a microscopic vision of the doubling (H.H. and Quilty) and mirroring that occurs in the roomy interior of the entire book (including Ray's Foreword), where even cars have their twins (p. 227); "the long hairy arm of coincidence" is said to have its unpredictable "twin limb" (p. 105); Mrs. Haze is echoed by the widow Mrs. Hays (p. 239); and obscure women of science mirror one another in spite of the almost 300 pages separating them (Blanche Schwarzmann: "White Blackman," and Melanie Weiss: "Black White"; see p. 302).

Double names, initials, and phonetic effects prevail throughout *Lolita,* whether the twinning is literal (Humbert Humbert, Vanessa van Ness, Quilty's Duk Duk Ranch, and H.H.'s alternate pseudonyms of "Otto Otto," "Mesmer Mesmer," and "Lambert Lambert"); or alliterative (Clare Quilty, Gaston Godin, Harold Haze, Bill Brown, and Clarence [Choate] Clark); or trickily alphabetical (John Ray, Jr.: J.R., Jr.). The double consonants of the almost infinite succession of humorously alliterative place names and points of interest H.H. visits are thus thematically consistent (Pierre Point, Hobby House, Hazy Hills, Kumfy Kabins, Raspberry Room, Chestnut Court, and so forth). Numbers even adhere to the pattern; H.H. imagines Lolita's unborn child "dreaming already in her of becoming a big shot and retiring around 2020 A.D." (p. 277). The name of "Harold D. Doublename" represents a summary phrase (p. 182), but the annotator's double initials are only a happy coincidence. For more on mirrors, see 119/2.

51/3 *Carmine, Rose:* see 56/1.

52/1 *Falter:* German; butterfly—and a companion of "Miss Phalen" (*pha-lène:* moth [56/2]) and the playwright "Schmetterling" (butterfly [301/5]). For a summary of the entomological allusions, see 6/1.

52/2 *Fantasia:* a corrected misprint (*s* instead of *z* in the 1958 edition). She is married on p. 289 (the "Murphy-Fantasia" wedding party).

52/3 *McFate, Aubrey:* a vagrant auditor, rather than a member of the class (see 56/1), though the reader may not realize it for four more pages. McFate's appearance in the middle of the class list undercuts the inviolable "reality" of much more than just the list. By placing the McFate allusions back-to-back on pp. 52 and 56, Nabokov gives the reader a fighting chance to make the association, and to realize its implications. It would be "easier" on the reader, of course, if the class list came *after* p. 56 (notes 251/1 and 253/1 limn similar effects). McFate's first name suggests Aubrey Beardsley (see 251/5), the "decadent" Art Nouveau artist (1872–1898) quite out of fashion when *Lolita* was written, and reveals another mother lode of verbal figurations: the invented town of "Beardsley," its school and college, and Gaston Godin (see 181/1). The self-reflexive authorial identification with Beardsley is, among other things, a serious literary joke aimed at the unfriendly critics, then and now, who consign Nabokov the gilt-edged prose stylist to Aubrey's party—the artistic dandies, the guilt-free Decadent School.

The Beardsley schools themselves may reflect and refract three actual institutions of learning in Wellesley, Mass. Professor Patrick F. Quinn, who taught English at Wellesley College (1949–1985), points to several links between Beardsley and the three women's schools in town (letter to the annotator, June 30, 1975). Dana Hall, a private secondary school, was for many years exclusively female, as was Pine Manor Junior College (it moved, c. 1970), and could be the prototypes for the Beardsley School. Wellesley College, where Nabokov taught in the forties, has a Founders Hall, which is "Maker Hall" in *Lolita* (p. 252). For about eighty years, Wellesley offered a required, yearlong Bible course, an unusual feature for an elite college; in *Lolita*, the course offering has been transposed to the Beardsley School (p. 189). Professor Quinn, by the way, is a distinguished Poe scholar. For Poe, see 9/2.

52/4 *Windmuller:* Louise and her father appear on p. 4; he on p. 290.

52/5 *bodyguard of roses:* classmates "Rose" and "Rosaline" serve as Lolita's rosy page-girls. The rose is of course the flower traditionally associated with gems, decorations, wine, perfume, and women of great charm and / or virtue. Lolita is continually linked with the flower. See 56/1. See also *Keys,* p. 118.

53/1 *Is "mask" the keyword?:* yes, because the masked author has just been mirrored, as it were, in the class list; see the Introduction and Chapter Twenty-six (109/1).

53/2 *charshaf:* a veil worn by Turkish women.

53/3 *Irving:* the reader may wonder why H.H. is sorry for "Flashman, Irving" (p. 52). "Poor Irving," said Nabokov, "he is the only Jew among all those Gentiles. Humbert identifies with the persecuted." See 261/4.

53/4 *ullulations:* or *ululation;* a loud, mournful, rhythmical howl.

53/5 *ribald sea monsters:* the intrusive bearded bathers of p. 13. "Annabel" and H.H.'s seasickness refer to Poe's poem. See 9/2.

53/6 *"Mais allez-y, allez-y!":* French; "But go ahead, go!"

54/1 *Dr. Blanche Schwarzmann:* mentioned by John Ray. See 5/3.

54/2 *libidream:* H.H.'s portmanteau of "libido" and "dream."

54/3 *Dorsal view:* belonging to, or situated on or near the back of an animal. The phrase is not a sentence, and it is followed by several other fragments. Style is definitely at issue here, in a chapter that deliberately mocks a jejune or degenerating prose—the clichés of popular "feminine" fiction; the half-baked writing of the diarist; verbal laziness of *any* kind that figuratively places Shakespeare in parentheses.

55/1 *manège:* French; tactics.

55/2 *tennis ball ... my ... darling:* Nabokov pairs the Poe allusion with a tennis ball because it is in the tennis scene that H.H. best captures her beauty (pp. 231–234)—Shakespeare out of parentheses, if you will and so to speak.

CHAPTER 12

55/3 *pederosis:* H.H.'s description of his condition. Although rare, the term exists; from the Greek *paid-*, meaning "child," plus *erōs*, "sexual love" (akin to *erasthai:* "to love, desire ardently"), plus Latin suffix, from Greek, *-ōsis*, an "abnormal or diseased condition" (e.g., *sclerosis*). *Pedophilia* is the more common word for H.H.'s malaise.

56/1 *Aubrey McFate ... devil of mine:* the devilish "force" responsible for H.H.'s misfortunes is invoked on pp. 52, 107, 116, 210, 211, 256. When H.H. perceives Quilty—the worst aspect of his McFate—as a "red-beast" or "red fiend," Nabokov is parodying that archetypal Double, the Devil. Red is Quilty's color, just as rose is associated with Annabel (39/3) and Lolita; her classmate's name, "Rose Carmine" (p. 51), defines the two motifs nicely. Its significance, however, has nothing to do with "symbolism"; the red and rose stipplings are the work of the author, rather than McFate, and add some vivid touches of color to the anthemion (see 32/7). Once pointed out, the color motif need not be identified further; but the reader is reminded again that Nabokov is no "symbolist." After reading the first draft of these Notes, Nabokov thought that this point had not been made clear enough, and, moved too by the annotator's loose play with some "red" images, wrote the following for my information, under the heading "A Note about Symbols and Colors *re* 'Annotated *Lolita.*' " It is included here because I think it is one of the most significant statements Nabokov made about his own art. He writes:

> There exist novelists and poets, and ecclesiastic writers, who deliberately use color terms, or numbers, in a strictly symbolic sense. The type of writer I am, half-painter, half-naturalist, finds the use of symbols hateful because it substitutes a dead general idea for a live specific impression. I am therefore puzzled and distressed by the significance you lend to the general idea of "red" in my book. When the intellect limits itself to the general notion, or primitive notion, of a certain color it deprives the senses of its shades. In different languages different colors were used in a general sense before shades were distinguished. (In French, for example, the "redness" of hair is now expressed by "*roux*" meaning rufous, or russet, or fulvous with a reddish cast.) For me the shades, or rather colors, of, say, a fox, a ruby, a carrot, a pink rose, a dark cherry, a flushed cheek, are as different as blue is from green or the royal purple of blood (Fr. "*pourpre*") from the English sense of violet blue. I think your students, your readers, should be taught to *see* things, to discriminate between visual shades as the author does, and not to lump them under such arbitrary labels as "red" (using it, moreover, as a sexual symbol, though actually the dominant shades in males are mauve—to bright blue, in certain monkeys). . . . Roses may be white, and even black-red. Only cartoonists, having three colors at their disposal, use red for hair, cheek and blood.

See 221/2 for further remarks on color.

56/2 *Miss Phalen:* from the French *phalène:* moth. For the entomological allusions, see 6/1.

CHAPTER 13

59/1 *friable:* easily crumbled or pulverized.

59/2 *parkled:* H.H.'s coinage.

60/1 *safely solipsized:* see 12/2. An important phrase (see second half of 16/6). The verbal form of *solipsist* is of course H.H.'s coinage—a most significant portmanteau suggesting that Lolita has been reduced in more than size, as H.H. comes to realize. Although H.H.'s "moral apotheosis" is expressed at the end of *Lolita,* hints of it are fleetingly glimpsed early on, shortly, when H.H. addresses the nymphet's solipsized condition: "What I had madly possessed was not she, but my own creation, an-other, fanciful Lolita—perhaps, more real than Lolita; overlapping, en-casing her; floating between me and her, and having no will, no consciousness—indeed, no life of her own" (p. 62).

60/2 *corpuscles of Krause:* after the German anatomist: minute sensory particles occurring in the mucous membranes of the genitalia. An au-thor's error has been corrected (*s* in Krause instead of *z* in the 1958 edition).

60/3 *seraglio:* the portion of a Moslem house reserved for the wives and harem.

62/1 *Drew his .32:* the revenge murder of Lolita which *doesn't* take place; see p. 280.

CHAPTER 14

62/2 *loan God:* from a cultural sequence (e.g., Greek-Roman, Hebrew-Christian); "lone" in the first mass paperback edition, and thus an "exis-tential image" to one critic.

63/1 *Dr. Quilty:* the "playwright" is his nephew (or cousin), Clare Quilty. For a summary of Quilty allusions, see 31/9.

64/1 *Shirley Holmes:* after Sir Arthur Conan Doyle's (1859–1930) famous detective hero, Sherlock Holmes (see 250/5). Between the ages of ten and fifteen, Nabokov was a Holmes devotee. That enthusiasm faded, though traces remain. "I spent a poor night in a charming, airy, prettily furnished room where neither window nor door closed properly, and where an omnibus edition of Sherlock Holmes which had pursued me for years supported a bedside lamp," writes the narrator of *Pnin,* at the end of the novel (p. 190). The narrator of *The Real Life of Sebastian Knight* "use[s] an old Sherlock Holmes stratagem" (p. 151); and, in *Despair,* Hermann addresses Conan Doyle directly: "What an opportunity, what a subject you missed! For you could have written one last tale concluding the whole Sherlock Holmes epic; one last episode beautifully setting off the rest; the murderer in that tale should have turned out to be not the one-legged bookkeeper, not the Chinaman Ching and not the woman in crimson, but the very chronicler of the crime stories, Dr. Watson himself—Watson, who, so to speak, knew what was Whatson. A staggering surprise for the reader" (pp. 121–122)—and a figurative description of several of Nabokov's own narrative strategies. "Was he in *Sherlock Holmes,* the fellow whose / Tracks pointed back when he reversed his shoes?" wonders John Shade in Canto One of *Pale Fire* (lines 27–28). After identifying Holmes in the Commentary, Kinbote says he "suspect[s] that our poet simply made up this Case of the Reversed Footprints" (p. 78), alluding to *The Hound of the Baskervilles* (1902). He is wrong, but his suspicion summarizes the way that Nabokov frequently parodies and transmutes the methods and themes of that genre, just as "Shirley Holmes" is a jocular reminder that *Lolita* is, among other things, a kind of mystery story demanding a considerable amount of armchair detection. See the remarks on Poe and the detective story, 9/2. For the penultimate moment in this "tale of ratiocination," see 272/1; and for a telling allusion to Holmes, drawn from *The Defense,* see 272/2.

CHAPTER 15

64/2 *Camp Q:* "Cue" is Quilty's nickname. "The 'Q,' " noted Nabokov, "had to be changed to 'Kilt' in the French translation because of the awful pun, Q = *cul!*" (which means "ass").

64/3 *Botticellian pink:* Sandro Botticelli (1444 or 1445–1510), master of the early Italian Renaissance, known for his tender renderings of sensual but melancholy femininity. That pink is most manifest in the vision of the three graces in his painting "Primavera," while the "wet, matted eyelashes" suggest his famous "The Birth of Venus," which H.H. invokes on pp. 270 and 274. In *Laughter in the Dark,* blind Albinus tries to transform incoherent sounds into colors: "It was the opposite of trying to imagine the kind of voices which Botticelli's angels had" (p. 242).

65/1 *her coccyx:* the end of the vertebral column.

65/2 *iliac:* anatomical word; pertaining to the *ilium,* "the dorsal and upper one of the three bones composing either lateral half of the pelvis."

66/1 *Catullus . . . forever:* Gaius Valerius Catullus (c. 84–54 B.C.), Roman lyric, erotic, and epigrammatic poet. H.H.'s *"that* Lolita, *my* Lolita" (p. 65) echoes Catullus's evocation of his enchanting Lesbia, as well as imitations such as "My sweetest Lesbia" (1601), by Thomas Campion (1567–1620), English poet. See 45/1 and 151/1.

66/2 *D.P.:* during and shortly after World War II, refugees were officially described as "Displaced Persons"; hence "D.P."'s.

66/3 *Berthe au Grand Pied:* Bertha (or Bertrade) with the Big Feet (or Bigfoot Bertha); the epithet is not pejorative. A French historical figure (d. 783), she was Pépin le Bref's wife and Charlemagne's mother, and is alluded to by François Villon in his ballad with the refrain *"Mais où sont les neiges d'antan?"*

66/4 *mais rien:* French; but nothing.

CHAPTER 16

67/1 *mon cher, cher monsieur:* French; my dear, dear sir.

67/2 *Départez:* the wrong French for "leave!" Correct: *Partez!*

68/1 *chéri:* French; darling.

68/2 *mon très, très cher:* French; my very, very dear.

69/1 *crooner's mug:* many younger readers of the rock-and-roll persuasion do not know that *to croon* is to "sing in half voice especially into a closely held microphone" (Webster's 3rd), a poor definition of the romantic style of ballad singing best represented by the oeuvre of Harry Lillis (Bing) Crosby (1904–1977), known affectionately as "The Groaner"; Frank Sinatra (1915–   ); and Mel Tormé (1925–   ). They are not mentioned by H.H. when he complains about pop singers (148/1). Nabokov's high standards prevailed quite instinctively, even on such foreign ground.

69/2 *Morell . . . "conquering hero":* Thomas Morell (1703–1784), an English classical scholar, wrote the song "See the Conquering Hero Comes." George Frederick Handel (1685–1759) used it in his oratorios *Joshua* and

Judas Maccabeus. Sung by a Chorus of Youths in *Joshua*, it begins, "See the conquering hero comes! Sound the trumpet, beat the drums" (Act III, scene 2). It was also used in later versions of Nathaniel Lee's (1653–1692) tragedy, *The Rival Queens* (1677), and is quoted in Joyce's *Ulysses* in reference to Molly's seducer, Blazes Boylan (1961 Random House edition, p. 264). It is apt that the "conquering hero" should be above Quilty's picture, since that motto predicts his victory. As for the c. 1949 magazine ad which is said to resemble H.H., his description of it is quite accurate. The ad is for Viyella robes, and is of some interest. It's reproduced in color in David Ogilvy, *Ogilvy on Advertising* (1983), p. 86. See the following page. For Joyce, see 4/11.

69/3 *A distinguished playwright . . . Drome:* Quilty. A *dromedary* is a one-humped camel, and H.H. is both playing with the familiar brand name and correcting the manufacturer's error: the beast on the cigarette wrapper is not a camel, strictly speaking. H.H.'s aside, "The resemblance was slight," refers to 43/8, where he is said to resemble Quilty. Note, too, that "Lo's chaste bed" is under Quilty. See 31/9 for a summary of Quilty allusions.

CHAPTER 17

70/1 *pavor nocturnus:* Latin; night panic. Quilty lives in "Pavor Manor" (p. 293).

70/2 *peine forte et dure:* French; strong and hard torture.

70/3 *Dostoevskian grin:* Fyodor Dostoevsky (1821–1881), the famous Russian novelist, was long one of Nabokov's primary targets. In the *Playboy* interview he said, "Non-Russian readers do not realize two things; that not all Russians love Dostoevsky as much as Americans do, and that most of those Russians who do, venerate him as a mystic and not as an artist. He was a prophet, a claptrap journalist and a slapdash comedian. I admit that some of his scenes, some of his tremendous, farcical rows are extraordinarily amusing. But his sensitive murderers and soulful prostitutes are not to be endured for one moment—by this reader anyway." "Heart-to-heart talks, confessions in the Dostoevskian manner are also not in my line," he writes in *Speak, Memory* (p. 286). But H.H. is the ultimate in "sensitive murderers," and by casting his tale as a "confession," Nabokov lets Dostoevsky lay down the rules and then beats "old Dusty" at his own game. See 40/6 for remarks on another convention allied with the confession—the literary diary.

Viyella robe by State o'Maine; breakfast-set by Wedgwood.

See The Conquering Hero Comes—in a Viyella® Robe!

Sound the trumpets, beat the drums, see the conquering hero comes—dressed to the nines in a Viyella robe, and armed with Sunday breakfast for his deserving bride. The superb thing about a Viyella bathrobe is that you can *wash* it. If it shrinks, we replace. Lamby-soft Viyella (rhymes with hi-fella) wears for *years*. A customer who bought a Viyella shirt eleven years ago tells us that he has had it washed and cleaned more than sixty times. "The colors are just as bright and distinct as when it was new . . . the only casualty throughout the years has been the loss of two buttons." Viyella robes (like the one our hero is wearing) come in authentic tartans, tattersalls, checks, stripes and plain colors. They weigh only 21 ounces and can be packed in your brief case next time you travel. $28.50 at fine stores everywhere. For the name of your nearest retailer write William Hollins & Company, Inc., 347 Madison Avenue, New York 17, New York. MU 4-7330.

70/4 *Well-read Humbert:* the lines he quotes are from Canto III, stanza 116 of *Childe Harold's Pilgrimage* (1812, 1816, 1818), by George Gordon, Lord Byron (1788–1824), English poet. These lines occur almost at the end of the Canto (lines 1080–1081), and are addressed to Ada, Harold's absent daughter. Byron was in Italy at this time, estranged from the wife he had married for the sake of tranquility and respectability—a gesture H.H. would no doubt appreciate, as he would sympathize with the difficulties occasioned by the amorous poet's incestuous relationship with his half sister. Dr. Byron is the Haze family physician, and he too has a daughter (see 95/2). But, as an unwitting accomplice to a seduction, he belies his name, for the sleeping pills he dispenses prove ineffective at The Enchanted Hunters hotel (see p. 128). Byron's works and Byron's Augusta Ada, a gifted girl in her own right, resonate in Nabokov's longest novel, *Ada,* as does the "Byronic" (and Chateaubriandesque) theme of incest; Ada Veen even has a bit part in a film called *Don Juan's Last Fling.* Nabokov's deep knowledge of Byron is made evident throughout his *Eugene Onegin* Commentary (see the "Byron" entry in the Index, Vol. IV).

70/5 *Charlotte:* the name of Werther's tragic love in *The Sorrows of Young Werther* (1774), by Johann Wolfgang von Goethe (1749–1832). The choice of a name is clearly ironic, since Goethe's Charlotte marries another. Weepy Werther, an artist of sorts, remains hopelessly in love with her and eventually takes his own life. "A faded charm still clings about this novel, which artistically is greatly inferior to Chateaubriand's *René* and even to Constant's *Adolphe,*" writes Nabokov in his *Eugene Onegin* Commentary (Vol. II, p. 345). See 76/1. Goethe is also invoked on 240/2. For Chateaubriand, see 145/4.

70/6 *quel mot:* French; what a word.

71/1 *incubus:* an evil spirit or demon, originally in personified representations of the nightmare, supposed to descend upon persons in their sleep, and especially to seek sexual intercourse with women. In the Middle Ages their existence was recognized by ecclesiastical and civil law. The epithet "Humbert the Cubus" is of course his own variant. For more on enchantments, see 16/6.

71/2 *mauvemail:* H.H.'s coinage; mauve is pale pinkish purple.

72/1 *"The orange . . . grave":* a parody of a "poetic" quotation.

72/2 *raree-show:* a show carried about in a box; a peep show.

72/3 *Une petite attention:* a nice thought (a favor).

73/1 *Incarnadine:* flesh-colored or bright pink. This word appears in a stanza from *The Rubáiyát;* see 262/8.

73/2 *eructations:* violent belches.

73/3 *by Pan!:* H.H.'s "by God!" In Greek mythology, a god of forests, flocks, and shepherds, having the horns and hoofs of a goat.

CHAPTER 18

74/1 *soi-disant:* French; so-called (also used on p. 147).

75/1 *a Turk:* Charlotte is not quite sure of H.H.'s "racial purity." Neither is Jean Farlow, who intercepts an anti-Semitic remark (p. 79), nor The Enchanted Hunters' management (p. 118). See 258/2 and 261/4.

75/2 *contretemps:* French; an embarrassing or awkward occurrence.

75/3 *rattles:* the sound-producing organs on a rattlesnake's tail.

75/4 *rubrique:* a newspaper section.

75/5 *"Edgar"* . . . *"writer and explorer":* Edgar A. Poe, whose *Narrative of A. Gordon Pym* was the product of an alleged polar expedition (see 31/5). For the Poe allusions, see 9/2.

75/6 *Peacock, Rainbow:* Thomas Love Peacock (1785–1866), English poet and novelist, whose name recalls the "Rainbow," or Arthur Rimbaud (1854–1891), French poet. After abandoning literature at the age of eighteen, Rimbaud traveled widely. In 1888 in Abyssinia, where he sold guns, the English called the ex-poet "trader Rainbow," as Nabokov notes in his *Eugene Onegin* Commentary (Vol. III, p. 412). For further allusions, see 163/6, 172/1, 250/7, and 278/1.

76/1 *Lottelita, Lolitchen:* H.H. toys with "Lotte," a diminutive of "Charlotte," and discerns *Lolita* in *Lotte* ("Lottelita"), which is also a phonetic transcription of American idiom and diction *(Lot of [Lo]lita). Lolitchen* is formed with the German diminutive ending -*chen.* H.H. no doubt recalls that Goethe's *Werther* calls his Charlotte "Lotte" and "Lottchen." See 70/5.

77/1 *ecru and ocher: ecru* is a grayish yellow that is greener and paler than chamois or old ivory. *Ocher* is a dark yellow color derived from or resembling ocher, a hydrated iron oxide.

78/1 *4640 Roosevelt Blvd . . . mattress:* the firm is Sears Roebuck Co., and the mattress in question will arrive at a grotesquely inappropriate moment on p. 105.

78/2 *the jovial dentist:* Clare Quilty's Uncle Ivor. Much later H.H. will learn from Lolita herself that Quilty met her through this association. On p. 272, H.H. recapitulates their confrontation: "Well, did I know that he was practically an old friend? That he had visited with his uncle in Ramsdale?—oh, years ago—and spoken at Mother's club, and had tugged and pulled her, Dolly . . . onto his lap . . ." An earlier draft of the novel contained Quilty's appearance before the ladies. See 31/9 for a summary of his appearances.

78/3 *such dainty ladies as Mrs. Glave:* from the unusual verb, "glaver;" "to palaver;" "to flatter; wheedle."

78/4 *arrière-pensée:* French; hidden thoughts, ulterior motives.

79/1 *interrupted Jean:* John is about to say "Jews," and Jean, suspecting that H.H. may be Jewish, tactfully interrupts. See 261/4.

CHAPTER 19

81/1 *A Guide to . . . Development:* the titles H.H. mentions are by turns invented (*Who's Who in the Limelight* [p. 31]; *Clowns and Columbines* [242/1]), actual (the other titles on p. 242; *Brute Force* [262/4]), or close approximations of existing works, as in this instance. A plethora of actual titles circle about this "fool's book" (e.g., *Guide to Child Development through the Beginning School Years* [1946]), and Nabokov seems to have created a central, summary title (though the exact title may yet exist). See 174/4.

CHAPTER 20

81/2 *Hourglass Lake . . . spelled:* earlier it was "Our Glass Lake" (see 43/3 and 45/2). H.H. doesn't correct "errors" in his "unrevised" draft. Whether right or wrong, both the names are significant, underscoring H.H.'s solipsism (the circumscribing mirror of "our glass") and obsession with time ("hourglass").

83/1 *the gesture:* it inspires the mock quotation, "look, Lord . . ." as if to demonstrate one's chains.

83/2 *duenna of my darling:* the echo of "Annabel Lee" is linked with *duenna*, "The chief lady in waiting on the queen of Spain" (Webster's 2nd).

83/3 *c'est moi qui décide:* French; it is I who decide.

86/1 *acrosonic:* a noise reaching to or past the sonic barrier. It would seem to be H.H.'s own word.

87/1 *shooting her lover . . . making him say "akh!":* a preview of Quilty's death. See 45/4 and 303/1. He may indeed have been "her lover," however fleetingly; "I knew your dear wife slightly," Quilty later admits to H.H. (p. 302).

87/2 *at first wince:* H.H.'s variant of "at first glance."

88/1 *Krestovski:* to give them one kind of scare or another; see 216/1.

89/1 *Cavall and Melampus:* the Farlows' dogs. "Cavall" comes from *cavallo* (a horse), and "Melampus" from the seer in Greek mythology who understood the tongue of dogs and introduced the worship of Dionysus. More specifically, noted Nabokov, the dogs are named after those of a famous person, though he was not certain who owned them. He thought it was Lord Byron, who had many bizarrely named dogs. In any event, these allusions are hardly within the cultural reach of the Farlows.

89/2 *Waterproof:* the wristwatch. See 272/1, where H.H. offers this interlude as a central clue to Quilty's identity.

89/3 *old Ivor . . . his nephew:* Clare Quilty. For a summary of allusions to Quilty, see 31/9.

CHAPTER 21

89/4 *"Ce qui . . . comme ça":* French; "What drives me crazy is the fact that I do not know what you are thinking about when you are like this."

90/1 *the ultimate sunburst:* in *Who's Who in the Limelight,* "Roland Pym" is said to have "Made debut in *Sunburst*" (see 31/7).

90/2 *Beaver Eaters:* a portmanteau of "Beefeaters" (the yeomen of the British royal guard) and their beaver hats. Some have seen this as an obvious obscene joke, but Nabokov did not intend one. "Moronic and oxymoronic," he said, remembering the guard's old reputation for male prostitution ("beaver" is of the female gender, innocent reader).

Chapter 22

93/1 *Euphemia:* from the Greek *euphēmos;* auspicious, sounding good.

94/1 *olisbos:* the leather phallos worn by participants in the Greek Dionysia.

94/2 *child of Dolly's age:* "Byron, Marguerite" (see p. 51). For Dr. Byron's namesake, see 70/4.

97/1 *my pin:* a coinage; H.H.'s favorite drink, a mixture of pineapple juice and gin (p. 72). He also refers to this "pin" on pp. 101 and 193.

Chapter 23

102/1 *savoir vivre:* French; good manners, good breeding.

103/1 *alembic:* anything used to distill or refine.

103/2 *Adieu, Marlene:* Dietrich; see 9/4.

Chapter 24

104/1 *simian:* monkey- or apelike. Nabokov is toying with the *Doppelgänger* convention of an evil self; H.H. should not be "simian" because *Quilty* is the bad one.

Chapter 25

105/1 *Eh bien, pas du tout!:* French; Well, not at all!

105/2 *Climax:* however broad the joke may be, there happen to be seven towns in the United States by this name (as well as a Lolita, Texas). Demon Veen, the father of *Ada's* hero, retreats to his "aunt's ranch near Lolita, Texas" (p. 14), a town which doubtless boasts no bookstore or library.

106/1 *stylized blood:* everything red is "stylized."

106/2 *argent: archaic;* silver, silvery, shining—as in French.

107/1 *Vee . . . and Bea:* see 43/5 and 19/9. For a summary of Poe allusions, see 9/2.

107/2 *glans:* anatomical word; the conical vascular body which forms the extremity of the penis.

107/3 *oolala black:* pseudo-French epithet for "sexy" black frills.

107/4 *anthropometric entry:* anthropometry is the science of measuring the human body and its parts.

108/1 *glaucous:* a pale yellowish-green hue.

108/2 *The Enchanted Hunters:* note the plural (H.H., Quilty, and, in another sense, the author). For "enchantment," see 45/3. Quilty names his play after the hotel (pp. 200–202) and adapts an anagram of it for one of his many pseudonyms (251/13); the married Lolita ends up living on "Hunter Road" (p. 268).

Chapter 26

109/1 *Heart, head—everything:* "Is 'mask' the keyword?" H.H. asked on p. 53 (see 4/4). As his narrative approaches the first conjugal night with Lolita, H.H. is overcome by anguish, and in the bare six lines of Chapter Twenty-six—the shortest "chapter" in the book—he loses control, and for a moment the mask drops. Not until the very end of the passage does the voice again sound like our Hum the Hummer, when the desperation of "Heart, head—everything" suddenly gives way to the resiliently comic command to the printer. In that one instant H.H.'s masking takes place before the reader, who gets a fleeting look into those "two hypnotic eyes" (to quote John Ray [p. 3]) and sees the pain in them. *Lolita* is so deeply moving a novel because of our sharp awareness of the great tension sustained between H.H.'s mute despair and his compensatory jollity. "Crime and Pun" is one of the titles the murderous narrator of *Despair* considers for his manuscript, and it would serve H.H. just as well, for language is as much a defense to him as chess is to Grandmaster Luzhin. But even when H.H. lets the mask slip, one glimpses only his desperation, not the "real" H.H. or the manipulative author. As Nabokov says in Chapter Five of *Gogol,* analogously discussing Akaky Akakyevich and the "holes" and "gaps" in the narrative texture of *The Overcoat:* "We did not expect that, amid the whirling masks, one mask would turn out to be a real face, or *at least the place where that face ought to be*" [italics mine—A.A.]. If the printer had obeyed H.H.'s request to fill the page with Lo's name, we'd have a twentieth-century equivalent of a totally self-reflexive blank or patterned page in Sterne's *Tristram Shandy* (1767).

CHAPTER 27

110/1 *redheaded . . . lad:* Charlie Holmes turns out to be Lolita's first lover (p. 137).

110/2 *moth or butterfly:* a reminder that H.H. is no entomologist. See 6/1. Nabokov stressed "Humbert's complete incapacity to differentiate between Rhopalocera and Heterocera."

111/1 *lentigo:* a freckly skin pigmentation.

111/2 *aux yeux battus:* French; with circles round one's eyes.

111/3 *plumbaceous umbrae:* Latin; leaden shadows.

111/4 *mägdlein:* German; little girl.

112/1 *Lepingville . . . nineteenth century:* as to the "identity" of this poet, Nabokov responded, "That poet was evidently Leping who used to go lepping (i.e., lepidoptera hunting) but that's about all anybody knows about him." See 141/1.

113/1 *backfisch:* German; an immature, adolescent girl; a teenager.

113/2 *simulacrum:* a sham; an unreal semblance.

113/3 *psychotherapist . . . rapist:* H.H. calls our attention to the rapist in the therapist. Nabokov similarly employs semantic constituents in *Despair*, when he poses a sensible question: "What is this jest in majesty? This ass in passion?" (p. 46).

113/4 *what shadow . . . after?:* in traditional *Doppelgänger* fiction the reprehensible self is often imagined as a shadow, as in Hans Christian Andersen's "The Shadow." H.H. constantly toys with the convention.

114/1 *Ensuite?:* French; then?

114/2 *shadowgraphs:* amateur X-ray pictures. The girls made pictures of each other's bones; not invented, but actual "educational" recreation at "progressive" camps c. 1950.

115/1 *"C'est bien tout?":* "Is that all?" The answer *"C'est"* ("It is") is incorrect French, a direct translation from English syntax.

116/1 *carbuncles:* medical; "a painful local inflammation of the subcutaneous tissue, larger and more serious than a boil; a pimple or red spot, due to intemperance." Originally, a jewel such as a ruby. H.H. is of course referring to the truck's parking lights.

117/1 *magic . . . rubious:* a corrected misprint ("rubous" in the 1958 edition). The rubylike convertible is Quilty's, a dark red shining in the rain and the night. His appearances are summarized in 31/9.

117/2 *frock-fold . . . Browning:* not a quotation, but an allusion to *Pippa Passes* (1841), a verse drama by Robert Browning, the English poet (1812–1889):

> On every side occurred suggestive germs
> Of that—the tree, the flower—or take the fruit—
> Some rosy shape, continuing the peach,
> Curved beewise o'er its bough; as rosy limbs,
> Depending, nestled in the leaves; and just
> From a cleft rose-peach the whole Dryad sprang. [lines 87–92]

A *Dryad* is a wood nymph (see 121/2). For nymph, see 16/6. For Browning, see 207/2, 242/1, and 245/1.

117/3 *cocker spaniel:* the old lady's dog (p. 118). See 246/1 and 261/4.

117/4 *porcine:* swinelike; the pig image is introduced in the first sentence of the previous paragraph.

118/1 *not Humberg:* H.H. corrects the desk clerk, who has coldly bestowed on him a Jewish-sounding name. The hotel is euphemistically restrictive (see 261/4). "Professor Hamburg" finds them "full up" (p. 261).

118/2 *Dr. Edgar H. Humbert and daughter:* H.H.'s *nom de registration* is in deference to Edgar A. Poe and *his* child bride (see 43/5). H.H. also uses the "Edgar" elsewhere (see 75/5 and 189/3). For the Poe allusions, see 9/2.

118/3 *A key (342!):* although H.H. is trying not to lose control of the language, as he did on p. 109, he (or *someone else*) is here managing to tell how H.H. was served by Mr. Swine, who is assisted by Mr. Potts, who can't find any cots, because Swine has dispatched them to the Swoons (see 212/2). A "key" to the meaning of this extraordinary verbal control is immediately provided by another "coincidence": the room number is the same as the Haze house number. H.H. will shortly offer a figurative key by placing the number within quotation marks, which is of course the only proper way to treat a fiction (p. 123). "McFate" produces "342" once more; see 248/2. Such coincidences serve a two-fold purpose: they at once point to the authorial consciousness that has plotted them, and can also be imagined as coordinates situated in time and space, marking the labyrinth from which a character cannot escape.

119/1 *Parody of a hotel corridor . . . and death: parody* to H.H. because nothing seems "real" to him on this most crucial of nights; *parody* to Nabokov because the world within a work of art *is* "unreal" (see Introduction). But to repeat Marianne Moore's well-known line, poetry is "imaginary gardens with real toads in them," and Nabokov's novel is a parody of death with real suffering in it—H.H.'s and Lolita's.

119/2 *a mirror:* the room is a little prison of mirrors, a metaphor for his solipsism and circumscribing obsession. " 'So that's the dead end' (the mirror you break your nose against)," an overwrought H.H. tells Lolita after catching her in a lie (p. 225). See 51/2 and 294/2. "In our earthly house, windows are replaced by mirrors," writes Nabokov in *The Gift* (p. 322). His characters continually confront mirrors where they had hoped to find windows, and the attempt to transcend solipsism is one of Nabokov's major themes. As a literal image and overriding metaphor, the mirror is central to the form and content of Nabokov's novels; in *Ada*, it describes the universe, for Antiterra's sibling planet Terra is imagined as a "distortive glass of our distorted glebe" (p. 18). If one perceives *Pale Fire* spatially, with John Shade's poem on the "left" and Charles Kinbote's Commentary on the "right," the poem is seen as an object to be perceived, and the Commentary becomes the world seen through the distorting prism of a mind—a monstrous concave mirror held up to an objective "reality." The narrator of *Despair* loathes mirrors, avoids them, and comments on those "monsters of mirrors," the "crooked ones," in which a man is stripped, squashed, or "pulled out like dough and then torn in two" (p. 21). Nabokov has placed these crooked reflectors everywhere in his fiction: Doubles and mock-Doubles, parodies and self-parodies (literature trapped in a prison of amusement-park mirrors), works within works, worlds refracting worlds, and words distorting words—that is, translations (art's "crazy-mirror," said Nabokov) and language games (see 34/2). *Pale Fire*'s invented language is "the tongue of the mirror," and the portmantoid pun is the principal mirror-language of *Lolita.* See 3/3.

119/3 *Enfin seuls:* French for "alone at last," the trite phrase of the honeymooner.

120/1 *lentor: archaic;* slowness.

120/2 *spoonerette:* a *spoonerism* is the accidental transposition of sounds in two or more words ("wight ray"). By acknowledging his spoonerism, H.H. reminds us what a wordsmith he is (in *Pale Fire* John Shade teaches at Wordsmith University). The affectionate suffix -*ette* may recall *majorette,* as well as the slang meaning of *spooner,* one who "necks" (or, as one dictionary archly puts it, "act[s] with silly and demonstrative fondness"). The suffix also parodies a recognizable and overused *préciosité* of Ronsard's, who in fact employed "*nymphette*" in one of his poems. See "*vermeillette*" (47/2) and Quilty's "barroomette" (p. 296).

120/3 *kitzelans:* lusting; from the German *kitzel,* "inordinate desire," and *kitzler,* "clitoris." See 250/11.

120/4 *seva ascendes . . . quidquam:* the language of Horace, Catullus, et al. (see 45/1) is appropriate to this modern, if hysterical, elegiast, whose "Latin" here turns out to be a curious mishmash of Latin, English, French, German, and Italian: "The sap ascendeth, pulsates, burning [*brulans,* from the French *brûler,* "to burn"], itching, most insane, elevator clattering, pausing, clattering, people in the corridor. No one but death would take this one [Lolita] away from me! Slender little girl, I thought most fondly, observing nothing at all." At moments of extreme crisis, H.H. croaks incomprehensibly, losing more than his expropriated English; for his attempts "to fix once for all the perilous magic of nymphets" (p. 134) almost resist language altogether, carrying him close to the edge of non-language and a figurative silence. Thus H.H. significantly announces this scene as a "Parody of silence" (p. 119), and, far from being nonsensical, the ensuing "Latin" is a parodic stream-of-consciousness affording a brief critical comment on a technique Nabokov found unsatisfactory, even in the novels of Joyce, whom he revered ("poor Stream of Consciousness, *marée noire* by now," writes Nabokov toward the end of a similar parody in *Ada* [p. 300]). "We think not in words but in shadows of words," Nabokov said. "James Joyce's mistake in those otherwise marvelous mental soliloquies of his consists in that he gives too much verbal body to thoughts" (*Playboy* interview). To Nabokov, the unconnected impressions and associations that impinge on the mind were irrational until they were consciously ordered and to order them in art is to fulfill virtually a moral obligation, for without rational language man has "grown a very / landfish, languageless, / a monster," as Thersites says of Ajax in Shakespeare's *Troilus and Cressida.* Even the imprisoned Cincinnatus, under sentence of death, is "already thinking of how to set up an alphabet" which might humanize the dystopian world of *Invitation to a Beheading* (p. 139). See the second half of 9/2.

121/1 *nota bene:* Latin; mark well. The 1958 edition incorrectly ran the two words together.

121/2 *dryads and trees:* see 117/2.

121/3 *writer fellow . . . ad:* Clare Quilty (see 69/2). "Dromes" is a corrected misprint ("Droms" in the 1958 edition). For allusions to Quilty, see 31/9.

121/4 *Femina:* Latin; woman.

122/1 *Purpills:* a contraction of "Papa's Purple Pills" from the previous paragraph.

CHAPTER 28

123/1 *le grand moment:* French; the great moment.

123/2 *hot hairy fist:* Quilty also has conspicuously hairy hands (p. 295).

123/3 *sicher ist sicher:* German; sure is sure.

123/4 *my uncle Gustave:* Gustave Trapp, sometimes a "cousin," whom H.H. mistakes for Quilty (see p. 139). A cousin of one's mother is both one's cousin and, in a sense, uncle.

124/1 *Jean-Jacques Humbert:* after Jean-Jacques Rousseau (1712–1778), Swiss-born French philosopher and author of the famous *Confessions.*

125/1 *one's dungeon . . . some rival devil:* Quilty, H.H.'s "rival devil," is staying at The Enchanted Hunters, and appears on the next page. The lust figuratively emanating from H.H.'s "dungeon" is objectified much later: "I had been keeping Clare Quilty's face masked in my dark dungeon" (see 290/2).

125/2 *comme on dit:* French; as they say.

125/3 *King Sigmund:* Sigmund Freud (1856–1939), founder of psychoanalysis. See 5/6 and 35/1.

126/1 *antiphony:* a musical response; a musical piece alternately sung by a choir divided into two parts.

126/2 *powdered bugs:* Nabokov said, "The 'powdered bugs' wheeling around the lamps are noctuids and other moths which look floury on the wing (hence 'millers,' which, however, may also come from the verb), as they mill in the electric light against the damp night's blackground. 'Bugs' is an Americanism for *any* insect. In England, it means generally bedbugs." For entomological allusions, see 6/1.

126/3 *somebody sitting . . . porch:* Quilty. Their verbal sparring on p. 127 telescopes their pursuit of one another and prefigures the physical struggle of pp. 293–305. The allusions to Quilty are summarized in 31/9.

127/1 *a rose, as the Persians say:* the fatidic flower and an allusion to *The Rubáiyát* (see 262/8).

127/2 *a blinding flash . . . can be deemed immortal:* for the photograph in question, see 263/1. H.H. was *not* immortalized.

CHAPTER 29

128/1 *entre nous soit dit:* French; just between you and me.

129/1 *grand Dieu:* French; good God!

129/2 *La Petite . . . Ridicule: The Sleeping Maiden or the Ridiculous Lover.* There is no picture by this name. The mock-title and subject matter parody eighteenth-century genre engravings.

130/1 *someone . . . beyond our bathroom:* Clare Quilty (see 248/4). Quilty also creates a "waterfall" on 294/4. For a summary of his appearances, see 31/9.

131/1 *A breeze from wonderland:* there are several references to *Alice in Wonderland* (1865) by Lewis Carroll, the pseudonym of Charles L. Dodgson (1832–1898), English writer, mathematician, and nympholept (see 264/1). "I always call him Lewis Carroll Carroll," said Nabokov, "because he was the first Humbert Humbert." Nabokov translated *Alice* into Russian (Berlin, 1923). "I got five dollars (quite a sum during the inflation in Germany)," he recalls (*Speak, Memory,* p. 283). In *The Real Life of Sebastian Knight,* a character speaks "in the elenctic tones of Lewis Carroll's caterpillar" (p. 123), while in *Ada,* "Ada in Wonderland" (p. 129), "Ada's adventures in Adaland" (p. 568), and the "titles" *Palace in Wonderland* (p. 53) and *Alice in the Camera Obscura* (p. 547) are variously invoked (the latter a play on the original title of *Laughter in the Dark*). "In common with many other English children (I was an English child) I have been always very fond of Carroll," he said in the *Wisconsin Studies* interview. "No, I do not think his invented language shares any roots with mine [in *Bend Sinister* and *Pale Fire*]. He has a pathetic affinity with H.H. but some odd scruple prevented me from alluding in *Lolita* to his wretched perversion and to those ambiguous photographs he took in dim rooms. He got away with it, as so many other Victorians got away with pederasty and nympholepsy. His were sad scrawny little nymphets, bedraggled and half-undressed, or rather semi-undraped, as if participating in some dusty and dreadful charade." But it might seem as though Nabokov *did* allude to Carroll in *Lolita*, through what might be called "the photography theme": H.H. cherishes his worn old photograph of Annabel, has in a sense been living with this "still," tries to make Lolita conform to it, and often laments his failure to capture her on film. Quilty's hobby is announced as "photography," and the unspeakable films he produces at the Duk Duk Ranch would seem to answer Carroll's wildest needs. Asked about this, Nabokov replied, "I did not consciously think of Carroll's hobby when I referred to the use of photography in *Lolita.* "

"I have only words to play with," moans H.H. (p. 32), and several readers have been tempted to call the ensuing wordplay "Joycean" — loosely enough, since "Carrollian" might do almost as well, given Nabokov's fondness for auditory wordplay and portmanteau words, and the fact that the latter usage was coined by Carroll. The family line is nicely established on Sebastian Knight's neatest book shelf, where *Alice in Wonderland* and *Ulysses* stand side by side, along with works by some of Nabokov's other favorite writers (Stevenson, Chekhov, Flaubert, Proust, Wells, and Shakespeare, who encloses the shelf at either end with *Hamlet* and *King Lear* [p. 41]). For Shakespeare, see 284/4.

132/1 *metamorphosing:* see 16/6.

CHAPTER 30

134/1 *emeritus read to by a boy:* an echo of the opening of Eliot's "Gerontion": "Here I am, an old man in a dry month,/Being read to by a boy . . ." See 16/3.

134/2 *shoat:* a young pig; a hog.

134/3 *callypygean slave . . . onyx:* or *callipygian;* "having shapely buttocks." *Onyx* is a variety of agate, a semiprecious stone. H.H. is no doubt here referring to *onyx marble* (alabaster). See 137/1.

134/4 *gonadal glow:* a gonad is a sexual gland; an ovary or testis. H.H. is evoking the neon tubing on the nether region of a 1947 Wurlitzer jukebox, an expensive "collectible" in 1991.

134/5 *canoeing, Coranting:* the latter is the participle of H.H.'s variant of *courant,* "a dance of Italian origin marked by quick running steps," and also dialectal English for "romping" and "carousing." H.H. is still in Volume *C* of the *Girl's Encyclopedia* (see p. 92).

CHAPTER 31

135/1 *Roman law . . . girl may marry at twelve:* the legal opinions offered in this paragraph move from fact to fiction (see 19/1). The first is true, though the legal question and its history are far more complex than H.H. would suggest. See Corbett, *The Roman Law of Marriage* (1930), pp. 51–52.

135/2 *adopted by the Church:* also true; see Bouscaren and Ellis, *Canon Law: A Text and Commentary* (1957), p. 513.

135/3 *still preserved . . . in some of the United States:* only in ten states (Colorado, Florida, Maine, Maryland, Massachusetts, Tennessee, Virginia, Idaho, Kansas, and Louisiana). See Vernier, *American Family Laws* (1931), pp. 115–117.

135/4 *fifteen is lawful everywhere:* not in Alaska, Arizona, California, Connecticut, Delaware, Illinois, Indiana, Michigan, Minnesota, Montana, Nebraska, Nevada, New Mexico, Ohio, Pennsylvania, West Virginia, or Wyoming, where the age is sixteen, or in New Hampshire or New Jersey, where it is eighteen. But there are exceptions granted if the girl is pregnant or if she is willing, over twelve, and the marriage has been consummated. Since none of these (save the consummation) apply to Lolita, it seems that H.H.'s confident legal scholarship has given way to dissembling. See Vernier, *ibid.,* pp. 116–118. Of course these laws pertain to H.H.'s day, and may have changed.

CHAPTER 32

135/5 *die Kleine:* German; the little one.

135/6 *moue:* grimace, facial contraction.

136/1 *sapphic diversions:* reference to the reputed lesbianism of the group associated with Sappho, Greek lyric poetess of Lesbos (c. 600 B.C.).

136/2 *Miranda twins:* in Lolita's class list, p. 52 (see 51/2).

137/1 *boat to Onyx or Eryx:* there are no such lakes. *Onyx* is often used for cameos, while *Eryx* refers to the ancient cult of Aphrodite (Venus) of Eryx, an Elymian settlement on a mountain above Drepana in western Sicily, built below their temple of Aphrodite (the goddess of love and beauty, to whom Lolita is often compared; "Venus came and went," says H.H. on p. 168; and the magazine picture of a surrealistic "plaster replica of the Venus di Milo, half-buried in sand" metaphorically projects Lolita's life with him [p. 58]). See 250/11, where scholarly H.H. obliquely informs the reader that the priestesses at the Temple of Eryx were prostitutes.

138/1 *I would not talk to strangers:* see 32/1 and 309/1, where the phrase echoes. The advice still holds.

138/2 *saturnalia:* the festival of Saturn in ancient Rome, celebrated with feasting and revelry; a licentious spectacle.

138/3 *A fellow of my age:* Quilty (see 31/9); the "blood-red armchair" should alert the reader. H.H. stresses their similar ages; see 218/1.

138/4 *Schwab's drugstore:* an author's error has been corrected (*a* instead of *o* in the 1958 edition). The Schwab's chain drugstores in Hollywood (now defunct) were a meeting place for film people and young aspirants. In the thirties and forties several subsequent stars were discovered there, some—according to folklore—while eating sundaes or drinking sodas.

139/1 *a fairytale vampire:* for the fairy-tale theme, see 31/3.

139/2 *le découvert:* French; the nude.

139/3 *immortal daemon . . . child:* see 16/6.

139/4 *Aunt Clare's place:* by mentioning Quilty's first name, H.H., a sly teaser, throws the reader something more than a hint. See 31/9 for a summary of Quilty allusions.

139/5 *hypothetical hospital:* "hypothetical" is the best word to use, since its name would be whatever H.H. chose to make it.

CHAPTER 33

141/1 *gay . . . Lepingville:* see 112/1. H.H.'s "lepping" is over; the town's name and gaiety mark the fact that, as Part One ends, H.H. secures his capture.

142/1 *swooners:* H.H.'s variant of the noun, its meaning expanded to include some garment that evokes a swoon. Teen-swooning, inspired by Frank Sinatra's crooning, was much in the news in the forties.

PART TWO
CHAPTER 1

145/1 *pharisaic:* self-righteous and censorious; resembling the Pharisees, a sect of the ancient Jews famed for its strict observance of ceremonies, rites, and traditions.

145/2 *earwitness:* a dictionary word (used as early as 1594) but amusing because no one ever says it.

145/3 *nous connûmes:* Flaubert uses the verb *connaître* in the literary tense *passé simple* when in *Madame Bovary* (1857) he is describing her unhappy experiments with all kinds of diversions, especially her lovers and their activities together. For other allusions, see 47/1, 202/2, and 265/2. Nabokov intends no allusion to Frédéric Moreau's travels in *L'Education sentimentale* (1869); "Not the education of the senses," he said, "a poor novel which I only vaguely remember." *Bovary* is funned in *King, Queen, Knave* and "Floeberg" burlesqued briefly in *Ada* (p. 128). Although Kinbote synchronizes Gradus's travels through space and time and the stages of Shade's composition of the poem *Pale Fire,* he nevertheless complains when Shade similarly alternates two themes: "the synchronization device has been already worked to death by Flaubert and Joyce" (p. 196).

145/4 *Chateaubriandesque trees:* the first European writers and painters who visited America were impressed by its great trees, and H.H. no doubt drew the image from *Atala* (1801), a separately published episode from *Le Génie du christianisme* (1802) by François-René de Chateaubriand (1768–1848), whose arrival in America is mentioned in *Pale Fire* (p. 247). In the *Eugene Onegin* Commentary, Nabokov calls *René*, another episode from *Le Génie*, "a work of genius by the greatest French writer of his time" (Vol. III, p. 98). See 70/5. Though unlabeled, there are many "Chateaubriandesque trees" in *Ada*'s Ardis Park, and by design, for Chateaubriand is to *Ada* what Poe and Mérimée are to *Lolita*. Van Veen reads Ada's copy of *Atala* (p. 89), and *René*, with its "subtle perfume of incest" (*Onegin* Commentary, Vol. III, p. 100), is alluded to directly (pp. 131 and 133). Mlle. Larivière, the Veens' grotesque governess, writes a novel and film scenario whose hero is named "René" (see pp. 198–199, 217, 249, and 424), and since "incest" and "insect" are anagrammatically linked (p. 85), a mosquito is named after Chateaubriand— Charles Chateaubriand, that is, "not related to the great poet and memoirist" (p. 106). For further discussion of Chateaubriand and *Ada*, see my article, "*Ada* Described," *TriQuarterly*, No. 17 (Winter 1970). For another Chateaubriand allusion in *Lolita*, see 210/1.

146/1 *non-Laodicean:* in Revelation 3:14–16, the Laodicean church is characterized as "lukewarm, and neither hot nor cold" in matters of religion.

146/2 *madamic:* H.H.'s coinage, referring to the madam, or proprietress, of a brothel.

146/3 *instars:* an insect or other anthropod in one of the forms assumed between molts. The pupa of a butterfly is an instar.

147/1 *do you remember, Miranda:* an echo of the opening lines and refrain of "Tarantella" (1923), a poem by Hilaire Belloc (1870–1953); "Do you remember an Inn, / Miranda? / Do you remember an Inn?" See p. 185.

148/1 *the nasal voices:* because "this book is being read, I assume, in the first years of 2000 A.D." (as H.H. says [p. 299]), readers not having had the benefit of a 1947–1952 adolescence may not be able to complete the names of the "invisibles" who serenaded her. "Rex" is a ringer, and "Sammy" refers to non-singer Sammy Kaye (1910–1987), whose very popular, very mediocre dance band featured a succession of lachrymose vocalists on hits such as 1947's "I'm Laughing on the Outside (But Crying on the Inside)," a title that splendidly summarizes H.H.'s rhetorical mask. The other singers are Jo Stafford (date of birth a secret), Edwin Jack "Eddie" Fisher (1928–), Tony Bennett (born Anthony Benedetto: 1926–), Peggy Lee (born Norma Egstrom: 1920–), Guy Mitchell (1925–), and Patti Page (born Clara Ann Fowler: 1927–), whose most successful recording, "The Tennessee Waltz" (1950), is commemorated in *Ada* with the mention of "a progressive poet in residence at Tennessee Waltz College" (p. 134). As Joyce says in *Finnegans Wake*, "Wipe your glosses with what you know." But this information isn't campy if you don't know who these "invisibles" are, and that their sentimental songs of love and romance were very corny, and backed by ludicrously fulsome string arrangements. Because Nabokov often uses a kind of shorthand to eviscerate Lo's popular culture, younger readers now need to be prepped; they actually believe that early fifties' pop music was "soft" rock-and-roll —as on the TV show *Happy Days*.

Study guide: *Your Hit Parade,* a series of record collections begun in 1988 by Time-Life Music, which will eventually cover every year of the forties and fifties. The disc for 1951 includes Patti Page's "Detour," Guy Mitchell's "My Heart Cries for You," and Tony Bennett's "Because of You" and "Cold, Cold Heart." The latter, an apostrophe to a cruel mistress, could be called a debased Petrarchan sonnet—just the kind of song H.H. would scorn. Play some of these hits while reading *Lolita*— as ironic descant, say, to the important reunion scene on p. 277, where H.H. says that one of her songs was throbbing on the radio as they talked. For an illustrated survey of teen culture, see Time-Life's volume, *This Fabulous Century: 1950–1960* (1970), especially for its facsimile pages from the sort of movie magazines that Lo and her pals consumed. The programmatic innocence that was proffered by these publications will come as a big surprise to younger readers, who expect scandal, and to aging scholars who have never before seen such stuff and only now can complete their education—really, if they want to understand the full reach of *Lolita*. "Patty," an author's error in the 1958 edition, has been changed to "Patti."

148/2 *Starasil:* an actual ointment.

148/3 *trochaic lilt:* in prosody, a *trochee* is a foot of two syllables, the first stressed or half-stressed, and the second unstressed.

148/4 *Huncan Dines:* the spoonerism hardly conceals Duncan Hines (1880–1959), author of such guidebooks as *Adventures in Good Eating, Lodging for a Night,* and *Duncan Hines' Food Odyssey.*

149/1 *chère Dolorès:* French; dear Dolores—an insulting translation for bilingual readers.

149/2 *comme . . . gentille:* French; as you know too well, my sweet one.

150/1 *rapist . . . therapist:* a slight variation of earlier wordplay; see 113/3. In *Ada,* thinkers who speculate on the existence of Terra are called "terrapists" (p. 341).

150/2 *by Polonius:* the talkative and complacent old man of *Hamlet.* The reference is probably to the warnings he gives his daughter, Ophelia, about the slippery ways of men. See 31/6.

150/3 *Mann Act:* the obvious "dreadful pun" is Mann: man. "Act" was not capitalized in the 1958 edition; the error has been corrected here.

151/1 *my Lolita . . . her Catullus:* the Latin love-poem motif; see 66/1.

151/2 *c'est tout:* French; that is all.

151/3 *thirty-nine other dopes:* forty, including Lo; the same number as the Ramsdale class (p. 51), and the sleepless nights (p. 109) — plotted "coincidences" all.

152/1 *crazy quilt of forty-eight states:* it is appropriate that Part Two's first allusion to Quilty should be this geographical metaphor, since H.H. and his nemesis pursue each other back and forth across "the crazy quilt." When all the journeys are ended, he is "quilted Quilty" (p. 306) and, once more, "the crazy quilt" (p. 307).

152/2 *inutile:* French; useless, unprofitable.

152/3 *Lorrain clouds:* Claude Gelée, known as Claude Lorrain (1600–1682), French painter who settled in Rome and established landscape painting as a respectable form. His open vistas and lyrical evocations of light and atmosphere influenced Poussin, among others. A character in *King, Queen, Knave* (1928) points at something "with the air of Rembrandt indicating a Claude Lorraine" (p. 91), a reminder of the consistency of Nabokov's vision.

152/4 *El Greco horizon . . . mummy-necked farmer:* the famous painter (1541?–1614?), born in Greece, schooled in Italy, resident of Spain. H.H. discovers in Kansas the turbulent Toledo landscapes of Greco and describes the farmer as though he were an "El Greco" — his elongated "mummy neck" is optically distorted in the manner of this artist. Since many early readers, especially the British and French, thought *Lolita* resolutely "anti-American," Nabokov urged me to note the book's tender landscape details, and the tribute paid to "the lovely, trustful, enormous country" (p. 176). H.H.'s tributes are of central importance. The "moral apotheosis" correctly sighted by John Ray (p. 5) is congruent with H.H.'s most rapturous description of the countryside (pp. 307–308), though the landscape described on p. 152 remains "two-dimensional" (H.H.'s phrase on p. 152) because it is essentially unpeopled (the farmer isn't human)—a purely aesthetic spectacle as opposed to the three-dimensional landscape on pp. 307–308. There, Nabokov completes the picture as a *novelist* rather than a dandy landscape artist or artificer.

153/1 *samara:* a dry, winged fruit, usually one-seeded, as in the ash or elm.

154/1 *ce qu'on appelle:* French; what one calls.

Chapter 2

154/2 *partie de plaisir:* French; outing, picnic.

154/3 *raison d'être:* French; the reason for being, the justification.

154/4 *John Galsworthy:* English novelist (1867–1933), author of *The Forsyte Saga* (1922).

155/1 *canthus:* the inner corner of the eye where the upper and lower eyelids meet.

155/2 *"Kurort" type:* German; health resort, watering place.

155/3 *roan back ... an orchestra of zoot-suiters with trumpets: Roan* is a color: chestnut interspersed with gray or white—said of a horse; also a low-grade sheepskin tanned and colored to imitate ungrained Morocco. Zoot suits were a "hep" male fashion of the forties that originated with the Hispanic "pachuco" gangs of Los Angeles in 1942. A zoot suit consisted of a porkpie hat, a wide-shouldered, thigh-length jacket, and billowy trousers that were tapered and "pegged" (bloused) at the bottom. A long watch-chain was optional. The humor of H.H.'s verbal cartoon turns on one's knowing that a sixteen-piece jazz band contained four or five trumpeters at most. Zoot, the saxophone-playing puppet on *The Muppets,* is not a tribute to fashion but to John Haley (Zoot) Sims (1925–1985), the great tenor saxophonist.

155/4 *author of "Trees":* Joyce Kilmer (1886–1918), American poet, best known for the sentimental poem which H.H. refers to here.

156/1 *bronzed owner of an expensive car:* although Quilty-hunters may find this man suspect, Nabokov said it is definitely not Quilty.

156/2 *lousy with . . . flies:* noted Nabokov: "The insects that poor Humbert mistakes for 'creeping white flies' are the biologically fascinating little moths of the genus *Pronuba* whose amiable and indispensable females transport the pollen that fertilizes the yucca flowers (see, what Humbert failed to do, 'Yucca Moth' in any good encyclopedia)." For entomological allusions, see 6/1.

156/3 *Independence . . . Abilene:* also a juxtaposition of the "starting points" of successive American presidents: Harry S. Truman (1884–1972) and Dwight D. Eisenhower (1890–1969).

156/4 *lilac . . . phallic:* H.H. continually reminds us that he has "only words to play with" (p. 32). His *phallic* is built on the semantic constituents of *lilac* and *Pharaonic* (of or pertaining to Pharaoh, the title of the sovereigns of ancient Egypt).

156/5 *lanugo:* anatomical word; in a restricted sense, the downy growth which covers the young of otherwise non-hairy animals.

156/6 *rufous:* a bright russet or brownish-orange hue.

156/7 *lucerne:* a deep-rooted European herb with bluish-purple flowers; in the United States usually called *alfalfa.*

157/1 *comme on dit:* French; as they say.

157/2 *hundreds of . . . hummingbirds:* these are not birds, noted Nabokov, "but hawkmoths which do move exactly like hummingbirds (which are neither gray nor nocturnal)." For entomological allusions, see 6/1.

157/3 *Shakespeare . . . New Mexico:* not invented; a mining town founded c. 1870 on property that had previously been involved in one of the largest unsuccessful mining speculations of the period in the Southwest. Now a "ghost town," it is no longer listed in any atlas.

157/4 *Florentine Bea's . . . contemporary:* Dante's Beatrice (see 19/9). A thirteenth-century mummy.

157/5 *Our twentieth Hell's Canyon:* see 296/5.

157/6 *winery in California . . . wine barrel:* it exists. Crossing over into Death Valley from Nevada, H.H. and Lolita travel down to Los Angeles and then wend their way northward up the California coast to Oregon (Crater Lake, p. 158). Most of H.H.'s observation's of "local color"

(Nabokov's phrase) will not be glossed unless they're particularly color-ful or obscure.

157/7 *Scotty's Castle:* an enormous and grotesque structure built in the twenties by Walter ("Death Valley") Scott, formerly with Buffalo Bill's Wild West Show. It is only half-completed because he ran out of funds when a mysterious "gold mine" was exhausted.

158/1 *R. L. Stevenson's footprint on an extinct volcano:* the Scottish writer (1850–1895) followed the woman he loved to California, where he lived for a year (1879–1880). In *From Scotland to Silverado,* James D. Hart, ed. (1966), collects his writing about the state. Stevenson is buried on the volcanic Mount Vaea in Samoa; but H.H., who may or may not know that, is here referring to his honeymoon stay on Mount St. Helena, California, generally thought to be an extinct volcano (it is in fact not one). There is a Robert Louis Stevenson Memorial there, but he left no actual footprint. H.H., having just noted "The ugly villas of handsome actresses," was no doubt more impressed by the footprints and hand-prints of movie stars immortalized in the cement pavements outside Grauman's Chinese Theatre in Hollywood. For further Stevenson allu-sions, see 184/2 and 206/3.

158/2 *Mission Dolores: good title for book:* this book, of course. The mission observed by H.H. exists, in San Francisco.

158/3 *festoons:* in architecture, a molded or carved ornament representing a festoon (a garland or wreath hanging in a curve). H.H. is observing the coastline of Monterey.

158/4 *Russian Gulch State Park:* in Sonoma, California; named by Russian colonists.

158/5 *The Bearded Woman read our jingle and now she is no longer single:* H.H. conflates a series of roadside advertising signs erected by the Burma Shave Company, or invents his own version. "The first form of sequential advertising," report Sally Henderson and Robert Landau in *Billboard Art* (1981), "the Burma Shave signs spoke to the public in a new way with both humor and wit. The small signs, installed at the roadside in sets of six, took approximately eighteen seconds to read when the car was traveling at a speed of thirty-five miles per hour." Burma Shave signs dotted the countryside from 1925 to 1963. Lolita would have been more interested in this cognate series: "The Bearded Lady / Tried A

Jar / She's Now a Famous / Movie Star / Burma Shave." Weathered old Burma Shave signs turn up today in "antique" stores, bathed in a very warm light indeed. Now that the old roads and their kitsch and clutter have given way to sleek super-highways and standardized conveniences, the once despised diners, gas stations, and one-of-a kind motels of the past have been deemed vernacular art and archeology by grieving nostalgists and students of a democratic culture. Picture-books such as John Margolies's *The End of the Road: Vanishing Highway Architecture in America* (1981) and Michael Wallis's *Route 66: The Mother Road* (1990), may also serve to document the vanishing cross-country quotidian world of *Lolita* and Jack Kerouac's more romanticized *On the Road* (1957). The photographs in Robert Frank's *The Americans* (1959) complement H.H.'s most melancholy rooms and ruminations, as he would put it.

158/6 *Christopher Columbus' flagship:* the zoo exists, in Evansville, Indiana. Its monkeys—kept out-of-doors on the ship from April to November —continue to be the zoo's most popular attraction.

158/7 *Little Rock, near a school:* rereading this passage in 1968, Nabokov called it "nicely prophetic" (the larger "row" over school desegregation, September 1957). For further "prophecy," see 226/3.

158/8 *à propos de rien:* French; not in relation to anything else; casually.

159/1 *town . . . first name:* "his" refers to Quilty. Clare, Michigan; an actual town.

159/2 *species . . . Homo pollex:* H.H. combines the familiar Latin *homo*, "the genus of mammals consisting of mankind," with *pollex*, or "thumb."

159/3 *viatic:* H.H. sustains his "scientific" vocabulary; a coinage from the Latin root *via. Viaticum* is English—an allowance for traveling expenses—but H.H. has gone back to the Latin word *viaticus*, which specifically refers to the road.

159/4 *priapically:* from Priapus, the god of procreation; see 42/4.

159/5 *man of my age . . . face à claques:* Quilty, with a "face that deserves to be slapped; an ugly, mischievous face." For an index to his appearances, see 31/9.

159/6 *concupiscence:* lustfulness.

159/7 *coulant un regard:* French; casting a sly glance.

160/1 *slow truck . . . road:* see 229/2; after an encounter with "Trapp" (Quilty), H.H. finds himself behind such a truck.

161/1 *natatoriums:* swimming pools.

161/2 *matitudinal:* H.H.'s coinage, from matin, an ecclesiastical duty performed early in the morning; or, though its usage is rare, a morning call or song (of birds).

161/3 *mais je divague:* French; but I am wandering away from the point; rambling.

162/1 *les yeux perdus:* French; a lost look in the eyes.

162/2 *oh Baudelaire!:* Charles Baudelaire (1821–1867), French poet. The image of the dream and the French phrases, *"brun adolescent"* ("dark [brown-haired] adolescent") and *"se tordre"* ("to undergo contortions" [erotic]), are drawn from Baudelaire's *Le Crépuscule du matin*, or "MorningTwilight" (1852): *"C'était l'heure où l'essaim des rêves malfaisants / Tord sur leurs oreillers les bruns adolescents"* ("It was the hour when a swarm of evil dreams contorts [or twists] dark [or swarthy] adolescents on their pillows"). For other Baudelaire allusions, see 262/1 and 284/3. "Poor Baudelaire" is evoked in a variant from Shade's poem in *Pale Fire* (p. 167); and Kinbote's gardener aspires "to read in the original Baudelaire and Dumas" (p. 291). The title of *Invitation to a Beheading* is drawn from Baudelaire's *L'Invitation au voyage*, which is variously evoked throughout the novel. The poem's opening lines are quoted and toyed with in *Ada* (p. 106).

162/3 *a famous coach . . . with a harem of ball boys:* a tennis star of the twenties (1893–1953), as famous in his sport as Red Grange and Babe Ruth were in theirs; winner of the American championship seven times, the Wimbledon title three times, and the U.S. doubles championship five times. In 1946 he was jailed on a morals charge, and H.H. and Lolita meet him after his tragic double life has become public knowledge, and only a few years before his death. Given the context, the prosaic phrase and vocation of "ball boy" becomes a pun. When asked if the deceased player should be identified by name, Nabokov imagined him now "consorting with ball boys . . . on Elysian turf. Shall we spare his shade?"

162/4 *Gobbert:* a corrected author's error (one *b* in the 1958 edition). André H. Gobbert was a French tennis champion c. World War I. "I saw him beaten by Patterson in 1919 or 1920 at Wimbledon," recalled Nabokov.

"He had a tremendous (old-fashioned) serve, but would double fault up to four times in a game. Big dark fellow, doubled with Decugis against Brookes and Patterson, I think" (see 234/1).

162/5 *ange gauche:* French; awkward angel.

163/1 *simulacrum:* an unreal semblance (a favorite word of H.H.'s; see pp. 113 and 175).

163/2 *a tall man:* a mirage of Quilty. The subsequent teasing ambiguity as to whether H.H.'s pursuer is "real" or an autoscopic hallucination (see p. 217) parodies Golyadkin, Jr., and the central problem of Dostoevsky's *The Double* (the narrator of *Despair* considers *The Double* as a title for his book, "But Russian literature possessed one already," he says [p. 201]). For Quilty, see 31/9.

163/3 *diaphanous:* delicate to the extent of being transparent or translucent.

163/4 *pavonine:* like a peacock; iridescent.

163/5 *oculate:* eye-spotted.

163/6 *ramparts of ancient Europe:* translation and paraphrase of line 84 of Rimbaud's *Le Bâteau ivre* ("The Drunken Boat" [1871]): *"Je regrette l'Europe aux anciens parapets"* ("I long for Europe with its ancient quays" [ramparts]). Rimbaud's use of *"parapets"* is shortly reinforced in an echo of the phrase (172/1). See 250/7 for another allusion to this poem. Nabokov translated it into Russian in *The Rudder*, December 16, 1928. Rimbaud's poem is transmuted, along with almost everything else, in *Ada*'s anti-world; Van Veen receives a message "in the Louvre right in front of Bosch's *Bâteau Ivre*, the one with a jester drinking in the riggings (poor old Dan [Veen] thought that it had something to do with Brant's satirical poem!)" (p. 331). Ada and Van know by heart Rimbaud's *Mémoire*, and it is one of two texts they use for their coded letters (p. 161). For more on Rimbaud, see 75/6.

164/1 *caravansaries:* from a Persian word; in the East, an inn in the form of a bare building surrounding a court, where caravans stop for the night.

165/1 *well-drawn . . . bobby-soxer: Penny,* the comic strip created by Harry Haenigsen in 1943. For other allusions to comic strips, see 217/5, 254/5, and 254/6. As responsive as he was scholarly, Nabokov the literary anatomist was also amused and delighted by "lower" forms of art, and was not above making selective use of such materials in his writing. No one, he laments in the Foreword to the revised *Speak, Memory*, "discovered the name [in the first edition] of a great cartoonist and a tribute to him in the last sentence of Section Two, Chapter Eleven. It is most embarrassing for a writer to have to point out such things himself" (p. 15). The tribute is to Otto Soglow, creator of *The Little King*: "The ranks of words I reviewed were again *so glow*ing, with their puffed-out little chests and trim uniforms . . . [italics mine—A.A.]" (p. 219). John Held, Jr., is also alluded to (p. 265). "Who will bother to notice," wonders Nabokov in the Introduction to *Bend Sinister*, "that the urchins in the yard (Chapter Seven) have been drawn by Saul Steinberg" (p. xviii). In *Ada*, an 1871 Sunday supplement of the *Kaluga Gazette* "feature[s] on its funnies page the now long defunct Goodnight Kids, Nicky and Pimpernella (sweet siblings who shared a narrow bed)"—based, in reality, on an old French comic strip (p. 6). At the end of *Ada*, ninety-seven-year-old Van Veen describes how he "look[s] forward with juvenile zest to the delightful effect of a spoonful of sodium bicarbonate dissolved in water that was sure to release three or four belches as big as the speech balloons in the 'funnies' of his boyhood" (p. 570).

165/2 *areolas:* the more-or-less shaded narrow areas around the nipples.

165/3 *recedent:* a heraldic term, to match *pursuant.*

165/4 *"We . . . in this bottle":* the "quip" derives from the fact that the mariners could not possibly know they lived in the Middle Ages, just as the reader of this annotation has no idea what the twenty-sixth century will call our epoch.

Chapter 3

166/1 *umber . . . Humberland:* the pun (see 3/3) turns on the not-uncommon place name of Northumberland (England; New Hampshire; Virginia; Pennsylvania).

166/2 *Frigid Queen . . . Princess:* the actual name of a milk bar, recorded by Nabokov in a little black notebook. The "Princess" alludes to "Annabel Lee" (9/7), who, fused with Freud, is once more in the novel's foreground: "the search for a Kingdom by the Sea, a Sublimated Riviera, or whatnot" (p. 167).

166/3 *hors concours:* out of the competition: when something is exhibited at a show (e.g., livestock, tulips) but is so superior to the rest of the exhibition that it is barred from receiving the awards or prizes.

166/4 *leporine fascination:* like a hare. The "able psychiatrist" is being hypnotized as a rabbit is by a serpent (H.H.).

167/1 *manatee:* any of several aquatic mammals, such as the sea cow.

168/1 *Arcadian . . . wilds:* from Arcadia, the idyllic rural region of Greece and the classic image of pastoral simplicity. "Even in Arcady am I, says Death in the tombal scripture," notes Kinbote in *Pale Fire* (p. 174).

168/2 *rill:* a very small brook.

168/3 *cabanes:* huts; simple dwellings.

168/4 *que dis-je:* French; what am I saying?

168/5 *marmot:* any rodent of the genus Marmota, such as the woodchuck.

168/6 *Venus came and went:* H.H. is being verbally playful about a sexual climax.

169/1 *un monsieur très bien:* French; a proper gentleman (a very pompous and bourgeois expression).

170/1 *hospitalized . . . by now:* reference to H.H.'s Western-style fight with Quilty on p. 299.

171/1 *strumstring:* H.H.'s coinage; the crooner is Gene Autry (1907–).

171/2 *harpies:* from classical mythology; foul creatures, part woman, part bird, that stole the souls of the dead, or defiled or seized their victims' food.

171/3 *orchideous masculinity:* belonging to the natural order of plants akin to genus *Orchis*. Its Greek etymology adds a comic dimension, for *orchis* means "testicle" as well as the plant. The *hideous* increases the humor.

172/1 *parapets of Europe:* a Rimbaud echo; see 163/6.

173/1 *Oriental tale:* invented by Nabokov.

173/2 *Beardsley:* after Aubrey Beardsley; see 52/3.

173/3 *Woerner's Treatise:* it exists, Nabokov told the annotator.

173/4 *A Girl of the Limberlost:* by Gene Stratton Porter (1863–1924), it was once a great favorite of schoolgirls (published 1914). *Little Women* (1869), by Louisa May Alcott (1832–1882), continues to be read.

174/1 *ganglia:* plural of *ganglion,* an anatomical and zoological word; "a mass of nerve tissue containing nerve cells, a nerve center"; a center of strength and energy.

174/2 *dans . . . l'âge:* French; in a mature age (when he is most robust).

174/3 *vieillard encore vert:* French; literally, "an old man still green"—that is, sexually potent.

174/4 *Know Your Own Daughter:* the "biblical title" is real, said Nabokov, although it has been impossible to document. Many similar titles exist, all lending themselves to *double-entendre:* Frances K. Martin, *Know Your Child* (1946); C. Lewis, *How Well Can We Know Our Children?* (1947); C. W. Young, *Know Your Pupil* (1945); and E. D. Adlerblum, *Know Your Child Through His Play* (1947). See 81/1.

174/5 *The Little Mermaid:* anyone familiar with this fairy tale by Hans Christian Andersen (1805–1875), the Danish fabulist, knows that H.H.'s gift has been carefully chosen, and that there are several ironies involved. The little mermaid longs to "enchant a mortal heart"—namely, the prince—and thus win an immortal soul. Lolita has succeeded all too well; but neither H.H., Quilty, nor her husband Dick Schiller, who will carry her off to Alaska, qualifies as prince in the fairy tale *Lolita.* At the end of Andersen's tale, the mermaid has been transposed into one of the freely circulating children of the air, who must float for three hundred years before they are admitted into the kingdom of heaven. But they can get in earlier, as one explains as the tale concludes: "Unseen we float into the houses of mortals where there are children, and for every day that we find a good child who makes his parents happy and deserves their love, God shortens our period of trial. The child does not know when we fly through the room, and when we smile over it with joy a year is taken from the three hundred. But if we see a naughty and wicked child, we must weep tears of sorrow, and each tear adds a day to our period of trial" (from *The Twelve Dancing Princesses and Other Fairy Tales,* Alfred and Mary Elizabeth David, eds., New York, 1964, p. 274). H.H., who later sheds "merman tears" (255/1), no doubt hopes that Lolita will take this to heart. See also *Keys,* p. 134n. For the fairy-tale theme, see 31/3.

174/6 *casé:* settled.

175/1 *27,000 miles:* see 31/15.

175/2 *rentier:* a man who lives from the interest of his invested capital (generally applies to an old, retired man).

175/3 *her bi-iliac garland still as brief as a lad's:* The bi-iliac are the two most prominent points of the crests of the iliac bones. H.H. is toying with the last line of "To an Athlete Dying Young" ("The garland briefer than a girl's") from *A Shropshire Lad* (1896), by A. E. Housman (1859–1936), the English poet and Cambridge classics don (see *Speak, Memory*, p. 273; *Pale Fire*, p. 269). The poem's aura is homosexual, but its theme of loss pertains to H.H., and his sense of youth's transience. *His* athlete (roller-skating, tennis) is figuratively dying in this passage; the nymphet is *growing.* H.H. can appreciate the double lives (Housman tried marriage), the anguish and legalized persecution suffered especially by homosexuals in England (Oscar Wilde was jailed in 1895). Gaston Godin's garret (181/4) is built on this Housman.

CHAPTER 4

176/1 *habitus:* a not uncommon Latin noun meaning moral condition, state, disposition, character, etc.

177/1 *Miss Cormorant:* she is named after the voracious sea bird.

177/2 *recueillement:* self-communion, "collectedness."

178/1 *harems and slaves:* of course she can care, and H.H. has compared her lot to theirs.

CHAPTER 5

179/1 *Lester . . . Fabian:* their respective first and final syllables form "lesbian" (see also *Keys*, p. 96). See 195/2 for a similar effect.

CHAPTER 6

181/1 *Gaston Godin:* his "Beardsley existence" (p. 183) is also figurative, for he might well have been drawn by Aubrey Beardsley. H.H.'s caricature resembles the famous cover drawing of "Ali Baba" (for a projected edition of *The Forty Thieves*, never undertaken [1897]), as well as Oscar

Wilde, whose post-prison alias is bestowed on H.H.'s car (see 227/4). Gaston is *fin de siècle* in many ways, as pp. 181–182 make clear.

181/2 *mes goûts:* French; my tastes.

181/3 *He always wore black:* H.H.'s attire; see p. 295.

181/4 *large photographs:* they constitute a veritable pantheon of homosexual artists: André Gide (1869–1951), French writer, author of *Les Faux-Monnayeurs* (*The Counterfeiters,* 1925), winner of the Nobel Prize in 1947; Pëtr Ilich Tchaikovsky (1840–1893), Russian composer, whose "vile" and "silly" opera *Eugene Onegin* Nabokov could not abide; *Onegin* Commentary, Vol. II, p. 333); Norman Douglas (1868–1952), English writer, author of *South Wind* (1917); Waslaw Nijinsky (1890–1950), Russian ballet dancer of Polish descent (see p. 302), afflicted with insanity, and an associate of Diaghilev (who in *Ada* is the ballet master Dangleleaf [p. 430]); and Marcel Proust (see 16/4).

181/5 *two other . . . writers:* one of whom, W. Somerset Maugham (1874–1965), author of *Of Human Bondage* (1915), would have been named had he not been still alive, said Nabokov. The other, Nabokov told me, is the Anglo-American poet W. H. Auden (1907–1973). "These poor people," says H.H. (p. 184).

182/1 *Oui, ils sont gentils:* French; Yes, they are nice.

182/2 *toiles:* French; canvasses (paintings).

182/3 *"Prenez . . . savourer":* "Please take one of these pears. The good lady who lives across the street gives me more than I can relish." (Gaston's French is pedantic and his prose properly decadent, especially in the following.)

182/4 *"Mississe Taille Lore . . . j'exécre":* "Mrs. Taylor [phonetically rendered to indicate Gaston's foreign accent] has just given me these beautiful flowers which I abhor."

182/5 *au roi!:* check!

183/1 *"Et toutes . . . bien?":* "How about all your little girls? Are they all right?"

183/2 *sale histoire . . . Naples, of all places:* the first phrase is French; compromising episode (sexual in nature), and it *should* have happened in Naples, once notorious for its willing young waterfront males, some of them prostitutes. The association of G.G. and H.H. is another "false scent" in the game, a trap for the reader who believes the psychiatric diagnosis of H.H. on p. 32 (" 'potentially homosexual' "). Several Freudians of my acquaintance *do* interpret nymphets as substitute boys.

183/3 *my school-girl nymphet had me in thrall:* H.H. is echoing Keats's "La Belle Dame sans Merci" (1820), from the stanza that describes the dream the narrator has after the Belle Dame has lulled him to sleep in her "elfin grot":

> I saw pale Kings, and Princes too,
> Pale warriors, death-pale were they all;
> They cried, "La belle dame sans merci
> Thee hath in thrall!"

H.H. the self-pitying dissembler here notes how his enchantress—technically, a witch—is draining him of his humanity as well as money: "With the human element dwindling . . ." (p. 183). La Slavska, the stage and cinema songstress of "The Assistant Producer" (1943), "was a Belle Dame with a good deal of Merci" (*Nabokov's Dozen,* p. 77).

CHAPTER 7

184/1 *painted roses:* the smallest details cohere; see 52/5.

184/2 *Treasure Island:* the children's classic (published 1883) by Robert Louis Stevenson. See 158/1.

184/3 *Whistler:* James McNeill Whistler (1834–1903), Anglo-American painter and etcher. The famous painting of his mother is actually titled "Arrangement in Grey and Black."

185/1 *cars . . . bars . . . barmen:* the fripperous internal rhymes burlesque Belloc's "Tarantella" (147/1): "And the cheers and the jeers of the young muleteers . . ." H.H. is paraphrasing his own verse; a complete version appears, in all its majesty, on pp. 255–257.

CHAPTER 8

185/2 *Star:* the newspaper's name was not italicized in the 1958 edition; the error has been corrected.

186/1 *time leaks:* spent with Quilty. For an index to his appearances, see 31/9.

187/1 *sly quip . . . Rigger:* The Right Reverend Rigger (in some versions "Reverend MacTrigger") figures in an old limerick that begins, "There was a right royal old nigger." "His five hundred wives / Had the time of their lives," and the rest is too obscene to appear here. But see Joyce's *Ulysses,* where Bloom quotes it (1961 Random House ed., pp. 171–172). For a summary of Joyce allusions, see 4/11.

188/1 *Argus-eyed:* "observant"; from the hundred-eyed monster of Greek mythology, who was set to watch Io, a maiden loved by Zeus. In *Laughter in the Dark,* Albinus meets his fatal love in the Argus cinema, where she is an usher (p. 22). "My back is Argus-eyed," says the speaker in "An Evening of Russian Poetry" (see 3/3). In *Pale Fire,* one of the aliases of the assassin Gradus is "d'Argus"; Hermann in *Despair* envisions "argus-eyed angels" (p. 101); the title character in *The Real Life of Sebastian Knight* "seems argus-eyed" (p. 95); Ada and Van dread "traveling together to Argus-eyed destinations" (*Ada,* p. 425), and Van, in search of the nature and meaning of Time, drives an "Argus" car (p. 551).

189/1 *celebrated actress:* an allusion to her resemblance to Marlene Dietrich; p. 103.

189/2 *ne montrez pas vos zhambes:* French; do not show your legs (*jambes* phonetically spelled to indicate an American accent—a recollection of Charlotte; see 44/1).

189/3 *Edgar:* in honor of Poe; see 75/5 and 118/2. For a summary of Poe allusions, see 9/2.

189/4 *hygienic evening in Providence:* at that time Providence, R.I., possessed a large redlight district.

CHAPTER 9

189/5 *Avis Chapman:* "When naming incidental characters," said Nabokov, "I like to give them some mnemonic handle, a private tag: thus 'Avis Chapman' which I mentally attached to the South-European butterfly *Callophrys avis* Chapman (where Chapman, of course, is the name of that butterfly's original describer)." For entomological allusions, see 6/1.

190/1 *save one . . . names are approximations:* Mona Dahl. Because she was Lolita's accomplice in deceit, a cover (or quilt!) for Quilty, H.H. takes his vengeance by revealing Mona's name to the world.

192/1 *Ball Zack:* Honoré de Balzac (1799–1850), French novelist.

CHAPTER 10

192/2 *my Lolita:* this brief chapter sounds an urgent chord in what might be called the "true love" theme. The succinct "Latin" locution (see 45 /1) is sounded on pp. 32, 44, 53, 66, 79, 80, 92, 111, 115, 128, 134, 154, 166, 167, 176, 190, 198, 199, 207, 231, 241, 247, 267, 277, 278, 284, 293, 309, 311. "My unique Lolita" (p. 183), "my lone light Lolita" (p. 285) and "my conventional Lolita" (p. 287) vary the pattern.

CHAPTER 11

193/1 *"Why, no,"* I *said:* the comma after *no* was omitted in the 1958 edition; the error has been corrected.

195/1 *teachers':* the apostrophe was omitted in the 1958 edition.

195/2 *Miss Horn . . . Miss Cole:* the first letters of the teachers' names have been transposed. "Corrected," the names combine to form an obscene verb. For their anagrammatic colleagues, see 179/1.

196/1 *The Hunted Enchanters:* "the author" is Quilty (see p. 200), though Pratt has the title wrong (*The Enchanted Hunters,* after the hotel and the nympholepts, common and uncommon varieties [see 108/2]). She is figuratively correct, however, since Quilty *is* hunting the enchanter (Lolita), and it is apt that Pratt, her keeper, should make this accurate "error." For a summary of Quilty allusions, see 31/9.

197/1 *She is in Mushroom:* the very astute reader of *Who's Who in the Limelight* knows this already; see 31/8, where the plant is identified as a phallic symbol.

197/2 *girls':* the apostrophe was omitted in the 1958 edition.

198/1 *Reynolds:* Joshua Reynolds (1723–1792), English painter. "The Age of Innocence" portrays a very young girl alone under a tree, in the wrong room here ("smelly" Mushroom).

198/2 *Baker:* George Pierce Baker (1866–1935) gave a famous course in playwriting at Harvard, and his *Dramatic Technique* (1919) was a popular text.

CHAPTER 12

198/3 *Dr. Ilse Tristramson:* Tristram[n] was the famous hero of Celtic legend, and the love of Tristram and Iseult has often been celebrated. The story of Tristram is in Sir Thomas Malory's *Morte D'arthur* (1485), Books Ten through Twelve. Matthew Arnold treated the theme in "Tristram and Iseult" (1852), Swinburne in "Tristram of Lyonesse" (1871), and Tennyson in "The Last Tournament" (1871). "Tristram in Movielove," notes H.H. (p. 254). Tristram's sons are the poets of love. The punning name of the physician who examines Lolita is in the spirit of a novel that is both a love story and a parody of love stories; but, more than that, it acknowledges Laurence Sterne, whose involuted and a-realistic *Tristram Shandy* (1767) might be called the first modern novel (for the *Shandy* reference, see also *Keys*, p. 96). The aesthetic kinship of Sterne and Joyce and Nabokov, which has nothing to do with "literary influence," is strong enough to call both *Ulysses* and *Lolita* "Tristram's sons." "I love Sterne but had not read him in my Russian period," said Nabokov (*Wisconsin Studies* interview). See 255/4 for another Sterne allusion and 109/1, where H.H.'s verbal play evokes Sterne.

198/4 *caloricity:* "the physiological ability to develop and maintain bodily heat."

198/5 *Venus febriculosa:* Latin; "slightly feverish Venus." Lolita's malady in mock-medicalese. See 137/1 for other references to the Roman goddess of love and beauty. See pp. 270 and 274 for allusions to Botticelli's famous painting of her.

199/1 *Doris Lee . . . Frederick Waugh:* The Doris Lee (1905–1983) painting under discussion is called "Noon." It shows a man with his hat over his face, asleep on a haystack, while in the foreground a girl and another man are making love beside a haystack (reproduced in *Life,* III, September 20, 1937). All of these artists are realistic painters, quite out of fashion in the nineteen–fifties. Grant Wood (1892–1942) is well-known for his meticulous renderings of eminently American subjects, especially for "American Gothic" (1930)—"good title for book"—the coolly sardonic portrait of a Midwestern farm couple. The subject matter of Peter Hurd

(1904–1984) is primarily Southwestern, including his portrait painting (his name became legend in 1967 when President Lyndon B. Johnson refused a Hurd portrait of him, calling it the "ugliest thing I ever saw"). Reginald Marsh (1898–1954) indefatigably chronicled the common (if not low) life of New York City, in a style more graphic than painterly (a misprint in his name has been corrected [*s* instead of *c* in the 1958 edition]). Frederick Waugh (1861–1940) concentrated on marine subjects. Like their maker (see 263/3), Nabokov's characters usually know a good deal about art and express their opinions freely. As an entomologist, Nabokov valued exactitude, but as a novelist and critic he scorned brilliant technique put to banal use. In *Pnin*, Mr. Lake thus teaches "That Dali is really Norman Rockwell's twin brother kidnaped by gypsies in babyhood" (p. 96).

CHAPTER 13

200/1 *Elizabethan:* that epoch's play-within-the-play is relevant here, for *The Enchanted Hunters* functions in the same manner (as do other "playlets" mentioned on p. 201, though the latter are of less significance). See 51/1 and the Introduction, p. xxx.

200/2 *Diana:* Roman moon goddess, patroness of hunting and virginity; identified with the Greek Artemis.

200/3 *suggested the play's title:* the title was of course suggested by Lolita's enchantment of H.H. and Quilty; their conversation at the hotel is on pp. 126–127. As happens so often in the universe of Nabokov's fiction, the title reflects or refracts a motif distant in time but not in space, insofar as "the poet . . . is the nucleus" of everything (*Speak, Memory*, p. 218). The year of his death, Sebastian Knight "is said to have been three times to see the same film—a perfectly insipid one called *The Enchanted Garden*" (*The Real Life of Sebastian Knight* [1941], p. 182). See Introduction, pp. xxix–xxx, lii, and, for typical examples, 3/3, 12/1, 188/1, and 240/1.

201/1 *Hansel and Gretel:* the three "playlets" are adaptations of fairy tales that have to do with deception or enchantment.

201/2 *Richard Roe:* a party to legal proceedings whose real name is unknown; the second party when two are unknown, just as "John Doe" is the first party. *Dorothy Doe* is an alliterative party of no legal significance.

201/3 *Maurice Vermont . . . Rumpelmeyer:* Nabokov said, "I vaguely but persistently feel that both Vermont and Rumpelmeyer exist!" (probably culled from a telephone directory). Whether "real" or not, these names were chosen because they are a play on (and with) the emperor's old clothes: *to rumple* (to form irregular folds) and the *Vermont,* a merino sheep having greatly exaggerated skin folds. *Maurice* points below to Maeterlinck, a purveyor of more pretentious fairy tales; while *Rumpelmeyer* also suggests Rumpelstiltskin, a fairy tale that is resolved only when the fair protagonist discovers the grotesque villain's name. For a similar moment in *Lolita,* see p. 272.

201/4 *Lenormand:* Henri René Lenormand (1882–1951). In the period between the two world wars, he was the center of those French dramatists concerned with subconscious motivation. He was regarded as a Freudian, but he claimed that his plays were based on emotional conflicts rather than on intellectual systems. Lenormand believed that all altruistic action was motivated by egoistic impulses. In his plays man is set in physical nature and climatic conditions are considered as a shaping force in human behavior. *Le Temps est un songe* (1919) and *À l'Ombre du mal* (1924) are among his best-known works. The allusion to Lenormand is generalized, said Nabokov. Although some of them are a parodist's delight, Nabokov had no specific Lenormand works in mind. Lenormand's play, *La Maison des Remparts,* features a girl named Lolita, but Nabokov never saw or read it.

201/5 *Maeterlinck:* the reputation of Maurice Maeterlinck (1862–1949) was at its height in the last decade of the nineteenth and the first decade of this century, when the Belgian-born writer's anti-naturalistic Symbolist plays exerted a wide influence. In an effort to communicate the mysteries of man's inner life and his relation to the universe, he created a theater of stasis, rich in atmosphere and short in action. He won the Nobel Prize for literature in 1911. Among his most famous plays are *Pelléas et Mélisande* (1892) and *L'Oiseau bleu* (1909): see 250/7 and 301/5. Invited to Hollywood by producer Louis B. Mayer in the thirties, he wrote a Symbolist screenplay. "The hero is a goddamn bee!" proclaimed the horrified Mayer.

201/6 *British dreamers:* Nabokov had in mind Sir James M. Barrie (1860–1937), Scottish novelist and dramatist who wrote *Peter Pan* (1904) and *A Kiss for Cinderella* (1916), and Lewis Carroll (see 131/3 and 264/1).

201/7 *a seventh Hunter:* see 249/2 and the Introduction, p. xxx. This Hunter is implicitly the author himself.

201/8 *elves:* for "elves" and the fairy-tale theme, see 31/3, which underscores the fact that the entertainment is indeed "the poet's invention."

202/1 *Was it?:* her euphoria is caused by the realization that Quilty has named his play in her honor.

CHAPTER 14

202/2 *Miss Emperor:* Mlle. Lempereur is Emma Bovary's music teacher. By pretending to go to lessons Emma is able to meet Léon in Rouen and deceive her husband (Part III, Chapter 5). See also *Keys,* p. 25. See 145/3 for Flaubert.

202/3 *Gustave's:* because Lolita has followed Emma's example, Flaubert (not Trapp) is still on H.H.'s mind.

203/1 *mon pauvre ami . . . saluent:* French; my poor fellow, I have never seen you again and although there is little likelihood of your seeing my book, allow me to tell you that I give you a very cordial handshake and that all my little girls send you greetings.

203/2 *d'un . . . contrit:* French; a look of contrived mortification.

203/3 *rehearsing . . . with Mona:* she meets Quilty here. See 31/9 for a summary of his appearances.

204/1 *pommettes:* cheekbones. A corrected author's error (not italicized in 1958 edition).

206/1 *haddocky:* fishy (akin to the cod); the adjectival use is H.H.'s.

206/2 *dackel:* German; a dachshund.

206/3 *Mr. Hyde:* in Robert Louis Stevenson's *Dr. Jekyll and Mr. Hyde* (1886), Hyde similarly knocks over a little girl. Note that H.H. identifies himself with the evil self of Stevenson's *Doppelgänger* tale. For Stevenson, see 158/1 and the Introduction, pp. lx–lxi and lxii.

207/1 *hurriedly hung up:* the conversation was with Quilty.

207/2 *Pim . . . Pippa:* an allusion to the play *Mr. Pim Passes By* (1919), by A.A. Milne (1882–1956), and to Browning's *Pippa Passes*. See also *Keys,*

p. 20. See 117/2 for another reference to *Pippa Passes,* and *Pale Fire,* p. 186. For *My Last Duchess*'s Fra Pandolf, see *Pale Fire,* p. 246.

207/3 *J'ai toujours... Dublinois:* "I have always admired the [*ormonde*] work of the sublime Dubliner." The sublime one is James Joyce, but *ormonde* does not exist in French; it refers to Dublin's Hotel Ormond (no *e*), whose restaurant provides the setting for the so-called "Sirens" episode of *Ulysses,* and whose name is a most Joycean pun—*hors* [*de ce*] *monde* ("out-of-this-world," a further tribute). (See also *Keys,* p. 20.) The reverential allusion is delivered obliquely in the requisite Joycean manner. Also in the Dubliner's spirit is the "jolls-joyce" car in which the hero of *Ada* rides in one scene (p. 473). See 4/11. In a 1966 National Educational Television network interview, Nabokov said the "greatest masterpieces of twentieth-century prose are, in this order: Joyce's *Ulysses;* Kafka's *Transformation;* Bely's *St. Petersburg;* and the first half of Proust's fairy tale, *In Search of Lost Time.*" "*On fait son grand Joyce* after doing one's *petit Proust,*" reads a parenthetical statement in *Ada,* added to the "manuscript" by gently derisive Ada herself, "In [her] lovely hand" (p. 169). When Véra Nabokov saw some of the opened pages of the annotator's copy of *Lolita,* the typeface barely visible beneath an overlay of comments in several colors of pencil and ink, she turned to her husband and said, "Darling, it looks like your copy of *Ulysses.*" Although there are strong artistic affinities between Joyce and Nabokov, he dismissed the possibility of formal "influence": "My first real contact with *Ulysses,* after a leering glimpse in the early 'twenties, was in the 'thirties at a time when I was definitely formed as a writer and immune to any literary influence. I studied *Ulysses* seriously only much later, in the 'fifties, when preparing my Cornell courses. That was the best part of the education I received at Cornell" (*Wisconsin Studies* interview). See 221/1.

In addition to admiring Joyce, Nabokov also knew him. "I saw [Joyce] a few times in Paris in the late thirties," recalled Nabokov. "Paul and Lucie Léon, close friends of his, were also old friends of mine. One night they brought him to a French lecture I had been asked to deliver on Pushkin under the auspices of Gabriel Marcel (it was later published in the *Nouvelle Revue Française*). I had happened to replace at the very last moment a Hungarian woman writer, very famous that winter, author of a bestselling novel, I remember its title, *La Rue du Chat qui Pêche,* but not the lady's name. A number of personal friends of mine, fearing that the sudden illness of the lady and a sudden discourse on Pushkin might result in a suddenly empty house, had done their best to round up the kind of audience they knew I would like to have. The house had, however, a pied aspect since some confusion had occurred among the lady's fans. The Hungarian consul mistook me for her husband and, as I entered, dashed towards me with the froth of condolence on his lips. Some people left as soon as I started to speak. A source of unforgettable consolation was the sight of Joyce sitting, arms folded and glasses glinting, in the midst of the Hungarian football team. Another time my wife and I had dinner with him at the Léons' followed by a long friendly evening of talk. I do not recall one word of it but my wife remembers that Joyce asked about the exact ingredients of *myod,* the Russian 'mead,' and everybody gave him a different answer."

Nabokov makes a Joycean appearance in Gisèle Freund and V. B. Carleton's *James Joyce in Paris: His Final Years* (New York, 1965). Pictured on pp. 44–45 is a meeting of the editorial board of the Parisian journal *Mesures.* Nine literati are shown gathered around a garden table, and a caption identifies the group, which includes Sylvia Beach, Adrienne Monnier, Henri Michaux, Jean Paulhan—and Jacques Audiberti, a tall, thin man standing in the back, looking down, his face in shadows, a trace of a smile suggesting some miraculous foreknowledge of the caption that twenty-eight years later would mistakenly identify him as "Audiberti," and in thus denying the existence of the already pseudonymous V. Sirin, would summarize the vicissitudes and spectral qualities of Russian émigré life, and cast him as The Mystery Man in the Garden, a role based on the nameless man in the brown macintosh, the mystery man of *Ulysses,* the "lankylooking galoot" (as Bloom calls him) whose name is misunderstood by a newspaper reporter as "M'Intosh," under which name he is immortalized. The photo is also included in *TriQuarterly* 17 (Winter 1970).

207/4 *C'est entendu?:* French; that's agreed?

207/5 *Lenore:* although Poe wrote a poem thusly titled, the primary allusion is to the title character in one of the most popular dramatic ballads of Gottfried August Bürger (1747–1794), German poet of the *Sturm und Drang* period. H.H. echoes the best-known line, in which Lenore and her ghostly lover ride off: *"Und hurre, hurre, hop, hop, hop, hop!..."* (line 149). See also *Keys,* p. 141n. The allusion is ironic, since Lenore grieves over her lover. Nabokov discusses the poem in the Commentary to his *Eugene Onegin* translation (Vol. III, pp. 153–154).

207/6 *qui ... temps:* French; who was taking his time.

CHAPTER 15

208/1 *Professor Chem:* for "Chemistry."

208/2 *edusively (placed!):* a portmanteau word; from *educible* (*educe:* "to draw forth; elicit"; see *Edusa*, p. 209), coined to rhyme with *effusively.* By punning on Edusa's name he manages to place her.

208/3 *the author:* Quilty. See 31/9.

209/1 *Edusa Gold:* named after the Clouded Yellow, a golden-orange European butterfly known at one time as *Colias edusa.* See 231/1. For entomological allusions, see 6/1.

209/2 *Some old woman:* Quilty; Lolita's diversionary ploy is successful; see 273/1.

209/3 *natural climax:* an echo of the "traumatic" experience; 13/3.

CHAPTER 16

210/1 *le montagnard émigré:* "the exiled mountaineer," the legend under a picture of Chateaubriand and the title of one of his *romances* (a sentimental ballad or song). An *émigré* is an expatriate; the word originally referred to Royalist fugitives from the French Revolution (such as Chateaubriand). *Le Montagnard émigré* was first published in 1806 and later included in Chateaubriand's story *Les Aventures du dernier Abencerage*, where the untitled verses are sung by a young French prisoner of war. Several of its lines are important in *Ada*, and appear literally at the center of the Ardis section; see pp. 138–139 and 141 (also see pp. 106, 192, 241, 342, 428, and 530). For more on Chateaubriand, see 145/4.

210/2 *Felis tigris goldsmithi:* taxonomic Latin: "Goldsmith's tiger" (*Felis:* genus; *tigris:* species; *goldsmithi:* subspecies), and allusion to line 356 of "The Deserted Village" (1770), by Oliver Goldsmith (c. 1730–1774): "where crouching tigers wait their hapless prey" (the animal is in fact a cougar rather than a tiger). "I found it and I named it, being versed / in taxonomic Latin," writes Nabokov in his poem "A Discovery" (6/1). Surely the same cannot be said of H.H., who is completely unversed in such matters (see Nabokov's remarks, 6/1).

210/3 *catalpas:* botanical term; "any of a small genus of American and Asiatic trees of the trumpet-creeper family."

210/4 *Nebraska . . . first whiff of the West:* a parody of the state's omnipresent pre-1960 slogan, "Nebraska—Where the West Begins!"

210/5 *Red Rock:* the initial rock is on p. 13. Nabokov told me that the image is in no way a reference to the "red rock" that appears in *The Waste Land* (l. 25)—mentioned now because several correspondents have inquired about this.

210/6 *caravansary:* see 164/1.

211/1 *detective tale:* one of the works of Maurice Leblanc (1864–1941), who was a kind of French Conan Doyle. See 250/5.

211/2 *persons unknown:* Quilty. For a summary of allusions to him, see 31/9.

211/3 *sign of Pegasus:* trademark of Mobil Oil; in Greek mythology, Pegasus is the winged horse sprung from Medusa at her death. Because a blow of his hoof brought forth Hippocrene, the fountain of the Muses, he is an emblem of poetic inspiration.

211/4 *that bug:* according to Nabokov, "this 'patient bug' is not necessarily a moth—it could be some clumsy big fly or miserable beetle." For entomological allusions, see 6/1.

212/1 *the Conche:* Shell Oil's trademark; in Greek mythology, the sea demigod Triton, son of Poseidon and Amphitrite, played a trumpet made of a conch. See 227/2.

212/2 *Chestnut Court:* throughout the novel, the smallest verbal units are undergoing a kind of metamorphosis (see 118/3). The chestnut trees below the motel are said to be "toylike," and H.H. is indeed toying with "Chestnuts." On p. 213, "Chestnut Court" becomes "Chestnut Castle," five lines later turns into "Chestnut Crest," and on p. 215 it returns to its "Chestnut Court" form; given a new context on p. 216, it becomes a horse. See 251/12, by which time it has become "Chestnut Lodge." As happens so often, Nabokov himself has described the process best: "The names Gogol invents are really nicknames which we surprise in the very act of turning into family names—and a metamorphosis is a thing always exciting to watch" (*Gogol,* p. 43).

212/3 *an elf-like girl on an insect-like bicycle:* H.H. has just mentioned that they are near Lolita's home town of Pisky ("pixie"; see 46/1); elves are thus indigenous to the region, and Nabokov has blended the fairy-tale theme with the entomological motif.

213/1 *Chestnut Castle:* see 212/2.

213/2 *"Bertoldo"* . . . *comedy:* the famous clown of Italian popular legend, who was the subject of a sixteenth-century collection of witty tales, *Vita di Bertoldo,* by Giulio Ceasare Croce. Bertoldo is planted here to show that H.H. could easily understand Quilty's later allusion to Italian comedy (p. 248).

213/3 *red hood:* Quilty; the devil's presence is more than fleeting; see 214/2. His appearances are summarized in 31/9.

213/4 *cod-piece fashion:* in the fifteenth and sixteenth centuries, a flap or bag, often ornamental, concealing an opening in the front of men's breeches; *cod-piece* is archaic for "penis" (often used by such writers as François Rabelais [c. 1490–1553], author of *Gargantua*).

214/1 *adolori* . . . *langueur:* "affected by love's languor." The phrase *"d'amoureuse langueur"* appears several times, with slight variations, in Ronsard's *Amours.* *"Adolori,"* a punning tribute to Lolita *(à Dolores),* is of course H.H.'s addition. See also *Keys,* p. 137n. See 47/2 for another Ronsard allusion.

214/2 *diabolical glow:* Quilty. She was with him at about the time H.H. was having his hair cut by the grotesque, tragic barber (p. 213).

215/1 *the shadow:* Quilty is continually identified as such.

CHAPTER 17

215/2 *Gros:* French; fat.

215/3 *"luizetta":* H.H.'s invention; from *louis d'or,* the French gold coin.

215/4 *the* . . . *life we all had rigged:* that "we all" (= H.H., Quilty, McFate, and Nabokov) involutes the narrative once more. See 32/7.

216/1 *burley* . . . *Krestovski:* see 88/1. The punning adjective summarizes his essence: *burly* (sturdy, stout) plus *burley* (an American tobacco, used in cigarettes and plugs).

CHAPTER 18

216/2 *Chestnuts and Colts:* freed from all modifiers (see 212/2), the trees, motels, and unstated brand names of the above pistols are here able to frolic together briefly as horses. "We are faced by the remarkable phenomenon of mere forms of speech directly giving rise to live creatures," as Nabokov says of *Dead Souls* (*Gogol,* p. 78).

217/1 *Aztec Red:* Quilty's "red shadow" and "red beast" (p. 219), characterized below as a "Red Yak."

217/2 *Jovian:* in Roman mythology, Jove (or Jupiter) is god of the sky.

217/3 *donc:* French; therefore.

217/4 *crepitating:* crackling.

217/5 *Jutting Chin . . . funnies:* the comic strip *Dick Tracy,* created by Chester Gould (1900–1985) in 1931.

218/1 *of my age . . . rosebud . . . mouth:* Quilty; the fact and the motif are familiar. H.H. had thought of growing such a mustache (48/1), and they also own similar bathrobes (p. 294).

219/1 *O lente . . . equi:* "O slowly run, horses of the night"; H.H.'s adjacent "translation" puns on the literal Latin (night mares). Less one *lente,* this line is from *The Tragical History of the Life and Death of Doctor Faustus* (V, ii, 140), by Christopher Marlowe (1564–1593). With only one hour left before eternal damnation, Faustus hopes for more time. H.H. does not try to "outspeed" Quilty, that latter-day Mephistopheles. See also *Keys,* pp. 31–32. For a similar pun—nightmares and stallions—see *Ada,* p. 214.

219/2 *viatic:* see 159/3.

220/1 *lady . . . lightning:* see 31/11. The allusions to *The Lady Who Loved Lightning* and "Fatface" anticipate the next passage, in which H.H. and Lolita attend Quilty's play. He and his collaborator are mentioned by name on p. 221 and even appear on stage.

220/2 *Soda, pop. 1001:* there is in California a Lake Soda, pop. unknown. The magical "1001" is well chosen. It is simultaneously a numerical mirroring (see 51/2) and an allusion to the fairy-tale theme (see 31/3) via another vertiginously involuted work, *The Thousand and One Nights.*

220/3 *flatus:* gas generated in the bowels or stomach.

220/4 *kurortish: Kurort* is German for "health resort" (see p. 155); the usage is H.H.'s own.

221/1 *children-colors . . . a passage in James Joyce:* the colors of the spectrum; the "living rainbow" mimed by the "seven little graces" on p. 220. It is from *Finnegans Wake.* The theme of the diversity and unity of all things is central to the constantly metamorphosing dream world of *Finnegans Wake.* The seven colors of the spectrum represent diversity and are most frequently personified by seven "rainbow girls" who oppose the archetypal mother, Anna Livia Plurabelle. The book opens with a reversed rainbow; the seven clauses in the second paragraph each contain a color, shifting from violet to red. Although not wrong, H.H.'s mention of a single "passage" is misleading because the motif is sustained throughout the *Wake.* To have the hateful Quilty "lift" from *Finnegans Wake* rather than *Ulysses* constitutes a rather private and thus thoroughly Joycean joke, based on Nabokov's low opinion of the book he calls *Punnigans Wake,* or, in *Bend Sinister,* keeping its vast liquidity in mind, *"Winnipeg Lake,* ripple 585, Vico Press edition" (p. 114). *"Ulysses* towers over the rest of Joyce's writings," said Nabokov, "and in comparison to its noble originality and unique lucidity of thought and style the unfortunate *Finnegans Wake* is nothing but a formless and dull mass of phony folklore, a cold pudding of a book, a persistent snore in the next room, most aggravating to the insomniac I am. . . . *Finnegans Wake*'s façade disguises a very conventional and drab tenement house, and only the infrequent snatches of heavenly intonations redeem it from utter insipidity. I know I am going to be excommunicated for this pronouncement" (*Wisconsin Studies* interview). Charles Kinbote sustains his maker's negative opinion: "it would have been unseemly for a monarch to appear in the robes of learning at a university lectern and present to rosy youths *Finnigan's* [*sic*—A.A.] *Wake* as a monstrous extension of Angus MacDiarmid's 'incoherent transactions' and of Southey's Lingo-Grande ('Dear Stumparumper,' etc.) . . ." (*Pale Fire,* p. 76).

Joyce himself helped to introduce Nabokov to *Finnegans Wake.* In Paris in 1937 or 1938, he gave Nabokov *Haveth Childers Everywhere* (1930), one of the fragments published before the *Wake* was completed. Future commentators will no doubt find several echoes of *Finnegans Wake* in *Lolita;* but it could hardly be otherwise, since Joyce's book is so inclusive, so monstrously allusive (Phineas Quimby appears on p. 536 of the *Wake* [standard American edition], and on p. 250 of *Lolita*—but who *doesn't* appear in *Finnegans Wake?*). Moreover, Joyce's punning mutations anticipate and echo sentences which are yet to be written. The hero of *Finnegans Wake* is HCE—Here Comes Everybody, Humphrey Chimpden Earwicker, usually just Humphrey (with a humped back). Since he is "Everyman," there are some forty humming variations of his name, and, "influences" aside, there is statistically reason enough for some of Nabokov's humorously distorted forms of "Humbert" to coincide with a few of Joyce's punning phonetic variants. Thus Nabokov's sartorially splendid "Homburg" (p. 109) complements Joyce's "Humborg" (p. 72, standard American edition), and Joyce's "Humfries" (p. 97) should surely be served with Nabokov's "Hamburg[s]" (pp. 109 and 261) —but these are all coincidences, said Nabokov, for, "Generally speaking, *FW* is a very small and blurry smudge on the mirror of my memory." The only persistent "smudge" is a trace of Anna Livia Plurabelle. In *Bend Sinister*, Ophelia is imagined "wrestling—or, as another rivermaid's father would have said, 'wrustling'—with the willow" (p. 113); and in *Ada*, the title character alludes to the music of the self-contained A.L.P. section: "Did he know Joyce's poem about the two washerwomen?" she wonders (p. 54). The "children-colors," however, constitute the only intentional allusion to *Finnegans Wake* in *Lolita*. For a summary of Joyce allusions, see 4/11.

221/2 *Orange . . . and Emerald:* when I asked Nabokov if he chose these particular colors because they are also the common names of a butterfly and a moth, respectively, Nabokov responded: "The Dubliner's rainbow of children on p. 221 would have been a meaningless muddying of metaphors had I tried to smuggle in a Pierid of the Southern States and a European moth. My only purpose here was to render a prismatic effect. May I point out (at the risk of being pretentious) that I do not see the colors of lepidoptera as I do those of less familiar things—girls, gardens, garbage (similarly, a chessplayer does not see white and black as white and black), and that, for instance, if I use 'morpho blue' I am thinking not of one of the many species of variously blue *Morpho* butterflies of South America, but of the ornaments made of bits of the showy wings of the commoner species. When a lepidopterist uses 'Blues,' a slangy but handy term, for a certain group of Lycaenids, he does not see that word in any color connection because he knows that the diagnostic undersides of their wings are not blue but dun, tan, grayish, etc., and that many Blues, especially in the female, are brown, not blue. In my case, the differentiation in artistic and scientific vision is particularly strong because I was really born a landscape painter, not a landless escape novelist as some think." For more on "blue," see 263/3; for a more generalized discussion of color, see 56/1.

222/1 *P. O. Wace and P. O. Elphinstone:* = P.O.W. and Poe, and the imprisonment theme.

223/1 *Ne manque . . . Qu'il t'y:* an allusion to Quilty and a parody of the classical alexandrine verse of seventeenth-century France, specifically of *Le Cid* (1636), by Pierre Corneille (1606–1684): "Do not fail to tell your suitor, Chimène, how beautiful the lake is, because he should take you there." Chimène is from *Le Cid,* but the line itself is invented. See also *Keys,* p. 71. For an index to Quilty references, see 31/9.

223/2 *the mysterious nastiness:* Mona knew all about Quilty and injected his name. H.H. is not supposed to understand, at the time, the planted *"qu'il t'y,"* though he suspects some nasty trick.

223/3 *à titre documentaire:* French; just for the record.

223/4 *Lo to behold:* H.H. toys with the worn interjection, "Lo and behold," as Lolita did much earlier (50/3).

224/1 *detective:* Trapp (Quilty).

224/2 *un ricanement:* French, a sneer.

224/3 *Alice Adams:* the title of a 1921 novel by Booth Tarkington (1869–1946) about a small-town girl who pines for better things.

225/1 *Browns:* "Browns" reappear on pp. 245, 251, and 253.

225/2 *Cokes:* the 1958 edition did not capitalize the trademark; the error has been corrected.

226/1 *intacta:* H.H. uses the Latin form of the common word "intact," but invokes its less common meaning, "untouched virgin."

226/2 *boy friend:* Quilty.

226/3 *bearded scholar:* "Another little bit of prophecy" (see 158/5), said Nabokov. "Lots of bearded young scholars around these days."

226/4 *la pomme de sa canne:* French; the round knob of a cane.

227/1 *Mirana:* H.H.'s father had owned a Mirana hotel; see 10/5.

227/2 *Proteus of the highway:* Quilty; from Greek mythology; a prophetic sea-god in Poseidon's service, who would assume different shapes when seized.

227/3 *remises:* carriage houses.

227/4 *Melmoth:* a triple allusion. There is no such car; it is named after the four-volume Gothic novel *Melmoth the Wanderer* (1820), by Charles Robert Maturin (1782–1824), Irish clergyman and writer (also identified in *Keys*, p. 31). In his *Eugene Onegin* Commentary, Nabokov calls Maturin's Melmoth a "gloomy vagabond" (Vol. II, p. 352). "The book, although superior to [Monk] Lewis and Mrs. Radcliffe, is essentially second-rate, and Pushkin's high regard for it (in the French version) is the echo of a French fashion," writes Nabokov (*ibid.*, p. 353). Nabokov's paraphrase of the "action" of *Melmoth the Wanderer (ibid.)* underscores the humor of naming H.H.'s car after it:

> [John Melmoth] and his uncle are descendants of the diabolical Melmoth the Traveler ("Where he treads, the earth is parched! Where he breathes, the air is fire! Where he feeds, the food is poison! Where he turns his glance, is lightning. . . . His presence converts bread and wine into matter as viperous as the suicide foam of the dying Judas . . ."). John discovers a moldering manuscript. What follows is a long tale full of tales within tales—shipwrecks, madhouses, Spanish cloisters—and here I begin to nod.
>
> . . . .
>
> Melmoth's nature is marked by pride, intellectual glorying, "a boundless aspiration after forbidden knowledge," and a sarcastic levity that makes of him "a Harlequin of the infernal regions." Maturin used up all the platitudes of Satanism, while remaining on the side of the conventional angels. His hero enters into an agreement with a Certain Person who grants him power over time, space, and matter (that Lesser Trinity) under the condition that he tempt wretches in their hour of extremity with deliverance if they exchange situations with him.

Maturin's novel most likely supplied Oscar Wilde (1854–1900) with his post-prison pseudonym of "Sebastian Melmoth." In addition, added

Nabokov, "Melmoth may come from Mellonella Moth (which breeds in beehives) or, more likely, from Meal Moth (which breeds in grain)." For entomological allusions, see 6/1.

227/5 *grays . . . his favorite cryptochromism:* a coinage; "secret colors." It is also an authorial favorite, in view of the puns on Haze, shadow, and ombre.

229/1 *"ordeal of the orb":* changing the tire.

229/2 *gigantic truck . . . impossible to pass:* a fear confirmed; see 160/1.

CHAPTER 20

229/3 *"Love Under the Lindens":* planted between famous plays by Henrik Ibsen (1828–1906) and Anton Chekhov (1860–1904) is a combination of *Desire Under the Elms* (1924), by Eugene O'Neill (1888–1953), and *Unter den Linden* (a boulevard in Berlin). See also *Keys,* p. 150n. The portmanteau title, credited to "Eelmann" (O'Neill plus Thomas Mann), is mentioned in *Ada* (p. 403). Nabokov's low opinion of O'Neill's *Mourning Becomes Electra* is expressed in *Gogol* (p. 55).

230/1 *flashlight:* a corrected author's error (instead of "torchlight" in the 1958 edition). The quotation marks which enclosed this extract in the 1958 edition have also been corrected.

230/2 *Cyrano . . . sleeping stranger:* after rereading this passage in 1968, Nabokov belatedly put words in H.H.'s mouth: "Cyrano's big nose. Cyranose. Sorry myself to have missed that portmantoid pun. 'A sleeping stranger,' " he added, "is enchanting and haunting." Edmond Rostand's famous play (1897) is based on the life of Cyrano de Bergerac (1619–1655), French writer and soldier. "Cyraniana" in *Ada* (p. 339) alludes to his most famous work, *Histoire comique des Etats et Empires de la Lune* (1656; modern edition: *A Voyage to the Moon*).

230/3 *petit rat:* a young ballet student at the Paris Opera (ages nine to fourteen).

231/1 *Electra:* "The name is based on that of a close ally of the Clouded Yellow butterfly," said Nabokov, "and has nothing to do with the Greek Electra." See 209/1. For entomological allusions, see 6/1.

232/1 *Ned Litam:* the anagrammatic (it reads backwards) pseudonym under which the great tennis player William T. (Bill) Tilden II wrote fiction. See 162/3, where Lolita takes lessons from him.

232/3 *endorsing a Dromedary:* like Quilty; see 69/2. Note how H.H. is continually providing oblique clues; see 31/9 for a summary of Quilty allusions.

232/3 *fifty-three:* the 1958 edition omitted the hyphen; the error has been corrected.

233/1 *susceptible to the magic of games . . . I saw the board:* H.H. is speaking for his maker, who would hope that the reader shares this limpid view of the gameboard that is *Lolita.*

233/2 *stratagems:* "beautiful word, stratagem—a treasure in a cave," writes Nabokov in *Gogol* (p. 59).

233/3 *tessellated:* laid with checkered work or adorned with mosaic.

233/4 *Champion, Colorado:* an actual town, chosen by Nabokov because this is a championship game—H.H.'s attempts to fix in prose the beauty of the nymphet.

234/1 *Decugis or Borman:* Max Decugis was a great European tennis player who often teamed with Gobbert (see 162/4). They were Wimbledon men's doubles champions in 1911. Paul de Borman was the Belgian champion in the first decade of this century. Nabokov recalled, "He was left-handed, and one of the first Europeans to use a sliced (or twist) service. There is a photograph of him in the Wallis Myers book on tennis (c. 1913)." I could not find the Myers book, but Decugis and Borman are discussed in George W. Beldman and P. A. Vaile's *Great Lawn Tennis Players* (New York, 1907). Beldman deplores Borman's lack of aggressiveness and poor position (resulting from the way he used his body to achieve his spins and cut shots), and writes of him, inimitably, "I do not know that he has a single perfect stroke, yet in every shot he made there was education for him who was able to take it" (pp. 350–351). Nabokov took it, and immortalized Borman in *Lolita.* At first wince (to quote H.H.), such minutiae may seem no better than Kinbotisms, but they are calmly offered as an example of the precise manner in which Nabokov's memory speaks to him and, as well, to suggest how he does indeed stock his "imaginary garden with real toads" (see 119/1). He was in fact a lifelong tennis enthusiast and supplemented his meagre income as an émigré by giving tennis lessons to wealthy Berliners. Not by chance does he have H.H. poeticize Lolita's tennis game, on a court invested with the geometric perfection that the painter Piet Mondrian (1872–1944) brought to rigorous abstractions that sometimes look like overviews of tennis courts.

234/2 *butterfly:* although Nabokov intended no "symbolism," it appears after H.H. has come as close to capturing Lolita's grace as he ever will. Nabokov only commented, "Butterflies are indeed inquisitive, and the dipping motion is characteristic of a number of genera." See 6/1.

234/3 *wimbles:* any of several instruments for boring holes.

234/4 *a syncope in the series:* an elision or loss of one or more letters or sounds from the middle of a word.

234/5 *Maffy On Say:* phonetic American pronunciation of *"ma fiancée."*

235/1 *purling:* gently murmuring, as a brook.

235/2 *three horrible Boschian cripples:* one of whom is Quilty. Hieronymous Bosch (c. 1450–1516), the great Flemish master of the grotesque, whose paintings abound in moral and physiological cripples. "And Flemish hells with porcupines and things" is a brief Boschian vision in the poem *Pale Fire* (line 226). On his deathbed, in *Ada*, Daniel Veen, an art collector and Bosch devotee, imagines that he is being put-upon by creatures from a Bosch painting, and dies "an odd Boschean death" (pp. 435–436). Nabokov then comments at length on the butterfly rendered at the center of Bosch's "Garden of Delights."

236/1 *That . . . intruder . . . a double:* Quilty; a pun: a double at tennis and a *Doppelgänger.* See 243/7.

CHAPTER 21

236/2 *red ball:* rolled by Quilty, who reappears on p. 237.

237/1 *Aztec Red:* H.H. remembers the color of Quilty's car. See 217/1.

237/2 *padded shield:* like the *olisbos* of 94/1; Quilty is seen as a grotesque Priapus who in this passage transforms nature into a veritable forest of phalli. *Priaps* (below) is H.H.'s usage.

CHAPTER 22

238/1 *Elphinstone:* where H.H. will lose his "elf"; see 31/3.

238/2 *Soyons logiques:* French; Let us be logical.

239/1 *saguaro:* a giant cactus with a thick stem and white flowers.

239/2 *fatamorganas:* mirages: see 10/5. A display in the fabulous department store in *King, Queen, Knave* offers "a Fata Morgana of coats" (p. 68).

239/3 *José Lizzarrabengoa:* Carmen's abandoned lover. See 45/3, 243/4, and 278/2.

239/4 *Etats Unis:* French; U.S.A.

239/5 *Mrs. Hays:* H.H. found Lo at Mrs. Haze's house, and will now lose her at the motor court of Mrs. Hays, also a widow.

240/1 *Blue:* from the common German name, "Blau." Dr. Starov, from the last chapter of *The Real Life of Sebastian Knight* (1941), and Dr. Blue combine in *Pale Fire* (1962) to form "The great Starover Blue [who] reviewed the role / Planets had played as landfalls of the soul" (lines 627–628). See 200/3.

240/2 *heterosexual Erlkönig in pursuit:* Quilty; an allusion to Goethe's poem *Erlkönig* ("Erlking"; king of the elves), in which spectral incarnations of the Erlking pursue a little boy who rides with his father through the dark and windy forest. Unable to possess the beloved boy, the Erlking wills his death. When the father arrives "safely" at the farmhouse, the child is dead in his arms. In *Pale Fire*, the Zemblan word *"alfear"* (Nabokov's coinage) is defined as "uncontrollable fear caused by elves" (p. 143); and a passage of John Shade's (lines 653–664) alludes to Goethe's poem, especially line 662, which Charles Kinbote likes enough to scan and then translate into Zemblan (p. 239). See the *Onegin* Commentary (Vol. II, p. 235). See also *Keys*, p. 138n. For "elf," see 31/3.

240/3 *"ague":* a violent chill.

241/1 *haute montagne:* French; above-timberline pastures.

241/2 *Lore . . . Rolas:* the importation of Basques and their vicious sheep dogs, and the place names (Lore, etc.) are "real," Nabokov having encountered them both in the Pyrenees and the Rockies. *"Que sais-je!"* is a French cliché ("and so forth," "or whatever").

241/3 *French perfume:* the Soleil Vert of p. 256.

241/4 *secret agent . . . or hallucination:* Quilty.

241/5 *Aurora:* the dawn, as personified by the Romans (Eos for the Greeks). The image of the "warmed hands" means the sun had hardly risen high enough to warm the hillside.

241/6 *lavender:* a mint cultivated on hillsides in Southern France, used for its fragrant oil.

242/1 *Clowns and Columbines . . . Tennis:* the first title is H.H.'s invention (the other titles exist). In the *commedia dell'arte* (see 213/2 and 248/6), the clown Pulcinella had a dual nature: witty, ironic, somewhat cruel, yet also silly, fawning, and timid. Columbine was the eternal coquette whose keen wit allows her to manipulate the most complex intrigues. She is the constant companion of Harlequin, the volatile, elusive character associated with Mercury as the patron of merchants, panderers, and thieves. The analogy with H.H., Lolita, and Quilty is clear. Helen Wills (1905–   ) was the greatest woman tennis player of the twenties and thirties, and her youthful championship and 1928 book, *Tennis,* are obviously meant to inspire Lolita further. The dance volumes are evidently there to inspire a new program of instruction and state of grace that H.H. will never get to see. The volume of Browning must contain *Pippa Passes* (see 117/2 and 207/2). The title character, a perambulating mill girl, is so good-natured that she keeps on singing, no matter what she sees.

242/2 *fundament jigging:* buttocks.

242/3 *a crumpled envelope:* the letter was from Quilty.

242/4 *chassé-croisé:* side stepping and re–side stepping each other.

243/1 *"Je croyais . . . doux":* "I thought that it was a *bill*— not a love-note" (a pun on *bill* and *billet doux*).

243/2 *Deseret News:* an actual newspaper in Utah.

243/3 *sister Ann:* it will be clear in a moment that H.H. is alluding to Charles Perrault's (1628–1703) fairy tale about Bluebeard, who murdered six wives. Hoping to be rescued by her two brothers, his seventh wife posts her sister Ann as sentinel; "Sister Ann, do you see anyone coming?" is her constant refrain. She finally does, and the "brutal brothers" slay Bluebeard. See also *Keys,* p. 48. When I was writing this note, I called to my wife in the adjacent room, asking her if she remembered all the details in *Bluebeard*. "I know the story," replied Karen, my seven-year-old daughter, running into the room (this was in 1967). I showed her the passage in *Lolita*, and, after helpfully identifying Sister Ann, she read H.H.'s dirge for Bluebeard. "Poor Bluebeard," she quoted. "*Poor* Bluebeard? He was *awful!* What kind of book *is* this?" For allusions to *Bluebeard* in *Ada*, see pp. 164 and 180, and in *King, Queen, Knave,* pp. 263–264. See 31/3.

243/4 *Est-ce que ... Carmen:* "Do you not love me any more, my Carmen?" José says this to Carmen in their penultimate confrontation (Chapter Three). José's very next beseechment is also quoted by H.H. (278/2). For Mérimée, see 45/3.

243/5 *plotting in Basque:* Carmen and José plot in Basque in the presence of her rich, uncomprehending English lover, whom José kills.

243/6 *Zemfirian:* "gypsy"; H.H.'s coinage, from the heroine of *The Gypsies* (1824, published 1827), the long poem by Russia's greatest poet, Aleksandr Pushkin (1799–1837). Another "Carmen" story, its hero Aleko kills both the treacherous Zemfira and her lover (also see *Keys,* p. 49). The poem is also an affirmation of a gypsy's freedom, which is another reason why H.H. says that the conspiratorial girls are speaking "Zemfirian," as well as Basque. Carmen is a gypsy too, and in her last moments proclaims this freedom; Ada is cast as Dolores, the fatal gypsy dancing girl in the film *Don Juan's Last Fling* (*Ada,* pp. 488–490).

243/7 *double game:* a pun; Nabokov is also playing it by leading the reader on with a *Doppelgänger* situation that parodies itself. See Introduction.

243/8 *father-substitute:* Quilty; a parody of the Freudian "transference" theory, whereby the daughter transfers her affections from her father to another, similar man, thus exorcising her Oedipal tension. Quilty is said to have indulged "snow"—argot for cocaine (top of p. 244).

244/1 *gitanilla:* a diminutive of *gitana,* Spanish for "Gypsy girl," used often in Mérimée's *Carmen*. In *Ada,* "Osberg" (Borges) is the author of *The Gitanilla,* a novel reminiscent of *Lolita* (see 9/1), and several allusions to Osberg and his influence on Van Veen are jokes aimed at the critics who yoke Nabokov and Borges. A revolving paperback stand (p. 371) offers *The Gitanilla* along with several volumes no doubt as racy (*Our Laddies* and *Clichy Clichés,* joke titles aimed at the pornographic works produced by *Lolita*'s first publisher, the Olympia Press).

244/2 *une belle . . . en bleu:* a beautiful lady all dressed in blue (a vision of the Virgin). "Visionary" nurse Mary is of Basque descent, and the Hautes-Pyrénées of her ancestors is in the same *département* (state) as Lourdes, where many little French girls have experienced visions of the blue-garbed Virgin, phenomena duly celebrated in the press and popular literature. Nabokov mocks a best-selling romance on the subject in *Bend Sinister*, Chapter Three: ". . . that remarkable cross between a certain kind of wafer and a lollipop, Louis Sontag's *Annunciata*, which started so well in the Caves of St. Barthelemy and ended in the funnies" (the object of this parody is Franz Werfel's *Song of Bernadette*).

245/1 *a saint:* the lines which follow parody the first half of the fourth stanza of Robert Browning's "Soliloquy of the Spanish Cloister" (1842):

> *Saint*, forsooth! While brown Dolores
> Squats outside the Convent bank
> With Sanchicha, telling stories,
> Steeping tresses in the tank . . .

For a summary of "While brown" gamesmanship, see 253/1. For Browning, see 117/2 and 207/2.

245/2 *a great holiday:* Fourth of July, 1949. "Independence Day—for Lolita," said Nabokov.

245/3 *like some sly fairy:* Frank may also have dallied with *his* Mrs. "Haze" (Hays). His tattoo of an elfin nymphet evokes the novel-length fairy-tale motif. See 31/1 for a summary. Her nakedness and "flower–crowned head" are in turn evocative of Polynesia.

245/4 *I would stay in bed all day:* like a king, especially if "I felt . . . Polynesian" (p. 246). The latter is a reference to the traditional family and clan division of Polynesian society, and the wide–ranging and complicated networks of ties overseen by the head of the clan who on some of the isles is a king over several islands. A good clan chief would certainly look into the disappearance of a daughter. The humor of the reference is also predicated on the importance of their incest taboos, which H.H. would obviously bypass. H.H. has doubtless read Margaret Mead's omnibus volume, *From the South Seas* (1939).

246/1 *Mr. Gustave . . . spaniel pup:* Lolita has told Quilty that H.H. has mistaken him for his uncle (or cousin), Gustave Trapp; Quilty has known this for some time (see 251/4). Lolita liked the old lady's cocker spaniel at The Enchanted Hunters (pp. 117–118; commented upon by H.H., 261/4), which eavesdropper Quilty may have recalled and thus bought her this pup. But one of his three hobbies is "pets" (p. 31). For references to him, see 31/9.

246/2 *Caddy Lack:* an obvious pun, but young readers, especially in A.D. 2000, may not know that in the 1947–1952 period the Cadillac was by far the most luxurious American car, and a "status symbol," though H.H. uses its vulgar diminutive ("Caddy") to suggest otherwise.

246/3 *maquette:* a small, preliminary model of something planned, such as a stage set.

246/4 *telestically:* with the projection of a purpose, with a definite end in view, inwardly expressed.

246/5 *bemazed: archaic;* bewildered, stupefied.

247/1 *my brother:* Quilty; see 249/1 and 251/13.

<h2 style="text-align:center">CHAPTER 23</h2>

247/2 *fiend's spoor:* Quilty's trail; a "spoor" is the track of a wild animal. The evil selves in Poe and Stevenson Double tales are of course animal-like. In "The Murders in the Rue Morgue" (1845) it *is* an animal.

247/3 *comme il faut:* French; good manners, decorum.

248/1 *Kawtagain:* "Caught again." Needless to say, there is no such town.

248/2 *342:* see 35/4 and 118/3 for the patterned "coincidence."

248/3 *N. Petit . . . Ill.:* abbreviated title of the illustrated French dictionary, *Nouveau Petit Larousse Illustré.* Lucette's "Little Larousse" in *Ada* is a pun on the French *rousse,* "red hair" (p. 368).

248/4 *a few paces from Lolita's pillow:* see 130/1.

248/5 *Ponderosa Lodge:* the return address on the letter received on p. 242.

248/6 *Dr. Gratiano . . . Mirandola, N.Y.:* in the *commedia dell' arte,* Doctor Gratiano is a philosopher, astronomer, man of letters, cabalist, barrister, grammarian, diplomat, and physician. When the doctor speaks, one cannot tell whether it is Latin or Low Breton, and he frequently delivers badly mangled quotations in Latin and Greek. His audiences usually must interrupt and thrash him in order to arrest the tide of "eloquence." The nonexistent "town" Mirandola has nothing to do with Pico, the Italian humanist, Nabokov said; like Forbeson, he was a minor character in Italian comedy. Nor, said Nabokov, did he intend any allusion to Mirandolina, the heroine of *Mine Hostess,* by Carlo Goldoni, Italian playwright. See 242/1.

249/1 *your brother:* H.H. has already said this of Quilty.

249/2 *an impossible balance:* a very important passage. The verbal figurations throughout *Lolita* demonstrate how Nabokov appears everywhere in the texture but never in the text, though the impersonator "come[s] damn close to it" (see 201/7), especially in the "cryptogrammic paper chase" on the next two pages. "Trapp" 's balancing act lucidly describes the performance of both the narrator and his creator, while the "thrashing anguish" also belongs to John Ray's "old-fashioned readers."

250/1 *logodaedaly* [p. 249] *and logomancy:* to prove that he is versed in *logodaedaly* (the arbitrary or capricious coining of words), H.H. the logomachist creates his own word from *logo* (word) plus the suffix *-mancy* ("divination in a [specified] manner").

250/2 *Quelquepart:* French; somewhere. Quilty must be there. See 251/5.

250/3 *fountain pen . . . repressed undinist . . . water nymphs in the Styx:* a most liquid passage. An *undine* is a female water spirit who could acquire a soul by marrying a mortal. "But," added Nabokov, "the main point here is that 'undinist' is a person (generally male) who is erotically excited by another person's (generally female) making water (Havelock Ellis was an 'undinist,' or 'fountainist,' and so was Leopold Bloom)." Ellis was the first to use the word this way, and H.H.—like Quilty, "an amateur of sex lore"—no doubt has read the section on "Undinism" in *Studies in the Psychology of Sex,* Vol. VII. In Greek mythology, the Styx is the main river of the lower world.

250/4 *passion . . . cryptogrammic paper chase:* Quilty is indeed a tease, but so is H.H., who punningly alludes to the "melancholy truth" about Quilty's virtual impotence (p. 298). Thus H.H. refers to Cue's "teasing," his "passion for tantalization" (that is, his main passion), and the "ejaculat[ion]" of "his fiendish conundrum." The summary word "cryptogrammic" includes "cryptogamic" ("belonging or relating to the non-flowering plants"), which alludes to his sexuality, as well as his cryptogames. These games may be more gratifying than some, since Quilty's literary sources are so broadly hinted at in the text.

250/5 *Arsène Lupin:* the creation of Maurice Leblanc (see 211/1). See also *Keys*, p. 12. Most of the allusions in the two-page "paper chase" are also identified in *Keys*, pp. 12–19. *Arsène Lupin contre Sherlock Holmes* (1908) and *Les Confidences d'Arsène Lupin* (1914) are typical of the many Lupin volumes. For Conan Doyle, see 64/1. Hermann, the narrator of *Despair*, wonders, "But what are they—Doyle, Dostoevsky, Leblanc, Wallace—what are all the great novelists who wrote of nimble criminals . . . in comparison with me? Blundering fools!" (p. 122).

250/6 *A. Person, Porlock:* in the note which he affixed to "Kubla Khan" (1816), Samuel Taylor Coleridge (1772–1834), the English poet, explains how his dream was interrupted: "At this moment he was unfortunately called out by a person on business from Porlock. . . ." H.H.'s "dream" has been interrupted with equal finality by Quilty. In "The Vane Sisters" (1959; in *Nabokov's Quartet* and *Tyrants Destroyed and Other Stories*), a story about psychic phenomena, there is an eccentric librarian named Porlock, "who in the last years of his dusty life had been engaged in examining old books for miraculous misprints such as the substitution of 'l' for the second 'h' in the word 'hither.' "

250/7 *touché, reader!:* H.H. grants that the reader "got" these "easy" pokes; Rimbaud's poem *Le Bâteau ivre* (see 163/6 and 172/1) and Maurice Maeterlinck's play *L'Oiseau bleu* have been transposed (see 201/5). H.H. has written a book on "Rainbow" (see 75/6 for the garbled newspaper report, which Quilty has evidently read). *Schmetterling* is German for butterfly (see p. 301), and Maeterlinck was in fact an amateur entomologist.

250/8 *D. Orgon, Elmira, NY:* Orgon is the husband of Elmire in *Tartuffe* (1664), by Molière (Jean Baptiste Poquelin [1622–1673]), French playwright and actor. The title character tries to seduce her. "Elmira" is of course an actual town, and the location of a college for women. Quilty was born in New Jersey and educated in New York (p. 31), and "D. Orgon" is an accurately transcribed phonetic rendering of the regional accent.

250/9 *Bumper, Sheridan:* Bumper is a character in *The School for Scandal* (1777), by Richard Sheridan (1751–1816), Irish playwright.

250/10 *Phineas Quimby, Lebanon, NH:* in mythology, Phineas provided Jason the directions to find the Golden Fleece; while Phineas Quimby (1802–1866) was an American pioneer in the field of mental healing, born in Lebanon, N.H. He initially specialized in mesmerism, and for several years gave public hypnotic exhibitions (1838–1847). H.H.'s coercion of both Lolita and the reader make him a latter-day specialist, and on p. 308 he says that "Mesmer Mesmer" was one of the possible pseudonyms he had considered for his narrative.

250/11 *Dr. Kitzler, Eryx, Miss.:* for *Kitzler*—H.H.'s tag, miraculously picked up by Quilty—see 120/3; for *Eryx*, the cult of Aphrodite, where "religious prostitution" was indeed practiced, see 137/1. The abbreviated form of Mississippi adds to the pun cluster an incongruous note of formality; "translated," it reads "Dr. Clitoris, Venus, Miss"— and "Miss Venus" is the archetypal if not the ultimate beauty contest winner.

251/1 *living vacationists:* "Johnny Randall of Ramble was a real person, I think (as was also Cecilia Dalrymple Ramble, p. 252)," said Nabokov, but the two are linked to form another verbal "coincidence."

251/2 *N. S. Aristoff . . . NY:* Catagela is the comic name of a town in the play *The Acharnians* (425 B.C.), by Aristophanes (445–385 B.C.). It is from a Greek word meaning "to deride."

251/3 *James . . . Hoaxton:* James Mavor Morell is one of the main characters in *Candida* (1894), a play by George Bernard Shaw (1856–1950). *Hoxton* (Shaw's spelling) is a place name therein. The additional *a* is well in the spirit of this "cryptogrammic paper chase," since Quilty is a permanent resident of "hoax town," and his maker has passed through that town more than once. Dreyer reads *Candida* in *King, Queen, Knave* (p. 263).

251/4 *G. Trapp, Geneva, NY.:* H.H.'s relative is Swiss, so nationalistic Quilty chooses a city found in America as well as in Switzerland.

251/5 *Aubrey Beardsley, Quelquepart Island:* "Aubrey McFate" (56/1) and the Beardsleyan motif (52/3; 181/1) are finally united by Quilty in "Quelquepàrt"—that is, "somewhere." This French mirrors a Mérimée tag that lies ahead (278/2).

251/6 *Lucas Picador:* in Mérimée's novella, Lucas the picador is Carmen's last lover; José, tired of killing her lovers, kills Carmen (see 45/3). In bullfighting, the picador is the member of the company who uses a lance to annoy and weaken the bull just prior to the kill. Although Quilty seems to cast himself as the picador, it is the tired bull who will ultimately make the kill.

251/7 *Merrymay, Pa. . . . my Carmen:* a pun; Mérimée. The abbreviated *Pennsylvania* is a pun that nicely capsules Lolita's insulting, mock-familiar tone, as though she were saying, "the merry May festival is now being celebrated by Quilty, *Dad.*" H.H.'s betrayed "pathetic endearments" are his frequent epithets from *Carmen*.

251/8 *Will Brown, Dolores, Colo.:* Quilty echoes H.H., whose "forsooth" acknowledges the "coincidence"; see 245/1 (*"Saint,* forsooth! While brown Dolores") and 253/1. For "Dolores, Colo.," see 9/5 and 296/4.

251/9 *Harold Haze:* Lolita's deceased father.

251/10 *Donald Quix:* this pseudonym is appropriate to the Sierras, because they constitute so elevated a target for a windmill-tilter such as Quixote.

251/11 *bodkin:* a stiletto or dagger.

251/12 *Chestnut Lodge:* although H.H. is very sensitive to numerical and verbal "combinations," he is no match for Quilty, who is acute enough to have had miraculous access to H.H.'s previous pages: "Chestnut Lodge" completes H.H.'s cycle of changes on "Chestnut" (see 212/2 and 216/2); the key to the Lodge is held by Nabokov.

251/13 *Ted Hunter, Cane, NH.:* an anagram of "Enchanted Hunter" (see 108 /2), it is as expertly done as "Vivian Darkbloom." Quilty's punning allusion to Cain is appropriate and indeed perceptive, since H.H. has just referred to him as his brother (see 247/1).

251/14 *interrelated combinations:* the letters and numerals on the first two license plates offer William Shakespeare's monograms and dates of birth and death (1564–1616). For Shakespeare, see 31/6 and 284/4. The letters on the second set of plates refer to Quilty and his nickname ("Cue"). Less obvious and most literally "cryptogrammic" are the numbers, which add up to a highly significant fifty-two. H.H. and Lolita spent a year on the road—that is, fifty-two weeks—and there are as many lines in the poem addressed to her on pp. 255–256. Ray's Foreword indicates that Lolita, H.H., and Quilty all die in 1952 (see p. 4). There are fifty-two cards in a deck, and the author of *King, Queen, Knave* still has a few up his sleeve, as he demonstrates here.

251/15 *cunningly contrived . . . a common denominator:* cunning or not, it *is* revealed, for it is quite impossible that either H.H. or Quilty could realize the full significance of the number fifty-two; only one person can, and the "common denominator" points to the author. The "paper chase" is contrived in the same spirit as Ray's Foreword (see 4/4), the entomological motif (see 6/1), the opening chapter (see 9/1 and 9/6), *Who's Who in the Limelight* (see 32/7 and 34/3), and the Ramsdale class list (see 51/1 and 52/3)—to name only the main clusters and interlacements of Nabokov's grand anthemion. Of course, many of the allusions are within Quilty's reach, and there are plausible explanations for his knowing certain things. But other details are extraordinary, and it is not simply a matter of Quilty's brain having "affinities with my own," as H.H. says (p. 249). How could Quilty know that earlier in these pages H.H. had used *"Kitzler,"* identified *"Aubrey"* as his *"McFate,"* toyed with Chestnuts, alluded to Eryx (and Venus), and quoted "While brown Dolores"? Quilty knows all this—and everything else—because Nabokov wants him to know it, and because Quilty and H.H. can be said to "exist" only insofar as they have been created by the same man. In its concentrated effect, the "paper chase" is to the last part of the novel what *Who's Who* is to the first.

CHAPTER 24

252/1 *garçon:* French; fellow.

253/1 *Bill Brown . . . Dolores:* see 245/1 and 251/8. This "Bill Brown" rings a final verbal change on H.H.'s "While brown Dolores" (245/1) and Quilty's "Horribly cruel" (says H.H.) guest book entry, "Will Brown" (251/8). The echoic cross-references are placed almost back-to-back in order to give the astute reader a chance to make the association. Seeing the veracity of the narrative collapse, but not willing to grant that fiction is artifice, and rightly feeling that any cruelty *is* at his expense, the reader may anxiously wonder *who* is responsible for *what* here. The author, is, of course, and Nabokov immediately mocks such doggedly persistent literalism by having H.H. hire Bill Brown, an imbecilic private detective, to check the names and addresses collected from those guest books —a gesture that can only be for the benefit of the literal-minded reader, since H.H. himself plainly considers the material "nonsense data." The "information" provides a non-solution that parodies the reader's need for a solution and our belief that either literature or life will ever reveal one, in the largest sense. A hyphen, omitted in 1958, has been added to Bill's age.

CHAPTER 25

253/2 *Dolorès Disparue:* see 32/2. In the first French edition of Proust's great novel, *Albertine disparue* is the next-to-last volume. The definitive Pléiade edition (1954) has restored Proust's own title for it, *La Fugitive* (it is called *The Sweet Cheat Gone* in the Moncrieff translation). See 16/4.

254/1 *daymares:* H.H.'s coinage.

254/2 *chambres garnies:* French; furnished rooms.

254/3 *auctioneered Viennese bric-à-brac:* Freudian trappings, secondhand symbols. See 5/6 and 274/4.

254/4 *que . . . cela:* French; how far away all this was!

254/5 *Comics:* the first two are generalized and invented comic strips.

254/6 *gagoon . . . kiddoid gnomide:* on a visit to Montreux in 1968, I mentioned to Nabokov that I had been unable to identify that "repulsive strip" for this edition. Nabokov could not remember its name, but, expanding upon H.H.'s description, he dated it (the late nineteen-forties), noted that the strip "had science-fiction overtones," and vividly recalled "a big gangster, and his very small, big-eyed, lemur-like dwarf wife wearing a lot of jewelry." Because even that failed to awaken this annotator's memory, the author provided the drawing shown on the facing page. A 1976 correspondent is certain that the strip was *Kerry Drake,* created in 1943 by Alfred Andriola, who featured *Dick Tracy*–like grotesques drawn in a Milton Caniff manner. For other comic strip allusions, see 164/1 and 217/5.

Gagoon is a portmanteau of *gag, goon,* and *baboon,* while *gnomide* draws on the common meaning of *gnome* (dwarf) and combines its original meaning (from the Greek: a general maxim, a saying) with the nearly synonymous *bromide* (a tiresome, commonplace person; a hackneyed expression). *Kiddoid* is also H.H.'s coinage. Because the *-oid* suffix (resembling, having the form of) is used in scientific terms formed on Greek words, its incongruous usage here becomes humorous (e.g., *anthropoid;* H.H.'s word is defined as "genus of kid"). See *hypnotoid,* p. 274.

254/7 *Et moi . . . génie:* "And I was offering you my genius!" A bogus quotation, echoing any French Romantic poet (e.g., Alfred de Musset [1810–1857]). H.H. the cultivated European purposefully invokes French —the language of culture or genius—in ironic contrast with visual and verbal fragments of American mass culture. He catches perfectly the slangy neologisms and staccato beat of such forgotten voices as the gossip columnist and radio broadcaster Walter Winchell (1897–1972): "Joe–Roe marital enigma is making yaps flap."

255/1 *merman:* a fabled marine male creature; the mermaid's counterpart. See 174/5. In *Pale Fire,* Odon, Zemblan actor and patriot, appears in *The Merman,* "a fine old melodrama" (p. 129).

255/2 *losing contact with reality:* for an earlier incarceration, see 34/3.

255/3 *something I composed:* H.H.'s "something" is generally light enough, especially in its humorously blatant rhymes, but its fifty-two lines are truly "composed" in the way they cohere with a larger pattern: the fifty-two weeks H.H. and Lo spend together on the road (August 1947–August 1948), the year of their deaths, and so forth (see 251/14).

255/4 *I cannot . . . starling:* a quotation from Laurence Sterne's *A Sentimental Journey through France and Italy* (1768). On a visit to Paris, Yorick the narrator takes lightly the infamous Bastille. But his attention is drawn to a caged talking starling: " 'I can't get out,' said the starling." He is unable to free the bird, whose constant refrain moves him deeply. It becomes a symbol of all enslavement and confinement, and, returning to his room, he imagines at length a solitary captive in the Bastille. He next explains how the starling was given to him and subsequently changed hands countless times; the reader has perhaps seen the bird, suggests Yorick. From that time, he adds, he has borne the starling as the crest to his coat of arms, which he includes in the text. It bears an uncaged bird (see the Penguin English Library edition [1967], pp. 94–100). The starling that had learned only those "four simple words" is most important because it partakes of *Lolita*'s origin, and its lament is at the book's center. *Lolita*'s initial inspiration, writes Nabokov, was "prompted by a newspaper story about an ape [in the Paris zoo] who, after months of coaxing by a scientist, produced the first drawing ever charcoaled by an animal: this sketch showed the bars of the poor creature's cage" (p. 311). H.H., the "aging ape" writing from prison, whose impossible love metaphorically connects him with that imprisoned animal, learns the language, in his fashion, and records his "imprisonment." His narrative is the "picture" of the bars of the poor creature's cage— and an orchestration of the starling's four simple words.

256/1 *vair:* gray; the pale color of miniver fur.

256/2 *Soleil Vert:* French; Green Sun.

256/3 *L'autre soir . . . de ta vie?:* "The other night, a cold *air* [italics mine —A.A.] from the opera forced me to take to my bed; / Broken note— he who puts his trust in it is quite foolish! / It is snowing, the decor collapses, Lolita! / Lolita, what have I done with your life?" The four lines are a splendid parody and pastiche of various kinds of French verse. The alexandrine verse of line one (see 223/1) scans perfectly in French. The *air froid* is an untranslatable pun (*air:* melody; draft or wind). Line two is a traditional saying, originating with Virgil, though it is in fact drawn here from *Le Roi s'amuse* (1832), a play by Victor Hugo:

> *Souvent femme varie,*
> *Bien fol est qui s'y fie!*
> *Une femme souvent*
> *N'est qu'une plume au vent.*

These lines are sung by the King, first in Act IV, scene ii, in a cabaret. The first two lines are repeated from off stage in Act V, scene iii, which informs Triboulet (or Rigoletto) that the King is still alive (he had planned to murder the King, but kills his daughter instead). The play was performed only once before being banned by royal decree. It is the source of Verdi's *Rigoletto* (1851); Piave adapted the words and Verdi was responsible only for the music. The French version, which H.H. undoubtedly knows, is *Rigoletto, ou Le Buffon du prince*. *Rigoletto* is appropriate, since, figuratively speaking, H.H. is in his own right a grotesque clown. For Hugo, see 10/7. Line three of H.H.'s pastiche is overly sonorous, but the burlesqued entreaty of line four manages to express both the "truth and a caricature of it" (the artistic intention of Fyodor in *The Gift*, p. 200).

257/1 *pederosis:* see 55/2.

CHAPTER 26

258/1 *ensellure:* French; the concave curve formed by the spine; in a woman, the lumbar incurvation.

258/2 *Babylonian blood:* H.H. is very coy in "racial" matters, and enjoys using euphemisms (e.g., "Turk," p. 75) in the manner of the Victorians, with their "Mediterranean types." See 261/4.

258/3 *depraved May:* echo of a well-known line in T. S. Eliot's "Gerontion": "In depraved May, dogwood and chestnut, flowering judas" (line 20). See 16/3.

258/4 *Blake:* after the English poet and engraver William Blake (1757–1827). The invented *Toylestown* is a pun commemorating his "London" (1794) —toil's town.

258/5 *burning . . . Tigermoth:* a play on Blake's "The Tiger" (1794)— "Tiger! Tiger! burning bright"—and a reference to the actual Tigermoth ("an Arctid," noted Nabokov). For entomological allusions, see 6/1.

258/6 *cavalier servant:* a knight who is vassal to his fair lady; a medieval archetype of courtly love.

259/1 *mulberry moth:* wrote Nabokov: "Rita's phrase 'Going round and round like a mulberry moth' combines rather pleasingly the 'round and round the mulberry tree' of the maypole song and the silk moth of China which breeds on mulberry." See 6/1.

259/2 *Valechka:* like Ritochka (p. 260), a Russian diminutive.

259/3 *Schlegel . . . Hegel:* Friedrich Schlegel (1772–1829) and Georg Wilhelm Friedrich Hegel (1770–1831), the German philosophers, form a nonsense rhyme.

259/4 *shams and shamans:* H.H. enjoys the fact that while shamans (conjurers, witch doctors) may be shams, the semantic similarities are also illusory; the former is Anglo-Saxon in origin, the latter Tungusic and Sanskritic. *Columbine* (two lines above in the text) was misspelled in the 1958 edition (*o* instead of *u*); it has been corrected.

259/5 *ancilla:* accessory, aid; literally, in Latin, "maidservant."

259/6 *Tartary:* from *Tartarus*, the infernal regions of mythology; any region, usually in European Russia and Asia, inhabited by the violent Tatar (or Tartar) tribes or hordes, who are mostly Turkic. The Tartar empire is restored in *Ada*'s Antiterra.

260/1 *Mnemosyne:* in Greek mythology, a Titaness, daughter of Uranus and Gaea. She is associated with memory or remembrance. The nine Muses resulted from her union with Zeus. In the Foreword to the revised *Speak, Memory,* Nabokov says, "I had planned to entitle the British edition *Speak, Mnemosyne* but was told that 'little old ladies would not want to ask for a book whose title they could not pronounce.' "

260/2 *Cantrip . . . Mimir:* a cantrip is a charm or spell, while Mimir is a giant in Norse mythology who lived by the well at the root of Yggdrasill, the great tree symbolizing the universe. By drinking its water, he knew the past and future.

260/3 *travaux:* French; works.

261/1 *très digne:* French; very dignified.

261/2 *souvenir . . . veux-tu?:* "memory, memory, what do you want of me?" The opening line (minus *"l'automne,"* the last word) of "Nevermore" (title in English), by Paul Verlaine (1844–1896). H.H. begins his next sentence with that last word. Memories awakened by The Enchanted Hunters bring this line to mind. Verlaine's poem ends with the poet telling his beloved that his most perfect day was when she charmingly murmured "*Le premier* oui"—her first yes (see also *Keys*, p. 33). For further Verlaine allusions, see 264/2 and 278/1. H.H. identifies with Verlaine, who was abandoned by his much younger (and homosexual) lover and traveling companion, Rimbaud. In *Pale Fire*, Kinbote recalls a visit to Nice, and "an old bearded bum . . . who stood like a statute of Verlaine with an unfastidious sea gull perched in profile on his matted hair" (p. 170). Ada and Van Veen are touched by "the long sobs of the violins," the opening lines of Verlaine's *Chanson d'automne* (1866), translated and quietly absorbed into the text of *Ada* (p. 411). Van's "assassin pun" (p. 541) puns on "*la Pointe assassine,*" line seventeen of Verlaine's *Art poétique* (1882). "Verlaine had been also a teacher somewhere / In England. And what about Baudelaire, / Alone in his Belgian hell?" writes Nabokov in "Exile," an uncollected poem (*The New Yorker*, October 24, 1942, p. 26). For Baudelaire, see 162/2.

261/3 *petite . . . accroupie:* nymphet crouching.

261/4 *spaniel . . . baptized:* the old lady's dog, with which Lolita had played (117/3). H.H. wonders if the hotel's policy of "NO DOGS" had been broken to accommodate Christian dogs, because "NEAR CHURCHES" was commonly used (c. 1940–1960) as a code sign, a discreet indication that only Gentiles were accepted. A similar *quid pro quo* occurs in the same hotel when "Humbert" is misunderstood and distorted into a Jewish-sounding "Humberg" (p. 118), just as "Professor Hamburg" now finds the hotel full. "Refugee" H.H. is often mistaken for a Jew; see p. 79, where John Farlow is on the point of making an anti-Semitic remark and is interrupted by sensitive Jean. Quilty thinks H.H. may be a "German refugee," and reminds him, "This is a Gentile's house, you know" (297/2).

Nabokov's father was an outspoken foe of anti-Semitism. He wrote "The Blood Bath of Kishinev," a famous protest against the 1903 pogrom, and was fined by the tsarist government for the fiery articles he wrote about the Beiliss trial (Maurice Samuel mentions him several times in his book on the Beiliss case, *Blood Accusation* [1966]—coincidentally published at the same time as Bernard Malamud's novel based on it, *The Fixer*—and quotes from Nabokov's reportage). Nabokov *fils* was also outraged by anti-Semitism, and, because his wife is Jewish, was sensitive to it in a most acutely personal way (witness the empathy for "poor Irving" [53/3]). Nabokov recalled going into a New England inn years ago, accompanied by his son and his son's friend. Opening the menu, Nabokov noticed therein the succinct stipulation "Gentiles Only." He called over the waitress and asked her what the management would do if there appeared at the door that very moment a bearded and berobed man, leading a mule bearing his pregnant wife, all of them dusty and tired from a long journey. "What . . . what are you talking about?" the waitress stammered. "I am talking about Jesus Christ!" exclaimed Nabokov, as he pointed to the phrase in question, rose from the table, and led his party from the restaurant. "My son was very proud of me," said Nabokov. In *Pale Fire*, Kinbote and Shade discuss prejudice at length (note to line 470; pp. 216–218).

262/1 *Reader! Bruder!:* German; "brother." An echo of the last line of *Au Lecteur*, the prefatory poem in Baudelaire's *Les Fleurs du mal* (1857): "—*Hypocrite lecteur,—mon semblable,—mon frère!*" ("Hypocrite reader —my fellow man—my brother."). See 162/2.

262/2 *the Gazette's . . . Dr. Braddock and his group:* see p. 127. *Gazette* was not italicized in the 1958 edition; the error has been corrected.

262/3 *portrait . . . as a . . . brute:* an obvious play on Joyce's *A Portrait of the Artist as a Young Man* (1916). In searching for a title for his manuscript, the narrator of *Despair* considers "Portrait of the Artist in a Mirror," but rejects it as "too jejune, too *à la mode*" (p. 201). For Joyce, see 4/11.

262/4 *Brute Force:* the actual title of a movie released by Universal Pictures in 1947, directed by Jules Dassin, and starring Burt Lancaster, Charles Bickford, and Yvonne De Carlo. *Possessed* was released in 1947 by Warner Brothers, directed by Curtis Bernhardt, and starring Joan Crawford, Van Heflin, and Raymond Massey. The titles gloss H.H.'s circumstances, and *Brute Force*—a prison film, which Nabokov thought he had seen—is thematically apt.

262/5 *Omen Faustum:* Latin; Lucky Omen, or Lucky Strike cigarettes (pointed out to me by the philologist and Latinist, Professor F. Colson Robinson), a companion to "Dromes" (p. 69); related to *dies faustus*, "a day of favorable omen," or, specifically, "a day on which Roman religious law permitted secular activities."

262/6 *58 Inchkeith Ave.:* obsolete for "inchworm" (or Looper), the *last* thing that should be used for the name of an avenue, since inchworms (the larvae of certain moths) destroy shade trees. For entomological allusions, see 6/1. Fifty-eight inches was Lolita's height at the outset of the novel (see 9/3).

262/7 *Dark Age:* the author is Quilty; see 31/13. *Dark Age* was not italicized in the 1958 edition. The misprint has been corrected.

262/8 *Wine, wine . . . for roses:* see 262/1. Quilty is toying with lines from the sixth stanza of Edward FitzGerald's translation of *The Rubáiyát* (1879), by Omar Khayyám (d. 1123?), Persian poet and mathematician:

> And David's lips are locked; but in divine
> High-piping Pehlevi, with "Wine! Wine! Wine!
> Red Wine!"—the Nightingale cries to the Rose
> That sallow cheek of hers to incarnadine.

The latter word was used earlier by H.H. (see 73/1), demonstrating once more that "the tone of [Quilty's] brain had affinities with my own" (p. 249).

263/1 *nothing of myself:* see 127/2; but Quilty's "spectral shoulder" has been immortalized. For a summary of allusions to Quilty, see 31/9.

263/2 *vin triste:* French; melancholy intoxication.

263/3 *Why blue:* when I asked Nabokov "why blue?" and whether it had anything to do with the butterflies commonly known as the "Blues," he replied: "What Rita does not understand is that a white surface, the chalk of that hotel, does look blue in a wash of light and shade on a vivid fall day, amid red foliage. H.H. is merely paying a tribute to French impressionist painters. He notes an optical miracle as E. B. White does somewhere when referring to the divine combination of 'red barn and blue snow.' It is the shock of color, not an intellectual blueprint or the shadow of a hobby . . . I was really born a landscape painter." See 221/2.

CHAPTER 27

264/1 *Alice-in-Wonderland:* for Lewis Carroll, see 131/1.

264/2 *Mes fenêtres:* French; "My windows," a mock title that parallels *Mes Hôpitaux* ("My Hospitals" [1892]) by Paul Verlaine, and in general parodies the traditional use of the possessive in autobiographical writing. See 261/2.

264/3 *"Savez . . . de vous?"*: French; "Do you know that, when she was ten, my little daughter was madly in love with you?"

264/4 *Proustianized and Procrusteanized*: from *Procrustean*; violently forced into conformity or inflexibly adapted to a system or idea. Procrustes was the legendary robber who made his victims fit a certain bed by stretching or cutting off their legs. Proust is also alluded to on pp. 16, 182, and 253. Similar wordplay occurs in *Ada* when Van Veen discusses Space and Time: "avoid the Proustian bed and the assassin pun" (p. 541); the latter phrase is also an allusion to Verlaine (see 261/2).

264/5 *late*: a corrected author's error (instead of "early" in the 1958 edition).

265/1 *tankard*: a tall, one-handled drinking vessel with a lid.

265/2 *Never will Emma rally . . . timely tear*: a reference to *Madame Bovary*, Part III, Chapter Eight, where Homais the pharmacist and Emma's two physicians, Bovary and Carnivet, frantically try to save her life. They summon the very distinguished Dr. Larivière, but he cannot do anything for her ("He was the Third Doctor," added Nabokov, "but that fairy tale Third did not work" [see 31/3]). Old Rouault, Emma's father ("Flaubert's father," because the author said, "Emma Bovary? *c'est moi!*"), arrives after she has died; his subsequent tears are not too "timely" (III, Chapter Nine). See 145/3.

266/1 *honeymonsoon*: a portmanteau; *honeymoon* plus *monsoon*, the periodic wind and rainy season of Southern Asia.

266/2 *them*: Lolita and her kidnaper.

Chapter 28

267/1 *Pas tout à fait*: French; not quite.

268/1 *handkerchief . . . from my sleeve*: an English fad of the twenties and thirties. Affected rarely today, even among the pseudo-sophisticated.

268/2 *Ah-ah-ah*: simply the sound of a three-folding "harmonica" door.

268/3 *Dick Skiller:* a phonetic rendering of the pronunciation of "Schiller," and a blending of "Dick's killer" and the street name.

268/4 *Hunter Road:* a streamlined Enchanted Hunters; see 108/2.

Chapter 29

269/1 *Personne ... Repersonne:* French; a humorous alliteration; "Nobody. I re-rang the bell. Re-nobody."

270/1 *invisible tennis racket:* he is measuring this wan young woman against his wondrous memory of the tennis-playing nymphet (pp. 231–234).

270/2 *russet Venus:* "The Birth of Venus"; see 64/3 and 274/1.

272/1 *Waterproof:* see 89/2; Jean Farlow almost mentions Clare Quilty's name as the chapter concludes. For further discussion, see the Introduction, pp. lxiii–lxiv. For allusions to Quilty, see 31/9.

272/2 *everything fell into order ... the pattern of branches ... the satisfaction of logical recognition:* this passage, and the novel's crystalline progression, are prefigured in *The Defense* (1930) when Nabokov describes the two books with which chessplayer Luzhin

had fallen in love for his whole life, holding them in his memory as if under a magnifying glass, and experiencing them so intensely that twenty years later, when he read them over again, he saw only a dryish paraphrase, an abridged edition, as if they had been outdistanced by the unrepeatable, immortal image that he had retained. But it was not a thirst for distant peregrinations that forced him to follow on the heels of Phileas Fogg, nor was it a boyish inclination for mysterious adventures that drew him to that house on Baker Street, where the lanky detective with the hawk profile, having given himself an injection of cocaine, would dreamily play the violin. Only much later did he clarify in his own mind what it was that had thrilled him so about these two books; it was that exact and relentlessly unfolding pattern: Phileas, the dummy in the top hat, wending his complex elegant way with its justifiable sacrifices, now on an elephant bought for a million, now on a ship of which half has to be burned for fuel; and Sherlock endowing logic with the glamour of a daydream, Sherlock composing a monograph on the ash of all known sorts of cigars and with this ash as with a talisman progressing through a crystal labyrinth of possible deductions to the one radiant conclusion. [pp. 33–34]

For more on Holmes, see 64/1.

272/3 *valetudinarian:* a person having a sick or weakly constitution.

272/4 *visited with his uncle . . . Mother's club:* see 78/1.

273/1 *sidetrack . . . female:* see 209/2.

273/2 *frileux:* chilly; susceptible of cold.

274/1 *Florentine:* Botticelli's Venus (p. 270).

274/2 *French . . . Dorset yokel . . . Austrian tailor:* the "salad of racial genes" mentioned on pp. 9 and 10, where a Swiss and "Danubian" dash is added. "I have carefully kept Russians out of it," noted Nabokov, "though I think his first wife had some Russian blood mixed with Polish." Similarly, there are very few specific allusions to Russian writers in *Lolita.*

274/3 *beast's lair:* Quilty.

274/4 *Viennese medicine man:* Freud. See 5/6.

274/5 *hypnotoid:* a variant of "hypnoid," of or pertaining to hypnosis.

275/1 *Streng verboten:* German; strictly forbidden.

275/2 *like her mother:* "Lolita's smoking manners were those of her mother," emphasized Nabokov. "I remember being very pleased with that little vision when composing it."

275/3 *Cue:* Quilty's nickname; see 4/9.

276/1 *Curious coincidence:* "Camp Q" (p. 64). It's no "coincidence" at all; someone in the know has planned it this way.

276/2 *Duk Duk:* an obscene Oriental word for copulation, sometimes rendered in English as *dak* or *dok,* from the Persian *dakk* (vice, evil condition) and *dokhtan* (to pierce). No less "an amateur of sex lore" (p. 250) than Quilty, H.H. gleaned this from a sixteenth-century work, *The Perfumed Garden of the Cheikh Nefzaoui, a Manual of Arabian Erotology* (1886), translated by Sir Richard Burton (1821–1890), the British explorer and Orientalist (the treatise is mentioned by name in *Ada,* pp. 351–352). Such recondite material reminds one of *Lolita's* reputation, among nonreaders, as a "pornographic novel," and also underscores how Nabokov has had the last laugh, in more ways than one. In *Speak, Memory*, Nabokov writes about the "delusive opening moves, false scents, [and] specious lines of play" which characterize the chess problem. The subject matter of *Lolita* is in itself a bravura and "delusive opening move" —a withdrawn promise of pornography (see 3/1). The first one hundred or so pages of *Lolita* are often erotic—Lolita on H.H.'s lap, for instance —but starting with the seduction scene, Nabokov withholds explicit sexual descriptions, while H.H., trying to draw the reader into the vortex of the parody, exhorts us to "Imagine me: I shall not exist if you do not imagine me" (p. 129). "I am not concerned with so-called 'sex' at all," H.H. says (p. 134); Nabokov, on the contrary, is very much concerned with it, but with the reader's expectations rather than H.H.'s machinations.

"Anybody can imagine those elements of animality," he said, and yet a great many readers wished that he had done it for them—enough to have kept *Lolita* at the top of the best-seller list for almost a year, although librarians reported that many readers never finished the novel. The critics and remedial readers who complain that the second half of *Lolita* is less interesting are not aware of the possible significance of their admission. Their desire for highbrow pornography is "doubled" in Clare Quilty, whose main hobby is making pornographic films. When Lolita tells H.H. that Quilty forced her to star in one of his unspeakable "sexcapades," more than one voyeuristic reader has unconsciously wished that Quilty had been the narrator, his unseen movie the novel. But the novel's "habit of metamorphosis" is consistent, for the erotica which seemed to be there and turned out not to be was in fact present all along, most modestly; and it is Nabokov's final joke on the subject, achieved at the expense of the very common reader. Although the requisite "copulation of clichés" (p. 313) doesn't occur in the novel proper, its substratum reveals some racy stuff indeed: "Duk Duk"; "Undinist" (250/3); "Dr. Kitzler, Eryx, Miss." (250/11); the quotations in French from Ronsard and Belleau (47/2 and 47/3); anagrammatic obscenities (195/2); foreign disguises (*souffler*, 277/1); and so forth—erotica under lock and key, buried deep in dictionaries and the library stacks. Until now, only a few furtive "amateur[s] of sex lore," law-abiding linguists, and quiet scholars—good family men, all—have had exclusive access to this realm. The "incidental Dick" and "hole" of p. 278 are in the open—democratic, available references—on the junior-high level.

276/3 *redhaired guy:* see p. 234.

276/4 *Sade's . . . start: Justine, or, The Misfortunes of Virtue* (1791), by the Marquis de Sade (1740–1814), "French soldier and pervert" (as *Webster's Second* defines him). Like *Lolita, Justine* is prefaced by a Foreword resolutely "moral" in tone (in some editions, however, these initial paragraphs are not formally identified as a "Foreword"). The title character is an extraordinarily resilient young girl who exists solely for the pleasures of an infinite succession of sadistic libertines. She undergoes an array of rapes, beatings, and tortures as monstrously imaginative as they are frequent. Quilty has done a screenplay of *Justine* (298/3).

277/1 *souffler:* to "blow."

277/2 *my Lolita:* the "Latin" tag (see 45/1 and 192/2) appropriately concludes this important paragraph (p. 278), as it will the entire novel (309/3).

277/3 *dreaming . . . of . . . 2020* A.D.: "2020" because he has perfect prevision; also a numerical reflection of the doubling that occurs throughout the novel (see 51/2).

278/1 *mon . . . radieux:* "my great radiant sin," a line from Verlaine's *Lunes* ("Moons"), part of the sequence titled *Laeti et errabundi,* in which the poet celebrates his liaison and travels with Rimbaud. Again, H.H. identifies with Verlaine, the abandoned lover, and casts Lo as the deceitful Carmen. For Rimbaud, see 75/6, 163/6, and 250/7; for more on Verlaine, 261/2.

278/2 *Changeons . . . séparés:* "Let's change [our] life, my Carmen, let us go live in some place where we shall never be separated"; from Mérimée (see 243/4)—José and Carmen's next-to-last interview. He has romantically offered America as the place where they will be able "to lead a quiet life." H.H. is more specific in matters of geography. The Mérimée phrase *"quelque part"* (p. 278) mirrors "Quelquepart Island" (251/5), another "coincidence" that allows the author to reveal his presence at the center of a crucial scene, a verbal plant akin to the appearance of McFate's "face" in the mirrorlike Ramsdale class list on p. 52. For Mérimée, see 45/3.

278/3 *And we shall live happily ever after:* H.H. holds out to Lolita the possibility of a stereotyped fairy-tale ending, even though the tale seems already to have ended in "Elphinstone" (238/1). For more on the fairy tale, see 31/3.

278/4 *Carmen . . . moi:* "Carmen, do you want to come with me?" A quotation from Mérimée; a most dramatic moment at the end of the novella (see also *Keys,* p. 51). Carmen *does* go with José, but after they ride off she says that she will never live with him again, and will only follow him to death. A tearful imploration fails, and he kills her.

278/5 *"you got it all wrong . . . your incidental Dick, and this awful hole:* obscene double entendres on his name and home, which may have been missed by speed-readers. More subtle is H.H.'s use of one last colloquialism, "got," as though this common touch would help him communicate with Lolita. Her adult coarseness is telescoped by the *"bucks"* and "honey" on p. 279.

279/1 *mon petit cadeau:* French; my little gift, the little something. His "4000 bucks" in 1952 meant a great deal more than in today's money. "For some odd reason," said Nabokov, "this paragraph, top of p. 279, is the most pathetic in the whole book; stings the canthus, or should sting it."

280/1 *fly to Jupiter:* they are going to Juneau, but to H.H. it might as well be the planet. Jupiter is veiled by haze, and Lolita dies in "Gray Star, a settlement in the remotest Northwest" (see 4/8).

280/2 *Carmencita . . . -je:* "my little Carmen [in Spanish], I asked her"; another quotation from Mérimée.

280/3 *fool thing a reader . . . suppose:* especially a consumer of pulp fiction and movies, or a learned reader who has kept *Carmen* in mind. The several *Carmen* allusions on nearby pages serve as very fresh bait. See 45/3. See also *Keys,* p. 52.

280/4 *my American . . . dead love:* "One of the few real, lyrical, heartfelt outbursts on H.H.'s part," said Nabokov.

CHAPTER 30

281/1 *pulled on . . . sweater:* H.H. dons Quilty's fate, as it were.

282/1 *genuflexion lubricity:* worshipful lasciviousness or lewdness.

282/2 *he:* Quilty. For allusions to him, see 31/9.

282/3 *shadowgraphs:* see 114/2.

CHAPTER 31

283/1 *lithophanic: lithophane* is porcelain impressed with figures made distinct by light (e.g., a lampshade).

283/2 *To quote an old poet:* he is invented, but his "message" is signal.

CHAPTER 32

284/1 *a garden and . . . a palace gate:* one of those rare moments when H.H. is "so tired of being cynical." He contemplates the hidden beauties of Lolita's soul, and the mood prefigures his realization of Lolita's loss, fully expressed on p. 308.

284/2 *stippled Hopkins:* Gerard Manley Hopkins (1844–1889), English poet. *Stippled:* dotted (see 43/1). Its use refers to Hopkins's "Pied Beauty" (1877): "Glory be to God for dappled things— . . . / For rose-moles all in stipple upon trout that swim."

284/3 *shorn Baudelaire:* H.H. is referring to what might be called the poet's dramatic baldness. In the self-portrait c. 1860 and in Carjat's photograph of 1863, his hair seems to have been torn from the head; and the sculpture by Raymond Duchamp Villon (1911) and the etched portrait by his brother Jacques Villon (1920) accentuate the great forehead and cranium. See 162/2.

284/4 *God or Shakespeare:* an echo of Stephen Dedalus's invocation of "God, the sun, Shakespeare," in the Nighttown section of *Ulysses* (1961 Random House edition, p. 505). For Joyce, see 4/11. "The verbal poetical texture of Shakespeare is the greatest the world has known, and is immensely superior to the structure of his plays as plays," said Nabokov. "With Shakespeare it is the metaphor that is the thing, not the play" (*Wisconsin Studies* interview). Although the problem has not yet been submitted to a computer, Shakespeare would seem to be the writer Nabokov invokes most frequently in his novels in English. The title of his story " 'That in Aleppo Once . . .' " (1943) is drawn from *Othello*. Part of Chapter Ten of *The Real Life of Sebastian Knight* and all of Chapter Seven of *Bend Sinister* are devoted to Shakespeare; he informs the center of *Pale Fire*, where streets of the Zemblan capital city are named Coriolanus Lane and Timon Alley. "Help me, Will," calls John Shade, searching for a title for his poem—and he does help, providing a passage from *Timon of Athens*. Nabokov translated into Russian Shakespeare's Sonnets XVII and XXVII (*The Rudder,* September 18, 1927), two excerpts from *Hamlet* (Act IV, scene vii, and Act V, scene i [*The Rudder,* October 19, 1930]), and Hamlet's most famous soliloquy (Act III, scene i [*The Rudder,* November 23, 1930]). Regarding *Hamlet,* see 31/6. For significant verbal play on *Richard* III, see 49/1.

284/5 *pentapod:* counting as fifth the monster's "foot of engorged brawn" (p. 283).

284/6 *turpid: rare;* foul, disgraceful.

284/7 *mais . . . t'aimais:* French; but I loved you, I loved you!

285/1 *azure-barred:* the motel's neon lights reaching their bed from the window.

285/2 *Avis:* Avis Byrd: a pun, since "Avis" is Latin for *bird,* and another verbal doubling ("bird bird").

287/1 *above Moulinet:* in the Alpes-Maritimes.

CHAPTER 33

287/2 *scintillas:* sparks.

287/3 *Bonzhur: (bonjour)* "good day," phonetically spelled to mimic Charlotte's poor French accent; see 44/1.

287/4 *Edward Grammar . . . had just been arrayed:* an actual crime, noted Nabokov, drawn from a newspaper, as was the case of Frank LaSalle on p. 289. By saying that Ed had been *arrayed,* instead of *arraigned,* H.H. punningly describes the imposing display. His name deliberately recalls that of Edward G. Robinson (1893–1973), who starred in numerous crime films.

288/1 *Turgenev:* Ivan Turgenev (1818–1883), Russian writer. H.H. is alluding to the sonata of love that pours out the window near the end of his novel *A Nest of Gentlefolk* (1859).

288/2 *plashed: to plash* is to form a wave so convex that it splashes over (maritime term).

289/1 *Murphy-Fantasia:* the marriage of Lolita's classmate Stella Fantasia (p. 52). Note the verbal play on "moon-faced" and "stellar [Stella] care" (see also *Keys,* p. 8). See 24/3 for more stellar play.

289/2 *mille grâces:* French; a thousand affectations.

290/1 *vient de:* French; just (for the immediate past).

290/2 *"Réveillez-vous . . . mourir":* French; "Wake-up, Laqueue [*La Que:* Cue; Quilty], it is now time to die!" A fake quotation, significant only for its reference to Quilty. The image of his residence in H.H.'s "dark dungeon" was introduced, in a more generalized way, at The Enchanted Hunters hotel (see 125/1).

290/3 *toad of a face:* a favorite pejorative image in Nabokov (see also *Keys,* p. 153n). "Toad" is the boyhood nickname of the dictator in *Bend Sinister.*

291/1 *Dr. Molnar:* the dentist's name aptly contains a molar; it is not, said Nabokov, an allusion to Ferenc Molnár, Hungarian playwright.

291/2 *six hundred:* at that time $600 was a huge sum for dentures.

292/1 *Full Blued:* simply a reference to its finish (p. 216).

CHAPTER 34

292/2 *Pavor:* Latin; panic, terror. The Manor on Grimm Road burlesques the Gothic castles of fairy tales, Poe's mouldering House of Usher, and the medieval settings in Maeterlinck.

293/1 *penele:* a coined adjective; "penis-like" (*penes* is a plural form).

293/2 *My Lolita!:* the penultimate elegiac "Latin" intonation. See 45/1.

293/3 *selenian:* of or relating to the moon.

293/4 *raised a gun:* a foreshadowing of Quilty's death; an echo of the murder prefiguration in Chapter Two of *Laughter in the Dark.*

CHAPTER 35

293/5 *Insomnia Lodge:* Nabokov's bravura reading of this chapter is not to be missed (Spoken Arts LP 902; Side Two includes seven poems, one in Russian). The recording is especially recommended for classroom use. The nuances of Nabokov's accent—Cambridge by way of old St. Petersburg, the French in perfect pitch—are a striking aural equivalent to the theme of exile in his work and the international nature of that art; and the gusto of his reading communicates vividly a sense of the man, as well as underscoring the comic tone of the novel. Experience has suggested that the latter is not always sufficiently appreciated by students who have grown up with TV, and don't always "get" the tone of a printed page. Where's the laugh–track when you need it?

294/1 *fairy tale:* the fairy-tale opening is appropriate, for this is the most fantastic chapter in the novel, as witnessed by the uncommon velocities and trajectories of the bullets H.H. will fire, and the extraordinary behavior of their target. H.H. inspects three bedrooms because that is the fairy-tale number. For more on the fairy tale, see 16/6, 31/3, and 303/2.

294/2 *deep mirrors:* Quilty literally lives in a house of mirrors, just as H.H. is figuratively imprisoned in one; see 51/2, 119/2, and below, where the mirror is held up to him and he sees a familiar bathrobe. For an index to Quilty's appearances, see 31/9.

294/3 *keys . . . locks . . . left hand:* the keys don't work because magic and terror prevail in the special world of Pavor Manor. See 303/2.

294/4 *brief waterfall:* Quilty has once before flushed the toilet thusly; see 130/1.

295/1 *Je suis . . . Brustère:* "I am Mr. Brewster," spelled in phonetic French.

296/1 *Punch:* the hook-nosed and hunchbacked principal character in the traditional "Punch and Judy" show (see Introduction and 32/7). Used here in the sense of "clown."

296/2 *vaterre:* "water," with a phonetic French spelling; slang for "water closet" (lavatory).

296/3 *Patagonia:* an actual town in Arizona.

296/4 *Dolores, Colo.:* Nabokov, the enchanted butterfly hunter, made one of his most important captures at Telluride, near Dolores, Colo., which is why he finally chose Dolores rather than Virginia as the proper name of his nymphet. Did you ever hear of a girl named "Telluride"? For Dolores, see 9/5. For a mordant blending of Proust and Dolores, see 253/2. For the butterfly in question, see 308/1 and 316/10.

296/5 *those calls:* but H.H. has in mind the fake call *Quilty* made on p. 235.

296/6 *La . . . Chair: The Pride of the Flesh,* not a noteworthy translation of *Proud Flesh,* which in French would be *Tissu bourgeonnant or Fongosité.*

296/7 *Wooly- . . . -are?:* a phonetic burlesque of American pronunciation: *"Voulez-vous boire?"* (French; "Do you want a drink?").

297/1 *une femme . . . cigarette:* "a woman is a woman but a Caporal is a cigarette." Quilty has made nonsense out of "The Betrothed," by Rudyard Kipling (1865–1936): "A million surplus Maggie are willing to bear the yoke / And a woman is only a woman, but a good cigar is a smoke" (see also *Keys*, p. 136n). The pun is on *corporal* (military rank) and *Caporal* (the brand name of a French cigarette).

297/2 *a Gentile's house:* for a summary of what could be termed "the anti-Semitism theme," see 261/4.

298/1 *"Vous . . . vieux":* French; "You are in a fine mess, my friend."

298/2 *"Alors . . . -on?":* French; "What do we do then?"

298/3 *Justine:* see 276/4.

299/1 *Because . . . a sinner:* a parody of T. S. Eliot's "Ash Wednesday" (1930): "Because I do not hope to turn again / Because I do not hope / Because I do not hope to turn. . . ." H.H.'s structural use of "Because" in the remainder of the poem echoes Eliot's. For Eliot, see 16/3.

300/1 *moulting:* animals and insects *moult;* to cast off hair, feathers, skin, etc., which is replaced by new growth.

300/2 *flavid:* yellowish or tawny-colored.

301/1 *rencontre:* French; meeting (duel).

301/2 *soyons raisonnables:* French; let us be reasonable.

301/3 *as the Bard said:* in *Macbeth* (V, vii, 19); and for this pun Quilty deserves to die.

301/4 *Vibrissa:* one of the stiff, bristly hairs which many animals have about their mouths (a cat's whiskers); also the similar feathers on a bird.

301/5 *Schmetterling:* German; butterfly. During a conversation with Nabokov, I singled out this moment in the H.H.-Quilty confrontation as a good example of the kind of humorous but telling detail whose significance critics often miss. Nabokov nodded and with complete seriousness said, "Yes. That's the most important phrase in the chapter." At first this may seem to be an extreme statement or leg-pull; but in the context of the involuted patterning it is perfectly just (see 32/7), for by mentioning the German word for *butterfly* Quilty has superimposed the author's watermark on the scene. Like the mention of Dolores, Colorado (296/4), this reference—the only butterfly in the chapter—points to the lawful obsession with Lepidoptera that makes Nabokov a fellow traveler with enchanted hunters as unsavory as H.H. and Quilty. This tack is summarized in 316/9. For Maeterlinck, the heavy-handed symbolist, see 201/5. For the entomological allusions, see 6/1.

302/1 *herculanita:* a very potent South American variety of heroin.

302/2 *Melanie Weiss:* "Black White"; from *melanin* ("black [pigmented]") and the German for "white"—and she does measure reality in black-and-white terms. Her work burlesques the researches of a famous woman anthropologist who also favored far Pacific isles. See 5/3 for the sisterly mirror reversal "Blanche Schwarzmann" ("White Blackman"), a verbal relationship that once again reveals the author's hand.

302/3 *Bagration . . . Barda Sea:* many islands in the Pacific were discovered by Russians, and named by them, but neither of these places exists. The first is after Prince Pëtr Ivanovich Bagration (1765–1812), the Russian General who fought with distinction against Napoleon at Borodino, where he was fatally wounded, in 1812. *Barda* is a vodka-distilling sop given to cattle in Russia. The "geographic" names offer an ironic tribute to Miss Weiss's heroic efforts.

302/4 *Feu:* French; Fire.

302/5 *Impredictable:* a portmanteau word; *unpredictable* plus *impredicable* (from *predicated*): "incapable of being categorized."

303/1 *a feminine "ah!":* see 45/4 and 87/1.

303/2 *trudging from room to room:* the keys jangling in H.H.'s pocket have not locked the rooms (see 294/3); a fairy tale and nightmare blended. Quilty's refusal to die mocks the Double story, and the idea that evil can be exorcized so easily.

304/1 *pink bubble:* see 17/1 for the original, figurative bubble.

305/1 *purple heap:* the color of his bathrobe and his prose.

305/2 *staged for me by Quilty:* see 31/8.

CHAPTER 36

306/1 *Thomas had something:* Thomas the Apostle, the "doubting" disciple of John 20:24, who refused to believe in the resurrection of Christ until he himself had touched the nail wounds. Asked if an allusion to Thomas Mann might also be intended here, Nabokov replied, "The other Tom had nothing."

307/1 *Hegelian synthesis:* the death of Charlotte is remembered here (the killer's car going up the slope; p. 97), blending with the whole story of Lolita, from the cows on the slope (p. 112) to her assumed death (if the reader reads the book, Lolita must be dead; see pp. 4, 280, and 309). This "Hegelian synthesis" realizes Quilty's "Elizabethan" play-within-the-novel, *The Enchanted Hunters,* which featured Lolita as a bewitching "farmer's daughter who imagines herself to be a woodland witch, or Diana" (p. 200), and seven hunters, six of them "red–capped, uniformly attired." A "last–minute kiss was to enforce the play's profound message, namely, that mirage and reality merge in love." (p. 201). When Humbert asks a pregnant and veiny-armed Lolita to go away with him, he demonstrates that the mirage of the past (the nymphic Lolita as his lost "Annabel") and the reality of the present (the Charlotte-like woman Lolita is becoming) *have* merged in love, a "synthesis linking up two dead women."

307/2 *beavenlogged system. . . . crisscrossing the crazy quilt:* Part Two's final reference to Quilty by name mirrors the section's first entry, "crazy quilt" (p. 152). We've seen that such "coincidences" limn H.H.'s entrapment, his particular obsessional McFate—"I cannot get out, said the starling"—and, of course, the author's presence. The book–length system of planned coincidences and harmonious authorial patterning can also stand as a metaphor for evidence of the cosmic Author's work, divine Revelation of some "heavenlogged system" (*logged* here means "to enter in a logbook," "any record of progress"). As for Nabokov's specific "system," *pantheism* is a just word—lofty, but hardly reductive.

308/1 *from my lofty slope:* Here, H.H. realizes that the sounds emanating from the mining town below were of one nature—children at play. "One could hear now and then, as if released, an almost articulate spurt of vivid laughter, or the crack of a bat, or the clutter of a toy wagon. . . . And then I knew that the hopelessly poignant thing was not Lolita's absence from my side, but the absence of her voice from that concord," and with these words, it is clear that H.H. has transcended his solipsism. "The rich, ore-like glitter of the city dump" (p. 307) pinpoints happy metamorphoses, especially H.H.'s progression as an ethical being. The pretty but two-dimensional "pregnant" landscape of p. 152 (reread the passage) has given birth to the concord of children, a three-dimensional conception because it includes people. Aesthetic, moral, and communal perspectives have cohered, as ideally they should. The image of the "heavenlogged system" on p. 307 posits a fourth–dimension, all of which is at a considerable remove from the one–dimensional landscape represented in the conventional "ancient American estampe" on p. 26. Humbert's is indeed a lofty perch.

The personal dimension of this signal passage is documented by a letter that Nabokov wrote to Edmund Wilson in September 1951, from Ithaca, N.Y., describing a successful quest for butterflies in Telluride, where, in July, he had caught the first identified female of *Lycaeides sublivens* Nabokov, though his letter isn't taxonomically specific about his finds. He does mention "a steep slope high above Telluride—quite an enchanted slope," and the mining town, "full of most helpful, charming people—and when you hike from there, which is 9000′, to 10000′, with the town and its tin roofs and self–conscious poplars lying toylike at the flat bottom of a *cul-de-sac* valley running into giant granite mountains, all you hear are the voices of children playing in the streets—delightful!" (*The Nabokov-Wilson Letters, 1940–1977* [1979], p. 265). The passage on pp. 307–308 of *Lolita*, which clearly echoes many of these words, may well have been composed shortly after this letter; the end of the novel *was* written at the outset. In any event, two kinds of wonder are conflated in *Lolita*'s version of the letter's lofty vision.

308/2 *Otto Otto:* queried about this name, Nabokov answered, "a doubled neutrality with something owlish about it."

308/3 *Mesmer:* after Franz or Friedrich Mesmer (1734–1815), the Austrian physician who established hypnotism. See 250/10.

308/4 *Lambert:* a step away from Humbert. No literary allusions intended.

308/5 *fifty-six days ago:* in the concluding paragraphs of *Lolita*, H.H. reasserts the verisimilar basis that has been belied everywhere in the preceding pages, linking the last three paragraphs of his manuscript with the first three paragraphs of "editor" John Ray's Foreword, creating an elegant pairing and extraordinary equipoise for which neither H.H. nor Ray is responsible (see 4/4).

309/1 *Do not talk to strangers:* in *Who's Who in the Limelight*, "Quine, Dolores" is said to have made her debut in *Never Talk to Strangers*, and on p. 138 H.H. advises Lolita similarly (see 32/1). "Coincidence" and design govern in things this small, to paraphrase Robert Frost's poem "Design" (1936), a bleak reversal of Nabokov's hopeful pantheistic vision.

309/2 *do not pity C.Q. . . . . aurochs and angels, the secret of durable pigments . . . my Lolita:* "durable pigments" preserve the angels in Old Master paintings. The "auroch" refers to the European bison, now virtually extinct, as is this definition, since it is omitted from Webster's 3rd. H.H.'s aurochs allude to those delicate and stylized images of bison that still are visible on the cave walls of Spain and France where they were painted ten to twenty thousand years ago. Their "durable pigments" are an inspiring idea and sight, even when the images are poorly reproduced in text books. But I would never have identified the auroch as such if Nabokov himself hadn't mentioned it to me during a 1974 conversation about the cave paintings of Lascaux. (The beleagured drawing instructor in Nabokov's 1938 story, "Tyrants Destroyed," who endures a totalitarian regime, finds some solace in his doctoral dissertation on the cave origins of painting.) But *Lolita*'s cave painting is too "Joycean," too obscure; "C.Q.," the final Quilty reference, is much fairer. With it, H.H.'s tone turns an unfamiliar shade. Although the narrative surface is still intact, the masked narrator does speak in a newly impersonal way. When asked if one is now supposed to "hear" a different voice, as at "the end" of so many of his novels (see Introduction), Nabokov said, "No, I did not mean to introduce a different voice. I did want, however, to convey a constriction of the narrator's sick heart, a warning spasm causing him to abridge names and hasten to conclude his tale before it was too late. I am glad I managed to achieve this remoteness of tone at the end" (*Wisconsin Studies* interview). This "remoteness" is appropriate, for Humbert's love and Nabokov's labors have become one. The final phrase sounds the "Latin" locution that has echoed through the narrative (see 45/1 and 192/2), and the last word of the novel, that fatal constriction, repeats the first: "Lolita." It is a fitting and final symmetry for this Byzantine edifice, this verbal equivalent of an ordered (divinely ordered?) universe. Fyodor, the young poet of *The Gift*, wonders, on a summer stroll, "what is concealed behind all this, behind the play, the sparkle, the thick, green greasepaint of the foliage? For there really is something, there is something! And one wants to offer thanks but there is no one to thank. The list of donations already made: 10,000 days—from Person Unknown" (p. 340).

ON A BOOK ENTITLED *LOLITA*

311/1 *ON . . . ENTITLED LOLITA:* this Afterword was written to accompany the generous excerpts from *Lolita* which appeared in the 1957 edition of *The Anchor Review*, the novel's American debut, made possible mainly by Jason Epstein and the review's editor, Melvin J. Lasky. It was appended to the Putnam's edition in 1958, and has since been included in most of the 25 or so translations.

311/2 *the poor creature's cage:* see 255/4. In *Pale Fire*, Kinbote tells John Shade, "with no Providence the soul must rely on the dust of its husk, on the experience gathered in the course of corporeal confinement, and cling childishly to small-town principles, local by-laws, and a personality consisting mainly of the shadows of its own prison bars" (pp. 226–227). Writing about Sirin—himself—in *Conclusive Evidence* (1951), in a sentence omitted from the second edition *(Speak, Memory)*, Nabokov says, "His best works are those in which he condemns his people to the solitary confinement of their souls" (p. 217). Nabokov employed the prison trope in many ways. See my Introduction, pp. xxii–xxiii.

311/3 *best . . . are not translated:* this of course is no longer true.

312/1 *destroyed it . . . after . . . 1940:* nor is this true. The story, titled "The Enchanter," unexpectedly turned up among his papers in 1964, a fifty-four-page typescript rather than the thirty pages of memory. Two passages were made available to Andrew Field for use in his study *Nabokov: His Life in Art* (Boston, 1967). Newly translated versions are quoted in the Introduction, pp. xxxvii–xxxviii.

312/2 *The book developed slowly:* its design and order of events, however, were clearly in mind early in its composition, said Nabokov, although various sections were written well out of sequence, as was customary with him. See Introduction, pp. xxxix–xl.

312/3 *"reality" (one of the few words which mean nothing without quotes):* in *Ada*, Nabokov writes, "It would not be sufficient to say that in his love-making with Ada [Van] discovered the pang, the *ogon*', the agony of supreme 'reality.' Reality, better say, lost the quotes it wore like claws . . ." (pp. 219–220).

314/1 *America:* a corrected misprint ("American" in the 1958 edition).

315/1 *Palearctic . . . Nearctic:* one of the four world faunal regions, the *Holarctic* (arctic and temperate zones), is subdivided into *Palearctic* (Europe and Asia) and *Nearctic* (North America). The "suburban lawn" and "mountain meadow" above are open country for a lepidopterist, notes Diana Butler in "Lolita Lepidoptera," *New World Writing 16*, p. 61. See 6/1 for a summary of all the entomological allusions.

316/1 *spring of 1955:* a corrected author's error (instead of "winter of 1954" in the 1958 edition).

316/2 *Mr. Taxovich:* Maximovich, the ex–White Russian colonel reduced to driving a taxi, is totally infatuated with H.H.'s first wife, Valeria. H.H. graciously lets her go. See pp. 28–30.

316/3 *class list of Ramsdale School:* it is most notable for the way it mirrors the artist who created it (see 51/1 ff.), and for "Flashman, Irving," who suffers quietly, the only Jew in a class of Gentiles (see 53/3).

316/4 *"waterproof":* When Jean Farlow notices that H.H. has gone swimming with his watch on, Charlotte reassures her, and dreamily relishes a miracle of modern technology: " 'Waterproof,' said Charlotte softly, making a fish mouth" (see p. 89). The word is also the clue H.H. uses to torment the reader who strains to learn the identity of Lolita's abductor (see 272/1), and one is thus reminded that *Lolita* is a very special kind of detective story (see 9/2).

316/5 *in slow motion . . . Humbert's gifts:* Lolita is remembered as an illusory creature in a dream, rather than as the object of H.H.'s lust (see p. 120), and the allusion to his gifts recalls his desperate bribery as well as its results.

316/6 *the pictures . . . of Gaston Godin:* furtive love is invoked; like the artists whose portraits dominate his garret, Gaston is clearly homosexual. See 181/4.

316/7 *the Kasbeam barber:* he talks of his son, dead for thirty years, as though he were still alive (see p. 213).

316/8 *Lolita playing tennis:* if ever H.H. succeeds in "fix[ing] once for all the perilous magic of nymphets" (p. 134), it is in this scene (see pp. 232–234).

316/9 *the hospital at Elphinstone . . . irretrievable Dolly Schiller dying in Gray Star:* Nabokov is referring to Lolita by her married name (see p. 4). Twin deaths are recorded: Lolita "dies" for H.H. when Quilty steals her from the hospital (pp. 238–247) and "dies" for Nabokov when the book is completed, and her image is irretrievable. But Lolita does not die *in* the book; as H.H. says, "I wish this memoir to be published only when Lolita is no longer alive" (p. 308). Her creator points beyond the novel's fictive time into the future, for he would agree with H.H.'s closing statement that art "is the only immortality you and I may share, my Lolita." It is important to note that none of these "secret points" is exclusively sexual. Rather, the images and characters all formulate varying states of isolation, loss, obsession, and ecstasy which generalize H.H.'s consuming passion; the concluding "co-ordinate," after all, places in their midst the author, butterfly net firmly in hand.

316/10 *tinkling sounds . . . Lycaeides sublivens Nabokov:* the final "co-ordinates" form a most interesting progression. The last "nerve of the novel" is in fact outside the novel and extends from the lepidopterist to the nympholept, who almost seem to pass one another on the same trail. H.H. also experiences a most pleasing unity of sounds coming from a valley town (pp. 307–308); and the butterfly in question was captured by Nabokov near Dolores, Colorado (see 9/5 and 296/4). Nabokov commented: "This Coloradian member of the subgenus *Lycaeides* (which I now place in the genus *Plebejus,* a grouping corresponding exactly in scope to my former concept of *Plebejinae*) was described by me as a subspecies of Tutt's '*argyrognomon*' (now known as *idas* L.), but is, in my present opinion, a distinct species." See 6/1.

316/11 *My private tragedy . . . my natural idiom:* the narrator of *The Real Life of Sebastian Knight* (Nabokov's first novel in English) says something very similar about Knight:

I know, I know as definitely as I know we had the same father, I know Sebastian's Russian was better and more natural to him than his English. I quite believe that by not speaking Russian for five years he may have forced himself into thinking he had forgotten it. But a language is a live physical thing which cannot be so easily dismissed. It should moreover be remembered that five years before his first book—that is, at the time he left Russia,—his English was as thin as mine. I have improved mine artificially years later (by dint of hard study abroad); he tried to let his thrive naturally in its own surroundings. It did thrive wonderfully but still I maintain that had he started to write in Russian, those particular linguistic throes would have been spared him. Let me add that I have in my possession a letter written by him not long before his death. And that short letter is couched in a Russian purer and richer than his English ever was, no matter what beauty of expression he attained in his books. [pp. 82–83].

Nabokov's "private tragedy" *is* our concern, for in varying degrees it involves us all. Nabokov's search for the language adequate to *Lolita* is H.H.'s search for the language that will reach Lolita; and it is a representative search, a heightened emblem of all of our attempts to communicate. " 'A penny for your thoughts,' I said, and she stretched out her palm at once" (p. 208). It is the almost insuperable distance between those thoughts and that palm which Nabokov has measured so accurately and so movingly in *Lolita:* the distance between people, the distance separating love from love-making, mirage from reality—the desperate extent of all human need and desire. "I have only words to play with," says H.H., and only words can bridge the gulf suggested by Lolita's palm. H.H. has failed once—"She would mail her vulnerability in trite brashness and boredom, whereas I use[d] for my desperately detached comments an artificial tone of voice that set my own teeth on edge" (p. 284)—but it is a necessary act of love to try, and perhaps Nabokov succeeds with the reader where H.H. failed with Lolita.

317/1 *frac-tails:* Nabokov wittily demonstrates that the "native illusionist" is now an internationalist: *frac* is French for "dress coat." It is just that Nabokov (and this edition) should conclude with a joke, however small, for, from behind "the bars of the poor creature's cage" (p. 311), desperate Humbert also exults. In *Gogol,* Nabokov notes how "one likes to recall that the difference between the comic side of things, and their cosmic side, depends upon one sibilant" (p. 142), a juxtaposition implicit in the early title, *Laughter in the Dark.* The title goes two ways: it records the laughter of the cosmic joker who has made a pawn of Albinus, blinding and tormenting him, but it also summarizes Nabokov's response to life, his course for survival. Toward the end of *Lolita,* the sick and despairing Humbert has finally tracked down Lolita, who is now the pregnant Mrs. Richard Schiller. He recalls how he rang the doorbell, ready to kill Dick. The bell seems to vibrate through his whole exhausted system, but suddenly Humbert takes his automatic French response to the sound and playfully twists it into verbal nonsense: "*Personne. Je resonne. Reper-sonne.* From what depth this re-nonsense?" he wonders (p. 269). It sounds from the depths of Vladimir Nabokov's profoundly humane comic vision, and the gusto of Humbert's narration, his punning language, his abundant delight in digressions, parodies, and games all attest to a comic vision that overrides the sadness or terror of everyday life.

and place for reading and study before that same fountain; now that same frustration began to reappear. He was the apostle who would frequently carve childiron Salzbur superb only humane facts; when a child passes of Halifax so sometime his painted large primer level a new delightbon discussions, precepts and manuscript from a resolve whom that inner cleaving subtler by reason of everything by

About Vladimir Nabokov

Vladimir Nabokov was born in St. Petersburg on April 23, 1899. His family fled to Germany in 1919, during the Bolshevik Revolution. Nabokov studied French and Russian literature at Trinity College, Cambridge, from 1919 to 1923, then lived in Berlin (1923–1937) and Paris (1937–1940), where he began writing, mainly in Russian, under the pseudonym Sirin. In 1940 he moved to the United States, where he pursued a brilliant literary career (as a poet, novelist, critic, and translator) while teaching literature at Stanford, Wellesley, Cornell, and Harvard. The monumental success of his novel *Lolita* (1955) enabled him to give up teaching and devote himself fully to his writing. In 1961 he moved to Montreux, Switzerland, where he died in 1977. Recognized as one of this century's master prose stylists in both Russian and English, he translated a number of his original English works—including *Lolita*—into Russian, and collaborated on English translations of his original Russian works.

About Alfred Appel, Jr.

Alfred Appel, Jr., was born in New York City on January 31, 1934, and raised on Long Island. He served for two years in the U. S. Army, and was educated at Cornell and Columbia, which granted him a Ph.D. degree in 1963. He has taught at Columbia, Stanford, and, since 1968, at Northwestern University, where he is presently Professor of English and American Culture. He has received Guggenheim and Rockefeller Foundation fellowships. The first edition of *The Annotated Lolita* was in print for twenty years and went through twelve printings. His other books include *Nabokov's Dark Cinema*, *Signs of Life*, and *The Art of Celebration: The Expression of Joy in Twentieth-Century Art, Literature, Photography, and Music*, forthcoming from Alfred A. Knopf.

VINTAGE INTERNATIONAL

VINTAGE INTERNATIONAL

_____ **The Sheltering Sky** by Paul Bowles $12.00   0-679-72979-8
_____ **An Act of Terror** by André Brink $14.00   0-679-74429-0
_____ **The Death of Virgil** by Hermann Broch $16.00   0-679-75548-9
_____ **Angels & Insects** by A.S. Byatt $12.00   0-679-75134-3
_____ **The Game** by A.S. Byatt $10.00   0-679-74256-5
_____ **Passions of the Mind** by A.S. Byatt $12.00   0-679-73678-6
_____ **Possession** by A.S. Byatt $12.00   0-679-73590-9
_____ **Sugar and Other Stories** by A.S. Byatt $10.00   0-679-74227-1
_____ **The Virgin in the Garden** by A.S. Byatt $12.00   0-679-73829-0
_____ **The Marriage of Cadmus and Harmony** $13.00   0-679-73348-5
     by Roberto Calasso
_____ **The Road to San Giovanni** by Italo Calvino $10.00   0-679-74348-0
_____ **Six Memos for the Next Millennium** by Italo Calvino $10.00   0-679-74237-9
_____ **Exile and the Kingdom** by Albert Camus $10.00   0-679-73385-X
_____ **The Fall** by Albert Camus $9.00   0-679-72022-7
_____ **The Myth of Sisyphus and Other Essays** $9.00   0-679-73373-6
     by Albert Camus
_____ **The Plague** by Albert Camus $10.00   0-679-72021-9
_____ **The Rebel** by Albert Camus $11.00   0-679-73384-1
_____ **The Stranger** by Albert Camus $8.00   0-679-72020-0
_____ **Answered Prayers** by Truman Capote $10.00   0-679-75182-3
_____ **Breakfast at Tiffany's** by Truman Capote $10.00   0-679-74565-3
_____ **The Grass Harp** by Truman Capote $10.00   0-679-74557-2
_____ **In Cold Blood** by Truman Capote $12.00   0-679-74558-0
_____ **Music for Chameleons** by Truman Capote $11.00   0-679-74566-1
_____ **Other Voices, Other Rooms** by Truman Capote $11.00   0-679-74564-5
_____ **The Fat Man in History** by Peter Carey $10.00   0-679-74332-4
_____ **The Tax Inspector** by Peter Carey $11.00   0-679-73598-4
_____ **Bullet Park** by John Cheever $11.00   0-679-73787-1
_____ **Falconer** by John Cheever $11.00   0-679-73786-3
_____ **Oh What a Paradise It Seems** by John Cheever $9.00   0-679-73785-5
_____ **The Wapshot Chronicle** by John Cheever $11.00   0-679-73899-1
_____ **The Wapshot Scandal** by John Cheever $11.00   0-679-73900-9
_____ **Age of Iron** by J.M. Coetzee $10.00   0-679-73292-6
_____ **After Henry** by Joan Didion $12.00   0-679-74539-4
_____ **A Book of Common Prayer** by Joan Didion $12.00   0-679-75486-5
_____ **Democracy** by Joan Didion $12.00   0-679-75485-7
_____ **Run River** by Joan Didion $11.00   0-679-75250-1
_____ **Salvador** by Joan Didion $9.00   0-679-75183-1
_____ **Anecdotes of Destiny and Ehrengard** by Isak Dinesen $12.00   0-679-74333-2
_____ **Last Tales** by Isak Dinesen $13.00   0-679-73640-9
_____ **Out of Africa and Shadows on the Grass** $12.00   0-679-72475-3
     by Isak Dinesen
_____ **Seven Gothic Tales** by Isak Dinesen $13.00   0-679-73641-7
_____ **Winter's Tales** by Isak Dinesen $12.00   0-679-74334-0
_____ **The Book of Daniel** by E.L. Doctorow $12.00   0-679-73657-3
_____ **Loon Lake** by E.L. Doctorow $11.00   0-679-73625-5
_____ **Ragtime** by E.L. Doctorow $12.00   0-679-73626-3
_____ **Welcome to Hard Times** by E.L. Doctorow $10.00   0-679-73627-1
_____ **World's Fair** by E.L. Doctorow $12.00   0-679-73628-X
_____ **Love, Pain, and the Whole Damn Thing** $9.00   0-679-72992-5
     by Doris Dörrie
_____ **Once Were Warriors** by Alan Duff $10.00   0-679-76181-0
_____ **The Assignment** by Friedrich Dürrenmatt $7.95   0-679-72233-5
_____ **Going to the Territory** by Ralph Ellison $13.00   0-679-76001-6
_____ **Invisible Man** by Ralph Ellison $11.00   0-679-72313-7

VINTAGE INTERNATIONAL

VINTAGE INTERNATIONAL

___ **Lolita** by Vladimir Nabokov	$10.00	0-679-72316-1
___ **Look at the Harlequins!** by Vladimir Nabokov	$12.00	0-679-72728-0
___ **Mary** by Vladimir Nabokov	$10.00	0-679-72620-9
___ **Pale Fire** by Vladimir Nabokov	$11.00	0-679-72342-0
___ **Pnin** by Vladimir Nabokov	$10.00	0-679-72341-2
___ **The Real Life of Sebastian Knight** by Vladimir Nabokov	$11.00	0-679-72726-4
___ **Speak, Memory** by Vladimir Nabokov	$13.00	0-679-72339-0
___ **Strong Opinions** by Vladimir Nabokov	$12.00	0-679-72609-8
___ **Transparent Things** by Vladimir Nabokov	$10.00	0-679-72541-5
___ **A Bend in the River** by V. S. Naipaul	$10.00	0-679-72202-5
___ **Guerrillas** by V. S. Naipaul	$12.00	0-679-73174-1
___ **A Turn in the South** by V. S. Naipaul	$11.00	0-679-72488-5
___ **A Way in the World** by V.S. Naipaul	$13.00	0-679-76166-7
___ **The English Patient** by Michael Ondaatje	$11.00	0-679-74520-3
___ **Running in the Family** by Michael Ondaatje	$10.00	0-679-74669-2
___ **Body Snatcher** by Juan Carlos Onetti	$13.00	0-679-73887-8
___ **Black Box** by Amos Oz	$11.00	0-679-72185-1
___ **My Michael** by Amos Oz	$11.00	0-679-72804-X
___ **The Slopes of Lebanon** by Amos Oz	$11.00	0-679-73144-X
___ **Metaphor and Memory** by Cynthia Ozick	$13.00	0-679-73425-2
___ **The Shawl** by Cynthia Ozick	$7.95	0-679-72926-7
___ **Dictionary of the Khazars** by Milorad Pavić		
male edition	$13.00	0-679-72461-3
female edition	$13.00	0-679-72754-X
___ **Truck Stop Rainbows** by Iva Pekárková	$11.00	0-679-74675-7
___ **Cambridge** by Caryl Phillips	$10.00	0-679-73689-1
___ **Crossing the River** by Caryl Phillips	$11.00	0-679-75794-5
___ **A State of Independence** by Caryl Phillips	$10.00	0-679-75930-1
___ **The Law of White Spaces** by Giorgio Pressburger	$10.00	0-679-75246-3
___ **Complete Collected Stories** by V. S. Pritchett	$22.00	0-679-73892-4
___ **Swann's Way** by Marcel Proust	$13.00	0-679-72009-X
___ **Kiss of the Spider Woman** by Manuel Puig	$11.00	0-679-72449-4
___ **Memoirs of an Anti-Semite** by Gregor von Rezzori	$12.00	0-679-73182-2
___ **The Orient-Express** by Gregor von Rezzori	$11.00	0-679-74822-9
___ **The Snows of Yesteryear** by Gregor von Rezzori	$10.95	0-679-73181-4
___ **The Notebooks of Malte Laurids Brigge** by Rainer Maria Rilke	$13.00	0-679-73245-4
___ **Selected Poetry** by Rainer Maria Rilke	$12.00	0-679-72201-7
___ **The Breast** by Philip Roth	$9.00	0-679-74901-2
___ **Goodbye, Columbus** by Philip Roth	$11.00	0-679-74826-1
___ **The Great American Novel** by Philip Roth	$13.00	0-679-74906-3
___ **My Life as a Man** by Philip Roth	$11.00	0-679-74827-X
___ **Operation Shylock** by Philip Roth	$12.00	0-679-75029-0
___ **Portnoy's Complaint** by Philip Roth	$11.00	0-679-75645-0
___ **The Professor of Desire** by Philip Roth	$10.00	0-679-74900-4
___ **When She Was Good** by Philip Roth	$12.00	0-679-75925-5
___ **Mating** by Norman Rush	$12.00	0-679-73709-X
___ **Whites** by Norman Rush	$10.00	0-679-73816-9
___ **Light Years** by James Salter	$13.00	0-679-74073-2
___ **The Age of Reason** by Jean-Paul Sartre	$13.00	0-679-73895-9
___ **No Exit and 3 Other Plays** by Jean-Paul Sartre	$10.00	0-679-72516-4
___ **The Reprieve** by Jean-Paul Sartre	$15.00	0-679-74078-3
___ **Troubled Sleep** by Jean-Paul Sartre	$12.00	0-679-74079-1
___ **Open Doors and Three Novellas** by Leonardo Sciascia	$12.00	0-679-73561-5
___ **Cock and Bull** by Will Self	$11.00	0-679-75092-4

VINTAGE INTERNATIONAL

___ My Idea of Fun by Will Self	$12.00	0-679-75093-2
___ All You Who Sleep Tonight by Vikram Seth	$7.00	0-679-73025-7
___ The Golden Gate by Vikram Seth	$13.00	0-679-73457-0
___ And Quiet Flows the Don by Mikhail Sholokhov	$15.00	0-679-72521-0
___ By Grand Central Station I Sat Down and Wept	$10.00	0-679-73804-5
by Elizabeth Smart		
___ In the Eye of the Sun by Ahdaf Soueif	$15.00	0-679-74932-2
___ Ake: The Years of Childhood by Wole Soyinka	$12.00	0-679-72540-7
___ Ìsarà: A Voyage Around "Essay" by Wole Soyinka	$9.95	0-679-73246-2
___ Children of Light by Robert Stone	$11.00	0-679-73593-3
___ A Flag for Sunrise by Robert Stone	$12.00	0-679-73762-6
___ Confessions of Nat Turner by William Styron	$12.00	0-679-73663-8
___ Lie Down in Darkness by William Styron	$12.00	0-679-73597-6
___ The Long March and In the Clap Shack	$12.00	0-679-73675-1
by William Styron		
___ Set This House on Fire by William Styron	$13.00	0-679-73674-3
___ Sophie's Choice by William Styron	$13.00	0-679-73637-9
___ This Quiet Dust by William Styron	$12.00	0-679-73596-8
___ A Tidewater Morning by William Styron	$9.00	0-679-75449-0
___ Confessions of Zeno by Italo Svevo	$12.00	0-679-72234-3
___ Ever After by Graham Swift	$11.00	0-679-74026-0
___ Learning to Swim by Graham Swift	$9.00	0-679-73978-5
___ Out of This World by Graham Swift	$10.00	0-679-74032-5
___ Shuttlecock by Graham Swift	$10.00	0-679-73933-5
___ The Sweet-Shop Owner by Graham Swift	$10.00	0-679-73980-7
___ Waterland by Graham Swift	$11.00	0-679-73979-3
___ The Beautiful Mrs. Seidenman	$9.95	0-679-73214-4
by Andrzej Szczypiorski		
___ Diary of a Mad Old Man by Junichiro Tanizaki	$10.00	0-679-73024-9
___ The Key by Junichiro Tanizaki	$11.00	0-679-73023-0
___ Quicksand by Junichiro Tanizaki	$11.00	0-679-76022-9
___ The Reed Cutter and Captain Shigemoto's Mother	$11.00	0-679-75791-0
by Junichiro Tanizaki		
___ On the Golden Porch by Tatyana Tolstaya	$11.00	0-679-72843-0
___ Sleepwalker in a Fog by Tatyana Tolstaya	$11.00	0-679-73063-X
___ The Real Life of Alejandro Mayta	$12.00	0-679-72478-8
by Mario Vargas Llosa		
___ The Eye of the Story by Eudora Welty	$11.00	0-679-73004-4
___ Losing Battles by Eudora Welty	$12.00	0-679-72882-1
___ The Optimist's Daughter by Eudora Welty	$9.00	0-679-72883-X
___ The Beautiful Room Is Empty by Edmund White	$11.00	0-679-75540-3
___ Forgetting Elena by Edmund White	$10.00	0-679-75573-X
___ The Passion by Jeanette Winterson	$10.00	0-679-72437-0
___ Sexing the Cherry by Jeanette Winterson	$10.00	0-679-73316-7
___ Written on the Body by Jeanette Winterson	$11.00	0-679-74447-9

Available at your bookstore or call toll-free to order: 1-800-793-2665.
Credit cards only. Prices subject to change.